ONE

In Which Jill Forces Herself on Herself and Begins

THE DAY BEFORE yesterday was my birthday and Josh boiled two lobsters in seawater and then baked a chocolate cake for the party later, so rich I wanted to eat it in tissue-paper slices. As the sun shone warm for late March, the first seedlings, the cress, broke through the ground in the garden we had plowed and planted last week. All day I was glad but curiously light and cut loose.

In midafternoon I suddenly knew why. When my mother last read my palm that summer I left home for good, she told me I would die between the ages of thirty-eight and forty-two. I had passed out of a zone of danger.

"How could you have believed her?" Josh asked.

I didn't: some child closeted in me did. As I ran out of the house yesterday at seven to drive to the airport with my head stuffed with the grit and sand of fatigue, something was nagging at me. All day in airports and bumpy planes, I hunched notebook in hand expecting a poem to issue from this curious itch, but it didn't.

I was met by three graduate students and taken to my motel. A workshop followed with some good questions and a chance to make a few political points, a potluck supper with the local women's center, my reading. I strode to the microphone in my velvet gown patterned like a starry night and knocked over the water pitcher as I adjusted the microphone—always preset too high. "We expected you to be taller," they said, as they always say. Then I went for their hearts. Passion out of accidental circumstance transcended is what they're buying.

Afterward at the reception, the timidity, the weirdness, the undulating snake dances of ego before me kept me on edge. "Aw, come off it," I wanted to say. "It's just this person, me. All those years when I made a living at part-time secretarial work, people like you wouldn't even say hello to me. What's the fuss?" They think I am the books solidified, but the books are the books. I'm just this round cranky tired woman who would rather be home in bed with Josh by now telling the beads of our days and making the amber of that reality shine with the heat of our bodies. Too much self-regard has never struck me as dignified: trying to twist over my shoulder to view my own behind. And it is not a mirror I want but a long view back. I feel as if I have come through rough terrain and across the wasteland around factories and down unmarked city streets without a map and I both know and do not know where I have been. I want to explain to somebody. To me? To Josh? The hypothetical gentle reader? For though I have crossed the danger zone alive, still at forty my life was wildly shaken by divorce, and if I find myself still myself now, that seems more of an accomplishment than it used to. I also find myself hard in love in a way I have to search far back in my life to match.

It is not that whole busy swarming life, then, I feel compelled to march through leading you in a crowd of tourists into the bazaar but those few years when I became the woman I have somehow in all weathers and colors of luck remained. I want to revisit that burned-over district where I learned to love—in friendship and in passion—and to work.

Today three planes end to end like rackety subway cars through the clouds have brought me home safe at last, so

I'm inclined to dawdle here where there is always wind fresh off the ocean and the sound of wind chimes and gulls crying and cats mewing on the wrong side of every door and one of our typewriters going. Whenever I get back, I wander in circles singing, so glad to be back, so glad to be back. Are you so damned sure you'd like to meet your young self face-to-face? Mother of what I am now, sucker, poser, kid rawer than I would like to admit and yet survivor, with the wariness and strong stomach of the scavenger. I can summon up pity for a battered alley kitten. Annoyance. Patronizing approval. The desire to stick my fingers in and make me prettier, cleaner, braver, better. But what I really feel penetrating my ribs like a knife is stark terror lest somehow entering that mind I'll be trapped back in that skinny sixteen-year-old body. I hardly got through the first time. My idea of hell is to be young again. Ladies and gentlemen, girls and boys, cats and dogs, have mercy on the candid for they get what they crave: an education.

To it, then. It's March of 1953. I am sixteen, soon to turn seventeen. The Korean War seems to be winding down; the Rosenbergs are convicted and waiting in prison; Eisenhower has been president since January and Washington emits clouds of grey fog on the news every night; times are pretty good in Detroit for the workers on the line. Give me a sprightly fife-and-drum accompaniment in the back of your head. She is—all right, all right—I am striding from tie to tie between tracks orange with rust while on my left run the shiny tracks on which still once an hour diesels streak by. Ragged stalks of last year's weeds swish against my jeans. Between the tracks puddles stand from yesterday's rain. Not even a rim of ice today. Mother was disinclined to put me into brassieres till high school, so I developed early a slouch and a walk to shield myself, a quick steady glide that still brings me in and out of rooms a little on the sly, for I am small, dark and move fast. Alone I swing along at a good clip past the back picket and wire fences of wooden houses turned in rows like soiled cupcakes to occupy what in my childhood had been a patch of industrial wilderness between the blocks where workers live and the factories where they work. When the UAW

(United Auto Workers) is out on strike, our neighborhood runs on empty and the men are testy on the street corners where their kids usually hang out.

In those trash-scarred prairies and thickets Callie and I used to play explorers and scientists and bank robbers and commandos. There we found a dead pheasant and held a funeral in spite of maggots, found trodden weeds and discarded condoms, found a nest of bunnies we could not save from a dog. Last year Callie got in trouble and quit school. Walking I mourn the Callie of twelve whose lanky tomboy rebellion alternated with keeping her nails long and purple and sulking over confession magazines we swiped from drugstores. The roar of a train hits me and I jump, not having heard it come up on the good track. Swoosh-click, swoosh-click the cars loom past, Santa Fe, Chesapeake, Southern Pacific. I wish I could go away, away.

Romantic freight trains of my childhood. Callie and I ran alongside yelling at the brakemen till they threw us pieces of chalk as big around as our starved wrists—chalk they wrote on the cars with. Best for hopscotch and writing dirty words on walls. Dreaming of oceans and mountains, I did not know our tracks were the Detroit Terminal Railroad, shunting goods from one dead end of the inner city to the other. Callie got sent up in '61 for shooting her husband with his own police special when he threw their daughter down the stairs. I think we could make a test case of it now but then all I could do was hitchhike for a visit. She got life.

I have walked a mile and I have another to go before I see my friend Howie. The gritty wind blows the heat and yelling of our tight house from me, at the same time that it cuts through me like a boning knife. We both live in inner city Detroit in predominantly Black neighborhoods, but mine used to be and still is somewhat Irish, Polish, Appalachian, and his used to be and still is somewhat Jewish. Going scalded to him from quarreling with my mother, I build vague tortuous expectations. I have something to tell him. What? Oh, something. A statement that will light the ash-grey sky, mesh my life and dreams, make someone, him, see me. Past the backs of factories I march with the steady thunk of pistons rattling in my knees. Hands stuffed in the pockets of a suede jacket from an old riding habit Mother bought at a rummage sale, I take comfort from the smell of stables and aging leather. I don't even remember what Mother and I quarreled about: it is a continual quarrel that began when I reached puberty.

Far past the factories I turn into Howie's neighborhood of many rooming houses. A chiropractor's sign winks from a wide bay in the bosom of a matronly grey house. Here's one with steamboat prow, newly painted a spanking yellow with maroon trim: TEMPLE OF TRUTH, REV. MADAME FUTURA, SPIRITUAL ADVISOR AND MYSTICAL PSYCHOLOGIST. ENTER AND FIND PEACE. Good old bulldog Howie entered and got in an argument with her secretary.

The wrought-iron gates of the Jewish cemetery stand wide under the awkward cobblestone arch. I peek in the office window. Empty, thank you. Howie's father is old and talking with him strains my scanty Yiddish. I am always nodding at phrases I don't quite understand, embarrassed to pretend. Howie says, "Why should you?" but that's worse. Excused from the gym class of the world, belonging to no team.

Just beyond an island of hemlocks the road divides into the cluttered plain of the necropolis, grey and white as an overexposed snapshot. Necropolis. Howie taught me that word. I say it over gloatingly as I ring the bell of the house. Impatiently I ring again. If you aren't home! I shiver with incremental cold and my calves ache. I should be wearing a winter coat but mine is a plaid in orange and purple with a decayed fur collar that belonged to my mother's friend Charlotte. Mother and I have been skirmishing about the coat for two years. If forced to wear it out of the house to school, I leave it at a girlfriend's house halfway. I get enough grief at school about how I dress to prefer a November-through-March head cold.

The door opens. His face is red and puffy, making him

look even younger. He is almost a year younger than I but
we're both seniors. "Jill . . . hey . . . You startled me. I was
dozing."

"You sleep too much." The close heat of the living room
makes my nose run. Light dies in front of the narrow
windows, before the compacted plush dark. "God, it's hot.
Can we open a window?"

"They like it hot. So I'll grow like a potted geranium."
He ambles past flexing his arms behind his head, his
square jaw pushing on his chest as he yawns. I always
forget how tall he is because he hasn't lost what his mother
insists is baby fat. The outlines of his strong low-slung
body and stubborn face are blurred. *With difficulty I con-
jure you. . . . You had not got your own face yet. I do
violence in fixing your later face to the broad but pudgy
boyish shoulders. I am afraid the face I see by now is the
photograph they kept reprinting. You looked when you
had just turned sixteen sometimes a sullen baby, sometimes
wizened against intrusion like an old man davening, sometimes bleak and sneering, fat boy who thought too much,
peering in.* Shaking off sleep he scrubs his knuckles against
his eyes. "My mother's taking Grandma to the doctor."

The furniture straining to the dark ceiling makes me
fidget. "Let's go outside."

We share a stone bench in the courtyard closed in by the
high outer wall, the walls of office and house. I like this
court where greenish urns hold withered stumps, a wheel-
barrow leans against the blank office wall beside flowerpots
stacked neatly in each other on the wobbly brick floor.
Traffic rumble pours over the wall with a steady bass
murmur like the cupped sea in a large shell. Howie talks
loudly about the Aristotle he's reading for Great Books. I
first met him in a section held in the main library, before I
had to quit for an after-school job. I cannot see Howie
often enough, but I'll never again see Beck, tall with curly
dark hair who talked with such vehemence and wit my
hands shook under the table and I could only contradict
him crankily. "What's his name—Beck?—does he still go?"

"Sure. He's an ass."

"Yeah? Beck is?" To speak his name is a stinging pleasure, but I would subside like a beached jellyfish if Howie guessed. We must allow no stickiness between us, no messages escaping my bottled inner world of itch and wonder, crush and rumor.

"Beck turns everything around to suit his jabber. Every idea's so simple when he gets done, you wonder why they went to the bother." He grimaces, looking guilty at the judgment.

I can't keep my news back longer. "Howie, I got the scholarship to the university. It came in today's mail."

"Good news." He takes out an old but carefully kept package of Luckies, offering it. "Are you going to Ann Arbor, then?"

"Will *they* let me?" I get up to pace the bricks. Howie doesn't understand. It's assumed in his family that he'll go to college. He's already accepted to Columbia. His grandmother has saved for years, put aside her husband's insurance money for the best education they can buy him. In my family it's all my idea. "I've been working summers but I'm two hundred short for the dorm. They make you live in it. Will my folks let me go? Will they give me the extra two hundred?"

He nods grimly. "How are you getting on with your mother?"

"Rotten. We had a fight just . . ." I sit down.

"Today?" The smoke creeps under his glasses. He waves it away. "What about?" He squints at me.

"Oh, everything. Loud and dull."

He blinks suspicion. "Like what?"

I busy myself with my cigarette. "Well, you. She says it's morbid to hang around here, because you live in a graveyard."

"I live in a house. " His grey eyes are blind and inturned. "That's what I used to say in school. I thought it was clever but it never did any good. The kids told stories about me and Papa chewing on the bones." As if for comfort he hauls out the lucky silver dollar his brother Milt brought him from Reno and fingers the eagle.

"I know." I do. When my childhood appears in dreams, my grade school is a prison, the kids tearing at each other in frustration and rage. It smells like piss and blood and cinders. My name Jill Stuart hangs on me queerly, prompting strangers to wonder if there was a mix-up in the hospital. I look like my mother and we both look like Jews from Kazan, where there's a heady admixture of Tartar. In grade school the kids could not decide whether to taunt me for looking Chinese or whether simply to torture me for being a kike. There was one other Jew, a Black girl named Sarah Altweiler. The authorities used to put us on hall guard together. At age ten or eleven, the humor did not escape us. The authorities were right, we got on well together standing back to back in our common freakhood. Then I would go home where if I mentioned anything in front of Dad he would rage at me that I'm not Jewish. I learned early that I had to keep my mouth shut with him and also that everybody is somewhat crazy, except me. And Sarah, maybe. She has frizzy hair of a fascinating metallic bronze and her skin is grey satin. The way our checkered blocks are gerrymandered, she now goes to the Black high school and I go to one still mostly white. I hardly ever see her any longer. *Years later of course she was the lodestar that pulled Howie South. At that funeral in Selma I stood with her.*

In hot silence Howie tosses the silver dollar, pockets it. We are alike, fat boy, skinny girl, staggering out of our brutal sickly childhoods with arms clutched full of books. How can we possibly draw comfort from each other, when we each look so unlike the stuff of dreams? I stamp out my butt and tuck it under a loose brick, bursting into what I know will draw him into safe abstract argument. "Howie, I've been reading Dos Passos' *U.S.A.*, and I think if we'd been grown-ups in the thirties, we'd both have been Communists—"

With fare borrowed from Howie I boarded a bus, hollow with the drunkenness of talking too much, too passionately, with no issue. The streetlights came on making night, and I'll get it for being late. Doggy houses crouching with your head between your paws, you look too working class to carry any magic. I can't imagine potent strangers behind your shades, just a geegaw lamp framed in the exact center of the window, like the one lit by now and waiting for me, still wrapped in its cellophane although four years old. Riviera Theater where I used to stand in line for Saturday matinee, two Westerns and six cartoons, and we'd hide in the john to see the adult show afterward. Now I read Freud and Marx. If I can't escape my parents, I can classify them.

I get off the bus into a sharp air flavored with a locomotive smell of soft coal burning from chimneys; only the better-off families have the new oil. Our street looks cluttered, the wooden two- and four-family flats with their porches banked like crossed arms, the bungalows jostled between, but it is gracious too, for every house has a square of lawn and a big shade tree. Suppertime, so no kids stand under the streetlights. No stopping to smoke a butt or pass a few jokes; no flash of guilt. I stopped hanging with my old gang when I began taking grades seriously, scribbling in my notebooks, saving for college. In all my dreams I am gone from this neighborhood, shot like a cannonball out of the narrow fear of being stuck here, knocked up early, in trouble with the law that always belonged to Them and not to Us, on the streets, fallen in the pits of drugs and booze down which I've already lost friends. From books I learned there is something else and I want it bad. When I talk with them I say, "I'm goin' to the Ra-veer-a Thee-ay-ter," for Riviera Theater, and I say, "Freddie didn't never ball me, he can shut his lyin' face or I'll shut it for him." When I talk to Howie, I talk in a way I learned off the radio. I know I am a fraud and that is part of my guilt. The rest ferments in the stories I carry inside. Everybody talks to me.

"Jill, he gets stinky drunk every doggone Saturday and look what he done to me. He pull't my hair from my scalp in a big ole handful and then he broke my tooth, see?" Callie opens her mouth wide, pointing.

"Jillie, that fuckin' john had hisself a billy club in his pocket. I thought that's his doing at first, you know, I was rubbing on him and I said, 'Sugar, you one well-hung dude!' "

The truth is I have only the vaguest notion what Marcie means in biological detail but all she wants is for me to listen. My mother broke me in early to doing that; practice makes a listener who can hold eye contact all evening. And go home with my head full of bloody sorrow like the garbage cans behind the butcher's shop.

"Two hunert in cold cash. Two meazly hunert. I got to get it. There's shitloads a money in numbers, Jill, I can do it if I can get just bankrolled but I owe that lying spade two hunert last week already." That's Freddie, who was my boyfriend at thirteen and fourteen when I ran with the gang.

Ooops, Dad isn't sitting in the front window with the newspaper: they're eating. She'll throw the kitchen at me. The streetlight shows up the chalky asbestos siding making the house ominously white and waiting. Crooked elbow of front porch waiting to grab me.

"Mother, I'm home." Smell of stew. Mother calls it beef stew, rich broth of succulent meat and vegetables. Dad won't eat lamb. I only found out I like lamb when the butcher got a new assistant and yelled at him, "No, she wants the usual stew meat for Stuart, that's the lamb."

"Mother," I repeat, "I'm home." Let's get it over. She stands in the kitchen washing glasses from the upper shelves, used only for company. Why? She thrusts a towel at me.

I do not speak in hope of avoiding a quarrel. Instead I try to pretend I do not notice the angry glint of her dark eyes, the menacing clatter in the sink. My shoulders hunch. The top of her glossy black always unruly hair comes to my chin, although I'm only five foot four. In spite of her floppy washdress splashed with bleached petunias, in spite of the cheap bras she wears limp before cutting down for me, in spite of a craving for sugar exceeded only by a craving for melodrama, her figure is impressive. Fat pads out the curves extravagantly—houri arch of hips and buttocks, pronounced waist, major pride of breasts. Her hands and feet are small and often swollen. Eyes dark as mine. Both with small straight noses. Her mouth is a Cupid's bow of which she is vain, deploring big mouths like mine. Her voice is low and pleasant but capable of great stridence. This is a house where everyone yells.

You see a plump coy energetic doll with mincing gait. I see the Great Devouring Mother, ogress big as a horizon sitting on my head. *"Your father,"* she begins, words always italicized, "is not home yet. Of course he hasn't called. We'll eat at midnight. Men! They think the food grows on the table, just pops out of the wood like toadstools from the ground."

Dad works for the city servicing the trolleys and trolleybuses the city is gradually replacing with buses (*as part of what appears from this late vantage point as a master plan for destroying its public transportation*). He is shop steward for his union and the senior wizard with the reputation of making any piece of junk run a day longer. My stomach growling, I keep looking for the stew, for it is not on top of the stove. The stove has been scrubbed immaculate and there is no food on it at all. Our hatbox kitchen is surprisingly modern, bristling with electric frypans and electric can openers with a huge slab of refrigerator lording it over the wobbly old table. Dad has no more ability to resist buying an electric shoe polisher than my mother does to resist a shocking pink two-dollar rummage sale sweater in size 14 that can surely be made to fit me if I put on fifty pounds.

I scan the last dusk for Dad's car to pull into the drive. It looks as if Mother has been digging up the edges of the lawn again for vegetables, putting out the first hardy seeds. She can make anything grow under the fall of the acid chemical rain from the yellow-brown skies of industrial Detroit. My father cherishes only grass, which means respectability to him, and they fight a war as long as the growing season, him running the lawn mower over her plants, her stealing a few inches by widening her beds. My skinny body is convulsed with hunger cramps. I try to think of the great ascetics, but the air is moist with the stew.

"Where did you go when you barged out of here?"

"For a walk."

"What did your friend Howie have to say?" She pulls the stopper and the soapy water goes slurping down.

No use denying. "He's reading Aristotle for Great Books."

"What makes them great? The filth?"

"That was Aristophanes who wrote the play you got mad at. You know sex is a part of living, so what's wrong with writing about it?" When I was younger, Mother read my books with me, but somewhere between *Rebecca of Sunnybrook Farm* and *Brave New World,* we parted company, and we have not forgiven each other. She is a compulsive reader who brings home armloads from the Gabriel Richard Public Library every two weeks, which she consumes late at night. A vast hunger for something. That same hunger that terrifies her in me. She is scared of the world and thinks if she punishes me first, I will be broken down enough to squeak through.

"Was Howie's mother home?"

"His father was." Anyway, he was probably around, out in the cemetery. I lie automatically.

"In the house?"

"In the office. Anyway we went outside."

"Because his dad was inside?"

"Because they keep the house too hot."

With a flirt of her head she shakes the hair from her eyes. "Howie's a sensible boy. You don't catch him running over here. Real Jewish boys mind their mothers."

"What's his mother got to do with it? This house is too small."

"Too small for what? You can entertain in the front room."

"You always listen."

"What have you got to say you're ashamed your own mother should hear?" As she sets the table I stand with clenched fists backed out of her way against the newspapers heaped waiting for her to go through to clip weird news stories for her collection. She lilts on in a sugar and vinegar voice, "Run, lie to Howie about how I mistreat you, because he'll believe you till he gets to know you better."

This is stupid. I want to walk out with a cool yawn and read the paper, but I cánnot tear myself from her. Younger I used to say, I tell everything to my mother: she would turn me out like her purse down to the crumbs and pennies. Now we live at war, our reconciliations brief and aching with sore love and rancid mistrust, one of us always shouting betrayal. "You think I have nothing to talk about but you? You aren't my universe."

"Your universe! Your pigsty!"

Imitation tough guy grin on my face I back against the papers. "Inside. The one place you can't pry."

"If you're this bad now, this defiant, what'd you be like if we sent you to college? You just want to get out of working and paying us back." Eyes lit up with that hard glint. I can't look that fierce; I know because I've tried before the mirror. Her fists prance between us. One step more and I'll sprawl on the papers. "You've had it easy. If you had to slave like me. Even your father finally sees through you. You used to be able to twist him around your finger, but—"

"I only want to be left alone! You want me a baby locked in a playpen. Whenever I like someone, you try to ruin it!"

"Like you? They laugh at you behind your back! Friends? How dare you slam out of here and go sneaking around a graveyard doing God-knows-what all day leaving me with a house to clean and then parade around in front of me giving yourself airs about friends!"

My tensions go all to silly laughter and I slide back, flailing for balance. Screaming she gropes on the table and scoops up a cup, sends it flying. I drop on the papers as the cup strikes the wall spraying shards of crockery. The grade door opens. I stop laughing and we both freeze. A look of quick complicity: the auslander comes. I scramble to my feet, sweeping fragments of cup under the papers, while she rushes to the cupboard for a new one.

Still he heard something. As he opens the door he looks swiftly at her and then hard at me, his grey eyes behind the gold-rimmed glasses cold and weighing. His deep voice is devoid of inflection. "Where's supper? I got held up at the shop."

If she takes the quarrel to him, he will squash it in a moment and me too. But she bustles round him, her voice an octave higher. "Malcolm, I'm sorry, I'm awfully sorry, but you know I couldn't start supper. Now I'll throw something together. Why don't you glance at the paper? I'll have it ready in a jiffy, some nice hamburgers."

Imperceptibly, I hope, I step backward and press the lever on the garbage can just enough to look inside. My stomach leaps. O lost and luscious stew still steaming on the brown paper.

TWO

The Cowbird Egg in the Eagles' Nest

W E SIT CRAMPED around the table. Our three chairs are jammed between chimney and basement door in space that a large chair would fill. This is a house built for people for whom respectability meant owning a house, but who couldn't finance more than a packing crate. Even tonight, however, the wobbly legs of the table bear up poorly under the load of side dishes: two kinds of bread, jellied beets, mashed potatoes, hamburgers and for dessert home-canned peaches and apple cake baked before our quarrel.

"Don't pick at your food!" Mother heaps my plate with potatoes made in a hurry, burned on the bottom and full of small hard lumps. "Eat!"

I feel too close to their elbows, exposed to the blast of their whims. At the first suspicious glance my appetite withers. Scrawny would-be changeling, at four I sat forever before a plate of cold congealing goo, condemned to stare at the orange o's of canned carrots until I got them down, threw them up or snuck them into the garbage. *Twenty-five years later the smell of canned spinach or overcooked peas, the sight of the slime-mold shapes of commercial gelatin*

15

*can force a rush of acid up my throat. Fortunately in the
life of a food snob such encounters are rare, but I still eat
too fast.*

In words of ritual I could intone with him, Dad says
with heavy jocularity, "I see you served a little meat with
the onions, Pearl." (*Plaintive.*) "I can't see fogging up the
natural taste of beef with that Eyetalian greenery."

(*Arch.*) "I just put a dash in for flavor." (*Martyred.*) "I
swear I don't know why I slave to set a good table plenty
of men would give their eyeteeth for and nothing but carping for reward."

Dad calls himself a meat-and-potatoes man and tries to
ignore the stomach he passed on to me, organ of emotion
and only secondarily of digestion. Between Mother and me
all is touch and wrestle, the love and hate thrust into relief.
Between Dad and me feelings mass themselves amorphous
but lowering. His hair turned silver early. His brows loom
and hairs bristle from his deep bony nose and glint on the
back of his long fine deeply scarred hands, stained as his
teeth with nicotine. The moments at the table as he wolfs
down his food and drinks his cup of black coffee are the
only times I ever see him without a cigarette. When he
rises from sleep where snores break shuddering from him, I
hear him in the morning hacking as he stumbles to his
dresser and then the rasp of a match as he lights his first
butt. He is a Celt who wants to be a Wasp and treats his
emotions like mice that infest our basement or the rats in
the garage, as vermin to be crushed in traps or poisoned
with bait. He will keep the peace if he can, but once
roused, his temper cleaves the house. Then he strikes out
with fists and feet, hitting and kicking hard so that what he
shatters then cannot be mended. When he hits me, he
always leaves bruises.

Dad comes from a small town. His mother spoke Welsh
as my buhbe spoke Russian and Yiddish; and as my
mother almost never speaks Yiddish, my father claims to
know no Welsh. If I know any Yiddish, it is because my
buhbe always spoke it when we were alone, and until she
died last year when I was fifteen, she always spent half the
summer with us. My father's father kept a dry-goods store

and although through his wife he was related to half the out-of-work miners in the country, he never let it queer his books. My mother, my father, they are the halves of two worlds that don't mix or even balance. Over the two families the same sky does not hang nor the same earth stretch underneath.

Mother was born of immigrant Russian Jews and grew up in the slums of four cities. She had seven brothers and four sisters, born before her eyes with the help of local midwives. At fifteen she had to leave school to go to work. At sixteen she married. At seventeen she was a widow. Her first husband Sam, just a year older, had a job at Carnegie Steel. When he fell into the molten ore, the company sent her an ingot to bury. She moved back the six blocks to her family just in time for my grandfather to be shot by Pinkertons. He was a union organizer. So my mother married Max Abel, a Philadelphia businessman steady and fifteen years older, and began to give her mother money.

Mother was still married to Max Abel when Dad met her, long a bachelor with the pleasures of cronies and barrooms and the loneliness of furnished rooms. How can I conjecture the bolt of lightning not unlike his temper that transfigured him to love her? Mistrust is mixed with their love and they fascinate each other in a stymied grappling years have confused but not eased. They fled Philadelphia for Detroit into the full onslaught of the Depression, convinced that it was their personal punishment. Love, the cannibal, presided over my cradle; it is small wonder I am scrupulous with my dinner.

They squabble still about how Mother takes her coffee sweet and light and Father takes his black. They are doing that halfheartedly and poking at the mass of papers on the table, the announcement of my scholarship, the forms I must fill out for the university on dormitory perference.

"Dormitory." Mother gives the papers a cuff. "Like a hotel?"

"They have hours, Mother. It's girls only. They lock us in at night." I try to short-circuit what I guess is her path of thought. She once worked as a chambermaid and associates hotels with drunken salesmen trying to corner her.

"Humpf. Wayne is a very good school. You just hop on a bus and you're there."

"Two buses."

The phone rings. Mother leaps up to pounce on it. "Leo!" I hear her moan. "It's Leo!" she tells us, eyes dancing. "I'll accept the charges, operator."

"Ask him how the underwater lot business is going," I say, but softly. Leo is my oldest brother. Both my brothers are Max's sons but Max has nothing to do with them. Leo's thirty, living in Toledo across the state border so he won't have to pay child support. I think he would have been rich long ago—the only passion I've ever discerned in him although he does keep marrying and marrying—but he's somehow too slippery even to hold on to his money. I like my brother Francis better, whom they call Frankie. At thirty, Leo is balding and portly and wears three-piece business suits that always look as if he borrowed them from somebody twenty pounds thinner. Francis has more style, but let's face it, it's gambler's style.

At twenty-seven when Francis comes home and walks down the street with me, the girls who don't know him yet all ask who my cute boyfriend is. He wears a loud shirt under a leather jacket and I remember his pegged pants and his zoot suit of a few years ago. I adore him, he can melt the heart in me to pure chocolate with a wink, but I wouldn't trust him with a five-dollar bill if I locked him in the bathroom with it. He'd smoke it if he couldn't lose it on a horse or a fight or a poker game. Francis has no luck. Everybody knows that but him. I can't quite trust him with secrets either. Unlike Leo, he loves me, I think, but Mother can turn him upside down and empty the pockets of his soul till my secrets come tumbling out along with his. I was a consummate flirt when I was younger but I have lost the knack and at sixteen he is the only man I flirt with.

"You did! That's wonderful," Mother burbles. She turns to us. "Leo's gone into the paint business! He got a whole carload of paint dirt cheap." She turns back to the phone. "You're right on the ball, Leo, that's my darling. Everybody paints their house in the spring. Why, we have to

paint inside ourselves. . . . Of course you can. When are
you coming home?"

Singed with jealousy, I rise to sneak out. Dad stops me,
clearing his throat. He has put on the reading glasses that
don't correct his farsightedness and is holding the application at arm's length. "What is this about Donna going to
the U. of Michigan also?"

"I guess so." Donna is his brother Hubie's youngest girl.
Donna Stuart. "She wrote me she was going."

"Did she ask you to live with her in this whatever-it-is,
rooming house?"

"She mentioned it," I say reluctantly. Getting away from
the family is more what I had in mind.

"It's good to be with kin." He frowns at the application.
He is also listening to the conversation with Leo.

I take the moment to skip out. I'll be called back for
dishes fast enough. We have only two bedrooms and mine
still looks as it did when Leo and Francis shared it—bunk
beds, two dressers in one of which Mother keeps sewing
supplies and out-of-season clothes. The door that looks like
a closet leads up to the attic, where I am headed. That is
my sanctuary. The bedroom I share with a busy sewing
machine and a mangle and the things that belong to my
brothers and Grandma when she visited has been mine
since I was six but it has never felt private. The attic
does.

Stifling hot in summer, close to freezing in winter, a
scene of boxes piled on boxes, this is my dusty heaven.
Running from the back window, which looks down on our
tiny yard full of flowers and clotheslines, to the chimney is
my room. The barriers were imaginary around my doll
beds. Boxes formed walls for those girls' clubs I used to
instigate, imitating books; they never met but once and
that meeting always taken up with making lists of all the
girls we wouldn't ask because of snotty wrongs they'd done
us, Callie and Shirley and me. Last year Dad put up beaver-
board partitions. For weeks an unfinished door leaned outside; finally I took it in and standing across several boxes it
serves as my desk. My books, my chair, my glider (late of
the front porch). Mine, mine, mine.

The rafters are the ceiling. Three walls are white. I ran out of paint so the fourth is stuck full of tacks to hold my gallery of reproductions clipped from *Life*, an arty Christmas card and maps, blueprints of escape. Love's body spread-eagled on the walls, red roads, black roads. New York, Paris, Athens, veins and nipples, loins and valleys of the abundant and mysterious world, I will come!

On the satisfyingly grainy flat of my desk in a welter of library books is my current notebook, full of poems scrawled with careful illegibility so their heresies cannot be spied (themes running heavily to death, unrequited passion and escape). I keep lists of classical music I hear and books I read and words that impress me (plangent, autodidact) not for the pleasure of lists, for little about me is orderly, but because the world of art and literature and ideas is a four-dimensional maze where I struggle a few turns from the entrance.

List of MEN WHOM I ADMIRE:

KARL MARX
LEON TROTSKY (I am not sectarian)
MOZART
GANDHI
LORD BYRON
PICASSO
MR. STEIN (My English teacher. I have written a sonnet
   sequence to him. He allows my sweated worship.)
GARIBALDI
ADLAI STEVENSON
VAN GOGH
FRANÇOIS VILLON
WILLIAM BLAKE
BUDDHA
N. BECK (ass?)
FRANZ SCHUBERT
J. S. BACH
LEONARD BERNSTEIN
TECUMSEH
MY GRANDFATHER DAVID HABENSKI

MARLON BRANDO
ALDOUS HUXLEY

I started a matching list of WOMEN WHOM I ADMIRE:

~~MY AUNT RIVA~~ (I crossed her out when she visited us
   last year and sided with my mother.)
SACAJAWEA
GEORGE SAND (I can't find any of her books in the library but I read about her in a biography of Chopin.)
ZIPPORA MENDEL (A sabra I met at the main library in
   the card catalog room. She had been a soldier and
   was studying to be an engineer.)
EMILY DICKINSON (Her poetry stuns me and she would
   understand about the attic.)

That's it. I feel embarrassed. I am tempted to add Eleanor
Roosevelt and Florence Nightingale but truthfully I am not
desirous of becoming either. Every so often I try to add to
that list, for whenever I contemplate it, it makes me feel
dreary.

Tucking my hands between my thighs for warmth, I lie
on the glider. I scarcely distinguish work and reverie, for
all my projects—poems, notes, diary, dreams, reading—
seem part of the same clandestine nether world. Does
it really exist someplace? I spend a lot of time adjusting
novels and biographies I read to invent roles for myself,
which takes ingenuity for a female Hamlet or a female
Count of Monte Cristo taxes my inventiveness. Hamlet gets
to hog the whole play, emoting in wonderful soliloquies I
can quote by heart and brandishing a sword and running
somebody through from time to time, but all Ophelia gets
is the mad scene and a mouthful of waterweed. This difficulty is a lump I cannot dislodge in the middle of my
mind. I cannot imagine myself one of those Others I am
curious about but largely ignorant of.

Girls when they talk to boys become different. The voice,
the expression, the way of laughing and talking and
standing of my girlfriends alter; they express different ideas
and even their gait changes. I do not know if I cannot or

will not do that; I only know I am afraid. Marriage does not figure in the tales I tell myself. I see it daily and it looks like a doom rather than a prize. Mother is always saying Riva was a dancer, but then she got married; Charlotte was a buyer for Crowley's, but then she got married. Glory and adventure are the prizes. And love. I despise my hunger for affection.

Loving is not exotic since I've always been in love with somebody and not infrequently somebody had a crush on me, although the two longings haven't coincided since age eight, unless you count Callie. I try not to.

I was eleven when an older girlfriend now on the streets hustling with Marcie seduced me. "Let's play house," she said and showed me how. In the next years I discovered that just about any of my girlfriends would play that game. I knew it was bad, but so were two thirds of our amusements. It did not seem worse than shoplifting from Woolworth's or looking through our mothers' drawers or letting air out of Old Man Kasmierov's tires because he called the cops when we skated on his smooth new driveway or filching cigarettes from our fathers' pockets and smoking them in the basement at school. It was casual sex, although I didn't know it was sex at all. At the same time we argued about exactly what men did to women and where babies came out. What boys did to you was real sex, scary, fascinating, murky.

Callie was my best friend from seventh through ninth grades. I seduced her in 7A. Alone of the girls she never called Sarah or me kike when she got mad. They called her a hillbilly. We went around together arm in arm talking about boys and went to the movies and cut out pictures of singers and actors to worship. I tried to do her homework regularly so she'd pass with me, but she felt more and more resentful of school. Callie talked Southern and the teachers gave her a hard time. She never had milk money or the other coins they pried out of us for savings bonds. Callie dressed what they called inappropriate. So did I, but my hand-me-downs were drab and attracted no attention unless the other white girls wanted to torture me. Callie's were from her older sister who worked as a cocktail waitress. Callie was always coming to school with or without a safety pin holding together décolleté that would in any case reveal nothing but rib cage.

Suddenly I writhe on the glider. When I was twelve I was given a new red nylon sweater for my birthday, which I wore to school. Nylon sweaters were new and cheap and bright and I was proud, for I'd never had anything like it. In the john, two girls held me down and took it off so the others could see if I was wearing falsies. The rest of the day the boys kept trying to pinch me. I was too ashamed to wear the sweater to school again.

I was stuck on Callie. I could not touch her that often without attachment, without emotion, without love. Is she good enough for me? I asked myself when I was feeling smart. Am I good enough for her? I asked when I was ashamed of my treacherous longings to get up and out of the neighborhood, when I had shown off in class, whenever I got 100 on a test she flunked. Callie was my little low down nest of belonging. I came to her with my sores and I tried to stand between her and the scorn that rapped against her daily. I nagged her to behave.

We were both running with the gang, but nobody knew of our secret attachment. What words did we have for it? It was as furtive as the fact that we both still sometimes played with our old dolls; as furtive as when Aunt Riva gave me a Valentine heart of chocolates and I shared it only with Callie, not with the gang; as furtive as the time Callie put on her mother's bra, stuffed it with tissues, painted her face and strolled along Grand River collecting wolf whistles and dragging me hunched over behind her clumping like a broken wagon.

Then one July afternoon we were playing poker for bottle caps at Dino's house, his parents being both at the bakery. I remember I was winning and in the excitement I was paying little attention until Dino and Callie went into the bedroom and shut the door. Even then I didn't worry until time passed and passed and Freddie and Sharkie started making jokes I didn't want to understand.

The game ended. I waited and waited for her. Freddie tried to get me to go upstairs with him. "Bug off," I said, beginning to feel sick with anxiety. It was getting near five and we both had to be home. Finally I banged on the door.

"Don't be a jackass," Freddie warned. "Dino'll bust you in the snoot if you barge in on him."

But they were done. Callie strolled out buttoning her blouse, while Dino did not bother to put his shirt on. He said a long good-bye at the door, kissing her sloppily, but did not offer to walk us home.

Right on the corner of Tireman by the drugstore we had a big fight. "Did you fuck him, Callie? Did you?"

"So what if I did?"

"You could get pregnant!"

"No, I can't. I never got the curse yet."

"Callie! Why did you want to do that?"

"Dino's cute. He's the cutest boy I know. You're just jealous. You like him too."

I was stung because I did have a crush on Dino. Everybody said Freddie was better-looking, but Dino was quicker in his words and his thoughts and how he moved. I associated him with my beautiful black-and-white tomcat Lightning I had till he was killed; but I could not imagine doing whatever Callie did with Lightning or Dino.

Callie took my arm. "You can have Freddie."

"I don't want Freddie! Why did you do that?"

"Let me be, Jill. I bet you could get Freddie. Easy."

"Besides, I got my periods. Last year."

Callie yanked her arm away. "You're just chicken! Just a baby chicken! But I'm growed up and I'm going to act like it."

I went home weeping through the alleys, so no one would see me. The bond between us snapped. Not only was Callie instantly absorbed in Dino, doting on him and fetching and taking his coarse lip, but she dropped me into unimportance, a bystander in her real life. A year later Dino passed her on to Sharkie, whose kid she had. Freddie wanted me to be his girl, so I was, but I wouldn't do more than neck with him.

I sit up on the glider, chafing my cold hands. Lately reading psychology books and adult novels, I found a label

for my adventuring. Am I sick? Am I depraved? "Am I an
L.?" I write in my notebook, scared to spell out lesbian.
Not only were our games wicked, it turns out, but they
were worse than regular terrifying real sex. I can hardly
believe that, but there it is in black and white, and I have
to trust books over my own unlikely and childish experiences. Perhaps I'm already crazy? I talk to myself, I make
up fantasies I care more for than my homework, and I am
not popular, blond or going steady—nothing a teenager
should be. I have never had a real date like I read about or
see on TV. I still miss Callie. Now she is changed forever
from the mischievous soulful runt who buried pheasants
with me to a housewife padding around in slip and feathered mules, a permanent whine in her voice and a puzzled
frown pulling at her wide mouth.

Francis' guitar is leaning against the wall in its battered
case, its female curves drawing my eyes. I am staring at it
in my usual vague welter of want and revulsion when the
door downstairs bangs open.

"Jillie? Are you hiding up there again? Who do you
think is going to wash your dishes for you? Santa Claus?"

When I climb down the steps, however, she is standing
at the bottom wrapped in the red kimono Francis brought
back from Japan. Her small mouth puckers with gloom. "I
can't decide what to wear. And my hair won't come right."

"It looks fine to me."

"Like a cat caught in a fan!" She puts a hand coquettishly to her throat. "You do it so well. And Charlotte's
hair will be all done. She goes to the beauty parlor every
Friday."

We spread dresses on the bed. "Say, isn't this new?"

She gives it a punishing slap. "Since when do I have a
penny to spend on myself? I picked it up on sale, ages
ago."

Letting the kimono slide from her plump shoulders she
beckons for the dress, turquoise with white flowers. I take
up the comb. "Your hair's in good form. You'll see, it'll
look fine." Page boy, handmaiden, mirror to my mother,
you see me in a role I have played since I was old enough
to sit up and say yes to her tales and complaints, in recent

years consciously disarming her wary jealousy by flattery.
Why she is jealous is opaque to me, for all I do with a
mirror is make faces. Even before my own reflection over
her head as she flirts with herself, I avert my eyes self-
consciously. I have seen my mother naked hundreds of
times, for she often calls me in to wash her back, but I
rarely see my father less than fully dressed. Even bathing
suits are unusual. In center city Detroit there is not a lot of
water around, even though when you look at the Great
Lakes on a map, we look as if we're afloat. Maybe twice a
summer we go to a beach. I am scared of the water, as of
so much else; I have all my mother's fears and a few extra.
Although I learned to swim in high school, I would feel
disloyal. Dad can swim but Mother can't. To swim would
be to desert her, clutching my hand, nervous in a foot of
water.

"So *he* wants you to share a room with the skinny blond
one." She snorts. "What's the use of going away to Ann
Arbor if you don't meet new people and make useful contacts? You never got on with your father's people anyhow."

He comes in, taking a tie from the door rack and whipping it playfully at her behind. He is impatient for the
company of men where a couple of drinks will loosen his
humor. He has strict notions what talk becomes a man:
baseball, football and hockey in their seasons, union matters and politics—if the other fellows are regular Democrats too. When he mentions Roosevelt his voice catches.
The thirties were his Armageddon. Although his work is
dirty, he puts on a suit as often as he can, for his father
taught him not to dress like a workman. "Yes, sir, we'll
beat the pants off Gene and Charlotte."

"Oh?" She turns, her eyes glinting anger. "So that's what
you'd like to do to Charlotte? I've always suspected as
much." It is impossible to tell if she is joking. Does she
know?

He gives his hair a quick rake and tosses the comb to his
bureau. "Hustle it up or they'll be asleep before we get
there." He looks well in a suit, for he is lean.

Mother chirps around him picking off lint. Suddenly her

eyes are doleful. "If Gene suggests playing for money, you put a stop to it. How much are you taking?"

He brushes ash from his lapel. "Don't worry about it."

"With the refrigerator and the TV still not paid for! It would shame us before the neighbors if they take them away!"

I stand at the front window while the Packard pulls from the driveway. My father will not drive a Ford or a GM car. He remembers how Bennett's Ford Service fired on the unemployed and how they beat the UAW people, mostly women, who came to leaflet outside the gate, breaking the back of one and fracturing another's skull. He describes the sit-down strikes at GM. We have Terraplanes, Hudsons, Studebakers until they fail one by one. "Henry Ford hated Jews," my mother whispers. "Ford was a union buster," my father mutters. History soaks into me.

Then I draw the blinds and swirl around. Empty, empty house. I run to do the dishes twice as fast as usual, so that the house is truly mine, without duty standing at my shoulder interrupting.

Done, flushed with the heat of the water, I grab a glass and clatter downstairs past the grade door that leads to the yard. Damp shadows lean on me breathing rotting potatoes as I hurry past the stout-armed furnace where firelight plays on the cement, dodging under the line where Dad's overalls drip, past his workbench and power tools, into the fruit cellar.

I love the bright jars, golden peaches, buff pears, dark berries, the quarts of tomato juice, the half-pints of strawberry and raspberry jam, although I hate the season when I help Mother put them up. *Superimposed images. September is my season for canning peaches. I like putting up the fruit I grow. I become my mother in joy. After thirty her strengths and virtues began to bloom in me, her dislike of waste, her witch's way with plants and birds and furry animals, her respect for sunlight and clean water and soil built well with compost.*

Dad's Christmas bottle of Old Grand Dad is hidden by a row of home-canned tomatoes. The damp creeps along my

arms, seeks the neck of my sweater. Taking care not to
disturb the dust I pour an inch in my tumbler, return the
bottle, return the tomato pints to their circles on the news-
paper-covered shelf, return myself tumbler in hand fleeing
the shadows upstairs.

I loll on the bumpy rust-colored couch that fills one
wall, sipping my prize and contemplating whether or not to
turn on the TV. In the curve of gradual acquisition of TVs
on our block, we were average. I was in the ninth grade.
Had we gotten it earlier, I am convinced I would not have
become a compulsive reader and thus the ability to study
my way out of here would have been closed to me. At first
we watched every night, but now it is theirs and I am
grateful to it for occupying them while I steal away into
my privacy. Still I have warm memories. During the Ke-
fauver hearings my besotted mother let me stay home from
school pretending the flu during the best parts so we could
watch together, mesmerized. "Not that the businessmen
aren't just as big crooks," she reminded me. "And the
senators are all in their pockets. All riches are robbery."
But she couldn't resist the spectacle. Our last period of
passionate rapprochement was during the recent trial of the
Rosenbergs. That scared my mother. We never spoke of it
in front of Dad. We didn't fight even about the books I
read and I stayed downstairs in the evenings. We are sure
they will be pardoned, still. They cannot kill a mother with
children over some nonsense with matchboxes. Dad does
not suspect how much radical identification she has passed
on. Not that she can argue a political position, but the
passion and loyalty she has given I can attach to a base of
reading and observation. Logic I learned from him. You
have to argue a case if you want anything out of him,
unless you proceed by indirection, as she always does.

Small room with aqua walls bedizened with pictures of
snow-capped mountains, with plaques of grapes (including
the one I was painting at day care when the Detroit race
riots came into our neighborhood), with hanging begonias
in planters shaped like puppies. The tormented pattern of
the rug struggles between runners of green and brown put

down where it has worn. Two corners are hung with knick-knack shelves of huddled china giraffes and elephants, gilded cups and saucers, wigwams, souvenirs of Mackinac Island, the Blue Hole, the Wisconsin Dells.

I march to the radio and turn on one of the benefits of Detroit, the CBC that pumps real music at me. This time I make it loud so it fills the house, an aquarium of music where I rise and sink, suddenly graceful. I leap and twirl and prance and kick until the music stops and I drop in a heap on the floor looking at the raw underside of the table. The edge of the tablecloth Buhbe crocheted hangs down all around. Would she still love me? Or would she judge me nasty as Mother does? Warm cinnamon lap, tales told all different from the way Mother told them, like turning the figures in a photograph around and seeing their backsides.

Slow and romantic violin. I dance but I am longing for *U.S.A.* which I am two thirds of the way through. Librarians so tight and clammy. That one wouldn't let me have *U.S.A.* without Mother's note. "My daughter Jill has my permission to read any book in the collections of the library. Only through wide and uncensored reading has a young person's mind . . ." I learned to forge notes by seventh grade, when Callie and I began to cut school occasionally.

I finish the bourbon, shuddering as I subside on the couch. I have a conviction that mixed drinks are inauthentic. The worse the bourbon stings my throat, the more adult it seems. He will be tall and brilliant and terribly witty. I love the word urbane, although I am not sure exactly what it means. "Bourbon is urbane," I say aloud, dressing him in a romantic ruffled white shirt and dark pants as his eyes focus on me intense and molten with an electrifying stare. The concert ends in applause and I switch off the radio. . . . I saw *To Have and Have Not* four times. That's how it ought to be, both the man and the woman wanting each other and dueling a little and making wisecracks but showing bravery and loyalty. I want to be brave. Maybe I can add Lauren Bacall to my list. I adore her. Yes, I'll do that, but not now. Silence chills the house.

The ceiling creaks into footsteps. The wind whines at the panes, trying the catches. I want my notebooks and my novel but I'm suddenly scared of the attic.

In my mind the tall and handsome stranger in the ruffled shirt is still standing there with smoldering eyes but suddenly he is close up and turns into Freddie that time he came in while I was here alone ironing my father's shirts. I see his face hard and angry and I remember the terror that gripped me on the kitchen floor when I realized he wasn't going to listen to my firm loud nos that time. Terror twitched me violently as a bad shock and I bucked under his weight, his hand fumbling at my breasts, hurting me. I punched him in the ear as hard as I could and then I twisted free and grabbed the hot iron. He backed off then. I still don't like to remember his face. How can I find any link between the music that stirs my emotions and the violent grappling that doesn't? Something's wrong with me.

Will no one ever love me? I am single and perverse. My fingers tingle but I don't know if I am stung with loneliness or overflowing to reach out in abundance. The squat black shape of the phone draws me. I can't call Howie because it's Friday night. The receiver sings in my hand. My few girlfriends are out on dates. I dial my own number except for two digits changed at random. Ring. Ring. Where, in what front hall or beside a bed, on a desk or kitchen wall? Harsh sound alerting their air.

"Hello?" Male voice, deep and a little too loud.

No matter. "Hello? Hello, I love you." Down with the receiver. My face burns my cold fingers. I am crazy.

I pin my hair under Francis' old wool cap. I have been growing my black hair over protest for two years and it comes partway down my back and ties on my head in a perfect knot. I slip on my suede jacket and stand a moment on the porch, checking the time and that I have my house key. If I get back by ten thirty, they will never know I have been out. My neighborhood is supposed to be dangerous, but I go about as I choose. I figure I run fast. In jeans and jacket and Francis' cap I pass for a boy. I know that too is somehow wicked but it gives me a free pass through these blocks.

I am off and running toward Callie's flat over the bake-shop on Joy Road. I don't bother to call. Callie will be there with her baby and it's much too early for Sharkie to come home. I'm ashamed of myself, running to what is left of her. She makes me sad, but the house I always think I want to myself makes me taste loneliness harsh as the bourbon. Callie will sulk at first but I'll listen to her complain about Sharkie and I'll dandle and admire baby Marilyn and tell Callie all the dirt I can remember about kids in school. I'll turn somersaults to stir her out of her sulk. I wonder if Callie has ever figured out what I learned out of books, that according to them, doctors and psychiatrists and judges, we were lovers and could go to jail. I'm not sure she remembers, except that sometimes she looks at me in a certain shrewd skeptical way that makes me feel as if all my weaknesses are hanging out. I am walking slowly but I go on. It's better than being alone, I guess.

THREE

A Round of Paints

Every day for two weeks it has rained. If I step off the sidewalk onto a lawn or curbside plot, the ground squishes. The attic roof leaks, maddeningly into a pail. Mold grows between my fingers and I cannot decide on anything. The dormitory forms are still downstairs, only half filled out. Almost I could give up. Do what they want. Drop my fantasies in the trash. Give up, give in and be loved. I do not know if they will let me have the two hundred I still lack, for I cannot interrupt their fighting and painting to find out.

Spring rouses the maniac painter in both my parents, but the major blame for the last week can be laid on Leo, who filled up the basement with cartons of paint in gallon cans. He is storing some of his inventory here, as it turns out not to be as easy as he had expected to move paint. I wonder if it is hot, but that suspicion never touches my parents. They are pleased to buy enough paint to float a barge at what Leo calls wholesale. With all that paint sitting in boxes, they can use any color they please.

Mother won turquoise walls for the living room over

Dad's light green but he used the light green in their bedroom, which made Mother furious as she says she can't
wear green. He says he didn't know she wore the bedroom
walls. My multiuse bedroom has been done by their mutual
choice in robin's-egg blue. They now fight fiercely over the
kitchen. Mother wants a lighter yellow with Chinese-red
cabinets, while he wants beige and blue. The kitchen has
become their sticking point. Neither will budge.

Today at last the clouds tear into high gauze and the sun
stands over Detroit like a daisy of fire. My parents spend
their Sunday morning fighting about the kitchen while I
hide upstairs, studying irregular Spanish verbs. Then I hear
my father walking over my head on the roof just before
Mother calls me down.

She has shoved her crisp hair under a fuchsia and yellow
bandanna—I swear half the clothes she wears she buys
with choked rage—and grinds the vacuum sweeper back
and forth on the rug. She shuts off the motor, letting the
sausage bag deflate with a sigh, and points to two steaming
buckets and a pile of rags. "Get started on the porch windows. You can reach the front-room windows if you stand
on the steps. Go on, get moving. Lollygagging around
while others work!"

My method of doing housework is to concentrate so
hard on a stirring tale in my head that I hardly notice what
I'm up to. It has advantages and disadvantages. With windows it works fine, for I note subconsciously when I have
got them clean while I imagine what Mr. Stein *should* have
said to me when I told him I got the scholarship to the
university. I know he knows I have a crush on him and in
my sourer moments I suspect him of enjoying it, but at
least nobody has seen the poems I have written to him.

> He is a needle, shiny, deeply thrust
> into my mind. My plans are broad and hard
> but blow like milkweed's silk seeds in a gust
> of wind before his will. I have no guard . . .

and on and on. He told me I had to stop writing what he
called free verse and start writing sonnets.

"What?" I am startled back.

Dad has come down the high ladder from the roof. Rubbing his wind-reddened neck, he sits on the steps to smoke. "Stiff. . . . Damn it, forgot the hammer. Go up and get it, would you?"

The dirty pink rag, Mother's old panties, hangs limp and steaming from my hand. "Up the ladder? To the roof?"

He grins with slight irritation. "It won't walk down."

"I'm sorry, but, you know . . . Climbing makes me sick."

"You give in to yourself." His eyes weigh on me, his teeth lock in his jaw. "You and your mother! Get it down."

"It's just . . ." Judge, mercy! "Maybe you could get it later?"

"No!" His big gnarled hands clasp on his knees as he glares.

He wanted a boy. At twelve I made the grand try, rowed him around twilight-curdled mosquito bogs, impaled the worm flesh, pulled hooks from my hair, stared at the bobber and itched. For months on end I sat itching and sweating and trying for a poker face, straight wooden tightlipped virtue, Robin to Batman, a real goy boy. I tell you, I tried.

His knuckles bleach as he grinds his fists on his knees. In a moment he will explode. I scuttle to the base of the ladder. "Please. Maybe I can do it later?"

He rises and I scramble up the first six rungs. One foot, then the other up beside it. My palms sweat against the wood. Nearer now to the chalky grooves of asbestos siding. Don't look down. I got all my fears from her and he never makes her do this! The ladder wobbles, swaying. The rungs bruise my breasts as I lean into it. My calves stretch taut to aching. A cramp: smash on the sidewalk below, legbone jutting through. Now I am up at the roof level, but how do I step over?

"I'm holding the ladder." His voice from right below. "Just walk onto the roof. Go ahead!"

Afraid he will shake the ladder in annoyance, I scuttle over onto the roof. It slants but I find I can rise slowly, tipsily. I am just above the level of the second floor on both sides and Le Roy next door, who's in tenth grade gapes out at me. I swagger down the roof tree to the chimney. There's the hammer. Nonchalantly I pick it up and swing it. I wish I could fly off into the big old elm tree in the yard, its buds greenish. Up here the neighborhood elms are impressive, an alternate spirit world above the streets. I wish I were a kite and the wind would lift me.

If I were a dead leaf thou mightest bear;
If I were a swift cloud to fly with thee;

My fifteenth year was Shelley's. He was the first poet I loved, before Walt Whitman. Before Keats. Before Emily.

"Jill! What's happening?"

Shit. What goes up must come down. I creep to the edge where below me the world rushes away in a cold waterfall of dizziness. He stands waiting. Closing my eyes I back into space, groping with my foot for the rung. Vacation in the mountains of Virginia, blue haze dissolving the horizon. On the ground Mother clutched her bead purse to her head shrieking, "You'll kill her!" Above me on the fire tower Dad tried to twist my paw loose. Halfway and petrified, I wished the mountain would close over this monkey in the middle.

I freeze partway down with the hammer clasped in one hand and my feet stuck to a rung. "Have you got it?" he calls. "Don't drop it. Remember, I'm holding the ladder."

"Coming!" Voice of chalk.

He takes the hammer as I step off, making a motion as if to slap me on the back. "Bet you'll be glad that old roof won't leak on you anymore."

My knees wobble. Where is the medal for cowards? I should be grateful instead of locked in my weird fears. "It'll be much better."

"It's nippy in spite of the sun. Let's see if we can rustle up some coffee." Buddies together, we go around to the grade door, avoiding the front room where Mother is still puffing and prancing like a toy dragon. He will protect me now for a while. I have paid my way.

"Dad . . ." I pour the coffee from the percolator into his

special tall blue mug. "I really want to go to the university, but I'm two hundred short. Are you going to be able to give it to me, do you think?"

He frowns, silent a long time. I don't dare ask anything else but sit and twitch. Finally he says, "Hubie's really sending Donna there?"

I nod fervently. He knows, but does he believe what he knows? "Donna always did better in school than Estelle." Her boring straight-laced older sister, married and living in Detroit. "Donna got a scholarship. Like me."

He pokes the applications. "You haven't finished filling these out."

"I thought I should wait to hear if I can go. If I tell Donna I'll room with her and then I cancel, she might end up with just anybody." Why do I always feel like an actor if I ask help from him? The role is awkward and shames me. When it all comes down, he has the real power. It's his money. Mother asks before she spends, but he never does. It took me years to understand that, because Mother seemed so strong when I was little. She was the sun, source of warmth and nourishment and life itself; all other planets and lights bobbed around her. Why should she lie to him and wheedle and plead? I couldn't comprehend it. Why was she strong before me but weak before him?

"Go ahead and tell her you'll share a room with her. We'll manage it."

I grab the forms and take them off to fill out, before he can change his mind.

When I come home from work Tuesday, Dad's car is in the garage. Home so early? All the furniture is back in place and Mother is dusting. She nods to me with a meek stricken air, her mouth pursed, her eyes lowered. Yet I feel a guarded smile in her silence. She dusts with coy gestures, as if resting with secret satisfaction in her plumpness. Smell of fresh paint. Did she finally get her way on the kitchen?

I don't see Dad. I walk to the kitchen door. "Jesus!"

She is at my shoulder instantly, pinching my upper arm. "*Shhh*! He's in the basement. He came home at noon in a temper, and then he did it. Don't say a word in front of him!"

Our cabinets are Chinese red, all right, and that wall is yellow. The wall by the driveway is pink. The back wall is buff. The wall behind the table is wildly striped with broad bands of turquoise, red, pink, blue, green, and white and black enamels. I cannot help giggling and suddenly she laughs with me, covering her mouth with her hand. "That man is a riot!" she says admiringly. "That man!"

General Custer High School: brick monolith, cold red whale where this Jonah grows thin on blubber. Bog-water soup stink of the lunchroom. Musty odor of the auditorium. Sportsmanship Assembly, our principal rolling his false teeth around in his mouth as he gurgles, "Boy-yahs and Gur-ruls," no more fights with broken bottles after the games. Bells for the period jangle off the puce ceiling and battered locks. Here boredom is sliced by the hour and the room and the tracking system. Here you take Boredom 1_x (which means you're tracked for college), followed by Boredom 2_x, and if you pass all the tests you get to move on to Advanced Boredom. Here if you ever, ever tell the truth you will be mocked, failed and sent to the principal's office. Note passed through me in civics: "Don't you think Jim is a doll? Did you ever go steady? Your friend, Wilma." Answer passed back through me. "Jim who? Yes once for 3 days with Bill McIver. Your friend, Sue." *The Custer Custodian* windowless office. There I, news editor, sit on a table swinging my legs and gossiping to put off going home.

Zipping my jacket, I push on the heavy double doors. The sky drips. The flag flaps at the top of its pole in the wet wind, clanking the ropes and metal rings that raise and lower it. Cars pull squealing from the lot and shoot into traffic. As I wait for my bus, a girl beside me shouts, "G'wan, ya never did! Don't hand me that BS." Blue lids, a silver streak in her brown hair, green nails. Hard bulge of calf above spike heels. She carries a freshman lit book, but I must look years younger. I feel barely female beside her. Like me she is protesting but I have created a gap I can

cross now only with difficulty. Still I am closer to her than
to those confident girls in pastel sweater sets and pleated
skirts who go steady with young men with orthodontically
corrected white teeth and campaign posters and button-
down shirts and blazers. I work with those girls on library
staff and other stupid extracurricular activities I have volunteered for since I figured out you were supposed to, to
get into college, but I don't know how to chat with them.
When I approach, they fall silent. I am the school radical
and they don't know what to make of me, except fun when
they can. I know they are comely, those boys, but they
move me no more than a handsome greyhound might. The
bland neat couples move off toward the parking lot or the
bus that goes west into the more middle-class section the
school also serves.

Books under one arm I hang from a strap near the back
door. At the back boys are shouting dirty cracks. One
sings:

I got a gal in Singapore,
          baby, honey,
I got a gal in Singapore,
She's nothing but a two-bit whore,
          honey, baby, mine.

I got a gal lays on a rock,
          baby, honey,
I got a gal lays on a rock,
All she does is suck my cock,
          honey, baby, mine.

The girl with the silver streak is close to tears shrieking,
"Shut your fucking mouth, Jerry, or I'll slap it shut!"

I hunch to my books. Why do they hate girls who do?
My daydreams twist like knives in me. I try not to fantasize about going away to school, not to blur it with false
expectations. What have I agreed to in Donna? Will she
spy on me to her parents and mine? Uncle Hubie is a
bully. The way he looks at Mother and me is chilling. I

have made common cause with Donna at weddings and funerals.

I haven't seen Donna since we were fourteen at Uncle Floyd's funeral, the only son-in-law and a miner. In the anthracite mine, they were working too far under the river and the river broke through. Four of them were killed. The river filled the mine and threw all my other cousins and second cousins and first cousins once removed, all the Welsh kin, out of work. I remember Aunt Elaine hunched over with grief as if she were sick to her stomach.

My thirteenth summer, Donna and I were in Cold Springs together. We climbed the mountain over town. We slept upstairs in an attic room and giggled all night. We swam in the old quarry and had supper just the two of us with Aunt Elaine and Uncle Floyd in Cokeville where he showed us the mine entrance and the great machines and the shifts pouring in and out. He fed us venison. When he was not working, he loved to be up on the mountain among the trees. Donna was small and blond with skin that burned in half an hour and seemed to tear on every fence we scaled, on every blackberry bush we picked from. I was always leading her into temptation, but I remember that she always went. I remember her crying when Uncle Hubie scolded her for getting blackberry juice on her white dress and for falling into a creek in her pink dress, but I don't remember her ever saying what would have been true, "Jill made me do it." I liked to show off before her intense blue eyes, the color of the flowers of the chicory that grows wild in vacant lots.

I loathe visiting my father's father, the old patriarch in his Cold Springs house built in 1889, where he reigns over the daughter who got stuck home to take care of him. Aunt Mary is now fifty-five and my grandfather eighty, but he still walks a mile to town and back every day although now the town has grown out to them. In recent years I have had the excuse of working summers and vacations. My father's family look down on Donna's mother as a Catholic. Uncle Hubie was working on the line at Flint Chevrolet when he met Aunt Louella, but now he is a foreman. He is on the side of management, so my father and Uncle Hubie argue some. Uncle Hubie bought a house in a white neighborhood. It is small but brick. I wonder if Donna has turned into one of those girls in pastel sweater sets.

When I walk in from school, one of the neighbors, Mrs. O'Meara, sits at the kitchen table with Mother. Mother reads palms on occasions when *she* chooses, but she will read tea leave on request. Before the gaudily striped wall Mother and Mrs. O'Meara lean forward with the earthen teapot from Buhbe between them, its bulging sides like the coat of a tabby, while around its broad base like off-spring the "interesting" cups are clustered.

"Chickie, have a cup of nice hot tea? It's Darjeeling."

"But will he marry her?" Mrs. O'Meara whines. She wants Mother's full attention. Small dogeyes wait. Mrs. O'Meara is as short as Mother. Like children playing tea party their feet do not reach the floor but curl around the chair rungs.

"There's no stopping him, he's that dead set on her." Mother sits straight, her shoulders thrusting back the chair.

"But if he leaves me I'll rattle around in that house."

"Youth and age! You've had your life." Mother fixes her sternly. "But if you made a little apartment upstairs so they'd have their own place, that'd be different. They can't be too eager to shell out for the rents the dirty landlords are gouging out of folks these days."

"Pearl! That's it." Mrs. O'Meara even smiles at me. "A little apartment upstairs. I could fix it up cute—"

"Time to put the chicken on." Mother bounces up. "Keep me posted." When her patience runs out, it disappears all at once. She is already slicing onioins, the knife flashing.

"Er, Pearl . . ." Mrs. O'Meara pauses at the head of the back stairs. When women come to consult Mother, they always come in the back way. "What happened to your kitchen walls? Who did that?"

"My oldest son Leo's gone into the paint business. He was just trying it out. Of course we'll paint over it this weekend."

"Trying it out?" Mrs. O'Meara stares at the striped wall hoping for some piece of gossip. Mother is as out of place in this neighborhood as a tawny lioness. She will not even follow Mrs. O'Meara's glance, only nodding matter-of-factly as she slices.

When Mrs. O'Meara has eased herself out, Mother shakes her head. "Silly old fool! I never tried to keep my sons tied to my apron strings. A son has got to go out on his own."

A daughter too. I do not contradict her, but Leo marries every two years. As Mother screamed at Francis last time he was home, he's stuck on "hanging your hat up with nothing but tramps and tarts."

I say only, "I'm going upstairs to study."

"Don't you want lunch?" The knife goes snick, snick.

"Ate a sandwich at school."

"Have another cup of tea while I put the chicken on."

"No thanks." The paint fumes are still strong, saturating even the attic stairs. I climb slowly, savoring the ascent above the house into my privacy. My eyes rise level with the floor and through the open door I see it, a broad yellow wall. My glider has been pushed to one side, my books piled haphazardly, my papers (rifled? read?) in a heap, my room turned inside out and painted a shrieking yellow. I leap to the doorway, sick but unbelieving. No. We are so locked in combat anything can serve as assault one on the other, presents, meals, even paint. Then I flung my school-books across the room and plummet down the steps.

She swirls from the oven to face me, her face tight with an imitation smile. "Doesn't it look cheerful? I worked all morning to surprise you."

"Like hell. How dare you take over the only thing I have?"

"Don't scream at me. Any normal person would thank me. Hiding up there day and night."

"Damn you! You'll do anything to hurt me. You try to eat me alive!"

"Don't talk to me that way, you little worm! There'll be no more rooting in dirty books like a pig in its sty!"

"You have no right! Surprise—knife in the back."

"Yowl! Yowl like a cat. You walk around with your head up your ass and your ears full of shit, you complete klutz, and then you wonder why you don't know anything!"

"I'll never forgive you for this! Never!"

I duck but not quick enough. The heel of her hand strikes me on the mouth, jolting my head back. "Forgive me? You poor blind ugly slut! You dirty little gutter worm living on your own shit!"

Crying already, stupid with rage and self-pity, I turn, jamming my hands over my ears and rush out. Running till my side jabs, then walking block after block, teeth chattering, sucking my swollen lip and clenching my fists, finally I wear my anger numb. Then indifferent and cold to the pit of my brain, cold through all my knotted muscles, I turn and walk home. I will get away. I will not give in to them. I will get away.

FOUR

Wherein We Learn That Snow
Leopards Bare Many Tales

WITH THE KEY I just signed for at the desk in the
lobby clotted with families and luggage among the rubber
plants, for the first time I enter the small double room.
Light from the courtyard pours between draperies of tomato burlap, roughening the texture of the white walls and
casting shadows from the plain blond furniture and the
heap of boxes and suitcases.

Mother bustles past to drop her load. "Well! So tiny.
Looks like a cell, chickie. You'd think for what they
charge . . ."

I start, a shock of instant contact meeting my cousin's
stare. For another moment she stands rigid in the corner
where she must have backed at our noisy approach, small
and flaxen with a hard pallor (why do I remember in the
zoo one spring afternoon with Howie meeting through the
intervening bars a snow leopard pacing alone round and
round?), before her high voice bursts from her frantic as a
trapped bird in inane family greetings.

Dad rumples his hair in disappointment. "Hubie and

Louella left? Kind of thought we might see them. Have supper. I said we should get an early start."

"That's your quilt on the bottom bunk?" Mother beams at Donna but the poppies of her hat jiggle ominously. "Of course you'll want to change around each month, to be fair."

Mother wants to unpack me, but parting makes Dad fidget. While they argue, Donna bats between them, joking nervously, and when we are left alone laughs even more frantically, trying so desperately to present a scatterbrained simple blithe facade that I am puzzled. She wears a little gold cross that Sunday on her pale blue sweater, but the next morning it is gone. The only time I find it thereafter is when I am rummaging in her top drawer for a clean pair of socks to borrow.

That first week we tiptoe around each other cautious as dynamiters. Her facade breaks off one brittle shard at a time. Two forces free Donna. One is me. I am a force. A power of joy moves through me those early weeks in the realm of my own sweet volition. I have grown a foot overnight. I sit up till two studying. When I finish my classwork, I read hers just to share, to gobble everything. I run to lectures, my face burning with the passion to listen, to consume, to take every course in the fat catalog simultaneously forever. I will learn French and Zoology, Chinese Thought and Physical Anthropology, The Hundred Years War and the World of Cervantes. Intimate rain caresses me. No one scolds me into golashes. I run bareheaded through streets pelted with bright minnow leaves swimming in the gutters. I stride past the dormitories, lamps blazing from each room as the huge buildings steam against the wind-buffeted lowering sky like ships of light, and no authority minds what I do as long as I am back by curfew. The bars are gone. I have leapt from my cage and no one shall entice me into a narrow room again. My energy makes Donna smile.

The second force? Her own desperation. I feel it as an electric crackling that builds till it burns across the gap like a voltage experiment in physics, when she cries at me, "Oh, you don't know! You don't know me. If you did, you'd walk out of this room!"

That is a sharp hook. I narrow my eyes at her astride her desk chair like Marlene Dietrich in *The Blue Angel*, with her corduroy skirt rucked up to show her beautiful legs—Donna's, not Marlene's—and I know I am being lured to ask questions. How delightful, that someone should want me to pay attention. By the fourth week I do not think of her as my cousin any longer; I have begun to think of her as my conspirator. We are poor, we are on scholarships, we are ill-dressed, we take the hard courses, we come from the wrong cities and addresses, we will not be rushed by sororities. On the rest of the corridor respectability is counted in the number of cashmere sweater sets and boyfriends with Greek addresses a virtuous girl keeps under or near but not on her bed. You go nine tenths of the way and get pinned. Donna always manages to have dates on the weekends but whatever she is looking for, the Kens and Bobs who have asked her out so far are not it. How am I suddenly aware of caste lines on our corridor? Donna is educating me in her awarenesses, as I in mine. She describes herself as a socialist, since last week.

Our talk is full of "musts" and "must nots," as in, "We must learn to act authentically with the opposite sex" (me), to Donna announcing right now, "We must get ourselves decent bras."

A decent bra in 1953 is nearer to an armor breastplate than to a silky froth of lingerie. It holds the breasts apart, forward and out as if setting up a couple of moon shots. We do not have such objects but Donna has it in mind that we need them. Buying them is beyond our means. I regularly steal food for us to supplement dormitory rations, but I can't see how to swipe bras which are kept under the counter downtown and doled out one by one to be tried. I have checked the situation, and in the process, with a resurgence of my old gang skill, swiped two sweaters, a black wool for me with a turtleneck and long sleeves and a navy blue for Donna. I did not think of them as being for either of us in particular, since we both wear the same sizes

in everything but bras and shoes, but Donna insisted ownership be established. I will work on her, I think. I lean
toward the communal. I would like everything in the room
to be both of ours.

Donna wears her new navy turtleneck, eyeing her neat
pale self in the mirror as she flattens the sleek bowl of her
moon-colored hair. "Devastating. If only it was cashmere."

I learn. Next time I will steal the right kind. I want to
please her. Pleasure makes her avid and fierce. Now she is
peering with a frown as she repeats, "We must have decent
bras."

I perch on the ledge by the casement windows open to
the gentle rain, feeling a sensual melancholy like a drug
cooling my veins. "Mmm," I say, "I can't make those
stores for a bra, ma Donna."

She looks at her watch, graduation present from a
former boyfriend. I think she graduated from him too.
"Almost midnight. We'll hit the laundry rooms."

"I don't know." I turn from the rain to face her. "Hitting a store is one thing."

"From those rich bitches? I'd love to hit them for real."

It's expulsion if we're caught, but that's beside the point.
I appreciate her class hatred that sharpens mine, but I wish
she didn't covet so fiercely what the others have. " 'Things
are in the saddle and ride man,' " I quote, but Donna
says, "Buggery! You wouldn't walk all hunched over if you
had a decent bra."

I set the ground rules: we can only rob girls whose wash
reveals their class to be very affluent and only if they have
on the line more of what we take. We can only use other
houses than our own. (Four houses connect through their
basements to each other. The outer doors are all booby-
trapped with alarms after ten thirty.) That last rule is for
fear somebody may recognize her stuff in our subsequent
washes. Down into the bowels of the hill we glide in our
bathrobes carrying laundry bags and books, as if to wash
and study. Donna takes on a bright tight look, her eyes
squinted behind her blue-rimmed glasses, her lips pulled
back to show her small good teeth. Where did she get good
teeth in our family? When I opened my mouth at the

physical examination for freshmen, the dentist yelped with glee and three times every week I have dental appointments for students to practice on my poor child's rotten and broken molars.

"Want to see *The Wild One* tomorrow night?"

She shakes her head no. "Going out with Bob."

"What for?" We check out a laundry meeting all our specs, except for size: 38A. Too bad. "You don't even like him."

"What's that got to do with it? He's better than nothing."

"I saw you necking with him outside," I say tentatively.

"So? I'm not fucking him, if that's what you think."

That she might hadn't occurred to me. "Why shouldn't you, if you want to?" I brazen it out, although the idea of her touching anybody she doesn't even like is ugly to me.

"You mean that?" She inspects another row of washing. "Name tags sewn in. I can get them out with a razor. This is your size. I thought you'd be involved with some guy yourself by now."

"Me? I wouldn't know how to go about it." I angle between her and the door, keeping watch.

"You aren't a virgin. You! You aren't!"

I shrug. "Now, if you could lose your cherry by thinking about it or reading about it or even writing about it . . ."

"I never expected it." She is disappointed in me. "Of course I'm a virgin."

She is lying. I am embarrassed. I feel as if I have failed her by lacking experience and failed her if she must lie to me. I say nothing but lead on to the next laundry room.

Football Saturday in late October, the dormitories, the hills of town are emptied. From the stadium two miles away the rhythmic shouts rise, a great roar going up through the brilliant air and jangling the nerves, suggesting to me who has already sampled the hard cider I carry on my hip a human sacrifice out of *The Golden Bough*. I also carry my notebook, while Donna totes rye bread, cheese and pears. We head into the Arboretum. Donna was here last night making out with Vincent, her newest. Across a ravine, brick apartments for married students show be-

tween salmon-leaved oaks. We sold our football tickets to
buy records. I have just discovered Bartok and what one of
us bites into, the other chews and swallows.

"In that black turtleneck and a good bra, you look sexy
today," she tells me.

I shrug. Making me over. Broad leaves webbed brown
on gold, scarlet slivers drift over the ruts of the dirt road.
"I don't want to get trapped in that kind of female caring.
To be blind with self-centeredness."

"Listen!" She stops short. In the sun her eyes are alcohol
flames. "If you aren't aware with your body, you might as
well die. You are self-conscious, but in a bad shy way."

"I'm two months old. I was just born and you're good
for me."

She lets out her high barking laugh. "Me? I'm the original corrupting influence."

Corrosive maybe. We strike against each other chipping
off the useless debris of our childhoods. With her tense
never quite completed motions she hurries down this road.
She has so little color in her skin and hair she should look
wan, but her pallor has an edge. "We define each other."

"Let's feed each other. I'm tired of walking." She points
out a path. "There's the plateau, for couples in a hurry. On
fine nights you can't walk without stepping on them."

We leave the road to climb a hill. Above the shrubs the
top is treeless, stiff with brown grass that crackles under us.
We pass the jug, as I watch small brown ants busy as rush
hour around their anthill. Mother from early childhood
trained me to see, to listen, to notice. She considered it
immoral not to be sharply observant, and used to make me
describe what I'd seen in detail to her. Together in secret
we would imitate how acquaintances talked. In recent
years appalled at my adolescence, my skimpy but undeni-
ably female growth, she retreated to instructions to chop
down curiosity, hang back, blind myself. I took refuge in
books and fantasies and now Donna is tearing at those
paper walls. As I realize I have truly left home, I can
remember how close Mother and I once were.

"You had something to show me," she murmurs.

I glanced at my notebook in the dead grass. "Not important."

"I could kick you, Stu. You want me to listen and I'm willing. Use the moment."

I take up the notebook, knowing I delay as much from fear as from modesty. "Called 'Day is for faces.'" I clear my throat and launch into a fast embarrassed gallop:

Over the abyss of each self
the face stretches its drumhead. . . .
Children with sticky fingers behind old sofas
whisper false secrets.
Slaughtered friends are strung up
like joints of beef in a freezer. . . .

I have stopped riming. Immediately the lid has blown off. Sweat beads my back as I race through the section where voices cry their confessions: the funeral of our common uncle, stealing, spying. Then:

In a house of cinders and bottle glass my alleywise friend
played father to me on her mother's bed.
Afterwards I washed my hands and stared in the mirror.
When I got home, waited for Mother to read me like a
    palm.
I knelt. "O God I won't ever again."
Till the next afternoon.

As I finish the poem, what Donna says, opening her eyes with her hand shadowing them, is, "I'm not a virgin, Stu."

I sit up, wondering if I should act surprised. "With Bob or what was his name?"

"With my own sister's husband."

"Jim?" His grinning freckled face. Him? "But how?"

She clenches her hands on the clumps of rough grass. Her voice rises muffled. "I came to stay with them in Detroit while she was having her baby. While she was in the hospital, Stu!"

In my own city these things occurred while I was in the

attic reading Freud. Estelle is older but I remember her
with blond angel curls, bouncing a blue ball. Perhaps I
recall not Estelle in the flesh but Uncle Edward the minister's home movies in which forever as in the mind of God,
Estelle pirouettes, in which Donna red-faced and grubby
drags a crippled doll and as she bursts into tears, her panties fall down: all uncles and aunts guffaw. "But how? Did
he just ask you, or what?"

"When we were making their bed." Quick rough sobs
shake her back. "I worship Estelle, I really do!" Her face
twists. Brown mascara stains her cheeks like rust as I try to
comfort her.

"Don't cry!" My hands are catcher's mitts. What was
story is suddenly factual pain. "You didn't mean to hurt
her. She doesn't know, right?"

"Isn't that worse? She loves me, because she doesn't
know."

"Then it doesn't hurt her," I say leadenly.

Sitting up she blows her nose. "But it happened again."

Capsized. In that moment a blunt weariness wilts my
bones. Air of damp baby, baby skin, baby hair. Her anguish has worn through and with keen appetite she pre-
pares fresh revelations. That electric springiness, the pain,
the turning, are equally real. "How?" I ask.

"Last summer, when they were visiting. Mother and Estelle went shopping that day, while Jim and I stayed with
baby. Jim came to my room. Afterward, he made me
promise I'd never tell Estelle and I'd never let him do it
again."

"Did you?"

"No." A small crooked grin. "We haven't been alone
since. And he's short-tempered with me. Stu, he blames
me."

"He has no right. He should never have done it if he was
going to make you feel guilty."

"He used to tease me. Call me baby doll. But Estelle has
always been wonderful. Mother never told me about periods. All she ever said about sex was, 'Men are beasts.'
When I got acne, it was Estelle who took me right to the
doctor to fix it."

"Donna, listen." Gripped by vision I squat. "Sex isn't dirty. Your brother-in-law is a hypocrite, and you had a bad first experience, that's all."

"It wasn't so bad. I mean during it. Afterward I felt like a piece of garbage. I even got religious again. I went to confession and I did almost everything Father Ross told me to, for penance. I got bored though. The second time I didn't bother. I don't believe in that crap anyhow."

"We'll be the good family for each other. We'll close ranks and help each other and undo the lies they teach us."

Her face has dried to a harsh whiteness, though her lids are swollen. "You don't think I'm rotten?"

"No more than me. We have to find a morality that works for us." Lolling back I touch my notebook and glow with power like a successful shaman. My poem changed the world and I am not alone.

But she is watching me with a little smile. "I'm glad I wasn't in your poem along with that Callie girl. I thought I might be."

It is as if I fall thirty feet as I sit. "In the poem?"

"Because of that time—you remember—when we slept upstairs together at Grandpa's—when I was fourteen and you were thirteen." She is watching me warily, her eyes large but that little smile not quite under control.

I know immediately that she is right. I can't tell her the truth, that I plain forgot. I think she would be insulted. I can't believe I seduced my own cousin during summer vacation, but at thirteen I didn't think of it as sex. It was just good old dirty fun. But she knows it's serious; she learned that too. We've both read psychology books. "I don't think I'm really a lesbian," I say meekly. I haven't the faintest idea what I am. An idiot who can forget seducing her cousin, obviously. I'm lucky she didn't squeal on me to the whole family. I'd be in prison or reform school or the loony bin.

"Of course not," she says soothingly. "I don't think you're really sick. But you must have some experience with men. It's lopsided. You started off wrong."

"I haven't done that in years. I had lots of boyfriends, in

the gang. I necked with Freddie a lot. And he tried to rape me once." Some credentials. The truth is I don't feel particularly feminine as defined by Mother and the girls in the dorm. I don't feel male either. I must be something else altogether, like a giraffe maybe. Who can tell the sex of that oak tree scattering acorns on the slope below us? The idea of being fertilized by the wind has a certain appeal when I make my way through the crowd of couples slobbering good night in the courtyard of the dormitory every night, as I return from a walk, a movie or the library.

"You just lack confidence," she pronounces, biting into a pear once she has inspected it. "If you act attractive, everybody treats you that way." She eats only fruit that satisfies her exacting standards. I eat the rest. "You eat everything mushy and battered that isn't squashed flat."

"Ah, but I draw the line at mold. We all have our principles." The blue of the sky is dimming. The air grows heavier and colder.

"Principles," she mutters. "I don't want to keep seeing Vincent. He's a little fascist. I have to act stupid with him."

"I don't think we should have anything to do with people we have to pretend with."

"I hate to stay in weekends."

"There are fourteen thousand men on this campus."

"What an idea." Breaking open the cheese, she tosses me a piece. "You know how to cheer me up. . . . He'll call tonight. You answer, say I'm out. Be evasive. Imply I'm on a date."

"Why not just tell him you don't want to see him?"

"That won't do. No, do it my way, won't you?"

"Okay," I mumble, nervous at the prospect. Giddy with cider we talk, we lie and talk and talk till the sun is a bonfire at the foot of our hill and we are chilly and hungry for even a dorm supper.

FIVE

What Women Are Made For

M ORNINGS WE LOAD our trays with desiccated eggs, toast, a pat of unidentifiable jelly, bitter coffee. Too sleepy to talk we bolt our food. Julie, who has a single room down the hall and does not eat breakfast, joins us for coffee. Then we hasten together out to the muddy path that runs above the women's athletic field. Clatter and clank of dishes, women pouring from every door to join the clotted processional downhill and up again. The wind at the brink blows the last wisps of sleep away, leaving us cranky and raw from late studying.

I trot wagging my tail to offer my themes to Professor Bishop. Long face running well up into his scarce hair, long liver-spotted hands whose deft red sarcasms dot my papers, he is the dyspeptic angel who guards the gate to my paradise of words. To seduce his wearily malicious surfeit of freshman prose. I tell him tales of my childhood. He assigns a theme on privilege: I write on Father. He assigns a theme on freedom: I write of Mother. "Amusing." "Astringent." The circus of my upbringing stands open for your delectation, Mr. Bishop, although my clowns turn somersaults in terror of your scorn, not at all sure why we are funny.

Slimy grappling in zoology lab. The diagrams in the manual are precise, but my frog holds only eggs. We are handed live frogs to pith their brains. My partner jabs nervously. Blood oozes on the frog's spotted back as it screams, kicking long and distorted like a saint from El Greco, in my partner's clumsy fist. Taut with fury I take the frog to drive in the needle, my hand wet with slime and blood. Proud of my successful brutality, I look up to see Donna charging out the door, the lanky lab assistant fluttering behind. "It's the waste," she says later. "Killing them and nobody learned a thing. Better to stab those hateful premed students." She is intransigent even in petty hatred, intense where I am mottled and curious.

I struggle through the central lobby in the liberal arts building known as the Fishbowl. Hot and disheveled I subside into a front seat in a wedge-shaped auditorium to gaze on my idol, Professor Donaldson. I had intended to take ancient or medieval history, ending up in American only because at registration I heard two students gossiping about what a pinko Donaldson is. His classes are standing room only, full to the legal limit of 440 and beyond with those formally or informally auditing.

He starts talking almost before he is in the door. He uses his jacket sleeve to erase what he scrawled earlier, occupying space he requires again. Slim, agile, he is over six feet tall but does not seem so because he droops, his head like a prize dahlia the stem cannot hold upright. I suspect he has grown his full auburn beard to look older than his students. Who could have expected the Pilgrim Fathers to have politics or the Revolutionary War to sound like a real revolution in Bolivia? Since last Wednesday he has broken his glasses. They are held at the hinge with tape I find endearing.

Saturday morning after looking up his address, I drag Donna off to gaze upon what turns out to be a Tudor-style red brick apartment house on North State Street altogether too bland and normal to suit my fantasies. The seventh time around the block, Donna who has never seen Donaldson but is willing to share my infatuation companionably, at last complains. But we are rewarded. He comes out with a woman wearing a trench coat much like his. Chestnut hair in a long single braid. They climb into his blue VW bug and drive off.

"At least you know he likes women," Donna says. "Can we go home?"

"She didn't look much older than me. She looks like a student."

"Twenty-two maybe. Gorgeous boots. Good tweed skirt. Money, I'd say." Donna has humored me but on the way back she begins to charge interest. "This is ridiculous. You're comfortable in these crushes. Running across town to spy on him. You could meet him if you wanted to. Just march up to him and preempt his attention."

"I couldn't," I mumble. "Why should he notice me? He has a thousand students at least."

"Wear your new black turtleneck."

"A third of his students have tits, Donna. I'm sure he's seen them before."

"You're defeatist, Stu. You can't drift along this way, having nice safe crushes on men from a distance of two hundred feet."

Why not? I'm not bored. I'm happy. When I explain this, she becomes more annoyed. "You talk about wanting to experience everything, but it's all rhetoric. You're scared."

The subtext of her argument is that I must prove myself normal, heterosexual. The reason for my resistance is half incompetence—I have not the tiniest notion how to begin —and half satisfaction. I have someone to love: Donna. I just want to read my books and listen to our music and run around town like a puppy set loose, taking in all the free concerts and cheap plays I can gobble and talk and talk and talk to her.

We do talk. "Defense" is the dirtiest word we know. We condemn racism and militarism and our parents; we make dramas of what we would say to McCarthy. We seek a

fluid openness in which to think means to speak and results
in being understood—immediately; in which to conceive of
an action is to be more than halfway toward doing. We try.
Our white room burns. Outside the air feels laxer.

We share a booth in the sweetshop across from the
dorms. Our coats are buttoned to the neck because we are
dressed only in skirts. Our blouses and underwear are
churning clean in the house laundry room. A foul supper
left us hungry. "So why sit and starve?" I demanded. Now
with the rough lining of my jacket chafing my nipples
tender and a newer dare on the table, I am torn between
the excitement of our games and the fear of how fast they
escalate.

"We need a teapot." She motions toward the metal pot
that just served us. "You struck out as a child. I just
blundered into trouble. I must learn to act."

"But if they catch us tonight?" Our booth is open to the
counter where the scrawny proprietor leans. Donna has
toward her slim body a cool functional pride I can admire
but not imitate.

"That's a weak shitless reason." She empties the pot into
her cup and crams it into her open purse. As she rises
and heads for the cashier, I stuff the ashtray, butts and
straw ends and all in my pocket, and hurry after. Damp
with sweat my fingers fumble the coins.

In the wet street we grin at each other. "What a nice
teapot, my dear," I lilt. "Has it been long in your family?"
I turn out my pocket and shake the mass of butts and
ashes into a puddle as she hops on a low wall and balanc-
ing struts past me. It electrifies me how what I say to her
does not return to me thoroughly chewed as with Howie
but leaps into action.

The snow swirls in the courtyard, large cotton candy
flakes Julie plays at trying to catch at our open casement
window. On the ledge where I so often curl or sprawl, she
is sitting, one leg in plaid wool slacks drawn up, one with
the booted foot flat on the floor. "You think we could have
missed them?" she asks in her deep cooing voice.

"She'd be up here by now."

Julie's short fawn-colored hair was done yesterday in stiff loopy curls and she keeps fingering it shyly but obsessively. "Perhaps he's taking her to supper."

"He's got no money. Besides, she *said* she'd come back." Last night Donna went out with an art student. Now we wait for our first look at this Lennie. "He's ugly in an attractive way," Donna told me. "He's subversive-looking. He grew up in a slum and he's *brilliant!*" Sophomore from Brooklyn, he's here like us on scholarship. I wonder if his being Jewish shows my influence.

"I don't know why we're making such a to-do about it," Julie murmurs sourly. "She finds a new one every three weeks." Julie comes from Bloomfield Hills, a wealthy suburb of Detroit I had never heard of until I came to college and discovered that was one of the few areas around Detroit you were allowed to be from. Julie's parents bought her culture along with horseback riding and skiing lessons, but she took to books and music too seriously to please them. She finds us vulgar but intelligent. I find her a lonely snob with vulnerable patches. She is tall and pear-shaped, blushes easily and hates herself for it. Now a cry bursts from her, her charm bracelet jangling. "Come here!"

I jump up, grazing my head on the upper bunk. Donna in her blue coat is walking twined around a boy just a little taller. Curly red hair thick as a fox brush and a luxuriant red beard halo his face in tangles. Jostling at the casement we wave madly. "Hey, Donna!" echoes through the court till she looks up grinning and waves and Lennie turns where she is pointing and waves too, his beard jogging as he calls out something.

Julie brings her hand to her mouth, palm out. "It's too much," she giggles. "He looks like a madman! Van Gogh crossed with a rabbit!" She laughs till her eyes are wet.

"Julie, so help me if you don't stop giggling I'll push you in the closet! Admire him for her!"

She shakes my hand off, subsiding. "You want me to tell her he's handsome?"

"Say . . . he looks interesting."

Donna rushes in, flinging her coat at her desk chair.

"People! What a wonderful afternoon!" Her fine hair clings to her scrubbed-looking cheeks. Her eyes squint up to blue slits of joy.

"What did you do?" I ask.

"We walked. Up- and downhill, walking in the beautiful clean sweet snow. Making tracks." She kicks off her shoes soaked dark. "What do you think of him? Isn't he wonderful? Isn't he wild-looking?"

"He looks interesting," Julie says primly, glancing at me.

"I'd love to meet him," I say. "Did he kiss you?"

"Hundreds of times. All up and down every hill." Her laugh barks, high and lively with delight. "His beard is soft, like cat's fur!"

Julie checks her slender gold watch. "Well, I must be off to Le Cercle Français. . . . Shall I see you at supper?"

As soon as the door closes behind her, Donna throws her arms around me in a violent shy hug, drawing back before I can respond and hopping past her chair. "He's marvelous, Stu. He knows everything! He's like you—quick and a little dogmatic and all warm and soft inside."

"You like him, Donna? This one you really like?"

"I love him."

"I'm glad. See, things are working out better already. This is the sort of man you want—somebody you can talk to." I pace the room, flapping my arms with excitement and truly I am not jealous. My love for her is at once humble, white hot and nonpossessive. I want the world for both of us. I want her to sail out on daily adventures of learning and doing and feeling and sail back into harbor with me at night to share and discuss.

She is staring in the mirror, bleak, cynical. "What am I doing with someone so wonderful? I'll just fuck up. Fat chance I could do anything right. I don't deserve him."

Tonight, Saturday night, I have a date with one Carl Forbes from my Spanish class. Donna supervises my dressing. "What does he look like, this Carl? Tall and blond?"

"Not bad at all." I do not know, because I had not paid

attention and after he asked me out, I was too shy to stare.

The buzzer sounds. I gasp, reaching for my purse before I realize what Donna says, "*Two* buzzes. That's Lennie. I was afraid he wouldn't get here in time."

I put my purse down with a thump. "In time for what?"

Smoothing her fine hair, she wrinkles her nose at me. "We want to see this gent. Give him our committee approval."

"No, Donna!" The door bangs behind her and I slump on the lower bunk, afraid to budge for fear I will muss myself. Still I am proud. I did this on my own. When the buzzer sounds for me and I trot down to the lobby, Lennie gives me a broad lewd wink as I cross to the sign-out desk. There Carl looms in a tweed overcoat, chesty and flat-footed with a ruddy, broadly handsome face. He takes my arm and we are off across campus to the movie.

"Well, how are you doing in old Spanish?"

"It's killing me," I say politely. I have been trying to read Neruda's *Canto General* on my own.

"Say that again! Where're you from?"

"Detroit. How about you?"

"Chagrin Falls. That's outside Cleveland."

This is not so hard. I begin to unwind. I can actually swallow and breathe. We are scarcely seated in the dark before the colored screen where the colors flash a Cinemascope epic of the Bible in living muscle power (I forgot to ask him what we were seeing), when his arm comes around my shoulders. A moment later he is whispering in my ear.

"I'm sorry. What did you say?"

"Nothing, honey." Still the lips move at my ear. When I feel his tongue I am surprised, then worried if my ear is clean. Pressed and pawed and nuzzled, I sit uncomfortably quiescent. His face looks strange and bloated close up. A belly dancer is performing with snakes. The king gossips in the ear of a wicked-looking bozo with a scimitar. I wish Carl would move away, but I do not want to offend him. Embarrassed into sticky rigidity, I watch slaves toil drag-

ging boulders until his hand closes tight and hot over my
right breast. I push his hand away. He moves it back. I
move it off and sit up, leaning away. The hand withdraws
to my shoulder. I breathe again. In five minutes the hand
has edged down. I tuck it between me and the seat to trap
it there.

Carl murmurs, "Don't you like that?"

"I don't know you."

"Don't you want to get acquainted?"

"Shhh!" from behind us. Moses is delivering the Gettys-
burg Address while Rome burns and the walls come tumbling down. If I close my eyes I cannot even see Carl's
face. When the hand pounces again, I twist the fingers
hard. I expect him to jump up in anger: let him go! But he
only begins nudging and nuzzling again. I must have hurt
him but he gives no sign. His attack feels half hostile. I
cannot believe he likes the little he knows of me.

As we leave, God's last stentorian commands echoing in
our ears, he says, "I know about a party. What do you say,
honey?"

I want to go home, but if he is not angry, perhaps I
should not be. This initial attack may be customary. I hate
to go home to Donna a complete failure. We trudge past
the shops of campus town at a quick march. We cut
through campus and slog on half a mile out Washtenaw. I
have no small talk to offer him while he hastens. I hear the
party as we approach a big white house set well back from
the street.

The living room is jammed. I would not step into this
hot noisy moil of strangers if he had not got hold of my
arm again. Girls sit on boys' laps and everyone sits on the
floor. A record player offers white dance music loudly. The
Four Sophomores. Dreary and the Dreamers. Stanley and
the Softheads. I like to dance: I learned in grade school
and that was one thing I loved to do with Freddie. We used
to do both Detroit- and Chicago-style jitterbug until we
dropped. Detroit is tighter; Chicago is stompier. But no
one here dances. There would hardly be room.

The girls look like those in the dorm, well dressed,

matching, neat as they talk in tight groups or lean glued to their escorts. Under the light fixture hung with balloons, a beer keg makes a puddle on the floor. Focusing on one of the banners I realize this is a fraternity house. I am disappointed. I expected luxury, but the furniture is old and battered.

From a private source Carl gets two paper cups of gin, shouting a few hellos as he bucks our way through to a back room. Only a nightlight thins the smoky gloom in a room just as crowded. No one looks up. I hear a few wet kisses, soft moaning, laughter. How strange that people go to a party to neck. Stumbling over legs and bottles, we sit in the only vacant corner, half under a desk.

"No!" I say. He gets more gin and tries again. I drink speedily what he hands me, so he won't see my grimaces. What am I doing in this hothouse, with this monster of persistence? Why does he imagine I will change my mind? I ask him.

"What do you think you'll do when you get married? Argue all night?"

"I'm not going to get married."

"Go on, every girl wants to get married."

"Bullshit. At any rate, this isn't marriage."

"How will you get to know fellows, if you act cold?"

Does he want to make me right on this floor? "I'm not cold. You're nuts." He is a dim looming shape. I begin to laugh weakly, helplessly.

He produces more gin. "What are you, a freshman?" When I nod, he says, "You'll change your tune. I'd like to meet you in a couple of years. Women are made for love." He gets up for more gin. As the moments pass and pass in groggy haze I realize he has abandoned me. I stumble to the bed and drag my coat from under a dozing boy.

I dodge through the living room, a blaze of impinging faces, popping balloons of talk. The door opens and shuts. The change is electric. The street is frozen, still. My feet are disconnected. Here I am hiding like a monkey in the tree behind my eyes and I've lost control of my feet but they trot along down there like friendly dogs, keeping me

company. I begin to run, sliding on ice, leaping around
corners to sink knee-deep in banks of snow with a crackling as I break through the icy crust. I jump to spank my
hand against a No Parking sign. Coming down, my heel
skids and I plump on my back. I can hardly rise for laughing. I cross campus galloping, bursting through a hedge to
skim across a parking lot. The sharp cold bites my skin as I
scoop up the snow, packing it to send wild blooping arcs at
the cars grinning at me.

"Hey! Stop that, you!" A university watchman runs at
me.

See him waddling. I pack a snowball and it sails out
keen and true, exploding on his neck. In surprise I stare till
he is almost on me, then break and run, bounding through
the far hedge. His heavy footsteps thud behind me but by
the time I run up dormitory hill I have outdistanced him. It
is easy to drop behind a thicket of bare lilacs along the
cemetery wall across from the oldest dormitory. The lights
on the dormitories blink twice, blink once and go out,
signaling curfew. I smile, listening cunningly for the watchman's steps. Finally I get up, brush the snow off and trot to
my dorm. The doors are locked and I must pound for the
assistant to let me in.

"Well. You're late." The woman looks me over. "What
happened to you?"

"I fell. Twisted my ankle." I limp cleverly to the desk
and sign in, then limp to the elevator. Up we sail so nice.
The doors open. I step dazed into a crowd. The hall is lined
with girls in robes and pajamas setting their hair in pin
curls, filing their nails. Waiting for me? Trial by jury.
Escape!

"You're late for the corridor meeting again, Stuart," the
trim grim blond standing in midhall raps out. "If it's not
one of you, it's the other."

With a show of dignity I brush the particles, dead leaves,
twigs from my coat. "Ladies, the democratic process means
a lot to me!" I am getting my wind. "The trouble with this
place is——"

Julie tugs hard and I sit with a thud between her and

Donna. My hands are grimy and cut with a slow ooze of blood from my palm. Through the long winter of the meeting I stare at the baseboard. Dulcie, the athletic chairman, is urging us to play soccer or field hockey. I raise my hand when others do. I sign a paper and pass it. My head aches.

Following Donna into our room, I snap off the overhead light. "Could you study by your desk lamp?"

"What made you late? You're not going to bed already?"

"I'm dead." I peel my clothes and let them drop.

Her chair clatters back. "Stu, did something happen with Carl? You'll feel better if you tell me."

The room churns slowly. I draw the blankets over me. "Carl?"

"Isn't that his name?"

"Carl. . . . I lost him at a party."

"Oh, Stu!"

"No, he was out of his mind." I expose my face from the heap of blanket. "I'm not cut out for dating. I'm sorry, I can't do it, Donna, that's all!" When she speaks again, I pretend not to hear.

I push open the door to Drake's, a place offering many teas and coffees, some jazz and dim booths, and walk into the dark brown air thick with smoke and conversation. Awkward at approaching strangers who lounge at home here, I slip nervously toward the back. Ah, Lennie: ruddy thatch, his strong teeth showing against this beard, he waves me over. As I slide in the bench on the opposite side from them he says, "Great news! I found an apartment with two other guys. I can move in February second."

"It's a drag now." Donna sighs with exasperation. "No place to go. We're never, never alone. We just sit on benches necking till we get pneumonia."

I had planned to tell Donna alone, but I pull out the pages with the red needlepoint of my English instructor around the edges. "Bishop gave me back 'Day is for faces.' "

"How did he like it?" She leans across the cups. Their interest is more than polite, for the voices from the pit now

tell about Donna's seduction by her brother-in-law and the
terror of her first period, along with Lennie's grandfather
dying of a heart attack on their stairs and the time Lennie
was beaten by a Puerto Rican gang who caught him crossing their turf. Their heads touch over the pages, flax and
red. I know what they read.

Miss Stuart, the accidents of adolescence are not the stuff
from which literature is honed. Personal outcries cannot
infect the critic with anything but dismay; and I doubt
whether the experiments of puberty could be so rendered
as to attract any audience but that of the confession
magazine. Outpouring such as this should be kept to
oneself.

Lennie slams the manuscript down. "Button-down fag!"
Donna blinks rapidly. "Accidents of puberty! That's all
there is."
"He wouldn't look at me. He thinks it's addressed to
him—you know, love me et cetera." Lean dry Mr. Bishop.
"Maybe it is melodramatic."
Lennie plants his hand on it—big for his size with crisp
paprika hairs. Through Donna I am conscious of his body.
"I'll show it to this poet I know. He'll give you a straight
crit of it."
I shake my head but Donna smiles. "He means Mike.
Mike has big brown eyes. He broods. I thought you said he
was coming?"
"What do you go aronnd noticing his eyes for? I'll put a
padlock on you." His big hand squeezes her shoulder, she
kisses his cheek. They are doggedly free in public affection,
so that I have learned to sit with blank face and continue
talking.
Outside Drake's I stamp my feet while they say good-
bye, good-bye. Then I notice. From the doorway across
State Street someone is watching. He shields his mouth to
light a cigarette but his gaze over his cupped hands is on
us. He is big-boned, slouched as he stands in the wind with
the collar of his ill-fitting old coat turned up around his

ears. That much I see in a series of quick glances. His gaze attracts me because of its intensity. Stubborn to stand in the icy swirl of the wind. As Lennie jogs off and Donna turns to leave with me, a motion in the corner of my eye halts me, grabbing Donna by a wild clutch.

"What's wrong? Forget something in Drake's?"

I cannot think what to answer. In the meantime he strides toward us with an exaggerated purposefulness that takes him through a drift and out the other side with snow clinging to his pants as if he could not be bothered to notice.

Donna sees him. "Oh, there's Mike. Late as usual."

He flicks his cigarette away and his hands seek refuge in the pockets of his oversized coat where they are clenched —I can feel that. "Know where I can find Lennie?"

Fraud, I think, you saw him go. That gave me courage to look. His hair is dark, not black like mine but the darkest of browns, the color of black coffee. Strange face with a sharp scar just beside the mouth, something sensuous you would want to touch, dark in his sallow skin. Strong face, the skull is strong, but the eyes draw me: large, bark brown, set deep and darkly shining.

"You just missed him." Donna makes a motion as if to scoop me forward. "By the way, have you two met?"

Damn you, Donna, you know!

"So you're Jill? What do you know!" His grin opens him up. "Lennie says you're a poet-ess."

"I write poems," I say in a fierce terrier voice.

"Stu." Donna gives me another nudge. "Show him the poem. She gave some of her stuff to her English professor and he wrote the nastiest note. Show him, Stu."

"I make nasty comments too." Mike thrusts his chin out.

"How exciting. I write nasty poems. I'm not asking favors." I am astonished that I bark back, but my poetry is one of the few parts of life where I feel brave.

Donna leans toward him flirtatiously. "Mike writes poems too. If he isn't scared to show them to you . . ."

"I'd like to read them," I say.

"With a fair trade." He steps back. "Send your stuff over with Lennie and I'll reciprocate." He strides off, the coat too large for him flapping and bucking.

"Donna, did he really mean it? Oh, why did I argue with him?"

"I thought he was intrigued."

"Honestly? You're just saying that to make me feel good? How could you tell?" And on and on till she writhes away from me. I pick over the short meeting until it is worn flat. When I finally do send a few poems over with Lennie (they live in the same men's dormitory), I have forgotten why I ever wanted to. Next week we go home for Christmas vacation. When it's over I'll have to remember to have Lennie get the poems back for me.

SIX

The Darkest Night of the Year

"ARE YOU TRYING to squash my foot? Watch where you're pushing, Malcolm!" As Mother peers around the old overstuffed chair they are wrestling to a corner, she sees me walking the drum table after them a leg at a time. "Jill, you clumsy lummox, look what you're doing to my carpet!"

Matt ambles out of my ex-room, which smells so strongly of bay rum after-shave I wonder if he drinks it. Skintight Levi's with tee shirt, blond hair in a ducktail, face bold or crude depending on how much he annoys me; in three days he has annoyed me a great deal. "Let me give you a hand, Mrs. S. Stand back!" He heaves the chair up. "Where do you want this old thing?"

Brusquely Dad says, "Against the windows."

"Malcolm, do you want it gloomy as a cave? It's bad enough with the house next door shutting off the light—"

Dad tilts back, his hands in his pockets. "Want me to ask them to move it?"

When I came home to find Matt the new boarder given

the run of the house I thought, Dad's found a son. But Dad barely tolerates him.

Matt chides her, "Temper, temper, Mrs. S. Let's dump it here."

Why doesn't she strike him dead? But she beams. "You're a real help to me. Now where's that stupid tree stand? I swear every year I won't be bothered with this silly business ever again."

Matt and Mother bought the tree. The truth is that Dad takes Christmas for granted—he grew up with it and he has never shopped for a present in his life—while for Mother it still shimmers with forbidden glamour in the presents, the tree, the cards. She liks the decorations and when I was younger she and I labored to make everything special. I can hardly join in the fuss now. During vacations I work a split shift at the phone company, nine to one and six to ten, as a long-distance operator on the noisy board. With my room rented and my attic hideaway off limits because it is entered and left through Matt's bedroom, I feel sorry for myself with a dry sneering intensity. Mother has arranged for me to sleep on the couch, but until Leo comes home around New Year's, I'll spend most of my time on the cot near the furnace where Francis sleeps when he's home. Late at night when Francis is around you can tell by the soulful guitar rising through the floorboards; however, Francis is reported to be maybe in Texas and maybe in Mexico but surely in trouble. Until Leo arrives, the cot is mine.

I sit cross-legged on it feeling sour and sophisticated when I get home around ten forty-five until I sleep long after midnight. No one says, Jill: how brilliant you are now, how dynamic, how mature! No one sees that I am changed. I can't wait for Donna to arrive; she is spending Christmas with her parents and then New Year's with her sister and brother-in-law. In the meantime I read Dostoevsky and smoke, dropping the ashes on the cement floor. This time at home I smoke openly while Mother howls. *Dearest Mother: After twenty years I apologize, I creep and crawl and whine apologies. The truth is you were often wrong about what I needed or wanted, but this time you*

*were right. Every time I watch my late adolescent self
lighting up with a self-satisfied smirk, I could reach over
my shoulder and stuff it in my ear. By thirty-five I will be
coughing blood with chronic bronchitis. Never will I forget
laboring for precious air, laboring and choking. I thought I
was blowing the sweet smoke of freedom but I was just
sucking the well-advertised death tit. About everything that
grows, you are almost always right.*

Leaving the sullen wind and cars passing sluggishly with
a wake of grimy slush, I trot under the cobblestone arch. I
am only a half hour late but Howie stands at the window
glaring. His eyes cross me and I know he has seen me but
he pretends no, looking at his watch. I ring the bell. Leisurely he slips on a pea jacket while I am still waiting at
the door. His mother answers it.

"Jill, little Jill," his mother gushes with her soft, slight
accent. She should talk. She is exactly my height and con-
siderably wider, still in her starchy nurse's uniform. Her
hair is light feathery brown under a fine hairnet, the eyes
behind pink-rimmed glasses wide and blue to take me in.
"What a lot of hair. You look like Rapunzel in the fairy
books. So how do you like college? How are you doing?"

"We're on the semester system so we won't get our
grades till the end of January. I think I'm doing okay."

"Howie got all A's."

He has finally buttoned his pea jacket, trying to edge
past his mother. "Let's go, then. Come on."

"Where are you going?" his mother bridles.

"Down to the library." He leads me out.

"But I just got home," his mother calls. "I haven't seen
you . . ."

"The library?" I ask when we're around the corner.
"You should have called me. I could meet you there as fast
as coming here."

"I want to get out of the house. Let's just walk."

I pace beside him while for several blocks we say nothing. At least there is pleasure in walking with him. I forgot
how quickly he walks, at my natural stride. I ask at last,
"So you like Columbia?"

"It's a good school but a lot of shits go there. Kids with money and an exaggerated sense of who they are and what that's worth. I got real tired being ritually pissed in those first months."

I glance at him. "But you're in New York, right? I've never been there. I'd give anything to see it."

He takes off his glasses, wipes them with a rumpled handkerchief and puts them away, a new mannerism performed with a smile that says, be amused but don't comment. "Aw, Jill, I haven't hardly been south of One Hundred and Tenth Street. I've had so much homework, I've hardly done a damn thing else."

I suddenly realize that Howie is premed, just like the awful competitive jerks Donna and I must put up with in zoology. That startles me so I squint sideways at him to see if he has undergone some disgusting change.

He catches my glance. "Notice anything different?"

"Different?" Same wide-set grey eyes, stubborn jaw, broad body . . .

"Maybe now." He walks ahead of me, turning with a shamed persistence.

"The pea jacket's new? It becomes you."

"I got it last year and you've seen it hundreds of times." He rubs his cheek. "I've grown an inch and a half."

"Since September? I haven't grown since fourteen."

"I'm physically slow. The only thing I ever did on time was start talking."

"And sometimes you're stingy with that." I smile. "For me the most exciting thing has been Donna. We both hate the same kind of hypocrisy and crap—"

"You've mentioned her. In fact half of every letter you write me is Donna."

"Talking to her shakes my ideas down. You have to meet her. She'll be in Detroit spending New Year's with her married sister."

"Okay." He shrugs. "If she wants to. Don't make a big thing of it."

"She'll want to. She's wonderful, Howie. We don't look like cousins. She has silky blond hair. She's so fair you expect her to glow in the dark."

"Why talk that way?" He frowns. "You said she has a boyfriend now."

I do not know what to say. Of course I had not thought of Howie for Donna. There's Lennie and if there wasn't, Howie is too young—ten months younger than I am and almost two years younger than Donna. No, I had not meant that at all.

"It's wet and cold. Look, I found this Syrian coffeehouse on Second. What do you say, Jill? Ever had Turkish coffee?"

"Never. Why not? We'll all be Semites together."

"Maybe we can start a local Jew-Arab peace offensive? You don't feel a little hypocritical, that word you're so fond of, planning to march in there and sit playing Italian no doubt?"

"You think they'll ask for a passport, Howie?"

"With your snub nose, you're used to getting away with passing, aren't you, Jill Stuart?"

"Well, do you announce you're a Jew every time you walk into a regular goyishe restaurant, Howie?"

We are off and racing, arguing. I had forgotten the pleasure of walking with him at full stride. I had forgotten the pleasure of arguing with him, proving myself step by step to tear what final meaning I can from his bulldog grip. We are still friends.

Mother sits captive audience darning Dad's socks. Across the table I crouch behind my anthropology notebook, reading her the words that will obliterate her prejudices. "If primitive is apelike, then hairiness is primitive. Which is hairiest of races? Mother! You aren't paying attention!" I want to take her with me. I can't help it, we shared so much in my childhood I still long to carry her off on my journeys. If she wants me to be like her, I also want her to be like me.

"Of course I am. I never had the least trouble with body hair. You ought to pluck your eyebrows—they're as heavy as your father's."

"Nobody plucks their eyebrows anymore, Mother!" The sock in her hand is canary yellow. "Whose sock is that?"

"This one? Oh . . . guess it's Matt's. Such a nice boy, it's a pleasure to have him around."

"Yeah, it's an insight into primitive man."

"You're jealous. It makes up to me a little of the pain of my two boys being so far from home. . . ." Halfheartedly. After all, Leo's around more than I am since his paint business went sour. He's always dancing across the border to avoid his creditors in Ohio and then running back to avoid his ex-wives in Michigan. Her beautiful brown eyes gloat on the socks. "I had an evening gown just that color."

"Does he actually wear those? And doesn't get stoned in the streets?"

"With the smartest bolero. I wonder if I haven't got a piece of it? Like your father says, I never throw anything away." She winks. "Bet I could dig it out. What say?"

Such kindness is cheap. "Sure. Take a look."

Sitting on Matt's floor with her short legs spread to make a lap, she empties scraps from the dresser that holds sewing supplies and summer clothes. She tries to stuff her arms into a yellow silk bolero already split in the seams. "I've gained so much. I put it on carrying you and never could get it off." She stares at my body. "I bet it'd fit you. *Try it.*"

I squeeze it over my shaggy pullover. Coaxingly she smoothes it flat. When she was married to Max Abel, obviously she had prettier and better clothes than she has now. "When I was your age, I had a short dress that color. Not as good as this silk, of course. I bought it for a party. He'd been to college, that young man. But when we arrived, every girl was wearing green. They told me it was Saint Patrick's Day. Those girls, dressed to kill and mean as can be. What did I know about their saints? I hate green— makes me red as a beet."

"Did they make fun of you?" I ran into clothes snobbery at school and if I cared they could wound me, those girls who read the language of label and line. Donna calls them bitches but she lies on the bed sometimes turning the pages of *Vogue* and staring with tense hunger at the mannequins.

"They tried. But I knew how to dance and flirt. Nothing obvious, but the way men like. Soon I had the men buzzing. Those girls turned green as their dresses." She will not bond with me around weakness, ever. "Men like a woman with a good figure, it's human nature." Her eyes walk over me like spiders. "Throw your shoulders back. Have you met any nice young men? Hasn't *anybody* asked you out?"

I scrape the bolero off. "Once or twice."

"With your sullen temper, I bet you argue their ears off. Learn to keep your mouth shut and smile. Hold your mouth tight like this, it'll look smaller. Show me how you smile at a boy."

I jump up. "I don't smile. Donna says my mouth isn't too big. And if it is, it's mine! I like me. Donna likes me."

Her eyes rest on me hard and hostile. "Donna! Donna! Donna! There's something really wrong with you. Something rotten."

Do not respond. No expression. Bacall in *To Have and Have Not* when the cop slaps her. Pride is being cool. "In this zoo, why ever not?" I fumble for a cigarette, light it with a kitchen match struck off my thumbnail, a new affectation I know will drive her crazy. I am suddenly thirteen again and miserable.

We sit at the back of the bus for privacy. Donna dabs at her eyes. "It's only five years since Jim graduated, but oh, they're disgustingly settled! He used to care about things, he was practically a socialist. But when I tried to tell them about Lennie, they made fun of him."

"How could they? They never met him."

"Because I said he has a beard and paints." She blows her nose hard. "I said, why should women have hours when the men don't? They both started in, parents wouldn't send their *children* to school if they weren't protected. I said, Don't you think people screw before ten thirty? That just makes it sordid. And they had the nerve to pretend to be shocked!"

"How are things between Jim and you?"

"Stu, you know what he did? Took me aside and gave me a horrid smug lecture on making men respect me. He said because I'm not Jewish, Lennie would just try to use me—Lennie! I'm more fed up with not having sex than Lennie is."

"Lennie loves you. Don't talk to them anymore about him." I pick at my jacket, feeling the cold ingroup pushing. Virtuous air of Aunt Jean saying broadly, "Why, when I showed him the house, he tried to jew me down." Donna is an accident of warm flesh.

"You're the only living soul I can talk to besides Lennie, and there are things I can't say to him."

"Have you told him about Jim?"

"Not yet. He's so *good*. I just can't."

I am all for honesty but she is too unhappy for me to pester with my scruples. I check my package, peering at the fiery red of the dress. With great mystery Donna took me to a hallway lined with dentists' offices where with the staring fixity of her confessions she swore me to secrecy. "Promise you won't tell! Nobody! Especially Julie. Promise!" Thus I was initiated into the resale shop where I bought a red wool dress with a V neck, simple in a way that even I can recognize as well-made, of a jersey that clings and flatters.

"Donna." I tap her arm. She is staring out the bus window at Awrey's factory where they bake the almond-tasting windmill cookies. "I want you to meet my old friend Howie. Tonight?"

"Some other time. I'm worn out. Just let me come home with you. They make me feel so bad about myself."

Dad and Leo are down in the basement. The whine of the electric jigsaw rises. Whenever it stops I hear them talking. They get on together, their conversation jingling with odd, unfitted facts like a pocketful of nails. Dad loves to know exactly how mechanical objects or processes work. Since Leo is always going into or out of some new business, Dad gets to question him about something and Leo gets to play expert answering.

I stand at the sink washing supper dishes. Mother and Donna and Matt sit around the lit tree in the living room. I expected Donna to keep me company while I wash. I long for her to come. Instead she hangs out in the living room acting just like the Donna of that first week at school, fluttery, vapid, with a dry silly giggle like marbles rattling in her throat. Matt seems to swell while she shrinks. He occupies more than a chair, preening, strutting even as he sits. Mother watches, coy, amused. Mother sits with her sewing in her lap but she is not sewing. The bits of their talk that I can hear over the saw and the dishes cause me to grind my teeth in helpless annoyance.

". . . just adore the way you customized your Hornet." As if Donna can tell a Ford from a Chevy any better than I can. Ha.

"Matt's real clever with his hands," my mother says flirtatiously. "He can make anything go." Then she spoils her innuendo by launching into an interminable story about what went wrong with the washing machine.

". . . oh, Jill studies a lot more than I do."

Traitor! As a matter of fact—with pleasure I hit a cracked plate on the drainboard and lay the two pieces neatly to one side—I study one hell of a lot less than you, Donna baby. I go for walks while you're bent over your books curled up like a porcupine with a bellyache. And I read my work and yours. Maybe that annoys her. I never considered that before. Maybe she thinks I am showing off. I just want to know everything she learns to share that too.

When I finally finish the dishes, it's time for me to go to work. Matt offers to drive me. The telephone office is about a mile and a half away. I'd love to turn down his offer, but I'm running late.

As we're walking out, Mother is saying to Donna, "After all, it's not like you're engaged to this boy from New York, right?" She picks up Donna's left hand. "But since you aren't, what's the harm seeing another fellow for a little fun? If he leaves you alone on New Year's Eve, that's his fault. He can't expect you to sit home when he hasn't even given you a ring. You're only young once."

Matt hasn't driven me three blocks before we're quarreling. "She won't go out with you! She won't. You don't see anything in her but a pretty blond, but she's intelligent. She won't!"

"You want to bet? I can tell when a girl's interested. I saw her looking me over."

"How could she miss you parading up and down, you peacock?"

"Watch your language, Snow White." He squeezes my knee. Promptly I bend his fingers back. "Ouch! Hey, I'm driving."

"Then drive. They taught me it takes two hands in driver training." Actually I never took it. You had to pay a fee. Dad kept saying he would teach me, but every lesson ended fast with me reduced by his annoyance to the physical equivalent of stammering, pulling all the wrong levers and treading hard on the accelerator instead of the brake.

"I could teach you a few things you don't learn at school. But you're scared of me."

"Just bored." I wondered I can sound so bright and hard when I *am* quite scared. I don't trust him in the dark or the light. "You can play my mother's son all you want—just keep out of my way."

"Your mother is one damn fine woman. Grow up a little."

"Doing my best. Just leave me and my friends alone."

"Your mother says it's okay if I take Donna out. So let's leave it up to the lady, why don't we? I'll ask her when I drive *her* home tonight."

They are all laughing at me. Mother and Matt. Now Donna is being drawn over to them.

New Year's Eve. When I walk in at ten forty-five, my parents are entertaining. Mother insists I take a hand in their canasta game. On my right sits Charlotte Ballard, kidskin face, brassy hair lacquered into rolls. She spends a fortune she doesn't have on that curlicue hair and the upkeep of her body armored like a fighting dinosaur. "Oh, Malcolm, what a nasty hand you gave me, you mean man!" Next is Dad. Mother sits between Gene Ballard's scraped red face, eyes tough and beaming, and Leo. I have to give it to Leo, he manages to look darkly handsome in a tan suit. On my left is his new girlfriend. Anita has ash-blond hair in a poodle cut and wears a dress covered with rows of tassels. She is on her best behavior, which involves getting a little tipsy, laughing at whatever the men say, in case it should be funny, and saying "Pardon my French," every time she says "Damn it."

I deal, watching the cards snap out. Francis taught me. He also taught me to cheat, but I don't feel like trying that, being out of practice. I settle for style over control. Poor Lennie, we're both betrayed tonight. Mustn't think that. Why shouldn't she go out with Matt? I could give her no reason on the phone, with Mother running the sweeper behind me. The nerves creep in my fingers like caterpillars.

On the porch beside Dad at midnight I hear the fire-crackers and bells beating at the sealed black sky. Make Matt come back now. Wait till he decants a few of his choice opinions on women, society, the good life. What can she want with him?

One twenty. Dad flashes around the table a look of quick boyish triumph, then card by card lays down a con-cealed hand. "Out!"

"You old smarty!" Mother pretends to slap at him. Bal-lard, stroking his horsehead tie, peers sideways at the scoop neck where her breasts gleam through black lace. Ballard used to be in the shop with Dad. Then he went to work as an electrician for a contractor laying out subdivisions north of the city. Now he is a contractor himself, a little sleazy, sometimes rolling in money and sometimes so broke he borrows from my parents.

On and on the night drags till two-thirty coffee. Finally the house is emptied of guests. Leo has gone off with Anita, the social lie being he will come in the back way later on. As I lie sleepless on the couch, only the porch light glows. Dad's snores buck the dark. My thoughts plod round like a donkey chained to a mill. Like Samson, eye-less in Gaza. I do not love Milton but he feels appropriate in the rotten night.

Matt's key in the lock. I rise on my elbow and fall back. The porch light hits the clock. Three thirty. I would like to

kill him silently and suddenly. Still the hair rises on my
nape as I hear the rustle of Mother's robe. "Matt," she
whispers, "you're late. I want a word with you."

"Did I wake you? Sorry. I was trying to make like a
mouse."

"I haven't slept. It's four, Matt."

The kitchen light falls on me briefly as she stands aside
to let him past, then pulls the swinging door to. Her face in
that flash hangs on in the dark, lines about her mouth
sharply incised, eyes anthracite, hair standing up like a
mass of rankled nerves. As I ease off the couch and creep
toward the door, I feel momentarily sorry for Matt. The
hiss of her voice and his answering confessional murmur
torture me as I pick my way over the creaking boards.
From the bedroom Dad's snores rise undiminished.

Mother grates, "But you promised!"

His reply is a mumble. Slowly I lean on the door, a
quarter inch, a half inch. "Don't deny it! Matt, I see it in
your face. Don't you sit there and lie bold-faced to me."

"But Mrs. S.—"

"You broke your promise to me!"

"God is my witness, I didn't mean to . . ." I can hardly
recognize this whining boy. "I'm only human, damn it."

Sparks dance on my clenched eyes. No.

"I knew I was right about that little bitch. But that
doesn't let you off the hook. I'll never trust you again,
Matt. I took you into my home—"

"You've been an ace. I don't deserve it. But I *tried* to
remember my promise, honest."

She clucks her tongue, saying more amiably, "Well, I
haven't lived this long without learning that when a man
takes advantage of a woman, it's because she asked for
it."

"Mrs. S., she's got more fire than I ever run across—"

"I was afraid of this. I've got an instinct about people."

"I swear I never meant to do it. I don't know how to say
this to you, decentlike, but she got me all worked up—"

My shoulder hits the door. Half blinded by the glare I
lunge. "You dirty liar!" I get him by the throat, seeing the

pink lipstick smeared on his collar. Mother seizes my arm as he pulls free.

Her hand goes back to strike me, then falls. "Shut up, you fool. You want to bring your father out? You won't go back to college if he gets wind of this!"

Letting my hands drop I meet her dark stare. Eyes burning back. But I win. She turns with a dismissing wave to Matt. "Get to bed. Quietly. Not a *word* about this tomorrow."

He sidles past and out. I switch off the light, not wanting to see her. My anger cools to a solid lump in my chest. I feel her at my elbow.

"I won't have you living with her. I knew it was something like this! If your father finds out, he'll drag you home so fast it'll make your head swim. You ask them to change your room."

I walk stiffly to the couch, a taste like rust in my mouth. Mother has given me a weapon. Dad did not want a roomer. With his sense of clan he will never forgive her if he finds out, and blame her twice over for concealing it. She hides the tea readings, the palm readings, and ill smelling home permanent she uses, sure in her heart she keeps him with plotting and subterfuge. I would be cruel to tell him but it is fight or give up the pretense of my own life. I will not change rooms.

How Donna has played into Mother's concealed hand. Matt was only the silly bait. Is there nothing more between women and men than the secret war of marriage, sex the economic counter or submission to the alley world of smut? Rigid I lie, my hands clenched on my belly. If sex is a war I am a conscientious objector: I will not play.

SEVEN

In Which Poet Meets Poet and
Words Are Exchanged

SUNDAY NIGHT, A note from Donna lies on my bunk. She has plumped up her pillow and mine for breasts and used my black hairbrush for pubic hair and her hand mirror for a face. On the belly of the doll a note says:

Stuiest:

Peter (a friend of Lennie's—he has lots of $ and his own apartment) is lending it to us for this evening till curfew. Peter's due back late. So tonight is our night at long last! Pray for me now and in the hour of our death —hopefully from overindulgence.

love, love love
ya Donna

An hour later Julie perches on my bunk, slicing fruit-cake. "If I eat it, I'll get fatter than I am. My mother! She scolds me I'm overweight and then gives me a two-pound brandied fruitcake to take back. Is that sabotage or not?"

Julie is dressed up in a new grey flannel suit with a ruffled blouse. I do not like her in suits as her body's opulence is all in baroque hips and ass and she looks stuffed into the suit. I would put her in gypsy skirts or pants. "I had supper with Van, but he had to go back to his dorm early to study. He must be the only person on campus studying tonight. . . . So you met Mike? Doesn't he have marvelous melting eyes? But his ears stick out like the handles on a sugar bowl, poor lamb. Don't they?"

"I didn't notice." I don't want to be vulnerable in front of Julie. "I only met him once for five minutes."

"Lennie's getting an apartment in a month, hmm? I wish Van would. To neck standing up gives me a backache. Tonight, *toute* daring he put his hand on my sweater and squeezed. Then he blushed, I swear it. Of course all he got a hand on was my padded Lovable perfect circle thirty-four A—but it's the spirit that counts."

"Why don't you seduce him, Julie?"

"I'm considering that. Otherwise he'll go away when he graduates. If we do it, he might marry me."

"Well, you have two years to work on him, right?"

"Year and a half. He'll make a decent living as a college professor. He's applying to several of the best graduate schools. . . . I think Mother doesn't really expect me to do any better. But how am I supposed to seduce him standing in the courtyard?"

"You have to ask Donna. I wouldn't know how to seduce him lying down in a bed." Unless he were a girl, I think wryly. I'm out of practice but at least I know where to start.

"Donna? She'd be amused. She doesn't care for other people's tacky problems."

"Try her some time." Defend! Though without conviction. Among women Donna relates only to me. I wonder briefly if I have higher status because of that long-ago act I have tried hard to recall.

At thirteen I was part tomboy and part bookworm, finding my community with the gang. At fourteen Donna was

pert rather than pretty, wild and shy with eight elbows
jutting out. She had a high cackling giggle and a bright red
nose peeling from sunburn. I wore my hair in braids still,
for one of my acts of rebellion that August—the month
after I was in Cold Springs with Donna—was to make
Callie cut them off. I would not tell Mother who had done
it, so was kept in for a week. Then my mother relented,
setting my hair in metal curlers. Now she is permanently
angry because I wear it long. Nobody has long hair now-
adays, she says, and she is almost right. It is considered
bohemian, which may be why I grew it, but I keep it long
because I love the way it feels, part cloak, part fan, part
mane, part security blanket.

Donna and I had sat that afternoon in the backseat
while my father drove and Uncle Hubie read the map. I
said to Donna, "Oh, my best friend Callie and I have the
most super game when we're alone." I was going to tell her
how we had taken to calling up names from the phone
book and pretending to be the Gallup Poll. We asked
whatever came into our minds (Does your dog wear pajamas? What do marshmallows make you think of when
you step on them?) until they hung up or we started giggling. It astonished us how many stupid questions people
would answer. Then I realized both dads had fallen silent.
If mine heard me tell that, I would be in trouble.

"What game?" she asked persistently.

I signaled to her to be quiet.

"What game?" she whispered, moving closer.

"Later," I muttered and began talking loudly about
swimming.

All day she kept asking me and I kept not being able to
tell her, at first for security reasons of family within ear-
shot, and then because nothing was adequate to the
buildup. By the time we got into bed that night I could
imagine only one game this inadvertent crescendo could
climax in. I did not decide to seduce my cousin but backed
myself into a corner where my pride required I produce
something to justify all the suspense. I remember my desperation and my solution but not that act. At fourteen

Donna was nothing special in bed and I forgot her. Now I love her far more than she loves me.

Donna comes in Sunday night just before curfew ablaze with content, so it is not until the next afternoon that I bring up what I heard on New Year's Eve.

"Please." I lean over her as she sits stunned, knuckles to her forehead. "Don't ever sleep with anyone like that—someone who's likely to talk inside the family."

"Who'd ever, ever think he'd go home and tell her?"

"You can't gamble like that. Mother wants to separate us—"

"Oh." Stark childish fright wrinkles her face but she makes her voice flat. "When are you moving out?"

"Never. Don't be absurd. I'll say the dorm is full."

Relief is immediately driven from her face. "Will she tell my mother?"

"I don't think so."

"But she might? I want to die! What'll happen to me?"

Her face is so drawn I am ashamed of scaring her. "Why would she? She's scared of scandal and my dad would be furious."

She turns from side to side, not looking at me. "Besides, we only petted."

"Aw come on. He didn't mean that."

"Men exaggerate. You'd know that if you knew anything at all about men!" Still she turns in her chair.

"Donna, he was too scared to lie."

"I didn't." She jumps up, twisting to face me. "I didn't. Don't you believe me?"

"Forget it." I start to turn away.

She screams, "Do you believe me?"

"No."

She throws herself at me, her nails clawing at my face. By reflex I set my feet and shove her off. She runs out, slamming the door. My arm. Above the elbow a double furrow fills with blood. Cat scratch. I touch my tongue to the ooze.

At my desk I sit chin on my cold hand. Could she be telling the truth? What difference does it make! My doubt is dangerous. I promised to take care of her, to accept her. Perhaps I must accept that certain moments are a nightmare played out.

The door opens. I keep still. "Stu? I'm sorry. I'm so sorry."

I get up, jerking at my sweater. "I'm sorry too."

"I couldn't stand it when you wouldn't believe me."

"I guess I wanted to hurt you. I'm sorry too."

"Then you believe me now?"

I do not know. How can I know, when the cost of resolution is too high? "Of course."

Quickly she gives me a hard hug and withdraws her body at once. "I wouldn't lie to you. I love you. You're the only female I can stand. The only relative! The only person who's ever, ever known me well and not made me feel like a piece of shit." She takes my arm to look at the scratch. "I'll get a Band-Aid."

"Scratches heal faster when they're exposed." But not all wounds. I'll shut up about Matt. I realize that this is the first time any person has ever told me that they love me. I feel too numb to enjoy it. "I'm too wound up to study. Let's go get a cup of hot chocolate across the street."

"Fine, but not across the street. At Drake's they make it with milk and two whole marshmallows." At her mirror she retouches her makeup with ritualistic gravity. I like her better without the coral lipstick and blue eye shadow, but she believes that unless she uses all eleven bottles on her dresser, she looks "washed out."

"Six months ago, I'd never have believed anyone could make me walk half a mile for hot chocolate with milk and real marshmallows." But I approve her joy in details. To be consciously sensual is part rebellion and part discipline that she is teaching me.

In the Union cafeteria patronized by faculty and the loosely connected factions of campus intellectuals, I sit with my books spread before me. I have given up trying to study and begun instead a letter to Howie:

I am writing this from the student Union while waiting to
meet Mike Loesser, a friend of Lennie, who it a poet also.

I feel as if I have been dying into total stupidity sitting here
waiting and waiting, without being able to think of one
sentence to set beside that opening. Mike has obviously
forgotten our . . . appointment.

Someone stands beside me. I look up—not as tall as he
had loomed in my mind but with posture more rigid as if
on guard. "Oh, hello." Lightly, brightly, ouch.

"Well, here I am."

"Yes. Well, yes." We have nothing to say. I knew it.

He flips his old coat over a chair. "I'll get coffee. Cream
or sugar?"

"Sugar, thanks."

When he returns he takes out the sheaf of my poems,
thumbs them looking stern.

"May I see your poems?"

"Damn." He snaps his fingers. "Forgot."

Like hell. At least I can look at him. Dark hair starting
far back as if to give his face more room but thick on the
crown. Tall forehead over the bulge of bone. Long full
mouth. Don't let me blush. His neck is thin and so are his
bony wrists that lead to the long-fingered hands. None of
his clothes fit: they droop and hang and wrinkle on him
with a forlorn carelessness. His navy sweater is good wool
but raveled at the elbows and cuffs. His bones are big but
his flesh is spare. His lashes brush his cheeks as he reads,
smiling now. What amuses you: me? Woman-mouse I
crouch behind a barricade of table nibbling with my eyes,
but if you make a sudden gesture or speak sharply I will
turn into an empty chair.

He fans the pages out like a hand of cars. "Nice images,
weird! But like nothing has happened since the imagist
manifesto. They lack form."

Will he tell me to write sonnets, like M.R Stein did? I
am not comfortable in sonnets. They fit me like girly
clothes, that pinch and make me walk as if I were holding
a bar of soap between my knees. "How should I be writ-

ing?" I am not ironic. Probably I have to take lessons in a whole new language.

He passes that off with a wave of his hand. "But this one, wild. Reminds me of the stuff I was doing when I came here. Violent, screaming, grotesque stuff. It's real weird that a girl wrote it."

"That's the one my instructor told me was for the confession magazines—though it's a compilation of various people's experiences, you understand. Including Lennie."

"All that *I* business." He plants his elbows on the table. "I want to make gadgets so hard and brutal and self-enclosed that after the wreck of this syphilization, some little green men with antennae instead of ears can come along and dig them out of the rubble—and dig them. You understand? You see?"

Gently I shake my head no. "Explain. What would you be communicating that wasn't one I to another I?"

He drains his cup and shoves it aside. "Whole lot of rot talking *literature*. Let our critics do the carping for us." He pauses, listening to the sound of that allusion, lost on me. Then, "How old are you?"

"Practically eighteen. And you?" I hear he's a junior.

"I'm twenty." He frowns, sitting back. "You see, I'm younger than I look."

Well, maybe. The prominent bones are set for the face of the man but the too spare flesh, the tumbled hair, the mobile hypersensitive mouth and eyes contradict him. "You're from Detroit too, aren't you?" Should I have admitted I've been asking Lennie about him?

He nods, tilts back in his chair as if figuring something out. "Near Eight Mile. But I grew up in the inner city, off Second. Till I was nine. That's a Negro neighborhood and it's tough."

I smile. Everybody from Detroit claims a tough neighborhood. "My friend Howie lives near there."

"Your friend? Is he here?"

"He got a scholarship to Columbia. In New York City."

"I know where Columbia is," he says acidly. "And I went to Cranbrook Institute. *I* had a scholarship there."

That's some kind of fancy private school out Woodward someplace. "Did you like it?"

"Bunch of future commuters and barbarian pricks and nancies who like to use pastels. But I had Cribbets for a year."

"What's cribbets?" Maybe it's a deficiency disease?

His mouth curves scornfully. "Arthur Cribbets has only had poems in the *Chicago Review* and the *Beloit Poetry Journal* and—dozens of places. That's all."

I hunch in my chair. The names that come out of him. He must despise me.

"He's writing the definitive book on Rimbaud. You know what he told me? 'The requisites for the literary life are to know how to discuss the other fellow's work without letting him know what you think and to stand on your hind legs and drink martinis.' "

"I don't think I'd like him."

"Of course not. He's queer." One eyebrow dips independently. I wish I could do that. I resolve to practice.

"Why do you say I wouldn't, just because he's homosexual?"

"You're a woman."

Woman: not girl. Thank you. "So what?"

"So you wouldn't abide him."

"All right, so I wouldn't be interested in him as a man, say, but I might like him as a friend or a teacher." I wish Arthur Cribbets, the jerk, was at this table so I might begin liking him ostentatiously right now.

"As a woman, you couldn't."

"As a human being, I could too. You think I'm a bigoted idiot?" Suddenly aware he is looking at my sweater, I draw back and fold my arms.

"You look like you're ready to bite." That grin.

Our glances knot. We stare for several gluey moments. Then I look away and down to the empty cups. "I've got to go. I'll miss supper," I say.

On the sidewalk out front, "Well, look . . ." He stands hunched against the wind. The light changes unleashing a pack of cars and bicycles.

"Thanks for looking at the poems."

"Sure." He tilts forward, half frowns. If he would say something about seeing me again. But why? He turns and is off, his head ducked, his coat flapping loose. I begin to walk fast and then trot, wishing I was already in my dormitory room, transported instantly to Donna so I can spill out to her verbatim, gestures illustrated and pauses marked, the afternoon. Then it will be real for me, secured, understood.

Finals swallow us and the new term begins. The second Monday I wake with a jolt. Donna is hanging her coat. "Sleeping! Don't you have a class, Stu?"

"Didn't feel like it." I sacrificed Spanish to her. I try to catch her expression, but she is combing her sleek hair. She is smiling as she turns, swirling her skirt, so I may ask, "How did it go last night?"

"Beautiful. Worth any risk." She curls up beside me, seductively happy. "No rush, no clock watching. Making love is different when you really sleep together. No wonder people get married! Sharing the apartment with his roommates doesn't give us terrific privacy, but it's still fine." She smiles teasingly. "You'll understand. . . . Hear anything from Mike?"

"Your mind is not working oversubtly." I have news but I hoard it. I want all her attention.

"Lennie is so warm. When he feels good, happiness just flows from him." She stretches, coiling on the rich red corduroy of the quilt in a patch of sun. "He's begun painting me. Posing is tedious, but he makes me feel beautiful." Raising her arm against the sun she squints at me. "How were things on the home front? Did anyone ask where I was?"

"Not a peep." I stretch, feeling for my loafers. "I went down well before closing and signed out an iron. While the attendant was getting it, I took your slip from the sign-out box and popped it into the in-box. I even rumpled up your bunk."

"I felt sad when I thought of you alone. But . . ." She gets up, brushing imaginary wrinkles from her skirt. "Lennie says Mike keeps asking questions."

"Like what?" We sit down at our side-by-side desks.

"Like who Howie is and was he your boyfriend." She runs her knuckles across her nose.

"Donna, Mike asked me out. To a concert Friday. All Bach."

She laughs, tapping my shoulder. "I know! Lennie says Mike has been trying to think up an excuse to see you—as if he couldn't just ask you."

"I can't imagine him acting that way." I kick my chair back and go to lean my forehead on the cold window. The glare of the sun, the melting snow staining the flagstones of the courtyard dark, seem suddenly more than I can bear. "He won't like me."

"Of course he will. He'd be an idiot. Besides, Lennie said just yesterday that you're stacked—"

"Tell Lennie . . . Oh, leave me alone." I grab my book and pull myself into it. Donna watches a moment, then shakes her head.

The flood of couples pours between the pillars of Hill Auditorium, eddies on the sidewalk, then trickles in all directions. He says, "How much time before the Greyzies lock you up?" Bass voice incisive when he chooses but inclining to a mumble.

"About an hour. Greyzies?"

"You know. Them. The greybeards, the deans and administrators and judges. The ones who own places and lock you out or lock you in. Want coffee or should we just walk?"

"Whatever you like." Shyness makes me malleable.

"Then, let's *walk*."

Even under the coat I can feel the redness of my dress in its maiden voyage. "You know more about music than I do."

"I was an infant prodigy on the violin till I petered out about age nine." We stroll past the fountain covered with its winter shed. He grips my arm. Through the layers of wool, the meat burns. Clearing his throat: "There's something here I want to show you."

"Good. What is it?" I must lean a little forward to see

his head against the streetlight. He stares ahead with a sullen glare, his mouth grim. Have I bored him?

"Nothing. Just a house. If the moon stays out."

I stare at the blue-white disco of the moon trailing wrack. "Don't look yet. Wait!" He orders. Then he turns me to our right. "It's just that wall."

We face a narrow court whose left and back walls are stucco broken only by a narrow balcony and the heavy grillwork that covers the ground-floor windows. At the back a yellow lantern casts dim patterns. Moonlight white-washes the nearer wall and slants across it the attenuated shadow of bare tree branches.

"Doesn't it look damned French?"

"I must have passed here dozens of times, but I never noticed."

"In the day it's nothing. An arty stucco box. But do you like it?"

"Yes, of course."

He jams his hand in his pockets. "It's futile."

"What is?"

"Trying to recapture an experience. You can't step in the same river twice, and it's no good."

"But I'm glad you showed me." Slowly we walk away.

"Really?"

"Yes!"

He grips my arm again. "What do you think of yourself as being—Jew or Gentile?"

"I'm a Jew. That's just what I am. Not by religion. But I also feel Welsh, some. I'm a mongrel."

"That's absurd. You can't be two contradictory things. I wondered when Lennie said your dam was—"

"My what?"

"Your dam. You object to the phrase?" His shoulders snap back, his voice deepens.

"Well, I call her Mother myself. Don't you think it sounds a little phony?"

"*Merde.* Just squeamishness. Why use one word for other animals and a special term for man? It's the same act, the same covering. We're all born from a female's hairy cunt." He voice raised in speechmaking.

"Do you think that's sad or something? Would you rather be born from your father's hairy skull?"

"My father's skull is rot and bone. He's dead."

"I didn't know." I'm clumsy. I have hurt him. Slowly we climb past a dark classroom building, forestry.

He says gruffly, "This is his coat. I'm tall as he was now, but it's still too big. I've got to develop into it."

The coat is old. He will have to blow himself up like a balloon if he wants to fill it before it falls apart. "When did he die, Mike?"

"When I was ten."

"Were you very close to him?"

"Close? He was my father." He raps his knuckles on the column of a streetlight. "I can hardly call up his face. What's gone is gone and you have to see you can't do anything about it. I'm trying to tell you. Do you think I'm making small talk?" He turns on me fiercely.

"I listen. Are you going to give me a test?"

"Consider it an exposure."

"Sounds like a disease."

"If you think I'm sick, consider it that." He stands boring at me with a strained demand.

I unclench my hands and let them drop. "I don't!"

"One never knows. You might be amusing yourself."

"Mike! I'm not that crafty. Amusing myself?"

"My father was a furrier but my mother just couldn't run the business. She almost went bankrupt and then she had to sell it. She put the money into a trust fund to send me through college."

"Are you an only child?" I ask.

"I had an older brother. He was twelve. He was killed in the same accident with my father. . . . Do you have siblings?"

"Two brothers. One's thirty-one and one's twenty-eight."

"So much older. How did that happen?"

"They're my mother's kids by a previous marriage. But I grew up with them. I mean they were both home till I was six."

"She's a widow?"

"No, divorced."

"Oh," he says as if I had confessed my mother is an ax murderer. What a funny mixture of being straight-laced and trying to *épater* the bourgeois. I do not understand his world that looks dark and overshadowed. We walk on to the brink of the hill.

Opposite us my dormitory blazes, where I will be swallowed. "Don't be annoyed. I didn't know about your father."

He halts to look hard at me. "You're an odd one." Then he grins.

"Sure, but all told, no odder than you."

"That makes us even." He tugs my hand and we run down the slope, plummeting pell-mell with our steps clattering off the retaining wall like a rain of pebbles.

EIGHT

The Temptation of Saint Jill

ON MY DRESSER Donna stands barefoot holding a huge jagged green nude to the wall, the fruit of her long sessions posing. "Do I have it straight?" she shouts over *Rite of Spring.*

"Straight enough." I sit bobbing to the music while sorting clean laundry. Saturday-morning bustle tickles me and I like our room with Lennie's garish canvases blazing from the white walls, replacing the Picasso blue and rose period reproductions every tenth girl in the dorm has put up. On my bunk Theo is flopped like a large cocker spaniel. She and Donna share the same coloring, both flaxen-haired and blue-eyed, but Theo has a permanent tan. She is five feet ten, her bones big but shapely. She is something of an athlete and something of a lush. Theo talks little as she hums to the music, wriggling her foot. Donna is more relaxed with Theo than with Julie.

"Your dresser's covered with powder. Have you been using mine?" Donna hops down lithely, dusting her soles.

"You told me I looked better in it. So I used it last night."

Donna looks sharply at the socks I'm putting away. "Hey, that's mine."

I toss her the balled pair. "Should have known. They didn't have holes."

"What do you mean? My socks aren't new like yours."

"Well, how would you like to get fucking socks for Christmas? And the rest of mine are darned so lumpy they give me blisters."

As the record finishes, Theo unwinds to return it to its folder.

"Thanks for bringing that by," I say. "Stravinsky is ace."

"Oh . . . if you want to keep it for a week?" Seeing my expression, she lays the record in my lap as I sit among the laundry. "I'm off to the pool."

Donna mocks a shudder. "Chlorine. Cold water."

Theo gives that big smile with her eyes sad. "I wish you'd come to a meet sometime. Hardly anyone does."

As Theo swings out, Donna turns with her arms full of socks, dumping them at my feet. "I'm proving my point. Look!" She drives her fist in, wriggling her fingers through two holes at me.

"Think I'm impressed! Look, taken at random." I hold a sock to the light. "Five separate holes. Count them!"

"Feel how lumpy this darn is. Feel!" She presses a sock into my palm. Our gazes meet and we burst out laughing, kneeling face-to-face over our wash. "If we were burning at the stake, we'd argue over who had a hotter fire," she says.

I get up to start the record over. "Suppose the music built and built and didn't resolve?"

She stands on one foot like a heron. "Do you think Theo's queer?"

"No," I say loudly. If I wonder too, that is one thing I will not share with Donna. "She's asexual. Something's broken."

"Her hymen?"

"Something more serious."

"I don't know, kid." She gives me that crooked grin with her eyes squinted. "It seems to be a pretty serious matter—

like preparing for your Ph.D. orals—for you to deal with yours. Did Mike kiss you last night?"

"Nope." I glare at the pile of books by Pound and Eliot he lent me. "He's forming my mind. He's giving me a liberal arts course. At the end of four years he'll kiss me and make me a proposition." I manage to sound flippant but then I spoil it, chewing anxiously on my thumbnail.

"Why don't you and Mike come with us tonight? We're going with Van and Julie to see *No Exit* at the Drama Society."

"Mike hates Sartre. I tried to talk him into going."

"Since Julie started seeing that grind Van, I spend more time with her than exactly thrills me. . . . Sometimes I think you've set out to gather in every misfit in this dormitory."

"What's a misfit, Donna? What are we trying to fit into?"

Donna softens, giving me a cuff on the shoulder. "I'll tell you what—you can borrow my black jumper tonight. You'll look great in that."

"Really, Donna?" In her clothes I feel magical.

"But don't get food stains on it or spill coffee on yourself."

"I won't eat or drink! I won't hardly sit down. I promise."

One of the lounges—bold and arid as an advertisement and patrolled by housemother and attendants who apply rules such as kissing with both feet on the floor—has been designed for coed studying. There Mike and I are entrenched the following Wednesday night, while I try to start a paper on the Cleveland administration, first or second. I am taking American history post—Civil War, but Donaldson is not teaching it and all the bubbles have gone out. Our lecturer Professor Grimes recites the text. Even the jokes are in the book. Yet the flunkies down front laugh loudly and take notes. On what? His ties? (*Bow.*) His part? (*On the right.*) Grimes drops snide references to what we may have mislearned. "Contrary to what you may have gathered, Lenin was not one of the Founding Fathers, heh, heh." He lectures on the violence of labor. My murdered grandfather mutters in my ear, violence is when *we* dare to fight back.

Mike looms across the table writing in his loose-leaf of tooled brown leather. The neat columns grow in his curious ornate hand with its curlicues and pothooks, leaned a little back as if a wind blew against its progress. That looseleaf contains something besides class notes. With a wicked and satisfied smile he alludes to it. "It's evil stuff. I can't let anyone see it."

A little before ten he slams it shut. "Let's take a stretch. We'll leave the junk here. Nobody'll steal it."

The snow has softened into a slow casual rain. He raises his big black umbrella, our hands touching on the bone handle. I ask, "What's the use writing a journal if you won't show it to anybody?"

"To get it all straight in my mind. So I can escape from those depths and begin again." He grins. "I call it, 'Love Letter to a Scar.' "

How can you call a diary anything, except Diary? Then one little question among the several hundred I am dying to ask him squirms out. "How did you get that scar? The little one beside your mouth."

"In a fight. . . ." He swaggers a little.

I don't believe it. One thing I like about Mike is that he isn't strutting and muscle-bound like Matt. He's skinny and completely unathletic. His only sport is weight lifting, he told me: he likes to lift a full glass and then an empty one. He may or may not drink as much as he suggests, but he never took to street fighting, I know it. That he was beaten up I can believe and I want to put my arms around him and tell him it's over, it's all right, and now he's where brains and not muscles count. "I think it's very distinguished."

"A dueling scar. My pal Davis and I fought once at Cranbrook when we were after the same girl. A dumb sexy blonde who sang opera."

"What was she like? Did you go out with her?"

He shrugs. "Davis made her. But he's a fairy anyhow.

He was always sucking up to Cribbets." His voice loud, drubbing me.

At the foot of the hill near the heating plant steam pours from a manhole billowing over the wet pavement. "Hell's down there. Sinners like us are turning on spits," he declaims.

"Sinners like you. I claim nothing."

His voice is polite and mild. "Are you a virgin, then? I think it's very nice. A woman's virginity is the finest gift she can give."

"Appropriate for birthdays and Christmas, as well as weddings?" I start walking rapidly. He is laughing at me and I hate it. Gauche, grass green he thinks me. "What's the damned time?"

He holds out his wrist. "Ten twenty."

"Come on. We'll just make it."

As he runs beside me uphill, "My books. Bring them out."

"I can't if I'm late. Hurry."

"If we don't make it . . . My journal. Don't read."

"You want . . . me to know you."

He stops short and turns. "If you read it, I'll know. If you read it, you'll be in my past. You'll become an entry."

"Like that?"

"Just like that."

"Don't threaten me, Mike."

He lets his umbrella fall to grab me by the shoulders. "Promise me you won't. Don't you understand what's happening?"

"No. I'm tired of mystery. I understand nothing."

"What's *happening*." He kisses me.

A hand on the nape of his neck, I kiss him back. His lips are cold and fresh, his hair wet. Drawing back we stare. His eyes hold me as if I floated on them. He fumbles at the buttons on my jacket and imitating I open his coat. The large buttons slide easily through the worn rotted holes. The wind cuts me and I shudder. He tries to draw the old coat around us like a tent but the wind flaps through. Together we fill the coat, our mouths joining again open.

As he lets me go and we begin to run, he repeats, "Promise!"

As I come in, Donna turns rubbing her eyes. "Late, Stu?"

"Six minutes." Tossing my wet jacket over a chair I put the loose-leaf on the dresser, lie down and begin to stare at it. "See that loose-leaf?"

"It's not hard to see. Mike's isn't it? Nice leather." When I only nod, she asks, "want me to kiss it?"

"You can flush it down the toilet."

"Are you mad at him?" She sits beside me, her face immediately tense with indignation. "What did he do?"

"Not mad. Hand me the cigarettes from my purse, won't you?" When I am with Mike I forget to smoke. I wonder sometimes how I remember to breathe, for I feel crammed into my eyes and ears and fingers, crowding hard at those windows looking to fall out at him. "In that lousy binder is a journal. He told me if I read it, I'd become an entry. No more Mike."

"Cute. Read it, of course, but don't tell him."

"He says he'd know if I read it."

"He's trying to scare you." She reaches for it.

"Don't."

Reddening, she swaggers away. "It's all yours." With a quick shuddery yawn she begins brushing her fine hair.

'He doesn't trust me. He doesn't realize how bloody broad-minded I am. Any experience carries prestige, even with a rhinoceros or his grandmother. He thinks I'm too gauche for the truth."

"You're making a crisis out of nothing. If you're interested—and you're practically quivering—read it. I bet it's boring. Now I'm going to bed." Her bare leg disappears into the upper bunk. "Worry about that stinking journal in the morning. I bet he isn't lying awake."

Hands clasped behind my neck, I lie taut, my nerves whining. Damn leather binder, rival, trusted over me.

I get up, cross to the dresser. The binder weighs heavily in my hands as I flip the pages so that I can see only the outside bottom corner of each. Pages of German glossed underneath, lecture notes, till finally I reach a closely written section. Mike in my hands. Phrases flash into view: "tormented by unfathomable lust . . ." "She, sitting in the chair, her pendulous . . ." breasts? Who? ". . . could not see in the dank fog more than the outline of the dark prow bearing down. . . ." ". . . His aquiline profile sneering. I fought to control my rage." I hear Mike's voice saying these scraps, his deep reading-aloud voice projecting. "Nevertheless, C's persistent efforts to intrigue me by hints of Wildean decadence . . ." "blood spurting from his opened veins like geysers . . ." ". . . hips swayed as if the power of the waves were in her . . ." I taste excitement like acid in my mouth. My palms leave damp patches. Disgusting. Mother in my attic room, rifling my papers. I snap the binder shut and toss it on the dresser.

When he comes by on Thursday after his classes to pick up his loose-leaf, he asks with a wide grin, his eyebrows shoved high, have I read the journal?

"No. I kept my promise."

"Good girl. I knew you would. You're honest."

But I could swear for an instant there's a slackening of disappointment in his face.

NINE

In Which Jill Considers the Teeth of the Lion

MARCH HAS TWO weathers, rain and snow, with sleet the median: frozen or half-and-half. The spongy earth sucks at our feet when we wander into the country. Branches drip like icy sores on our heads. We have no place to sit or stand or lean out of the rasping wind and the sniveling skies. Hands joined in Mike's pocket, we walk between buildings that are great honeycombs of privacy from which we are shut out. We shuttle through the university searching a room some careless janitor left unlocked.

I know his days; I can see the buildings of campus and the streets of town like a chessboard where he alone moves crowned through the ranks of professors and pawns. At seven forty-five each morning I call to wake him. Now I must get up. I do not understand why he wants me to do this, as he is often too sleepy to say more than, "Morning, pumpkin. Damn, I'm sleepy. Up till three."

Whenever our schedules can be wrenched to touch, we meet. Five minutes in the Diag, a square in front of the library where many paths of campus converge, five minutes in the drafty vestibule of the old romance languages build-

ing. Sometimes over coffee in the Union he shows me a
poem. First he reads it in that special loud voice. Then he
lets me look.

Hinc illae lacrimae

At the windows dusted with grime he stood,
The stained shade flapping limply at half mast.
Disgust sat on his head like a monk's hood
As he gazed upon the land of his brief past
And briefer future. He dreamed of knightly good
But found within and out mere nightly nast-
iness of men who rutted, cheated as they could.
There boredom stretched its dominion smoking, vast:

The city prone with black thighs spread
to naked sport lit only by the lewd
and bloodshot sign that blinked inside his head.
The razor at his wrist first sipped, then chewed.
The new mouths in the spare flesh outspewed,
vomiting him whiter than the bed.

If I ask too many questions or am not quick enough in
praise, or praise the wrong elements, he withdraws, hiding
in his loose clothes. Carefully I proffer my reactions,
grooming them to his pleasure.

One night prowling between homes where the blue glim-
mer of television shows through windows, we find a garage
with doors ajar. Outside an icy drizzle falls, but in here the
air is dry with a keen cold smell of paint and gasoline. We
wedge ourselves between the grille of a Ford and a lawn
mower leaning tipsily against the back wall. Coats unbut-
toned we press together. "We're safe for a bit," he murmurs. "We've shut the Greyzies out."

When I am with him time hangs in a queer stasis. We
move into a dark pocket where there are only intensities of
touch and stare. I keep my lids wide as we kiss, watching
his eyes flow into one large eye. The Cyclops, we call it.
His sliding hands cradle my belly, close over my breasts. I
cling, hands groping at the taut bow of his backbone. I
draw back and touch his eyelids with my tongue. Ice

breaking in the veins and marrow loosing a flood of want, my body bends to him. He conjures me into motion unsensual, ascetic as an arrow eating its arc in air toward its target.

He mumbles in my hair. "Do you have any doubts?"

"Doubts?" I repeat, confused. We have argued about religion several times.

"Look. Either I love you or I'm crazy. Do you love me?"

I rock back against the car, clenching my hands on the cold grille. "That word! So fancy. I don't know. I think so. . . ." I trace his cheek. "Love is what stuck my parents together, gouging each other. Love is what Mother calls it when she reads my mail or my diary. . . . How can you tell?"

"I know. That's how."

"I don't think I ever really loved anybody but Donna before—"

"Maybe you are queer."

"Don't be jealous of her. She brought us together."

We leave the garage. As we cross the street a car passes, casting our shadows forward, great long-legged creatures with one fat joined arm. But Mike stalks in injured silence, staring ahead.

"Stu, what do you think you're doing?" Donna kicks off her boots to pad over with a plaintive smile. "I brought you a roll from supper and an apple."

"I reach out of bed. "Thanks."

"Are you sick? Did Mike do something?"

She has interrupted a prolonged fantasy on the meaning of those scraps of his journal I stole with my eyes, shamefully. I said I did not read it, but I read those fragments. C.: Cribbets? The singer he referred to, what happened between them? Whose pendulous breasts? Maybe I am just too naive for him. I roll off the bed quilt and fall onto the floor. My head bumps but I will not give my stupidity the consolation of rubbing it. "I'm such an idiot, Donna. Am I in love?"

"Holy mother, how do I know? Don't you think so?

You've used the word yourself. You're mooning like a twelve-year-old."

"I used it in its loose sense—like I love tangerines or Blake. You love Lennie?"

"Yes. And how!"

"What do you mean?"

She ruffles my hair. "I like to go to bed with him. I want to make him happy. If I don't see him, I miss him. I'd marry him tomorrow if my folks wouldn't blow a fuse. But none of that means the same as saying I love him."

I run my nail along the radiator face, then catching her expression, stop. "I want experience. I want to use my life fully. But what I've fought for, waited for and finally got now is a little freedom."

"You think he's going to put you in a cage?"

"Love says, mine. Love says, I could eat you up. Love says, stay as you are, be my own private thing, don't you dare have ideas I don't share. Love has just got to gobble the other, bones and all, crunch. I don't want to do that. I sure don't want it done to me!"

She straddles her chair facing me, her navy skirt riding up. "What do you feel when you look at him?"

I reach for my jacket. "Nothing."

"Nothing? Then you're not in love."

"I mean there isn't any me. It's as if I evaporated."

"Where are you going? Don't you want me to come with you?"

"Sorry for all this. I promise to come home sane."

"Stu. If this is making you unhappy . . ." She taps her foot. "Don't run away. Forget the sullen bastard!"

Most of the doors stand open on the corridor with after-supper traffic in and out. A buzzer rasps and a tall auburn-haired woman trips out to answer the phone, acrobatically running up the zipper on her skintight sheath dress over the girdle and waist cincher as she ankles past. Some back-seat part of me would like to be courted at length and succumb with grace. Love on the rest of the corridor is pin-swapping, dulcet fraternity serenades, the swish of cocktail dresses, odorless corsages of small orchids. Why must I take decisions like a coal truck on a rutty road? Yet even as I pity myself, I remember our athletic chairman, Dulcie, with her lean competence and perennial tan, took an overdose of sleeping pills between semesters. The maid found her, Dulcie's stomach was pumped and she spends several hours a week seeing a psychiatrist at the Neuro-Psychiatric Institute. She has taken off the engagement ring with the karat and a half diamond. Dulcie will not tell anybody what happened, so rumors are still proliferating.

The wide sky over the athletic field is deep blue, clear as a note from a tuning fork. In the west the bell tower and smokestacks of the heating plant, the bare upreaching trees, stand in two-dimensional obsidian sharp silhouettes against a lemon horizon. But what use is it to feel beauty if I have no one to share it with? An old lack. Have I got so used to loneliness I fight against breaching it? My mother has always called me a coward.

As I cross campus most buildings are dark, but for a slot of lights in a lab in the chemistry building, a vista of bleak halls where a Black janitor pushes a broom. I live in a white world now, I realize. Only two Black women in my whole dormitory and guess what, they room together although they clearly come from different parts of the country and cannot have requested each other. On the dormitory application they ask for a photograph and they also ask race. A stench of formaldehyde blows out the vent on the natural sciences building. Well, except as I live and act I am a sort of fetal pig myself, pink belly of shriveled innocence like the poor creatures we dissected in zoology for our lab final.

I turn away from campus through the streets of the town, the grey and white wooden houses, the arching oaks and maples. This is an attractive town, more spacious than my old neighborhood, one reason I like to walk here. Less often now because seeing Mike takes time. In a grey church a service is going on: in midweek? I thought they did that on Sunday. Light blends through stained-glass figures, tall and stoop-shouldered with faces in yellow fishbowls. All men, so it's Protestant. At least the Catholics have a lady or two. A smell of drains around churches. How can something holy be clammy? What I find holy is the radiance of the particular, this light, this tree, the uniqueness of a face. Donna's. His. When something moves me I want to seize it in my mind and write a poem that can make that energy happen again.

I remember going to church in Cold Springs at Uncle Edward the minister's church. We had no choice. Grandfather, Uncle Edward, Aunt Jean and Aunt Mary all assumed real human beings were Presbyterians. I tried to mesh in childhood. Everybody in our neighborhood seemed to go to some damned church except for Callie and me. She lent herself to my games, content with her urchin's wistful smile that a field should be a jungle or a Dakota encampment or an arctic tundra, if I said so. I lent myself to her home movies. "See, you got a gun and you twist my arm and tell me I got to. But at first I give you a real hard struggle. Then you push me down and you make me do it. Okay?" That virginity she was to give up so readily to Dino had fought first through the Perils of Pauline, only to submit on a heap of corpses under machine-gun fire with a bomb behind her head. Callie's old room—before she got pregnant and had to marry Sharkie—shines in my head like a stained-glass window in blues, yellows and whites, her white bedstead, the blue glass pitcher I won for her at St. Luke's carnival, a plastic doll dressed as a bride that we swiped at Kresge's. When a train passed, the springs hummed like rails. I loved her, awkwardly, clumsily, patchily; but never told her so.

I find I have turned and walked toward Mike's dormitory. Its lights rise over the wing of the Union. As I round the corner, I slow to a sedate walk. I do love him. I don't believe in forever or clutching, but I love him. I'll tell him right now. His dormitory has the same red-brick facade as mine but sprouts more wings and is much taller and bigger. Nine stories of men: embarrassing.

The anonymous rows of lights usurp the sky. Worse, as I cross the street to enter the court, I see that every wing has an entrance. Of course, the boys had no curfew; they don't sign in and out as we do. I see no women around. Women are not allowed in the men's rooms any more than they are in ours, but women do not go to the men's quarters as men

come to ours to fetch us and return us again. Perhaps there
is no desk to summon him? I imagine blundering through
corridors, stumbling panicked into wrong rooms, mocked,
laughed at. This place feels off limits. A guy leans out his
fourth-floor window.

"Hey, honey. Looking for me? What are you looking
for? You want it, honey?"

Although I pretend I cannot hear him, I turn away. I
imagine yelling out loud, "Mike! Mike!" until I hear my
voice bouncing off the walls and my neck heats as if I'd
done it. How do I know he's home? I realize with a spongy
sinking in my gut that I am not going to have the nerve to
barge through the nearest door and ask directions. I cannot
wish him out of that blazing rabbit warren. I am already
turning as I think, I should have just walked in.

I go back to my dormitory but I cannot yet face Donna.
She represents a set of demands. The first, that I become
involved with a man, I have fulfilled. The second, that my
involvement mirror hers with Lennie, I am just beginning
to reject. She does not want me as obsessed with Mike as I
am becoming. I consider Julie and reject her, for I am in
no mood for clever chatter or gossip. I go into the next
house and head for Theo's single room.

Theo's laconic, "Come," brings me in to find her lying
on the floor listening to a violin concerto. "Wieniawski,"
she offers, reading my curiosity. "Talk or listen?"

"Listen," I say, pleased at her company and her silence.
She offers me vodka from a rubbing alcohol bottle. I hate
vodka but think it would be gauche to admit that. I take a
big gulp and manage to swallow, although I must blink
hard to keep my eyes from watering.

When the record finishes I ask, "Have you ever been in
love?"

Theo sits up on a tan elbow and stares. "Me?"

"Is someone else here?"

"Ummm," she says noncommittally. Then she blurts
out, "Yeah."

"Did you love them a lot?"

"Too much."

"Did they love you?"

She coughs a laugh. "No. It was my psychoanalyst."

"Your psychoanalyst? Oh, transference."

"Yeah, he encouraged that. It was healthy and I had sexual problems, he explained, that could only be worked out by him. On top."

"You're kidding. A doctor? Who was he?"

"Never mind the name. I'm still scared of him."

"What are you scared of?" I hardly believe this.

"Jill, he and my parents had me committed. I had to spend a year in a loony bin before I figured out I should take back my story. I agreed it was hysteria and I was just making it all up about him forking me three days a week on the couch in his office."

"He made you do that?"

Theo shrugs, reaching for the rubbing alcohol bottle. "If this was really what it says, we'd go blind."

I choke. How do I know what's in the bottle?

Theo gives me a weak smile. "It was his idea. I was scared. But then I was in loooooove with him. Like a clam on a fork."

"But haven't you ever loved anybody else, I mean, in real life?"

"Pablo Casals. I want to be a cello. . . . That was my real life, old bean. This is my afterlife."

"But you got away from them."

"Not so far. Not so very far at all. Alan the doctor of my soul is in New York and so are my parents. You can fly there and eat supper with them. The wonders of technology."

"You didn't grow up in New York?"

"With a Kansas drawl? My father as he succeeds moves eastward. We moved to Manhattan when I was fourteen."

"But you're twenty." Mike's age. "You'll be twenty-one soon and then they can't touch you."

"Old bean, I'll never be an adult. They can always commit me. I've been certified a loony and loony is what I am. Every time I get kicked out of another school for drinking, they threaten me. Alan tells them how sick I am. The only terms I'm here on is I see this chum of his Dr. Atwood three times a week."

"What does he do?"

"Classic Freudian. Sits and hides his yawns. I know how to make the hour go by like a dripping faucet. I am careful. I am cool. All I have to do is keep my lies straight.

I decide I will not confide in Theo about Mike. As I go upstairs to Donna I remember her crack about collecting misfits. Yet Dulcie seemed one who fit in superbly, her future with its clauses spelled out like an insurance policy. All women are misfits, I think; we do not fit into this world without amputations.

A thaw quickens the air. The sky is busy; the sun appears like a blessing between clouds and touches my face. At four I am to meet Mike. Meantime I browse for Donna's birthday present. I've almost decided to get the collected Dylan Thomas poems when I think, If I give her a book she'll be flattered in her mind, but if I give her something pretty, she'll be glad all the way through. So I buy the Thomas for me and having no money left I saunter off to steal her present. What will please her truly I cannot afford anyhow. With a high tight tingle in my chest I amble in the trench coat only slightly stained and now repaired in the hem that Donna and I found in the Nearly New Shoppe just off Main Street last week. I have not repaired the right pocket, which is bottomless and empties into the hem.

Once I have secured it, I run with the present and the boughten book (dog with a bird in my mouth) to a bench I like over the railroad tracks. I like to be conscious of Detroit in one direction, Chicago in the other. Finally surfeited with poetry, I scrawl a quick letter to Howie quoting fatly and ordering him to buy the Thomas.

Spring vacation is only 2 weeks. Glad we're getting off at the same time. I'm in love with Mike. He comes from Detroit too—not that you'd think so to meet him. He's *erudite*. He's fantastically brilliant. It's a big blowy day here and soon I'll meet him. In the meantime I move carefully so as not to knock people's houses over. Remember to get hold of the Thomas immediately.

Your roommate sounds like a real jerk. If he keeps bugging everyone, why don't you send *his* name to McCarthy as a pinko-commie-dupe and let him see how much he enjoys his hero in action! If he does that again, why don't you tear up one of *his* books and see how he likes it?

We are so shy signing our letters that we both use the ploy of writing to the bottom of the page so there's room only for the name squeezed in. But love makes me strong in my other loves and I sign it with a flourish above my name.

Mike already sits at a table in the Union. I rush through the line to get my coffee. When I bring it over he is slipping my Thomas from its bag. His brows rear up. "So?"

I smile. "I went to get Donna a present, but greed ran away with me. 'The force that through the green fuse drives the flower drives—' "

"*Merde.* He was an actor, not a man of letters."

"I like those poems."

"You would. He's a decadent romantic and that draws you."

"Decadent, am I? I thought I was just badly read."

His hands rest with the knuckles heavy as judges, holding the book wrestled flat. " 'Into her lying down head.' That's all you need!" His mouth drops, he rolls his eyes.

" 'through the rippled drum of the hair buried ear;
    and Noah's rekindled now unkind dove
        Flew man-bearing there. . . .

Rekindled now unkind dove—all to rime eventually with love, as maybe we suspected? Hairy embroidery. You don't care what it means. You want to get drunk on the words."

I try to tug the book from under his fist. Already he has mangled that poem so I won't be able to read it without hearing his voice turning it to rant. "Give it to me. If you don't like it, you have no right to ruin it for me."

He plants his fist harder. "No right? How could I ruin it unless I'm right?"

"You can spoil anything saying it that way."

"You want to take it and hide with it! Like a secret drinker away in a corner smacking your lips."

"Are you jealous of a book?"

"Why not? That actor! If you loved me you'd understand. Why can't I hate anything you stare at and run off to and prefer to me? You spend yourself on everything."

"I do love you!"

"Sure." His teeth are clenched. He has hardened his face to a mask of derision on which my message is spent without effect. "You love me alongside of Donna and your idol Professor Donaldson and that boy you write to and your old dead cats."

The table sinks and I am strapped to my chair. "No. I love you. Listen." Tears burn my cheeks. "Do you want me to hate everybody else?" If only I had not signed the letter, love. "What can I say? I love you."

"More than the others?"

"Much more." I feel guilty. What does that mean?

"More than your parents?"

I nod.

"More than God?"

"I don't believe in any god."

More gently he says, "You have to. Otherwise it's just ants on an anthill. It just all comes to dust." He leans back in his chair.

He did not ask about Donna; that is a relief. In that lull I feel the stares. Scarecrow with dripping eyes I sit in a ring of watchful tables. In public nakedness I expiate my cowardice in not daring to enter his dormitory last night. If I had told my love then, this would not have occurred. He came ready to find fault with me.

He prods my hand on the table, the fingers one by one. "So we belong to each other now?"

Belong frightens me but I nod.

"If you love me, throw that book away."

"I can't. That would be wasteful."

"I'll return it. Get you something you should have."

I do not like this but I have no energy left to fight.

He sandwiches my book into the center of his pile, calling my attention to his leather binder. "Paulsen, my writing teacher, didn't like the journal. Too imitative, says he, the bastard. But I was getting tired of it anyhow."

The binder is noticeably thinner. "You didn't throw it away!"

"A purge." He snaps his fingers. "It was going good up to the point where my best character J.—for *je, naturellement*—kills himself by taking off his clothes and walking into Lake Michigan. But Paulsen, the creep, said that was too much like Virginia Woolf's suicide. I'm going back to poetry anyhow. Prose is too slack. It's for amateurs." He yanks his coat on, picking up the books.

That journal I agonized over was fiction. I'd like to break a chair on his head. He waits but I sit on, trying to think up something nasty enough to puncture him. Then remembering what I came to tell him today, I jump up. We walk out past the tables where certain stares follows us, as we proceed much too slowly toward the refuge of the hall.

TEN

Life Goes to a Party

W E HAVE ALREADY been thrown out of a dark conference room in Angell Hall to walk the rain-pelted streets under Mike's big umbrella. Watch how we walk, pressed together in concert, movements synchronized, thighs together, my shoulder floating on his arm. In a dark tango through the puddles I follow him, experiencing myself as small and soft, as if my body had changed suddenly. Under a tree we kiss and the slow drip of the branches blesses our heads. Luck is with us and in only the third building we find an auditorium left unlocked. A scuffling down near the stage halts us with our hands frozen together.

"Mice," he whispers. I sit on his lap and slowly we resume building up each other's body from the dark. I am so accustomed to the damp frieze of his coat against my cheek I cannot imagine how it would feel to be parted by thinner membranes. Flesh is a distant smoothness strained toward. This intense yearning will be interrupted in five minutes, sometimes in twenty, by janitor or campus cop or other students. I learn his body in small patches.

* * *

Tonight Donna is eating her birthday supper at Lennie's while I finish a paper due tomorrow, before we go home for spring vacation. Easter is early this year. When I am done, I am to join Mike, Donna and Lennie at a party Peter is giving in the apartment where Donna and Lennie first slept together the night after Christmas vacation. How my life has changed since then, and Donna's too.

A block of loose-jointed rambling wooden houses and thick-waisted oaks. The number in my hand matches a plain grey house with a wooden fire escape. Timidly I give the front door a push. It opens on a wide entry hall where an English bike is padlocked to the banister. Through a door ajar come guitars and voices singing a work song raggedly. I stand in the hall feeling the clean fragrant air of the spring night clinging to me, longing to go on walking through the roomy darkness past lighted houses with my thoughts for company. Then a couple enters and pushes past, arguing. "Well, maybe there are worse things than cutting a few classes," the woman snaps. "Such as being terrified ever to cut a class." It is Julie with Van. Then she sees me and forces a smile. "Are you lost, Jill? Peter lives here."

Van nods at me. I always feel he does not quite approve. In some way I am not appropriate. Mostly he gives me curt little nods from his blond-mustached eminence, sometimes a little jerk of his clenched pipe. He comes from Kalamazoo, where his father works in a paper mill. Sometimes I think he is afraid if he talks to me, our common class background will be apparent to everyone. In they go, Julie with her arm in mine sweeping me along. Her taffeta dress rustles. That worries me. My red warrior is at the cleaners, finally, and I am wearing my black turtleneck with my best black corduroy pants, an outfit put together out of some image in the back of my mind of French existentialists and set off with a long double loop of my mother's bloodred beads from the twenties I used to wear when I played dress-up with Callie.

In a moment I see that for once and accidentally I fit in. The women are mostly not dressed as the image party suggests, in spike heels and swishing dresses. "Rather bo-

hemian," Van mutters, responding to Julie's elbow by helping her off with her coat. "Didn't expect that of Peter."

"In his Prince Hal in Eastcheap phase," Julie murmurs,
peering around. Kids sit on the floor, playing guitars, ban-
jos, bongos, nodding their heads and faking the words. "In
college it is permitted to slum a little."

"I didn't know you knew Peter?"

"Not personally," Julie says. "But I know who he is."

"Who is he?" I mean that literally, looking at the dim
room crowded with people.

Van floats above us and all this. His interests end in
1800. His passion is Dryden. All since is arriviste.

"Forest Crecy's son," Julie says primly. "I never heard
of any other Crecys, but they're an old Detroit family."

"Crazy Louey's Bargain Used Cars," I say equally
primly. "Deals on Wheels. West Chicago and Grand
River."

"In Detroit there are only the Forest Crecys—they've
been around since fur-trading days."

In the next room I can see people standing in groups
talking, but the folksingers are easier on my shyness. This
is the only music actually sung and played in our peer
group. Pop music is crooners soggily serenading our parents. White rock music belongs to the high-school crowd
none of us were in with. Black music I knew only because
I lived in a partly Black neighborhood. We think folk
music is real, gritty, authentic. We like songs about old
labor struggles. With relief I see Lennie propped against a
radiator with a guitar that looks too big for him, his head
flung back and his red beard wagging as he sings with wide-
open mouth. Lennie, my longlost friend, I could kiss you
for providing me with a goal in this room. I can even take
my time climbing over legs and drinks, noticing that although your voice is hoarse, your hands are quick and
loving on the strings. I stand smiling while you finish with
a flourish, then flash your teeth as if in surprise.

"I didn't know you played. Where's Donna?"

"Here someplace." He glances around. "Mike's boozing
it up in the next room."

So far through a forest of shoulders. I sit against the radiator. Soon I will make my trek, soon. Clearly among the folksingers are two stars, who play the best and know all the songs. A woman who plays the banjo hard and skillfully is singing in a good full contralto, a tall woman with long straight heavy chestnut hair hanging like a cloak about her shoulders. Her face is sharp, pert, pretty in an asymmetrical way. I have the feeling I have seen her before, but I do not know where. She is somewhat older than I am and sings with ready confidence. Alberta, they call her. "Alberta, play 'East Virginee.'" "Alberta, 'Los Quatro Generales.'" The other performer is swarthy, broad-shouldered, good-looking, with teeth that seem to cancel out the rest of his face. He sings very loud but very well and they call him Rob.

Time to look for Mike and Donna. The next room is brighter and spotted with intent clumps, a few stranded on the rim like me, but glass in hand trying to look preoccupied. By the door to the kitchen Mike is talking with two men, one tawnily gorgeous, the other older in seedy-looking tweeds. As I come up, the tawny one is saying, "Salinger as the American Flaubert—if I hear that once more I shall puke. All those little borax freshmen running around with *Catcher* under their arms, thinking they've found their soul in paperback."

I wish Mike would introduce me. All he does is put his arm around me and go on talking. Now I cannot follow them, for they are discussing someone who wrote letters to the tawny man, Stone. He has a face that seems all profile, one he keeps exhibiting by turning his head to and fro like an electric fan, his mane flopping as he blows out words and hauteur.

Mike drawls, "If you really have those letters, how come you never printed them?"

The man in tweed flaps his elbows. "Couldn't get permission, eh, Stone?"

"I wouldn't know, since I certainly never tried. Don't you think it would be a little cheap to trade on his name?"

I will never understand. I do not like their fencing, but I

mistrust my dislike since entering it is beyond me. Mike is probably five years younger than Stone and ten years younger than the other, yet they treat him as an equal because he plays well. The knowledge that sets up the game, I want that.

A slight blond boy, conservatively dressed so that what I notice first in this motley arguing crowd are his detachment and his tailoring, stops to greet Mike, then looks leisurely and carefully at me. "I'm Peter Crecy." Our host.

Mike turns to say before I can, "This is Jill." His arm drops to my waist, hugging me against him.

"Of course." Peter smiles briefly. His blue eyes behind glasses are as fresh and paler than Donna's. He seems to have no inhibition against staring. Mike stands a moment suspended between us and the others, then with a scowl of despair, turns back to Stone. Peter says, "I've seen you crying in the Union with Mike," as he might say, "I've seen you having coffee."

Off balance I ask, "Do you know where my roommate is?"

He laughs dryly. "Might if you told me her name."

"Sorry. Donna Stuart."

"She's holding court in the kitchen. But you're Stuart too, aren't you? You can't be sisters."

"All men are sisters." I break from Mike to slip past Peter.

"The light and dark sides of the moon." Peter does not move to let me past. Instead he shifts his trim athletic body to brush against me. "What's on the dark side of the moon?"

"More green cheese." I wriggle past.

Mike calls after, "Our gin's in the refrigerator. Bring it back."

Donna's sharp sawing laugh. She perches on the Formica table letting her legs kick but does not see me at first because she is flirting with one of the teaching assistants from the English department.

"Happy Birthday, ketsale," I say, Grandma's endearment surprising me.

"I'm so glad to see you! Mike gave me a Bach cantata, isn't that nice? But see, I'm wearing my sweater you gave me. The first cashmere I ever had." Her baby face puckers. "Feel, how soft!"

A pullover with a round collar, the color of her eyes. Her face glows above it. "What are you drinking, ma Donna?"

"First it was Rhine wine. Then beer. Now it's Scotch. I love it and Peter got it out for me because it's my birthday. He has a whole cabinet of liquor but he keeps it locked." She leans conspiratorially and I think she means to whisper but instead she shouts in my ear, "Peter's rich!"

"And tight," a guy pouring water into trays at the sink adds. Donna mutters that he is Peter's roommate, whose name she has forgotten. She slides off the table to jiggle my elbow. "Come to the john with me."

After the door shuts she says, "I've been flirting with Peter and his nothing roommate and even with Rob Prewitt when he came in the kitchen, guitar and all." She sits down on the toilet. "I must pee quietly because the kitchen is full of men," she says gravely.

"I doubt they're listening. Men don't listen to us even when we talk." I am still irritated that Mike did not introduce me.

"I shouldn't have left Lennie, should I? Stu, he gave me a phonograph. He's so sweet I could cry!"

I lean on the bathtub rim. "Where did he get the money?"

"I thought it was so sad when Mike gave me a record, because if anything happened to your changer and it hardly works now, I'd never be able to listen to it again. The phonograph was here when we arrived, on the kitchen table. Lennie said, 'Peter's got so much dough he even has a phonograph in the kitchen. Crecy, be a good guy. Give the girl a break and let her have it.'" At the sink she daubs at her face. "Know what I'm going to do? I'm going to be honest and tell him about Jim tonight. Make a clean breast."

"You mean you didn't? Not ever?"

"If he doesn't love me then, I won't bother him. I'll give him back the phonograph and go away." Her shoulders droop pathetically.

"Go on, he isn't going to stop loving you for some old story."

"But, suppose he does mind?"

I take her hand. Clay cold. "You have to get it out of the way sometime."

"Out of the way, yes." She combs her fine hair. "How do you like Peter?"

I shrug. "Actually I don't."

"He makes me wonder what he's like in bed."

I snort. "Thorns and ice cubes."

She grins. "That's how little you know." She pushes me out of the bathroom ahead of her, facing the second room. Then she says, "Whoops. I've been off the job too long!"

Lennie has come into the second room. Perched on the arm of his chair and almost in his lap, laughing with gross-good-natured flirtation is a young woman in a gaudy homemade-looking orange and gold and purple dress, gypsyish with several bead necklaces that slither forward as she plays with Lennie's beard. "Who's she?" I ask.

"Stephanie Barboulis, the greedy Greek. Some bitch who's always trying to get him, ever since he used her for a model." Donna darts forward with a falsetto laugh.

I turn back to fetch the drinks I was sent for. The refrigerator is jammed with bottles but ours is easy to find, a half-empty bottle of Gordon's Gin stamped across the label with Mike's name and address. While I am mixing gin and tonic a familiar voice says, "Miss Stuart. What are you making?"

"Gin and tonic—the only drink I know how to mix. Want one?" I am damned if I am going to address him as Professor Donaldson at a party. I really would mix one for him, Mike's gin and all. As I look up into his auburn-bearded face my old puppy worship floods me warmly.

"No, I'm a wino. Booze makes me drunk all at once. Very unfashionable, but there you have it."

"I miss you. Professor Grimes is an old fart who's so far right he wants the monarchy restored." I rarely think be-

fore I speak, I decide. I open my mouth and the words like
dear little furry vampire bats fly out. Professor Grimes is
probably his best friend. I know it is not done to criticize
the faculty to each other.

"With himself as king? I thought he wanted to be pope."

"No. There's no fun being infallible if you have to use
somebody else's book."

"Never mind." He smiles at me. He is so much taller he
must crane way over. The last time I talked to him was
when I ran into him on campus the week after the final
and he told me I had gotten the highest score on the test.
Pure lust in action. I didn't say that; tonight I almost
could. "The semester's half over. Are you going to major in
history? Why don't you take my labor seminar?"

The folksinging has broken up and the guy Rob Prewitt
in the buffalo plaid shirt moseys up still clutching his guitar,
saying loudly, "I intend to. Are you starting with the
Knights of Labor?"

I could bounce a bottle off Rob Prewitt's head. I don't
remember him in that class but I suppose I rarely noticed
anybody but Donaldson. Rob is so self-assured I hate him.
Stealing my moment.

"With the first strike. That was before the revolution . . ."

I have lost his attention and Mike looms to grip my arm.
"Where have you been?"

"Talking—like you."

He tugs me along. "Let's find some privacy." The first
bedroom is occupied by a couple having a fight, Julie and
Van. Julie stands at the window kneading her taffeta skirt
in her hands.

"Please leave us," she hisses.

The second bedroom is empty. Shutting the door, he
starts tossing coats from the bed to the floor. How much
has he had to drink—all the missing gin? The bed clear, he
drops on it. I take a seat gingerly.

"Don't be coy. I've been wanting you desperately all
night."

"You've been too busy playing games."

"I have to keep up my contacts." Smiling at his own
pomposity, he sweeps me down beside him.

I try to distract him from his heavy drowsy ardor. "Who is that Stone?"

"Grant Stone? Got a rich mother and Spore Press. I've been trying to bug him into printing me but he just teases. He's a first-class asshole."

"What makes him a first-class one?"

"Most assholes are stupid. He knows, but he's out for himself." In long gestures his hands trace over me.

"That makes me second-class."

"That makes you soft." He smooths my hair on the pillow, letting himself down till his weight covers me. Hot and cold, yes and no, run arpeggios on my skin. Then for the first time yet familiarly the knot tightens, the hot hollow cramp of wanting. I stare at the ceiling where a lamp makes a wide dim circle on the plaster rippled by strips of lathing. His zipper. Laughter, a surf of conversation, a thump followed by breaking glass. Something presses against my thigh I know by counting his hands must be his phallus.

"Mike . . . somebody will come in."

"I locked the door."

"That's worse."

He closes my hand around it, thick and stumpy. To tear my flesh. I hold it where he placed my hand, scared silly of moving, while he kisses me. His organ is fatter and harder than I had expected and I cannot, cannot understand where it will fit in me.

"Well, don't hold it like a garden hose."

I laugh. "You were so damn tickled I'm a virgin."

He shakes me. "Don't giggle! What we're doing isn't funny."

"Mike, I can't help being nervous." I pull from him, fixing my sweater and pants with choppy gestures.

He cradles me against him. "I want you so much."

"But not just anyplace, not like dogs on a sidewalk."

"I'm not ashamed."

"I can't feel alone with you. I can't relax here. Are you angry?"

He stands tucking his shirt in, shaking his pants down. "During vacation I'll get the car. Then we'll be alone." His fingers graze my cheek as we step back into the party. "Next week in Detroit, pumpkin. One more week."

I look around to see if everybody is watching. Only Julie gives me a look of arched brows, as she steps into her coat. Rob Prewitt is playing the guitar again, with Stephanie sitting on the arm of his chair while he sings directly to her. Donaldson stands with his arm around the pert woman who played the banjo. I know now where I saw her, leaving his apartment that morning. I like the way Alberta looks. She is almost as tall as Donaldson and she does not lean on him but has her arm around his waist as his is around hers, standing there foursquare on her feet. I resolve to stop sticking to Mike's side like a melting snowbank. I watch them, puzzled. I am passionately in love with Mike, yet for a moment there in the kitchen I would have done anything to capture Donaldson's attention. I wanted him too. What does that mean? I'll have to ask Donna.

Donna is just hanging her coat as I walk in. "Well, bella Donna, it's after midnight and not your birthday any longer, but be happy still!" I kiss her cheek.

She leans her cold forehead against mine. "I'm sober now."

"Hung over?"

"I'm fine. It was a very nice evening." Voice quiet, gritty. She stares down at her skirt, unzipping it carefully as if it were on a mannequin.

"What's wrong? Did you tell Lennie about Jim?"

She folds the new sweater into a plastic bag. "Yes."

"What happened?"

She puts her bra and panties into her laundry bag. Naked she stands brushing her corn tassel hair, her small sharp breasts pulled high. "Nothing."

"Nothing?"

"He took it like a lollipop." She slips into her plaid robe and starts for the john down the hall. "He simply looked grave and said he was sure my sister would forgive me if she knew the circumstances. Then he started talking about abstract expressionism."

"Well, aren't you glad to have it out of the way?" I push open the door into the room with the row of toilets and row of sinks.

"Out of the way?" Beside me she brushes her teeth, spits, stares into the sink. "I guess I counted on that. It didn't mean a thing to him! He didn't understand."

Confession and absolution. A ritual we play. Lennie couldn't respond, is that it? I feel guilty as if I had deceived her, made promises about the world I cannot force it to keep.

When we returned to our room Julie is waiting, perched against the cream-of-tomato-colored draperies in her severe navy wool bathrobe piped with green. Sometimes I look at Julie and see someone dressed by a mother who does not love her, with a good deal of money to spend. I have a brief moment of feeling caught between clients, because Julie clearly has feelings about the evening to spill too.

"We didn't mean to walk in on you two." I sit at my desk, equidistant from Donna lying in an S shape on her bunk and Julie perched rigidly on the window ledge. "You didn't look too happy."

"Couldn't you expect a man who's supposed to be in love with you and can drive perfectly well and knows how to take buses anyhow, to be able to come and see you during a ten-day vacation? From Kalamazoo to my house is maybe four hours! He acts as if I'm requesting he visit me in Antarctica!"

"You want your parents to meet him?"

"They met him when they visited. But I want him to come to the house and view them in their natural habitat. Besides, I must move this along. It's stalled in the tentative phase."

"Are you sure you want Van?"

"Why not?" She pats at her tightly curled hair.

"Why not become a nun?" Donna snaps in response.

"Episcopalian nuns are too weird. Besides, I look like something undercooked in black. . . . You were in the bedroom with Mike a long time, Jill. Well?"

"Well, what? It wasn't that long. In the middle of a party?"

"If you really loved him, you wouldn't care," Donna says.

"Loving him isn't the same as being able to get excited," I say and an injured silence exudes from her. "I can't help wanting a time that feels right."

"I see. A rigid honesty does for me. If you don't think discussing certain things with Lennie was harder than just going to bed with him, you're crazy!"

Julie smiles a little mournfully, her brown eyes soft but her mouth pursed into a smirk. "We must both use our vacations, Jill, to get ourselves properly deflowered like Donna."

Bull's-eye, because Donna has just remembered she told Julie she was a virgin; a statement Julie disbelieved anyhow. Donna doesn't care enough to keep her lies straight with Julie. I have a moment of seeing the whole dormitory as a minefield of sexual hypocrisy, all women lying to each other about what they are doing or not doing with boys they also lie to, because the boys lie to and about them. "I don't think of it as a flower or a cauliflower," I say. "Just an accident I want to correct by willpower."

"That ain't what does it, sweetie." Donna sits up, cheerfully vulgar. "I say the two of you will come back from spring vacation just as you're going forth, prepared to talk about *it* every night for the next three hundred and sixty-four nights."

"To judge from what I heard of his torrid journal, at least Mike will know what he's about," Julie says. "You won't have to seduce him."

Donna is still angry at me: because Lennie didn't absolve her, because Julie is in the room, because she accidentally told Julie the truth. Because she is tired and wants to be asleep and we are clearly going to talk for a while. Because we all have to go home separated from our boyfriends and our little support group, and none of us want to.

Donna bounds up off the bed to pace, her snow leopard mode, all icy speed. Julie and I watch her bemused, our heads turning. Then she drops astride her desk chair and faces us, estranged from her by our inexperience. "Julie, you want it handed to you on a silver platter. If you do want him, get him. What's stopping you? Put your hand on his prick if you have to. Rub against him. Sit on his lap and wriggle. Nothing easier, if you really want him. People don't usually issue engraved invitations to have affairs with them. Not black tie. . . . And you, Jill, you're just scared of men. You talk and talk and talk about honesty and integrity and then you find some picky reason why it's honest and full of integrity to be scared shitless! I feel sorry for Mike."

I feel as if Donna has kicked me in the belly. I blink very hard. Julie looks resolutely impassive, watching. Donna goes on, smiling sourly: "I bet each of you a dinner you won't do it. That's what men of the better social classes usually pay for it, isn't it? A restaurant dinner?"

"In the restaurant of our choice?" Julie asks.

"No. The restaurant of my choice. I'm the one who's going to be taken out. Twice."

I agree to the bet, annoyed. Donna doesn't perceive Mike clearly or she wouldn't bother pushing. Me, I wish everybody began fucking each other when we were in kindergarten, to avoid this anxious nonsense.

ELEVEN
Hot Pastrami on Wry

"WHAT CAN I do, Mrs. S.?" Matt sits head in hands at the kitchen table. "I'm flat broke. But I swear I'll pay you for last month, somehow."

Mother washes, I dry, while Dad lies on the couch with the television on. Mother shakes the crisp unruly hair from her eyes. "Now, I'm not worried about that. But a big strong boy like you ought to be able to find work."

"I tried, Mrs. S. Don't I get up every morning stinking early no matter how it kills me and go the rounds? Do I lie in bed? Do I wait for them to come to me?"

How much like one of the family he sounds with that self-righteous rhetoric. Even begun to use his hands. Your best friends won't tell you, Matt, but you've been assimilated.

"They're laying off from the auto plants. And in the offices all they ask is, have you done your service and have you got your degree—and they don't mean no high-school diploma."

"It's a fact," Dad shouts from the front room. "A high-school diploma doesn't mean what it did. They keep them

125

in school too long anyhow." He has grown tolerant of
Matt. Sometimes he lets him cower in the basement, helping at the workbench as I used to. But only sometimes.

Mother's eyes narrow. "Did you go to all those places I
circled in red crayon in the Sunday paper?"

I dry the pots now, hurrying to finish so I can dress for
Mike. I know where Matt spends his days. I saw him with
Freddie's younger brother and Le Roy next door rebuilding
the engine on a hot rod at the garage where Sharkie works.
Matt ducked behind the raised hood when Sharkie came
out to yell at me, "Hey, Tits, how's it goin'?" the way he
does.

Matt half rises. "I'll join the army. Let them take me! I'll
go down and enlist tomorrow. . . ." He trails off, waiting.

Head cocked, birdlike, she deliberates. "That might be
your best bet, Matt. Both my boys were in the army."

Sure, and Leo came out a con man and Francis spent six
months in stockade and pulled a dishonorable. What games
they play. She'll never let him out from under her thumb. I
grab the bathroom, racing for the hot water left from
dishes. Although I turn on the water in the tub and strew
the floor with clothing to mark possession, when I pass him
in the hall he will not respond to my stuck-out tongue. He
shuffles along with his shoulders sagging in the tee shirt, all
the fight wilted from him.

I put on my black shirtdress I bought two summers ago
when I had a job at Sam's Cutrate Department Store downtown, quickly so that Mother will not appear and realize I
am not wearing a slip. Then I sit at her vanity hoping for
inspiration. I arch my neck, strain as tall as I can before
the mirror. The rite of unity that will forge us into one. On
my face the pale intensity of decision. Maybe I should
borrow Mother's powder. Rachel No. 2. The act of love—
such a taut phrase. I feel like the heroine of a novel or an
opera. I should speak in verse.

She sits at the mirror in the last pared minutes
of growing cool and separate as a birch tree
while the moth of fear beats at her throat. . . .

In her throat! Is pared too precious?

"Well, honey, a date." Mother shuts the door with a clanging of hangers, a swishing of Dad's ties. "What are you mooning about?"

If I ignore her, will she leave? Fat chance.

"Black! Why try to look drab?" She pokes at my shoulder.

I hang back from her touch. "I'm light. I can wear it." Why do I always defend?

"You'd think your parents had died, black black black! Wait till you have your fill of funerals." She sinks on the bed staring at me, her face reflected in the mirror next to my own. Her small lips are pursed as if over something sour. "What's he going to do—this boy—Michael?"

"Teach in a college."

"Um. Teachers don't make much."

"I'm not going to marry him, Mother!" I feel stirred up already, as if she could reach a long spoon into my guts. She is always making arbitrary naive statements about the outside world. The faculty makes a lot more than my father, but she is firmly convinced colleges are raddled by genteel poverty.

"Can't I make a simple statement?" She picks a loose hair from my shoulders. "What's his father do?"

"He's dead."

"Poor boy." She pinches my arm whispering, "He's Jewish?"

I nod.

She eyes herself in the mirror. "Your father won't like that. Orthodox?" She fluffs her hair.

"No."

"You know what a bother it was with Grandma. Papa used to say you need new ways in a new land. He could read five languages and his English was perfect. *She* never learned to talk right."

Actually I liked her food requirements, for they meant we ate differently and had to go down to the old Jewish neighborhood where Howie lives to shop. When Grandma came in the summer was the only time I ever had bagels, stuffed cabbage, smoked whitefish, ruggeleh. "Mike is studying German and French."

She lets her hands fall on her thighs. "Never could see what good it did Papa, selling door to door, packing fish. Then getting himself killed and leaving us with all those kids. It's a hard life, it's a dog eat dog, and don't let those professors tell you different." She sits staring, then flares up as if I had contradicted her. "But he was a brilliant man, and don't you forget it! A scholar and a man of action! A Jew who cared about everyone, even the Polacks, the shvartzehs. Too much he cared and ended up dead for it." She touches my hair. A spark snaps to her hand. "Let me cut your hair the way I wore it at your age. Your face would look so sweet, chickie."

The seductive power of the coaxing voice: give in, give in and all will be lovey-warm in the Garden of Was. I dare not remember how I loved her when I was small enough for her lap. "Mike likes it this way." Why must she stare with that shrewd yearning not for me but through me, to make me a phantom acting out her dreams?

"He's handing you a line. So, what do you talk to him about? You have to know what to say and what not to say to a boy."

"Mother, I talk to him just like I talk to Donna. To anyone."

"You have to know how to flirt, Jill. Didn't you learn anything from me?"

"I believe in being honest with men," I snap, roused finally. She always gets through in the end and I start to talk. "I'm not going to pretend I'm somebody else with him. I think if you're straight with men, they'll be straight with you."

"You poor idiot. Stick with that line and you'll end up raped and dead in a ditch with your throat slit."

The doorbell sounds with its three chimes, the middle one cracked, ding thunk dong. I run for the door.

"Now you hurry." She nudges past me in the turn, patting her hair. Dad is already shaking Mike's hand, both looking grim as captains going down with the ship, when

Mother bounces up rosy with curiosity. "This must be Michael! Jill's talked so much about you."

"How do you do?" Mike could not look stiffer if he were nailed to the wall. His face frozen with blind formality, he stares straight ahead, sitting in a chair by the television. He is closed against this house, judging it. I ache for the wheel-shaped antimacassars on the bony arms of the sagging couch, for the gilt peacocks strutting on the high sills, the gaudy china chaos of the knickknack shelves, the souvenirs of the Blue Hole and Wisconsin Dells. He does not know how to read the meaning of this sacred battleground, this stuffed palace. Bedecked with flounces and gadgets, this house floats like a bubble on my parents' pride. Never have they seemed as vulnerable, Mother forward on the couch, Dad well back behind a cloud of smoke, wondering why I could not remain ten and at least pretend to be a boy. Dad clears his throat. "What are you studying in school?" His voice implies that any answer carries shame.

"Literature, sir. I'm an English major.

Mother pouts. "Your mother, what does she do?"

"She's a social worker."

My protectiveness flops over as I read the strain incised around his mouth and eyes. "We'll be late for the show." I grab my coat, colliding with Mike as he jumps nervously to help.

"Jill!" Mother clucks her tongue. "Now, Michael, I know we don't have to tell you not to keep Jillie out too late. I'm sure you're a nice boy and you understand we'll be worrying. You won't drive too fast."

I can feel us turning into cartoon teenagers under her bright glance. Finally we are out, with Mike trotting me to his mother's aging Dodge. "Oh, isn't it good to be out of there?" He does not answer. "What have you been doing?" Still no answer. He must be angry because my parents asked too many questions. He drives as if shaking off a pursuer, turning down random side streets in erratic but widening circles north and west, past my high school, up Wyoming, over Plymouth to Schaefer. Nervousness sits like a third person between us. This is not our good silence.

I can think of nothing to say that might unfreeze his face. He does not love me. His family has stolen him back.

He says finally, "Say something!"

"What do you want me to say?"

"You don't know? Think." He jabs his butt at the ashtray and a shower of red sparks streams down. "We're lost."

"We're near Fenkell." Actually it is not possible to get lost in this whole quadrant of Detroit. Everything is laid out in a grid, the numbers going up hugely but rationally. The main drags are lined with shops and factories and the streets between are set with little or bigger houses.

He drives more slowly, slumped forward. He looks straight ahead and I press against the window. "What have I done?" I ask.

"Maybe that's it—the whole business of expectation and reality. Imagination *wilts* into fact. . . ."

A train crosses before us, lights flashing and bells clanging on the grade crossing. A ball of cold slick quicksilver forms in my stomach. It is over. He does not want me.

"Suppose we dare suicide now, before we've tested the reality? Who knows how disappointed we'll be."

The train clatters past, empty cars. As the gates rise and we bump over the crossing, the street darkens ahead, small factories and warehouses with blank dismal facades. All I understand is that he does not want me.

"Answer me! Are you here? Are you bored?"

"I'm miserable. What do you want? I'm here, I'm willing. Why are you punishing me?" I lean my cheek on the glass. Vista of an empty parking lot.

"Why don't you say it? Or don't you?"

"Say what?"

"What would I want? Except that you love me. If you do."

I stare at him in his hostile slouch over the wheel. "Of course I love you. What else am I doing here?"

Beside the loading ramp of a dark building he parks. "Why didn't you say it?"

"When? You never gave me a chance."

"You climb in the car and sit as far away as you can—"

"But you . . . Let's begin again. Good evening, Mike."

"God, I've missed you these three days. From the time I get up in the morning, and it's not your voice waking me over the telephone . . ."

Dark, but for the faint bluish streetlight, the glow of the watch he takes off and stows on the dash. A metallic silence around the drumming of his fingers on the wheel. He reaches over to touch my shoulder, and shyly we kiss. Slow undersea caresses as we act out our lack of haste. My breath feels heavy. He kisses my throat, his silky hair against my lips. Under his hands the pulse thickens in my breasts. The buttons of his shirt are small and meek to my fingers, self-effacing. Underneath he is nude, with ticklish brass hairs. "Why do you have a hollow in the center of your chest?"

"Why . . ." he teases. "Why don't you?"

To free each of us is different. He pushes my dress up, we pull his trousers down, unpeeling like the skin from an orange. His underwear is surprisingly familiar, for it's like what Mother buys on sale for me, cotton, white, childish. I tug clumsily and he springs free. Almost comical: Francis gave me a jack-in-the-box once. You slid the top off and a hammer sprang up and tapped your fingers.

Gently he strokes my belly. "You're made of moon."

I do not know what to do with my panties hanging at my ankles, for he is drawing me down and they hobble me. I scrunch them in a ball and put them in my purse. Gravely he fixes himself in position, the bones of his spare hips pinning me. I can feel his penis pushed tight against me, but somehow it will not go in. He bumps and butts against me, till the excitement dies and I begin to hurt.

Is that hurting you?"

"A little."

"Look, am I in the right spot?"

I am scared that he is forcing the wrong opening. "I don't know. Can't you tell?"

"Maybe you should guide me in."

"But, Mike, I don't know how!"

"What did you do with all those little chippies?"

I cannot explain that I know perfectly well where my clitoris is, although I never had a name for it till recently; but none of our pleasures involved penetration and I have never poked anything into me. I have never yet used a tampon, for my mother would not have them in the house and the rudimentary diagrams in the manuals for teenagers do not seem to correlate with my body. How can he speak so harshly to me? "You're the one supposed to know how."

He groans, "I can't believe it. Okay, brace yourself." He tries a quick lunge and bangs his back against the wheel. The horn toots. I can't hold back an outcry as he knocks against me bruisingly.

"Merde!" He sits up, rubbing his back. "The damn wheel's sticking in my spine. Let's get in back."

Holding his trousers, he opens the door and I stumble after him into the back, there to begin all over again from the first kiss, as if rehearsing. But it does hurt. It hurts like hot hell, and still he pounds away and still my flesh denies him entrance.

"Oh, I do want to. I don't know what's wrong, Mike. Maybe I'm misshapen." Then trying to joke because tears are dripping down my cheeks, and my flesh stings and shrinks from him, "Are you sure you know what you're doing?"

He wilts between my thighs. "If you wanted an expert, you should have picked one."

"What happened?"

He draws back with a deflating sigh. "I've lost it." We lean together, my head on his shoulder, hot and weary with vexation. He strokes my hair. I reach for my cigarettes and light one that we pass back and forth.

"Mike, am I different from other women physically?"

"How do I know?"

"Haven't you—"

"I've had just as much experience as you've had." He turns his head away.

"Please, look at me. I'm glad. Because we're even, then."

"You're trying to make the best of it."

"You should be glad too, dear. If you had a past, I'd drive you crazy with questions."

He hugs me. "Still, like all new objects you should come with a set of instructions." Drawing me closer, "The old man's raised his bruised and bloody head again, but let's try another position. Sit on me. Then you can exert as much pressure as you can take, and when it hurts too much, you can stop and rest."

At least this way we can smile at each other. I dig my knees into the upholstery and brace myself. He slips down and we fumble him back. The sweat breaks out in the small of my back. "Damn it. Damn it. Damn it. Do you suppose I have a cast-iron hymen?"

Braced too, he strains against me. "Close to it. I don't think I'll be able to piss for a week."

Even the laughter hurts and with pain ragged and hot I can feel myself tearing, while the blood spreads wet along my thigh.

"Ah, dearest," he says, "don't bite clean through my neck. My head will fall off."

"Sorry . . . Mike, I can't, I'm no good. I can't!"

"Hey, are you bleeding? We must have done it!"

"Either that, or we drilled a hole." Then because I feel ripped and sore and the hot drip of blood scares me, "Mike, I'm sorry. I've got to draw back."

"I'm half limp anyhow. And to think taking maidenheads has been the great sport of the Western world. Makes you wonder what some people call fun."

I slide off his lap, seating myself gingerly. "Oy, it hurts to sit. Do you have a handkerchief?"

"Look! We've gone clear through the seat."

We stare at the dark stain. "What can we do? At least I'm wearing black."

"I think there's cleaning fluid in the garage. I'll try to get it out tonight so she won't see it."

"Suppose you can't?"

He shrugs. "Tough. It'll stay there, then."

We dab at the stain, but it only sinks into the upholstery. "There I am all over your mother's backseat."

"Well, at least we got through, old friend." He grips my shoulder. "You're a good soldier. Want to call it quits for tonight? I'm for a hot pastrami sandwich."

"I think I've had it, if you don't mind." I follow him around to the front seat, and we put ourselves together. "What time is it?"

"Only eleven." He smiles crookedly. "We'll get you back by twelve thirty. That's within the rules, isn't it?"

Howie zips up his jacket as we walk under the cobblestone arch. His parents go to bed early and for the last half hour his mother has been yawning around fiddling with window shades. But now that we're outside I can no longer put off telling him. I cannot walk beside him under false pretenses. "Howie, I don't know how you'll feel—we've never talked about it. I hope you won't be shocked. I'm not a virgin any longer."

He slows down, his chin doubled against his throat. "You . . ." I can feel him searching for the right phrase. ". . . had sex with him? That Mike Loesser?"

"Well, does that bother you?" A tough disinterested voice I'm trying to squeeze from my throat.

"Theoretically I have no objections. The double standard sucks."

"Theoretically?"

He kicks a pebble tracked out from the drive. "He sounds sold on himself. Like that guy Beck at Great Books you used to have a crush on."

"I never did! Besides you haven't met Mike."

"Well, you talk about him all the time." He nudges his pebble from a lawn back to the sidewalk to kick it again. "Be *careful*, anyhow." He turns and with his fist hits me in the upper arm.

Startled I rub my arm and stare at him. He breaks from me, running to leap and smack his hand against the suspended bus-stop sign. Then he swings around the pole and comes jogging back to boom at me, " 'If I were tickled by the rub of love . . .' who knows how I'd act? Maybe it's good. Anyhow, I got Dylan Thomas, like you said. First he seemed weird. But Sandy had a record of him reading and it turned my head around—"

"Sandy?"

"This cat I know. He's twenty, he goes to Harlem all the time to hear jazz. He blows saxophone. Anyhow, once I heard Thomas perform, I began to dig the stuff."

That argot annoys me, fake from him. He grew up in a Black neighborhood and now's he's going to Harlem as a tourist and imitating the speech of Black musicians. "Thomas is fine at his best, in six or seven poems," I announce in my crispest CBC accent. "But Eliot's really major. This is the age of Eliot, and you can't understand it without him." I lean against the pole. "Thomas is awfully uneven."

"Since when are you crazy for what's fashionable?"

"I'm not talking about fashion but fundamentals. Pound and Eliot are our fathers—"

"Pound was a Fascist. He did broadcasts for Mussolini."

"You're kidding."

"The hell I am. Ask Mike. That's where all this shit is coming from, isn't it? Pound's anti-Semitic. I read his fucking poems too when you said to."

"But, Howie, you can't just like somebody because they sound good on a record—" The bus pulls up with a grinding of gears, startling us. I turn and jump on, fumbling for change. The doors close, the bus lurches forward. When I turn Howie is calling something after me.

He's stubborn when he gets an idea between his teeth. I plump into a seat. I'm not chained to an opinion just because I spouted it once in a letter. Imagine him trying to tell me I like Eliot because he's fashionable. I like the way his lines stay, his slow music works on me. The rhythms sink in. But I didn't say that—I said he was important. I haven't read any Thomas since Mike took the book from me. The two scenes hang counterpoised, Mike using the fulcrum of his anger on me. I'm a fraud and a fool. I jump up and pull the cord.

As soon as my feet hit the curb I began running. It's torture not to be back with Howie instantly, to have to carry my apology bouncing loose in me, to be saying it over and over to myself. The pad I'm wearing chafes my thighs. The bleeding has slowed down. Half a mile to go back to the cemetery. I have a strong guilty fear that what Howie said about Pound will turn out to be true. It wouldn't matter to Mike: why wouldn't it? Because he hates politics. Boring, he says. He is anti-communist by rote, because his heroes are. I am political in a way not currently meshing with what I do, but part of my basic equipment. I don't think poets' ideas are irrelevant to the effect or power of their work. Something in Mike's heroes must be deeply flawed, although I cannot prove it to him yet.

As I trot under the arch, the houselights are out but for one on the second floor. His room? His parents must have gone to bed. I can't ring the bell, then. I can't cart my apology home either. Must set things right. I'll call Howie down. I stoop and gather a handful of gravel from the drive and toss it at the lighted window. The gravel scatters and strikes aimlessly over the bricks. Too weightless. I go back and search for a handful of larger pebbles. Howie would have to be deaf to miss these. Carefully I toss one, aiming at the sash so I won't break the glass. The pebble hits and falls by the door. I more or less have the range now, and several more pebbles tick off. Is his bed by the window? I have never been upstairs. He's sure to hear me. The curtain swirls against the square of light, parts. I gather my breath to call softly. His father's ridged and sagging face, toothless now, the words gummy with spittle. "Who's that? You get out of here."

I am already running past the corner of the house, the gravel flying up as I cut around the office. The old man's gummy bellow of indignation pursues me. "Hoodlums!"

Again we stop on a side street, this time an area of little houses and big trees. We are afraid of parks, because the cops patrol them. Before we settle on this spot, we venture out of the car to walk hand in hand around the block, checking its solitude. In the way the streets are laid out, parallel but not equidistant, in a small barn that still stands behind a house back from the road, in the many lots with gardens laid out, we can see the village this section must have been before the city grew around it. We wonder what lost name it called itself, wanting to swaddle it in sentiment as we would not the village itself. We walk farther than we meant to. Then slowly, slowly we wander back to the car.

Dry cleaning fluid hangs over the upholstery. An anonymous brown stain marks the backseat. His mother said nothing. We are afraid to speak. The crackle of the condom. Pungent smell: the oilcloth of sailboats that used to cover the kitchen table. Or the smell of children's raincoats.

He smiles at that. "It is a raincoat."

Turned sideways he hides his face against my breasts. Then without looking at each other we slide together. (Doggedly in the bathroom I crammed the better part of a jar of petroleum jelly into myself.) He sets the movement and I follow clumsily. I do not want to think but cannot help it. This jouncing up and down. This localized petty jouncing is what I wondered about by the hour? All our loving and straining and groping toward this. We bounce mechanically as a merry-go-round horse. It hurts a little, a localized irritation, a sense of being stretched. Only that.

Just one more lie that society springs on you. No wonder they want you to wait till marriage: who'd bother? I draw back a little, raise my cheek from his to look into his face. But he is strained, curiously strained, his eyes shut tight, his hands clenched on my hips. Am I hurting him? But then deep in me a kicking, blunt pulsation and as I watch he opens, flowers, a glistening softness spreading in his face. With a deep inturned smile his mouth softens, his eyes open. A laughing moan rounds his throat and he hugs me and inside, where for a moment I can't locate him and tense my muscles involuntarily seeking, a vessel throbs and I cannot tell whose pulse that is, the hidden birdlike throbbing. His grip melts on me as he leans back and shakes his head, and throughout his arms and thighs a loosening warmth flows. He is radiant in his pleasure and I have caused this thing to be.

"Ah, Jill," he mumbles, "you almost killed me."

"I could feel you." Kissing his cheek and eyes and throat and hair. "I could feel you!"

TWELVE

The Round World and the Hidden Place

JULIE AND I show each other literature papers for criticism. Donna, who has decided to major in art history, stays out of this exchange, but Julie and I relish argument. I have come to her single room with the same bland blond furniture as ours but neat as ours never is. Her bed is covered with a navy corduroy spread pulled taut as a pool table, with a stuffed poodle bright-eyed against the extra cushions that turn it into a couch. As we sit primly at opposite ends she tells me she learned to make her bed correctly in camp. A camp to me is where my brothers went when they got drafted, where they did learn to make beds, although with Leo you'd be surprised how fast he forgot.

"But everyone goes to camp." She stares.

"I never knew anyone who went." Camp must be where kids learned the corny songs they sing at what are supposed to be jolly college evenings: "John Jacob Jingleheimer Schmidt," "Rise and Shine," "Taps," "Smiling Through."

"But that's what you do in the summer. This summer I'll

return as a camp counselor. That's what you do after
you're too old to be a kid at camp." Julie is nonetheless in
a friendly mood. She brings out a jar of smoked rainbow
trout pâté to spread on melba toast from one of the CARE
packages her mother mails. I eat the bounty as if accustomed, for I am always hungry.

Julie wants to open a new subject. Her method makes
me feel whatever it is bumping like a shark beneath the
floorboards. I have to idle along and wait for it to emerge,
teeth gleaming. She did not have sex with Van during
spring vacation. As she put it, "The matter simply could
not come up!" Julie makes fun of her love life; she assumes
that if she is involved in a scene, it must be somewhat
ludicrous. Laughing at herself before others get a chance.
A pervasive loneliness in Julie makes me patient with her,
a loneliness scarcely abraded by Van, her family, the other
girls she chatters with, her heavy load of classes, Le Cercle
Français, the literary magazine to whose meetings I go
with her. She does not write and has gravitated toward the
unappreciated function of advertising manager. Other staff
members are astounded when she succeeds in selling ads to
local merchants. We cannot think of any reason they
should place ads with us.

"I wish you'd come riding with me Saturday or Sunday
mornings. It's quite inexpensive here 'and the trails are
beautiful."

"Ride? Ride what?"

"You needn't prove your proletarian origins hourly.
You'd love it if you tried it. It gives you such power, such
energy!" Eyes gleaming, she flushes.

"Energy? How come?" Myself up on a horse like a cop
or a bronze general?

She sits bolt upright. "This powerful beast is lending you
his strength. You and a magnificent animal move as one.
You're ten feet tall and you can gallop!"

I have never actually touched a horse or an elephant
either. I am intrigued. "How cheap is cheap?"

"Just three dollars an hour."

"At the phone company, I get a dollar thirty-seven an

hour on long distance. The damn horses make more an hour than I do."

While Julie is silent, I wait. I don't think horses are the hidden agenda. With her middle finger she wipes the can of pâté and licks it as delicately as my old tuxedo cat. "Have you ever thought about nuclear holocaust, Jill?"

"Oh, every night between twelve and one. What's up?" I have a flash of delighted surprise. I have heard of Ban the Bomb marches. Could Julie be interested?

"Remember around December when we had one of those tedious crises, and for about a week everyone went around thinking the Russians might be about to drop the Bomb?"

"So what else is new? That's our childhood, in a sentence." I was in grade school when they began making us crouch under desks with our eyes covered against the blast; when they began marching us down into the cellar to stand under the steam pipes, where I would sarcastically point out that if even a tiny bomb fell nearby we'd be instantly cooked. Actually Mother set the style of sarcasm. When we were led on a tour of Uncle Edward the minister's bomb shelter—the only one that anyone we knew had or could afford—my mother muttered running her nail along the rusty cans, "Well, chickie, they'll have a hot time dying of botulism and rheumatism if they don't kill each other first. Rather'n be cooped up in a root cellar with your uncle Edward, I'd take my chances with the Russians. Canned pork and beans, they're going to gas each other to death."

Still the early jets would zoom overhead in Detroit rattling the dishes in the cabinets. In high school I wrote poems about waiting for the death to rain fiery down, since you could not tell Ours from Theirs if missiles collided overhead and the difference seemed academic. Who would ever know who pushed the final button? When I look through my poetry notebook from high school, half the poems talk about fire bombing, a world in ruins. We grew up expecting Armageddon any afternoon in the midst of bland tedium.

"Suppose you didn't go with the first blast? Highways clogged with millions of refugees. No gas. Cars stalling, abandoned. Food running out, water contaminated in the cities . . ."

After reading Hersey's *Hiroshima* I had nightmares. I was coming in low over the broad Detroit River, its brimming plain of water choked with gutted ships, some still aflame, floating corpses charred like wood. The waves had an oily sluggishness and as I swooped lower I could see dead fish belly up among the torn and cooked bodies glutting the river. No, I think, no. "With the fallout, better to die sooner."

"How would you know how much you'd catch?" She shakes her head impatiently. "Van and I hatched a plan in December I've been thinking about on and off ever since. He loves to ride, too. That's how we met. The idea is to head for the riding stables and take each a horse to ride and a couple to carry supplies. Then, head out."

I stare at her. "People die of overexposure. People starve if they're lost in the woods of the Upper Peninsula for a week."

"Horses eat grass. Even in winter, I'd wager you could dig enough grass from under the crust of snow." A petulance in her voice. A slight whining of insistence. "One possibility is to head north at once. That's why I have that map of Michigan up." She points.

I grunt noncommittally. Her nails are lacquered a cautious petal pink. Those hands are going to wrest a living from the wilderness?

"The other possibility is to ride west, give Chicago a wide bypass and go up through Wisconsin into Canada— north into unoccupied territory. To start over. Sanely. With horses and supplies. You can plow with horses, you can haul wood with them."

"It'd take years. You'd starve. *You* can't eat grass."

"I was a girl scout until I was fifteen. I know how to live off the land. I can tell edible from poisonous plants. Imagine starting over, Jill. That's when I felt closest to Van. He seemed so decisive then. I could almost see the two of us

riding off with a great pillar of smoke still hanging in the
sky—about to launch a new world."

"Adam and Eve, isn't it? Or the desert island. Making up
a world from nothing with a man." But to create such
charnal privacy, the universal chaos is which she can imagine herself at last freed from constraints of class, family,
sex roles, social expectations.

"Jill, don't you want to survive? You're a battler. That's
why I want you to come ride with me. You ought to
learn how."

She has a lot invested in this fantasy; I hope she will not
regret airing it, but it stinks of the decay that comes from
opening a closed place. "People would try to stop you and
you'd have to kill. For what? To squat in the damp woods
rubbing two sticks together and giving birth in a lean-to?" I
slide off the neat bed. "Besides, if they're taking out Ford's,
they'd get us anyhow. See you later."

"If there is a later," she says sourly as I slip out the
door.

Mike holds out his watch. "I'm supposed to be discussing a passage of Rilke. Sharp knows I'm missing becasue
the class is small."

"Shhh. Don't remind me where I ought to be."

"You can borrow botany and history notes. It's not the
same."

We cross a loop of road to climb between cherries in
white bloom. "Maybe you shouldn't cut so often, then."

"How can you say that? I do it to be with you."

My hand in his is the pivot. The buds have cracked open,
the distance is hazy with green. As we cross a meadow,
brittle stalks of old weed snap underfoot and we crush the
pliant shoots. I imagine popping a sapling in my mouth;
the wood would have a cool crisp taste like celery from
Mother's garden and the buds would taste sharp and a little
bitter.

We run up a grassy slope to the flattened top. Where we
lay last time is marked by a fresh heap of beer cans. I step
back. "It's spoiled."

He looks back at the path. "Any path is likely to be worn by people. We'd have to make our own."

"That's it. Our own path. A place for loving that's ours."

We race down the slope. By a contorted tree he waits for me to catch up. The fleshy purple blossoms sprout from black wood and stark spines without relief of leaves. "A witch tree," he pronounces.

"Look, it has a name." A weathered Latin label hangs at the first branching.

"The Arb's grotesque." Pulling off a blossom he fixes it in my hair as we strike off through a valley of beeches.

I must give you a sense of its bounty, this nurtured plot of well-used Arboretum. A dirt road branches through the wooded hills from the entrances: a back door for hobos by the burning dump, a formal entrance for Sunday drivers where fraternity row and rangy rooming houses begin to give way to wide-lawned residences that parents nod at from their cars, substance approving of substance—the route that winds down from a view of the river coiling like a scythe through the countryside and the two sentinel hospitals, University and the Veterans Administration, on opposite banks stolid in the distance. But the entrance worn by lovers is below the dorms, the route between ravine and cemetery that funnels into that first wide place that alone has a common name, the plateau; the other hills, ravine of rocks and green-eyed creek, submarine cove of waist-high ferns, hollow of slithering willows pocket dark, have names only for those who have lain and printed themselves on that earth.

In the afternoons of spring and fall botany classes troop through behind their hearty instructors, taking notes and flushing couples from the thickets. Trees grow lofty here. Rumor has it the hills are accretions of old condoms, and perhaps the cast sperm has quickened the soil. At night we grope hand in hand while nymphs sigh in the tall and spooky trees and the flesh of lovers stuns from the dark like gardenias. No, you cannot visit this place. You cannot enter merely by walking downhill. You have to be so young you're still scared by dark stairs. You have to believe sex is wicked and splendid magic. You have to be desperate and needy to taste the flavor of these trees and bushes, playground of drifters, joggers, botany field trips, fraternity beer parties, edgy delinquents with switchblades hot and shiny in their pockets, sunbathers, picnickers with babies and fried chicken but always and ever by sun and by moon and by rain under the cover of the leaves and the overarching branches, the lovers rustle.

We stand at the forking of the road at the foot of a steep rocky hill. He pulls me up. I scramble after clutching at roots. We climb to a shallow bowl of Scotch pines. The shaggy poles rise straight with patches of russet wood showing through the bark. The sun slants through the high branches to make bright patches on the floor, thick and soft with blanched needles. He circles the rim with his head jutting forward. "Great site for a fort. It commands the road." He stares at me and something tightens in his face. "Completely alone. If you yelled, no one would hear." Tentatively he puts his hands on my throat, then hard. "Aren't you afraid?"

I smile. "No."

"You trust me." He turns away, kicking at the needles. "I wonder how much? Even here we've been preceded."

Ashes beneath the needles. "At least a season old."

He nudges the old ashes. "This is our hearth."

"Maybe we could build a little fire and cook supper here sometimes."

"Right. Get those flat stones from the hillside." He plunges over the rim and I follow, crashing through the thickets. The first stone I try to dislodge is embedded too deep but the second gives as I haul, sending a leggy thing scurrying. He is setting two level stones side by side. Sweat breaks out along my back, my hands are bruised, but the ring grows. Finally he fits the last stone in.

He sprawls, and after a last survey, I join him. Labor has made the place ours. "Bet we could build a shack," he says. "Why not? Two crazy poets gone back to nature. Once a month we trot out, me with a grandfather beard

down to the waist and you in nothing but your long black
hair, and order a few supplies. 'Deliver them to the front
gate of the Arb, please.' "

I rest my head on his arm. Interwoven branches. Slashes
of late afternoon sky. "We could gather berries and nuts.
Plant a little garden."

He draws me closer. "Can't you see us all ragged and
fierce and hairy? There'd be rumors—wild hermits, live in
trees and throw rocks at strangers. We'd set traps for rabbits. Somebody'd catch sight of us running along all shaggy
like Bigfoot. . . ."

Gently I brush the needles from his hair. When his eyes
gloat on me with that dark somber shining, I am beautiful.
The ground prickles, scented with resin. Above branches
rub and dip. No footsteps to set us misbuttoning, only the
chatter of a squirrel, the pulse of bird wings. Weight my
body rounds to. This time before he enters, he touches me,
fumbling with powerful effect. It has never occurred to me
that he could touch me, for that seemed to me to belong to
those distant pleasurable games everyone seems to agree
are more dangerous than drag racing. Then he moves in
me alive and warm as if he turned and leapt. I close my
eyes and our bodies swell huge. Deep and elongated we
grow rushing backward like fast trains. Half afraid of the
hot lick of urgency I clutch him, the scratchy flame that
catches and fades, catches and fades in my cupped distorted upward-striving body.

Then I am freed falling backward while the star streaks,
hovers burning and finally explodes and the streamers flare
through my thighs and breasts and arms, the sparks hang
and die one by one. It feels right, it feels familiar, it feels
ancient.

When he has come and slides out of me, condom dragging, I say, "Mike, I came. I did. I really did."

"I knew we'd break through soon. What's it like for
you?"

I loll in my muscles, warm as bathwater. Effort to talk.
The completeness of pleasure separates us. "Heat . . . urgency."

"For me too." He settles curled against me. "Must be the same."

"Stupid we can't know. I'd like to crawl into your fingers and look out through your eyes."

"You haven't read Plato but he puts it nicely. We were round animals once, but the gods got jealous and split us. So we're all trying to find our other proper half."

"Mike . . . the way you touched me first? I liked that."

"Oh." He is silent. "The guys told me to try that when I said you weren't coming."

I sit up, clutching at my scattered clothes. *"What guys?"*

"The guys in the dorm."

"How could you discuss me with them?"

He grins. "They're envious because I'm getting laid regular. My stock has shot up. You're telling me you don't talk about sex with Donna or Julie?"

"But not what we do."

He shrugs. "Actually it may have been Lennie's idea. It's easy, once you get the knack of it."

I sit still clutching my sweater. All over town he has been discussing my body and its habits. I want to crawl into the earth. I sit on, trying to plane down my shame roughly so I can fit past. I will brazen it out with all of them. What else can I do?

Churchgoing students in heels and suits tap by staring at Lennie's painting and at me drumming my feet on the wall beside the dormitory. The green and empty athletic field stretches away, a little haze shimmering over it in the onslaught of the already pounding sun. From the tennis courts comes the regular pock-pock of volleying. Of all the times for Donna's parents to pay a surprise visit! This is the weekend of the May Festival and both Mike and I are reading along with eight other poets this afternoon. I was in the bathroom throwing up from nervousness when Uncle Hubie and Aunt Louella suddenly arrived. Now there is no time for me to fret about my first public appearance as poet. I had to sneak the two canvases down the back stairs and wait outside for Lennie. Finally, there's

Lennie in his leather jacket and red beard bucking the
churchgoing flow. He waves back, stepping up his jouncing
walk.

"Donna's parents came. She didn't want them to see the
nudes, not just yet."

He cocks his head. "Wait here. I'll be back."

"Where are you going? Hey!"

"To meet her folks."

I grab his arm. "Don't do that to her. Let her find the
nerve herself to tell them. She will."

"When? What's hanging her up?" He squints at me.
"Does she think it was easy to tell my mother?"

"Today she'll tell them. She promised. Let her do it her
way."

He runs his finger along the stretcher. "You always stick
by each other. Don't you?"

Uncle Hubie puts down his fork. "Lennie. What kind of
a name is that?" His hair still brown on top makes me
realize how much Dad's has silvered.

"It's short for Leonard." Donna's gaze touches me for
strength. "Just a nickname."

"Leonard," Uncle Hubie repeats. He and Aunt Louella
look at me and away. "From New York, you say? New
York City?"

Will they ask it while I sit here? We are dining at the
Colonial House where students come only with parents.
The waitresses wear black dresses and rustly aprons. As
Aunt Louella eats breast of chicken, she darts glances at
her daughter. They are alike only in their almost albino
coloring. Aunt Louella is a paper-thin woman awkward as
a damaged grasshopper and prone to wringing her hands
nervously. Her voice is a rising whine. Something in her is
always trembling. "Is he a nice boy?"

"Oh, yes," Donna says fervently. "He's very nice."
Under the table our hands clutch.

Aunt Louella's gaze shifts to her daughter and away, as
if she feared to look at Donna too long. Hubie and Louella
are both unprepossessing human beings, Uncle Hubie the
least attractive of the Stuart men with his underslung jaw

and eyes perpetually squinting. How did they give birth to Donna? They view her with suspicion, as too attractive to be safe. He face has ordinary sharp prettiness, but her skin, her body, her hair are luminous. Aunt Louella stammers, "I mean, really *nice*?"

I nod wildly. "And intelligent." Mistake: Aunt Louella ducks her head sadly and Uncle Hubie looks grimmer.

Tryouts for the poetry reading were held on four consecutive afternoons. Although I went to hear Mike, he was in class taking a test when I did my stint before a jury of the editors of the literary magazine and two of the faculty who teach creative writing. People glance at me half with pity as I take my place in the row of straight chairs lined up across the back of the small stage, for I am obviously, very obviously, the youngest, the greenest, the wettest of the poets. Seven of the poets are men, all eight feet tall and bearded. Several are Korean War vets in school on the GI Bill, with wife and children in the audience scowling at the other performers. One of the other women is also married; her husband and two sons sit blinking and waiting. The other is a suave and beautiful senior, daughter of a professor, about whom Mike entertains sexual fantasies, trying to prompt me into jealousy.

I know Dylan Thomas started or restarted poetry readings, and I go to any and all the university sponsors. Because of the Hopwood Awards and a writing program and an English department renowned as a bastion of the New Criticism, lots of writers come here and lots hang around Ann Arbor. I know I am out way past my depth. On the platform I clutch my arms so that my hands will not visibly shake. In my lap the pages of my couple of poems vibrate on their own as if a small earthquake had its epicenter right under me. Mike sits beside me but he is busy making his mean tough faces, chin pulled way in and eyes glaring.

Mrs. Starini reads first, poems about her sons, her husband, her domestic labors. I wonder why she is first, since she has published several poems already. *Only now thinking about it from the distance of years do I understand the editors, the other poets, despised her for her domestic*

*themes and for being dumpy. She was punished for lacking
appeal to their gonads.* I listen, scared. I try to tame the
audience as Mike instructed me by staring from face to
face. I find Donna in the second row with Lennie. No
parents. What happened? I will read to her. I am saved.
Julie and Van are sitting on the aisle. There's Alberta
Mann with her shiny hair wound in long braids around her
oval head, a grave expectant expression on her olive face,
but Donaldson is not with her. Damn it. I want him to be
here. Maybe he'll come late? She has saved a seat next to
her. Her big feed bag purse sits on it like a dog.

The second poet is one of the teaching fellows. He reads
dreadfully in a thick mumble poems on obscure points of
philosophy, but the committee did not dare leave him out
because he is a favorite son of the Resident Critic and is
also noted for his acid attacks on everybody else. The
knowing audience is still trickling in, many coming late to
miss the losers—including of course me.

I stand. For a moment I think I will not be able to hike
the last mile to the microphone, gleaming in a shaft of
sunlight like a battle pike. I am wearing a dress Donna
picked out, a dark burnt orange skirt and pale pink bodice,
Grecian-looking I think with the criss-crossed halves of its
bodice above a fitted waist and full skirt. She paid for half
of it as a birthday present and I paid for the second half.
Mike is behind me but I feel as if I am reading to him, for
he has not heard this poem. I felt shy about showing it.

Love, I grew up lopsided,
jaded by proxy. Not dis- but merely un-
illusioned, by hearsay and wide reading
made cynical, already without innocence,
only ignorance and fear my dowry.

How can I explain this to me?
My days have shot up
with clutching elevator intensity.
I lean on the hands of clocks
to will you out of buildings. . . .

I read to Donna, who sits still and unblinking as if her concentration sustained me crossing an abyss on a tight-rope. In her lap her hands are clutched, washing themselves like her mother's.

> I want to empty myself out for you,
> have you swallow my history, memorize my ages.
> Hold my desires and small pleasures between your palms
> till they glow warm from your body
> like beads from a broken amber necklace.
> I want to take your will like your tongue
> in my mouth and feel it stirring.

The amber necklace is Aunt Riva's and had been Buhbe's. I develop enough courage to glance swiftly into the audience. Theo has come in and sits at the back, out of place in dirty tennis shorts with her racquet beside her chair. She sits nodding her head like an old woman, unselfconsciously enjoying the sound. Donaldson never came. Alberta's purse still perches on the chair.

> Love, go slowly.
> I am a chandelier suspended by a single wire.
> Love, go strongly. If you hesitate
> I will constrict violently and crush myself
> like an imploding egg. . . .

Suddenly I am done. I flee the microphone. People are applauding, politely I suppose. I can tell from the way the other poets look at me that I am not writing the way you are supposed to, but the glare Mike wears upsets me. He didn't like the poem? I do not hear the next two because I am still trying to figure out if I did all right and why Mike frowned. I sit shaking like a dish of aspic, sour and quivering. I cannot believe I read my love poem before all these strangers; yet it did not feel personal.

Now Mike seizes the microphone and launches into his first poem. His voice fills the room, deep, resonant but carefully devoid of any emotion except perhaps scorn:

. . . like maggots crawling through the rotting meat
Pale, omnivorous they ooze along
Behind their busy teeth. The dead are sweet
to them. . . .

That's about professors. Sometimes I can figure the poems
out. The next is about suicide which he considers the most
poetic subject. People talk a lot about gratuitous acts.
Everybody is reading Camus's *L'Etranger*. Even if they
read it in English, they call it *L'Etranger*. I consider that
character a creep, but I don't dare say so again. Gratuitous
is a lovely word. Stealing is gratuitous. Besides there being
simply no way I could stay in college without stealing most
of my textbooks and supplies and incidental clothing, I am
partial to that moment when my skin becomes all eyes.
*Years later kids in the antiwar movement will call me
bourgeois when I habitually refuse to join their ideologi-
cally motivated shoplifting. But I don't have to do it anymore, I say. I don't have to anymore. I figure I wore out
my luck years ago when I needed it.*

Thus the hatchet crashes making hash of mommy,
How it flashes rising like a sun.
How it dongs on bone like a churchbell.
Now the blood leaps up in laughing come.

That's called "The Triumph of the Familial Ax," about
Lizzie Borden. After Mike reads he stands glaring at the
audience. There are two obvious factions, those who ap-
plaud and those who ostentatiously do not. I glare at them
too.

One of the eight-foot-tall giants reads, a sonnet of im-
peccably stony address to Saint Sebastian. Gilt-edged security poems on Brancusi, Fragonard and God. Then the
pretty senior Kate reads, all her material drawn from fairy
tales, mythologizing her life, her lovers. It is strange and
foggy but not uninteresting. She reads in a clear slightly
affected voice. Mike looks at her with that expression partway between a leer and a sneer that annoys me. He calls
her a castrating woman. She has a racy reputation, al-

though as far as I can tell she has done little to deserve it besides write an occasional poem that suggests a knowledge of the other sex. She is not here with anyone; she has not taken any of them as lovers. Perhaps that is her crime. A professor's daughter, she is at home in Ann Arbor and just a little independent. Grant Stone reads last, a series of sestinas. If anything is more boring than a sestina, it's several sestinas. A gaggle of geese. A sunday of sestinas. Then he reads some short rhymed poems:

Complaint of the Much Married Woman
I gave myself to various men
but they always gave me back again.

Everyone is so happy to get to laugh that he receives roaring applause. With a leonine grin he stands and drinks it in.

Afterward he strides up to me. "I did so enjoy your reading. It was . . . hypnotic. . . . 'I want to feel your will stirring in my mouth.' How marvelously phallic."

I am quite sure I have not been complimented. Mike separates us at once, arm around my waist tugging me back to a fierce argument about whether his work is prosy. One young man quotes Yvor Winters, one Hugh Kenner, one John Crowe Ransom, one plays it safe with Eliot. In a way Mike's poems mean to irritate and thus their fury validates him.

As we walk out I have to ask, "Did you like my poem?"

"It's soft, pumpkin. Too soft to waste on those jerks. . . . Of course it's formless and silly. It isn't art, naturally. You ought to have just given it to me. No point pouring it out on assholes."

Donna waits outside and we head for the dorm together for supper. I take her arm. "How was I?"

"I thought you were terrific," she says loyally. "You read too fast but with some feeling. At least your poems are about something human."

"Didn't I sound naive?"

"Only a little." She squeezes my arm back.

"Did your parents like Lennie?"

"Oh, they had to go back home. They had a dinner date. They only came up for lunch."

"They didn't want to meet him, after all that?"

"Meeting them is hardly a pleasure I'm keeping from him, now, is it? I told them. That's the big step. . . . We've been getting on so well, Lennie and I. Last night we had an hour alone in the apartment and we were lying in bed just after we made love. He told me I looked like a Modigliani nude."

"What?" But I heard her. "Er, Donna, this is going to sound weird, but yesterday in the Arb Mike told me I looked like a Modigliani nude."

We look at each other in disbelief. "Fuck them," she says. "Do you think they get together over a beer and make up what they're going to say to us?"

"It was Lennie's birthday last week. I know Mike gave him a book. You get only one guess what it must have been."

I am right, I know, they are innocent of collusion and yet we both feel cheated of our compliments.

The round world. The sense of community. We sit in vast overheated amphitheaters where the bald head of the professor shines at the bottom of the toboggan slide distant and cold as the moon while his words move into our ears and out our fingers. With electronically sensitive pencils we mark slots on multiple-choice tests and are issued our ranking. Education? That comes from each other. We go in a fierce noisy knot through exhibits and galleries while Lennie teaches us to see. We dismiss chunks of culture and gobble others. Books unknown to the departments of the university buzz wasplike between us, forming our language. Music is a passion and the structure of darkened rooms. We bang our ideas against each other. Lennie paints us in a red sea leaping like dolphins. None of us like the way we look but we each think Lennie did a fine job capturing the others. For two weeks everything we cook on Lennie's stove is yellow with curry powder. We discover avocados. We put capers in spaghetti. We make up plays starring us.

* * *

The sun hangs like a tangerine in the long-needled boughs of our Arb room. The cupboard is a round cookie tin buried flush with the ground. It contains two saucers from my dorm, two spoons, a salt shaker from the Union, a can opener, a book of matches and an extra packet of condoms. Sometimes we study here. The late light slants a deep smoky red between the poles of the Sctoch pines and gilds the eddying gnats. We eat supper of tuna fish with sliced onion and rye bread. The soft dusk liquefies, leaving the sky still milky. Sometimes we hear a couple talking on the road; sometimes headlights brush the shrubs of the slope, but we are safe above. Sex is easy now as talking.

THIRTEEN
The Worm in the Eden's Apple

THE TIME I'VE wasted! The sweet term spent and the reckoning of finals due. From my endless literary arguments with Julie I had matter enough on Faulkner to grind out my term paper, but with my back to the wall in the top bunk and my knees drawn up, I devour the Spanish-American War according to Grimes. One fifteen. Smoke hangs just under the ceiling. Whenever I finish a chapter and pause to abstract it, I become aware of Donna making unnecessary excursions to desk or closet, getting up and down with sighs and scrapings. I know she wants to talk but I refuse to meet her overacted restlessness. The spring creaks as she tosses, sits up, flings herself prone again.

What was the damned immigration act called, the first that began the design to keep out people like my grandparents, all the dark-haired and dark-skinned? My mind blanks, gears momentarily locking. Donna hates the way I study, my mad concentration, but without a scholarship I would be back in my dead-end neighborhood like a boxcar struck broiling on a siding. I view myself as a professional student: not that I mean to go on in academia like Mike but that it is my present work and I study for a living. Below Donna sets up a muffled sobbing. Damn you, let me be! "Is something wrong?"

She sobs louder.

What is the McCarran-Walter Act? No, that was recent, designed to keep out people like me, subversives, prophets, agitators, wild poets. What was the first act that slammed the golden door? When did Eden forbid the wretched of the earth? Marking my place, I clamber down. "What's wrong?"

Arching her back she grasps the posts that support the bunk. "I want to die! I want to die, I'm so scared!"

"Come on, you know your stuff. Finals are just con games."

"Finals?" She sits up, scrubbing her eyes. "I'm eight days overdue."

"Are you sure?"

"You sound like Lennie! You think I can't count?"

I hold my own belly. "What a rotten time for it."

"How can I concentrate?" Her pale lashes are matted. "What will happen to me? He leaves for New York next week. I have to go home to Flint."

I lean my forehead against the bunk. "Aren't there lab tests?"

"Lennie's finding out. I have so little time if it's true." She locks her arms around her knees. "If I am, how will we ever get the money?"

"How much do we need? I have twenty-some."

"Lennie's roommate knows of a doctor who does them. At least two hundred, he thinks. Maybe two fifty."

"Mike must have something. What about Lennie?"

"Not much, twenty or so, but he figures he can borrow more and sell books. Stu, I'm scared. Think of it growing inside. Peter has money but Lennie says he's tight. Peter always thinks everybody's trying to use him." She blows her nose hard. "I have twenty-eight and I can get ten from Estelle by telling her I have to see a dentist. She's big on getting her teeth fixed."

"Two hundred! After his last exam I'll hit Mike. I can't risk throwing him off stride." I squat at the shelves. "We could sell our books too." I squelch a pang of anticipatory loss. "It can't be true!"

"Yeah, like getting struck by lightning. Why me?"

I put my arm around her shoulders. "We'll get pledges, but don't believe it."

"Suppose something goes wrong? Suppose I bleed to death? Do they cut you open?"

"Shhh. We'll go to a real doctor." She feels breakable. Through the straw of her hair her pink scalp shows faintly, damp with sweat.

"So much money down the rathole. You know I think if I went to Peter and asked him myself, I bet he'd loan me money." Slowly her body relaxes. "I'd have the nerve, I know I would. The hair of the dog—you wouldn't think I'd get ideas about men."

My arm around her shoulders is beginning to ache. "You can ask him." Peter: air of polite chill, the planting of a dart. What does she see in him?

"Stu, life is so simple for those fireproof pink bitches down the hall. They give nothing, they never get hurt. Or am I just jealous because they're innocent?"

"What's innocent about them—their politics? The candles they burn before Saint McCarthy? Their pocketbooks?"

"Their idea of conflict is being on a diet, or giving up chocolates for Lent." Her hands tighten on her belly. "What am I going to do? I keep seeing pregnant women in the street like whales."

I rise. "Lennie and I will worry about money. You just study." Shoving the drapery aside, I lean out. Smell of damp grass. A bell dongs. "Two, already. Try to sleep." I feel soggy yet I can still touch a core of alert concentration like a scalpel embedded in a sponge. Ah, the Chinese Exclusion Act of 1882—that's when it began. People with my eyes. Across the court a light winks out. Our friends in their beds must pay a bit of the price to buy Donna free. In trouble how we need goodwill, far more than we have ever earned.

Dear Jill,

No, nothing is wrong here. Matt finally left just in time for your mother to get your room ready. In a huff he went down and enlisted. Your mother burned her hand ironing, which is why she hasn't written.

I am glad to be done with roomers for a while. We did not find the ideal. According to your mother he would not smoke, drink, entertain callers, use the bathroom facilities, receive or make phone calls. He would leave 7 a.m. and not return till 10 p.m., when he would go directly to bed or sit quietly without burning electricity.

Have you been following the baseball season? I think if they don't develop more strength in the bullpen, the Tigers are in trouble. Don't stay up late. A little study at a time is better than haste at the end.

Love, Dad

In the stream of students, Mike appears from his German final. I jump from the grass. "Over here! How did you do?"

"Don't ask. Don't talk about it." He strikes a match that goes out, strikes another. "Hopped up with Dexedrine. I must have filled three bluebooks."

The benches along the walks are empty, the campus a quiet park. Most students have left and the rest are buried in study halls or exam rooms. I grip his arm. "Donna went for a pregnancy test today." And didn't come back. We were to spend the early afternoon selling our books.

"What?" He breaks stride.

"She's fourteen days late."

He whistles. "They must have been careless."

"Donna says no. They always use a condom, like us."

He walks more quickly uphill, past a girl wheeling a trunk. We no longer touch as we walk.

I have twenty-two dollars. Donna has thirty and Lennie has twenty-four and he borrowed forty. What can you spare us?"

"What are you talking about?"

"For her abortion, if she is pregnant. We need at least two hundred, maybe two fifty. Can you borrow anything? How about hitting your friend Van?" My words tumble out. I have patiently held this in till the end of finals. "She'll save what she can this summer, working, and pay us all back in the fall."

"You want me to give her money for an abortion?"

"A loan. Not a gift. She can pay you back first."

"And you assume I'll chip right in." He strides along swinging his arms in an exaggerated way, lines pulling at his forehead.

I skip to catch up. "We're only taking pledges. She's off getting a lab test." We pass my dorm on the way to the Arb.

"I won't help finance murder."

"Aw, come on, Mike. Murder? Don't be legalistic!" The casements are open, the draperies on our windows drawn against the sun as I left them. Suppose she panicked and didn't take the test, another day lost with time running out?

"You're no nitwit. It's murder no matter how you slice it."

We cross and begin the descent to the Arb. "Having a baby you don't want is slower murder. For both of you."

"If you don't believe life is sacred, nothing's left. It just all comes to death and eating a banana is just like knifing your father."

"Bullshit, Mike! That's just words. A fancy position for a man to take, I mean it. I care about Donna. I'm willing for chickens and cows to die to feed her, and this embryo to keep her free."

"Shut up and listen. It was in the papers, a man robbed a grocery. He held up the grocer with a gun and to scare him, he fired in the air. The bullet went through a curtain and killed the man's wife, who was hiding there."

"Donna's real. An embryo's only potential. I don't want any baby born ever who isn't wanted, chosen, waited for."

"Like that man, you want to kill someone you've never seen."

"It's her body—don't you see that? She's no incubator,

neither am I. What do you want her to do—have the baby and quit school? Go on welfare? Ask Lennie to marry her? Kill herself?"

"That's her business. What do you expect from someone who'd fool around in their own family?"

"What was that— How do you know about her brother-in-law?"

"Lennie, of course."

"He told you? How could he!"

"He's a decent guy. The story shocked him. She's got the morals of an alley cat."

"Why are you so highfaluting moral all of a sudden? What are we going here to do but fuck, just like them!"

"It's not the same." He grabs me by the shoulders. "And you're not the same as that little shikseh bitch!"

"Mike, don't even start that! I'm a mongrel and don't forget it. You're as bad as her parents."

"Just because she's your cousin you don't have to worship her. She's always trying to undermine me."

"Mike, she wanted me to like you. You're crazy!"

"What did you call me?" He moves to block my path, glaring.

I have been shouting at him. That scares me. I swallow my voice small and say, "I mean irrational about this."

"PUMPKIN INFORMS ME I'm irrational!" His voice is mild with a forced control worse than rage. "I told you my reasons while you just moan hysterically about that bitch. You want to break laws and take ridiculous risks that could get us all into trouble. Haven't you said you know I'm the more intelligent?"

I am a little shocked. He knows more than I do. I've said that. "Sometimes I can be right. I don't want any child born who isn't wanted. Really wanted."

"Better to kill him unseen?"

" 'Man's happiest lot is not to be'—didn't you quote that Sophocles at me when you were going on about the ecstasy of suicide?" How did these privet leaves get into my hand? I am tearing them. The sunlight cuts my eyes like broken glass. "Those sperm you slough off in the bushes or flush away—murder? Nature is waste. Women—Donna and I—

can breed fifteen, twenty children from our wombs like litters of puppies before we die of exhaustion."

"Nature is waste! Jill's doing her own thinking now. First you scream at me and call me insane—"

I reek misery. "I'm sorry. I said I'm sorry." It comes down to him siding with fathers, the heavy-bearded fathers of his imagination who say no to women and turn us to pillars of salt.

"Why should you run around begging money to cover her?"

"I'm responsible for her. She's my best friend."

"What about me? We're back to Plato's round men. Either your missing half is me or you're a lesbian and your other half is Donna. There's that bad experience with Callie you told me about."

A dank weight of hopelessness settles in me. What was bad about it? It was the only warm thing in my life when I hated school, when I felt a misfit, when my mother no longer held or caressed me, for I had become sickly and skinny and too smart and uppity. "I love you. How can you refuse to believe that?"

"If you really love me, if you loved me as much as I love you, other people wouldn't matter. You wouldn't carry on about her."

"She's in trouble! If you love somebody, why should it make you despise other people? I don't believe that!"

"Because you don't love me as much as I love you. You're scattered. All I need in this life are you, that letter Pound wrote me and a handful of truly great poems."

I would say food, water, a little sleep. Talk. Writing. Do I *need* him? What does it mean to be needed? "You won't help us, so let's just forget it."

He stands hunched over me. "Suppose I tell you not to interfere?"

"You can't. I have to follow my own conscience."

"Against what you admit are my right reasons? Even if I ask you not to?"

Right reasons? Alien moralizing. He tries to twist me in his hands. "I have to."

"Because you don't love me enough to do what I ask."

"Mike! Stop it!" I explode into tears and after watching me weep, he puts his arms around me, stroking my hair and murmuring, "There, pumpkin, there's my baby." What are words for if I cannot make him hear me? He plays the father when I cry. As we walk off across the plateau he cradles my hand in his and hums, as if because I cried and he did not, he has won.

He stops short. "Is that rain?"

A light pattering in the trees. "Must be the wind."

"Must be." We walk on. Then he flings out his arm to stop me. "Hey!"

Before my face a wizened caterpillar the color of a dried leaf turns slowly in midair. I stumble back. From the caterpillar a filament reaches into the leaves overhead. "That's the sound. These trees are being eaten up. Let's get out of here."

"There's noplace to go. Maybe they don't eat pine needles," he says.

We pick our way through crackling woods where leaves break off and float down, past a small maple shrouded in gauze webs. Under the pines no caterpillars hang, at last, only mosquitoes that whine around us. To keep them off we light a small illegal fire of twigs inside our hearth. Under the smoke we lie on our bellies eating partly cooked, partly raw hot dogs, charred on the outside and cold at the center.

Then on the needles we move in toward each other as so many times. Love is a heavy thing, I think, still worrying at the hard bone, *need*. What does it mean to need someone? It feels to me like being turned or turning him into a thing.

As I walk wearily along the corridor, no splashing, no singing, no laughter comes from the shower room. Luggage waits outside doors. Near our door the drive of Bartók's Second Piano Concerto comes muffled. As I open the door it hits me pulsing. In bra and pajama bottoms, Donna is doing a bump and grindy ballet.

"Hey, what?" I stare at her. "Are you okay?"

Her face crinkled in a grin, she throws her arms around

me, breathing sour wine. "I started! Right after we left the doctor's office." She stops to catch her breath. "Oh, Stu, I'm so happy I'm out of my mind!"

"But where were you?"

"I got such horrible cramps I had to lie down at Lennie's. I'm still cramping and bleeding in gouts, but I'm so full of aspirin and wine I don't feel a thing. Have some Chianti—it's on my desk."

I fill one of the plastic cups we use for instant coffee. "What a relief. Donna, hallelujah! We're safe."

"Everybody's been such good guys to me." Donna shuts the volume down by half. Turning to me, her face folds in on itself. "This summer scares me, Stu. Nothing's duller than Flint in the summer. Except Flint in the winter."

"Please don't get in any trouble. Please. Read and make money. Don't even talk to a man."

"There's no one to talk to. How can I get into trouble in Flint? I'll miss Lennie like crazy."

Already his green nudes are gone and Mike's tomes returned. The cozy network of our life will be dismantled tomorrow and we'll leave this nest as bare as we found it. "I'll miss you, Donna. I'm a little scared too. Next summer, maybe, let's go to school."

She sits rubbing her belly. "I think I'll take another couple of aspirins. What a long lonely summer it's going to be. . . ."

FOURTEEN

It's a Good Sign When a Boy Takes You to Meet His Mother

SHORT BROTHERS TELEVISION has showrooms downstairs, but I work upstairs behind a bank of files at a desk covered with phones. The directory open before me, I dial each number in succession. When someone answers, I place the receiver next to a phonograph on which a record plays over and over a spiel about turning your old TV in now for a new set at a record-breaking-all-time-low price. Most people hang up. Some talk back but I am forbidden to speak, even to that poor grandmother who stuttered, "Hello, please? Speak slow, please. I can't hear good. My son, you want my son?"

I went out hunting for this job in full regalia, including my weddings-funerals-and-job-hunting hat, white gloves to carry, for they belong to Mother and do not fit my hands, and white pumps from my high-school graduation. As I dial the number and wait, dial the number and wait, I see Mother in the bright morning sunlight of my bedroom running sheets and towels through the mangle (she irons everything, including my father's underwear and her own). She slid in an unironed towel, slid out an ironed one from

165

the other end of the roller, folded and flipped it neatly behind her to the pile on the table. Her movement was beautiful, a severe and deft dance of the hands and torso, but her hand on the lever of the mangle with that livid purple burn hurt me when I looked at it. Did she feel guilty for forcing Matt out? Is that why she burned herself?

While I ate breakfast, she stood at the stove running through her litany of how if I hadn't spent all that money on silly college courses, I could have been taking a secretarial course and bringing home good money by now. I am out of practice at tuning people out. Away I mostly listened, except to Professor Grimes, friend to robber barons. Haughty receptionists, grim supervisors, typing tests with the stopwatch going, that would be my day. Lying about experience, lying about college. Then the boring routine that would eat the summer.

As I hobbled on my tight pumps to the door, "Smile!" she exhorted, trotting after me. "Keep your back straight. Don't answer back. Write clearly! Eat lunch in a nice clean place!" Suddenly she whispered in my ear, clutching my arm, "When they ask religion, say Episcopalian." Her cheeks were scored with the effort of pushing that thought into me. "Episcopalian, Jill! Remember, they can't tell."

I am back at my desk with all the phones, dialing while the strident insect voice on the record reiterates with undiminished enthusiasm the opportunity for low budget terms. She had to lie to get a job, and not about college. She is a figure shaped by troubles I will never have to know. Sometimes I do listen, even if what I hear isn't what she is trying to tell me.

"Mike, someone's coming." I twist off him and pull my skirt down. A man leaning on a cane steps through the pool of streetlight toward us.

"Don't tear from me like that. You half kill me."

"But he'd have seen us."

"How many people look into parked cars as they pass?" Dry stubborn tone. "How slow he walks, old man on a hot night. Missed a chance to give him a thrill."

I wish he could guess how someone passing wrings the desire from me, but I can't say that again. I'll provoke another scene.

"If I were a sculptor, I'd spend a year just doing old men." He caresses my neck absently. "The character is there, the smile and frown lines, yet they're more animal too—the hawk or bulldog or monkey trying to come through."

"I like that." Burrowing. So tired, up since seven.

His face breaks into a sly grin. "Confess I was working that up in a poem. Truth is, I talk to you all day inside my skull."

I catch my breath as we come together, but I cannot give over. I stare past his shoulder, turn cautiously so he will not notice. Someone by the bushes? My thighs ache. Headlights hit us casting the twin shadow of our heads on the backseat. I bury my face in his shoulder. The car sweeps by and its taillights dwindle in the rear window. Did they see? Oh, make it not matter. He gives a long throaty sigh as he loosens his hold. "Ah. Was that good for you too?"

I have not come in so long that last night he accused me of not loving him. We had a scene for two hours. I do not know what to say. How can he not tell whether I come? With another woman, I could always tell. But I can't face a scene. "Yes, I came." False sounding. I add quickly, "What did you do today?"

"Got up about eleven. Read some D. H. Lawrence. After lunch I hung around waiting for a call that never came."

"Mrs. Papich sent me to the post office and the printers."

"Then I went swimming with a guy from the neighborhood. He thinks I'm a big shot now because I get laid every day."

"You told him?"

He sits up. "Why not? You tell people."

"How could you say that? Getting laid. Like getting your hair cut."

"I wouldn't boast about getting my hair cut six times a week. What do you want me to say—I'm passionately in love, Reginald, hold my hand. A man can't go around talking like that, pumpkin, it wouldn't give him any points. What's the big male dream? Every night a new plush woman, and in the morning, off with her head."

"All you want is a lump of meat."

"You might be surprised what a man does want. I'll tell you a story." His voice comes slow, singsong. "My cousin Sheldon was in Germany right after the war. He had this girl who'd do *anything*. Any thing he asked and thank him for it. He says American women are cold and greedy. He hated to come back."

"Why didn't he bring her home with him?"

"She was a whore. That isn't the point. He told me she was heaven and everything was downhill ever since." He draws me to him so that my head tucks under his chin and his hands close loosely over my breasts.

"Some heaven in other people's rubble."

"You want him to pretend he didn't like it?"

"Why are we arguing about your cousin? Don't I please you?"

"There's one thing ever so nice you won't do. You won't let me come in without that damn armor."

Bump. We have arrived. "I'm afraid."

"Of what? I wouldn't come. It would be soft." He murmurs against my throat, his fingers arguing in the small of my back. "All those clothes. We never really touch."

"Suppose you came without meaning to?"

"I won't stay that long. Just so we'd really be together for a moment." When I am silent, he coaxes, "Don't you want that too? To do that for me? D. H. Lawrence says . . ."

Undressing I find my period has started. I circle the date on the calendar on my dresser before I pad to the bathroom.

Standing under the cool patter I weigh my soapy breasts in my hands. What do I feel like to him? Ashamed I turn the shower punishingly colder. Sometimes the girl of last year stands in me sneering, Don't you ever think of anything else any longer? Bore!

A light tap.

I hunch forward. "I'm in the shower. Out in a minute."

Mother comes in anyway. "Thought you might like to use the lavender soap since you're stepping out."

I stand with my knees pressed foolishly. The breeze from the open door raises goose pimples. "Thanks."

"It's nice to have something special." Her gaze moves over me like a fly walking. Abruptly she leaves.

Again, while I am dawdling in front of the mirror, she sits on my bed with a sigh, fanning her skirt. "Spite of that rain, didn't cool down much. What are you doing tonight?"

"I don't know." I keep my head bent.

"Do you usually see a movie?"

"Sometimes."

"What do you do the other evenings?"

I shrug. "We ride around. We talk. We have coffee."

"Don't you ever go dancing?"

"Dancing? No."

"Your father and I used to go to the Aragon Ballroom every Saturday. He used to be a fine dancer." Smiling bitterly she fans her skirt. "You'd never know it now. Michael ought to get more dressed up when he comes calling."

"He doesn't have many clothes."

"His mother should take better care. Have you met her yet? It's a good sign when a boy takes you to meet his mother." Leaning forward she smiles as she did in the bathroom, her tongue wetting her lips. "Is he affectionate, Jill?"

How can she ask such questions? "What do you mean?"

"Is he affectionate with you?" Her forehead puckers over a soft tentative smile.

"He's very intelligent."

Her hands rise and fall. "Do you *care* for him?"

"I like him fine." I wait for the sense of betrayal. Overpowering it is a greater sense of being trapped in a damp constricting curiosity.

"You see so much of each other."

"Who else is there? Howie stayed in New York, at summer school."

"When I was a girl, I dated several boys. It's not good to spend too much time with one—they get demanding."

Finally safe in the car I say to Mike, "You were late. Mother started grilling me—"

"Her too? How did you guess to get dressed up? Mother wants to meet you."

"Oh." A lump forms in my middle. "Why, all of a sudden?"

"We've been having a dogfight. That's why I was late."

"About me?"

"Among other things." He grimaces. "No importance."

I know Mike's neighborhood because we eat in a deli there, on Seven Mile Road, where the woman behind the counter winks and pretends she will teach me to cook. Mike's neighborhood is where the Jews moved after Howie's neighborhood, upwardly mobile out of the ghetto but not wealthy. His street seems wider and flatter than mine. The lawns are deeper, the lots bigger and the houses mostly sprawl, farther apart. He parks in front of one of the oldest houses on the block, rather mangy stucco, vaguely Spanish, with the grass long above a For Sale sign in Mike's best printing. "You didn't say she was selling the house." They will move? Where?

"She puts that sign out every so often. Nobody wants to pay what she asks for it. She still imagines it's the house it was when my father was alive, instead of everything slowly falling apart."

I can't rid myself of the feeling of being watched, but we walk into a dark living room. I can see lights toward the back of the house. I follow him through large somber rooms past a polished dining room table, past dishes and silver pieces spaced on display in a breakfront. Beyond is a sunporch where I suspect from the litter of books and sewing, they do their living. Of the two women in wicker armchairs, which is his mother? They sit forward for a few seconds staring past Mike at me with such force I want to retreat into the dark, before they sit back with small inquisitive company smiles.

Mike's face hardens into annoyance. "Well, Aunt Ban,"

he says to the much taller and leaner woman with cropped grey hair and the severely humorous face I associate with teachers, "what's wrong, the whole clan couldn't make it?"

The corners of her long mouth dip. "Just visiting. Now won't you introduce the young lady?"

"Mother, Aunt Ban, this is Jill."

"Miss Loesser," Aunt Ban corrects him. "And this is Jill . . ."

"Stuart," I reply.

"I remembered it was something Scottish," his mother says. "It's so nice that you could come." An old-woman so erect only her nape touches the chair back, she is hardly an inch taller than my mother and must weigh a third less. Her hair streaked with grey is turned neatly under. Her makeup is pallid, her glasses colorless, her dress brown. In spite of the heat she wears the sort of thing I put on to go to work. Yet she seems girlish because of her slenderness, her firm calves, her large but shapely hands (like Mike's) curled on the arms of her chair. I am wilting in the swampy night where no breath stirs, but she sits in her private air-conditioned space, motioning us to the settee.

"Jill," Aunt Ban repeats, "an unusual name these days. So English. Is that a name in your father's family?"

"No. My Aunt Riva—my mother's sister—was in vaude-ville—"

"Vaudeville?" Mrs. Loesser repeats.

Did I say jail by accident? That's where my brother is, in Mexico, but never mind.

"What did she do?" Aunt Ban asks, mildly titillated.

Did I say she worked in a whorehouse? What's with these people? All the Jews of my childhood were in show business, politics, the unions or in trouble. "Oh, she jug-gled. Anyhow one time she got a part in a musical—just when I was born. It was the Depression and everybody was out of work but her. I was named for the character she played." Because she was our benefactor at the time and paid for the doctor. Aunt Riva is generous with the whole bedraggled family when she's got anything to be generous with. I have known Jews who were down and out and Jews who were flush, but never any who really thought they were or ought to be respectable like this. It occurs to me my stereotypes are taking a beating today.

Well, that silence steaming in midfloor like a pile of freshly dropped horse dung takes care of my first and last names: thank my parents I have no middle name. His hands clasped between his knees, Mike slumps with a tense furrow across his forehead. The women look at me with polite expectancy: this evening feels like Cold Springs when we visit Aunt Jean the minister's wife who sits with a wound-up little smile waiting for Mother and me to do something terribly Jewish like crucify her collie Tam Tam. I hear Mother's whisper, "Do you suppose she boils the teacups after we leave?"

"Michael, why don't you bring us iced tea?"

A warning look from him. They want to catch me alone. "Anything else to drink?"

"I believe Sue Ellen made a pitcher of lemonade. But bring the tea for your aunt and myself."

"Sue Ellen?" I ask.

"The maid." He rises with exaggerated fatigue. "Come on, you can carry the glasses."

"Your guests don't want to run errands," his mother says but I hasten after. Mike has hardly any clothes, yet he does not work and they have a maid. The kitchen is stuffed with twenty-year-old appliances my mother would pity. The refrigerator is half empty, nothing to tempt noshing. "Mike, what does the maid *do*? Is she pretty?"

"She's fifty, coal black and big as a house." Against the refrigerator door he kisses me roughly, asserting something.

Instead of just filling glasses, serving is complicated. "Mike as head of household will pour," Mrs. Loesser says crisply.

He serves his aunt first but she frowns. "All that time in the kitchen and you forgot my lemon?"

"Sorry." Chin lowered he strides out and back. Then without looking up he sloshes tea into glasses and passes them out.

"Isn't it stifling? Aren't you glad you don't have to teach in this weather, Ban?" his mother says.

I ask, "What do you teach?"

"General science," Mike answers, giving her his best smile. "Any good snakes this year, Ban?"

"As a matter of fact, yes, I have a lovely blue racer. Would you like it for the summer?"

"Ban! You know Michael. Don't tempt him. All his life he's brought home strays. All manner of lost creatures from heaven knows where." The small pursed smile does not change.

What can I do but pretend I do not understand?

His mother's hands are braced over the ends of the wicker chair arms. Her gaze moves leisurely off my shoes to my face. My old winter flats. I have to fight the impulse to tuck my feet under the settee. "You're attending the university also?"

"Yes. I'll be a sophomore in the fall."

Aunt Ban smiles faintly. "Are you planning to do anything in particular?"

"I write."

"So many young people seem to want to be authors," she says dryly. "What do you intend to write about?"

Mike's mother says gently, "Ban, I'm sure growing up in a rooming house, one must encounter many unusual situations."

"I didn't grow up in a rooming house, Mrs. Loesser. Perhaps you're thinking of Thomas Wolfe?"

"I'm sorry. That must be another friend of Michael's. It would be an awkward position for a young girl." She sips her tea. "We had hoped to send Michael to a good Eastern school for his last two years . . ."

Aunt Ban nods brisk agreement.

". . . but I suppose that will have to wait for graduate school."

"You've years of schooling ahead of you, boy," Aunt Ban says with fierce good humor. "A long hard pull. You must apply yourself. This last semester's grades disappointed us. . . ."

His fingers strum his knees as he looks from one to the other with the expression of an alert and earnest boy.

Aunt Ban nods at the table where his leather binder lies. "How's the Proust going?"

"What?"

"Didn't you tell me you were going to read Proust in the original this summer?"

His voice is mild as when he is most angry. I suddenly understand that is what his mother does. "I admit it sounds like the sort of thing I'm apt to say." He gets up. "I'll put a record on."

"It's late, Michael," his mother says. "Sounds carry with the windows open. Perhaps you've lost perspective, you've been keeping such late hours."

He paces around the porch once, twice, then stoops to pull a violin from under the settee.

"Michael, did you take that out here again? The damp air will warp it."

"I was practicing." Tucking it under his chin, he runs the bow over the squawking strings. "This was my father's but I began learning on it when I was five. I caught on quickly and they thought I'd be a prodigy. But I petered out."

"Michael!" His mother shakes her head. "No one wanted you to be a prodigy, of all things. You hated to practice. Your father never intended for you to be anything but a doctor."

The bow chafes in agony against the strings. His eyes glow dark. "I remember differently."

"Prodigy!" She clicks her tongue, smiling with real amusement. "Then play if you like. If it wouldn't bore your friend."

"It's too damned hot." Picking up the case roughly he takes the violin into the house. A moment later, a drawer slams. The gazes of the two women meet in amused tolerance, and at that moment I quite hate them.

July 10, 1954

Dear Stu,

Somehow I haven't had the energy to answer. The less I do, the less I can do. Like oversleeping and waking up

exhausted. I write Lennie every night. We keep in touch
—but oh the frustration!

I found a cruddy job as receptionist in a dental building.
I swear I'll never waste a summer this way again. How
dependent we are on a few lousy dollars—all the difference between freedom and compulsion!

I've been reading Colette (in translation but don't tell
Julie if you see her) and C. Wright Mills. I realized I
had decided to be an art historian because of Lennie.
My own interests lie more in the direction of sociology,
as you've said yourself indirectly. I feel very class conscious, fascinated by interactions of people and groups.
I think I may major in soc. What think you?

You don't know how lucky you are to be with Mike,
able to act your love instead of trying to ship it through
the mails. I'd give *anything* to be with dear Lennie for
just two hours in the old apartment, or even a fast
twenty minutes! I'm minding my own business, hear,
and patronizing the local library. One of the dentists
isn't bad looking in a Gregory Peckish way, but who
needs someone used to saying, Open a little wider,
please, this won't hurt . . . much. Growing claws to fight
with parents. Growing hoarse with no one to talk to. I
miss you like crazy & our room & dearest sweetest Lennie & even those necking machines on the corridor with
their plastic hymens and cashmere brains! Write soon.
Tell me some good things to read.

Love, Donna

He lies along the seat with his knees raised and his heavy
head in my lap. Through my cotton dress I can feel his
breath. The slice of waning moon is up to roof level between the houses, ripe cantaloupe. It rained all day before
clearing, leaving the city washed. Trees purl and riffle with
the sound of a stream rushing over us. The houses of his
neighborhood are drowned in darkness. His lids droop, his
mouth relaxes. Suppose we lay in that house in a room on

the second floor with the casements flung open level with the elm leaves? He would turn in his sleep murmuring and I'd lean on my arm to watch over him as he settled again. . . . My head lurches forward. Must not sleep! "What time is it?"

"Ummmmm." He stirs, noses into my waist.

I reach for his wrist but he hides the watch under him. "Mike, it's late."

He yawns with a voluptuous heave of his shoulders. "Always damned late."

"Mother spoke to me again about staying out so long."

"Likewise and then some." He scrubs his knuckles across his eyes. "After I drop you off I feel raw. I hardly ever get to sleep before it's light."

"I wish we could just once sleep and wake in the same bed."

"When I was a kid I caught the flu. They piled the bed with quilts so I'd sweat it out. When I leave you, I have to burn you out of my system before I can sleep." His eyes are wide open, black. "Listen, I love you."

"I love you." Words are too feeble to relieve the pressure in my chest. I can only run my hands over his heavy-boned face and say it again and again. Quarrels rub me raw and weary. My parents find me an irritant. Every day I hate my job more. At home I feel as if I have been forced back into early adolescence with no community, no friends, no support group. I am losing my sense of myself. Only with him is there any tenderness and communication.

FIFTEEN
What the Tea Leaves Said

SATURDAY I GET up to find Mother at the kitchen table—cleared except for the teapot, a cup and an ashtray—smoking her semiannual cigarette. On her vanity she keeps a wooden chest of gold-tipped Russian cigarettes Uncle Murray the small-time comedian gave her when I was a toddler. Although she is not a smoker, he guessed their exotic appearance would take them out of the category of what she calls "that filthy habit." A year goes by while she never takes a cigarette out. Then one evening after supper on a day that feels no more unusual than any other, she appears with a slender brown cylinder cupped elegantly between her fingers, acting in her own movie. Then I see in her the young beauty from the slums, studying seductive graces in darkened theaters. All she had to save herself was encompassed in being female.

"It's late for breakfast," she says. "There's tuna fish salad for lunch."

"You could have got me up."

"You were out so late, I was sure you must be tired."

"It's the weekend," I say in automatic defensiveness.

While I eat, wisps of smoke from the scant tobacco curl from the cylinder as if blown through a straw. She is so silent I look at her with surprise, but she seems absorbed in her ritual. Not till she has tapped out the gilt mouthpiece does she rouse herself, then to pour me tea.

Leaves float thickly in the cup. "You forgot the strainer."

"So I did. I'll read the leaves for you."

I shrug, embarrassed. She read my palm when they brought me home from the hospital but never since. When I was little and jealous of the women in the kitchen, I used to beg her to read the leaves for me. "Jill's going to like to go to school this year and she's going to be a good girl and help her mother cheerfully." "Am I going to get a bike?" "That isn't clear yet," she would say sadly, meaning the money was iffy.

She takes the cup to brood over it. I lean my cheek on my hand, a yawn stretching my jaws. Maybe I'll sunbathe in the yard and read *Sons and Lovers* if she doesn't make me help clean the house. I'm pallid next to Mike. Then she shoves the cup toward me, a wave of tea sloshing out. She stares and I stare back until I say, "So, what's up? You see the sign of the hangman in the cup?"

"No. The sign of the beast."

Oh, we're in for some nasty weather. "Come on, Mother. Maybe I can have a cup of coffee instead."

"I cannot be mistaken." She stabs her finger at the cup. "You're sleeping with him—with that boy."

The room settles into new shapes. "What?" I cannot help following her finger to the bottom of the cup.

Her lip curls. "You heard me."

I force a sticky smile. "I don't believe I heard correctly." I consider saying she damn well knows I sleep here, but playing with language strikes me as inadvisable, given her expression.

"You're sleeping with that boy!"

"Mike, I suppose? God, Mother, you used to think Howie and I—"

"Do you have the nerve to call on Him? We raise our children to have them lie to our faces. Carrying on like a bitch in the alley!"

I jump from my chair. "Stop it! I'm going outside."

She brings her fist down, rattling the cups. "Sit down! Do you want the neighbors to hear?"

I sit, my stomach hardening. I do in fact hear the whirl of an electric mixer. Mrs. McAllen next door must be baking a cake.

"Not that they don't guess already with you coming in at two every morning." She swells with rage. "You've given yourself to him not once but many times. You've been playing me for a fool, carrying on behind my back. Traitor to your mother!"

Fascinated I stare. Then I snap to. "What do you want?"

"Don't try to brazen it out! You think I'm blind, I can't see it in the leaves?"

"You see what you want."

"How can you sit and eat my food, knowing what you've done? Have you no pride? My daughter, my only daughter, a slut."

"I have lots of pride." I clamp shut. Only by lying can I protect. "You've been accusing me since I was twelve. Lay off it. I've been working hard all week and I don't need a lousy weekend."

"Can you deny it? Look me in the eyes."

I meet her angry gaze. "Sure."

"Now I know you're lost." She pulls a folded paper from her apron and throws it down.

Gingerly I lift it. Donna's handwriting.

July 10, 1954

Dear Stu,
Somehow I haven't had the energy to answer. The less I do, the less I can do. Like oversleeping and waking up exhausted. I write Lennie every night. . . .

Relief courses through me like cool water. "This is just Donna's last letter."

She jabs the page. "Can you deny what it says right there?"

"How'd you get hold of this? It's mine."

"You think you're clever, but let me tell you, there's no

one stupid enough they don't know to look in an underwear drawer."

"It's personal. It was addressed to me."

"I wouldn't boast." She jabs at it. "Read this."

I follow her finger.

You don't know how lucky you are to be with Mike,
able to act your love instead of trying to ship it through
the mails. . . .

"What's wrong with that?" I ask.

"To be able to *act* your love?" Her voice lilts with sarcasm. "To *be with* dear Lennie for just two hours in the
old apartment, or even a fast twenty minutes? You think I
don't know what that means?"

"She misses Lennie. She's in love. It's nice."

"What do you know about love, slut? Dirt, that's what
you know."

"Quit it." I push my chair back and rise.

"Keep your voice down." She rises too, leaning so close
her breath burns my cheek. "You told me you didn't care
for him but he'll do, won't he?"

"What I feel is none of your business. I'm going out." I
start to slip past but she flings out her arm.

"Sit down, or I'll show the detective's report to your
father." She smiles tightly at my cry. "I had the two of you
followed by a detective these past ten days."

My skin burns with nakedness. "I don't believe you."

"You've been acting so strange since you came home—"

"No, you never spent money for that. It's too absurd!"

"Twenty-five dollars a night it cost me out of my own
money from Matt. Burke's Detective Agency, you can
look them up in the phone book."

"I don't believe you!" I repeated louder. "What a tall
story!"

She marches past me to grab her white beaded purse,
fumbling in it. "Here. That's the man. You saw him last
week when you and Michael were leaving just as he was
arriving."

It is a business card.

Thomas E. Burke Detective Agency
Confidential Investigation
Civil—Criminal—Domestic
2525 Woodward Avenue, Suite 14A
KL 5-8500

licensed   24 hour service
bonded   surveillance
over 25 years experience

Scrawled on the card is a name in ballpoint, Roy Nastasian. I am numb. My nerves ring but I feel nothing. I feel deaf. She really did.

"In that boy's car," Mother cries. "In parks and fields and alleys and ditches!"

"What does a place matter? How could you spy on me?"

"Have you no pride at all? Are you a bitch, to receive any male who comes sniffing?"

"That is the worst thing you've ever done."

"Are you through lying?"

"I'm not ashamed. You made it shameful."

"I always held myself too high!" She thrusts out her hands. "Did he tell you he loved you? Hot air is cheap. Men pay a prostitute but what did he give you?"

"What I gave him. I love him."

"Love!" She spits it through her teeth. "That's a joke."

"I'm proud of him and he makes me proud of myself."

"If a man loves you, if he cares for you, he respects you too much. He'll marry to have you."

"I don't want to be *had*. Respect that doesn't touch? How do I know if I want to marry him?"

"Marriages aren't made in bed, you poor fool."

"I don't share your values. I have to live my life by my own sense of right and wrong—"

She rises. "Call him."

"What for?"

"I want to talk to him tonight. I won't be surprised if he runs out, but if he cares for you—at all—he'll come."

I follow her into the living room. "You don't believe he

loves me." I reach for the phone, stop. "Are you going to listen?"

"Surely you don't expect me to trust you now."

I replace the receiver. "Then I won't call."

"Then I will."

I huddle toward the phone, dialing. The phone rings, rings. Let him be out.

"Hello?" Groggily. Voice thick as when I used to wake him at school.

"Mike, listen—"

"You woke me." He yawns. 'What time is it?"

"One. My mother just talked to me. She knows about us."

"Knows what?"

"About us. Yes, she's right here."

"What are you talking about?"

"She *knows*. She's standing here now. She accused me."

"What the hell?" I can see him shaking his head trying to wake up. "About us having sex?"

"Yes."

"You denied it, of course."

"For a long while."

"You didn't admit anything! Are you out of your mind?"

"She had us followed by a detective."

"*Merde!*" A long silence.

"Mike."

"You should still have denied it. What a mess!"

She leans against the jamb with a cold flickering smile. "Tell him to come over this evening."

"Mike, she wants you to come over tonight."

"Does she think I'm feebleminded?"

"Mike! She wants to talk to you. You have to come."

"Walk into that house. And 'talk' to her?"

"She said you won't because you don't care for me."

"What's wrong with you? Do I have to prove it to your mother?" He groans. "Why did you admit it?"

Mother stirs restlessly. "Is he coming or not?"

"Just a minute," I say to her, cupping the receiver. Then to him, "Are you coming, Mike? Please!"

"All right, I'll try to get there by eight. *Merde alors*, you sure got us in the soup. Don't say anything else. We'll see whether I can't repair the damage."

Hanging up I face her. "He's coming at eight." The harsh glaring anger has returned to her eyes but I pull free. "I'm going upstairs."

"Just so you get out of my sight!" She swirls past and slams the door of her bedroom. The springs of her bed wince sharply.

Dad's face is ruddy and beaming. His hair looks whiter by contrast with the burn from a day's fishing. "Ever see a prettier string of blue-gills? How come you made pork chops, then?"

Mother says, "I'll cook them tomorrow."

I push the food around my plate, waiting till I can leave the table.

"Your mother wouldn't let me get you up, or I'd have taken you along." He grins. "We took a dip afterwards to cool off. Water was fine. Poor old Gene didn't catch but one sunfish, and that was undersize." He helps himself to more potatoes. "Best to eat them fresh caught."

Mother sits low in her chair, her cheeks puffy. "I didn't have the strength to clean them."

He frowns at her. "Feeling under the weather, Pearl?"

She shakes her head.

His deep voice trembles with awkward gentleness, like his hands at some delicate work. "Sure you aren't sick? The heat's got you down."

"I'll explain after supper." She shakes her head, her face screwing up as if she will cry.

She cannot mean to tell him! She must have planned some story to get him out of the way. But as I start to clear the table, she says, "Better go upstairs. He'll take this hard. I don't know what he'll do to you."

Through the doorway he squats in front of the television. "What are you going to tell him?"

"What?" The lines in her face pull down. "What you told me."

"Mother, you can't."

"I have to. I don't look forward to it."

"Don't do it, then. Why? It's none of his business."

"Because if he figues it out, he'll blame me." She wipes the hair from her forehead. "He'll think I connived."

I turn and run upstairs, to hurl myself on the glider. Though I strain to hear, I catch only the murmur of voices mixed with the television. Then the television stops but the voices go on. She is a woman and sensual. Her mother had too many babies and she helped them into bloody birth. At ten she looked fifteen. Her hungry reading exposes her to some ideas, some breadth of living. But he has never indicated to me that sex exists. Love is not a word he uses. His judgment is the fall of a headman's ax.

The broken triad of gongs at last. As I start down, aware of how disheveled I feel, my eagerness to see Mike slides away. The world is wide, in all directions more attractive than this house. A rope of sheets out the window. They come to search. Ten years later a postcard from Manila, Jill the beachcomber. Now my parents will never approve of me, never accept me, never love me. Blown. But nothing I did was ever what they wanted. Wrong child.

Mike is posed stiffly in the rust armchair that rubs knees with the green, where Mother perches, her hands twisted in her lap. She has changed into her good blue dress and powdered her face, but her hair is wild. I look last and unwillingly at Dad in his usual chair in front of the windows. His face is a mask of cold fury. I seat myself on the couch toward the kitchen, the farthest point available.

"Now that this thing has come out, I intend to settle it this evening." Dad's voice catches. He sits heavily, addressing himself to a copper plaque above Mike of a galleon in full sail. "The worst has happened. We can keep shame to a minimum."

"I don't think we've done anything for which we need feel ashamed," Mike begins in his reading aloud voice. "There's been some misunderstanding."

"I misunderstand nothing." The lines tauten in Father's cheeks. "We will not talk about that."

"Mr. Stuart, Jill is old enough to know her own mind—"

"She's my daughter and my dependent, and this is my house." Father's hand quivers as he lights a cigarette. "A wrong has been committed against society, against us. It must be set right."

Those two hundred dollars: a dependent. But I can't make enough this summer to pay the whole dorm this year either. All my muscles clench as if pulling the words from Mike, for I want him to answer them, to make them understand. "Ideas change, sir. Jill doesn't think what we did wrong any more than I do."

"We're right," I burst out. "I can't live by a morality I don't believe in, I don't approve of. I don't try to make you act the way I do, but you grew up in a different world than I have to live in. You grew up right after World War One. They didn't even have cars—"

"Keep quiet," my father bellows. "You've forfeited your right to be heard." He does not glance at me.

"Suppose I'd done something really bad like robbing Mrs. Coyle of her Social Security check or running over a kid playing in the street! For two people to make love just isn't a crime!"

"There's nothing you can say! Be quiet!" My father's fists clench. For a moment there is silence. Everyone stares at the floor. Why doesn't Mike speak up? They'll listen to him.

Mother blazes at me, "Were you a virgin? Was he the first?"

My face prickles. I rub my fingers against the worn nap.

"Answer me. Were you a virgin, Jill?"

"What difference does that make? So was he."

Mike throws me an awful look.

"Are you lying to me? I wish I could believe you. Finding his nod has not released our stares he says finally, "Yes."

My only value to them. Broken like a vase.

"The only thing to do . . ." Father's gaze rebounds from our faces and comes to rest on the blank television. "What must be done . . ." His eyes behind gold rims are winter ponds. The new burn from the day fishing has condensed to hectic red splotches. "You'll be married as soon as possible."

Mike stirs. "I never promised to marry her."

"I never promised to marry him either!" I squawk. We will never escape this place. We will be staked here sweating forever.

"I'll bet you were careful not to promise anything!" Mother bends toward Mike. "Taking advantage of her— you can see she hasn't the sense to come in out of the rain. What did you intend?"

He thrusts his chin out, straining with exasperation. "We didn't intend anything! We like seeing each other, talking, spending time. I suppose we might get married someday when I have my doctorate, but that's irrelevant."

"I wonder how irrelevant your mother will find it when I show her the detective's report."

Father writhes in his chair scattering ash. Mike stares at Mother in frank hostility, each measuring the other's will. "You know I wouldn't have my mother see it. She'd die before she'd have anything to do with sordid matters like detectives."

"You should have thought of that before you began carrying on. You can drop that high-and-mighty manner right now."

"How can you do this to me? Don't you see Mike's right? I don't want to get married! It's the last thing I want."

"It's too late for that." Father lurches forward, clasping his hands till the knuckles stand out in ridges. "You chose each other and you'll have to make the best of it. Though God knows this is not what I'd have chosen. Or you for a son-in-law."

Mike asks quietly, "Are you going to put me through school?"

Father turns to glare directly at him, the light bristling off his white stubble. "What?"

"If I marry a girl who isn't Jewish—in fact if I marry at all now—my family will disown me and stop support."

"You should have thought of that before you messed around with Jill," Mother spits. "She was Jewish enough for you all this time."

Mike slumps negligently, drawling, "But don't you see, if they stop support, I don't care if they read your damned reports. I'll lose them anyhow. What does it matter whether they disown me because you drag dirt into my mother's house, or because I marry a wife she doesn't approve of?"

He has escaped them. How can they talk as if I'm an object whose ownership is debated? The loser will lead me off.

Father sits dreadfully still. "Get out!"

"Wait, Malcolm." Mother regards Mike from her lashes. "You object because you'll lose your mother's and aunt's support?"

"That's the situation, in a nutshell."

"Anything's more important to you than Jill. I understand. All right, good-bye, and I'll call the police if you ever come near her again."

"No!" My voice rings in my ears. I say again, "No! You can't do this."

"That's not true," Mike says. "How do you expect me to support her, by working in a factory?"

Dad says, "I supported my wife for twenty years without benefit of schooling. And we had the discipline to wait."

She was married to somebody else, but I cannot use those weapons on them. I know their vulnerabilities. "You made Leo get married, you and the Haleckis, when you caught him with Joanie. What did that last, eighteen months? What kind of satisfaction can there be forcing people to get married who don't want to? I won't marry Mike if he quits school."

"You'll do as you're told," Father says.

"I don't care. I'd rather die than make him quit."

Mike looks at me with warmth for the first time. "You heard what she said. We're united on this."

"You'll die too?" Mother smiles. "I have a better idea. Get married secretly, and no one needs to know till you graduate."

"But . . ." I can see the surprise hit him. "How do I know you'll keep it a secret?"

Father puts out his butt in the full ashtray, grinding and grinding. "You expect us to boast about it?"

"Suppose you got angry? How do I know you wouldn't take it to my family?"

Mother says, "We'd give our word."

From the set of Mike's lips I can taste his enjoyment. "Would you take mine?"

"What kind of a guarantee . . ." Mother begins.

Bartering. He sits bolted into himself. A cold slick of humiliation dirties me.

". . . at least my master's. . . ."

Let the roof fall and crush us to silence. We are insects, all.

". . . put it in writing with a lawyer . . ."

The reddish tree of life on the machine-made Oriental rug writhes like the twisted nerves in my flesh. On the knickknack shelf a blue china cat washes herself with cool dignity. Remember Lightning, my tuxedo tom, always coming home with an ear torn or a cheek clawed open, but in my lap he would lie purring himself to and from sleep. I wrote stories about his heroic exploits modeled on the Lad, a Dog stories and almost believed them.

"Jill, are you listening?" Mother asks sharply. "We agree not to disclose your marriage before Mike gets his Ph.D., unless you get pregnant. If we break the promise, we pay his tuition till he finishes."

Are they mad? Where would they get the money anyhow? They don't even pay my college costs, and my grades are better than his anyhow, which makes him furious. "Is this what you want?"

"Want!" Mother snorts. "This is the last thing I ever wanted."

"Will you send me back to school?"

"What for?" Mother looks uneasily at Father who sits contemplating his fingers. "Do you think you deserve it? Besides, you're getting married. What's the point?"

I am on my feet. Married off to a man who does not want me. The aqua walls and their pale faces are riddled with specks, red then black spots widening. The dining room table lurches toward me, slams me on the hip. I run for the bathroom. I grip the sink and propped on stiff arms vomit my small supper, my tuna fish lunch and undigested, acid, finally air.

Mother stands in the doorway hugging herself. "Jill, are you all right?"

All right? All wrong. When I come out she stands by the dining room table, holding herself. "About college, Jill. We'll see. After you're married."

Thin, shadowless I wait. I want to be unconscious.

She peers into my face. "Mike wants to talk to you. Do you want to go for an hour's drive?"

Out of the house, yes. They walk us to the door and standing a foot apart look after us down to the car. I huddle against the window. My throat feels scraped, my mouth tastes of mouthwash and acid. His face set with anger he takes corners squealing as I bump against the door and slide away. Rounding corners, through an alley, across tracks. "I think I've shaken him."

I try to rouse myself. "What?"

"The detective. Nobody's behind us." He halts on a side street by a big brick house where we have often parked, where we have elaborated fantasies of our life together in that house.

"If they're following, mightn't they come here?" The familiarity disgusts. I cannot escape the sense that someone watches.

"I hope he shows up." He drives his fist into his palm. "I'll break his damn nose and knock his teeth down his throat."

I cannot believe we will see Nastasian except in nightmare. Our old patterns are severed; I cannot move. Noticing he scowls. "Come here." He pulls me to be kissed: an assertion, without pleasure. He draws back to hunch over the wheel, drumming his fingers. "You've made a fine mess of things! Why didn't you keep denying?"

"I'm sorry."

"Why didn't you act shocked, oh Mother, how could you say such things, and run from the room?"

"Then your mother would have the reports by now. She wouldn't have believed me acting like that anyhow."

"Did you want this to happen?"

"You act as if you hate me!"

"What do you expect me to say, Gee, Mrs. Stuart, I'd be tickled pink to take your daughter off your hands? Just wrap her up to go."

"Don't you see how this humiliates me? I don't want to get married like this!"

"We won't, then."

"Then what's to become of us?"

He scratches his head. "I'll think about it. We'll outwit her yet."

"She's shrewd, Mike."

"Obviously." Again he drums his fingers. "Must be a way. Got to get advice. Cribbets, maybe. I can trust him to keep his mouth shut."

"Your old high-school teacher?"

"The poet. I'll think of something. Trust me."

I must believe he will. Tonight he was caught off guard.

"If he's watching, let him get his eyes full." He moves toward me.

The street is empty, ominously still under the streetlights. As so many times we make love in gestures repetition has made natural, yet I feel a shade of awkwardness, of actions more willed than felt. I am conscious of every movement, of even the faint caress of his cuff against my ankle. His hand on my breast is violent. As if he sensed me freshly, we are more passionate, yet colder. We grate electrically. For this simple act my parents hate me. They think you need a license for it. I remember the bloody empalement, how he put his arm around me and called me a good soldier. The time in the pines when my pleasure was born. Tonight a tautness in him does not yield, pounding into me and holding back. From time to time a wince of anger slants across his face; I too cannot escape remembering.

SIXTEEN
Jill Witnesses a Joust

THE NEXT MORNING I sit bolt upright at five thirty. The room blazes with light but no one stands over me. Then I remember. I cannot stay in this bed. Fear drives me upstairs to the glider—the fear of seeing my parents and being seen. I doze and wake sweating while the small noises of the house seep through the floorboards: the toilet flushing, the refrigerator door closing, the rough timbre of Dad's voice, Mother's contralto answering. I cannot sense time, for always the same oppression squats on my chest. Through the open window children's cries in a game of hide-and-seek flutter like white and yellow moths. A lawn mower chirrs. Faintly the odor of frying fish wafts up. Why should the knowledge of joy be accounted a crime? They suffer and I suffer and this house is too narrow.

The phone rings nasal through the floor. Then the door opens at the foot of the stairs. "Jill?" Mother calls. "Telephone. It's Mike."

Too uneasy to take a seat, I stand. "Hello?"

"Are you alone?"

The whine of the saw locates Dad in the basement, but Mother is dusting the knickknack shelves. "No. Will I see you tonight?"

"We're going to my aunt's. Try to get to a pay phone before six. I've been thinking."

"Did you come up with something?" Faint spurt of hope.

"The first shock was worn off. A cheap trick like that catches you off guard."

"I'll try to."

When I hang up Mother says, "You might as well eat. There's leftover fish I can warm up."

"No thanks."

"If you don't eat you'll get sick and I'll end up taking care of you. Stop feeling sorry for yourself. You made your bed and you'll lie in it."

Too lethargic to argue I follow her to the kitchen. "I'm not hungry. Is there any cheese? Any ripe tomatoes yet?"

"Is he coming tonight to give his answer?"

"Mike has to visit relatives."

"Any port in a storm." She turns on the burner under the coffee pot. "I'm so tired I could keel over. Even your father couldn't sleep."

Reek of fish from the frying pan. "Maybe I should leave."

"I remember the last time you did. You got plenty tired of Heinemann's garage."

I was ten. After the first few hours already waiting to be found, not knowing Mrs. Heinemann had called Mother and been told to leave me there till I got ready to come out. Defeat. I chew cottage cheese and cherry tomatoes.

"Of course if your friend wants to support you in that grand style he pretends to be accustomed to, wearing torn shirts . . ."

The kitchen door swings open. "Pearl, what did you do with that ant powder?" He halts and a wave of shock freezes him as if seeing me alive were too much. Then he leans forward with his jaw shaking and shoves the table at me. I jump from the chair. Mother's voice breaks in high warning, "Malcolm!"

His voice rips from him, "Guttersnipe!"

"You hate me! But I'm not sorry!" I run scalded from the room.

As I grab my wallet Mother comes after me. "Where are you going? If you leave, you'll regret it all the days of your life."

"I'm going for a walk." I let the front door slam and bound down the walk, something torn loose inside me. Mangled tissue. Guttersnipe. Worse to imagine what that stands for he cannot bring himself to say.

Marcie is sunning herself on her second-story porch with her shades on and old shorts, not yet duded up in her whore clothes. She gives me a slight nod. Since I went away to college nobody talks to me. Even Freddie doesn't spill me his money troubles. I feel like a double outcast. My old gang wouldn't bug me for fucking Mike; they'd shrug and say, What else? Where do my parents get their weird morality? I was the last virgin my age on the block. Mother adored Freddie. She was always making chocolate chip cookies for him, and if he didn't rape me on the kitchen floor, it was only because I took a hot iron to him. I thought fucking Mike was supposed to prove I'm a healthy normal female. I need a woman friend bad. Donna's miles and miles away. Julie's in a suburb I can't get to without a car. Theo's in New York, in a town called Southampton.

Three girls walk arm in arm ahead of me into the corner drugstore, their little butts in shorts twitching consciously, their chatter loud. "He whistled at me yesterday by Sharkie's Garage!" "Frieda was petting with him in the balcony during Doris Day." The girls stop at the soda fountain while I pass on to the empty phone booth at the back.

His mother answers. "Who's calling please? I'll see if he's at home."

I slide the door open for a little air. The grip of the phone soothes me. He has a plan.

"How's it going, pumpkin?"

"Don't talk about it. It's good to hear your voice. Can you get away tonight?"

"It's good strategy to delay a few days. Let them see they can't push me. I called Cribbets and I'm seeing him Friday."

"Don't wait till next weekend to give them some sort of answer, Mike." How long can I hide in the attic? I fear my father.

"Look, she's trying to marry you off. The old comedy routine. She's not about to send away the only suitor."

"That's not true! They're furious and they're ashamed."

"She knew what was going on. Since the first night she had us tailed, she's just been waiting to trap me good. I'm surprised she didn't marry you off to one of the boarders before this."

"Stop it!" I pull the door shut. "You're worse than she is! I'm still the same person, I haven't changed."

"It's still the same relationship, too. You went to bed with me because you wanted to, not so I'd marry you. Didn't you?"

"Of course. I was proud to love you. You don't know how this humiliates me." The booth closes in with its stale air. I slide the door open an inch and lean my nose to the crack.

"It's a tacky working-class ritual, marry-'em-off. Like a low comedy movie about hillbillies."

"It hurts them, too. They're trying to see your point of view, with the contract thing."

"Great. Like a taxi to your execution."

I shut the door. "You've said a hundred times you love me. Why is it an execution to marry me?"

"I don't want to get married."

"No more do I. But what can we do? What can we do?"

"Don't fly off the handle. I told you I've been thinking, and you haven't even asked me what I came up with."

"Tell me." I slide the door open and stretch out my legs.

"So simple I'm surprised we didn't think of it last night. Just move out."

"Leave them?"

"Right. Get a little apartment over here. Won't that be soft?"

"Not very. What will I live on?"

"Well, you're working, aren't you?"

"I bring home fifty-eight a week. And what about school?"

"In the fall you can get a job there. We'll still be together."

"Mike, I can't make enough to pay the dorm, and the university won't let girls live out. If I have to live off what I'm earning, I'll be broke in September when school opens."

He sighs with exasperation. "Minor points we can work out. The main thing is to get you out of that hell and them off our backs."

I close the door, a damp depression creeping like fog up my spine. "I can't see how it would help me." Working for prevailing slave wages in Ann Arbor, seeing my friends for an occasional evening now and then when they aren't busy, asking them for reading lists. I'd have to be self-educated like my aunt Sarah, smartest of my mother's sisters, who reads *The World Almanac* cover to cover, head full of unconnected facts she tries to tell you, like what's the world's longest suspension bridge. Aunt Sarah is a bookkeeper. "Why should I do all the suffering?"

"They're your parents."

"She's right, you don't care what happens to me!"

"How dare you say that? After what I went through for you last night, where do you get the nerve?"

"Mike, I'm sorry!"

"This is a test of whether you love me, if you'll leave them and follow me."

"All I need are tests. Why can't we do it the other way? Then we can go on just as we are and both go back to school."

"You want me to buy this shotgun marriage?"

"I could go through with it, and I don't want to any more than you do."

He does not reply for a long time. "Look, pumpkin, get

out of the house and call me tomorrow. I'll come by Tuesday or Wednesday."

"Tuesday's better. My father has a union meeting. One less to contend with."

"All right, but you be thinking over my plan. You could get a little apartment with a big bed. See if you don't agree."

At the end of a mine tunnel, this airless hopeless booth.

At Short Brothers I have graduated to typing bills for those low-budget credit terms. All day every day I fill in name, address, monthly payment and whether the poor sucker is overdue yet, but I no longer watch the clock. I hate to go home. Lunch hour as I wander the streets of yellow and pink houses with carports and carriage lights on posts, I wonder how a woman comes to want to be shut up in a box to keep it clean and fill it with newer and newer objects. Children are hope only if you know what you hope for. Is love only a honey-sticky trap so that there may be more children? Then why did the world grow when I fell in love? I do not know a girl who does not say, I don't want to live like my mother, I don't want to be like my mother. Is it our mothers, ourselves or our men who mold us?

"Don't try to tell me everybody does it." Mother snaps her head back. "I've been around the world some in my time, and I'm not impressed by would-be sophisticates."

Mike and Mother sit in the rust and green chairs with a pitcher of iced lemonade on the end table. I was amazed when she brought it in, but they launched right at each other. Now the pitcher stands almost empty. They sip lemonade between speeches like debaters.

"Look, Mrs. Stuart, we aren't children to be disposed of as you happen to think right. Sex has for each person only the significance he attaches to it himself."

"Oh?" Mother purses her lips. "And what significance would it have if Jill gets pregnant?"

"That's impossible, since of course I've taken every precaution to protect her."

Mother tosses her head with a theatrical laugh. "If you'd been married as long as I have and known as many women straddled with brats by oh-so-careful men, you'd know how funny that sounds."

"I can only say they were not careful enough."

"There's only one sure cure and that's a little virtue."

"Mother, you talk as if all virtue means is not having sex." I lean forward to draw their attention from glaring at each other. "Women are human too. Virtue's more complicated. There's honesty and compassion and generosity and courage—"

"And lying to your mother. I understand."

"Yes, if knowing means you interfere. You try to control me."

"Jill, let me answer her." Mike makes a slicing gesture. "This is between the two of us."

"You'd never have done this to her if her father was Jewish. You think that excuses you?"

He rakes his hand through his hair. "I don't need excuses! Can't you see that?"

Several cold moments she looks at him. "There's a snake like you behind every young girl's troubles. My sister Sarah wasted seven years on a bad actor who drank and chased around and deserted her with a child, finally, in the middle of Georgia. You remind me of him! That same look. You think whatever you want you can take, and no one has a right to ask you for the price."

"Mama, he's not like that! And I'm not on sale, I don't have a price."

"You don't know what he's like." She turns, her eyes bright with pleading. "You're blind to him. But I see and it breaks my heart to have you mixed up with him."

"You run on about virtue," he says, "but you connived to let us go right along till you had the evidence you wanted. If you were so concerned for your daughter's virtue, you'd have questioned her instead of hiring detectives. I want to see those reports. I'll bet you knew ten days ago what was going on."

Mother nods, an aloof judging motion. "So you want to see the reports."

"I insist on it."

"You think you're smart, but you're a credulous fool."

He lowers his head, his shoulders tensing. "What do you mean?"

"No detectives, no reports." She crosses her legs, letting her foot swing freely.

No detectives. A chunk of the world falls out. No detectives, and yet the wound does not close. It still haunts me that we lay down together and thought we were alone, while the bushes were full of eyes. "But you showed me that detective's card. He was here. I saw him."

"Roy Nastasian? Sure he was. Eunice is after Leo for the child support again. Mr. Nastasian was trying to find out where Leo is."

"Mother! Why did you say you'd done it? Why?"

"To save time. I knew you'd deny it, and he would deny after you stopped. I figured that Mr. Nastasian would be hanging around trying to catch Leo, so he might give you a good scare by accident. I told him Leo had a car like yours."

"God, of all the stupid things!" Mike drives his fist into his palm. "She took you in and you took me in. Fine!"

"But she showed me his card. I saw him here."

"Go ahead, blame her." Mother smiles tightly. "A man like you always blames the woman."

Damn Leo! At the same time I feel a pang of kinship; the Haleckis and my parents made him and Joanie get married, starting Leo off on his marrying tic.

Mother says, "You think you're so smart you're invisible. Keeping her out till all hours of the night and her never able to tell me what you've been doing. I went to examine her panties in the hamper to see what she'd been up to, and she'd washed them all by hand. I knew it then. And just listening to her on the phone, yes, Mike, yes, Mike, I'm sorry your lordship, all sugar."

"What do you expect her to say with you listening? She defers to me because she knows me."

I can hardly tell their furious strained faces apart. They enjoy this fight, I realize suddenly. They prove their strength in grappling. They look alike. Each performs with satisfaction.

"You think you're strong, but you're a weakling," she taunts. "A man isn't a man because he seduced a few girls, but because he takes on the responsibilities of a man. You're a hardheaded arrogant boy."

"Jill knows better than to listen to your malice."

Mother sits straight, her feet barely reaching the floor. "I can tell when she's gone out and called you, because she comes back with her face all swollen up from crying. That's how you love her."

"I don't have to justify myself to you."

"She's my daughter and I'll protect her as long as there's breath in my body!"

"Who's to protect her from you?"

They talk of love, love but mean power, and they look alike.

"We don't have to listen to your malice." He jumps to his feet. "Jill, let's get out of here."

I stand up.

"Where? Where will you take her?" Mother cries. "Into some alley? I will not let her leave this house."

"You can't stop us. Jill, come on."

I take a step and halt. "I don't understand. What do you want me to do, Mike?"

"I want you to walk out of here with me."

"Jillie, don't do it!" Mother starts out of her chair twisting her hands. "My baby, don't go with him!"

"Walk out with me." His face strained in a grimace of angry pleading.

"But, Mike, what will we do? Will you go home then? Will you move out and we'll live together?"

"Don't listen to him, chickie." Mother wrings my arm. "He doesn't care. He just wants to show his power over you. He wants to take you from me."

"You were the one trying to give me away! Will you both shut up? Do I have to prove I belong to somebody? I'm me, look! I'm alive! I'm a person."

Mike sinks back. "You have her all riled up, with your shrieking. Listen, tell this woman you love me."

"I love you. I do love him."

"Then why doesn't he marry you?" Mother collapses in the chair. "Why doesn't he show he cares for you?"

Mike takes his head in his hands. "My head is splitting. I have such a bad headache I can't think any longer."

"Do you want an aspirin?"

"Bring me two. With cold water."

Fetching them I stand beside him. In his temple a vein beats. I raise my hand to stroke him but let it drop as I see Mother over his shoulder, bowed goddess of loneliness. Her mouth draws toward her small pert nose, her eyes squint. "Do you want something, Mother?"

"I feel so faint. Can't you open the windows some more?"

I push the windows behind Dad's empty chair as high as they go. "Is that better?"

"A little." She touches her eyelids. "I haven't had a decent night's sleep since this thing started. I worry and worry."

Remembering their tense threatening postures, I dare not step back for fear of upsetting this peaceful equilibrium.

Mike stirs first, squaring his shoulders, pulling in his jaw to make a double chin. "So there were no detectives, if I can believe you now."

Mother tightens. "That makes no difference. This can't drag on longer."

"Don't try to rush me!"

"You were in an awful hurry before. All right, you sit alone and think about it. But you won't see Jill anymore."

I imagine him in that dark stucco house, digested into his family. "No. We need to see each other. We need to decide together."

"He only makes you unhappy."

"He has a right to!" My hands twist and leap. She doesn't understand, she can't see. He is the one who loved me. The one I promised myself: the dark, willful, brilliant and moody idol of my dreams, my own Heathcliff-Hamlet-Byron-Count of Monte Cristo.

"Till Saturday, then. Promise me you won't try to see him secretly."

I turned to Mike but his face is heavy and sullen. He stares at his worn loafers. I turn back to Mother. "I promise."

SEVENTEEN

In Which Nothing Becomes Something and Something Becomes Everything

---

I HAVE SWORN I would not check again until two and I have held out, but the other promise I forced on myself —that I would not hope—I cannot keep. As I bolt the stall door, I whimper to myself, of course I have not started, not yet. When I look at my panties and see nothing, a cold nausea slides through me. I was sure this time. I felt the blood. Donna was fourteen days late and I am only eleven. Given the mute embroiled misery in which I stew, no wonder my period is off. Yet I am afraid.

As I pass her desk the older secretary Mrs. Papich looks up with her stubby fingers poised on the keys. "Do you have the runs?"

I nod, looking meek.

"That's the third day you've spent dashing to the powder room. Better see a doctor, doll, before the boss gets annoyed."

The only way he'll know is if you tell him, toad. She identifies with Short Brothers, concerned to sweat every minute's ill-paid labor out of me. Yet when she asked yesterday how I like the job, my voice came out so fervently that she was taken aback. Papich, I would slaughter pigs all day to keep out of the house. Violent closet scenes, how could I, why did I, bitch, my baby, shameless, ruined your life. . . .

Rain drums on the rafters of the attic. In the west thunder growls, the tail of the storm approaching. Storms come over Detroit immense, thunder rolling in huge blocks down the sky, the rain coming straight down in vast sheets.

July 27, 1954

Dear Stu,

I couldn't make head or tails of your letter. I don't see how Aunt Pearl could have misconstrued my last letter so! I'm sure I didn't say anything of that sort. I know you and Mike just date as good friends. She must have misinterpreted something I said for a joke. . . .

Donna, Donna, don't you understand this is no use? I suppose I am to leave this where Mother can find it, as if it could fool her in the easiest of times. I would ten times rather have a real letter from you, meant for me and not Mother.

I fold and toss it in the wastebasket. In a white flash the backyard elm stands out with its leaves combed all one way by the force of the rain. I stick a sheet in my typewriter,

July 31, 1954

Dear Donna,

propping my head on one hand. Where to begin. That my period is fifteen days overdue? I can no more set that down than I can say it aloud. Should I tell her my father stalks the house like the ghost of Hamlet's father and that we are lucky to get through a meal? That Mike and Mother cannot decide whether it is worse to lose a debate to the other or to get stuck with me?

I rest my cheek on the metal of the typewriter, as remote from Donna as if it were ten years since we lived in the white room and talked our lives to each other. The simple telling has lost its magic. What can she do in Flint but worry about me? Absence is absolute. I yank the page from the machine and toss it after her letter. Immediately she seems even farther. A sheet of lightning, a crack and tumbling thud of thunder, and the light flickers in the rafters where a small moth knocks its cigar tip body against the bulb. I half want to go down to fight with them, for the human contact; I cannot go. The friction of their gazes wears me down.

"You know what old Cribbets said to me?" Mike slumps behind the wheel, his head bowed on his chest.

His tone, playful in a chilly way, sets me on edge. I wait.

"Breaking a hymen is not quite like breaking the rose window at Chartres. Don't take yourself too seriously, Loesser. End quote."

"Breaking his neck would be even more fun. I made less of a fuss about my virginity than you did."

"If you hadn't told your parents I took it, what would they have to wail about?"

"You want me to say there were forty others first?"

He turns his palms up in a shrug. "He also advised me in future to pick mistresses from women who've left home."

"If I'm your mistress, how come I have to go to work every day?" My neck creeps. He is trying to pick a quarrel. "It would have been more convenient if we'd met in three or four years, but which of us could say we weren't ready?"

He sighs loudly looking out. Then his face comes to life. "Say, look at those!" Two women in white shorts go cycling by. He strains to look after them. "Nothing beats a girl with a big ass."

Which excludes me. "Are you tired of me, Mike?" Unreal question.

"Tired in what way?"

Why doesn't he deny my nightmare question? "Any way."

"I'm more than tired of your parents."

I cannot believe this scene. We took a wrong turning and this is by accident; we can still retrace our steps back into loving. How his eyes burned dark when he said he

loved me. He has not looked that way lately. But if somebody loves you, if you're really loved, how can it just stop?
I can't believe it. I can't.

"Cribbets says the worst thing for a writer is to get
involved. A writer needs wide experience but he must keep
part of himself detached."

If he loved me and I am still me, why can't he love me?
I haven't changed. "Oh? Did you bring your notebook
tonight?"

"I don't expect you to agree. Every woman resents a
man's independence. She wants him hanging at her breast
like a baby."

"I write as much as you do. And you're not independent.
I come closer to supporting myself than you do."

"Inevitably, you're a woman first. And most of what you
write is just *merde*."

"Oh? You never said that before."

"It was implied in everything I explained to you about
aesthetic theory. You don't expect me to take it seriously.
Do you realize I've spent years thinking about aesthetics?
Planning my career?"

"Mike, if you want to end it, say so. Don't poison it."

"Don't be melodramatic."

"Don't you understand they won't send me to school if
we weren't married? You won't see me. I won't be around."

"Move out. You're eighteen."

"If I leave I can't go back. They're my parents!"

"You've enough parents to spread all around the city
and have enough left over to free all the orphans. He's
living in the Victorian Age and she's a power-mad witch."

I should keep quiet, I know. "Mike, won't you marry
me? I have no skin left. Why do you make me beg?"

He stares ahead, his arm with the muscles knotted hard
against my touch. I slide away to the door. "Sorry. I'm
upset. You'd better take me home."

"I didn't say I wouldn't marry you."

"Of course." A rock in my gut: the embryo? "Take me
home anyhow." I will never tell him, after tonight.

"We haven't fucked yet."

"I don't want to."

"Oh? After all the trouble you got me into? Don't try those withholding games on me. You think I'll come around, then. No thanks. Come here."

That night I experience sex as pure pain.

As I come up the walk with the steam of rush hour still printed on my skin, my wrinkled dress, Mother peeks out the window. "You're late," she says nervously.

"The bus broke down." I sit wearily across the table, taking up a knife to peel potatoes.

"Jill." Her tongue pink and rough as a cat's darts out to lick her lips. "Do you want to marry him?"

"I never did." I wince. "That's not apropos, is it?"

"I don't think this one would be."

"It's a long time, marriage."

"I've been thinking. We could send you someplace else to school, if you'd give him up. . . ." She trails off questioningly. We look at each other with a frank bald weariness.

"It's late to apply."

"You could get into Wayne."

"It's not as good a school as the university."

"He isn't worth the pain, honey. He's weak."

The protest rises in my throat, sinks back.

"You'll get over him. You'll be more careful, won't you? I can't stand to see you look so pale."

"You don't look so hot either." The scroll of peel uncurls from my knife. "Why did you have to interfere?"

"You weren't happy. I could see you weren't."

"I was. You think I'm happy now?"

"We could send you someplace else to school. Away from him."

"Berkeley?"

"So far? Well . . . Sarah's in Sacramento. They have a college there too. You could work till February and then go."

"Would Father agree?"

"He hates Mike."

"He hates me too."

"Don't say such things." She rubs her nose. "He's tired.

He wants it over and done with. We could bring him around."

"I don't know." The sectioned potato bleeds chalky juice that makes my palm itch. A live thing one cuts up. Trust me, she coaxes, and then what?

"You're young," she whispers. "How can a man tell you aren't a virgin if you hold yourself tight? I never told Max about Sam. Being a widow at seventeen, it was too much! Being supposed to wear black and never go dancing. He never would've known if your uncle Murray hadn't dropped it. Then I persuaded Max the marriage had never been, what do you call it?"

"It'd be selling out what we had. You and I will never agree about what that love meant to me." Past tense. I hear myself.

"You had a sordid affair in cars and fields and God knows where, like thieves. Don't glamorize your mistakes when I'm trying to help."

"We see things so differently. I can't take a bribe to break with him. I have to choose it." I also can't trust her. They won't send me anyplace except out to work at a dead-end job. They want nothing good for me, nothing I want for myself, not an education, not freedom, not compatible friends, not love, not a chance to write.

Her eyes flash narrowly as she slices the potato into smaller and smaller chunks. "Think about it, Jill. Think it over."

"Are you alone? I have news." Mike's voice slurs with excitement.

"They're on the porch. Can you hear if I speak this softly?" I want to ask what happened to him last night, that he didn't come at eight, but I don't dare.

"Night before last I talked to my cousin Sheldon. He said to tell Mother, that she wouldn't kick me out. So I did it."

"What did she say?" I hold my stomach.

He laughs shortly. "That's why I couldn't call yesterday."

"Does she want to see me today? Should I come over?"

"She's tearing her hair that I ever brought you in the house. She says your parents haven't a leg to stand on. She called her brother-in-law, he's a lawyer."

"They haven't been talking law, Mike."

"She locked up the car and threatened to take a leave of absence to watch me."

Why does he sound so flattered by the fuss? My hand on the phone does not sweat because it is too cold. "Planning to stay home?"

"I'll get over in a few days, when she cools down. But I'm glad I made a clean breast of it, finally. Throwing myself on the mercy of the court. The relatives are up in arms, phone calls and visits and summonses! They haven't been this riled up since Sheldon got caught cheating on an exam."

"I can't talk anymore. Good night."

I walk toward the bathroom to be sick. Twenty-nine days and no period. Twenty-nine mornings with that razor edge cutting me from sleep, twenty-nine days of seizing hope from every cramp and twinge, looking always for the blood that does not come. Red is the invisible color of hope.

Saturday morning I wake to see Mother standing by my dresser holding my calendar. Her face is hard. "Jill, are you with child?"

I swing out of bed, clutching my old pajama bottoms with one hand. "I don't know."

"How late are you?"

She can count it too. "Thirty-two days."

"Why didn't you tell me?"

I heist up my pajamas. "Are you kidding?"

"Do you have other symptoms?"

"Nausea. I've been throwing up."

"Do your breasts itch?"

They begin at once, O psychosomatic me. "I'm late because of the turmoil."

She shakes her head briskly. "A month late? Never. You're regular, like all the rest of my family."

Outside a mad robin chirrups in the tree. "You think I'm pregnant?"

"I knew it! You disobeyed me, going behind my back. Now you've brought this down on yourself."

"If you try to make me marry him now I'll leave this house." I step closer to her clenching my free hand.

"Does he know?"

"No! And he won't either. I'll walk out and you'll never see me again. You won't know whether I'm alive or dead, but I'll never marry him."

We stand with our faces a handsbreadth apart while her black eyes try to force mine to flinch. I will not be put down.

"We have to talk fast. Your father's in the yard gabbing with old man Wilensky. You don't want to be saddled with a fatherless child!"

"I don't want it. I want an abortion."

"No! They're dirty men, Jill. They charge a fortune and they blackmail you."

"We needn't give our right names."

"It's against the law. You can go to jail. Your father would kill me!"

"People go to them all the time and don't get caught."

"Half the time they don't do it right. No!" Her hands seek each other in her apron, her gaze darts about the room. "They butcher you so you can't have babies after."

"Mother! I'll take my chances. I've got to."

"No. You've made your bed and you'll lie in it." She shifts from foot to foot, her face twitching. "All right. I'll tell you what to do."

"Mother, a doctor knows what to do. I don't want to kill myself."

"Then have the bastard if you won't listen to me." She turns and pushes past me.

I grab her arm. "Mother, don't!"

"Will you listen, then? I'll tell you what to do." She rakes me with her gaze. "You've always been a weakling and a coward. Sickly since you were seven. You'll have to do this for yourself. You'll do what I say or I'll wash my hands of you. If you go running around to doctors, and you can't trust a one of them, only in it for the money, I'll tell your father and he'll make you have it."

"All right." I sit on the bedside clutching my stomach. Fish cold.

"Don't think it's easy. It's hard, hard."

"You'll see that I'm strong enough." The bile wells in my throat and I swallow it down. "Tell me what to do."

EIGHTEEN
The Agon

STEAM CLOUDS THE mirror, coalescing on the yellow wall and running down in rivulets. While the tub fills I sit on the toilet seat staring at my belly smooth and flat from harsh laxatives. Under the cushion of fat lurks the womb, spongy fist that will not open while in it cells divide and divide. The steam swirling hot from the tub smothers me as this body goes its animal way. I seldom felt feminine: I felt neuter. An angel of words. I could imagine myself a Hamlet, a Trotsky, a Donne. I thought I was projects, accomplishments, tastes: I am only an envelope of guts. This is what it is to be female, to be trapped. This sac of busy cells has its own private rhythms of creation and decay, its viruses and cancers, its twenty-eight-day reminders of birth and death. My body can be taken over and used against my will as if I were a hall to be rented out. Hot baths with Epsom salts, hot baths with pennyroyal; I am parboiled and still pregnant.

I loved and got caught and that phrase has teeth. Like my mother to cuddle a dark-haired girl-child and suckle it

211

on my frustration and beat it for my hungers and bind it for my loneliness. To sacrifice myself for a girl-child whom I will try to teach to sacrifice herself, a chain of female suffering. I lower myself into the scalding tub, groan, heave out, plop back. In the cannibal pot I stew. Only I will know how I sometimes dream of that small changeling dribbling love on my breasts and how sick is that dream quivering with power. It would love me, poor bastard; it would have to.

"We're just as good as his folks." Mother scrubs at the pot furiously.

"Good we may or may not be, but it's a matter of class." I am sweeping the floor.

"We're just as middle class as they are. We own our house. We own our car, only two years old and paid up. What's wrong with him?"

I don't know how to sort out what I feel, such a welter of pity and love and irritation. "Sure, everybody's middle class, right? But some are more middle class than others." I have been reading Orwell.

She looks at me in blank rage, standing there with her worn posied housedress soaked through with dishwater, wearing old grey tennis shoes and Orlon socks yellow with washing, and she waits for me to tell her why Mike and family consider us a few steps down the social ladder. Is this what I went to college to learn? "I will not, I will not marry him, so it doesn't matter, does it? What they think."

From the dark porch my parents watch the street arguing about Milton Berle, whom they watch every week and every week quarrel over. My mother says he works hard; my father says the network bosses are fools to pay him thousands for putting on women's dresses and making faces. I think Father suspects Milton Berle is Uncle Murray in disguise and waits for Berle to try to touch him for a twenty. Alto and baritone my parents' muted descant rises over the cars dragging at the corner and squealing down the street, enters the stifling kitchen where Mike stares into his cup. He yawns, flexing. "You don't understand, Jill.

She doesn't put me through scenes. The family's civilized. It's just the barbs. My cousin Sheldon saying, Sex for a homely girl is just her substitute for a pretty girl's flirtation."

"Do you think I'm homely, all of a sudden?"

"My aunt told him you were. Mother thinks you look Oriental. That with roomers in the house, your real father—"

"I won't hear!" I jam my hands over my ears.

He pulls them down. "I'm supposed to keep this poison in? At Uncle's last night they had a simpering piece from Swarthmore dangling in front of me the whole time."

"I hate them!"

"You can't. We come as a set. Now I've been considering how we can show them. How we can get my mother to stop making fun of pumpkin and see her good points the way I do."

Skinny birdwoman, cold and fleshless. "Your mother and I love and hate in polar opposition. I can't be me and please her. Why should I crawl?"

His eyebrows climb his forehead. "A strange tone for someone begging to be part of that family."

"I'm not begging now."

"That's a fact. Where does this hard line come from?"

"From me. I'm not interested in marriage any longer."

"So you set yourself against me. Going to show how stubborn you can be." That silky voice. "I want the pumpkin to be good, but she's trying to be a stone instead. So you can arch your back and stand up to me. Do you know what I can stand?" Taking the cigarette from his lips he pushes it against the palm of his left hand. He turns it back and forth, his gaze on me. The sparks flare against his palm and shower into his lap.

"Stop. Mike, stop it!" I tug at his wrist. He grinds the lit cigarette into his palm until I shudder with convulsive weeping. "Stop it, oh god, please, Mike!"

At last he snuffs it in the ashtray. "Shall I do it again?"

"No, Mike, please!"

"Do you think that hurt as much as what you said?"

"I'm sorry."

"Why do you cry if you don't care?"

"I do!"

Footsteps. I wipe my eyes but Father sees. "Any coffee left?"

"I think so." I fetch the pot from the stove and pour it.

He looks and looks at Mike. "You'll have plenty of time to make her cry if you do marry. Why don't you go home now?"

The house is quiet except for Dad's snoring. I sit nude on the old glider in the attic smoking a last cigarette. Maybe Mother doesn't really know how. It's not working. My eyes chafe as if the sockets fit too tight. That trick with the cigarette. Must he always break me down to get his way? I cry away my reason.

Flinching I bring the cigarette to my palm. *One*, I will count slowly. *Two*, so hot it feels not hot but sharp, *three*, like a needle. No, broader. *Four*, a drill lighting up a nerve. *Five*, shouldn't concentrate on it, one illuminated point. *Six*. Maybe if I do this, I can abort myself. *Seven*. Then never again will he be able to break me down with a cheap trick, *eight*, although I won't tell him I did it too. It would just up the ante. Still if he tries it again, *nine*, I will remind myself it's not so bad. Even longer I could. *Ten*. I grind the butt out.

I roll into bed, hanging my hand over the side with the palm still convinced the cigarette is eating it. I will not let him squash me.

Mother sits on the couch, her thighs spread wearily. "You aren't trying hard enough."

All the furniture is shoved back to back. I let the rust chair stay blocking the passage to the dining room and drop in it in humid collapse. "How can I try harder?"

"If you want this baby, say so. But don't fool around."

"Mother, damn it, I've lost twelve pounds with laxatives and taking those vile herbs and throwing up and jumping off porches."

She snorts. "You can't diet a baby away."

"I've lifted and heaved and jumped and pocked and twisted and boiled myself."

She looks at her plump hands red with washing. "I don't know . . ."

"Mother, maybe it isn't going to work. Let's go to a doctor. Please."

"And end up in jail? Never. You do it yourself, they can't prove it on you. They can't take you to court."

"I'm sick as a dog. I can't stand without dizziness. I almost passed out climbing the stairs at work yesterday. But nothing happens!"

"Keep your voice down." She taps her foot. Her thighs quiver nervously under the washdress. "There's another way. But it's bad for the heart."

"Anything."

She turns her head away. "We'll get you quinine and you take that and then the next day a mustard bath. If that fails you have to open the womb yourself. There's no more time."

I am watched all the time at home but at work since I have given up lunch I have time to get my rolls of quarters at the bank and shut myself up in a pay phone on a corner. I am calling New York.

"Is Lennie there?" I ask the woman who answers. "I'm a friend from school."

"What friend?"

"My name is Jill."

"I thought maybe you were that Donna. Lennie's been expecting her to call. Just a minute."

I thought he might be home because he works as a waiter six nights a week from four to twelve.

"Jill!" he roars. "What's up? Anything wrong with Donna?"

"No, I haven't seen her. Listen, Lennie what was the name and phone number of that doctor who does abortions?"

"What's wrong, you in trouble?"

He's a friend of Mike's rather than mine. "No, it's a friend of mine from the neighborhood. I told her I knew somebody."

"Just a minute. I got it written down somewhere." He disappears off the line while the operator coos, "Please signal when through." Meaning I have run past three minutes. Lennie, hurry up!

Finally he comes back. "Yeah, well he's Dr. Lytton Manning in Dexter. You call and say you need to have a growth removed. That's the phrase."

"He's got some sense of humor, that man."

"Yeah, well you bring one hundred dollars in cash in an envelope and you give it to the receptionist. Then she gives you a date. You pay the other two hundred when you go in. You give it to the receptionist the same way."

"Three hundred dollars?"

"That's it. So how are you otherwise? How's Mike? I wrote him but the bugger never answered me."

"He's fine," I say limply. "Listen I'm on my lunch hour."

"Well, have a ball. See you at school."

Maybe. I walk very slowly back to work. Three hundred: that's what I've earned for six weeks' work. It would eat up my fall payment for the goddamned dormitory where we are forced to live. Plus I would have to manage to get to Dexter, Michigan, twice. Hopeless.

On my next two lunch hours I see a doctor a day. Each gynecologist examines me, painfully, and tells me I am pregnant. I try out my routine, including telling each of them I will kill myself. They tell me they can call the police; they tell me I must have the baby; they charge me one ten dollars and one fifteen; they lecture me on morality. I am late back to work both days.

Is there any point being me? After turning up the water heater I stand in the kitchen. Mother weeds the garden, kneeling among the tomato plants lined up in their shagginess against the south-facing wall of Dad's garage. Why wait to bear this child or die tomorrow in a blood-bath? For all my pride, I have been to the auction block and returned unsold. My love rots like old meat. If Mike can-

not finally love me, whoever will? Why persist in studying
out my agony? She got me quinine; we have the mustard.
Last remedies.

From the holder over the stove I take the sharpest knife
and unbutton my blouse. Black-ridged handle, long bright
blade. Can't cut my breasts. Slide between. My heart beats
there against my fingertips, against the point of metal. I
dare you. If you don't do it, it's because you're scared.
Mother has often called me coward. In the gang I would
take any dare to duck that label.

I prop my arms on the Formica counter. Forgotten anything? A note. Dearly beloved, I grew weary of it all. Bye-
bye, yours affectionately, Jill. Give Donna my bankbook.
Nuisance, Mother will find the body. To evaporate cleanly.
Melodrama. Last words, a literary influence. I must have
learned something from all this exercise. Now Mother
weeds the bean plants. The elm leaves glow. A sparrow
lights among the sweet pea vines on the fence. On the sill
before me three tomatoes and a peach are ripening. Sunlight blanches the fuzz over the blush of the skin, rounded
fruit, deeply grooved as flesh. My mouth waters.

I give a sudden lurch and the knife enters. Before I can
control my reaction, I pull the blade out, letting the blood
course down, dark, running. It hurts! I watch the blood
well out. Think, damn it. Life doesn't mean, only people
mean. I wanted so much. If only my mouth would stop
watering. I can smell that peach faintly. Have to swallow. I
should close my eyes and push the knife in to the hilt, but I
cannot make myself. All the peaches I will never eat. I
haven't ever tasted a fruit that wasn't good in its way,
pears, Bartlett and Anjou and russet, honeydew melon pale
pistachio green; no wonder paradise is a grove of fruit
trees. Dusty purple plums, grapes splitting with juice. I
haven't had any black or red raspberries this summer. With
cream.

In spite of all, sun and peaches, young beans from the
garden, I wipe the knife and put it back. If I die tomorrow,
I die. The blood from my chest wound is staining my jeans.
I mop it with a paper towel, which I then push against
me as compress. It is soaking through. As soon as the

bleeding stops, I will eat this peach. Now I will go to work attacking my body in earnest.

Thursday night. I am half dead and nausea is a constant state, my heart is beating erratically, and yet I am still pregnant. Upstairs in the hot and airless attic, I prepare to follow Mother's last instructions. Through the floorboards the hoofbeats and gunshots of a Western arise. "Don't cry out," my mother warned me. "Keep your mouth shut." Squatting in the ruins of my old sanctuary, by force I open my womb.

If it were even a couple of years ago I would tell you more, but if I do so now, desperate young girls, desperate middle-aged women, the victims of rape, incest, battering, far more numerous than we like to believe, all the women who simply do not believe in catching a baby as you might the flu or pneumonia, would be tempted to do as I did, just because I survived it but barely. There have to be better ways. I cannot include a recipe for action that is likely to kill you.

Friday I do not go to work because finally hard pain wakes me and my fingers on the pillow show wet and red. Now in my belly giant hands twist. Contractions. Wryly I realize what I did not understand: that I am going into labor. My ears ring, the room hangs speckled as I gape at it. Five minutes, five hours? I swell and split until I cannot lie on my back or my right side or my left side but writhe like a landed fish on the dock gasping for oxygen. The lowered shades and the blue-and-white curtains rise and fall, rise and fall languidly. The air lies like a warm damp towel on my sweating face. I knead my body trying to squeeze the pain out. Occasionally Mother comes in, speaks.

"What?" My ears buzz.

"How is it?"

"Bad."

She unwinds the sheets from my legs and tucks them in far away at the foot. Biting her lips she stands over me, then hurries away.

The pains deepen. Pain is bigger than I am; I drown in

it. The contractions sharpen and ease in regular quickening waves but under the crests continuing is a substantial mass of pain always deepening. When I cry out, Mother comes at once and glares at me, drawing back her hand as if she will slap me. I know I must be silent and so I am. I twist my hands, thrash in bed, writhe.

Twenty-odd years later pain makes me mute. Since that day I have never recovered my voice when pain touches me hard. When I burn my thigh, when I cut my hand deeply, when I drop the typewriter on my foot, my vocal cords seize up as they never do in anger or danger. I weep but cannot speak until the pain ebbs.

In my mouth, a bitter ragged taste. Black fungus on the tongue, the taste of dying. All the blood is rushing from me, I feel it flowing. Forever, pain wrings me and the blood bubbles out. "Mother!" Why doesn't she come? Has she run away? "Mother?"

She trots in. "Shhhh! Don't make noise."

"I was calling. Not noise. Help me up." I am being squashed. The press closes on me. Got to move. Leaning on her I drag into the bathroom. "Go away. Wait outside."

She backs from me hesitantly. Fear rises from her like the smell of sweat.

"Shut door!" Vomit hot and acid charges up my throat. Back uphill to bed, leaning. Blood runs down my legs, red footsteps across the throw rug. I sink into bed. Pain sings in my ears like a choir of giant and hungry mosquitoes. My hands knead my body as if they could pinch out sensation. I ring like a cracked bell, bong, bong, pulling my guts out with it, all, out and down and down. . .

I open my eyes as if tearing open a package. Cling to the light. If I go under I won't make it back. I touch the freshly formed scab between my breasts and laugh silently. Now when I am really boiling in death's muddy river, I swim, I thrash to stay alive. The histrionics with the knife have no more to do with it than our games in the vacant lots with dime-store guns had to do with war. The blue-and-white curtains wave good-bye with bored flops. How much blood boils out, bright, beautiful on the sheets, huge rose that blooms from me. Mother peers down, hands plucking at her apron, lips moving. "You're so pale, chickie, your lips are white. What to do. . . . Oh God, dear God, don't let her die. She's punished enough now. Listen to me!"

Punished. I want to laugh. We are always in different stories.

"Push, Jill!" She squeezes my arm. "Push it out of you. Bear down. You have to push it out!"

I hear myself moan far away. Her hand covers my mouth and nose. I stop making the sound and she lets me breathe. She paces biting her thumb, tugging at her hair. Through the whine of pain I cannot hear, but her lips mutter ceaselessly. Sweat hisses through my pores. Blood scalds my thighs. I thrash. My belly ripples spasmodically. The bed buckles, kicks under me. Must go. Something is forcing me. I heave over the side and crumple. "Bathroom. Must."

She pulls me up screaming, "Stand up! I can't carry you!" The mirror dandles me dead white, a grey face. My vision burns out speckled. The room swings into black. "Jill, don't fall. I can't hold you!"

I hang my head till the light seeps back. Must sit, must. Stumbling I trip on rubbery tissue, dark and clotted. Long hell corridor swinging, closing like a press. Must.

The bathroom floor is cold against me as I squat. A nail drives in blow after blow. Push on it. Must.

Slowly the room slides back. The contractions ebb, rise serrated, ebb. Gradually my body quiets like a pond long after a rock. I pull myself up.

"Did you pass it, Jill?"

"Yes." Back to bed. "Blood's pouring out."

"Raise your legs."

"Can't."

She props a mound of rags under me.

"I'm cold.

"It's hot in here." She fans herself.

The air across the sill freezes me. "I'm cold."

She shuts the window. "Is that better?"

My teeth are chattering. "I'm cold."

"I don't want to spoil the blanket. Everything's soaked." She hovers, then sighs and pulls it up.

The curtains hang limp and straight. Done, all done. The amber light spreads over my eyes, lukewarm and smooth and syrupy. I sink and settle, I unfold. My ears still ring but pain has let me drop from its claws. I lie where I have fallen not quite sure I am alive but glad anyhow. Beautiful the light red through heavy lids. Let me float down to the bottom, all the way down. . . .

When I wake, Mother sits at the sewing machine darning socks, watching. "How do you feel?"

I touch myself gingerly. "I'm still bleeding but it's not running out."

"Do you feel okay otherwise?"

"A shadow. Breathing is hard."

"Let me bring you lunch."

"I don't want it."

"You've got to take something. Milk, maybe?" She smooths the sheet.

"I can't."

"Do you want to see him?"

"Yes, but don't tell him I did it. Say I miscarried."

"You're sure you want to see him?"

"Yes." Then as she rises I add, "I'm filthy. The bed, me. I'm stuck to the sheets."

I cannot lift myself but with the sponge we clean me. I can roll to one side if she pushes. Then rest. The clean sheets feel cool as peony petals. I drowse and wake. Water runs in the tub. Mother scrubs furiously at the floor I float detached, an escaped balloon borne on gentle high currents. Occasionally a small pain spreads in light ripples and then quiets. Euphoria.

Mike stands awkwardly, one hand on the jamb. He crosses as if walking on ice and leans over me. His lips move.

"You have to speak loud."

"What is it, Jill? What happened to you?"

"It's all over."

"She said you miscarried."

I nod.

"That's impossible. You can't have been pregnant."

"I was."

"Have you seen a doctor?"

"They said I was pregnant."

"I mean today."

"No. Don't want any now. Not any longer."

"I'm taking care of her," Mother says from the door.

"You're not trained. I'll call a doctor."

I strain to hear them. "Don't let him, Mother."

"Do you want to bring more shame on her?" Mother hugs herself. "No! I won't have it."

The bed dips under his weight. "Pumpkin." He strokes the hair back from my face. "If she opens a can of soup, will you let me feed you?"

Dozing, I know when he returns because his arm goes around me. Every time I open my mouth, soup fills it. A thick creamy taste vaguely of chicken comes into being. The soup forms a hot lake in my midriff, anchoring me so that I stop floating and once more lie in bed.

Through the wall comes rhythmic sloshing from the tub where Mother is trying to wash the sheets, the throw rug, the towels, the rags, so that the blood will not set as stains before she puts them in the wringer-type machine downstairs. A streak of sun from the edge of the shade lights on his ruffled hair. He looks so young, I wonder I never noticed it before. How could he help being weak, poor boy trying to become his father. He craves authority, rules, patriarchs to tell him how to cope. Only I cannot trust him anymore.

"Hello there, pumpkin. Feeling better?"

"Uh-huh. Get me a brush."

"Lie still like a good kitten and I'll do it." He brushes my hair gingerly and pins it up in an amateur lump. "There. How's that? You gave me a scare when I came in. But you're better, aren't you?"

I nod.

"How did your arms get so thin? You have to eat more."

"It's over now." And I won. I won my life back. My body, my self. I did it.

Gently he slips his hand through the throat of my pajamas, over my shoulders and breasts. "Take better care. Don't let that woman drive you to the wall."

"She helped me as much as she could let herself."

Weightlessly his hand moves over my breasts. As I look at him bent close, the brown eyes grave and luminous, the strong arches of his cheeks, a slow bolt of desire pierces me. It hurts. If I were not weak, I would take him in my arms. Hard to believe he has been mine, the long bones of his arm, the nutmeg hairs of his body and the mahogany hair of his head. I am glad to have seen him once more like this, suffused with the love I gave readily, readily.

At four, half an hour later, Mother sends him home and I sleep. But at five she bends over me. "Jill, get dressed. It's time for your father."

"I can't move. Let me sleep."

"Get up!" She shakes my arm. "You can't be lying there when he comes. He'll want to know what's wrong."

"Say I'm sick."

"Sick with what?"

"The flu. A stomach virus."

"Nonsense. He'll get suspicious and kill us both. Get up."

"I can't!" I jerk from her. "Leave me alone."

When Father comes home, I sit propped in a chair in the living room dressed in too big skirt and too loose blouse with a magazine hanging open in my lap, still slowly bleeding.

Brooklyn, 1963. The doctor botched the abortion and she is hemorrhaging. I am one of a group of women who help other women secure abortions. Sometime I'll explain the name we use, collectively. Now this woman, fat, gentle, in her late thirties and the mother of five, is bleeding like a slaughtered pig—like I did. I pack her vagina with ice. I hold her against me, a woman twice my size and twice my body weight, and rock her like a baby. She feels cold as my hands, as the ice I have stuffed into improvised bags of Turkish towels between her thighs. Live, live, I whisper to her, dear one, sweetheart, angel darling, live. Only live.

*Through the whole night we are together until dawn finds
her still alive and the bleeding under control. In the morning we return her to out-of-work husband and clamoring
children.*

*Chicago, 1969. I am meeting with an outlaw abortion
group, women who perform safe and cheap abortions for
other women. The best doctor we had, in Pennsylvania,
has been busted and faces prison. We are in trouble, but
trouble is our whole reason for being. In my files are
names and prices and directions for contacting abortionists
in eighteen states. I even have information on Mexico and
Guatemala. You never know when some woman may desperately need it.*

*New York, 1970. We are marching, tens of thousands of
us, through the streets of New York shouting for legal
abortion for all of us. Half the march I spend with older
women. I am sure every one of us has had an illegal
abortion or aborted ourselves. We are criminals. Then part
of the time I march with the highschool women. They
make up slogans and shout a lot. We are many and angry
and beautiful as we run along. At the square there are too
many speeches and we all get cold and my nose runs, but
no one can stop us any longer. We will be free. Women
will not pay in blood for love. Children will not be born
unchosen, unwanted, unloved.*

The following Saturday Mother calls a meeting. While
my father stares at his joined hands, she reads out an oath
for a year's chastity, which she has me type in triplicate
just like the invoices at Short Brothers I am back typing
five days a week.

Shaking his head, Mike reads it over. "What do you say?
Are you going to sign this thing, Jill?"

What a Biblical ring the oath has. "If I do not keep this
Oath, may my right hand wither and my strength rot, may
I never bear or beget living children and may my brain
decay. . . ." It's easy to tell Mother wrote it. I meet his
gaze. I say all three of you are acting in private plays. A
great indifference grinds my thoughts to dust. Love is a

word like the words on this paper, while I have learned no words bind beyond the noon of their saying. I also know that under my anemic indifference beats a will to live my own life strong enough to carry me through them and away. I will escape you all. I will choose what I do.

"Sure. Why not?"

Under the sickly light of the fluorescent fixture on the kitchen ceiling, with formality and silence we sign the oath. I write my name large, wanting to giggle. Three times. I get a copy, Mike gets a copy, they keep the original. One copy for both of them, they being one legal married body. Afterward Mother serves iced lemonade.

NINETEEN

Hardscrabble Year

I ARRIVE IN THE white room with tomato-soup curtains as graceful, as vigorous as a run-over cat. In Donna's appalled stare I read my ghastliness. I weigh ninety-two pounds dressed. My skin is bluish grey. I suffer from anemia, colitis, eczema, toothache and insomnia. The first week I find two jobs. Financial independence is my deity; I will achieve it at any cost except my studies. This is the year that everything I touch turns into A's, for I am only happy when utterly distant from my emotions. Four nights a week I work the dormitory switchboard plugging couples into each other. All day Saturday I take part in a psychology department experiment on ESP; I am fascinating to them because I regularly display negative correlation. When another subject sits in the next room trying to send me images on the special cards (circles, triangles, squares), I get them all wrong, whereas almost everybody gets at least a quarter of them right by chance. I block the images. I do not bother to explain about my mother. I let myself be studied and collect my dollar and a quarter an hour.

I go out with men who ask me, and many do. For the first time in my life I am naturally cold. I have not recovered an interest in sex, which seems to me a device for converting will and energy into passivity and flesh. Dating abrades the nerves but kills time, not quite as well as drinking which I do with Theo other evenings after the switchboard. In Theo I find a vast tolerance at once warm and cold: cold because nothing grows in that waste, and warm because she means me well. Compulsively at a certain level of drunkenness I tell her my summer again and again. Do I imagine I will wear it out? At a further degree of alcohol in the brain I escape into pure energy and final numbness.

At my desk I am finishing a paper on *Twelfth Night*, my favorite Shakespeare comedy with its mutable sex roles. November, but the day shimmers like painted cellophane under a glazed blue sky. After a week of icy rain the air is almost warm and I have the casements open. Now I watch Donna and Lennie trot briskly across the court, red beard and leather jacket, sleek blond cap of hair and blue wool coat. As they dance about each other gesturing, Lennie stomps in a puddle. I laugh and lean out to call to them under the lee of the building. Their sharp voices rise and I shut up.

"I am not your mother! If you want to wear dirty shirts, stink up the world. I won't be made to feel bitchy about it, I won't!" Donna's voice cuts high and thin. "Do I ask you to do my laundry?"

"It was you who lost the laundry slip and now you blame me. If you yell at me again in front of my roommates . . ." Lennie trails off, sulking. "That's castrating."

"It wasn't *my* laundry slip. It was *yours*. And we're never alone!"

"Can I afford to move out? Will you live with me if I do?"

I am bent over my paper as Donna bursts in. She flings her coat on the floor and herself on my bunk. "I just had a fight with Lennie again. He's always trying to make me feel guilty! If he catches a cold, he makes me feel I've done it to him."

"Be careful. A little patience with each other . . ."

"We keep fighting about you and Mike. As if Mike had a side. Men are so blind. Mike tells him how you got him in trouble with his family, trying to force him to marry you, and then dumping him. That's how he tells it all over town."

"Julie keeps me posted," I say dryly, looking out the window. "Lennie's still waiting in the courtyard."

"He is?" She gets up to look, beside me. "Idiot!" But she grins as she pokes into the sleeves of her coat. "Stubborn as a rock!"

The long grey winter settles in like a wolf feeding on a carcass. Julie talks about diaphragms. She is still not having sex with Van but they have progressed to fumbled petting. She believes in looking ahead, especially since, as she says, my case illustrates what happens when you depend on the man to take care. Van progresses no further as the months lengthen like icicles and drop of their own weight, but Donna and I discuss diaphragms frequently. Finally I make an appointment, although I have no immediate need.

It is Christmas vacation and I make the appointment for the afternoon between my split shifts at the telephone company on December 24. I give my real name and say I am going to be married.

"Where's your engagement ring?" The gynecologist asks. He is fifty and frowns at me.

"We don't want to waste money on that. We're both students."

He gives me a tight-lipped smile. "When you're married, you come back with a ring and a license, and I'll fit you. We don't fit unmarried women."

He charges me fifteen dollars and I go home with a stomachache. I will not be that stupid again. I consult Donna. We go to the dime store together the second half of Christmas vacation, while she's visiting her sister and brother-in-law. We pick out gold-colored bands. We pick out glass engagement rings. We make appointments back to back for the thirtieth of December. I am "Mrs. Mary

Moore" from Yeats's poem and my husband is Henry.
Donna is Mrs. Leonard Rose: Lennie's bride for a day. We
leave with our prescriptions and fill them together. I adore
my diaphragm, neat with its pellucid dome in its compact.
I cherish it in my jewelry box as I will in a few years
cherish my first passport, as something magical that permits passage out.

My mother has bribed me to have my hair cut, paying
for a real stylist down on Washington Boulevard, the most
nearly fashionable downtown address. With the malls just
beginning to erode downtown Detroit, Washington Boulevard is still an area where Mother goes nervously muttering, at the last minute trying to talk me into doing it at one
of the department stores, Hudson's, Crowley's. Why am I
willing? To destroy the last vestiges of the woman Mike
had? Perhaps. No one wears her hair long except Alberta
Mann and a few folksingers. I will try this accommodation,
while refusing most others.

The stylist is impressed by my hair, although he chops it
off willingly. He asks if I want it. I say yes and then forget
and he chases me half a block carrying it in a paper bag.
Mother and I sell it to a wigmaker. They say if it were not
black it would be worth more.

Slipping the nail file back in its leather case, Julie joins
her arms around her knees drawn up in tailored slacks.
"Last night in the Union, Mike sat down with Van and me.
He'd been drinking gin and he looked ghastly."

"Would he look better if he'd been drinking imported
Scotch? Why say it like that? I can't stop his drinking."

"Do you want to?"

"What has it to do with me? I haven't talked to him in
weeks."

"He says it has everything to do with you."

To sit back I move a white plush dog with bells on
nose and tail. Her room is paralyzingly neat, one Mondrian
and one Klee reproduction matted on the wall, blue scarf
on her dresser with cosmetics edge to edge, a row of pots
and candleholders from gift shops equidistant along the

window ledge and top of her bookcase. "Do you believe
that, kid? That I'm working voodoo on him, like that shit
he told Lennie?"

"The excess is part of the young Rimbaud pose anyhow," she says, adding to my blank look, "you should have
read Rimbaud last year to know what he's up to. I know
you don't read French well, but you could have found a
decent translation." Faint air of letting me in on a secret.
"He is brilliant, you know. I have an IQ of a hundred and
sixty and I can't follow him at times."

"That's because a lot of the time he doesn't make sense."

"You can't imagine what my high school was like. They
wanted us adjusted, one jolly community of interests and
green-clipped lawns. They acted as if I'd scored high to
upset them. It was much too high—for a girl."

"My mother has a mistrust of intellect too. She suspects
that brains are inherently subversive and dangerous and
they get you dead. But you're away from home, Julie.
Really away."

"Oh? Am I? I'll go back. A commuting husband and
three point five maladjusted children with braces on their
teeth going to child therapists and riding school."

"If you don't want it, don't buy back in. Join the circus.
Join the WACS. Join the Communist party. Join a nun-
nery." She makes me feel as if I'm sinking in down. I get
up, pace to the window and back. "Visit scenic Antarctica.
Work on a goat farm. Go on the streets." I hear myself
bellowing and fling myself down to ask mildly, "So how's
old Van anyhow? Have you had his sour cherry yet?"

Quickly she moves the plush dog out of the path of my
descending rear. "Never. I'm hoping his blood will thaw
with the spring, if it ever, ever comes. I swear, Mike makes
me think Van isn't alive sometimes. . . . But at least Van's
trustworthy. He'd never talk about me. I'm too bourgeois
to stand to have someone boasting about me the way Mike
did about you."

"What are you talking about?"

Her plucked brows rise. "Van told me when Mike used
to come back from the Arb last year, he'd come into the

room where his friends were playing bridge and he'd make a sign—"

My body grows hot. "What kind of sign?"

"For the number of times, he'd hold up so many fingers."

A hot coal burns in my chest. I could kill him. Those men laughed at me while I waltzed around on his arm like Juliet. "He treated me like a whore."

As I am returning to my room to find Donna, it occurs to me Julie will of course repeat that to Mike. "Jill says you treated her like a whore." Why do I come to suffer under her cold curious gaze? Yet I will return obsessed to hear what she knows of the backside of my great love.

My first civil rights action is meek. Eighteen of us gather in the blowing sleet to picket a local restaurant. Donna, Lennie and I march arm in arm. Donaldson is involved, which prompts Donna to try to awake my old crush on him, but I love her and no one else. My love for Donna is a small furry muff my buhbe gave me when I was five, ragged but still eloquent of another time and country, wherein my hands sought, to find only each other, but nonetheless were warmer.

In 1955 we are only cautiously radicals "of sorts," a professor in the zoology department having been fired after the last House Un-American Activities Committee incursion into Michigan for being "an avowed Marxist." I go regularly to a study group where we look earnestly into each other's eyes. Even to discuss civil rights or social change feels dangerous. The FBI may burst in the door; one of us may be an agent. A student in the Labor Youth League (membership of four) found out his girlfriend had been scared by the FBI into providing lists of everyone who attended his frequent parties. All of us know stories of teachers who lost their jobs because they once signed a petition for the starving children of Ethiopia or the bombed villages of Spain, thus revealing themselves Premature Anti-Fascists. The FBI agents visit the morgue of the school newspaper to read old editorials in case whoever they are investigating once wrote something critical of The

American Way of Life. Ideas feel incredibly potent in this thick atmosphere. Passing along a copy of Gunnar Myrdal's *An American Dilemma* or J. P. Thompson's *History of the English Working Class* feels like a brave political act.

We are PAF: the Political Alternatives Forum. Even that bland label has to most ears a harshly subversive sound and I cannot pull Donna or Lennie in with me. Lennie doesn't trust me—I am the evil bitch who wounded his poet. Donna claims to find the discussion dull, though she comes with me occasionally. "All those men and only two women!" Alberta Mann is the other woman, Donaldson's girlfriend. Donaldson is our faculty sponsor, so we can be a recognized student group to stage our little protests, show an occasional film (*Battleship Potemkin, The Grapes of Wrath, Open City*), bring in a progressive folksinger, that is when we can get approval. We have to pass through two deans and a vice-president to sponsor Pete Seeger. We also hold forums on H-bomb testing, abolition of dormitory hours for women, the U.S. Marine invasion of Guatemala. At those timid meetings I live for a few moments in a world larger than that bounded by dormitory and classroom.

My birthday. I no longer have time for the hours and hours of slow work at dental school, so I am going to an outside dentist. My birthday present from my parents is their paying my March dental bill. My only real presents are Pablo Casals playing two Bach partitas for unaccompanied cello from Theo and from Donna a black-and-umber cotton circle skirt. My parents don't call. The day passes rather grimly with a midterm in Shakespeare. Donna comes home at four and carries me off into the desultory snow.

"It ought to be spring, it's spring by the calendar. We'll make it be spring," she announces. Coffee laced with brandy in a thermos, a blanket snuck out from her bunk, a little wheel of Camembert and part of a roast chicken: we dine in the snow of Island Park tucked in a bend of the

Huron River. "Happy birthday, sweetie," she tells me. "It's got to get better from now on. Right? Right."

In the snow littering down in big unhurried discs we find two swings twisted up for the winter but not taken off, and unwind their chains. Side by side we swing far back, far up and out.

"Donna, Donna, this is wonderful. It's flying. I want to fly." Again. Swinging high, high in an arc. I remember it from childhood. I always loved it. It's sensual, the most arousing thing I have done in months. The blood pounds in me. The combination of caffeine and alcohol makes me energetically drunken so that I feel I could release the swing and sail out over the river, whose ice has broken but not melted.

We lie on the blanket afterward finishing the coffee with brandy, the chicken. "What happened to me, I survived it, didn't I? So I'm not really weak, I'm not a coward, I'm not worthless."

"You survived, Stu. I didn't feel too sure at first, but I'm sure now. You're all here again. Whoever said you were weak? Even since we were kids, you've been one tough customer."

"Aw, Donna, you're just easy to fool." I know she cannot afford this celebration, that it is purchased by giving up something else, and I am doubly grateful. She gave me my birthday.

During spring vacation Donna goes to New York with Lennie. When I get back from Detroit, her luggage waits in the room, but not Donna. Squeals, giggles, romping in the hall. Dormitory life lacks dignity, I think. There has to be an alternative. I resolve to investigate. Close to curfew, Donna runs in. "You're finally back!" Dropping her purse she hugs me, her sharp chin against my cheek.

"How was New York?"

"Oh." She hangs up her coat, giving it a careful brushing. "We have to live there, Stu. It's the most real city." Her voice sounds forced. Her skin is blue with fatigue under the eyes.

"Is anything wrong? Were his parents mean to you?"

She winces. "They were so sweet I was embarrassed. Let's get a soda downstairs. I'm dying of thirst."

In the corridor the house athletic chairman Dulcie is heaving her suitcase out for a janitor. She gives us a grin half antagonistic, half patronizing. "Well, well, the James sisters. What trouble are you up to?"

"Now, podner, we don't look for trouble, it looks for us. And when it finds us, even trouble runs."

Donna jabs irritably at the elevator button. "Why do you answer them? She does think we're sisters, by the way."

Seep of pleasure. In the mirror opposite the elevator we are framed. "Like negative and photo—me dark and you light."

"Outside." She strikes the down button with her fist. "I got away from Lennie to wander through stores along Fifth Avenue. Lord and Taylor's. Bonwit's." We ride down. "Money must take the hard edges off living. Beauty in the most casual objects. Small pleasures greasing the way to big ones."

"We're not likely to find out." I don't want Donna traveling through expensive stores in a daydream I cannot share. "Start craving those things and you're hooked."

"Start?" She laughs, a parched cough. We pass the row of dark dining rooms to the cubicle where the machines glow. As she uncaps her soda and tilts the bottle, lines of strain stand out.

"Donna, what happened in New York?"

"Nothing." She walks rapidly back. "Nothing that happens to me has any importance, because I'm a piece of shit!"

"Did you have a fight with Lennie?"

Her mouth curls as if she will laugh but instead she bursts into sobbing, grinding her palms into her eyes. I take the soda and steer her into the dark dining room, past the tables to the ledge that runs below the tall windows. "Shhh, Donna, please." I stroke her, soothe her. "Don't cry. . . .

What is it, tell me? What happened?" Droning on I persist, until exhausted she leans her cheek on the pane letting the breath from her parted lips steam across the glass.

"Why couldn't he let me love him my own way? Why does he have to try to make me into his mother? All the time his eyes on me pleading. I'm not like his mother, I'm not a self-sacrificing lap!"

"Why should you be? But you'll make up."

"I made sure that can't happen. Stu, he's all the time trying to pull the reactions he wants from me. I had to fight not to be deliberately Midwestern. And in museums!" Her voice climbs in a tight spiral. "Sometimes I think he has no taste but what's a defense for his own work. But I can't tell—he's ruined it for me. I can't stand paintings any longer. Something in me shuts off."

"What did you fight about? His work?"

"Tonight I told him I was sick to death of him." Her voice breaks. Her hands claw at her arms. "I told him about Matt. Oh, say I lied. So what? Sometimes you hound me worse than he does."

I guess I knew, for I feel nothing. "He reacted badly?"

"He said, but *why*? I said, because I wanted to. Because I was tired of waiting for him to find a bed. Because Matt had a good build." She laughs like glass breaking. "Besides it was a foot long. I wasn't so much excited as curious."

"Was he good?"

"Too fast. But it was an experience, like being charged by a buffalo herd. I don't think I like big pricks, but how was I to know beforehand?" She rubs her eyes roughly. "I don't *know* why I did it. I don't know! I make up reasons. I do things like I'm falling downhill, and then I make up reasons. Lennie said he'd ignored my past because I was lonely and everybody needs love. He did ignore it—why wasn't that enough for me? I must be a complete bitch."

Actually he didn't ignore it, but this is no time to pass on that painful hearsay. Outside a fine rain is visible only around each lamppost. I drum my fingers on the window pole beside us on the ledge. If the weather ever warms, it's used to open the upper tier of windows over the big plate-glass picture windows. "Because instant acceptance is un-real. Because we're arrogant enough to feel what we've done we have to digest and understand to grow—"

"You make it clean." She shakes her head, her hair whipping. "I hurt him. We? Why not say I'm sick." She rakes her hands hard into her scalp. "I disgust myself."

"Easy, Donna. When you stop loving, what can you do but get out? That's what you told me about Mike."

She glares. "Lennie says it's your fault."

"Me? But why?"

"He says you're possessive and dependent, since you don't have a man."

"Oh? How would he know what I depend on?" I hunch forward.

"And Mike told him that old stuff about those girls."

Including you, which neither of them knows. We are silent a few moments while she kicks her foot punishingly against the wall, thud, thud, jarring me. "I'll just keep doing this, won't I, fucking things up till I'm too fat and washed out to fool a man into thinking he wants me." The tears start again. "Everything that's nice, I spoil. I make everything dirty! It's me that's wrong, just me!"

"Donna, it takes two to fight. Don't torment yourself." I have a feeling that she is working herself into a frenzy of self-punishment.

She slides off the ledge. "You're in bed with someone and suddenly you wonder why you're there going through the gestures. That terrible blankness. Then I get crazy, I get dirty and mean."

"I know that blankness." I try to touch her shoulder.

She shakes free. "You don't know this rage. You don't know how sick I am. I want to break up everything—"

"Come, calm down, Donna. Come on. . . ." I sound exaggeratedly flat. I try to establish eye contact. I try to take her hand.

"I'd like to smash that window! That big expensive window on this goddamned stupid warehouse-dormitory!"

I try to grasp her arm and pull her along. "Let's go upstairs. My mother made a cake."

She thrusts me away. "So sure I won't?" She grabs the window pole.

"Come on, Donna." I turn toward the door. "Stop it. Let's go upstairs and talk there."

She raises the pole. I lurch back to stop her, but she is swinging it wildly by the end with the hook, the metal hilt whirring through the air. I duck just in time, throwing myself flat. With a sharp report like a pistol shot the hilt strikes the glass, opening a crack that travels from the impact point to the top. Then she lets the pole drop, staring at the streamered star where the hilt struck, the long crack. She looks dazed.

I rise cautiously, brushing myself. "Oy, gevalt. What for?"

"But . . . you didn't believe I'd do it." Small wondering voice.

Hearing someone in the hall, I scuttle among the tables to ease the door shut. Then I cross to the pole, picking it from the glass splinters to wipe on my jeans. No fingerprints.

"Must you play detective?" She runs to the door, eager to escape.

"We better take the steps up. Don't forget your soda." We listen till the hall is safe, then climb to our room.

"I'm beat," she says firmly. "Soon as I shower, I'm getting into bed."

"I'll study downstairs, but I'll shower first." I take my robe and towel. "What did I do with my soap?"

"You were supposed to get some in Detroit."

"I forgot. Can I use yours tonight?"

"You always leave it in the puddle so it gets gooey. I like my soap firm."

"I'll be careful." Her scolding assures me that she is done smashing things and that our life resumes.

"All right, but don't forget to buy soap tomorrow. You can't expect me to remember everything for you. Your red dress still needs cleaning."

With robe and towels slung over our shoulders, I follow her down the hall carrying the plastic soap dish like a chalice before me.

* * *

We were staying one town along the Sogne Fjord from
Flåm after taking the narrow-gauge toylike train down
from the swirling snow of the pass in and through the
mountains in corkscrew tunnels past hundreds of waterfalls
to sea level, a thin strand where there wasn't any land at all
between mountain and deep water. The lodge had only a
few couples staying; we were the only Americans. Those
days were the last mild weather of the year before the
arctic cold moved over it all. A short distance inland and a
short distance uphill winter had swept down. Here all the
windows were open on the fjord and, on the landward side
of the pension, to the apple orchard whose leaves were
changing color, duller than the apples that hung there and
littered the ground.

The couple in the room just below us, whose porch lay
right under our window, were French. Josh, who does not
speak French (his Norwegian after two weeks was con-
fined to where are the toilets, please, and thank you),
could not understand why I had begun to glare at him. In
fact we had fought, wept, reconciled and made love and
were outside with our feet hanging off a rock staring at a
ship putting out from the small dock in Flåm while the
spray from a cascade drifted over us, when I grasped it.
The tone of their arguments got me, that couple below.

They were intellectuals, some shade of left. He was engaged in a vast continuous proof of his superiority to her
for which every event of the day, every object encountered,
every newspaper discussed, formed the matter. He was
busy crushing her and she was busy striving to avoid his
anger. She read him all day like a weather map and moved
accordingly, retreating off the edge into weak smiles and
silence.

That tourist was much better at torture than Mike had
been, I realized. He didn't have to raise his voice to lash
her with anger. If you asked, they would say they were in
love. He preferred victory over her to whatever other battle
he might have engaged in, with state or party. Josh and I
sat up talking and reading timetables and drinking the cognac we carried in our suitcase. Josh pointed out I am not

married (no longer married) to the man downstairs and then he hiked to Flåm to buy tickets on the steamer at 6 A.M. In the morning we were both cranky and snarled as we dragged our suitcase and L. L. Bean shoulder bag all the way to Flåm and the ferry slip.

Once we were out on the water in the pearly fog of dawn, I kissed his hands. I had escaped Mike again. I had escaped from that marriage again. We were voyaging together, our fourth year in the fall, and I could love without confusing it with having a tooth drilled without novocaine. Josh scolded me for confounding past and present as we ate our apples and cheese, shivering on the deck. We had to go back to Oslo soon anyhow, where my Norwegian publishers were expecting us.

That night in the Hotel Terminus in Bergen I woke in the darkness hearing that man's cold voice relentlessly proving her wrong, but it was only the rain, the cold steady rain of Bergen. I wanted to wake Josh and tell him I did not confound the past with the present but the past was the compost that fed the present and the worm that curled inside eating away its sweet wholeness. The past confounded me only when I believed it was passed and dismissed it. I love this man so hard it scared me, resurrecting old fears to walk through me again wearing faces and clothes I had forgotten I ever possessed. I am a person to whom sex comes easily and pleasantly and love hard; friendship is common and important, intellectual and political passion my daily bread, but sexual passion conjoined with love rare. Now I was with my friend who is my lover and I went back to sleep again.

TWENTY

In Which Both Jill and Donna
Try a Change of Altitude

BY SPRING I have figured out that Donna and I should
move into one of the cooperative houses owned and run
by students, a federation that attracts those of us who need
cheap accommodation, foreign students looking for company and those attracted by the progressive aura. The one
that has room for us needs a great deal of work over the
summer, but by September—the beginning of our junior
year—we can move in.

Our housemother is Alberta Mann, at twenty-six considered mature enough to get a stipend from the university
for living here and exercising supposed discipline. Alberta
comes from New York, where her father is a lawyer whom
HUAC has pestered, although that does not seem to have
destroyed his practice, mostly in labor and civil rights
cases. When he is working on a case that excites him, he
still calls to give her bulletins, but carefully, always assuming as Alberta does that the phone is tapped. Alberta fell in
love with a Black law student she met at a National Student Association conference when she was nineteen. Their

marriage was annulled but Alberta did not return to school for another year. At that time she felt her father was a hypocrite to oppose her marriage, but she no longer thinks so; it was a disaster. The next year she met Donaldson. Now Alberta is in the last year of law school, having a hard time but persisting doggedly. Since her long affair with Donaldson seems to have come to a ragged ending, she has taken an interest in no other man. Their political work throws them together too much for her to have the opportunity to recover.

My only defeat was in failing to persuade Theo to move with us; I still don't understand why. I don't mind crossing campus to her, but inevitably I see less of her in the late evenings, which have been our intimate time. I didn't expect Julie to move into these frowsy accommodations, but I did think Theo would. She claims to be too lazy. I drink now with Alberta, who is fond of bourbon. I think of the bourbon I buy as Old Overcoat, the cheapest brand that tastes as though it were cooked up last night out of caramelized straw. Alberta buys Wild Turkey and shares it with me. Her husband of three months taught her to drink bourbon, she says; her family drinks Scotch and martinis. Alberta has the single room next to the white corner double that Donna and I share. Alberta's room is sumptuous, heavy fabrics, interesting textures of burlap curtains, velvet spread, corduroy-cushioned Danish chair, tones of mustard and gold and dark woodsy brown. Donna seldom drinks. She is high and giggly or melancholy after two shots; she disapproves of my drinking and tells me I stink when I come in to go to bed.

Now Donna stands in front of the full-length mirror she found in a secondhand store, putting her hands on her hips and turning to watch the line of the tight skirt over her small pert ass. "See, I can get into it finally." *It* is a black sheath dress she bought at a rummage sale, narrow enough to fit tightly on a barber pole.

"Yeah, after starving yourself for two weeks."

She rests her hands on her hipbones. "Americans eat too much." Usually no matter how wonderfully luminous her

skin, Donna greets the mirror as if it were the eye of an
enemy. But today she allows herself a pursed smile of
pleasure. Even with her skinniness the dress is so tight it
requires a girdle and hobbles her so that she must take
tiny, tiny steps like a windup Chinese doll. The effect,
however, is what I'd call sophisticated and that's what she's
aiming for.

"What kind of party is it?"

"Sal's just having some friends from the department and
a few grad students to meet Edmund Rosco while he's in
town." Her voice still cannot quite say "Sal" naturally. It
sticks out of the sentence like a flashbulb going off as her
voice rises a little in controlled anxiety.

I don't ask if she wants me to come; I know better.
Salvatore Spinellosa is her private adventure, a foreign cor-
respondent usually attached to the *Washington Post,* here
for a term as distinguished visiting lion. He teaches one
seminar and gives a few lectures while he writes a book on
the Middle East. He is in his forties with hair as black as
mine, silvered over his ears. Six feet tall, he carries his
potbelly well. He has gradually covered Donna's dresser
with French perfume I dip into when I dare. I know she is
going to buy a safe and lock it away from me eventually,
but I cannot resist. I like to smell my body with the musk
of perfume rising.

Donna is wearing a bra based on the design of a medieval iron maiden, pushing her up and out into the décolleté. Now grinning at me in the mirror, she hangs her little
gold cross around her neck.

"Holy shit," I mutter. "Didn't know you still had that."

"It's real gold," she says defensively but she is eyeing
herself with wicked satisfaction. "It gives him an extra
frisson."

"I suppose he needs all the help he can get." I do not
believe Donna is in love with Big Sal, although she
staunchly insists that she is, and I am furious with him
for being the occasion of her lying to me.

"He's a man of many talents," Donna says. "Some of
them above the waist and some of them below."

"Oh. You mean he digests well." I hate her forcing her body into the confines of the dress. I hate her hobbling across the floor on four-inch spike heels to dip carefully, holding her breath, to retrieve the velvet envelope of evening purse he gave her.

"Maybe you've forgotten what else men can do." She hobbles out while I am still trying to think of a retort.

Because his father is dying of cancer of the stomach, Howie has transferred from Columbia to Michigan. He has bought himself an old grey Plymouth he manages to keep running; weekends he commutes into Detroit to visit his father in the hospital and to do what he can for his mother and grandmother. Often I have coffee in the Union with him, Dick Weisbuch and Bolognese, who share with me a writing class and a course in the metaphysical poets and share with Howie and me membership in the PAF.

Has Howie changed? I study him as he sits with his elbows thumped on the table before him. Built like a fort, Donna said caressingly, but awfully young. He has matured over the past two years, jaw, neck and wide shoulders carved from the earlier fat. Sometimes he moves with confidence; sometimes he shambles like a bear in captivity. He is dogmatic and shy at once, hiding his constant worrying over his father as if embarrassed by his own grief. Monday, after a weekend of sitting by his father's hospital bed and of soothing his mother and grandmother and cleaning out the gutters on the house and putting up storm windows, he drags back to school exhausted. The two halves of his life do not mesh.

He likes to ride Bolognese, who lives alone in a rooming house on Packard, goes to bed at eight and rises at four to write cold electric fables. Lean, olive-skinned and neat, Bolognese views the world with icy mistrust.

"Listen, you cold bastard," Howie says genially, "you're locking yourself in a closet like Emily Dickinson. I see a great spinsterhood ahead."

"Good work comes from inside," Bolognese drawls. "With great effort."

"Sure. Like a starving man trying to shit."

Bolognese sits with fingers hooked over the table edge. The closest he comes to registering warmth is during their battles. "I see. The great doctor is going to close his office at five, kiss his fingers to his dying patients and go night-clubbing. A time for work and a time for play, or how to be piss-poor mediocre all the time."

"When I have fifty grandchildren singing me happy birthday, you'll be dead from overwork and they'll put a pretty marble stone over you for the pigeons to shit on."

"The two of you can do my research." Bolognese includes Howie and me in a wry glance. "You're both so good at getting what you want. And Dick can eat for me."

"Now you're both right." Dick is a mediator who thinks if we all married and ate good home-cooked meals, we'd be as plump and cozy as he is. Dick has a baby, financial troubles and the surest future: he will finish his Ph.D. and write "on the side" while teaching. I think his optimism greater than mine. I enjoy sitting with them and joining in their rivalries, particularly pleased to be here not through the patronage of any of them, nobody's girl, but by proved competence. Occasionally Donna comes along as she will to PAF meetings, but the boys flirt with her, competing awkwardly, while the tone of insult puts her off. She calls Bolognese the Undertaker's Assistant, and I laugh. But I respect him. He is serious about writing. Like me, he has no nets under him, no family with money. He works hard, he reads whatever I show him and says straight out what he likes and dislikes.

Peter across the table: clean-limbed English schoolboy. Clipped blond hair, black-rimmed glasses strident on the young mask of clearskinned slightly fragile face. Hard to believe he has six years on me or that he is a graduate student in particle physics, working here with Glaser who invented the bubble chamber. He slides the Mosel across the checkered cloth. "The sauerbraten must have been good tonight. I like the girls with hearty appetites." We are in a dark booth at the Old German.

"You've found one." I still work the dormitory switchboard, forcing me to miss meals at my co-op. We have shared four suppers, a movie or a play, then a drive back to my house where Peter double-parked, slid over for a mannered kiss and departed.

"Not surprising. Like pregnant women, we both eat for two. Ourselves and our neuroses," he announces.

"To make them grow?"

Earnest face except for that deepening groove beside the mouth. "Takes less energy to go straight ahead than forward in circles." He traces epicircles on the cloth.

"And less to sit still. What do you mean?"

"That's a proposition of geometry you grasp intuitively, or not at all."

"You're awfully arbitrary, Peter."

"But 'awfully' right." He refills the wineglasses.

With the sense of being rebuffed I chatter, "It's strange to drink in public. Whose ID card do I have?"

Quick grin. Point for him. "No idea who the girl is."

"One more thing I should grasp intuitively?"

"I have a friend in the lost and found. Operators are useful."

"If they don't operate on you. Or do you have a license yourself?"

He says sharply, "The knife goes across the bread-and-butter plate. Not on the table."

"You should have taken out a sorority girl."

"No reason you can't eat like one. To your advantage. After all, aren't you a social climber?"

"Like hell I am."

"You told me you're the first in your family to go to college. Working-class neighborhood. Going back there after college?"

"I can't." I am not about to explain my last summer in Detroit. "I'm a freak there now. What I aspire to is the society of compatible freaks."

He pours more wine. "Culture's nice but expensive."

"Not to make it. All it costs is paper and time."

"You don't want clothes that show a little taste? For a change." He can't resist little jabs. "A hi-fi that doesn't cook the music? Wine on the dinner table?"

"I bring out the inquisitor in you. Why?"

A flash of reaction across the high boyish forehead, the thin supple mouth with a groove like a scar of thought on either side. "You don't know yourself."

Old introspective me? "That's where you're wrong."

Two-finger signal to the waiter. "You're too busy reacting to take the time off. I'd gather you've had little enough to react to."

As he pays I finish my wine hurriedly, but walking out to his '51 Ford, he seems to have forgotten our conversation. Why doesn't he annoy me more, with his attacks and feints? I suppose he arouses my curiosity. What's behind all this? I experience an intellect that is cold but tactile.

Finally, waiting for a stoplight he asks, "How many sisters?"

"None."

"Jealous mother?"

"Of me? Hardly. Just possessive. Where are we going?"

"I ask because it's obvious those absurd ambitions and intellectualizing are compensation mechanisms you've picked up because she's made you insecure as a woman."

"Is any living thing secure? You must be a Freudian."

"Of course," he says. "In science you learn to prefer the most elegant explanation. It's the simplest cause-and-effect pattern."

"I find it a religious system in which everything means something else, as in Christian interpretation of the Torah. Whatever any poor bozo does prefigures Christ. In Freud you go on a long heroic quest journey into your psyche just to become normal—which is clearly not the norm—or healthy, which is clearly an unlikely state."

But he has stopped listening. "Bastard," he mutters as a red MG cuts us off. "Like to take it out from under him. A Jag or a Porsche, that'd be worth driving. But will he do that for me?"

"That guy? Do you know him?"

"My old man's never given me one thing I want. This fat-assed tin can. Burns oil like a furnace." He drives as if forcing the car through barricades. I am to learn that *HE* said with force through the teeth means his father. Finally Peter parks on a street hemmed in with Victorian rooming houses whose eaves almost touch.

"This isn't where you lived when I came to one of your parties."

Into the dim hall smelling of soft coal and overshoes. "Who could guess what was under that hair jungle?" He slides a wooden panel into a wall enough for us to step into what must have been the parlor, then slides it to. In the solid dark I can make out nothing, so stand waiting for a light. Instead, stepping up behind, he wraps his arms around me. His lips moving on my neck, he murmurs, "What a waste of time to find fault with you. When I hold you like this, you're perfect."

Schmaltz. Am I to stand in this cave while he nibbles my neck? He turns me to face him, letting our coats slide to the floor. Taste of wine on our tongues. I am half dizzy with the heat eddying in the room. We lock together. The breath catches in my throat, my hands want to wander on his back. Do I like him? The dark and winy warmth moves me, the curious movement of his mouth not passionate, no, but sensual, thorough. Perhaps what Donna speculated about. Finally it is he who steps back, switching on a lamp that sends a thick muted light through the room, then tossing our coats on a desk chair. A slice is cut off by an angled corner fireplace with a speaker in the grate and the mantel lined with records. I thumb through them.

He drops in a tubular chrome and leather chair, the only sitting chair and so out of place with the other fifty-year-old pieces I know he must have brought it from home. "What do you want to hear? Name it. But don't touch the turntable."

Yet another bookcase full. I have never seen so many records outside a store. "This Scarlatti I never heard. And Ives—who's he?"

"Relax. You have to be improving yourself even when you're supposed to be having fun."

"To satisfy my curiosity is more fun than you think."

"There's always so much more. You can't eat history in one gulp."

But in several? To sit I must choose the bed or lift both coats from the desk chair. I wander a circuit. Tennis racquet in a press, book on chess openings with the place marked with somebody's IOU for fifty dollars. Although he has turned the music so loud it crowds the room, his voice cuts it easily, clear with a rough undercadence, a hidden throatiness as if some part of him tried to hold it back. "The way you look around makes me feel I should have been more careful of the objects in my room."

"Sorry. I'm a cat in a new house."

"You don't feel safe till you've checked the exits?"

With a sticky smile I perch on the bed. "Cats are always on the wrong side of any door. They like all doors to stay open."

"Whereas I like them shut?" Lithely in his stocking feet he crosses to the mantel and takes a bottle of brandy and two glasses from behind the records. He holds the glasses to the light, blows in them with a quick shamefaced smile.

Kicking off my shoes I sit back. Now that I am used to the volume of the music, I like it, a warm liquid beating in waves across the room but miraculously leaving all in place. The special quality of this room affects me, deep, with close walls and high ceiling and drawn draperies. Habitat of a neat comfort-loving but not overly clean man. The atmosphere is of an organic interior, the inside of an ear, a sybaritically furnished stomach.

He lets himself down beside me and pours the brandy. He is going to kiss me again; strange to feel that impending and yet sit as if I did not guess. The record finishes and in the moment before the next drops, we freeze. Unreal that I should be waiting for him to move in on me, unable to relate what is coming to him or to myself.

"You have a sensual profile." His hands coast down my face. "Soft."

Mike's word. "Why do you imagine I don't know myself?"

A smile deepens the grooves along his mouth. Taking off his glasses, he reaches past to put them on the nightstand. Then still leaning across he takes me in his arms and with his cool smooth cheek against mine says, "Because you don't know who you are or why you do what you do or what you really want." His tongue licks at my ear caressingly.

I sit primly trying to carry on the conversation. "And you do?"

"There's more than one way to talk." His lids half shut, veined leaves of a blue-white tree. His palm is suddenly hard on my back to guide me down. A cold shark-fin of fears cuts the surface.

I jerk back. "I'm sorry but this is too pat. I'm dense but not this dense."

He sits up, dusting his blond brush. "What am I supposed to do, come on shaggy? Hiya, Jill, let's go to bed."

I take my Luckies from my purse. "I'd better leave now."

"I'm not taking you home yet."

"I know how to walk." I reach for my coat.

He gets there first, quick on his feet. "What would you do if you had, say, two months to live?"

"Do?" I stop a charged half foot from him. "I'd write seriously again." Mike persuaded me I couldn't write. I have only slowly begun again by taking the course with Bolognese and Weisbuch.

With an impatient gesture. "Would you stay? Be that curious?"

"What's the price of staying?"

He takes a step forward and I catch my breath, but he spins me by the elbow toward his desk. "What are you afraid of? You won't even flirt most of the time."

"I don't play games."

"Too senile?" He lets my elbow go but the grasp of his fingers tingles. "I'll bet you could learn. I do nothing else." He broods over his desk. Then he takes up an inlaid wooden board and an Indian box of chess pieces and carries them to the bed, jerking the chocolate spread smooth. Uncertainly I tag after.

"Here's a game you can start on tonight. First the movement of the pieces." In short impatient sentences he instructs me. He does not touch me again till the perfunctory kiss in the idling car outside my co-op.

TWENTY-ONE

On Various Kinds of Separations

"HE SAID HE was separated. That's what he told me. Being separated from his wife—that means something, doesn't it?" Donna sits astride her desk chair, her face wizened with pain.

"Separated by six hundred miles. Are they really coming here?" I am proofreading a paper on the Platonic influence on Sir Philip Sydney.

"That's why he doesn't want to see me during the holidays. And after I made up all those excuses to my parents and Estelle. Now I have to go home. What's the point hanging around Ann Arbor? Worrying I'm going to run into Sal on the street with his wife and kiddies."

On the back of the door hangs a dress he bought her, electric blue with a fishtail. I never knew a man could buy dresses. My father hands my mother twenty dollars and tells her to get herself a present. Once he bought a new garbage can for her birthday; he thought that was funny. Mike used to give me books. Donna is supposed to yank on her girdle and waist cincher and iron-maiden bra and wriggle over to his party for their final appearance as a couple until his wife and two daughters have gone back to Arlington, Virginia. He never comes to the house to pick her up. He gives her cab money to come and go. She is already late and when he called she had me tell him she was in the shower and couldn't come to the phone. She is made up carefully and enclosed in her armored carapace of bone, elastic and rubber, but she has not pulled on the dress.

"Come on, stay home with me," I plead. "We never kill time together and just talk anymore."

"Aren't you seeing Peter?"

"He's gone off to Grosse Pointe. His older brother just had a baby and I think they're gilding it or whatever they do to the first boy baby in each generation—lay down a magnum of old money for it?"

"You're not that interested in him? Are you?"

"He isn't open with me."

"I thought maybe you liked his being a physicist. But I didn't think he was your type."

"My type is not yet in production."

She gets up and takes the dress off its hanger. "It is gorgeous. Be a pity not to wear it at least this once."

"Donna, don't go. Stay with me tonight. Let's talk. I've been writing a lot again and I'd love to show you."

With a quick shudder she dives into the dress and begins working it down. "It'd be too depressing, sitting home on a Saturday night."

After midnight, she returns giddy. "I'm so glad I went, Stu. I had a wonderful time. He told me he's going to work things out with his wife—he says he really is separated but the children want to see him at Christmas. He just isn't ready for me to meet them until all the details of the divorce have been worked out."

"Donna, if Wanda upstairs came in and said that about some married man she was seeing, what would you think?"

"You don't like Sal. You've been jealous about him from the beginning."

"Granted. But jealousy has a sharp eye for flaws. Real ones."

She smiles crookedly in the mirror, touching the newly

processed fluff of her cottony hair. "You're just surprised I could get him. A celebrity. Someone who could have any woman on this campus!"

A strenuous politeness in my parents' house. My mother fetches out a bottle of Mogen David from the linen closet. "I always like a little wine during the holidays." She beams, her face a caricature of the pleasure she longs to feel. "Your father doesn't appreciate it. That smalltown streak."

Wine is Valpolicella or a California red to me, not this cough syrup, but my novice snobbishness is disgusting. Am I scared of losing the little status I've gained if I respond to an incorrect cue? "I'd love a glass of wine."

She stands by the stove with her arms loosely folded. "Christmas is fun even if we do have to do it at midnight after your job." Her gaze, fixed on the drawn blinds, turns opaque. "How I used to envy Gentiles their Christmas. I was so tired getting up from the table still hungry so the little kids and Papa could eat. Nothing ever clean or nice or new or right. All I want is to live like a human being." She groans, her hands dropping to her sides. "Like a mensch. They won't let you live."

"But now do you have what you want?" I have grown up thin on the milk of her discontent, and yet I do not know its source.

"We have to get back to your father. He always feels so lonely when he hears us talking in the kitchen together."

"Does he?" I wonder if that is not one of her myths. I wish I could see my father's love just once through some medium other than Mother's interpretation.

Peter drives in from Grosse Pointe Shores to see me. He is polite but clearly wary of my famous boy-eating parents. With my father he talks football successfully. With the rise of professional football leagues, my father finds it acceptable as he never did when it was primarily a college sport. Peter tells me I am to go with him to a party at his parents' country club on my evening off. He is amused at the idea. Mother sniffs after him with mistrustful approval.

"Well, he's better than that Mike Loesser." She peers

sideways, washing dishes, and waits for a reaction. "Doesn't it bother you that you can't wear heels? He's so short. But of course I wouldn't let what anyone else says trouble me . . . that is, if I really cared about him."

"Right you are."

"He thinks he's a good catch."

I shrug. "Could be." Shut face. My skin is leather.

Peter that afternoon takes me off to watch some friends of his bobsled in competition. On the way back he is glum. "Had a pinsticking contest with the old man. Oh, to be born from a bottle! He tried to forbid me bringing you to the country club."

"But they haven't met me."

"They've asked questions. He keeps discoursing about inappropriate discrepancies in background." He takes his narrow head in his hands. "Ties up with his general attack. Whatever I do is wrong and must be done only to irritate them."

"Does he want you to come into his business instead of being a physicist?"

"He wouldn't trust me to design a privy."

"I don't understand."

"Forest Crecy, architect. Hell and gone successful. You had to know that." He glares suspicion.

The next day he calls just as I'm off to my late shift at the telephone company. "You don't care that much about going, so let's forget it. It'll be goddamn dull. I got us tickets to the road company of *West Side Story*. A matinee because of your ludicrous job."

When he comes to pick me up he drives a gleaming white Sprite. "Not what I wanted, but a hell of a lot better than that garbage wagon, right? They couldn't find a cheaper sports job, but at least it's a real car. He says, maybe, maybe if I don't rack this one up, he'll get me a Porsche for my Ph.D. The bastard. Next year I'll have a job and I'll buy myself a goddamned silver Porsche."

Saucy white bribe. I hold my hair down and we are off like a playful hornet. A game with me as his sacrifice pawn. He boasts that his parents refuse categorically to sanction his relationship with me. I want to giggle. What relationship? His small well-made hands grip the wheel as he plays racing driver. I bet he even makes faces in the mirror while he shaves.

I ache with weariness as I lie on the glider in the attic, its grubby plastic worn to my body. My parents sleep. Sometimes I like the feeling of sitting up alone but tonight it gives me the sense of being more isolated than I care for. I snap on the little radio to the CBC. Mozart, yes, clarinet concerto, K. 622. Ignoring that my recognition is based on Lennie's having given Donna the record, how nice is my exactitude. I, Jill, daughter of Flicka, Bride of Franken- stein, rise from the morass of bubble gum and comic books and Saturday Roy Rogers matinees. What a triumph of will over environment. It was Mr. Stein, the high-school En- glish teacher who took such an interest in my poetry and sadistic pleasure in my crush on him, who taught me to say Mo-tsart instead of Mo-zart, a habit which has, my friends, become almost second nature. I am even now working to perfect the short o into what sounds to my Midwestern ears like harrible, preferred by New Yorkers on campus and my desk dictionary. What do I want? I ache through all my body and that can't be only the telephone company, uncomfortable as the switchboard is, swarming with roaches.

> O Western wind, when wilt thou blow,
> That the small rain down can rain?
> Christ, that my love were in my arms
> And I in my bed again!

A clean sweet sinking hurt those words leave. I sat in honors class while they explicated that poem—what we do to poems—and worried and worried over that phrase "the small rain." Finally I had to stick my hand up and say that due to the subject of the poem I thought it might allude to orgasm. I have never heard a silence as hot and wet as that one, broken a full minute later when our button-

down, black-umbrella-toting professor let out his pursed
lips, "That is a very interesting interpretation . . . *Miss
Stuart* . . . though perhaps a bit pornographic for our
purposes."

Four lines like four powerful straight blows on the head
of a nail to the brain. Where did you read your dreams?
An early addiction to the romantic poets, who could not
live out their verses either. Pain is aesthetic only at a distance. When Julie lent me *Axel's Castle* and there I read
what Mike said that first night we made love, I felt conned.
Maybe the solution is simply to have sex without building
castles over it—friends who sometimes copulate. Do I
know?

Sad, muted horn from the street. A foreign car in this
neighborhood? Sound that quivers on my nerves. The
junkman passing in the alley with his limp hat hanging
over his tobacco face, the reins slack on his lap, the grey
horse plodding. The big green wheels of his cart creaked
while he lifted what looked like a wooden egg to his mouth
and blew a questing entreaty. The other kids called him the
sheeny, but when Mother heard me use that phrase, she
had a talk with me. After that with self-attentive shame I
stood by the hollyhocks and watched him lurch past, each
shambling clop of the horse, each lunge of the big wheels
over a broken brick or bottle shaking him limp as a tree
but leaving him as finally rooted in his seat.

Backs of garages, rat tunnels, igloo garbage containers
for the apartment houses, tiger lilies sprung from asphalt:
the alley was my childhood boulevard. It led kitty-corner
to the four-family where Joey lived. Skinny, dark, quick as
a squirrel, he had the somber eyes and the grimace taut
and bitter even at seven of the hard-luck fighter. When I
was five, he asked me to marry him; Mother said I
couldn't because he was Catholic. . . . I can see myself
dawdling in the alley the day his family moved, until finally he came out, looked at me over the fence and then
rushed back in. I burst into tears and fled down our basement to smear myself with coal dust. I have always been in

love, in continual sequence since the dawn of memory. Whether that is my sickness or my health, I cannot guess.

By the time I get back to school January 3, Theo has already been expelled from the university.

"They caught her with Dulcie," Donna tells me, half scandalized, half amused. "Imagine Dulcie—that sexless officious thing!"

"Now I understand why Theo wouldn't move into the co-op with us. But what happened to Theo? Where the hell is she?"

"They expelled her so fast she was gone before anyone even heard. I mean, there's nothing scares them like catching a couple of women together. With girls being forced to live in the dorms, the deans are weak in the knees that the watchful rich daddies will pull their daughters out. So Theo hardly had time to put her clothes on before she was on her way back to New York."

I try to find out where she is, but no one wants to be overheard admitting to having known her. I am politely dismissed, even hung up on. Dulcie has been sent home to Pontiac, but I can't even get her number. I spent quiet times on the dorm switchboard pestering everybody I can think of. My only help is Julie. Oddly enough Julie does not worry about guilt by association. She assumes she is above suspicion. Friday she visits my co-op room with news.

"Theo's parents wired her money for a plane ticket home. Then they committed her to one of those posh funny farms in Connecticut."

"A nuthouse?"

"Only the highest quality nuts. Mostly women drying out, I expect. Sort of like a fat farm with bars."

"Find out the name of it, okay?"

"I'll try. I saw Mike yesterday—we have the same seminar in Ronsard. You can't even sneeze in English. Anyhow . . ."

Lately I seem to be bleeding internally. Donna is over at Sal's. Their romance has heated up after Christmas and

I have noticed catalogs for American University and George Washington on her desk although she has said nothing to me about following him East.

But Julie is watching me carefully. "You spent a lot of time with Theo, in her room. I guess you're missing her?"

Oh, we have arrived. "If you mean did I know she liked women, no. We never talked about sex."

"What did you talk about?"

"Death and music and trouble and music and booze and music."

"She was always playing records. A female jock with tastes for Handel and Bartók."

"She taught me a lot about music, Julie. I do miss her."

"Her or her record collection?"

"Both, I guess." I take the easy way out Julie offers me, wondering why it feels so shitty to lie. I am also lying when I say I never guessed that Theo was attracted to women. Any woman who has ever loved another has a special sensitivity to that openness.

"It's so . . . *dégoûtant*. . ." Julie muses. "What could they possibly do? Rub themselves together like sticks?"

"Ah, perhaps you should try out what men and women do before you judge what women and women do," I say, dangerously I am aware. Julie never did seduce Van nor pry an engagement ring out of him. Now Van is at Yale studying comparative literature and writing letters back to Mike about how stimulating it all is. Van got a fellowship but Mike's grades are not exceptional enough. His family would have to cough up the money for him to join Van.

"Perhaps I should," she says and actually blushes.

The end of term, the end of classes, finals and new trauma. Big Sal says good-bye to his class and leaves without telling Donna anything. Instead she receives by messenger a dozen yellow roses with a card saying, "My own sweet rose, it's been great and I'll always love you. S." A package arrives from his secretary with all the things she had left at his apartment packed neatly in it, robe, diaphragm, perfume, hairbrush, nylons. A week later a second and last package comes from Garfinkel's in Washington containing a negligee. The note says, "In fondest memory to my darling girl, S."

I have never seen a negligee before. It is pale blue and silky with much lace. Donna carts it out in the backyard. There we pour gasoline on it and burn it ritually.

TWENTY-TWO

Any Storm in a Port

"IF PAUL ISN'T there I'll throw a fit." Donna tugs at her sweater. She is back to dressing like a college girl, while the fancy black and fancy blue sheaths hang in plastic at the back of our closet. "All the graduate students in poli sci go for the free cookies. Oh, why does he stare all the time and not ask me out?" Paul is in one of her classes.

The political science department's weekly tea. Donna is a political science major now, a legacy from Big Sal. "Perhaps he's shy, baby. Take it easy. You're not over, you know, what happened yet."

With a sigh she takes my hand in her cold palms and squeezes it hard. "I feel old, Stu, old. How long before I get hold of my life?"

"Living's a slippery thing, ma Donna. We're novices."

She turns back to the mirror to glare at her reflection. "Can't even tell what I want. One week I'm a political scientist. The next, I'll be a prominent critic. Then I think I should study science. But whatever I turn to, it never feels real because it's still just me. Sometimes all I want is a good screw. Sometimes to kill myself—me and a dozen others."

"Good. Let's make a list."

"Think you wouldn't be on it?" Her lips pull back. "You don't know me! The day you see, you'll hate me too. Sal saw through me."

"Garbage. Your damn sin and confession upbringing makes you fear hell where there's only mistakes and impatience and people bumping on each other." I get up and put my arm around her gingerly, to comfort without alarm. "We're just learning our ABCs of intimacy."

She dodges my arm. "We're all such shits. We'll find out what you'll accept, when it hurts you, someday."

"Donna. Slow down. You run from me. You run from man to man. Why can't we take walks? Read poetry? Sit and talk to each other?"

"You never talk to anybody until midnight and then with a glass of bourbon in your fist. . . . Stu, walk me over. I feel like such an ass, chasing this jerk."

The snow blows down the street, blinding us, clotting in our lashes. She walks with one blue-gloved hand protecting her cheek. "How's Peter? Aren't you sleeping with him yet?"

"He hasn't tried again." Although I always carry my diaphragm with me when I see him, that is only as a failsafe device. I have no particular desire for Peter. Strange how startled he was when I mentioned Donna had dated an Indian student. "What happened to that guy Sol?" he asked. Peter never did get Sal's name straight.

"Maybe he can't get it up!" Her high laugh is chopped by the wind. In the Fishbowl lobby she gives me a glance of appeal. "Do I look all right?"

Facing the plate glass I sit on a bench to watch the storm. Almost time for my writing class. Hypnotically the snow pelts down while students pass sliding on the tile streaked with dark prints. Donna is hard to live with. She pursues violent attractions, abandons them with disgust, sets herself impossible tasks and derides her failures. Why can't I help?

Donaldson stands in front of me grinning before I focus on him. "Such concentration. Do you write in public like Sartre?"

"No, I sleep in public with my eyes open, like a cat." That loudmouth folksinger Rob Prewitt is with him and winks at me. Hanging on Rob's plaid arm is someone who looks vaguely familiar and who greets me by name. Smooth bronze hair, wide hips and plump arms bared under a kind of cape. Dressed like a gypsy in full-flounced skirt, peasant blouse, coarse stockings peeping out, big gold hoops, she stands out in the press of students.

"Hiya . . . Stephanie." The name comes back. Peter's party long ago. We chatter brief banalities about PAF and then I watch them off. Lennie enters sponging snow from his head and beard. Our gazes dodge, slide guiltily back. He plods toward me, drying his glasses on his denim shirt. "How're things?"

"Fine, Lennie. How's your work going?"

"Okay. I'm taking figure drawing with Russo—good man."

"Good."

"Mike is doing a little better," he says aggressively, as if giving me an up-to-the-minute report on an accident victim. "He's got a room by himself on Division. He's drinking but he made up his incompletes." He shoves his hands deep in his leather jacket, rocking on his boot heels. "And how's Peter Crecy?"

I get up to face him, resting my knee on the bench. "Fine. When I have supper with him tonight, I'll tell him you asked."

No, that sour grin is not of embarrassment nor accusation but an old man's expression, a knowing grimace of humor rooted in pain. He turns on his heel and sidles off with a backhanded wave. I look after him, judged. Faithful still to Donna? Our common ark of love on the cocoa sea he painted has gone down, and none of us doing right well by ourselves. Yet I would not go back into that tight place.

We are supposed to be planning a PAF forum this afternoon, but Bolognese came back from the dean of students with the absolute refusal of our speaker, a lawyer considered tainted by his appearance before HUAC. Donaldson sets his auburn hair on end, ruffling it. "We'll just have to be our own forum on this one, then. We can't let them scare us off the issue."

Howie is discussing the need to dramatize the issues, when Alberta pops out of her seat. She is so excited she has unwound her dark yellow scarf and waves it like a banner. "We'll be HUAC ourselves! We'll be the committee and we'll visit campus and hold hearings!"

"A play," I say. "We'll write a farce and put it on."

We decide to base our satire on the mad tea party in Alice with the Red Queen thrown in. Bolognese and I with Donaldson's help will do the writing and everybody will make suggestions and act in it. I feel out of breath just sitting here. My wrists and throat pound as they do when I run uphill or when I am writing and an idea carries me racing forward so I forget myself entirely. Suddenly it is six thirty. I forgot to ask Howie to let me see his watch and now I'll be forty-five minutes late meeting Peter.

I trot to the Union but he is not there waiting. Now what? I run to his house. The snow has stopped and the sky is clear up to the polestar glittering. The wind breathes ice on my cheeks.

Rooming houses lurk under the night sky on Division. February ice. As I pass one of the tall houses a movement in a corner room catches my gaze. A thin arm reaches through the couple of inches of open window to tap ash from a cigarette. The face drifts into the light in profile, then is thrust back laughing. Mike. A glimpse then of someone in the room, a flash of bright pink. His arm pulls the shade leaving me with my prying face of surprise angled up. Did he see me under the streetlamp?

I clatter up Peter's steps gritty with rock salt. Through the draperies light shows from his room. I slip into the pocket of hall and bang on the door. "Peter!"

Nothing. I feel as if he is inside yet he does not answer. Why did I assume he would come back here? I give the door a last thump, then leave a note. I swing by the Union once more and then I go home.

I am still waiting in my room for him to get in touch when Donna comes in with her blue wool coat draped over one shoulder. She looks sharply at me but does not speak.

"What I've done! The PAF meeting ran late and I missed meeting Peter at the Union. How do I do these stupid things? But we had a great idea—"

"Why make such a fuss?" She turns her back, brushing her hair with vehement strokes. She is wearing it extremely short, a cap fitted to her head.

"But he'll be angry, he always thinks I do things on purpose."

"If you couldn't remember you had a date with him, obviously you don't care."

"I just got caught up in the meeting. We're going to put on a play about HUAC. Bolognese and Donaldson and I are going to write it, hey? Come on, Donna, what's wrong with you anyhow?"

"I'm tired is all."

"You're tired a lot lately."

"What's that supposed to mean?" She swings around, glaring.

"Mean? You're irritable. Did you eat with Paul? Are you going out with him?"

She draws a hand across her forehead. "Oh, him. He's married."

"How do you know?"

"He was at the tea, all right. Gossiping about the high cost of babies."

"Donna, I'm sorry. Where were you, then?"

"Curse men who don't wear rings." She raises her head and seeing me waiting for an answer, winces with irritation. "Out! Out, mother mine by appointment of who?"

"Sorry. But what can I do about Peter?" I pace. "Maybe I should have waited at his place. Now no supper. I'm hungry."

Her hands attack her hair. "I don't care! Just don't go on about it!"

Martyred I stride in injured silence to the closet for a can of sardines, open them at my desk.

"That smell! The room stinks of fish."

I will not turn around. Why is she so cross with me?

She raises the window to the cold air. "Living with you is like hanging on to a seesaw."

I finish the sardines and drop the can in the wastebasket.

"Are you going to leave that in here to stink?"

"Even I don't eat tin. Get off my back, Donna."

"I want to." She leans tensely against the door. "I want to live with someone else."

"What?"

"I want to move out of this room. Living with you is too hard on me. You drive me crazy!"

For a moment I feel nothing. Then pain begins to resonate. "You want to move out? To live with somebody else?"

She nods. "I have to. Understand, Stu, I have to."

"Sure thing." I take my towel and toothbrush and cross the hall to the john. Can't believe. I stand at the stained sink facing the mirror, foaming white mouth in a fixed grin taking the toothbrush. I thought she needed me. Thought she wanted the way we strike on each other and nurture each other. Fool. People get tired of you. Vampire. Magpie. Fool. You want too much, you lean too hard, you spill your guts on the floor. Even my parents can't stand me. Nobody can.

She stands at the window with a taut nervous smile. Her painted nails click on the ledge. "We interfere with each other. You're always wanting to talk when I should be working. You don't need to study the way I do."

"Fuck it, Donna, if you didn't keep changing fields, you could take a normal load of courses. You're damned smart. Why didn't you say something to me about what was bugging you?"

"What good would it do? You can't stop. Then your stuff all over. You make me feel guilty because I'm neat—"

Petty reasons stinging like black flies. "Shut up!"

"Don't yell at me, Stuart. I'm trying to be reasonable!"

I am crazy with rage, I want to pound her face in. My anger terrifies me. My voice issues from me in my old gutter nasality, "Shut up, you motherfuckin' whore, shut your shitass face!"

"Don't scream! You demand too much. You jab at me and probe. You try to run my life. You try to drag me along to everything you do—"

I grope behind me, grasp something. Throw it hard overhand. A box of powder slams off the wall and shimmers down on her. A cry chokes in her throat as her arm snaps up to shield her face. Then she is sneezing, turning blindly in a swirl of settling powder. I grab my coat and run out.

Running, running blindly, I pause at last to ask myself after a few blocks, where? On State Street I duck into the drugstore to call Howie. No answer. I walk back along State to the Union and circle the tables. Mike sits with his tooled leather binder open before him. Grant Stone sprawls low in a tilted chair, running his hand through his florid hair, yawning. Julie sits primly on Mike's right working on a French translation. The arm of her pink sweater rests against Mike's arm in its old unraveling sweater. Oh. My goodness. Well.

Cold, it's cold outside. My jacket leaks through its poor seams. Where? Where else? At the corner of Peter's street a car grinds in frozen slush. As I climb his steps, the engine still grunts, the wheels still spin. Through his closed door music permeates the hall. I knock. Creak of bedsprings and then his voice. "Who is it?"

"Jill. Let me in."

He slides the door aside. His face is blank and sullen. He looks seven years old and sulking. "What do you want?"

"Sorry I missed you. . . ." The heat swells in my lungs. Padded cave of room. On the chocolate spread the impress of his body, a slit envelope, pages of a letter.

"I've eaten," he says bluntly but takes my coat. "What are you doing here?"

"Pure desperation." My head tilts forward on its stalk.

He turns my face toward him. "What happened to you?"

"Donna just told me she wants to move out." I pull from him, leaning on the mantel over the grate where the speaker blows Stravinsky in my face. "It hurts."

"Did she say why? What did she tell you, exactly?"

I shake my head. The end of something I loved. "She gave stupid reasons, like I'm messy and I talk too much."

"You probably do."

"So?" I wheel between the furniture waving my arms. "I'm me. I love her. She should care more!"

"Maybe she doesn't love you. Maybe your love is a burden to her." A nervy alertness in his face and in the tense hunch of his shoulders under a tee shirt, he sits yoga fashion holding the soles of his narrow feet. As I pace his eyes blue as Donna's fix on me tauntingly.

"What have I done to her? Only cared. She's sick of me."

"You're so naive. Must take a lot of work to stay that way."

"If you don't want to listen, throw me out. I'm set to bleed for the night."

He rubs his feet in sensual kneading. "It'd be so easy to comfort you."

"Don't bet on it."

"I do. Jill, I do."

"She wants to study? Bull. She wastes more time than I do."

He rocks back, chin against chest. "Cut the surface. Of course she didn't give the real reason."

I stop pacing. "Since I've been seeing you, she's resented it. How blind I am. You're attracted to her and she's attracted to you. What am I doing in the middle?"

"You say I'm attracted to her?"

"It's clear from the way you talk about her, ask after her."

"I couldn't . . . wouldn't push her out of bed. But she's more mixed up than I can handle."

"We're a lot alike."

"Hardly." He makes a fist and stares at it. "Considered it when I noticed her running around with Lennie. Obviously not going to stick to that poor twerp. Pure rebellion."

"Why not now?"

"She's too mixed up, I tell you. Too stormy." He catches my arm. "You're my size."

"Poor reason. If you'd rather have her, go after her."

"I don't want to." His arms tighten around me. "You're trying to put me off, but remember, you came to me tonight. I've been waiting for this."

"It's just pain, you know." My tears soak into his shoulder. Emptiness expands in my chest till I feel as if I am floating. I can even observe that he seems to enjoy my crying as if it released something in him. His hands move on my back, my arms, hands cradling and stroking and soothing, hand curious and avid of me, hands exploring my breasts, my thighs. So be it. His tongue catches the last tears. I lie back and look at him. In a moment of silence the record changes. "What's that?"

His cheek resting on my breast, he listens. "Prokofiev. Second violin concerto." He smiles. "Sometimes it's like pushing buttons, how predictable your reactions are."

"Why bother, then?"

"I want you."

The words echo through, tap tap on my spine. "Why?"

He smiles as he bends to my mouth. Long kiss carrying me backward on a slow swell. I want to be carried. I lie loosely as he undresses me, even perversely applying my limp leverage against him. But finally free of clothes, the first impact stops my breath in the ice-hot shock of flesh on flesh. My skin is charged with static. His body against me in the lamp glow seems hammered of some warm pale metal, hard, sleek and hairless. I desire him. Attempting to control my reactions, I say to myself, See, this is Lust. I am glad for the break when I stop to put in my diaphragm. I realize abruptly that Mike and I never were naked together. As Peter nibbles on my breast, an image lights my closed lids of that flash of pink in Mike's room and his thin arm pulling down the shade. Julie got what she wanted finally, although I wonder if she wants Mike entire.

I am so busy exploring my reactions and defending myself against them (what do I think will stoop and sweep me away?) that I am slow to realize he has pulled back, his face sullen. He contracts as if he were being unborn beside me, returning to fetus. I fold my arms around him comfortingly as he grinds his face into my breasts. He is not erect. He cannot pump himself erect.

"If you don't want to, Peter . . . You know it's not necessary."

"Damn it, damn it," he mutters. "You don't understand. It doesn't mean anything. I can't explain. It's absurd. It's just the body. The damn stupid body. It's mechanical."

I lie weary in a bubble of calm, my arms tiring as I hold him flung over me. Slowly his muscles loosen and at length he rolls onto his back. "What I really want, I can't have, it seems."

I touch his mouth for answer. Long blond lashes almost invisible, mauve-veined lids. He has hooked something in me. He will not meet my gaze but turns the clock to face him. "Better dress. Time to take you home."

Not to leave him like this. "Would you like me to stay?"

"After that, you want to? Won't they catch you?"

"I didn't even sign out." The truth is, Alberta is my friend before she's my housemother, and she slipped me my own key awhile ago. Probably because we work together politically and because she respects my class background and my putting myself through school, she considers me mature above the other inhabitants. Of course I think her a great judge of character. I don't doubt that Donna would cover for me anyhow.

He rolls away to lie with his hands under his head. Just a slit of sharp blue like a knife edge glints under the lids. "I was about to write a letter when you arrived."

I am used to being naked with Donna, and that seems to extend to feeling natural with him. "The pages on the bed."

"That's Sue's last letter. I've been going with her on and off for years. She graduated from Wellesley last year. Now she has a dippy job as a buyer for a shop her aunt has an interest in."

"Do you love her?"

The record finishes, letting a glacial silence in. Down in his throat he groans once, whether from pain or annoyance I cannot tell. "At this point it's a formal engagement or good-bye. I can't string her along any further. That's what I was trying to decide."

"Did you?"

Hand closing on my shoulder. "In a sense does it matter whom I marry, long as she's healthy, functional and good-looking? Got to have a home, children. Why not?"

"What is Sue like?"

"Light brown hair, hazel eyes. Pretty since she was a baby. Good sailor, good swimmer. Won a trophy in a meet once. Nice legs. No sense of humor but lots of poise. I took her virginity and so what?"

"Did she take yours?"

"Not bloody likely. I had my cousin when we were fifteen. . . . But Sue's absolutely rooted in family and the Grosse Pointers. I have New York visions. I'm working on landing a job at Brookhaven National Labs." He kneels, a hand on my stomach. "Feel used, because I didn't tell you? You can still leave."

"What's the difference? You don't love me."

"Try to make me?"

"Maybe."

"It won't be worth it if you don't. Casual sex depresses me. I had quite enough that year I lived with those two losers in the music department and played *la vie bohème*. Gave parties for all the campus arty-farties to come and drink up my booze and patronize me. . . . I could have had you that first night I brought you here. But I wanted to wait till you came around to me."

Till I got desperate enough? Curious enough? I know I am with him to avoid Donna. "Are you sleepy? I am."

His sleek shoulders hunch as he reaches for the light switch. "We'll talk about it all in the morning."

I am glad for the warmth of his smooth body beside me and glad for his indifference. Someone who cared would not let me cover my eyes, and I cannot stand to see the pain and rage that burn through my mind leaving shame and devastation behind.

"Good night, Peter."

"G'night."

TWENTY-THREE

Chicken Potpie and the Pastel Egg

THE DRIP OF icicles. The radiator burbles. Whatever I shouted, whoever I argued with in the room of sleep I've lost now. Only a phrase remains, the mirror is broken. All my fantasies have left me. He groaned, ground his teeth. Once his outflung arm struck me. Now in light sleep his face has a sensual innocence, death mask of a fallen seraph. I start as the clock radio turns on Vivaldi from the university station. When I face him he is watching under his lashes.

"Hello." Hand drifting over me. "The name is Jill, isn't it?"

Games. "The name's Penelope and I'm Queen of the Fleas."

His drowsy face broods on me. "Good body. You look better out of your clothes."

"I don't expect to be courted this early in the morning."

A laugh sticks in his throat. "I'm not the first to tell you that."

Actually he is. I swing out of bed reaching for my scattered clothes.

"What are you doing?"

"I have a nine o'clock class."

"Right here. Don't try to run out on me now." He slides out after me, moving lightly on his feet. His menace makes me smile as he circles, his face wary, his penis quite erect now. I have a moment to contemplate him and what I will do before he seizes me. No doubt he is stronger but I would, if I meant to get out of here, clout him with the lamp or the radio, not my small fists. I did start something last night, and that my mood of masochism and passivity has tightened into a harder resolution this morning does not wipe out his usefulness then. I guess I owe him one. I let him pull me roughly down on the bed. His face grim, determined, he acts out a scene of brute mastery. I am something soft he is conquering. Holding my wrists in one hand over my head he pokes at me, thrusts in finally. I don't think he knows a lot about exciting a woman. It hurts when he enters but not much or long. Light small body on me hammering. I am warmed by the tussle as if he had held me tenderly. I move with him and he releases my wrists. His face relaxes.

He starts and stops and rides up on me carefully. He is very controlled, to use that phrase of Donna's, and yet gone, grim in purpose, totally rapt. No sound but the bed creaking and the Vivaldi still tripping along. I cannot let go, conscious always of his different hard body athletic and determined and adjusting itself to me, bearing in, riding up. The phallus as tool, sex as technique. I am sore with disuse, my thighs aching. I am sleepy, hungry, cranky. He goes on. Heat rises from us. An announcer speaks. A Haydn quartet begins. Then a loose partial pleasure fans out and hangs on, a slow wholly muscular release. Finally he comes, moaning through clenched teeth. I am glad I still have my diaphragm in from last night.

"You didn't really want to leave, you see," he says.

"Looks that way."

"I didn't hurt you?" He is smiling in tentative enjoyment.

I shake my head no. He feels good and keeps giving me little proprietary pokes and taps as we dress. On our way toward campus the snow is soft and rotten underfoot, the

air spongy. The sun leaks intermittently between torn
clouds. "Breakfast at the Union?" he says. "Sort of public
announcement, what the hell? Why are you so quiet? It's
man who's supposed to be sad after coitus. Woman is
supposed to be smug."

Lennie in a booth looks up from *The Times* and Professor Bishop, comp. one, gives me a damp hello as we pass
the table where he sits alone eating stewed prunes. After
my eleven o'clock class I will go home, cut my afternoon
classes and sleep. Peter's smooth mask across the table is a
void I refuse to fill with fantasy or false hope. He eats
methodically, slicing his fried eggs into neat parallelograms
and spearing them with his fork. Good-bye, kid, it's been
fun, he'll say, and be surprised when I am not hurt. I am
oddly content sitting here, easy in my body. I do not hate
myself; I do not even hate Donna. I feel at home in my
flesh and I want to survive. I am a step further from Mike
and that summer.

He spears the last yolk-smeared parallelogram, finishes
his toasted English muffin. "I've decided to break off with
Sue."

"Sue?" Far away a pasteboard woman shrivels.

His hand clutches the cup. His forehead seams. "I have
only a short time here. I make my second try at my orals
soon. Then off to wherever I land a job. The sons of
successes are always such poor little shits. I'll never be
more than an indifferent physicist. Sometimes I wish I'd
picked something easier, but I had the talent for math early
on and it seemed like something to quell *him* with. The
lightnings of the atom grasped in my puny fist."

"Do you really admire his buildings?" He showed me
pictures, and some in concrete reality when we were last in
Detroit. Monolithic, hierarchic office buildings decked with
poured fretwork like frozen rage. Pompous ill-tempered
monuments to corporate wealth. They are Assyrian, I think,
without the massively phallic power of their winged bulls.

He waves that question away. "We can take this time
and see what happens. No promises. I am what I am! Try
each other on for size and see how it shakes down."

Careful as it is, this proposition stuns me. "You want a

relationship with me?" Relationship: the jargon of our world. The relationship of two parallel lines.

"Why not? Try it on for a while." His gaze rests on me, sullen. He is actually tense with waiting.

Reaching through mounds of gauze I take his hand and pry it from where it curls around the cup. Deep in my head something opens. "Why not? It'll be spring soon."

"But no promises."

How have I touched him? "Peter, if you were going out with Sue for so long, how come you didn't take her to your country club dance at Christmas?"

"I did, finally. But I didn't want to."

"What did you tell her?"

"About you? The truth. That you were this weird little black-haired exotic Jewish intellectual I might be very interested in." With a paper napkin he blots his lips. "I told you I've never been in love with her."

I see the logic neatly: he doesn't love me either, so how then will this be different? He chases false expectancies, disproved before he tries them. But maybe not: I am not from his world. Maybe I do offer him a way out and a chance at feeling? My calm after all is grounded in getting laid not an hour ago, and I feel loyal to his neat hard body if nothing else. I have to mend myself, I have to survive. And I am still curious. I kiss him and go off to my course in the metaphysical poets, where Dick tells me I look lovely, lovely, he repeats.

What are we protesting in our corner, Dick and Bolognese and I? Partly our arrogance unites us, for English is a hierarchical department and as writers we talk with a fierce authority totally unrecognized by faculty and fellow students. Literature is the stuff on which grades are honed to most of the class. Every time papers or tests are returned, a bitter hush falls. On the way out we're sure to be stopped by better-behaved students clutching their typescripts or bluebooks with the hopeful sally, "What grade did you get?" and the almost audible prayer, O Lord of Justice, let it be lower than mine! We are taught the narrowly defined Tradition, we are taught Structure, we are taught levels of Ambiguity. We are taught that works of art refer exclusively to other works of art and exist in Platonic space. Emotion before art is dirty. We are taught to explicate poems and analyze novels and locate Christ figures and creation myths and Fisher Kings and imagery of the Mass. Sometimes I look up and expect to see stained-glass windows on our classroom. Somewhere over our heads like a grail vision lurks a correct interpretation and a correct style to couch it in. We pick up the irony in the air before we comprehend what there is to be ironic about.

With our skins Dick and Bolognese and I perceive that if we accept, if we acquiesce, we will never create a new good thing out of our wasted heat; so in our corner we give battle. Dick struggles because he is given to trusting his own reactions and cannot be bent past a point close to his centers of appetite and strong Jewish family feeling: Bolognese and I because we feel ourselves in the service of a muse that is part art and part politics and part rebellion and part identity; we fear being wooed into the neat progressions and intricate small proprietary diversions of academia. Our best weapon is the wrong question. Our second-best weapon is bad manners. We make economic and biographical interpretations. We compare authors to others we've read in translation: heresy. We ask long questions and on occasion try to make speeches. We sulk and exchange notes.

Eight years later, paranoid hallucinations one dead summer in Detroit after he lost an editorial job. Bolognese's semiliterate parents sign the paper so that electroshock may burn the originality from that beautiful lizard brain. He calculates now for tenure at the small college in central Michigan where he teaches, where all his ingenuity goes into elaborate decoys to keep others from guessing the time spent in the state institution. Dick has settled with his family in San Diego, where he is doing quite well as a technical writer for the electronics industry. He has four bright and active children whose photographs he sends me every Rosh Hashonah in a card. The third, Fay, who calls herself after her nickname Feygele, is writing better poetry than her daddy ever did, but he does not like it because it is lesbian love poetry.

We want another university. Bolognese says we want a permanent Symposium, to be drunk on ideas. I am sitting in with them and Howie on Donaldson's class, auditing it, for this year he and Grimes have switched and he is doing the second half of American history. In that class we run before Donaldson like hunting dogs. We love him not because he is a good performer, for he is not. He goes off on side trips all by himself. He alludes to things he has never explained and never explains them. He puts charts on the board and charges on before we can copy them. He gets involved in questions from the floor and forgets to finish his lecture. But he speaks to us. He makes sense. As we copy his words we do not shut off our minds or shut out our lives. His view of mad autonomous corporations gobbling the riches of those with less fancy weapons is not a world we can live in: but we do not find our world one we can with conscience live in as we find it.

His classroom is not a gallery where we are invited to stand before one painting at a time, told what to see, asked for our cued responses, told to move on. Howie says Donaldson thinks the shortest way between two points is to fall down the stairs, but he comes, he listens, he rehashes the lecture with me afterward. Bolognese says Donaldson's lectures represent the collision of Marx and the Marx Brothers, but he never sleeps as he does in our other classes, head tilted so the light reflects off his glasses, skinny hands pressed prayerfully to his nose, propping his head up. I am a little in love with fiery Donaldson again. When I am around him, I always seem to be hot or cold, sweating or freezing. Sometimes when we of PAF become mired in long procedural haggling till I am bored with what I see as the need of the men to argue ritually with each other over all petty points, ego tintinnabulating against ego like toy rapiers, I sit and try to undress him, but I never manage. He is too tall and skinny. I find only bones. The last time his parents visited he shaved his beard to make peace with them and he is suddenly younger looking. It amuses me that a professor should have still to please his parents. That gorgeous face like a ship's prow lean and questing over a leather-covered skeleton. Yet if he touches my arm, I burn for half an hour.

Dick, Bolognese and I sit shoulder to shoulder again in writing class where discussions are carried on by all with the impetus of those duels from the Saturday swashbucklers of our childhood, the Errol Flynn costumed chases with swordplay from precipice to roof beam, turret to ledge with great style and sickening vertigo. Here the safe hierarchy of the literature classes dissolves like wet pasteboard. Is imitation virtue? If Wordsworth wrote this way about daffodils, why can't I? Who wrote the rules? Why can't pigs fly?

Here the bright boy scout who can run through the thorny interstices of Donne's imagery bearing aloft the torch of inquiry gets a thrill from bleating out lines like:

Truth is a holy temple fire,
A light to guide and to inspire,
Leading Mankind ever higher
Through pitfalls deep and straights most dire. . . .

O dreary backwaters and rabbitlands of home, I want to be killing the Grandfathers, I want to be going at Them with an ax to clear the road, and here sit Bolognese and I quivering to defend *The Love Song of J. Alfred Prufrock* as legitimate poetry.

The class is divided too into virgins and us. We sit in sweaty-palmed anonymity (anonymity tattering until in response to insult we rise naked in assertion, dripping expletives) while our sexual obsessions and accidents splash over the Puritan granite. I leave class damp with argument, hot with vexation, sore with ambition, wound to a pitch that could only achieve satisfaction in the instantaneous output of a six-volume Bildungsroman. Ugggggh! Ah there. Boxed to be sold.

Therefore I do not cut my classes to sleep, as I had imagined. When I finally trudge wearily back to our room, Donna sits at her desk toweling her hair dry. "Nobody noticed you stayed out all night," she says in a compressed voice.

"Hot dog."

"You were with . . . Peter? Or?"

"Of course." I smile. She smiles. I think of strangling her, thin neck in my hands, bones as light as those of a fish.

She stands oddly braced against the closet door. "Stu . . . there's something you may not know . . . I think."

"There's a lot I don't know, Donna." I use my street-kid voice and manner to hold her off.

"Something I did."

One more confession. I have had enough of them. She can keep it, pickle it, can it, eat it for breakfast. "I guess it'll stay that way, then. I cook tonight, so let me at that Spanish rice." I go past her and out.

I sit in the only comfortable chair watching, resting my sore muscles while Howie unpacks. His room is in a third-floor corner, part of it fitted into a tower. I am relaxed, easy in his presence, my arms and back pleasantly tired from moving him. "What happened to you yesterday? You weren't at Donaldson's lecture."

"Another operation on the old man." He stoops to the suitcase to gather an armful of socks. "If I was a medical student already, they'd give me the straight shit. Now I have to pussyfoot around while they sweet-talk us. Mother has to get it from them, because she's a nurse. It'd be a lot better if they told me and I figured out how to say it to her. She's coming apart at the seams."

"She's a lot younger than your father."

"She lost her own family. They make all these mother-in-law jokes, but my mother moved into a family and she calls my bobbishe 'mother' and means it. She was born in Germany and got out early . . . so my father and his mother mean everything to her. . . ."

Listening, I watch him. Good strong curve of back, broad shoulders. Light thick hair on his arms where his sleeves are rolled up. Twilight pours in through the semi-circle of tower windows, liquid, tangible, the color of lilacs. Spring thaw. Birds are screaming outside, excited at the longer twilight, the growing warmth. It's mud time. "So how is your father, really? The sixth operation. I can't imagine living through all that."

"Who can?" He shrugs. "He's dying and it takes a long time. That's what it amounts to. A lot of pain, for nothing."

"It's getting to you."

"Goddamn it, how could it not?"

"It's good for you to admit it. Mostly you won't."

"Oh, to you. Don't ask me about it in the Union. I have to keep things in their boxes. . . . I'm hungry. Could you look at the bag of stuff Bobbishe sent back with me? Maybe there's something you can heat up on the hot plate."

With a sigh I slide out of the chair and go look. "Kidney beans. I can make chili. My brother Francis taught me. I'll get some ground beef, an onion, some spices at the corner, and be back. Give me some money."

While I am cooking, the smell of the chili powder reminds me again of Francis. Last time I was in Detroit, a package had come for me from Mexico. Inside was a wooden box with cacti etched on the side. When I opened the sliding top, a toy rattlesnake swung up and bit me on the hand. He's always sending me things like that, when he remembers I exist. I'm permanently twelve years old in Francis' mind. The last letter I wrote to him came back. Leo is marrying again to what my mother calls a hillbilly singer who lives in a trailer. Mother says she has a big bosom but buck teeth. Leo always introduces his wives to Mother; Francis never brings his girlfriends home. Mother never likes Leo's wives until after he has left them, when she counts up their good points, commiserates with them by the hour on the telephone and oversees all her grandchildren zealously, explaining to their mothers how to raise them and buying them presents she can't afford.

"I ran into Peter Crecy in the Union yesterday." Howie does not turn around as he speaks, dumping his shaving supplies on the bureau top with a clatter. "Challenged me to a chess match. Of course he beat me again. Then he climbed on the board and crowed."

"Why play him? You knew he could beat you."

"I didn't consider my manhood at stake."

"What's eating you, buddy?"

He comes to stand by the couch, arms folded on his chest. "What do you mean?"

"The way you talk about him. Always by his full name. Always in that tone, as if holding him by tongs."

"He practically referred to you as his mistress."

I laugh. "Oh my! He was too cheap even to give me a birthday present." Then I see I have shocked him, that he did not believe Peter. My big mouth. Why should it matter? "I think maybe you still believe in bad girls and good girls."

"That clod. That fidgety little clod!" His hands twitch. "I don't believe it!"

"It's not an article of belief. I am not in the habit of clearing my lovers with my friends."

"Maybe you should," he growls. "That smug suburban fink." Sinking heavily in the dusty mohair easy chair. "Maybe you're right, anybody's better than nobody."

"I never said that!" I finish browning the chopped meat and onions and add them to the chili. I clear my throat. "Howie. Can I ask you something?"

"I've paid for it. And last year I had a girlfriend in New York, before everything fell in and they started cutting up my old man." He is being tough again.

"Paid for it?" Marcie comes to mind. I imagine her got up in her lurid cruising outfit flagging down Howie. I know how whores talk about johns. All johns are ugly.

He nods. "The first time. I was hanging around Woodward. She said ten dollars and I turned out my pockets. She settled for seven twenty-one and the lucky silver dollar Milt brought me from Reno."

"The first time?"

"And the second and the third and so on. I never knew I could have a girlfriend till last year."

"Do you miss her? Your girlfriend in New York?"

"Sure." He shrugs. "Not really. We had trouble talking. If we could find something we could talk about like a movie or something from class—I met her in chemistry— we'd beat it to death because after that there'd be this awful silence while I tried to think of something, football, the weather, anything to talk to her about."

That reminds me of being thirteen and trying to talk to boys. I know I have replaced Donna with Howie, as she has withdrawn from me. I cannot talk with Howie on the same wavelength of intimacy or honesty I could talk with Donna because he is after all not a woman. On the other hand we share a political life. If you asked me who my best friend is, for the first time since I left home I would not answer you, Donna. I would say, Howie. He is my best friend. I would never say, Peter. He is my lover now, but he is not my friend.

"You have no sense of reality." Peter shakes a stream of sugar into his coffee. "You think you can pile your neuroses in a closet and go waltzing around. You think you'll never have to work on yourself and deal with your problems."

"I don't think sitting in a room talking to some guy at health service is dealing with my problems. What do you really get out of therapy?" He goes to a guy in Detroit twice a week.

"Self-knowledge. Coping. Besides, therapy is just a stop-gap measure. Once I land a good job, I'm going into the real thing."

"Huh?" I am eating my chicken potpie, looking vainly for chicken among the potatoes, carrots, peas and gravy. Chicken potpie is memory food. It makes me think of traveling with my parents when I was little, since it was a dish I never got at home and often ordered in diners or those small-town restaurants called Martha's Home Cooking. *In civil rights and early writing days when I was poor I ate frozen chicken and frozen turkey and frozen beef pot-pies by the dozens. Those years are marked in potpie containers and the starchy contents in my stomach. Once I ate smelt for ten days because a vast bag of it was on sale, frozen, in a Chicago supermarket. But that's another fishy story. Peanut butter. A vast heap of spaghetti with a little dab of sauce.*

"I'm searching for a good analyst." He eyes me through his blond lashes. He looks forward to analysis much as I did to my first sex: it will be moving, awesome and change

his essence. "I want a good one. I'm prepared to buck
down for a long haul. That will be my real education."

"In what?"

"All we ever know: self. I'm ready for it." Then a fe
moments later he tells me, "You take yourself too se
ously. All those compensation mechanisms because you'
not fulfilling yourself as a woman. You refuse to wo
within your limitations."

"I know my physical limitations. If I have less than fo
hours' sleep, I concentrate badly. I know my body ca
betray me, by getting pregnant—"

"What? I thought you were using the diaphragm. Wh
is this?"

"Theoretically, Peter. I'm speaking theoretically." I u
the diaphragm with a passion equal to if not exceeding th
with which I enjoy sex.

"Because if you get yourself into that state, don't sta
hearing wedding bells. I know a good abortionist in D
troit."

"Do you? What's his name?" I take out my Spani
notebook and prepare to take down the name.

"What for? What's up?"

"Nothing, Peter, relax. It's just that somebody's alwa
needing the information." I don't exactly know why I a
ways write down that information, but I have started kee
ing names, approximate fees and instructions in the ba
of my Spanish notebook. There has to be someone wl
knows, I figure, and I am willing to be that woman.

"Where you ought to be going is to my man at heal
service. Landauer. That would do you wonders."

"I should go offer up my secrets to the enemy? I shou
say, You haven't got me yet, but here's my valuable gut
you'd like to do a better job on me next time? Besides
can't afford it, even with their sliding scale."

He calls me paranoid. When supper is over he pays t
cashier for his meal and walks out. "Peter, you forg
me."

"You can buy your own supper. Why should I pay a
the time? We aren't married yet."

"I wouldn't have eaten so much if I'd known I had to pay."

"Just out for what you can get, see?" He is only half kidding. Part of him believes everybody is out to take him. I am almost mad enough to stalk off. But what will happen if I do? He will pick up another girl and swindle her into bed. He will get laid, I will get none, and he will have the satisfaction of demonstrating he does not need me. Therefore I follow him. The trouble is I always do want to be fed. Whenever he takes me out I eat as much as I dare, making up for my missed meals. Hunger is a wind that blows through me most of the time. As I sharpen into life again, I am hungry for food, hungry for work, hungry for learning, hungry for love, hungry for sex, hungry for friendship. I experience my self as a clamorous need, a volume level of desire turned too high.

What holds me is the sense of Peter as a prisoner in the finely molded cage of bone that is his skull. What captures me is the elaborate game he constructs around me, traps and lures and attacks and feints and withdrawals. What brings me back to him is the sex, athletic, physically complicated but emotionally simple as a good workout. He is full of experiments. We are always laboring in strange yogic positions. He bites harder than I like, he uses his fists and elbows. It leaves me pleasantly used and with an interest in my body's health. My mind labels elements sadistic, elements masochistic, but I feel nonetheless perfectly safe.

If he would touch me before he came in, if he would eat me, I would come better, but he says wanting that shows I am sexually immature and stuck in the clitoral phase of development. If I was a real woman, he says, I would not need stimulation. He has learned that certain things you do in bed are healthy and certain things are forbidden because unhealthy under his Freudian code. I don't know who assigned all the point values but they have nothing to do with what feels good to me. He is also uncomfortably (for me) aware that I want sex oftener than he does. Though I try to be subtle in my expression of desire, he is quick to sense a source of power and at times he enjoys deferring

my pleasure more than taking his own. That too is interes
ing, so unlike Mike that I unlearn my barely formed ge
eralizations about male sexuality. I also learn more abo
my own. Wanting him more than he wants me makes n
aware of myself as actor, as agent, even if frustrated. Lyi
caressing him tonight wondering if we will or we won't,
think of Alberta who always talks about sex as somethin
men do to you. She is passionately active politically, pa
sionately passive sexually, I surmise from our late nig
conversations over the Wild Turkey.

Tonight we do. He is semiviolent, battering on me as
I were a door that could admit him to oblivion, a tunn
through which he could pass prick first to Somewhere Els
Relaxing afterward with his sleek-skinned neat boc
against me, his eggshell head sullen with pleasure at n
breast, I am moved for him and his inturned pain.

"I'm no good," he mutters. "I'll never be any good. F
anything. For anybody. There's something deeply crook
in me, all the way through. I'm a runt. That's what *he* us
to say. I'm shorter than he is. How can you be shorter th
your father? Every generation gets taller. *He's* five fe
eight. Gene, my brother, is five feet ten. I'm a throwback.
get lost in crowds. Nobody ever looks at me and thinks, I
must be brilliant. I've never had love at first sight. I do
deserve it, maybe. Then or ever. I've never had real lov
I've never been loved and I never will be loved . . . becau
there's something deeply wrong with me."

"Peter," I hold him like a petulant child, "you just ne
to open up. That's all. Reach out! Of course you can I
loved. Don't I love you?"

He snorts and sits up, staring at me with narrowed eye
"You what?"

I hadn't paid much attention to what I said; now I fe
stuck with it. So what? Loving is easy; it grows on fema
trees. Love comes up thick and abundant and ordinary
grass. You can love anybody if you want to. "I said I lo
you. I want you to feel better about yourself."

"I *knew* you could love me. I had that sense." He ru
his nose, almost glaring. "I knew you could! Ha. Then wh
can't you learn to play chess?"

"I can't put that much effort into a game. My mind wanders off to poems I'm working on or papers I'm writing," I say apologetically. "You have lots of people to play chess with."

"But we have to share more things. I have to develop you."

Like the fields populated in my childhood with pheasants and rabbits developed into dreary little tract houses, I think, but then I am pleased as I consider that is after all his way of caring. He is opening up, he is cracking open, my beautiful pastel egg.

A couple of mornings later as I am eating breakfast in the Union with Howie, I feel a cumulative dissatisfaction like an itch between my shoulder blades: intolerable to sit in the Union across the room from Mike three or four times a week and never speak. We are dawdling over our second cups of coffee when Mike takes a table, attended by Julie and Grant Stone.

With unkind heartiness Howie, who never drinks too much, asks, "Hung over?"

"In a sense. I was thinking about Mike." A knot of old emotions and an ongoing curiosity that is part concern. I feel as if I've become unauthentic in his presence; his gaze makes me an actor. "I haven't spoken with him in months."

"Not that long since you spoke *about* him."

I look at Howie's broad serious face on which the lines that will score the forehead are already faintly etched by his frown of worry. I know how often I think of Mike and how little by comparison I speak of him.

"Know what you do?" He persists as if poking a stick through bars at me, I think. "Use that rotten experience to protect yourself against anything really meaningful with a man."

"I hadn't noticed a line had formed." But I am staring across. Perhaps Howie is right and I make every man, every imagined coupling, stand in contrast to my myth of first and total love, secure in its wrapping of violence and tragedy from inner decay. I must make Mike into a person I can size up. "This is absurd. I'll say hello to him."

"He may not answer. Finish your coffee and let's go visit Bolognese, if he'll let us in. He has a new story."

"I want to know how Mike is." A little opposition gives me impetus. Mike watches me coming with a sly look that I'll bet is a bastard to maintain. I cross a tilted slab of stage, feeling too many eyes on me. I scramble through their gazes awkward as a damaged puppy, swaggering and recoiling at once. My notoriety is something I try to pretend I do not know about. I do not even know if I am supposed to be clown, menace, femme fatale, or culture hero-ine.

"Mistress Stuart, how's your boneyard friend?"

"Howie, you mean? Just fine. Hi, Julie. Hi, Grant."

Julie purses her lips looking hard at me. She cannot quite bring herself to smile.

"If he's doing jes' fine you must not be done picking his brains or his bones yet." Mike raises his left eyebrow in that old gesture. For almost two years his presence has maddened me. It is irritating that the beloved should continue to look and act as the beloved did, and no longer be loved. It is as if they persist in the old tricks in order to tease you for your credulity or to flog you for having failed in your loving. Mike seems a parody of himself, but I must force myself to see him now. His presence has solidified. He sits like a Chinese sage, the bones in his head and body not padded by the weight he has put on but confirmed. An ironic line already shaping his mouth, he looks more than a couple of years older than the man I loved. His clothes are new, a black Shetland pullover that sharpens his pallor, grey flannel pants that actually fit. The collar of the shirt that shows between outthrust chin and new sweater is not frayed. His hair is somewhat longer, tumbling over forehead and collar, that dark, dark brown just a shade lighter than mine.

I peer at Julie, who puts her hand quite deliberately over his on the carved wooden tabletop. Grant Stone, winking at me, puts his hand over Mike's other hand, but Julie is watching me and does not notice. Mike endures both passions with equanimity. In a slow drawl, his gaze beating into mine, he says, "I hear that your hero's risking his head. Or at least his chair."

It takes me a few minutes to understand he means Donaldson may be in trouble if we put on our HUAC farce. I do not bother to ask how he knows I sit in on Donaldson's class, because his acquaintances always spy on me and report back. "So, what are you doing this summer, Julie?" I ask ingenuously, making eye contact. "You're graduating, right?"

"We're not sure yet. Mike has been accepted to Yale but he didn't get a fellowship. We're thinking of going to graduate school here or at Northwestern. I'm accepted both places too."

What a married sounding *We*. No ring on that possessive hand. Mike looks into outer or inner space. Grant Stone says in Mae West style, "You ought to come up and see *me* sometime. I'm a broad-minded fellow and curious as hell. The world's my thing." He glances at Mike. "Don't mind him glowering. He treats everybody as his serf."

"*We*—and that is the royal WE—" Mike announces, glaring at his family left and right, "We may go off to Madagascar and eat fried monkeys. We may retire to a Tibetan lamasery. We may sign up as a lighthouse keeper. We may go off to Morocco and screw Arab boys. We may go off to Antarctica and screw ourselves. Aren't you bored, Jill? I think you look bored."

"That's just my morning expression." Howie is putting on his yellow oilskin slicker and I must hurry to catch him. "Hey, wait for me."

"My breakfast is not only eaten but digested. I got tired of being put in storage."

Have I pushed him too far? "Please don't be moody. You haven't the ego to do it like the master over there."

To my relief he turns back to me. "Arf."

"He says Donaldson is going to get fired because of our play."

"Arf!" Loudly. Several heads turn. "Arf arf!"

"Has rehearsing the play turned you cuckoo?"

"Making faithful dog noises. You're so easy to embarrass. I don't think Donaldson will be fired. McCarthy's fallen. The tide's turning. Two years ago, maybe. We're too late to be brave, kid." We hike off toward Bolognese. "They've won what they wanted—they broke the Left. Nothing remains but a few study groups and some folk-singers. Donaldson's too popular to be got rid of easily." Howie loves to sound cynical. I am not so sure.

TWENTY-FOUR
Le déjeuner sur l'herbe

A̲T̲ FIRST DONNA is pleased with her new lover
Charlie. He is twenty-four. ("A man ought to be a little
older, Stu, because boys our own age just don't know
enough to keep us interested. But I admit Sal was *too* much
older. He couldn't take me seriously.") Charlie is pleasant-
looking. His voice has some rough honey in it I can always
recognize when I answer the phone and he asks for her.
He dotes on her. Being a graduate student who works for
a sociologist, he has no money. In April he stole daffodils
from his professor's garden. In May he picks bouquets of
lilacs from the hedge outside the astronomy building, their
rich sexual fragrance dyeing the air in our room for a week
before they droop.

Tonight Donna sits painting on a face, with brushes,
pots, powders, unguents spread out in a semicircle. She
does her work slowly and with many wry grimaces. The
dollface she will create is much admired by men, but in
truth I prefer her scrubbed face with its albino pallor and
sharp bones. "You seeing Charlie?" I asked.

289

"Who else?" She shrugs in her plaid bathrobe. "Want to switch?"

"I grin. "Afraid not."

"You like *him* now, don't you? You're hooked."

"Good word—hooked. He's like a stainless-steel fish-hook in my gut. . . . Did you talk Wanda into switching rooms?" I try to sound indifferent. Every day I expect Donna to move.

"I decided I couldn't take her roommate Billy Sue."

"Are you sorry you moved into this house?"

"It's cheaper than the dorm and a lot looser. But who wants to live with a bunch of females?"

"Jesus, Donna, I sure wouldn't want to live with four-teen men. They'd all leave the toilet seat up and expect you to pick their socks off the floor."

"Men—not boys—men have something to offer—in fact, the world. If you want to learn anything, you have to learn it from a man," she says sententiously, beginning to brush on mascara.

It's certainly true that the only woman who has taught us at the university was in Romance languages. "But you don't think we've given each other a lot? And what are you learning from Charlie?"

"Sadism." She snorts and then swings around straddling her chair to face me with a sudden sharp giggle.

"He's sadistic?"

"No, silly. He's a spaniel. I swear I've got the worst of Lennie again—that guilt. Except that Charlie isn't as good at making me writhe with it. . . . Is that the choice, Stu? A choice between letting a man use you like a tube of tooth-paste, or using him?" She looks rakish with one of her eyes mascaraed in rusty brown and the other lashed invisibly blond.

"I guess I want to know if loving has to be fatal. Can you love somebody only a little and survive fine, but if you both really love each other, then he tries to bash you into the ground?"

She sighs. "*La belle dame sans merci* is fine if you're the pale knight interestingly loitering or littering your bloody hillside. But it's a bone-crushing bore being *la belle dame*. You just sit there sneering all day and working in your bitchy little touches. It's an art form but a limited one, like decoupage or pasting shells on lampshades."

"The knight is even more boring. Suffering is overrated as an exercise program for the soul. I wasn't human for a year after Mike."

She nods, smiling crookedly. "But isn't Peter sadistic, a bit? I sense that . . . tang in him."

"He tries." If I loved him the way I loved Mike, I would be in deep trouble; he would tear me into little pieces. But I love him only as much as is proper: more than he cares for me but with a clear sense of how he fits into the fervent chaos of my life. One at a time he jabs his finger into my piddly fears and childhood muddles and pus-filled vanities. He wants to defeat me and possess me. He wants to prove himself right and me wrong. I could warn him that bed is a poor place for arguing with me. I walk away from him into the war of attitudes in my classes, into hard argument with Bolognese and Dick and Howie, into the grimy fiddling of my various jobs, into my endless rebudgeting and borrowing and paying back and cadging meals. When I think of him, it is in brief sexual images like a muscle spasm.

The composite flower of the house absorbs me. When I have half an hour I sit in the kitchen spreading my net of curiosity and talk hard to whoever walks in: the Thai physics student we call Sally, with her mind glinting from its sharp edges like an industrial diamond and her little laugh with her hand coyly across her mouth; fat Wanda, the house clown and arbitrator; Billy Sue, who ran away from a stepfather who raped her only to find misery with a truck driver. Now she works her way through ed school. I am drawn to her because she reminds me of Callie, but she combines Sunday piety with anti-Semitism she has learned to deny but can't resist showing. Lynn is a hearty big-voiced folksinger, one of those women in whom I catch appealing glimpses of the independent tomboy of eleven or twelve, at that age when a strong girl is still a physical match for a boy. She falls in love and unrequited misery with charismatic men—including Donaldson and Rob Prewitt.

I hear them often playing and singing a couple of nights a week in the living room: Alberta, Lynn and sometimes Rob Prewitt, who drops by with or without his girlfriend Stephanie, who is thinking of moving in next fall. *When I hear Beatles songs I date events of the sixties. Rock music calls up a summer, a party, a friend, a trip cross-country, a political era. Folk songs are pegged to the fifties. Alberta, who has not touched a banjo in fifteen years and whose youngest son is drummer in a punk band called Toxic Shock, would be astonished if she knew how often it is her voice I hear singing the blues or old ballads:*

> Hangs-a-man, Hangs-a-man,
> Slack your rope awhile.
> Think I see my father coming,
> Riding many a mile.
>
> Oh father have you brought me gold
> Or have you paid my fee?
> Or have you come to see me hanging,
> Hanging on the gallow's tree.
>
> No, I have not brought you gold.
> I have not paid your fee.
> Yes, I have come to see you hanging,
> Hanging on the gallow's tree.

Then the mother comes and she's coming to see the hanging too, and the brother and so on. Then finally the true love comes, and he's got the money to buy her off so she won't hang. I sang that song along with them with conviction till the last verse when I'd kind of peter out. Surely I had believed True Love would save you from your family, but that hadn't exactly panned out. In my world if a female friend didn't manage to scrape up the money somewhere, you hung and everybody applauded. The only saving factor in the grim exigencies of dating and mating was the feeble conspiracies of women who would pity each other at least briefly.

The house is noisy enough so that if I didn't keep late hours I would have trouble writing papers or poems, but it provides me with automatic intimacy. In any moment of despair or loneliness, I can find someone whose conversation, whose presence and peculiar song of self will draw me outward and ease that central ache I can label, sometimes ignore but never quite cure.

"It belonged to Everett Carmichael," Peter explains. At my blank stare, he does his equivalent of throwing up his hands: his delicate lids quiver. "My noble savage. I can't decide if it's annoying or refreshing trying to talk to someone who can't read the social map."

"So who was Everett Carmichael?" Maybe the moose whose head eyes us. I thought only in cartoons did people have animal heads mounted on their walls. My uncle Floyd who used to hunt in the mine-hollowed mountains around Cold Springs had a freezer full of venison by mid-December but never a head or antlers.

"He held one of the patents on the vacuum cleaner. But that doesn't say who he was. The symphony was his passion. That was one reason why it was decent when we were growing up."

"They used to take us from grade school," I remember suddenly. "To the Masonic Temple. They'd play Saint-Saëns *Carnival of the Animals* and talk about the woodwinds and the percussion. I loved it. It was sumptuous sitting in the dark. . . ." Peter has stopped listening. "So how come you can use this guy's house?"

"It *was* his hunting lodge. Now it's my uncle's but they hardly use it. It is a little . . . overblown."

It actually reminds me of a small wooden church with its high ceiling and the gallery around the top. Up there are cubbyhole-sized bedrooms but they're too drafty. We're sleeping downstairs, near the wood stove and the view of the broad wind-ruffled lake. From the obviously modern glass wall at the lake end of the living room, you could almost believe this is still wilderness; but when we take out the little sailboat he calls a catboat, we can see other cabins tucked among the pines. Still the lake is hardly what I'd call crowded, even for Memorial Day weekend, although yesterday some water skiers were out with two motorboats late in the afternoon.

I am not sure whether we're supposed to be here or not, because Peter creates an aura of forbidding me to ask. We stopped at a real-estate office in a nearby town. Leaving me in the car, he walked in and got the key. The people there, Peter said, see to the maintenance of the old house. Peter had called ahead and the water was turned on, the refrigerator running. It was magical to arrive at six o'clock with our supermarket groceries at a house in the woods at the end of a long bumpy and arbitrarily winding road and find the lights on and the house humming to itself, sitting there under its gingerbread. I expected a witch or the three bears. Instead all those old dead heads regard us, elks and stags with mournful glass eyes and a solitary bear with a leathery mouth open on mean teeth, little pig eyes still contemplating its murderer's just desserts.

Now we lie in bed trying to provoke each other to rise first into the cold that leaks through the wooden walls and rises from the stone floor. Finally I make a deal with him that I will start breakfast if he will light the fire, gone out during the night. In a lean-to against the north wall, neatly piled logs in very short lengths reach to the ceiling. Somebody cut it. I would lay a bet it was not his uncle.

Peter kneels in front of the green enamel Jotul stove with its bas-relief of a naked woman being serenaded by a man in bohemian attire who strums a guitar. The stove is pretty but the picture bothers me. Why is she naked? Why isn't he naked? She will get covered with mosquito bites. If it's cool enough for him to be comfortable in his ample garments, she must have gooseflesh and tomorrow a cold. What is he singing to her? Eskimo immolation songs for isolating old ladies on ice floes? Peter and I have never before shacked up together. He has the disconcerting habit of tweaking or grabbing parts of my body at random moments that makes me feel clumsy and overripe, like a dish of fruit in the middle of a dinner table.

I shiver over eggs sputtering in the iron skillet, the thick Canadian bacon he likes that is new to me. He assumes I know how to cook. My cooking to date has consisted of opening cans of sardines or scrambling eggs when my parents were away or when my working caused me to miss my father's mealtimes, and the simple preparations at the co-op, following instructions and easy recipes from our house steward. Peter makes precise requests and I supply imprecise results. He knows exactly what he wants to appear on his brown quail china plate—bacon crisp but not burnt; eggs thickened to the texture of good hollandaise sauce; toast caramel brown; coffee black and sweet—but I know neither what he means, being unused to fine distinctions in food, nor how to produce what he wants inside the massive frying pan.

Then wrapped in sweaters against the early morning chill we take scraps of toast to the dock, coaxing minnows from among the fronds of waterweed. White froth touches our shoes as the wavelets lap in and I toss crumbs to the fish.

As the day warms we drop layers of clothing and take out the catboat. I scramble to obey him, confused but game. It is odd to be out on a field of water with so much water under us, making me feel entirely out of place and elated. We skim and turn and skid over and execute maneuvers he devises while I feel like part of a sea gull. Then at last he is content to drift gently before the breeze. I dabble my hand over the side to feel the tug of the water. Smoky green reeds poke from a submerged sandbar. Near shore I can see the rippled bottom. The sky floats milky over us. How have I touched him? Flat blue eyes, thin nose with pinched nostrils, supple mouth, exquisite hands pared and functional as the design of suspension bridges. Each body I love has its own aesthetic, I am discovering, its own proper scale and metaphors, its fruit and flower and mineral and seasonal imagery.

Under the suddenly full leaves of late May we walk around the lake among greens that look freshly painted, the colors still not dry. He carries field glasses, his light meter, lenses and camera. He poses me against the bole of a tree, lying in the grass, kneeling by a brown and piny brook. The air is clear. That we hear voices across the water now and then or see the two motorboats with the water skiers darting behind only sharpens our privacy. Eating regularly and sleeping long nights make me feel fresh as the lake. We toast marshmallows in the stove and once again he orders me to play chess with him.

"We're a sex machine," he says with that throttled laugh. And, "From the back your body looks like a boy's." He enters my vagina from behind. That excites him. "Boy in back and girl in front—you're a frigging hermaphrodite."

Later my head rests on his abdomen as he strokes my hair, but when I bend to kiss him on his half-erect prick, his hand on my nape squeezes hard to stop me. "That's too personal." The word lodges like a splinter in my chest.

Afternoon. Rain hits the wind-ruffled lake. He has spread out his photographic gear on the table. As he cleans his lenses he whistles a Telemann air for flute. I keep wanting to hear the flute instead. I go upstairs to get away, installing myself in a monastic cube of bedroom that faces the water. I say to myself, Today I will work. Something not him to save me from despair.

Is he a void I try to fill?

Is he a need I try to answer?

Your back sleek and sealed against my
begging fingers   groping fingers   hungering fingers
sealed.   ice smooth   coiled porcupine

A pebble takes warmth from the tongue.

A pebble sucks warmth from the tongue.   Too active.

A pebble warms on the tongue
but cannot feed me. I return
it to the beach where it lies cold.

I shudder. Well, that's one view of our relationship. But Peter is no rock—too active, manipulating, prodding, poking, setting up minidramas. Through money he controls our environment. No, my poem is neat self-aggrandizement. I am warm and he is cold. I am open and he is shut. Ah, the couple on the stove. I am naked, vulnerable, supine. He is clothed, protected, upright.

We dance together, naked woman
and man in full armor, clanking.
When he presses me tight to his
bosom, mine is impaled
on a protective spike. If
you love me you'll kiss me
he says and knocks out my teeth.
If you love me you'll save
me from this imprisonment he
says as he fits a new point
to his lance and climbs
on his horse and charges. You
didn't really love me
he mutters to my corpse;
that's why I'm still locked
in here. Oh, the love
of women is weak. It sure
is my blood sings like gnats
in the evening as he
goes clanking off.

I feel like calling it "Man in a Can," but I know better than to be flip. I can't bring it to class anyhow. It isn't in stanzas or regular meter and has no neat literary references and no ambiguity at all.

My inky palm. Wind scuds the rain over the lake in waves over breaking waves. Peter as abstraction and Peter tinkering with his equipment. Work is a room where every object has a significant place, a room where I can have what I want or at least name what I have and name what I want. Without work I am too small. My writing justifies me: what am I doing here? Writing two poems. All is not waste. I am the alchemist, turning leaden failure into golden work. Even as I wrote that of him in a moment of recoil, I believe that trapped in him is a man struggling to reach the air. If I didn't expect from moment to moment that man to break through, I would not be here beside this northern lake.

How can these people, his uncle, leave such a pretty house to itself? Unlike the summer cottages my parents used to rent from ads in the papers for my father's two-week vacations, this house is not furnished with battered mismatched pieces. Even the dishes are good china. How can they just leave good things here in the woods? How come they don't bother being here?

"They don't use this place much anymore," Peter explains as we curl up on the leather sofa by the stove. "It used to be nice, but it's a bit spoiled." He gestures at the lake where the sun is setting behind the far woods.

Spoiled. I think of the treat it was for us if we got to rent a cabin in a row of cabins, three rooms and an extra cot on the porch. A rowboat was a big deal. Now his uncle has a house in St. Thomas. That's in the Virgin Islands, Peter explains. They go there in the winter. In the summer they prefer Maine. I could stay here, I fantasize. Just stay here, with this house around me alone in all this space and I'd write and write. Would I be scared alone in the woods? I have no idea; I've never been allowed to find out. Imagine, to have places you can go off by yourself and be alone in a pleasant comfortable space. I catch a glimpse of the fact that Peter has brought me here because nobody in the family cares about this place; they are holding on to it as an investment when the land will be developed. Yet what is rustic to him is one of my first glimpses of what I would call luxury. All my life I have been crowded for space. Wedged in, jammed together, smelling and hearing each other. The silence of this place enters me through my ears and gives me enormous mental space to fill with words. What a privilege to enter this green world full of other creatures whom people have given names I do not know, neither the labels nor the furred, feathered or needled and labels call to mind, making precise what I see as quick blurs.

Sun tints the morning to a painted egg. Rippled straw-colored sand. Filmy jade weeds. Silver in the weathered boards of the dock where I sit on a pier. On the rim of my vision he squints through his camera. "Look to the left and up. A little more." I stare at a boathouse, a low uninteresting building. I try to look interested. He says, "I see things you don't see yourself. Things others can't see. I'm going to prove they exist." Touching me through the lens.

Now he has me wade into the water with my jeans rolled up, water so cold my bones wail. He poses me against the same pier with my hands behind me. "I used to be interested in textures," he mutters. "The way a fly would see a book or an apple. But now I'm photographing dreams." He uses the word a lot. This morning at breakfast he cradled his hot mug against his cheek, telling me, "I've got to get my dreams straight."

Standing up to my knees in ice water assuming a posture of bondage and feeling like a fool—parody of a fashion model, with my sweater pulled tight against my breasts and my back all goose pimples—I say, "What did you mean about getting your dreams straight?" Conversation turns me from object into agent again.

"It's time. It's that or die inside, like my sister, like my brother. Are you going to help?"

At first I think he means his nightmares. In sleep he grinds his teeth, mutters curses, rolls from side to side struggling.

His hands move on his forehead soothing. The camera hangs like an outsized necklace. "I talk crooked and expect you to hear straight. But I make sense, if you'd listen!" He turns abruptly and stalks away, leaving me to scramble out, my teeth chattering. "Know what the old man said when I told him I wasn't going to the traditional clan picnic? If you take another of your joyrides, don't expect me to bail you out. You'd think I was a playboy! That's how he talks to me. I racked up a car once when I was seventeen, and he's still counting the pennies."

"You have to leave home. You never really have. Even going to Michigan, you're within striking distance. Don't take the job in Detroit, if you don't get the one in Brookhaven. Go to California."

"You're right—you see it! Yeah, my brother thinks he's such a big man because he does a bad imitation of what my father turns out. My sister lives a mile away. We're an old Michigan family, they say. Here long before the Fords —the salt Fords, they're older than the Henry Fords. Yeah, I say, we were here a long time, a bunch of drunken French trappers cheating the Indians out of their furs and drinking bad rum and knocking up squaws. That bugs them. . . . You want to live on Long Island?"

"What's it like? I've never even been to New York City."

"We ought to go together. We will!"

"Will we?" I hardly dare believe but wish he means it.

"Scarface never lies, baby. My word is good as a bond. A tax-free municipal bond." He is pleased with me. Gradually he has been loosening. We are making it a lot, for us; he is talking a lot. Sometimes he even embraces me when we are not in bed. "We'll go this summer. If I get the job, you can come see me for long weekends."

The knot is hard and green . . . *is* too weak

I write upstairs.

> The knot tucks itself there
> hard and green. If you grow
> impatient and slice into it
> you expose an intricacy
> that rots fast. But if you wait
> the sun opens it slowly
> one petal at a time among
> its thorns, my yellow rose.

During supper he begins to close on himself a little. As I clear the dishes he takes his narrow head in his hands. "I'm getting a headache." He slumps forward. I stand behind him massaging his temples as I have learned to do. "More . . . more . . . there."

At last he mutters, "Better. I'm a sick man. Will you

bury me with soft hands? Hey, baby, want me to tell you a story?"

"I'm listening." We sit on cushions in front of the wood stove. Glinting dully the eyes of the decapitated watch us.

"I saw a sleazy movie on TV last time I was home. Pepe le Moko is the big cheese in the Casbah, where he's got everything—almost—that he needs. The cops can't touch him. He's safe inside. But he falls for a broad from the outside. The cops send her away. To get her back, he has to leave his walls. The cops get him. End of Pepe."

"Who are the cops? Your father?"

"No, the same as Pepe and the girl." He rubs his forehead slowly. "Say the supplies are running out inside the Casbah and the walls are growing higher. All the time."

"Suppose she didn't run."

"She has to. She can't survive inside his walls."

"He doesn't need his walls with her. She won't hurt him. She isn't anybody's cops."

He laughs.

"All she wants is to pass in and out freely! All she wants is for him to come out when he wants to. All she wants is to love him!"

"We'll see." He smiles at my vehemence. "We'll see. We'll take things as they come." His lucid gaze lifts to my face. "Go see if there's any scotch in the cabinet. My headache's gone. Or if they left any cognac. That would be too much luck."

Sunday night I return well pleased with Peter and myself. See, I have opened my frog and a prince is stepping out. The images that flood my mind when I think of Peter are moving and gentle: his face stripped of mask, showing emotion, half fearful, half tender.

Our door is shut, and when I try to open it, I find it bolted from the inside. Donna can't be fucking somebody right in the house? But the opening door frames her in her old plaid bathrobe, hair damp from the shower clinging to her fragile skull. Her scrubbed face crinkles with excitement. She comes very close to me, crossing a boundary of physical contact that has existed since she told me she wanted to be free of me. "Shut it quick," she whispers.

"Are you hiding?"

"If you don't want her around, I'll try to get someone to take her."

I look around. "Who?"

"Shhh." She pads barefoot to her closet.

I look over her shoulder. Curled on Donna's blanket a young cat lies washing its matted black coat, plainly pregnant and starved to the bone. The cat raises her triangular head from her raw side. Her ears flatten. Her yellow eyes wait on me. "Hello. Where did you get her?"

"In the alley by Campus Drugs. I was walking off a depression. Wasn't easy making friends." She shows me her scored arm.

"Did you break up with Charlie?"

"Yes. I can't do it. I have to be alone for a while. I have to get a sense of myself back. . . . Poor girl." She kneels to stroke the bony head gingerly. "You can see she had a home till they kicked her out—how clean she tries to be."

The cat leans to her hand but watches me warily always. I get down on my haunches and blink my eyes, averting my gaze like a cat. "Welcome, new roommate. Can we get away with it?"

"There'll be a house meeting about it," Donna says grimly. "You could try to line up votes, you're good at that. I hate people! They get a cat and they don't want to pay to have it spayed so it gets pregnant—of course—and then they punish it by throwing it out to starve to death. Female sexuality bugs people. We're supposed to produce babies on request and not otherwise and orgasms on request and only in both cases with our proper wedded husbands."

I advance my hand to be sniffed. I smell interesting, like the lake and the woods and the cabin. And sex. "Poor body. What'll we name her?"

"Don't be sentimental." Donna reties her robe firmly. "Cats don't have names. Or if they do, we don't speak the language any more than you or I can pronounce Sally's real Thai name. Doesn't she have nice lines?"

"And so many. Dig those vertebrae. Count those ribs."

"So we keep her?"

"Till you move out," I say, wary myself like the cat.

She stands before me, emphasizing the awkwardness by putting her weight on one foot, holding the other ankle up behind her to grasp. "I know I've been dreadful. I hate how I've been. I want to stop. Don't leave me just when I'm reforming."

Our gazes push away like opposing magnets. "Am I leaving?"

"It's just that my A's never felt as big as your A's. Except for Sal, and then it turned out he was just using me, my men are never as interesting as your men. As soon as something belongs to me, I begin to disrespect it. I began to disrespect you because you loved me. But I want to stop!"

I lean on my braced hands. "I want us to be close again."

"So do I, Stu." Her hands clasp themselves behind her back. "I want us to stay together."

I squeeze my wrist. Pulse, a slow fountain of hope. "I'll keep my stuff neater. And I'll cut down on the drinking. You learn out of books and movies that's what you're supposed to do when you're a writer. I think I'm over the brunt of my bang-up. Really."

"Take me back, Stu?"

"Who said you'd gone anyplace?"

But she had. She had. We name the cat Eurydice. You bet your next rent payment I'm not going to spoil anything by taking a sharp look backward, to hell where we've just been.

TWENTY-FIVE

Game Called on Account of Pain

HOWIE LEAPS ON the table, dressed in a checkered business suit stuffed to make him rotund. He belts out his big song in a surprisingly decent baritone:

"I am the judge.
I am the jury.
Kiss my behind
Or you'll feel my fury!

We got subpoenas.
Immunity too.
You can't touch us
While we cream you."

Donaldson and Rob Prewitt play the other HU-WHACK members. Bolognese enacts a stool pigeon, Dick and Alberta, the witnesses. I play the dormouse member of HU-WHACK. I fall asleep and slide out of my chair and tip over the papers. Every so often I wake up ostentatiously and shout, "Hold the witness in contempt. Hold everybody in contempt. Hang 'em all." It has been unanimously agreed that under no circumstances do I sing. Donna plays

304

the committee's secretary, a part created for Stephanie that requires only that Donna undulate around in a tight skirt showing her legs whenever possible. Stephanie and Rob broke up. Rob has been flirting with Donna, but she is not interested. Alberta has a way of watching Donaldson when he is not looking at her. The person who watches Alberta is Howie. He sings:

"I call up the teachers,
I call up the hams.
From lions they turn
into little white lambs.
Baaaa! Baaaa! Baaaa! Baaaaa! Humbug."

We have a full house for our decidedly amateur production. Basically the daring of attacking HUAC would produce laughs even if we weren't funny we are breaking a taboo. It's hot in here under the lights in my dormouse papier-mâché head. Now Donaldson, in his ordinary clothes skinny as death but improbably handsome, sidles up to Alberta to sing:

"Oh tell me now in forty-two
Did you sign a petition I'm asking you?"

How can he not love her? Wearing a sort of red girl scout uniform with shorts, she looks healthy, radiant, strong enough to fight at a barricade and carry him off to safety, if necessary. She sings:

"How can I recall, Representative dear.
I was nine years old, that very year."

Donaldson: he is thin as Bolognese who stands near him on the stage, whispering in his ear like Iago but altogether lacking his magnetic presence. Donaldson is tall and negligently tweedy. His quintessential outfit is a good Harris Tweed sports jacket worn with a flannel shirt and chinos. Women want to tidy him up. Bolognese is ageless; Donaldson at thirty-four (Alberta told me his age) is boyish.

Since he shaved off his beard, he seems closer to us. I guess that's why he grew it. He sings:

"There are Commies of ten,
premature anti-Fascists of six,
dwarfs, midgets and trolls:
we know their tricks.

There are babies today
agitating in bed
whose bottoms are pink
and faces, red!"

Alberta pirouettes. She has enormous stage presence. That surprises me, but then she is a folksinger and lacks only her banjo.

"Oh, I was a red diaper baby.
I even had a Paul Robeson doll.
Now you think I will squeal on my parents,
But blood is much thicker than gall!"

They generate electricity, this used-to-be couple. How could he prefer anyone to her? Alberta is plain good. She's bright and political and caring. If ever I saw a wife going to waste, that's Alberta. She even takes care of me, but she's her daddy's girl and she loves only daddies. When I'm sick she makes me tea with much lemon and a dash of bourbon so I sweat out my fever. She gives me vitamin pills and sometimes a scarf or necklace she has grown tired of. I adore being taken care of by Alberta, and I bet he did too. I think she will make a great lawyer.

Donaldson appears all head. His long lean body calls no attention to itself, but is only a stand to hang his leonine head on, the large eyes fixed on infinity. He slumps there like an outsized right parenthesis, yet he too radiates energy, not physical like Alberta's but intellectual. In droves we fall for his brilliance, but can you bed down with intellect? Alberta is not a profoundly sexual woman. Being in love is everything for her, rare and absolute, and sex comes along like an awkward wagon dragging behind.

The curtains close and as the audience begins to clap I step out, waving them to momentary silence. "Dear friends," I cry, "if you think this was a farce, you are dead right. Let's laugh it off the face of our country." I bow, the curtains part and the cast all come forward. We are a big hit.

Applause, you can get drunk on it and then it's gone at once while I stand backstage waiting my turn for the little dressing room so I can climb out of the dormouse pelt (left from a production of *Peter and the Wolf*) and the papier-mâché head Alberta made, that I plan to hang on my wall. Howie is ebullient. He bounds up to Alberta to hug her awkwardly. I bet he's been plotting all night to do that. "You were great!"

"We were all not half bad," she says mildly, disengaging herself. "Let's hear it for the writers!"

"We had a full house." Dick, our treasurer, speaks happily. "We made our expenses back and we'll finish out the year with a little extra in the kitty for the first time ever."

At the party Donna stays close to me and does not pick anyone up. Peter is off in New York on a job interview. It is not that I do not miss him, but suddenly I have a lot more time this weekend. Relationships do eat up the hours. Donna enjoyed being in the play, even as an afterthought. She has been studying hard for finals already. Charlie calls her every day. I hear the conversations when I can't avoid it. Sometimes she brings the phone into our room on its long cord.

All the conversations are variations on his asking, "But why won't you see me any longer?" She says, "But I don't love you." He says, "But you didn't love me before and you slept with me anyhow." She, "That was a problem." He, "You'll come to love me. Because I love you." She, "Charlie, you don't even know me. I never acted natural with you. I don't know if I'm capable of loving anyone. Go find yourself someone better than me. It won't be hard."

This nub end of the school year I feel happy. Donna, Peter, Howie, my writing, my classes, my jobs, my political activity: all the golden balls float in the June light like perfect clouds. I am a juggler who has finally mastered

her best trick. I am happy in my love for Donna which I
call sisterly and in my love for Howie which I call brotherly
and in my love for Peter which I call sexual and nurturing.
I am even happy in my growing fondness for Minouska,
who was named Eurydice, a name she refuses. She comes
to Minouska, one of my grandma's pet names for me.
She stands beside my desk chair mewing plaintively, requir-
ing me to pat my thigh six times repeating her name before she will sail up and land, belly dragging, and turn
three, four times to curl up right over my cunt purring.

Obviously, I have helped Peter. He is more human, more
open. He will take a job in New York, where I may go
after I graduate in a year. In the meantime we can see each
other vacations. We have a kind of grace together now, not
the all-consuming relationship Mike was, but a model of
how it should be for a mature adult, I tell myself.

When I am happy and when I am unhappy I draw
people. When I am ordinarily involved and working and
solving or failing problems, I am or seem less accessible.
When I am opened liked an oyster to the tides of grief or
when I open myself to the rich flood of joy, people come to
me. Tonight whenever I turn from Donna who stays close,
Donaldson is beside me. He is looking at me a lot as
Alberta looks at him and Howie looks at her.

I begin to drink heavily for the first time since Donna
and I reconciled. I feel as if the will and the pain of the
people in the room push on me, closing in like falling
furniture, something so tangible that the air thickens with
fears and wishes. I loathe this feeling of being skinless and
peeled to others' needs.

Why should the misfortunes of love and sexuality seem
like a vast metaphysical disease to me, as if I saw deep
cracks in things and under this ordinary badly furnished
room of Dick and Carole Weisbuch, the terrors of outer
space at the temperature of absolute zero yawn?

"Heavens, that dress must be made of iron. You've had
it since I met you," Julie says. She has materialized before
me in a shirtdress of pale green silk.

My gaze slides past her to scan the room. Finally I have
to ask, "How are you? . . . Is Mike with you?"

"Mike is off at Yale for the weekend, whither his family is sending him in the fall. To get him away from me." She sounds almost proud, but adds with immediate brute justice, "Of course he didn't have to go."

"Maybe he felt he did," I offer. Relief stuns me. Not to run into him ever again. "He feels very obligated to them."

"He didn't feel very obligated to me. . . . He complained I'm too inhibited in bed. You were a virgin, weren't you? I don't know what the difference could be."

"I have no idea." I suppress an urge to giggle. Can we be having this conversation? But Julie has always been completely open about sex, as if anything that happens to her has to be a shared joke.

"I don't think he ever really fell in love with me. I don't know why. He loved *you*, after all. It seems to me he could have loved me if he'd wanted to. After all, I could talk to him about his work and I can read all the languages he can. I would have helped him in his work; I would have loved that."

"Maybe it'll work out still. Once he's through school."

"Mike? I'm sure he has somebody else already." She points. "I have a new boyfriend. Carl Forbes. He's from Chagrin Falls and my father's gotten him a job already in the accounting section at the General Motors offices in Newtown."

I follow her finger. The guy is tall, ruddily handsome and vaguely familiar. I wonder if he was in one of my classes. Accounting? Maybe a lecture. "That's wonderful," I say. "Are you serious about him?"

"Jill! Are you drunk? Look at my finger."

All that pointing. Oh. A chunky diamond on a white gold ring. "But you just broke up with Mike?" Did I fall into a time warp?

"He's more my speed, I think. He's *very* experienced with women but he's not too bright. In some ways that's a winning combination. He knows he's foundering. . . . Jill, everybody makes jokes about women getting the senior jitters, but I discovered some men get it. Graduating can scare them too. I've done all right." Observing him growing a little too animated over Donna, she heads for him.

Although when Donaldson casually puts his hand on my arm—and touching for him is never casual—my arm glows like a lightning bug with a cool yearning flame, I cannot look back into his hazel eyes under those auburn curls. I pretend I do not understand. I pretend I do not notice. I cannot hurt Alberta. Although I am so fascinated by him I would like to follow him home like a puppy dog, I ignore all signals. Stupidity covers me like a bird whose owner has thrown a blanket over its cage. Nothing must happen, I mutter in my head and laugh too loud and drink too much. Nothing will happen!

Nothing does. Except when I am standing by Julie and her new boyfriend, Carl, he puts his hand on her ass and murmurs, "Baby, women are made for love." I recognize him then. My first college date.

Peter returns from his interview at Brookhaven sour and depressed. He has not been turned down but he has not been hired. Essentially he has been told maybe, by and by. The job offer in Detroit is industrial. Boring, he says. Detroit Edison is planning a fancy new breeder reactor near Monroe, to be named for Enrico Fermi, one of Peter's heroes, but he still does not want to work in industry or in Detroit. He views himself as defeated. In his new job he will start at more money than my father ever saw, but I know how little that salary seems to Peter, who has no experience at living within any means he provides himself and for whom almost anything he can earn as a physicist must seem minimal. Since the psychoanalyst of his choice is on Long Island, he must put off entering analysis too. I am ready to comfort him but confused. I was keyed up to say good-bye. I was set to endure having his slender hard body wrenched from me and only the cold comfort of letters and occasional phone calls.

Now I am reprieved. I feel a muggy mixture of delight and resentment as summer school gets under way. The truth is I arranged my summer to comfort me for his loss and made a number of commitments and arrangements that depend on my having more time than I am likely to with Peter in Detroit. On the other hand, we have been doing much better. My angel clam has opened to me, so why stop when I'm making progress? He moved out of his dark comfortable room in June and is now living with his parents while he hunts for an apartment.

The weekend after July 4 he takes me home for the first time. I am geared up to meet his parents, a stomachache all the way in the Sprite, but it turns out he has an apartment of his own in the sprawling multileveled family enclave. We climb a fight of steps to a second-floor door on its own little terrace. Peter has a large living room with a view out the far end to the lake, St. Clair—littlest of the Great Lakes chain but quite big enough. You can't see Canada across it.

When we came across the border from Detroit to Grosse Pointe Woods, the world changed. My city is a Black city. This is a white world, to an even greater degree than Ann Arbor, which after all has the old Black neighborhood around Detroit Street sloping toward the river and a smattering of Asian and Black students. But here the only Blacks I see are maids getting off work for the day, dragging their tired feet down to the bus stop. The Grosse Pointe suburbs are fancy, but in spite of the big trees, no greener than the city. In Detroit lush wild jungles sprout on any vacant lot in the slums. Here in fact nature is under strict control; armies of gardeners prune the hedges and lop back the trees and uproot the hardy weeds for expanses of flat lawn glinting under sprinklers. The houses seem to be vying in grandeur, pretension and size. Even the small lots sprout enormous houses.

In Grosse Pointe proper, a few blocks only, the streets wander down to the water where the biggest houses of all preen themselves before their view. But in Grosse Pointe Shores, the lake lies across a busy street from the houses and is almost inaccessible, marked with signs that forbid parking, stopping, swimming, fishing and would dearly like to forbid you looking. The signs proclaim all these activities dangerous, as the gentle sand beach slopes away gleaming in the sun like clean kitchen lineoleum that nobody walks on. In order to keep the hoi polloi of Detroit from

shlepping out here to use the beaches, the inhabitants are
willing to sacrifice their own use.

"So what do you do when you're dying for a swim? Use
the pool?" I had noticed one near the house, kidney-shaped
and vast.

"The yacht club. Everybody goes there." He points
toward the left. He explains that within a mile radius there
are various country clubs, boating clubs, yacht clubs. "The
Detroit, the Crescent, the Grosse Pointe—you can't walk
two blocks without hitting a fence."

I wander around the living room, much neater than his
old room. He has been reading the *Detroit News, Playboy*,
and a physics journal. A couple of big glossy books of
photographs lie on the glass-topped coffee table, the rya
rug showing through. Five photographs of me are arranged
in aluminum frames on the wall over the pale nubby couch
among perhaps twenty others of women and of landscapes.

When he sees me staring at the wall, he motions me to
sit on the couch. He fans out photographs—eight by tens
on matte paper—over the coffee table.

"See?" he asks insistently. "I caught it. The things I
perceive that you don't even realize are in you. Now you
can tell what I meant about photographing dreams."

Maybe. The photographs are of professional caliber and
the young woman in them could be a model or a starlet.
She is all soft invitation, gentle radiance shimmering from
her flesh like watered silk. Every curve invites with the
passive gorgeousness of a ripe peach. For a moment I fall
in love with myself on the table as he mixes martinis,
watching me in the mirror over the little bar. My god, I
think, is that me? I don't spend a lot of time staring in a
mirror and nothing in my life ever prepared me to find
myself or to be found by anyone else beautiful. Is that
what he means by not knowing myself? In a fine clear
moment of narcissism I could wish to fuck that body on
the paper. But that isn't me in any useful sense. I do see
myself in the bathroom mirror mornings with my eyes half
open, my lips curled in a sneer of only partially diluted
exhaustion. I meet myself scratching my ass and picking
my nose. I am the cold hard intellect that improves my

scholarship a step at a time until I am able to pay for far
more than my tuition in the fall, so that for the first time
since I stopped begging the difference from my parents, I
will not have to work while I go to school this September.
The dormouse is as much and no more me than these faces
that are all lush softness. He has taken my backbone out so
I do not scrap or snap. If I were truly that passive plum of
a woman, Freddie would have had me on the kitchen floor
at age fourteen while the iron burned through my father's
shirts above. Today I would be where Callie is, pregnant
again, longing to move out of a three-room walk-up, at
best working in the typing pool of a local office.

I don't know in what words to praise them. "They're
beautiful," I say. "Much more than I am just walking
around."

"You're such a mess, Jill. Half blind faith and half self-
hatred."

But I prefer myself to these perfect images. "Can I have
copies?"

"They're for you. So you can remember how I see you.
So you can keep in mind the woman you could be with me,
for me. I have my own copies, framed. I put the best ones
up on the wall this week."

As we sip our martinis, he keeps glancing from me to
the photographs, searching for confirmation of what he
shot and processed.

When he has downed a couple of drinks he grips me by
the elbow. "Okay. Time to meet Mother."

"I thought we came upstairs to avoid her?"

"I like to keep my options open."

His mother is lying on a white-painted wrought-iron
chaise longue cushioned in aquamarine. She is about
Peter's height and as thin. She has less belly than I do.
Bones and suntan, she wears a beige bikini, sunglasses with
a graduated mauve tint. Her hair is just the faintest shade
yellower than Donna's. I am surprised to see that it is
probably as long as mine used to be, worn up in an elaborated French knot. Her expression I cannot tell behind
the sunglasses. Her lips part in a small discreet smile and

she extends her hand, but not to shake because she waves limply.

"Yvonne mentioned that Peter had brought someone up." She nods then at the pool. "Did you want to swim?"

"I didn't bring my suit. I wish I had."

"There might be something in the changing room that would fit you." She peers at me. "Perhaps not."

Peter is fidgeting and she turns her invisible gaze on him. "Petey, you look unhealthy. It's well into July and you look as if you'd just crawled out of a cave."

"Very few physicists spend the whole summer on the beach."

"Oh nonsense. You don't even have a position yet. There's nothing to prevent you enjoying the club facilities with your friends. Your friends here," she amends, obviously nervous he may decide to take me. "In Maine we'll get you back into shape."

"What's this about Maine?" I ask him when a maid brings out a phone to her and we retire to the other end of the pool.

"They want me to go with them."

"Are you going?"

"Perhaps. I don't know, Jill. Depends on what happens at Argonne Labs next week. Maybe they'll hire me immediately and I'll move to Chicago. If not we'll work out a way for you to spend some time in Maine."

I don't even bother arguing. I am in summer school and working and I wouldn't have the money for a jaunt. Before going out to supper, upstairs while Peter slips on his sports jacket, he says, "Well, I did it, didn't I? Introduced you to Mother?" Pointedly he hands the photographs to me, as if accusing me of forgetting them.

As we wait for our prime ribs, he fans out the photos again, looking quizzically from them to me. I have learned to eat my beef rare; otherwise he mocks me. It was an acquired taste but it has taken; if I ever ate a steak alone, I would now eat it rare. I have not been able to learn to like martinis but that forms no obstacle tonight as we are drinking beer—he legally and I on the old fake ID furnished by him when we first began to go out together. He fingers the photographs so obsessively I half expect him to take them back, but as we are getting up, once again he pushes them toward me.

As it turns out I don't see much of Peter during the summer. After he is not hired by Argonne, he has until August 10 when his job at Detroit Edison officially begins. He vacations in Maine with his family until he must return for work.

Summer in Ann Arbor: the air is heavy as wet wool. Breathing is an effort you must force on yourself. The humidity is an absolute. We live as if in the back room of a laundry. How often Donna and I say in the tenative cool of the morning that we will hike out to the country after class, that we will hitch a ride to go swimming, that we will pack a picnic supper for ourselves. How often when afternoon lies over us like a vast hot sea of lasitude on whose bottom we barely crawl, we decide after all we will just stay home and sit on the porch. We see a lot of movies the summer of 1956, because the theater is air-conditioned. Minouska's favorite place is the bathtub when not in use; she spreads out full length like a drawn bow of blackness seeking the cool the porcelain can offer. One wet night she gives birth, straining and striving, purring and uttering deep cries, and forces out with long pauses one black kitty, one grey tabby and one dead black and white. We will have to find homes for them in the fall.

Early in August I realize that Donna has in the space of a week withdrawn from me, but I am inclined to put it down to her usual obsession with coming finals, the long paper she is writing for political science on Hobbes (the legacy of Big Sal), the questionnaire she has been designing for sociology (her minor) and the therapy she has begun. I spend more time with Alberta who will be leaving soon for New York.

When Peter returns from Maine, on the weekend he checks us into a motel as Mr. and Mrs. Fender. "But why?" I ask him.

He grunts. "Scarface doesn't leave tracks, baby. He don't leave evidence for the feds." He has even brought a small leather suitcase, although it contains only his shaving gear, a change of underwear and a clean shirt.

The motel is my first. Being Mrs. Fender for a night feels a little exciting, a little sordid. But for whom is this caution exercised? After I leave him Sunday I find myself disappointed. Our communication has suffered attrition, making me work twice as hard to get half as much response from him.

The next weekend we go swimming Saturday at Silver Lake and then eat at the Old German downtown, our favorite restaurant in Ann Arbor. "I'm moved into my new pad," he announces. "Good-bye to the parental stockade."

"Are we going there tonight?"

"Why not?"

As we drive into the city in his Sprite, he glances at me sharply. "You're letting your hair grow," he accuses.

I nod. "I missed the weight. Every couple of weeks I had to get it cut. But I'm leaving the front short. You'll like it once it's grown out a little."

"Did you start therapy yet?"

"Aw, Peter, come on. When do I have time? Or money?" Or the desire, if the truth were spoken. When I remember telling my mother I was always going to be honest with men I was involved with, I sigh. A little I understand her calling me naive.

"Why don't you go to the therapist that Donna's seeing?"

"We couldn't both go to the same guy. How did you know Donna's gone into therapy?"

"Oh. When I was waiting for you. Last week. She told me."

"She likes the guy," I say to be agreeable.

"What do you mean? Transference?"

"No. Just that she feels comfortable with him."

Peter's apartment is on the tenth floor of a newish high-rise on the river, although his apartment does not face that way. It has only two rooms and a balcony just big enough for a deck chair and a plant that has already died. It faces a similar high-rise next door with its tiers of similar balconies. Peter had left the air-conditioning on so that the living room with its kitchenette separated by a counter is marvelously cool and inviting. He pours us each a martini from a pitcher ready mixed in the refrigerator. I take one gulp and leave it on the counter. He carries his into the bedroom and strips off his jacket, shirt and pants between sips.

"My period started last night," I announce sheepishly. He doesn't enjoy making love during the first two days of my period. He claims there is a smell and not enough friction.

"You must not want to make it with me." He stares with his flat blue eyes, lying on the bed in his briefs with his hands behind his head, elbows out.

"That's not true. I want to at least as much as you do. And you know it!" I perch on the bed's edge, still dressed.

"That's what you say, not what your unconscious means."

"Come on, Peter. Periods come. It's my time of the month, right on the full moon."

"You let me visit this weekend knowing that and then you kept me dangling all day."

"But I *wanted* to see you. You can't drive up during the week. We could make love anyhow. It doesn't always have to be perfect, does it?" I cross to the plate-glass window and peer out between the draperies. The sky is pale lavender with high diffused clouds. Inside the air conditioner purrs, making me cool for the first time all week.

He seems to agree, for when I approach the bedside, he catches my wrist and tugs me so the springs wince under my fall. I grin over his shoulder at the fierceness of his attack. He does want it and tonight he won't tease me, feinting, withdrawing, changing his mind.

As I undress he asks, "Who have you been seeing?"

"Seeing? You mean friends?"

"You don't think for one minute that's who I mean."

"I haven't been seeing any men besides friends, if that's what you're asking me."

"Being faithful to me?" He grins. "What do you think that will get you?"

In a flash of annoyance I answer with dangerous honesty, "Nothing much but I've been busy. I haven't had the time to spare."

"I fucked Sue a couple of times." He sits up watching me. "The sex is just the way it was. A trifle dull."

Peter never kisses or cuddles as much as I like. Tonight I miss that more than I usually do either because we have been apart long enough for me to lose taking his habits for granted or because I have really missed him. I feel untouched. I want to be held and caressed even more than I want sex itself. Peter, however, is not in a tender mood. His eyes stay open as he watches me. Again it occurs to me that I disappoint him. Perhaps he has been daydreaming about me in the past month with the aid of those photographs that are much closer to what he wants than I am. We were doing well back in June. He had begun to warm toward me, to loosen. His family is not good for him, and not being able to get a job he wanted has shaken his confidence. I try to force contact by making conversation, to slow down his progression toward fucking. "It was lovely to swim together. You're sure in the water—powerful."

He laughs. "You sure aren't. You're clumsy. How did you learn to swim? From imitating a paddleboat?"

I draw back, scalded. I have no idea how I look in the water, having never considered swimming an aesthetic performance, like dancing; certainly growing up in center city Detroit I had little practice.

"And that bathing suit. It must once have been red, huh? It looks like a barn that needs painting. Did you borrow it from your mother?" He's having fun. Being witty puts him in a good humor as he nibbles on my shoulder.

"If you don't like that one, get me another." I try to keep the bitterness from salting my voice. "I'm open to improvement in the bathing suit department—say of Jacobson's?"

"My little gold digger," he mutters. "I'd have to pick it out, wouldn't I? You have no taste. You'd confuse a dishrag with a bathing suit."

They say you have no taste when what they mean is you have no money and no status objects bought by money. I grow inert. His hands claw at me metallically, the feeds of a machine.

"I think you wear those preposterous clothes to try to trick me into outfitting you," he says, prodding. He wants me to grow upset and deny his charge vehemently, as I usually do. "That weird milkmaid dotty dress. Nobody wears clothes like that."

"My dress? I thought you'd like it." My bathing suit is old, but my dress I found just last week in the Nearly New Shoppe, a full-skirted peasant with a scoop neckline in a blue-and-white paisley. It is a quintessential summer dress to me, easy fitting and sensual. Not knowing what he sees wrong with it makes me feel lost.

"I know what I like—some hot sex. If not one way, then the other," he says in a loud jolly voice, turning me onto my belly. I think he means to enter my vagina from the back, but instead he falls over me pushing against my buttocks, thrusting hard. While I am pinned under him, he forces his prick into my ass.

"Ow!" I try to shake him off.

"Come on. It's no good fucking the other way. Just lie still. I'll do the work."

"It hurts!"

"Only when you tense up. If it doesn't hurt the other way, it won't hurt this way. Don't be a prude. I've done this a dozen times with Sue."

It hurts; it hurts a lot. I feel dry and torn. Every stroke rubs me raw. Also I feel disregarded, as if my cunt is being bypassed with contempt. I feel extraordinarily used, lying there with a thumping within me that feels partially familiar and partially odd. I am no longer sexually excited. I am angry and bored and in pain. It wasn't my choice. He didn't give me a choice.

After what feels like half an hour he comes, flooding me. I remember being forced to have an enema in childhood; that sense of being full in the colon where fullness feels wrong. He goes off to shower while I lie feeling extremely sorry for myself. When he comes out of the bathroom I pass him to run the water for a bath and he gives me a quick embrace as if nothing out of the ordinary had occurred. I stay in the tub until the water has cooled to

tepid. I don't want to leave the bathroom. I don't want to
have to talk to him.

When I finally edge by to pick up my clothes and put
them on, he is lying in his madras bathrobe watching the
Tigers play the Cleveland Indians.

"I didn't like that," I say.

"I did." He grins. "Come on, you liked it fine. You just
think you shouldn't."

"No, I didn't like it. It hurt. You didn't ask me first."

"You never did that before?"

"No."

"Well, I got one of your cherries, then." He laughs
shortly, in a good mood. His eyes are on the pitcher as he
winds up. The images from the television set are reflected
twice on his glasses. I want to have a fight with him but I
feel torn in my body and my esteem at once, and it is hard
to fight satisfactorily with someone who is watching a television program. I march over and interpose myself.

"I'm upset. Can't you see that?"

"I can't see through you, that's for sure." He sits up on
the edge of the bed, scowling.

Suddenly I have no stomach for the fight; I feel too raw.
I turn and start out of the bedroom, hoping he will come
after me and make it less demeaning. Apologize. Make up.
Instead he calls after me, "You left your drink on the
counter. When you get it, bring me a refill."

I am in no hurry to oblige him. I wander around the
beige and terra-cotta living room with its Danish pieces,
the coffee table from his old apartment at home. All the
photographs in their aluminum frames including me glori-
fied. I am not comfortable here. I want to go home.

I take orange juice from the refrigerator and pour the
martini into it to make it palatable to me. Then I pour him
a drink from the pitcher into a clean glass from the open
shelves over the counter. As I sit at the counter with my
drink, idly I pick up pages of a letter lying there in plain
view. Then I stare. Then I begin to read, for the handwriting is immediately familiar.

Dearest Peter,

    I am already missing you desperately.

I stop and read the date. August 12. Last week.

Dearest Peter,

    I am already missing you desperately. Desperately. I know you are angry because of my decision. But it isn't a decision, my darling, so much as a matter of holding the fort a bit while your reach *your* decision. I can't go on like this.

    You must speak to her. I can't deceive her day in and day out. The last three weeks has been more than I can endure. It has to be your choice and you must go ahead and make it, but you also have to be honest with her and tell her about us.

I feel deceived. I feel like a fool, disregarded and thrust aside. I read slowly, my eyes moving through syrup. I have forever to read Donna's letter to the man she obviously loves.

    My therapist is supportive of my feelings. He says it's very healthy that I wouldn't go to bed with you just yet. He says it would be very destructive for me to do so without some kind of emotional commitment on your part. Remember how badly it turned out for us when we rushed ahead violently before!

Before. When? Suddenly I know. Not exactly how or what but I know that when Donna wanted to move out on me in the winter, that was the secret subtext. Peter, Peter and Peter. The room is slowly revolving on a turntable. The pages fall from my hand to the floor like outsized snowflakes but they do not melt. I walk out the sliding door onto the balcony and stand there, the humid air thick as feathers in spite of the breeze off the river. I don't belong here. At all.

    I don't go back and read the rest of the letter. Instead I return it carefully to where I found it. I have read enough.

I trudge back to the bedroom. "Peter." He does not look at me.

"Where's my drink?"

"I think we've run out of gas. I didn't like tonight and I don't feel good about you."

Now he faces me with a slight grin. He gets up to turn the sound off on the baseball game. "What makes you say that suddenly?"

Now I know what I had subliminally suspected: he left the letter there for me. "It isn't sudden." I won't trust him with the information that I read Donna's letter, for he might use it on her. "All evening we've been trying to make each other be somebody different. I want you to be open and giving. You want me to be soft and malleable."

"It's clear, isn't it?" he asks eagerly. "That I don't love Jill. Only what Jill could be. And you could!"

"Would you mind taking me home?"

"After the game," he says. "It's the top of the seventh."

Alberta's clan summers near me. She married late but well. Manny and Alberta still listen when the other talks and still watch each other across rooms. Manny's specialty is labor law and he has come and gone from the government with the changing administrations over the last twenty years—in with the Democrats and out with the Republicans. Alberta's base remains New York with her law firm and their kids, so that some years they have lived together and some years they have lived mostly apart, but they have persisted.

Alberta has matured well. She is a big woman, buxom but not fat. She and Manny jog, sail their little boat and play softball with the kids. Her hair is long and iron grey, her skin olive and smooth still. She talks louder than she used to because she has trouble with her hearing, dating from an antiwar demonstration in New York when the Tactical Police suddenly attacked her line of march and clubbed her unconscious. I always talk to her left side when I can maneuver around.

Summers, her house on Gull Pond is full of her three children, the oldest nineteen, the youngest fourteen, their friends, friends of hers and Manny's, her parents, Manny's mother. We meet at Newcomb Hollow when I finish work for the day and walk toting our beach chairs till the crowd thins. Then we sit talking, staring out to sea, while around us her family chaos breaks and subsides. We share private walks and improvised picnics, always with more kids than we counted before. Summers are our less political times. The rest of the year we talk once a week in spite of the long-distance rates, sometimes on business and sometimes for pleasure.

Thus in March on a day the damned weather had turned and pissed on Josh and me with a wet nasty snowstorm right after we plowed, when the phone rang later at night than I like to answer it, I wasn't surprised as she boomed at me, "Kiddie, it's time to go to Washington again. Faster than inflation we got to move. Those bastards are planning to kill us." She read me the text of a proposed constitutional amendment to outlaw abortion and then the draft of an ad to be run in protest.

"I'll call Theo," I offered. "But in the morning. You New York slickers don't respect the hours country mice keep."

"Violins, please—fiddles? Faddle. You don't like the statement, I can tell."

"I'm not crazy about it."

"Oh. And what's wrong with it?"

"Too much dead rhetoric. I'll work on it in the morning."

I figured you'd feel called upon to rewrite it. Can't you do it tonight?"

"Brain rot sets in with sunset, Alberta. After supper, I turn into a pumpkin above the shoulders. . . . Years ago, I had a lover who called me that. You never knew him."

"What were you, then, five? I saw your ex yesterday."

My tongue curled with that sour wash of disappointment. "Ah, with the heir to his wife's fortune?" Trying for the light note and failing, not from loss or sorrow but pure disappointment of trust and hope pulverized.

"No, with two big bags from Zabar's, actually. I ducked into the Bagel Wheel to avoid him—he always looks so

hangdog when he sees me. . . . Jill, never mind. He'd been a sourpuss for years. Josh loves you a lot more than he ever will. It shows."

"But for how long?" I moaned and felt ashamed. "I thought I was done fretting about men. For years my passions were literature and politics—and tomatoes. Never underestimate tomatoes as a suitable object for passion. . . . What time can I call you in the morning?"

After I hung up, I couldn't sort out if I felt depressed because of contemplating how after fourteen years of intimacy in open comradeship, my life had been torn open; or if I was depressed because of contemplating how the forces of the right were planning to tear women apart. Two steps forward and one step back and sometimes two steps back and then one sideways feinting dodge and then a leap forward. I know we must take the long view. Still I do not know a feminist who began married who ended married, at least to the same man. So who said it was going to be easy? Never me.

Like my old cat, I have lost a few teeth in battle. Like my young cat, I am crazy to play and have my belly rubbed. I have given myself in love now new and dangerously and I give myself into battle as the forces of reaction darken the skies and the heat loss of the world seems to quicken. A cold late spring nonetheless comes. After all, I know about cycles and epicycles. I know what happened to the various safe and dangerous choices my friends made the first time around.

I couldn't get the words out of my head and in fact I worked on the statement until two thirty. But I always do wake at seven anyhow so I called Theo when I went downstairs ahead of Josh to run the well's copper out and then put on a kettle for coffee. She always rises early too.

Theo is silver, silver and teak. She looks years older than she is, but she still looks good. She is thin and wiry with the brittleness of an ex-alcoholic who is aware that is a choice that she makes again every day. She knows a great deal about nutrition but she is also a food faddist with a satchel full of supplements she urges you to try. Theo is a *therapist specializing in alcohol and drug problems, because what else does she know more about, except music? Her avocation is building and repairing flutes. Her country living room is half grand piano and half wood stove. When she was busted at an antinuke demonstration last winter, her current lover—a musicologist at Bennington—discovered the bondage of feeding Theo's horse, Theo's chickens, Theo's nanny goat, Theo's five cats, Theo's two terriers, Theo's resident bird population and Theo's friendly skunk. She tends to see her lovers in town. Although her house smells like a stable, I love to visit because I too enjoy animal company and when she is off at work, I bang on her piano and play her records loud. The horse, however, overawes me.*

It was Alberta who got Theo out at last. In those days Theo was a mess, incoherent, depressed, addicted to tranquilizers. That first year we wondered if we had made a naive mistake. The women's movement gave Theo a spine. I can still remember how off-putting the younger women found Theo. With their worries as the mother of young children or their raw political savvy and fury against the male organizers who had denied them the equality they were fighting for for others, they saw Theo as some potty, boozy dowager aunt meandering on. But they learned. And she did.

"Enough of press releases," Theo announced that morning. "We need a traveling exhibit. Part art, part circus."

Unusual suggestions always fire me. "A huge wall-sized quilt made of the flower faces of dead women."

"You know, we can silk-screen photos right on fabric. I'm serious. And little memorials. And a lot about children, what happens to children who aren't wanted. A lot about child abuse and the sexual abuse of children. My dear, in a week I collect enough information about the ravages of children to fill a hall."

When you live in the country, everything political starts on the phone. Where does it end? It doesn't, silly. You end. It doesn't.

TWENTY-SIX
What Is Taken and What Is Taken Away

THE DRIVE BACK is interminable. I look out the window while Peter makes resolute small talk, seeming elated. When we finally arrive at the co-op, I half expect him to bound in ahead of me to find Donna, but he says nothing except, "We'll keep in touch."

"I'm sure," I say grimly and climb the front porch steps. The old house stands with its doors and windows flung wide uttering light to the humid night. As I walk from room to room calling names, I find lights left on over desks with books spread open, lights over dressers with cosmetics awry as if the inhabitants had been all enchanted away. Minouska comes meowing tail high to meet me: I alone have escaped to tell you. She takes me to her kittens and behold, their eyes are open.

A door slams. I go warily to meet whoever it is: Alberta, who is studying for her New York bar exams. Too soon she will leave. "Nobody's home," I say.

"I am. You are. Are we nobody? I just went down to the corner for some tampons. Ever since I'm not with Donnie, I forget when my periods are."

I cannot quite bring myself to tell her my evening. I say only, "I just broke up with my boyfriend, the jerk."

"You can't marry somebody who doesn't share your politics, anyhow, so why waste your time? Oh, Howie called from Detroit. He left a message for you to call him back whenever you got in. He said whenever you got in, three times. And here you are early."

I don't recognize the number—not his family's house, not the hospital. I dial and the phone is answered, "Feldman's Mortuary, can I be of service?"

"Is Howie Dahlberg there?" I talk standing. It hurts to sit down. When Howie comes on I ask, "Your father?"

"He died this afternoon. The funeral's tomorrow at two. Would you come in?"

"Sure," I say immediately and then wish I hadn't. I don't really want to go. "You want me there especially?"

"Would I ask if I didn't?"

I waver a moment and then loyalty overcomes me. He is my source of strength, my buddy. "Where is it? Should I wear black?"

After I hang up I realize I have offered no consolation in conventional formulae or gracious original poetry. None. He wanted none. He is businesslike, numbed into performance. I do not in the least feel like taking the bus into Detroit tomorrow like a pool ball bounced off the walls in some game I don't control. But what the hell. Let him get from me what he needs. He's entitled.

I go back to my room slowly, my knees loose-hinged, and get down on my hunkers to watch Minouska with her all-black and her gray water-marked tabby kitten suckling. We are going to have to find homes for them, a seige that will take all the skill, flirtation and shrewdness we can muster. Then I want to have Minouska spayed. Donna hesitates, identifying. Donna.

I hear the screen door open downstairs and somehow I know that this time it is Donna. I get to my feet. On the way across the room to my bed (we have twin beds here) I glimpse myself in her long mirrow. What's wrong with this dress? I still don't know. I still think it's sexy. I have a vulgar passion for low necklines, perhaps because my breasts were the first part of me ever admired and I myself tended to seek comfort in them, as now, when I bow my head and my hands close each on one. Why should I, who wait to confront her, feel guilty?

Donna flings through the door, starting as she sees me. "Aren't you early?"

"That is true."

She yanks her shirtdress over her head and lets it drop, kicks off her sandals. "I've hit bottom."

"A loose surge of disbelief, a colder rising tide of fore-knowledge. "What now?" I fight the urge to stop my ears.

With hasty motions she strips. "I picked up a town boy and screwed him." Her lips pull back over her small per-fect teeth. "I hope I get syphilis." She runs across the hall to the bathroom.

Her mattress-ticking shirtdress slowly deflates. Picking up her towel and robe, I follow. Without covering her hair she plunges under the shower, then pulls the curtain closed.

I stand outside, hands crossed over my chest. I question, she answers. What good does it do? I don't want to listen. "A town boy?"

Her eye appears at the parting of the yellow plastic curtain. "I felt so lonely. No one to talk to." She ducks back.

Because I was with Peter? Does that make it my fault? Was I too dense, too self-involved to notice what was hap-pening? If I stayed with her, would that help? "How did it happen?"

She peers out. "I had an appointment with Professor MacLean this morning to talk about my project for sociol-ogy. I'd drawn up a questionnaire about women's attitudes toward each other—things we talk about—to do a study in the dorms. He thought it was a joke."

"Donna, who are you punishing? Him? You? Me?" My voice spirals up. I pull the curtain open to look at her.

She faces into the full splatter of the shower. "I saw him looking at posters outside a movie. He seemed . . . big, defeated. Gypped."

Laughter rattles in my head. "May you never feel sorry for a horse."

"I wanted someone lonelier than me. Somebody *I* could pity. Somebody where I could feel I was better than him." The water is turned off and her hands grope for the towel, which I hold out. "I didn't know I was going to fuck him till I did. So ugly!"

Wrapped to the neck in her plaid robe she pushes past me and climbs into bed, leaving only her eyes exposed. It occurs to me to tell her the kittens have opened their eyes, but that seems irrelevant even to me, who feel like a wineglass broken into forty shards of thin curved glass.

"I have a date with him tomorrow," she says.

"You're not meeting him again?"

"He knows where I live, Stu. He walked me home."

"I'll say you're not here."

"No." Her hands tug at the sheet. "He said he had a friend. Come with me, Stu."

"Howie's father died. I'm going into Detroit for the funeral."

"Why?"

I want to say because he asked me, but she is asking too. Instead I say, "Donna, you don't have to punish yourself any longer. Peter and I broke up tonight."

She sits up abruptly. Her face scrubbed raw beneath the skullcap of wet hair, she looks frightened. "Did he . . . I mean, who broke it off?"

"He left your letter in the kitchen for me to find. On the counter."

"Oh." She seems afraid to ask anything. She does not deny having been there.

"I read the first page. But I didn't let him know. He may suspect, but he doesn't know. Then we broke up by mutual consent. So, if you want him, he's all yours."

"Are you furious with me?"

"Why didn't you tell me you were seeing him?"

"He made me promise not to tell you. He said he needed time to make up his mind. He says you overreact to everything."

"He could make you promise, but he couldn't make you keep that promise. I don't give a shit about him, Donna! Why didn't you level with me?"

"You don't love him. Otherwise I never would have."

"Oh, Donna, I was attached enough. But he dispensed with that. It was my period tonight and he doesn't care for blood, so he fucked me in the ass."

"In the ass." Her eyes narrow with interest. "I've never done that. . . ."

"Be my guest. I don't think I'll shit without pain for days. My goddamned ass is bleeding, which is why I'm lying like this."

"You broke up with him because of *that*?"

"I broke up with him because he wants me to be somebody else. I broke up with him because he's cold at the core. Because he has a hard sadistic streak up his middle. He's a no-win game, Donna. He makes you try to get him to love you, but you're never quite good enough. He broke up with me because the game's worn out with me and he wants to play it with you."

"Oh, Stu, you and Peter are a mismatched pair. I never could understand why it dragged on. He and I are much more alike."

"Last spring, what exactly happened?"

"Oh, he told you about that?"

"He told me nothing. I asked him nothing. You tell me."

"After that graduate student I had the crush on turned out to be married, I went to the Union and there was Peter, waiting for you as it turned out. I sat down, we started talking. You didn't show up. I don't know how it happened but we left together and went right back to his place and fell into bed."

"I wasn't sleeping with him yet. Why didn't you just get involved then?"

"We had a fight five minutes later. The intensity scared him. He made a crack about Lennie, how Lennie was a loser and I'd never had any experience with a man I couldn't push around. I lost my temper and we lit into each other." She seems glad to talk. Sliding out of bed clutching her damp plaid robe around her, she stands over me, hovering. "Stu, understand. It's not like any other man for me."

"You don't know what it's going to be like."

"But you don't either, Stu. He and I, we hit it off hard and fierce. I get at something in him nobody else can—he told me that."

He offers every woman a little come-on. To you only can I tell this tale of my secret sorrows and you only can save me.

I look skeptical enough for her to rush on, "It isn't like anybody else for me. It has all the fierceness of when I fall into lust with somebody I shouldn't touch. Then all the tenderness I felt for Lennie. Peter won't see I truly loved Lennie, but I did. He just never got to me sexually the way those mean studs do."

"That is a lot to base on one quick fuck and a blowout."

"But I know I can be faithful to him. It's real. Oh god, if only I'd known what you were going to tell me tonight! Now I've blown it. If he knew, he'd dump me like that." She snaps her fingers.

"Take the bus into Detroit with me. See your sister. See him. Come to the funeral. It'll keep you out of trouble. When you aren't here, the guy will know you don't care to see him again."

"No. I can't bear to face my therapist and tell him what a mess I got myself into. I've done it already, Stu. What good will running do?"

"Avoid a repetition."

"I won't do it again. I won't! You'll see. I have to prove that. I have to prove it to myself."

"You can't unfuck him, Donna."

"Yes, I can. I can get myself back from him. This time I'll face the ugly thing I've done and take control. Then I'll be safe. I'll know I can control myself and it won't ever happen again."

"Donna, you can't make this guy act out a little magic play with you."

"I'll act cold and say I'm miserable and shocked. I'll make a big fuss about how awful I feel. I'll tell him I can't go to Mass tomorrow because of what we did—he's brought up Catholic too. I know how to get at him."

"I don't want you to go! It's crazy."

"It's not crazy. And I'm not. I won't be crazy and sick. I don't want to be out of control. I have a chance to fix my life now, to prove I'm not a rotten nymphomaniac, and to get what I want. Come with me, Stu! Please."

"No! It's stupid. I promised Howie I'd go to the funeral. I'll get a ride back in with him and be here by eight or so."

She lies in her bed, turned to the wall. Minouska springs up and climbs over her. She cradles her cheek in the cat's black flank. I would like to shake Donna from her rigidity. "Donna, listen," I begin. She does not open her eyes or acknowledge me. Her breathing is deep and regular but as I bend over her, her lids quiver. I decide I will go sit in a hot bath for my ass in spite of the warmth of the night. I turn away and take Joyce's *Ulysses* off to the tub to read. When I finally go to bed, she really is asleep, snoring softly, a placid, secure sound.

Some people look smaller in grief: Howie's grandmother. She seems to weigh sixty pounds and have as much substance at the grave as a furled black umbrella. Some people come loose from their center and spread out: Howie's mother looks as if she had gained thirty pounds and as if her arms had grown long and gangly, pulling partly out of their sockets. Her dress hangs in back. She leans on Milton, Howie's older brother who fought in Korea and didn't want to be a doctor and works for a plumbing and heating firm. Milt looks vague in the cemetery, as if worrying about something distant, his bills, his children, his wife. He holds Mrs. Dahlberg with an arm around her shoulder and by rote he gives comfort, but his eyes are distracted.

Standing beside me, Howie has hardly spoken. I greeted him when I arrived at the synagogue, just in time for the service. I sat toward the rear. The room was only a third full. From the conversations I overheard afterward, I realized many of the mourners were in the funeral business and couldn't help judging the job critically.

This familiar cemetery is now a graveyard where the dead are put away rather than a promenade where I go to argue and debate with Howie, to confess and to question. The sky flattens us like a steam iron. I sweat in my black shirtdress. When I touch my scalp, I burn my hand. About thirty of us are gathered at the grave.

I take Howie's hand, like grasping a piece of stone in the shade. He lets me keep his hand, but he is so rigid I think if he bent over, he would be permanently creased into that new shape like a cardboard cutout. Sweat stands out on his broad forehead but his hand is cold marble. A monarch butterfly zigzags across an avenue among the mausoleums toward us where we stand on the plain of small crowded graves. Right across from me I read:

REBECCA MOSHER
BELOVED WIFE OF AARON MOSHER
LOVING MOTHER OF SANFORD, SHEILA AND ROBERT

1898–1942

A Hebrew inscription underneath I cannot read. A short life.

It is Howie's turn to step forward and toss in a handful of dirt. I like the literalness of the gesture. Several wreaths, rather fancy, friends in the business. Howie looms beside me again. People are saying goodbye. We walk among the Mogen Davids, and the stone flowers in stone urns and the modern high-gloss slabs of dark granite streamlined as if to rush off somewhere in eternity. He says, "We'll have to get out of the house now. I'll have to help her look. Milt doesn't have room for both her and Grandma."

"Why move so fast?"

"Because the house comes with the custodial job. The new guy's been good about not moving in while Papa was in the hospital. . . . Now finally my family won't live in a cemetery." He smiles wryly. "A bit late to improve my social life in high school."

He wants me to drive back and is astonished that I don't know how. "I'll teach you," he promises. "I wish I had already."

We are close and yet silent. He has the radio tuned to a Black station and the R & B thrums my body. For long moments I forget to be serious and loll there in the hot car, enjoying the music, enjoying being driven through the flat summer with the windows open and my hair blowing. We stop to eat at a Greek place in Ypsilanti, the industrial town next to Ann Arbor where Kaiser-Frazer just shut down. Neither of us can slip back into a collegiate setting yet. At five forty-five the restaurant is half empty. We both want wine badly but Howie does not succeed in ordering it. He will not be twenty-one until he finishes the university.

"Come on," I say in exasperation to the old waiter. "We just buried his father. We just came from the funeral."

"The law's the law," the old waiter tells us mournfully, but he lets me order retsina on my fake ID. We sit in a booth and drink wine from the same squat glass.

"Where'd you get that?" He picks up the ID. "Doesn't look like you."

"Peter gave it to me. As I broke up with him yesterday, you can skip the obligatory vomiting and stomping. . . . You're still numb, aren't you?"

He nods. "I've walked through it all. I can't let myself feel yet. I'd fall apart—like Mother. You can't have everybody fall apart. I took the best role, being practical, making arrangements." He finishes a glass by himself. "Why does this taste like something you should use to take paint off a door?"

"Will you ever let yourself feel it?"

"Of course. Just not right now."

I don't understand where emotions go if you deny them. Do they wither or molder or gather strength underground? Being nervous this evening makes me less warm and comforting than I want to be. I want to be graciously distracting, but all the time I am worrying about Donna and resenting worrying about her.

Probably she didn't go out with the towny. Probably Peter called and she's seeing him. Right now they are in bed together celebrating my removal from that charged space between them. I can't say that my presence did Howie any good today, but his mother appreciated it and I owe him many good turns. It was me he asked to keep him company through the funeral and the burial, not Dick, not Bolognese. I am a little proud.

Maybe he would rather have asked Alberta on whom he has a crush worthy if totally futile. Alberta is as conventional in her ideas about love and marriage as she is radical in her economic politics, and would never consider a man seven years her junior. A sect is a religion that only a few people belong to and a crush is a love that is felt only by one, I think, minimizing labels for what we don't happen to share. My eyes keep straying to the big Pepsi-Cola clock over the door to the kitchen. I do wonder where Donna is. With Peter, of course. He'd want to see her today. Off with the old and on with the new. It's just all going to be awkward as a full chamber pot in the middle of our bedroom floor.

I suddenly realize Julie got married that summer to Carl. But when? I can't remember that. It was hot and Julie kept worrying that it would rain. All I have is a snapshot of the three of us. Julie is grinning and has her arms around both of us. Her dress is white tulle and sticks out alarmingly. I remember she wore three or four crinolines under it, the stiff petticoats that were fashionable then and stiffened by allowing sugar water to dry on them. There am I on her left in the notorious dress. Looking at it now I still don't understand what Peter was objecting to, but many years and a couple of husbands have taught me that when somebody wants out, even the caviar is too salty. On the right, Donna stands shielding her eyes from the sun. Something strange is happening to the old snapshots and Donna is fading. You cannot read her features at all because she

*and the landscape behind her are escaping from the paper
into a featureless glare. In the next photo beside it, Julie
awkwardly holds Carl, Jr., wrapped in a blanket, as she
stands in front of a brand-new tract house.*

I am sure Donna will be in our room. Across the hall
someone is taking a bath. Wanda is chatting on the phone.
Upstairs on the third floor Ravel's *Boléro* plays loud. She is
not in our room.

When Wanda hangs up, I grab her. "Do me a favor. I
beg you."

"Absolutely, kid." She grins, sitting spread-legged in
paint-stained jeans on the stairs. "Name your poison. Who
do you want bumped off?"

"Quite a few people, actually, but I'll settle for one
phone call. If you call the number I give you in Detroit,
just ask if Donna's there. If he asks who you are, just say
you're a friend from her house. If you get her on the
phone, just ask where I am, you're trying to find me. I'm
just trying to locate her."

"So why can't you call her yourself?"

"Because of the male person who may answer the
phone. Do it for me, Wanda."

"Okay, toots. But remember, the celibate life is the simple life." She dials Peter's number. Donna is not there but
Peter is. So much for that gambit.

I go back to our room. My scalp is lead. The backs of
my hands itch. Every time I look at the clock it is ten after
nine. I have to fight the desire to call Howie and urge him
to come back to keep me company. I have made Minouska
nervous till she prowls the room like my black anxiety
embodied. I cluck and call but she will not come. Only
flattens her ears and stares, flicking her skinny tail. She
keeps counting her two kittens. I no longer even wish
Donna back, but only that I did not suspect where she
is.

I am scared to the bone now. What is she doing to
herself, and do I have to watch, to participate? Tendrils
creep in my neck, tightening around my eyes. Glass ash-

tray heaped with butts. The one I stole from the sweetshop long ago to match her boosted teapot. Spiral that has not come to rest. I chain-smoke till my mouth stinks.

The door opens slowly. Stiffly, fists clenched, Donna stands with her head hanging forward as if it were loose. The pen falls from my hand. She steps into the room and then gripping my desk chair, vomits. She turns, shaking her head, to walk a few steps and sit on the edge of her twin bed. Her chin is stained with something dark and caked. Blood? As she writhes sideways and begins vomiting again, I shove the wastebasket before her. Long after her stomach is empty she gags, her muscles jerking.

I sponge her face, take off the crumpled dress, torn in the hem, bodice smeared with dust and grease. Then I clean the floor, the chair, the basket. Smell of vomit thick in the room. I open the windows high. "What happened?" Ritualistic phrase. I ask in her dreams. Her teeth are chattering. Swollen spots that will be bruises mark her arm that lies limp on the sheet. Her panties are missing and on her brassiere are spots of what has to be blood, although it does not seem to be from her breasts. I reject this nightmare in which I lay out her body, smoothing the sheet. I am exhausted. Her face is badly swollen.

"What happened?" I repeat. "Are you hurt?"

"Yes. No. I don't know."

"Are you bleeding anywhere?"

"I don't know." She writhes in the bed. "My back hurts bad."

Gently I turn her over. More bruises. A cut on her right buttock. I get antiseptic and sponge it.

When I turn her back to face me, her eyes focus for the first time. "He had a car tonight." Voice small and pallid, wondering. "I said I had to talk to him."

"I thought you'd see Peter tonight."

"He didn't call. I couldn't see him, being guilty. . . . I went through the whole routine how I was ashamed and I'd never done anything like it. I tried to flatter him, saying I got carried away." She pauses. "My mouth tastes awful."

"Want a glass of water? Tea? I could make you tea?"

"I couldn't keep it down. . . . He said we'd go eat a pizza and talk. Then he parked by the river. I got scared. I left his car. He came after. He wanted to and I wouldn't."

"Why didn't you leave?"

"We were out of town by the river. He caught me by the arm and he wouldn't let go of me. I kept telling him to take me home. He kept saying I did it with him once already so what difference did it make?" She stops, leaning to spit blood into the basket. "He kept on."

"Did he break a tooth?"

"I can't tell yet. I fought so hard, Stu! I never thought men could really rape you, if you fought." She twisted under the sheet. "He wouldn't stop. I held him off till my arms were so sore I couldn't raise them. God, my back hurts. I think I pulled something."

"Let me call a doctor. Or take you to health service."

"No! I'm too ashamed. I don't want this on a record."

"Why should you be ashamed? You didn't rape him."

"I couldn't scream. I can't explain. I was afraid to. I was afraid he'd kill me if I screamed. He kept slapping my face when I tried to bite him. I had a nosebleed."

The blood on her brassiere. "Donna, Donna . . ." I take her head in my lap. As if the touch released her, she begins to cry. Tears soak through my skirt, fitting it to my thigh like a warm poultice. I hug her frail head. "Donna, it's all right now. You're safe. And you didn't give in." I hardly listen to what I mumble. Tears flow across my thigh like blood from a female wound. At last she is inert and her breathing eases. Thinking she is asleep, I pick up her clothing to deal with it, but she stirs again.

"Afterward I got up as soon as I could move and I started to walk toward town. He kept insisting I get in the car. I wouldn't. But then I was scared to walk on with my clothes all torn and messed up and my mouth bleeding, in the dark. Finally I did get in the car. Then when we drove into town, at a traffic light, I jumped out. He left the car there and ran right after me down the street."

"Did he catch you?"

"No. I had a real head start by the time he parked. But I

could hear him yelling. Stu go look out the window and see if he's still there, outside the house."

The streetlight falls on a couple embracing under the low boughs of a sugar maple. "No one's there."

Restlessly she stirs, passes her hand over her eyes. "It's terrifying to feel helpless. That someone can just take you and use you like that."

"It hurt?"

"Like being torn. How it must hurt those young girls, virgins." She holds the pillow against her. "But I didn't give in!"

"You didn't." I stroke her hair. "Don't talk. Lie still."

"Promise you won't tell anyone. Ever. Ever!"

"Donna, I won't, but why? Being raped is terrible and painful, but you didn't do anything wrong."

"Everybody makes jokes about it. Everybody thinks that's what you really want. I didn't want it. I didn't want him. I hated him. I was scared of him. I was terrified lying there. I was terrified he'd do something even worse and cut me up or kill me. I was sure he was going to kill me and leave my body there."

I stroke her head, her thin silky hair. "Shhhh," I say. "I'll never tell anyone. Never." The night is small and hot with a lid like a casserole holding us. In a dull soothing voice I try to lull her, stroking. "Tomorrow is Monday and the week begins. I have a paper due on Donne's 'Extasie.' My lecturer Fells spent the hour Friday deciding Donne had never achieved a true mystical experience—such as I'm sure he does every morning before breakfast on dry toast—and could be dismissed as a Catholic manqué." Donna snorts, her body unclenching slightly. My tongue clacks in my mouth like a dried piece of leather. "Fells's method is to work our way through the body of somebody's work, like Donne, logging as we go, finding the flaws in all the supposed great works, until one or two absolutely perfect masterpieces are left standing, and then move on with our chain saws to the next mountain."

The toilet flushes again and again, our housemates clatter upstairs. Minouska comes to explore her, sniffing. Goes back to her kittens. Donna's fine hair tangles under my hand. Finally she sleeps. Maybe she does need Peter. Maybe he can do better than I at keeping her alive and well. I seem to have failed her. I sit on while the amorous lowing of the front-porch leavetaking rises and falls, a gelid grey despair weighting me quiet and still.

TWENTY-SEVEN

Old Allies Waver and New Alliances Form

MONDAY DONNA DOES not go to her classes. Exhausted, she lies in bed. I tell the other inhabitants of the co-op that she has a summer cold. No one is markedly curious. It is the end of August and some of the women like Donna and me will be here in the fall, some like Alberta are just finishing up and ready to leave Ann Arbor and some are only taking summer courses. The house has a loose disjointed feel, so that no one pays as close attention to others' welfare as in the winter. Her bruises and weeping are invisible.

Monday evening after supper while Donna is napping, a teacher here for the summer calls up the stairwell, "Donna Stuart, Donna Stuart, you have a visitor."

Peter? Grimly, making myself smile ferociously at the treads, I march down. The guy standing in the hall is not familiar to me. Then he is. I know exactly who he is, about five nine and big-boned, his hair in a blond ducktail. For a moment he reminds me of Matt, but Matt soft in the waist and slope-shouldered. Awkward in the hall. "You get the hell out of here," I say. "You've done enough to her!" I stop three steps from the bottom to keep some height on him.

"Who're you? Where's Donna?"

"Sick in bed from what you did to her, what do you think? You son of a bitch. I'm her cousin. If you ever show your face around here again—"

"Go on, what do you know about it? She went out with me twice."

A coat tree stands in the corner of the hall. As I glare at him, I am suddenly moving forward past him to seize it, raincoats, umbrellas and all, and swing it. It hits him a glancing blow on the shoulder, tumbling him backward into the wall. I swing the wooden coat tree around again and he is out the door and down the steps. I follow to the screen door, weak in the knees, my rage gone as it came, out of nowhere, to nowhere. "And don't come back!" I yell, wanting to sound fierce.

The guy at the wheel of the silver convertible out front is laughing as my victim climbs in the other side. Then the dark-haired driver takes off with the obligatory screech. I pick up the raincoats and umbrellas scattered over the hall. The teacher stands in the doorway to the living room, watching me with an expression of alarm. "As you were," I say to the coat tree as I stand it in its corner.

I feel better as I climb upstairs, less helpless. Donna sits up. "Where were you?" she asks.

"Just talking to Howie."

"You like being one of the boys." She shakes her head sadly. "Don't think they ultimately unsex you?"

"Nobody else can either give me my sex or take it from me," I say companionably, perching on the edge of her bed. "Want some tea now?"

When I hear that Francis is home for Labor Day, I make immediate arrangements to drive in with Howie, who is moving his mother and grandmother into a small garden apartment out Seven Mile Road, about a mile and a quarter from where Mike's mother lives.

When I walk into the tiny square living room, Francis is

sprawled on the sofa with his feet hooked over the arm reading *The Racing Form*. He glances up and looks me over. Rolling onto his elbow with his lazy grin, he then recognizes me. "Goddamn it's you," he says accusingly. "Jill!"

I hug him but he is stiff with me. Skinny, skinny. Because I am so pleased to see him with his tough grace, his way of moving and sitting, never even flicking the ash from his butt without style, it is a while before I notice how bad he looks. "Where's Mom and Dad?" I drop on the couch turned sideways to absorb as much of him as possible.

"Doing the shopping. . . . So, you're a coed? You're going to college and taking courses and rah-rah football games and all that?"

"Aw come on, Francis. I sell my football tickets—"

"Yeah! I could get a good price for them, if I'm around."

"I'd like that. Francis, what happened to you? Where were you?" I count years on my fingers. I haven't seen him since I was fifteen. "When I wrote you at that Texas address, the letters just came back."

"I was in business down Méjico way . . ." he says. Then he looks at me, his dark eyes that are my mother's and mine squinting with wry amusement. "Actually I got busted."

"You were in jail?"

"In Durango."

"That's in Mexico or Texas?"

"That's in hell, that's where it is. But don't you tell her. This is strictly between you and I."

"I wouldn't dream of telling." But I bet you tell Mother yourself. "How long have you been out?"

"About six months. If I would've come up any sooner, she'd have smelled the jail on me. When I crawled out of there on my belly I looked like a starved rat."

"You look fine now," I say, part truth, part lie. He's a good-looking man on a small-framed lithe model. His curly black hair is receding a little and he is so thin I could cut my face on his chin. He looks years older than he ought, older than Leo, lines around the eyes, lines scoring the mouth. As soon as Mother gets some weight back on him, he will look more like himself. I tell him about the HUAC play we put on and what we're doing in PAF, for Francis is the only one in the family I like to talk politics with. He's a left-wing anarchist.

Now he's skeptical. "Bunch of college kids, what's the point? They won't do nothing. Now you put that on at Ford's, you're getting someplace."

"You have to reach everyone," I argue. "College is where I am. A lot of people go now, Francis, not just rich kids. Donaldson, our faculty sponsor, points out that most people graduating college will be working for wages. They'll be doing cleaner work than their parents but with no more power or control."

"Is he the guy she said you got mixed up with?"

"Professor Donaldson? Of course not. What was she telling you anyhow?"

"Some guy knocked you up and wouldn't get hitched then. Why didn't you come back home?"

"What for, Francis? I didn't have the baby. Why don't you move back home? It's a little dull here for both of us, right?"

"It's not the same thing," he says stubbornly, making me wonder if Mother has set him to trying to talk me back to Detroit. "I'm not about to get knocked up."

"No Francis, you look more like you been knocked down and knocked out. I am not about to get pregnant anymore either."

"Yeah? You telling me you learned your lesson and you're running around on the loose and you don't go near no guys?"

"No. I'm telling you I got myself a diaphragm. Now lay off, Francis. I haven't asked about your sex life, in jail or out."

"Jesus," he says. "I go away for a while and everything turns to shit. You think you know what you're doing. I've known a hell of a lot of women, and I know what happens to girls who think they can hit the road like men."

"Aw come on, Francis, you've known a hell of a lot of

whores. And so have I. We both have had good friends on
the street—"

"Your old pal Marcie . . ." He draws his finger across
his throat.

"What do you mean? Somebody beat up on her?"

"Dead. Two weeks ago. Guess you don't keep up with
home."

"Who killed her?" It occurs to me as I say it that I'm
being silly. But what disease kills a twenty-year-old? Car
accident?

"She killed her. ODed. Too pure horse rode her into the
wall." We both contemplate the wall before us. "You see
what comes down."

"I don't sell my body. School's interesting—I'm not so
bored I need to do drugs. I'm financially independent of
Mother and Dad."

"Mom says they send you twenty-five a month."

"I sure can use it. But you're not imagining that pays for
anything essential. Francis, you been home a couple of
days and already you think you know more about my life
than I do. That's like Leo."

"Bullshit. She's worried sick about you."

"Now let her worry about you." I point to his guitar in
the corner. "Learn any Mexican songs?"

"I don't know who's worse out of tune, that or me." He
flexes his fingers on his knees.

"What did you get busted for?"

"None of your business, little sister. You never ask that."
He laughs shortly. "Just a little of my business." He feels
the sharp edge of his chin. "I was in a fight."

He could well have been and yet I do not believe him.
For getting in a fight, they don't put you in jail that long.
We all have bad tempers and strike out, but never with the
loss of reason it takes to maim or kill, unless it was self-
defense. He offers me a beer and I sip politely. I want
Francis to admire me, how I have grown, how I have
changed, and to treat me as an equal at last. But I don't
think he is going to. I want to wrest approval from him. I
have pulled myself way uphill from the tortured self-doubt-

ing cowardly waif he last saw. He must approve of me; he must.

Things remain awkward, good by flashes. The best time is Labor Day when Francis and I leave the union picnic early for one given by his Italian anarchist friends. The food is better with wine instead of beer. Francis even dances with me. As always he is a graceful dancer but now I can keep up with him. Well behaved, a perfect sister, I flirt with the old men and not with the young ones and generally act with only a splinter of myself.

As I climb the steps of the co-op with my suitcase and return to Howie's car for a box of food from home, I am curious. A new graduate student housemother. Half the house will be strangers. As I lug the suitcase upstairs, an orange-haired girl in shorts is standing on a chair in my room doing something to the ceiling fixture. "Hi," I say, "can I help? What are you doing to our light?"

"I'm just putting on a new shade. No, thanks. I can do it. Are you going to live in the house too?"

"Er. Did Donna switch off rooms to another one?"

"No, this is her room. Hey, Donna!"

She hurries from the bathroom scrubbing a towel over her wet hair. "Stu? How was Detroit?"

"What's up here?"

"This is Rosellen, Stu. Rosellen's going to live with me. Our schedules are in such conflict—you're up so late and out so often. But there's a great single room on third. I hauled your stuff up there and moved you in. You can have it to yourself."

I stare at her. "To myself."

"You know how I fuss about neatness." Finally she looks me in the face. "You know it won't work. The two of us in one little room again. We need some space, desperately."

Rosellen looks from one to the other, smoothing her bangs. "You used to room rogether? I mean, I could move—"

"No, no," I say. "Fine." I pick up my suitcase.

"Donna follows me into the hall, asking softly, "You're not angry?"

"Angry?" I shake my head. The only feeling I can locate is guilty relief and a little amusement that she should have moved me into a room by myself: if not her for companion, none. I climb slowly, turned inward and waiting for the lurch of my heart, but only that shoddy relief spreads like a flowering weed. Our great experiment in honest intensity is declaring bankruptcy. Our sisterhood has been proved fictional. She isn't my burden any longer. If there is to be a recording of loss, it does not come then.

I walk around the third-floor hall. First door, Wanda typing. She waves. Then comes the little room under the eaves I thought Donna meant, but inside a young woman is giving herself a home permanent. In the third room a heavyset girl is doing exercises with thuds that shake the bottle on the dresser, while Lynn tunes a guitar. Last door shut. I knock. Walk into a burst of Greek dance music. My books are piled on the floor. The closet door stands wide and I see my clothes hanging there. The Greek record is playing on my little turntable. In the rocker sits Stephanie Barboulis, feet curled under her, marking time to the beat with her plump shoulders.

"Welcome!" She smiles from under thick bronze lashes. "I saw your cousin moving your stuff next door, so I commandeered you. I persuaded Joyce, whom I'd agreed to live with just the day before, that she really wanted to live alone. I couldn't manage her, really, she's a prude. She kisses a poodle doll with bells on before she goes to sleep."

"How do you know I don't? Actually I prefer Basque sheep dogs. I bet you could have bought me direct from Donna, cheap."

"Because you're a poet. I used to see you in the Union with the great Mike Loesser and that wild-looking painter, Lennie. I posed for him once, you know. I think he had a crush on me."

"I used to see you around with Rob Prewitt."

"It's a mistake to go out with performers, they're in love

with themselves and everybody chases them." Her straight sleek hair falls shoulder length, exposing her broad face with thick straight brows and big brown eyes with light green flecks in them, like little fish, I think. She wears a finely embroidered peasant blouse with drawstring neck. As she laughs it goes plunging off one shoulder.

Out of my suitcase I pull a bottle of white lightning I bought from Freddie. Freddie is working for a guy who runs a still in his garage. Francis and I went there together to buy cheap booze. Finally the only way Francis acknowledges my grown-up status is that he will drink with me, on the porch late at night drinking the corn likker out of a brown bag under the glider, as if that fooled Mother inside watching TV.

Chin out I announce policy. "I never make my bed. I keep late hours. My desk is messy but I'll chop off your fingers if you touch it." Reversing old promises to Donna.

"Of course. She throws up her arms, hopping out of the rocker to come skipping barefoot across to me. "Don't worry! Why don't we have a drink? To celebrate the new conspiracy of Stuart and Barboulis."

The tyrant in me blossoms. "Connivers, freeloaders and arty bums." I pour a finger of the rotgut into two kitchen tumblers.

"Yassou." Stephanie takes a healthy swallow and gags. "I guess I don't care too much for it. Not much flavor."

The flavor of molten steel. It tastes like my mother's first husband, I think, but keep that to myself as I nod patronizingly. "Take small sips." The green-flecked eyes admire. I look around. She has been unpacking out of an ancient black steamer trunk. "You know, we won't be able to breathe till you get that monster trunk out. We better get Wanda to help us."

"I have a date with a man I met buying books." Pouring a palmful of cologne she rubs it in her hair. "I prefer older men, don't you? He's a graduate student in sociology. I'll get him to move it down."

"Instant captivity? I bet we live with it for a month."

Smiling broadly she hitches up her petticoat into the

waistband of her skirt to keep it from showing where the elastic is shot. "Don't bet. Wouldn't want to take money off a poet. We each have our little talents."

By suppertime, the trunk is moved.

We whitewash the sloping walls and make curtains of red burlap with the bottoms cut raggedly. Our clutters blend. We pool food, clothes, strategies for survival. Together we sneak into the astronomy department tea for free doughnuts, sociology tea for coffee cake, and when one of us goes out to supper, she brings home extra rolls in her purse. Stephanie lives on a slim allowance plus her summer bank balance, I on my new scholarship and a monthly pittance for working two evenings and Saturdays in the library.

Yes, we do fine. But I always hear Donna's laugh bark in the hall and I question with a rawness in my chest what she is reacting to. I am always passing her door to see her bent fiercely over her work, making me wonder what is striking pleasure or defiance from her. Minouska, glossy and sinuous, curling at her feet or on her lap, comes up to see me far oftener than Donna does. I tell myself watching Donna chop gizzards in the kitchen that I've been replaced by good girl scout Rosellen and a cat. Every Friday after her last class, Donna packs a small suitcase and I hear the hornet buzz of the Sprite arriving. Peter waits and she runs out to him. Sunday evening he returns her. Out of some surprising delicacy, he rarely enters the house. If I did not see her driven off by him every Friday and returned every Sunday, I would not know they were involved.

The core of falsity in the search for love: a woman gives herself to a man as if that got rid of the problem of making an identity, with a most personal god to reward, pardon or damn. No matter who holds me in his arms my eyes are brown, my teeth poor, my poems unwritten; I must conclude I am more honest alone. On the dustheap and junkyard of my desk I prop my elbows. I will find my work. I have talked and talked, smeared my world with borrowed words and made nothing truly new. Let love strike like lightning if it wants me. I have enough else to learn.

* * *

As I return to the co-op just at curfew, Stephanie is saying good night on the porch to Roger Ardis, a lean paper clip of a man with a wispy beard that reminds me of lichen. Whatever he is saying makes her laugh bubble up frequently, but she breaks from him to follow me inside. My sweater, her skirt, my striped knee socks, her glass beads, if ownership remains. We clatter upstairs. I start blocking out a paper on *A Portrait of the Artist as a Young Man*. Facing me she opens a book but her eyes fix on the window. A pencil loosely held between her blunt fingers with their nails of burnt orange taps, taps.

As we undress she says, "I don't normally confide in women, they're so catty and hypocritical. I mean, you can't shout the truth out the window, but you have to tell it to yourself, no? How many affairs have you had?"

"With men? One that meant something—Mike—and one that only worked at it."

"Is that counting your boyfriend?"

"No such beast." Turning out the light, I crawl into the lower bunk

"That guy I always see you with? Broad-shouldered, with curly hair and glasses. He was in that play—the one I was supposed to be in but Donna stole my part after Rob broke up with me."

"That's Howie. I've known him since high school. Listen, I'm not getting mixed up with anybody. It breaks my back."

"I thought you'd had lots more!" The springs groan as she rolls over to peer down through the dark. "I'd heard you'd slept with *everybody* in PAF. I must say I wondered about Bolognese. But I suppose if you were making it a complete set?"

"Untrue." I am a little alarmed. "A complete set of nothing. Never touched one of them."

"He's actually sort of intriguing. I wonder if his skin is cold. He makes me think of Count Dracula."

"He's very bright," I say loyally. "And political."

"Then no trespassing for me! I had enough of that with

Rob. He used to call me his vacation. But he treated me as a child-mistress—he's only twenty-four. He was never serious with me. It was perfectly evident he wasn't even thinking of marrying me."

"Did you want to marry him? If you don't share his politics—"

"Of course not. A folksinger? I wanted him to want to. Can you imagine what my pa would say? He's looking for a suitable husband for me. Greek, about forty-five and in business. I'll fight that battle when I get to it. He'll leave me in peace as long as I stay in college. But don't you think Donaldson is cute?"

"I adore him. But I always think of him as being permanently on some level involved with Alberta Mann."

"It's true, they almost did get married. But then he wouldn't. I bet he's hard to pin down! Don't tell anybody else I'm not a virgin, okay?"

"In this house? Besides, nobody's likely to think you're one."

"It's one thing to suspect. Never tell a woman anything you don't want a man you're interested in to know." She sighs. "So you don't think there are many? Rosellen wipes the toilet seat before she takes a crap because she honestly believes that's how you get VD. Donna sure isn't. . . ." Stephanie's voice drifts down through my drowsiness, counting me to sleep with numbered maidenheads.

Donna pats herself with bath powder, staring, absorbed, at the pale radiance of her thighs. "Whenever I run into you, you're with Howie lately."

"Why not? He's my best friend." I climb into the full bathtub.

"I'm sorry you didn't end up with a single." She shaves her leg in the basin, stroking the flesh gingerly with a razor. "Honestly, I really thought you would. I moved your stuff into that single and I don't know what happened."

"I like old Stephanie. She's alive."

"Is *that* it? See if you can get her to cut down on the dime-store jewelry and the—gasp—dime-store perfume."

"That's her style. It works for her just fine." And how can you take girl scout Rosellen, big-eyed and banged and ready for Junior Achievement? A life on the Welcome Wagon. I start to laugh suddenly, wanting to make Donna see how ludicrous we are, both naked as worms with the words proceeding between us in carefully wrapped packages.

Maybe she does see. "I know that Roger Ardis. He had a wife. It may be he's misplaced her. . . . Damn!" Blood bubbles from her calf. She dabs wildly at the cut with toilet paper, panicked.

"Let it coagulate," I say. "It'll stop by itself."

"It's not stopping." Setting down the razor she rubs steam from the mirror, eyeing herself in that hostile appraisal. "I want to get married! Tomorrow isn't soon enough. I want it done with. I'm sick of this. Julie's pregnant already and I'm still running in circles."

Stephanie sticks her head in. "Greetings. Get out of the tub and let me in, or I'll be late."

"There's no hot water. This is hardly tepid."

Wrapped in her mandarin robe she plumps down on the toilet seat. "Guess I'll stay dirty. Back to the earth."

Resolutely ignoring Stephanie, Donna continues, "Sick of meaningless shopping around for a decent relationship. Beginning and beginning and losing it all every time. I feel too old for this. I want it out of the way. I want to move on! This business of dating and affairs and breaking up consumes my life when I ought to be free to move into a profession. It's mounting an offensive on two fronts at once." She dabs at the still bleeding cut.

"Bullshit." I pull the stopper and climb out. "You never can *have* anybody, like you put them in a box and go on to bigger things. Plus you're talking about market-economy sex: you invest in somebody and lose. Like what have you lost and what can you win? Loving is an action. You can't have love, you can only do it."

A brief smile like a grimace. "Fine rhetoric, Stu. I do mean to *have* something, for a change. I've been had, quite enough."

"If you think adding Peter's problems to your own will simplify your problems, you haven't discovered life inside the Chinese box factory."

"When you really love someone, it's simpler to be married." She wraps a towel around her and goes out, leaving the door ajar, her leg still bleeding.

Stephanie shuts it. "Paleface is getting the senior jitters."

"It's a mood. Buy now, pay later." What does Donna want from me, an hour of intimacy a week to keep in shape?

"I'll never understand why you're so close. Family ties are gratuitous to me. I have a kid sister and a married sister and they're no more like me than two strangers." Cheerfully, squishing upstairs before me in loose slippers, "Besides, blondes fade early, you know."

At the turn I look back. The door to her room open, Donna lies on the bed wrapped in the towel. With her cheek cradled in the cat's flank she strokes while Minouska carefully washes her flaxen head, licking and pausing to sneeze and trying to settle the fine hair. The look on Donna's face scares me, while Minouska shudders with pleasure. She has fallen into good times. Five days a week she is Donna's only intimate. Weekends she comes up to me, plaintive, questing, looking for Donna around and around the room before she settles for my lap or my bunk.

"There's got to be a cutoff point. There's got to." Howie eats the pizza as fast as I do but he is glowering.

"It'd be easier if you weren't so close to home."

"Well, I'm not going to med school here whatever happens."

"What's keeping them in Detroit?"

"My mother's job and my grandmother's circle of friends. She must have forty old ladies she visits with. My mother's more isolated. She has friends on the job only. . . . Ah, Jill, I've given them a year. I can't carry them anymore. I can't."

"Why do you feel so guilty?"

"Wouldn't you?" He takes another slice.

"I've had to put space between me and my parents. There's distance anyhow between me and my father—we've never been intimate. He didn't take much interest in a girl-child. My mother, it's more like after a divorce. Puberty separated us." Growing a rival woman's body, that was my sin. The blood came between us as if I had begun menstruating to fault her. No more hugging, no more being kissed and cuddled. Suddenly it was all, "Sit with your knees together, are you trying to show men everything you've got?" And, "Exactly where did you go after school? It doesn't take two hours to go to the corner and back." No more the posy in her garden, I was something to be policed, both evil in myself and potentially inspiring of evil from men.

"I love my folks. I want to go on having a decent relationship with them. I don't want to live you do." He rakes his hand through his tight curls. "I want to feel connected. But I'm drained. I haven't done a goddamn thing for a year but my classes and them."

"Why can't you just say that to them?"

"Jill, I try. I think Milt should carry the ball for a while. He says he's got his own family. I say I'll never get a family at this rate. I'll never even get laid."

I laugh. "Well, if you stop going to Detroit every weekend, that should be easy enough around here."

He changes the subject. "Dick told me Donaldson called a PAF meeting for next Thursday. It won't seem like the same old organization without Alberta. By the way, have you heard from her?"

"She passed her bar exam." The pizza is gone. We both poke for crumbs. "I had a bit of a crush on her too, Howie, but it was equally hopeless for both of us, frankly."

Some men when they are angry lower their heads as if to charge. Others throw their heads back and glare down their noses at you. A few, like Howie, turn to stone. "I do not think," he says slowly, "that misadventures with a couple of idiots make you an expert on men and women. Thinking they do gets you in more trouble than if you simply admitted to yourself a couple of accidents don't make anyone fit to teach driving training courses."

"Pardon me for surviving. Of course it's all wonderfully easy for those born lucky. Or is it only born male? I'll give you no more advice at all. Fall down your own flights of steps." Like Donna. I am viewed by everyone as a complete failure in love.

TWENTY-EIGHT
Of the City of Brotherly Love

T HE SURFACE WITH Stephanie is hectic. She rushes
in with skirts flying and tosses her clothes in the general
direction of her bunk. "Five minutes to get ready," she
shouts, taking whatever's at hand, hers or mine, bracelets
jangling and petticoat askew. She hums as she hikes up
her bra an extra inch, rubs a palmful of perfume into her
bronze hair and clatters tinkling downstairs shouting back
instructions about what to tell various men if they call.
For some time Roger Ardis has prevailed in these messages
and in person.

Tonight, Thursday, she curls in the rocker wrapped in a
screaming pink Mexican shawl. She loves bright exotic
things, Indian bangles, Moroccan blouses, Guatemalan
embroideries. Unlike Donna, she will not try to look like
Princess Grace or Marilyn Monroe, but has opted out of
that game altogether. *Of course in the late sixties when
Stephanie's choice became mass fashion, she knew everything about such clothes and started her shop.* "Roger says
he'll get a divorce as soon as Dorothy agrees. Besides, he's

amusing." She clasps her hands behind her head with a savoring smile. "He's giving a party Saturday. Naturally you're invited."

"Thanks, but I hate parties and I have work to do."

She stretches, sauntering to the window. Watching her own reflection on the dark pane she plays with the cord on the halfway shade. "I'm a trifle nervous. I'm sleeping with him as no doubt you've guessed. Don't read me any lectures on married men."

"None forthcoming."

"I didn't mean to." She makes a noose to hang her thumb. "The ways he tried to finagle me into bed amused me so much, I forgot to defend myself. He's a clever beastie." She pulls the cord tight on her thumb till it reddens and swells.

The expression of her sensuality differs markedly from Donna's white heat attraction and ascetic repulsion. "Still, the situation sounds rickety. Be careful."

Over her plump shoulder she smiles at me. "Of what? My reputation?" She yanks her thumb free. "You'll come, won't you?"

"Stephanie, I don't want to."

"Stu, you've got to. For me."

"Please don't call me that."

"*She* does." She flings herself into the rocker. "This will be my first official appearance under the inspection of the old friends who know his wife Dorothy. I'm scared."

"If I'm not at a party to pick someone up, what am I doing? I'll just get drunk and stupid."

"Flirt with someone from your classes. Get a date to bring you." She sighs with exasperation. "Can't you find anyone? I want your backing, Jill. I can't believe you won't turn up some sort of man by Saturday night!"

Little choice for tonight but my red dress, veteran of several years' campaigns. I am repairing the hem when I hear footsteps climbing. Stephanie forgot something?

"I saw your roommate leaving and thought I might come up." Donna's voice breaks high.

I lay the dress on the upper bunk, my nerves stirring as if a cold wind hit them. "Saturday night and you're here?"

"Yes. . . ." She notices the dress laid out. "You have a date?"

"I'm going to a party at Roger Ardis', but not for an hour."

"Stu, do you hate me?"

"Hate you?" I grope for an answer. "No."

"But you're hurt."

"You're hurting yourself."

"I need him, Stu!"

Outside a fine rain is slipping down; I can hear it in the silence between us. "You have him. Don't you?"

"He wants me to meet his parents next weekend. This weekend he's at their house 'preparing' them."

"Have they agreed to meet you?"

She nods. "Official invitation." She pulls from the pocket of her robe a much fingered but still fairly stiff sheet of notepaper, beige with dark brown printing at the top. It is an invitation from Peter's mother to visit them, indeed. One paragraph.

Why is Donna less unsuitable than me? "Should I wish you luck? Like they should all die of typhus before next Friday."

"I'm scared witless. . . . Did you used to get sick about going to visit in Cold Springs?"

Tall gaunt house. "It was stifling. I couldn't breathe. Except when you were there too."

"They daunted me. All those rooms. Elephantine furniture. That big oak staircase, each pillar a tree. Those acres of starched lace curtains."

"And one shriveled lamb chop for supper."

"I could always feel the aunts and Grandfather thinking I wasn't good enough."

"But at least you're blond, kid. The right genes."

"Once when I was little I was sitting on one of those worn plush chairs in the diningroom with my legs dangling, waiting for my mother to get me. I was picking my nose dreamily and I picked out a boogie. I didn't have a hankie so I stuck it on the underside of the chair—and Aunt Mary materialized, in the doorway." Donna holds herself. " 'We don't do that,' she said, '*you dirty little girl.*' "

"They never hurt me because I didn't want them. I wanted my mother's family, my magnificent aunt Riva with her husbands and her hats. My aunt Sarah with her permanent California suntan."

"Oh, my mother's family." Her lips curl from her teeth. "Washboard poor. One of my aunts didn't even have a toilet in the apartment in Flint—it was in the hall. Tow-headed morons sucking their thumbs. Every generation or two they strain real hard and produce a nun who sees angels."

"It's true, the Stuarts are respectable. Took us to screw that."

"Stu, my period's late."

"It should have been Tuesday."

"That's not bad. You've been later than that before."

She looks awkward in Stephanie's rocker, small for it, thin. Her hands grip the arms as if she might suddenly fly up and out. "I know, I know. But I'm scared."

"Why?"

"Because Peter only started sleeping with me recently and I've been using the diaphragm. He kept putting it off at first, I think to punish me for making him wait this summer. He's never going to believe I'm pregnant by him. And you know if I'm knocked up, it isn't Peter."

"From that guy?"

"When he raped me, he didn't use anything."

"Oh." We look at each other. "Get a test."

"It's early. . . . I'll make an appointment. Will you go with me?"

I want to tell her to ask Peter, to ask Rosellen, but then I think, Oh shit, we are connected. "Sure."

"Then you don't hate me?"

"Donna, why him? Why Peter?"

"He's everything I try to be and can't quite bring off. He's bright, he's cool, he's at ease in the world. It belongs to him. He knows as if by instinct what to wear and what to say and where to go and how to be. He has a profession that's important and everybody respects it, but it doesn't consume him. He lives . . . with grace."

I can't think of a damned thing to say, but I wonder if she is involved with the same man I thought I knew.

Her voice flat, she asks, "Do you think he'll marry me?"

"His parents make the rules. Don't expect fair treatment. I doubt if he'll ever break with them."

"Because of the money." She nods, yet I feel the words do not penetrate. "Stu, do you suppose I could go to Roger's party? I'd like to be with people tonight."

"Sure. Why not? But I'm not going till Howie comes by for me."

"I think I'll go right over. I know where he lives, by the bell tower. I'm too nervous to sit still."

After she leaves I dress mechanically. For a few minutes there we touched noses and sniffed as cats will, convinced we were each learning something.

Howie leans on the newel-post. I could warm my hands at his grin as at a brazier of glowing coals. "Very pretty. That's a new dress?"

He has never seen it. A pang, as if I have put something over on him. I take his arm. The rain is fine and penetrating with a cold ammonia smell. Leaves float in the puddles, fish belly up. As I cling to Howie's solid arm worrying out loud about Donna, my blood thaws and races, warming me back to hope.

"Of course if she's really fallen for that nebbish, she won't listen to a thing you say," Howie says. "Sure you want to go to this party?"

"I promised Stephanie." Like Donna I want to be digested into a crowd. I want a loose easy alcohol high. I want to chatter and flirt and evaporate.

I dig out the address, wondering if I got it wrong. We are heading among a mix of university and town buildings near the bell tower. Then we come to a standstill in front of a courtyard. A yellowish bulb in a wrought-iron cage throws its light on the opposing stucco wall, where ivy climbs among the windows: Mike's "damned French" scene that first night. I stop abruptly.

Howie turns. "Changed your mind?"

I'm being a superstitious idiot. A tantalizing babble leaks from the windows of a second-floor apartment, open to the October air. What do I expect to happen at parties? Some encounter? Some transformation? I am drawn, a fly to flypaper, by the press of bodies. "We can always leave in half an hour if we're bored," I offer.

Stephanie dashes to meet us, jiggling my arm in excitement. "Look what a mob we have! This is the party of the month, obviously. If you don't see the booze you want, yell, and I'll steal it. Roger even had a whole turkey roasted. I've been having a ball playing hostess."

Roger leers at me, plucking at the non-colored lichen on his chin, his eyes bright as shards of broken glass. "Jill Stuart, eh, Stephanie goes on about you by the hour. You have her thoroughly conned."

Uncomfortably close to the truth. The apartment is civilized for a graduate student's, for they usually live in warrens like overpopulated and underfed rabbits. He has only the pallor. The furniture is turn-of-the-century with nouveau art touches—glass vases, a lamp base, some Beardsley reproductions. Some person actually exercised a dominant taste in this room, with its grey walls and maroon and navy accents, a taste that hints of money, of leisure, of confidence.

Rosellen tagged along with Donna, whom Charlie, her boyfriend of last spring, has expropriated. They are all sitting on a plush couch with Donna in the middle. Charlie is doing an imitation of the sociology department chairman while the two women laugh wildly. Howie goes off to the kitchenette to open our wine.

"Hi, Jill. How're you doing?" With a tremor of surprise I look into Lennie's lean rabbinical face. He appears any age in a dark suit, his beard longer and more formal.

He backs away from my cry of welcome, his eyes suspicious. "This is my girlfriend."

No name given. Clinging to his side she is dark and shy

as the running shadow of a doe. An exchange of still
greetings. Then with a squirm of shyness she draws his
attention and they walk off. I look to see if Donna has
noticed him, but she is shrieking with that steel mirth.
Charlie is her necessary evil tonight. He watches her with
pride and a daddy's darling look; she does not glance at
him, but looks around. They are all drinking screwdrivers
from a pitcher Charlie mixed. Rosellen, not used to alcohol, has a belligerent uneasy gaze as if she felt something
dangerous inside beginning to hurt. Myself, I am drinking
whatever anyone offers me. I have had a glass of red wine
from Bolognese, with whom I talk about *Being and Noth-
ingness*, which we are both trudging through, a labor of
love. The two of us, to the amusement and contempt of
Dick and Howie, have taken to calling ourselves existentialists.

Then I have a glass of white camel's urine offered by
Dick. Then I have a Scotch from Grant Stone, who carries
the only real flask I have ever seen, inlaid with silver. He
leans into me. "Spore Press is always looking for . . .
eager young writers."

"To plant your spores in?" I ask, already too drunk to be
polite. I don't believe he'd publish me no matter what. If I
believed for a moment he might, I would lack the courage
to insult him.

I have been considered pretty too short a time not to
relish the casual lust of men eyeing me. Like Stephanie, I
can enjoy being looked at, for it is novel and makes me
want to giggle as if I am getting away with something,
knowing that it is really me under the coat of flesh. But
sometimes I cannot handle the brute hostility that peeps
out of the lust, that taint of despisal. I have a glass of
purple passion punch (grapefruit juice, Mogen David wine
and lab alcohol, a local specialty that mutates genes with
each sip) offered by a vaguely familiar man who promptly
tries to pinch my right breast and does not like being
kicked in the shin. Howie is making his own way through
the party, talking now intently to Bolognese who is permanently bent over the diminishing turkey. I appeal to Howie
with my eyes to come, for I feel a little too vulnerable.

"Did you want to be rescued?" he asks, plowing through to me.

"Actually, yes."

"Anything in particular?"

"Everything in its particulars."

Immediately before us Roger leaps up from his wing-back chair. The newcomers are the tall ash-blond Dorothy Ardis and a local dentist Dr. Ashburnham, who grasps her elbow with clothespin fingers. She leans away from the dentist, smiling blandly at Roger, gazing about with large maple-walnut eyes. She surveys the room, touching her fur collar to her throat, strolling among the suddenly invisible guests from the navy plush couch to the Beardsleys. "Why, you have your auntie's furniture out of storage. And so neat. When did you start being neat?"

"I cleaned it," Stephanie mutters to me. "Did he invite her? I'll kill him."

"I'm surviving." Roger walks on Dorothy's free side, his chin grazing her collar. "I've learned to make spaghetti. But tell me, how do I keep the refrigerator from turning into an igloo?"

With a slow smile Howie looks after her stately strut of a crane, a long-necked and long-legged water bird. "She's beautiful. Who is she?"

I answer, "His soon-to-be-ex-wife Dorothy."

"He can't do this to me. He'll introduce me, or I'll break his neck publicly. They'll hose the pieces off the ceiling." Putting on a glittery smile Stephanie marches after them into the kitchenette.

I have lost my glass, so Howie and I drink from the bottle in turns. He asks, "Is Roger trying to make his wife jealous? Or is he just being friendly in a friendly divorce?"

"Your guess is worth mud, like mine. He's a bastard, I think."

Dorothy has handed her coat to her escort and is peering into cupboards while Roger watches her like a dirty movie. The room is contracting, people stretching to the ceiling in poses of fun-house-mirror despair. Donna is pinned to the wall by a spidery man, all arms and legs, surrounding her with his outsized paunch rubbing against her breasts. She looks about to faint, while a cracked smile of immolation distorts her face. Charlie watches with bleak sadness past Rosellen, who lies half sprawled across him, crying.

"I shouldn't drink. I shouldn't go to parties. It unpeels my skin," I tell Howie. That midnight moment has arrived when my skull is lifted off and on the wet grey convolutions of my brain are printed directly the misunderstandings and mismatings in this room. "It's hopeless."

He takes the bottle from me. "So stop."

Stephanie is gallantly trailing the married couple, bringing up the rear with the dentist. Charlie has taken Donna by the hand but she pulls from him. "I'm just starting to have fun!" she whines. Her face is sharp with forced gaiety. Her eyes pass blindly over me. She will never listen.

"I don't know why I feel so naked, looking at people." I sway forward, bump Howie's arm. Room, a funnel of wrong noises.

"You want to leave?"

"Yes . . . but . . . I feel sick." I hate the room, the people with open sores jostling each other. I push blindly at him until he guides me into the hall, shutting the door of the apartment behind us. The sudden chill, the dimness of the stairway bulb suspended like a dying sun in limbo, the collapsing of roar into murmur, only increase my dizziness. He looks so familiar bending over me—"Are you sick? Jill? Do you want air?"—that I burst into tears. As he puts his arms around me, I burrow into his chest and cry harder against his sweater.

His chest is warm through the wool. Warm and broad. If I move forward half an inch, it will be a simple embrace. He is holding his breath. The tears dry on my face as I stand and desire rips at me as if I had walked into a giant cactus. "There, there," he mumbles. Points of heat flare where we touch. If I raise my face, I could kiss his mouth. Want to. But like this? Sodden, stupid, like grabbing a hotwater bottle. Desperate as Donna grabbing at Charlie. I stand suspended in desire holding my breath till my fingers and breasts ache. I wince against his chest and step back.

"Sorry, Howie. I'm a sloppy drunk."

He takes a step toward me, pauses. "I'll get our coats. Are you really all right?"

I nod but do not get out of his way. I stand against the door. With every muscle I wish he would take hold of me. Maybe he is my rational choice, but I can't make that choice for both of us. The door opens and I almost fall in. Stephanie pushes past me, slamming it.

"Jill! I'm glad you're here. I thought you'd left."

"We're leaving now."

"That dirty low-down rat!"

"What did he do?"

She wrings her hands with anger. "He wants me to pretend to go home and come back after. And clean up, I suppose! He's playing a double game. I'm through!"

"Get your coats." Howie steers us each by an elbow. "I'll see you home."

As we are putting on our wraps, Roger strolls up. "Leaving already? Things are just getting started."

"I do have hours. I'll run along with Jill and Howie."

As he leans close to speak in her ear, she smiles through matted lashes. "Sure, honey. See you later." As we walk down she twirls her scarf, laughing theatrically. "How long will he wait up? Not long enough. I hope Dorothy divorces him and marries her dentist. She strikes me as a cavity that could well be filled with gold."

Through the quiet streets we compete in laughter. Alcohol simmers in my brain. At the door Howie and I have no moment for private leave-taking that might connect with what almost did or didn't happen in the hall.

I lie on my bunk with questions circling and bobbing and pursuing like a race of carousel horses. If he is attracted to me, wouldn't he have made a move? But I could not. I did not dare. If I let him know that I want him and he only likes me as a friend . . . I feel hollow. He could stop being my friend. I need him as a friend.

Stephanie climbs into the upper bunk. "I can see why you like that guy Howie. He has a good sense of humor."

Will he laugh at me? I clutch the pillow as the bed swoops backward. I drink too much, I talk too much!

Discipline. The bed rushes backward through the night like a crack express. Occasionally Stephanie sobs in the dark. I must think hard about him. Am I crazy, am I sick, am I corrupt suddenly to want him, after all these years? I don't think I ever touched him before, except for holding his hand at his father's funeral. Please bed, lie still. Oh, but I wish he had reached out, there in the hall.

TWENTY-NINE

Procrastination Must Be a Genetic Trait

MONDAY NIGHT OR rather 1:40 A.M. Tuesday a week and a half later, the cheap alarm I have carried into the kitchen with me ticks like a headache. My thick lids swell. I am sodden with instant coffee tasting of burnt cork. Sleep weights my brain while I try to atone, my neglect of the eighteenth century. Tomorrow morning an exam yawns. What have I been doing? Writing a verse play—a proper bitter cud of two lovers and how they died to each other, couched in the Bluebeard myth. Instead of the course's prescribed readings, I have consumed not a taste of Pepys but the whole diary, mounds of Rochester, Defoe, Pope . . . and now all night I must read the dreary rounds of those dull worthies who will stock the examination. In the middle of Thomson's *Winter* it is winter indeed. Shenstone, Warton, Pomfret . . . eating excelsior. My chin slides forward, coming to rest on *The Task*.

"Sleeping in that position will give you backache." Donna carries in a typewriter with books and erasable bond balanced on top.

"Procrastination must be a genetic trait."

"I didn't get any work done this weekend."

"You met them? How did it go?"

She shrugs. Face scrubbed clean. The skin around her eyes is blue and papery with fatigue. "Can't say yet. They didn't poison me. I'm not what they want, but I may be what they'll accept." She yawns.

I yawn. We work in silence, facing over the kitchen table. When she rises in forty minutes to put on water for tea, she asks, yawning again, "Stephanie's giving up on Roger Ardis?"

"With bells and banners."

She nods. "Is she going out with your friend Howie, then?"

"Howie?" I am wide awake. "What makes you ask?"

"I saw her sit down with him in the Union yesterday. She was her . . . uh, animated self. Meaning she didn't completely crawl across the table to sit on his lap but nearly."

Could I ask him casually, What do you think of Stephanie? But suppose he hasn't yet? Donna is waiting patiently, and I am glad of the bedrock empathy that brings her to me with the observation, just in case it's relevant, and lets me say bluntly, "Thanks," instead of having to pretend the news does not matter. Stephanie never mentioned meeting him. I have exams this week, a paper due, a summons home I will feel guilty if I ignore. Mother has been in terrible pain with her teeth, the same rotten set she passed on to me. Francis made an appointment for her at some clinic downtown on Saturday morning but he wants me to come in and accompany her. I have to take the bus into Detroit Friday evening. What do I want from Howie? What do I dare want with him? What can I have? I would like to hypnotize him into answering me before proceeding.

"What have you been doing with Howie? Waiting for him to grow up and get broken in? A dangerous business."

"I can't be sure what I want." Loyalty to the cemetery afternoons, the dialectical fencing, the love that was all words. "You can't just add sex to what you have with a friend and see how it flies."

"Once you would have said, why not?"

"Meaning the taste of blood has made me a coward? But, Donna, I never said, *why not*, to you."

"Why not?" She grins, looking years younger. "Sometimes I used to feel you were on the verge of asking or whatever."

"Same reason as with Howie," I say untruthfully, for Howie never put pressure on me to become sexually involved with other people. Howie may think I am out of character or out of line, but he will not judge me sick. Theo, as far as I know, is still behind bars for asking that question. Donna is flirting a little with me tonight. "Did your period start?"

"Not yet," she answers with no surprise at my lack of transition. The subject is on her mind all of the time. "I'm supposed to get the results of the test tomorrow."

"Did you tell Peter?"

She laughs, something catching in her throat—a rusty bike chain. We sit face-to-face again, and again we work in silence for half an hour. Then I break my concentration to rummage through the large refrigerator, looking for leftovers legitimate to nibble on. A dish of wilted salad. Some zucchini casserole no one could endure. She leans back in her seat watching me with a friendly gaze.

How was their place?" I ask. "Like the delivery boy, I got as far as the door."

"Beautiful, Stu!" Her eyes widen. "On four levels, with a courtyard where they retained an oak. Fieldstone fireplaces. Spanish tiles in the kitchen. Every bedroom has its own huge john. Abstract epressionist paintings the size of billboards in a living room you could use for a dorm lounge. Fabulous view of the lake. A maid and a part-time woman too. Darkroom fancier than my mother's kitchen. A pool table. What I can't get over is the details—like inlaid boxes of English Oval cigarettes put out for guests. My room had Early American antiques. A pair of tiny French poodles that belong to his mother called Droit and Gauche . . ." She stops abruptly. I can feel her editing the speech. Never again will she gush about Peter's family. "They live quite comfortably."

Well, Peter should have enough money to support if not
a tree in the bedroom and two maids, at least an army of
Oval Early American poodles smoking handcrafted hook-
ahs and dropping the expressionist ashes in Lake St. Clair.
Although she sees Peter bringing her into the Cinderella
world, I am sure she sees him as the jewel of that world,
her own glass prince. "Would you be comfortable around
them, Donna?"

"But we won't be around them. We're going to live in
New York. That's my secret bottom line. I have to get him
away from them and I know it—I'm not as blind as you
think—but what's going to happen if I'm pregnant? I can't
bear to think about it and I can't think about anything
else."

"How much money do you have?" This litany, this litany. I go through it every four months with some woman
and I have gone through it with Donna before. How much
money, what shall we do, who do you know, and will they
do it and how much humiliation and pain will it cost and
will they do it in time? At least on this occasion I am
prepared. "Donna, I have a list of abortionists. You don't
mean to have it, right?"

"Are you kidding? I'd strangle a baby that looked like
. . . that goon. I hate to go downtown now. I'm always
afraid I'll see him. Once I did, Stu. Really. It was him."

"Where?"

"On Ashley downtown there's a bar called Ovid's. I saw
him coming out of there when Peter was getting his car
gassed up across the street." She shudders visibly, goose
pimples on her forearms. "I have a hundred dollars. I put it
away gradually. I wanted to buy some clothes, good
clothes."

"I have twenty-three. That's it. But I could borrow
some."

"How much do we need?"

"If the doctor in Dexter will do it, three fifty. I haven't
checked his prices this fall." Bleakly we look at each other.
"Don't worry, we'll get it," I say heartily. She is my friend
again. In some subterranean cavern awakens the hope of

winning her back. I will save her, I myself, not Peter. I will
go to Detroit and be good to my mother and make her love
me. I will come back and seduce Howie magically without
his realizing I am seducing him: he will think it is his idea.
I will find the money somewhere and save Donna. Everybody will love me, because I am good and indispensable.

Beside me on the bus my mother fumes in her old musk-
rat coat with her hair standing up like angry black flames
around the red toque. I have forced her to go. What intox-
ication to find I can assert and insist now, as if absence
had turned into authority! She argued, she pleaded, she
made excuses. She said she had a headache, a stomachache. Her feet hurt. Next week would be better. Ah, the
sharp salty pleasure of forcing somebody to do something
you consider good for her. I am mothering my mother with
all the harsh efficiency she has often used on me. For your
own good, I croon. "Why I go to the dentist all the time. I
practically spent my first semester in dental school. Because *you* never took me to the dentist, I had the worst
teeth they'd ever seen." Make her feel guilty. Then do for
her what she wouldn't do for me. Oh, the pleasure of
growing up. I always knew I'd like being an adult.

Dr. McMeel is downtown in an old building where we
sit for almost an hour before she is called in. I have a
feeling this dentist was picked out by price, but he may be
the only dentist Francis found out about by asking—where,
at the corner bar? I shouldn't blame him. At least he
made the appointment. My father has done nothing but
put pressure on her and pooh-pooh her fears, as I have
been doing. This guy does a volume business with a clientele that is mostly poor and mostly Black.

Well-thumbed copies of *Life* and *The Saturday Evening
Post* and two ancient *National Geographic*s somebody has
ripped pictures out of. I have my homework. I do it for an
hour and then for another. What is happening? We've been
here since nine forty-five. Now it's one and I'm hungry. I
begin to wonder if there is another exit. Perhaps, confused,
she left by a different door. Feeling like an idiot, I ask the

receptionist, who makes me feel more idiotic. I return to my seat. Probably Mother has Dr. McMeel telling her his life story.

When she comes out, she is staggering. She walks as if by brute willpower, one step forward, pause, then the next step forward. Her mouth is smeared with caked blood where she holds a mass of wadded tissues. "And this is the prescription, Mrs. Stuart. You get this filled downstairs."

She will not look at the receptionist. I take the prescription.

"And that will be seventy-five for the extractions, Mrs. Stuart, and twenty down."

I count the cash out of her purse, a clump of wadded-up bills, fives and tens and ones folded together in a bulging coin-purse. The last six dollars I pay in coins.

"Your teeth will be ready next Wednesday."

She leans on me in the hall, her face turned away. I ask, "What did he do to you?"

"Leave me alone!" Her voice is funny, a husky lisp with a hint of coyness.

"Did he give you novocaine?" I try to look at her but she keeps her face turned from me. I am almost carrying her. I realize as we reach the street I am never going to succeed in dragging her to the bus. "Mother, can you stand here? Lean on the lamppost. Please. I'm going to get a cab."

"Ha." She turns her head away from me. "Who nees? Wase sa money."

I have to force her into the taxi. "Mother! What did he do to you?"

Her cheeks sag, suddenly flaccid. She looks older than she looked this morning. I cannot stand her pain. "Puhd 'em all." She turns away from me, holding the wad of bloody tissues to her mouth.

"He did what?" But I figure it out. "He pulled some teeth?" I had some pulled when I was sixteen, but since I went to college, they don't seem to pull teeth. They do all kinds of fancy and time-consuming work, but rarely do they extract.

"All! All!" She bares her bleeding gums at me. Her

mouth is full of dark blood welling. Her eyes burn with rage.

"But why?"

That night I eat alone with my father. She is staying in bed. Occasionally the springs wince and she gives voice to a broken muttering, a formless lament that rises and falls again behind the closed door. All day she has taken nothing but weak tea. I cannot endure seeing her look old. I don't want her to put on that strange ravaged face. Suddenly she seems made of eggshell and rice paper. Sharp edges everywhere she could be blown against. Myself the sharpest edge.

My father and I try to make conversation. We discuss the Tigers. The last team I followed was six years earlier, but I try. He talks about the Russians with a plaintive irritation, as if I were somehow in the confidence of Khrushchev. Lacking common subjects we fish for neutral ones and come to a series of dead ends like a set of roads paved near Cold Springs for a suburban development that was laid out but never built up after the mines closed. We go up each cul-de-sac and find nothing and hastily return. Finally we talk about the weather earnestly. It is a wet fall, yes, and a cool one and not much sun. Yes. Then he finds a subject: the virtues of polyester. Mother has bought him some polyester shirts and Orlon socks and he describes their superiority. Listening, I realize how Donna has educated me in inappropriate snobbery. I may have only five shirts and three of them from the Nearly New Shoppe, but they are all cotton or silk.

By Sunday Mother gets up. She is not capable of lying long in bed no matter how she feels. She makes regular meals for my father and me (Francis has moved in with a friend in Ecorse, a working-class suburb; he has got a job at Great Lakes Steel) while she eats consommé. I go down to the corner store on Joy Road to get her some jars of baby food. At table a hectic bitterness works in her, pulling the corners of her small mouth down, pinching her nose. *I am not going to render her speech as she sounded. We could figure out what she was saying, well enough.*

"My anniversary present," she calls the bridge being made for her. She has never stopped minding that my father won't observe their anniversary. "That's what your father gave me for Halloween. Now I'm an old witch." She droops, her short neck bent. "I can't eat this slop!"

Dad puts down his fork. "Suppose I cut the beef up fine, Pearl?" His voice is shy and tender. We avoid each other's gaze, conspirators who robbed her of her teeth.

"I think that dentist was a quack." She picks at the baby food, a tear running down the groove beside her nose. Without my demon appetite I would flee the table. "I saw those teeth he pulled, my teeth! There was a lot left on some of them."

"But you were in pain." He pleads with her. "You were lying awake nights with the pain."

"I let him go ahead because I was sick and tired of both of you badgering me. He said it was cheaper to pull them than to fill them, and it'd only take two visits. Otherwise I'd have to go down there for months."

I want to lay my head down on the table and weep. What is the use arguing with her now, as my father becomes entangled in doing? The teeth are pulled. Even now I wonder why. Were they that bad? Was he a man who saw no reason to bother with a woman without money, like the dentist who pulled three of mine when I was sixteen? Did she really do it to save money? That's possible. It's painfully hard for her to spend money on herself. Of course, I think, it isn't her money. She does not work for money, she works for free, and that makes all the difference.

When I get off the bus with my suitcase and basket of food, it's ten thirty. I do not head for my co-op but go directly to Howie's. As I walk between houses muffled in fog, the blocks feel elongated. I walk and walk and walk. This weekend has peeled a skin from me, leaving me raw to my hope. Brother me no brothers. I go without plans or prepared speeches. On the bus I would not permit myself a fantasy. I only know that I want him but that I do not mean to impose that wanting on him, that I am unwilling for the least fence of reticence or awkwardness to build between us because of my sudden lust. I have no idea how to bring off this miracle of indirection and discretion but trust to blind luck. Indeed! Shall I walk in, take off my coat and then the rest of my clothes to stand there naked? "Hey, Howie, what does this make you think of?"

I halt in the fog. No light shines from his corner room. He must be out. Damn. Well, I could wait awhile in the hall. Maybe he's napping. I climb the stairs to rap on his door. "Howie? Howie, are you home?" I shift from one foot to the other in the dim hall.

Sounds. A line of light suddenly marks the door. He is home! "Jill? Is that you?"

"The very same. Let me in."

"Just a minute." He adds something I can't catch. Absurdly electric with excitement, I turn to and fro in the hall, urging him silently to hurry, hurry. As the door swings open, Stephanie dances across the room barefoot, tucking her blouse in. With a breathless laugh she combs her hair back with her fingers. "You got my note? Good. Howie came by to see if you were back, so we went to supper." She laughs again, not nervously but in high spirits. "How was Detroit?"

I want to bellow my disappointment but I must speak sweetly not to spill my envious guts on the floor. "No, I didn't get your note." I had better play this straight, for they will see the luggage in a moment. "I stopped by on my way from the bus—my arm's breaking. By the way, we're both just in time not to be late." My chest feels tight and dry. I lick my lips, staring around the room.

"Late?" She swirls, that overflowing exuberance in her movements. "Guess it is time."

Too late for me. She says, "Come, walk us home and help Jill carry her junk." Running to step into her boots, in passing she rumples his hair. He ducks and our gazes meet, shy off. So, that is that. I point out his glasses on the nightstand and he puts them on.

Beside me as we walk back she starts sentences and leaves them unfinished, breaks from us to twirl around to face us. Howie yawns on the far side of her.

When we are alone, she hurls herself into the rocker, wrapping the Mexican shawl around her shoulders against our room's chill. "He's a strange complex man. More so than Rob or Roger, even if he is young. I'd always been attracted to older men. This is a new breakthrough for me."

"Actually he's younger than you are," I say with weak malice.

"But he's strong, even if he hasn't that commanding manner." She cocks her head waiting for me to agree. "Stu, don't tell him about Roger. I said I never really slept with him."

After what he heard? "But why?"

She plays with the shawl's fringe. "That's too recent. I'm sure he liked it better this way." She sighs, rubbing the shawl against her cheek. "I hope you won't think I'm . . . callow. But I was exaggerating about sleeping with Rob. I didn't want you to know how inexperienced I was. . . ."

My head flips like a coin. Rob but not Roger for Howie; Roger but not Rob for me; and for her? I don't know that I buy it at all. Rob has certainly been to bed with Lynn and several other women I know, and Stephanie went out with him for over a year.

"I was a virgin with Roger. Wasn't that a stupid beginning?" She pulls the shawl up to cover her face. "My father, do you know I'm afraid of him? He'd kill me if he knew. What a botch he's made of me. Praising me, oh Papa's little darling, the prettiest one, who'd better mind Papa or she'll get her arm broken."

Her voice urgent, sibilant. Casting a spell. "Stephanie, you have left home, after all. . . ."

"Nonsense. You don't leave that easy where I come from. Don't interrupt! And don't tell anyone, ever. Ever since I was a child I've wakened at night and seen him standing by the foot of my bed staring at me. He still makes me sit in his lap when he gives me my allowance. In high school he kept telling me how dirty boys were. They'll want to get under your dress. He's out of his mind. I wonder I'm not." She lowers the shawl, twisting it. "To get free of him! I've never told this to anyone, I won't again. At Roger's, whenever there was a step in the hall, I used to sit up in bed terrified it was him. A man for me has to be strong. Strong enough to throw Papa downstairs the way he threw me down when I was foolish enough to accept a date in high school." She stops short, taking a breath that escapes in that bubbling laugh, and I breathe again. Her story has beaten me into a submission of the imagination. She lets the shawl drop, sitting up. "Yes, look at me. You see how much I need Howie!"

I sit dazzled. Then I remember a fact nibbling my mind: she has two sisters. Stephanie, I'm sure it's all true but also exaggerated for effect. "Have you told him this?"

"No, and I never will. You think I want to scare him off? He'll save me, without knowing he has. I mean to do this one right."

Poor Howie or not? "Right, how?"

"Because it's going to be a long haul. He's bound for medical school. I won't be a drag on him—I hate women who cling and strangle men. My mother's like that. I mean to be civilized."

"It's only just happened. You may want a man, but is it Howie?" *Me*, he came to see tonight, *me*, I want to shout, but it is too late to complain. I have only my own procrastination and quibbling to blame. The next man I'm interested in I'll jump first and think about it afterward.

Kicking off her boots, she tucks her feet under her. The flush that marked her face in his room warms it again. "He'll be a handful. He's stubborn and not at all broken in. No woman has rubbed down his sharp corners yet. Demanding and independent as a porcupine. I'll hold him on a very loose rein." She hugs her knees. Her restlessness tortures me, all this energy struck into heat by him. "You must tell me everything you know about him—everything!"

"Nobody's the same with two people. We've been friends, and that's a different matter."

"And you'll go on being friends. You'll see—I won't interfere with you in the least. If you hadn't been friends, how would I have met him? Even if the two of you were together one time and got drunk or something and ended up in bed, I'd understand. I don't expect him to be faithful to me one hundred percent."

"Don't be absurd." I stand up and begin unpacking. "It isn't that kind of relationship."

"I know," she says soothingly. "I'm just trying to explain how I feel. I mean, two people can't pledge to be absolutely everything to each other forever. I don't want him to feel I kept him from anything he wanted or thought for a while he wanted."

"Agreed. But you might be more jealous than you imagine. One can rationalize and reason till the sky falls in and mean it, and still be blind jealous," I say with real feeling.

"I'm sure you're right. . . . He fascinates me. I knew something good was going to happen. It was time, it had to. I want so much to break out! I hope I'm wise enough to hold on to him."

Against my will and my desire, I almost hope so too.

I know that one of these damned days I am going to be forced to have my phone unlisted, but I put it off because it seems like giving up on being a real person. Besides, I want sponsors to find me for readings because that's a lot of my income. Unfortunately strangers call up all times of the day and night, surprised that when they want to tell me their feelings or ask personal questions because they imagine they know me as I do not imagine I know them, I turn out to be in the bathtub or asleep and cranky or eating supper with my mouth full of potatoes.

The worst is when somebody arrives on the doorstep. That morning, eleven thirty actually, when I've usually been at my typewriter for a couple of hours already, Josh and I were both naked and screaming at each other about who said who ought to go on a diet. If I'm interrupted in midfight, I would prefer to be overheard arguing politics or philosophy and not whether Josh or I implied the other was carrying five or six pounds extra around the belly.

We have tempers and we screech a lot, unlike my last husband who thought if you expressed hostility aloud (instead of quietly acting it out for the next decade), the trees would wither in a quarter of a mile radius and the song-

*birds drop dead feet up. Josh and I have fights where we
both swear we are about to drive off in the night or kill
ourselves; we have silly fights like this one make up at once
in bed, where we belonged right then.*

*"I'm never going to eat anything," my Roaring Boy was
bellowing. "I'm going to starve myself to death!"*

"Hello? Hi?" The voice came through the screen door.

*We looked. Josh said with slightly crushed urbanity—
both of us being more modest of our privacy than of our
privates—"Hi there. Er, who are you looking for?" Hoping
it was our summer neighbors.*

"Jill, of course."

That didn't mean anything. They all call me Jill.

*"Yes," I said. "Look, I like people to call before they
appear." I did let her in, naked as I was, because I never
know if they're in real trouble. Sometimes women who call
really need something I can give or pass along or provide,
like concrete help. I have the normal capacity to feel smug
after being of assistance. But most times it's ego knocking.*

*"I hitchhiked from New York today. I thought mother
would find the note and call you by now. . . ." She was
following me into my bedroom, when I turned to snarl,
"Sit in the living room, please. I'll be back in five minutes."*

*Josh slumped on the bed, having carefully shut the door.
"Oh, here I am your groupie from Indianapolis who just
happened to be on vacation nearby and I've brought a four-
thousand-page manuscript I plan to read aloud. Here we
are a whole coven of us and we're about to make a druidi-
cal sacrifice of a blue goat on your front lawn. Here I am,
an all-A student, writing a term paper on you, and I've
come to ask you to fill out a forty-six-page questionnaire
on your religious and philosophical beliefs for my research."*

*"Shhhh. Since I'm not offering you around for lunch,
why don't you put your pants back on?"*

*The bastard excused himself, offering to go to town for
the mail. I strode out but our visitor had disappeared into
the kitchen. She sat on the table swinging her foot, absently picking up breakfast crumbs with her forefinger.
"Don't you know me, Aunt Jill?"*

*I looked carefully. Frankie died unfathering so far as I
know, but Leo had six kids by various marriages. She
didn't resemble my nieces by Leo, all black-haired with the
family eyes and handsome. Her hair was sandy and kinky,
close to her head. She was big-boned, a little awkward, her
face not formed yet. She wore cutoffs and a shirt tied
under the breasts to leave her waist bare. I shuddered to
think she had hitchhiked from New York dressed that way.
"Karlie?" I ventured.*

"You didn't recognize me because I've changed a lot."

*"When I saw you last you were still a kid." She would be
eighteen in three months. I gave her lunch while she
worked her way up to telling my why she had suddenly
appeared here.*

*"I never knew him." She pouted, perching on the edge of
my kitchen table, butt two inches from the butter dish.
If I moved it, she would be judgmental. She reeked of
discontent and judgment. I stared at her, hoping to read
her father in her face, finding him mostly in her body. "But
your mother certainly did. You're proof of that."*

*"But . . . I want to know what he was really like. Ben
was two, and even he doesn't have any real memories. But
I wasn't even born yet!" She sounded affronted.*

*"Does Stephanie know you've come to see me?" When
Stephanie chatted on long distance Monday night about
her husband and their boutique and her impossible daughter (the one before me, not the nine-year-old Tamara), she
said nothing of an impending visit. Stephanie and I always
talk of getting together, but we do better on the phone. In
person we jar each other.*

*"What business is it of hers? I travel on my own. I don't
need to ask permission. . . . Besides, I left a note."*

*Her eyes were Stephanie's but lighter. Her hair was cer-
tainly his. I noticed she wore under the tied yellow shirt a
Mogen David on a chain. I know she was not raised Jewish. "What do you want to know, that was worth risking
your ass to hitchhike here?"*

*"I didn't come alone," she said reluctantly. "My boy-
friend's at the beach. . . . What was he like? Oh, don't tell
me he was brave and political and a hero and all that shit.*

I've grown up with him, like some stupid icon you burn candles in front of, like *Agios Georgios* killing the dragon on the wall at Grandma's. I can't stand it! He wasn't thinking about me when he got himself killed, and here I am saddled with him forever!"

"Why me? And won't you have more cheese? Another bagel?" Friends brought them to me from New York and I froze them. If I'd known Karlie was coming, I'd have given her a shopping list.

"The *Lightning Elegies*—they're to him?"

"Did Stephanie tell you that? No. To somebody else."

"Well, because it says the guy died too young."

"They were to a woman who died even younger. Another friend."

"Oh. . . . But you were his big affair, right? That's what I've picked up, around."

"We were friends, Karlie. Friends from the time we were sixteen. When I was your age, he was my best friend."

THIRTY
Donna Calls It Slumming, Jill
Calls It Down-Home

I CAN REMEMBER WHEN Ann Arbor felt marvelous, a book of a thousand pages containing all I did not know and longed to. Now it is merely a small city whose least collegiate sections I prefer, the Black and working-class blocks that remind me of Detroit. I am corresponding with Alberta and planning to move to New York in June. The green pastoral hills of Ann Arbor bore me.

I am strolling along Ashley with money heavy on my mind, four hundred dollars to be exact, when dead ahead of me on the sidewalk outside a bar known as a towny hangout I see him, Donna's rapist. As I turn to avoid him and his friends, it infuriates me. Why should his presence force me off a sidewalk in broad daylight? I walk on toward the three men. A moment later I begin to regret my bravado. One of the guys, his black hair preened into a Presley pompadour, is looking at me. He wears a style that is absolutely a class uniform: Levi's, black leather jacket with studs, motorcycle cap. Nobody at the university dresses that way. He stares straight at me and to the rapist he says, "Hey, Buddy, you better run for it. Here comes the broad that beat you up."

"Aw, shit, Kemp, she didn't do nothing. I didn't want to hit her, that's all."

By the time I realize they are not going to let me slip by, it is too late to do anything but persist. After all we grow out of the same street life. I can't act chicken any more than they can. I have two seconds to figure out a defense, and that must issue from my emotional boil which is closer to anger than fear. "Yeah, Buddy," I say but keep eye contact with the leader. He was driving the car that day. "You're a big headache to me. You knocked my cousin up. She's supposed to marry her boyfriend and she's in a lot of trouble because of what you made her do."

"Big deal. So she gets married with a belly. Her and everybody else."

"She can't get married. She told you she didn't sleep with guys. She doesn't do it with her boyfriend. So it can't be passed off as his."

"Don't look at me. I ain't claiming it either."

All the guys laugh. I keep looking at Kemp. "I'm going to get her an operation, from that doctor in Dexter. But her folks don't have money. We're both in this place on scholarships. So if you want to know why I'm mad at you, I got a good reason, 'cause I don't know where to get that money."

"Get lost," Kemp says to his friends. "Hang out in Ovid's," he pronounces it Oveed's. "I'll see you later."

They obey him. I do not walk off. I am curious about what he is going to say. He does not say anything but takes my elbow in a firm but by no means rough grip and steers me across the street to the silver convertible I recognize. He opens the door on my side. "No dice," I say. "No reason to make it two for two. I got enough problems."

"Never used force on a female in my life. In my opinion, guys who got to do that, they don't know their prick from a baseball bat. You're safe with me, if you want to be safe." He strolls around to climb in his side.

Standing there I surprise myself by grinning broadly. What is it? A little Francis, a little Dino. He moves with the grace of a man whose body is his only asset. Whatever he saw in me in the last five minutes I have also seen in him. I get in, thinking I am being both stupid and reckless. As he turns the ignition on, the car radio begins to play hard driving rock. The great boat of the car swings out into the street and lurches off. The music is loud; we do not talk.

In ten minutes we are on a country road. I must be out of my mind. Casually I reach into my purse and arrange my keys (the key to the co-op that Alberta gave me, the keys to my parents' house, the key to the room where PAF meets) between my knuckles. An empty Stroh's Bohemian Ale bottle lies on the floor. I put my foot on it to roll it within grabbing distance.

He pulls up at a dead end on a bluff overlooking a wide bend of the river. The sun is setting and the scene would be pretty if I wasn't scared. He broods on it. "What are you going to do for money?"

"I don't know," I say. "I've been trying to borrow some."

"You could make it hustling."

"Shit on that. I saw too much of that hard life when I was home. I won't do that, even for her."

"You could make a lot of money that way. Fast."

"I don't want to use myself that way. I'd rather steal the money than whore for it."

He laughs. "You'd rather steal it. You think that's easy to do?"

"No. But acceptable. Why?"

"Just curious." He grins at me. His eyes are the color of my mother's (flash of guilt, her lost teeth), of mine. His skin is darker. He has strong teeth but an incisor is discolored, probably from being struck. His hands rest on the wheel, lightly. "I like this place."

"I've never been here."

"Bet there's a lot around here you never seen."

"I bet you're right."

"I respect your coming to me. I respect that. You got

guts." He gives the wheel a chop with the side of his hand.

He thought I came down that street on purpose. "Guts or naïveté? What is it?"

"You still a little scared?"

"Why not?"

"You're not going to pull that number your cousin did. Say you're a virgin."

"What has that got to do with it? You think because I balled one man, I got to ball every man who thinks he wants to? How would you like it if you had to ball any woman anytime she thought you ought to?"

"You only had one man?"

"Two."

"Want to make it three?" He extends his arm along the back of the seat.

"My mind's on money, not sex."

"Like you say, you won't hustle for money. But if I told you I'd help you get the money, you'd ball me."

He's not stupid. I draw my legs up and face him on the bench of the seat. I cannot help but smile. "What do you do? Who are you? Were you born in town? Is Kemp your first or last name?"

"The sun's down. I like to get out in the country. When I was a kid, there was a lot more country here. Not so many fancy professors' houses. More rabbits and pheasant. Even some deer. Ever had deer meat?"

"My uncle Floyd used to give it to us. He worked in the mines in Pennsylvania and when he was off work, he liked being in the woods."

"I work in an optics factory. Ball-busting work. Gives you a headache so your scalp could break open like a cracked tomato. Buddy works there too and Ray. One good thing is we go through it together."

"Buddy really hurt her. It was no joke. She was covered with bruises and her back was so sore she had to stay flat for two days."

Kemp shrugs. "Buddy's a horse's ass. You give him something, he won't let go of it."

"You never did answer me your name. What do you think I'll do if I know it?"

"I don't want to ball you here. In the car. I want to take you back to my house. See, if you want to talk, we got to go to bed. Because otherwise we don't have enough of a basis in common. Right?"

"Orville Wright. It'll never get off the ground."

"Sure it will. All you got to say is yes."

"Otherwise will you take me back to town?"

"Right back where you live. Think I'd dump you here? One time I found a girl walking down the road, eleven thirty at night with her blouse tore. Some dude from the basketball team did it to her. Tore her blouse because she wouldn't fuck him. So he just dumped her out of the car in the middle of Lodi township."

"You going to tell me you rescued her?"

"Sure. Why not? Besides, she wasn't my type. Too skinny. Flat all over. And she was shaking. I don't like broads that scare easy."

I don't want to go back to the co-op where Stephanie is gloating about Howie and Donna is worrying about Peter. Besides, he feels so curiously down-home. If I had got involved with Kemp at fifteen, it would have been fatal; but at twenty, I suspect I can have him if I want and survive handily. "Who lives in your house?" I don't want a gang bang set up on me.

"Just me. I'm on my own. You'll be surprised. I live good." He switches on the engine and the lights. Suddenly it is night.

"Could we eat first? I'm hungry. I usually am."

"How about spaghetti and meatballs? At my place. I bet I cook better than you do."

"No contest." I sit back. Whatever crazy thing I am doing, I am doing it.

Kemp has a little house on a gravel road you get to by going way out West Liberty until you begin to see working farms. He has a bedroom and a combination living room-kitchen heated by a wood stove. Outside, the neatly split wood is stacked. It's homey and certainly as clean as I keep my room back at the co-op.

Times blur. With Kemp few sharp scenes form. The first time was more awkward than the succeeding times, but our conversation always occurred in spurts.

Kemp is no reprise of my childhood delinquents, for country and city blend and collide in him. He grows tomatoes, lettuce and eggplants in his garden. The sweet and the hot peppers are around the corner from each other. He says the hot peppers are male and the sweet peppers are female, and if you put them in the same bed, the males get at the females and make them hot too. Between my first and second visits, we have a frost. He pulls up the tomato plants entire and hangs them from the rafters. The hot peppers he dries. The sweet ones fill the refrigerator. He chars them at the flame in the wood stove, then braises them in olive oil.

He is the first really good cook I have met. I think from an occasional pot of sumptuous rosemary chicken or manicotti that appears after he has been at home, that his mother taught him. He's a bastard; Kemp was his father's last name, a married truck driver. His father gave his mother money when Kemp was little but after the man went away to the army, they never heard from him again. His mother waited all through the war; then in 1946 when Kemp was eleven, she married a man who worked in the same plant. She was thirty then and she had three more children in rapid succession, lost a couple and finished with one more at thirty-eight. Kemp has two half brothers and two half sisters. We agree that connection through the mother is strong.

Because he was a boy and already beginning to run with the other guys and pull away from home when his siblings began to appear in an almost annual harvest, he did not feel stuck with them. He loves to appear laden with presents, playing Kemp the magnificent. He struts like a dark rooster, adored by everybody except his mother's husband Jerry, who is awkward with him. Kemp doesn't mind. "Julietta," he says, his name for me since he finds Jill too Wasp, "I owe him a big one. He got me off the hook." Because he feels he lives better than they do, he tastes a little guilt: hence the constant presents. "If she hadn't of married that poor tired old horse, I'd still be handing over half of my paycheck, still paying on a mortgage from the year one for a house at least that old." One of the presents he takes to his siblings this week are brother and sister kittens—Minouska's offspring.

He is cock of the walk, he is king of his cronies, so he may indulge himself in cooking. He cooks and I wash dishes. He is as fussy as my mother that I get them clean, but he is better than my mother at teaching me to cook. She wanted my help without wanting to share her skills. Most of what he cooks is Italian, but if we eat out and he tastes something he likes, he attempts to reproduce it. Because he didn't learn from books, he lacks the vocabulary I will acquire later. When he is telling me to do some assistant's job, he will say, "You put it on the soft fry," in teaching me how to sauté onions instead of frying them to brown plastic shards. He calls it a soft fry because it leaves food soft.

Because he likes to eat well, because he likes to carry presents to his two half brothers and his two half sisters who lack too many things for the list ever to sustain a serious dent no matter how fervid his generosity, because his mother has a bad chronic cough, because nobody knows more how to enjoy what there is before him to enjoy, he supplements his income from the optics factory with thieving.

He has a good mind that has passed through public school with its ignorance of books or the world of culture never enduring abrasion. He has not read a book since he left school except for a try at *Tropic of Cancer* in a battered and imported paperback, because he was told it was dirty. Betsy, one of the whores who hang out at Ovid's, gave it to him. Her clientele is university professors. Certainly she reads more contemporary fiction than anybody I ever found teaching in the department of English.

His intelligence finds its outlet not only in cooking but in stealing. For an amateur thief, he is careful and successful. His impulses play themselves out with women. I am one of three or four he is seeing. "A little of this, a little of that, it's more fun," he tells me, waiting to see if I will play jealous. I am not; I do not. A little of Kemp is just perfect, once or twice a week.

I am saddened that my adventures must be with men. If I walked into Ovid's by myself, I could not stay. I would be harassed till I left. I could never sit in on conversations. If I came in alone, the whores would never chat with me. If I wandered the seedy Ann Arbor underworld he moves so grandly through, unpleasant and violent things would happen to me. Following after Kemp Tomaso Fuselli I walk through walls. Sometimes I am visible; sometimes I am invisible. In both modes I listen and watch and I am fed.

With Donna's education in small snobberies and the university's education in major snobberies, I have been forgetting something of myself I want to remember. Furthermore, in the world of the university, men who are drawn to me still know that a blond Wasp dressed by Peck and Peck would be more desirable. Here my Oriental eyes and glittering black hair mean less than my body. I feel myself my mother's daughter in a strong new way, even as I worry about her when I am trying to sleep. Kemp's friends define me as smart, but that does not make me asexual as it did in high school. My being smart redounds to Kemp's credit. He shows me off like a new car.

What do I flee to in Kemp's shack? Sex, you say? Nonsense. He is too involved in his own pleasure to be great in bed. If he manages to put off coming long enough, he is a delightful and sensual lover, but when he feels like coming, he comes. That tension makes it hard for me, since I never know if I let myself mount in excitement whether he will pull the plug. Then I am barely able to control a desire to bite off his head. I form the conviction that that is why the female praying mantis turns and attacks the male in mid-act. He has probably just prematurely come. To a woman who reaches orgasm in intercourse, all ejaculation before her climax is premature. He does not make me come any other way and at that point in my and our common history, I do not know I can ask for that.

But I like being in bed with Kemp because his personality doesn't change. He doesn't get deadly intent or infantile or weird. He makes me laugh in bed. My most intense pleasure with him is at table. What I like best is that although we talk a lot, here the intellect is not primary. I live among people who think that analyzing something is an action, who think that if they have dissected why they have done something that makes it permissible to do it again, who think that a label gives possession, that when they have identified a sharp-shinned hawk they know something of hawkness—wooing high in the air and sinking with talons locked, swooping on live prey and tasting the fresh blood spurt hot, feeling with each extended feather the warm and cold shift of the winds and the sculpture of the invisible masses of moving air. Dealing in words, I try to remember how far they go and where they leave off. Hungry for food for my brain, I try to remember all the other ways of knowing that coexist. Kemp is good for me, but I cannot persuade Donna or Stephanie.

"Slumming," Donna calls it. "You've given way to a decadent romanticism. You've seen too many James Dean movies."

"This one doesn't pout. He enjoys life like a baby."

"It's a giant step backward! What did you struggle to stay in college for? You're going to get torn to ribbons."

"Actually I think you're playing a more dangerous game."

She drops her face into her hands. "Where are we going to get the money? Where?"

"I'll find it. Trust me."

"Where? Last time we could ask our friends. But if Peter gets wind of this, I've had it."

A vague desire to write him a poison-pen letter crosses my mind, but I expect their engagement to collapse from within. I do not tell Donna that Kemp offered last Saturday to give me the money. I can't take it. What he said in the car that first night stays in my head, and I will not take the money because I am sleeping with him. I will earn it somehow. If I pretended to myself I was borrowing the money, I could never pay Kemp back, and I'd be bound to him. As I chug along, the virtues of financial independence clarify. I will take nothing from Kemp except his company and cooking.

I have not told Donna that Kemp is Buddy's buddy, but I know she senses a connection, a betrayal. But I will get the money to buy her abortion and that will justify my adventure.

Donna argues, "But it can't *go* anywhere with Kemp."

"Did Mike go anywhere? Yes, to Yale. Did Peter? Yes, up you."

"As a one-night stand, Stu, I can see it. We all have our violent flings. A mud bath now and then. But to go on seeing him, as if he were a . . . a real possibility!"

"I'm not husband hunting and I don't find him dirty. He treats me better than Peter did. I feel better before, during and after."

She shakes her head, not believing me. She feels guilty, as if by taking Peter she has condemned me to what she sees as the depths of degradation. "Why do you want to go back where we came from?"

"I can't go back. But I can use some time there, Donna."

The subject rubs her sore. When she looks at me now, she stares with the anxiety I used to beam at her. I am not displeased. Her caring emerges in the attempt to argue me out of Kemp, bully me, psychologize me. Every day she produces fresh reasons. I imagine her sitting in boring classes making notes on how she will dissuade me of my folly. Every week she tells me about a great new therapist.

Stephanie has decided to treat Kemp as one of my poetic aberrations. "Verlaine and Rimbaud liked to hang around gangsters," she tells me. "It's a phase. You'll get bored. It's like when I was dating that hockey player. You can put up with just hockey, hockey, hockey for a limited time. . . . Not that your hoodlum isn't handsome as the devil—looks like old photos of my papa except for the nose. I don't wonder you succumbed. But you can't just go on with it."

I have committed a class sin, a crime against upward mobility expected of and by my friends. The potential for shock of my love life during my senior year has not begun to exhaust itself.

I can't remember whose idea it was that the movers and shakers of PAF should meet at Donaldson's apartment for a potluck: probably Dick Weisbuch, who lives with his wife and baby and who arrives with a decent tuna and noodle casserole made by his stay-at-home wife. But if you ask five men and two women, all students, to bring stuff for a potluck supper, you end up with one tuna noodle casserole, two loaves of bread and four bottles of cheap red wine.

This is my shining hour. Recently I watched Kemp make fettuccine, glory from such minima: noodles, eggs, cream, a little cheese. I can do it if I try; and I do. This wins me the gratitude of six other hungry people and the barely divided attention of Donaldson. As the meeting is breaking up, he says quietly, "Stay and help me clean up, why don't you? I'll give you a ride home."

This is hardly an invitation I can refuse. The annoying part is that I cannot sort out if I am being asked teacher to student, comrade to comrade, or—if I am brazen in examining my scarcely formed suspicions—perhaps from romantic interest? The cleaning is over in half an hour, for we ate on paper plates. I feel a little manipulated as he conducts a postmortem of a dull meeting. I experience him as being entirely in control of what will or won't happen, so that even my suspicions feel disloyal and crude.

"Would you like coffee?" he asks.

On a sudden aggressive impulse, born out of frustration at the awkwardness, I ask, "What is your name? I know Alberta called you Donnie."

"Just a nickname. My given name is Gerrit." He sits at the kitchen table with an empty cup before him, to excuse his idleness. Of all the men I have known he is the most indifferent to his surroundings. The apartment is rented furnished in boxy blond modern. He has added only a couple of Käthe Kollwitz prints, a George Grosz exhibition poster and several thousand books and periodicals. He still lives in the vaguely Tudor apartment house where I spied on him when I was a freshman.

I face him across a Formica-topped table, like a little lunch counter. "You don't like the name much?"

"Gerrit? I didn't when I was younger. I thought it was affected. But nobody's used it in so long, it's as if I'd lost it. You could call me that or Jerry—my sisters call me that."

"I'll use Gerrit." I am not about to call him anything other than Donaldson in meetings, no matter what. How the hell is he going to make a pass at me across a Formica table? If I were planning a move, I would have kept us on our feet or sat us down on his perfectly comfortable couch. Or is he the type who says, Let's do it, all verbal?

Nothing happens. Except in Gerrit's mind. When he takes me back to my co-op he kisses me good night. Two days later he takes me to a showing of a film made of Raymond Radiguet's *Devil in the Flesh*.

So I have two "lovers." I perfunctorily sign out for Detroit whenever I spend a night with Kemp. Our new housemother, a graduate student, is no special friend, but finding me already in possession of my own key and accustomed to independence, she acquiesced and I have her pleasantly cowed. I avoid making an issue of my habits by observing minimal forms. I sign in and out, even if what I sign does not correspond to my activities.

We tramp through the fall woods while Kemp picks late mushrooms to use in a spaghetti sauce—tomatoes, tomato paste and sauce, a dash of cinnamon, some red wine, a garlic clove mashed with the back of the stirring spoon, basil added late—and we drive in his barge of a car to country bars to dance.

His eyes are beautiful in their darkness. The irises turn translucent when he is happy and opaque in his angrier moods. If he believed I really exist with my own hungers, he would be a good lover. He is a true solipsist, I think, but his charm saves him, rooted in an ease with himself and what he likes. The world scrapes him raw enough to save him from complacency. His body draws my hands, the lithe power in his satiny back. Some nights when I sleep alone I have erotic dreams about him, yet nothing in our lovemaking matches what I sense could happen. Neither of us speaks of love, a reticence I find delightful. Love is not much on my mind. I know which man I could love and my path is away from meddling with Howie and Stephanie. I tell myself I have Kemp for my body and Gerrit for my mind.

Gerrit has not slept with me. As Mike used to, he lends me books. He expects me to cook, which I sometimes do, trying out on him what I learn from Kemp. I prefer eating with Kemp. I am willing to cook occasionally, but a long day in school and a long evening in the kitchen are not my delight. We see every art movie that comes to town. I have always gone to the movies. Now I discuss "the cinema," as if they were all one long foreign film. He subscribes to periodicals that analyze movies. His French and his German are superb, at least in reading, although when I hear him speak French, I always have to ask him to repeat because I can't tell what language he is pronouncing as Milwaukee English. He even reads some Russian. I learn vocabularies for film and a wider political vocabulary. His leonine head moves me as it always did and I walk teetering on the verge of falling for him hard. His coldness holds me back. I cannot find the fire in the private man that moves me in his public self. My hands reach out and come back empty.

He feels guilty about Alberta, a sore I seem to lurch into but actually touch intentionally. I need to understand. I still judge him for not keeping her. He loses his temper by growing taller and colder. The temperature drops forty degrees in two minutes while ice crystals form in his eyes.

Stephanie and Howie spend every evening together, except the Tuesday nights PAF meets. When she has gone to him, her afterimage haunts the room. She paces, shaking her sleek hair back and talking compulsively of him. I hallucinate them in bed. Jealousy scalds me. Ever since I was in Detroit, too, I am haunted by myself as my mother's heir and successor, of how the energy and vitality in her were leeched away by the grind of surviving. I have a vision of myself just before sleep as a mountain composed of millions of women, keening, begging, demanding the fulfillment denied them. All their thwarted wills flow through me.

* * *

"You still want to make some money?" Kemp is brushing his hair in the bathroom mirror. It takes him ten minutes to arrange it to his satisfaction. He likes brushing mine for the sensual pleasure.

"You know it." I bring up the subject with tedious regularity because my panic is fed by Donna's. It is soon or never. If I don't get money some other way, I will have to put the bite on both men.

"If you got the guts for it." He eyes himself in the mirror as critically as Donna.

"Try me." I sound more confident than I am. Money, money. The hills of Ann Arbor feel lately like compacted bills. The booze that flows one weekend in a fraternity house would buy Donna free.

"I'm thinking on it," he says cagily. "If your nerve's good. Because once you're in on this, you're in."

My mind summons up images of bank robberies, technicolor shootouts starring Randolph Scott and John Wayne; then my mind plays black-and-white gangster movies. Rat-a-tat-tat and James Cagney dies in the gutter. Edward G. Robinson is machine-gunned into a wall. I see stocking masks, fast black sedans taking off with a screech of rubber.

"It's a dental supply place."

"Dental supply?" I am almost outraged.

"Babe, they put gold in teeth, right? But mostly we're after drills, drill bits, equipment. I got a connection wants a load of it, but it's pretty specific."

"We're going to steal dentists' drills? You're putting me on."

"This is a right deal. The best kind. Where you got a buyer and you got a supplier. Now I've been looking over a place the orders go out from and it's a piece of cake. In a block of offices. The night watchman makes his rounds every two hours. We'd have an hour and a half safe."

"Don't they have an alarm?"

"That's my business. I got myself a key made but I have to check it out—make sure it works and see if a key triggers alarms. Tonight we have to make a spot check."

"What do you want me for? Is that why you've been teaching me to drive?"

"Julietta, you don't drive that well." He laughs. "I got a list of what my man needs and Saturday night when we do the job you got to find what's on it so the boys can move it out."

"A list? Of things like drills?"

"All kinds of fancy expensive stuff. He—the man—can sell it in Detroit. Costs a fortune for dentists to set up in business. We're doing them a favor."

"But I don't know anything about dentists."

"I'm giving you a list. The boxes'll be labeled."

"And I get a cut of what he pays you?"

"A fifth."

He gets two shares. "That's because I'm the contact with our man and 'cause I do the headwork. Without me, nothing happens."

I am to meet him at eleven tonight. I sit through Friday classes in a stupor. "Miss Stuart, I realize your thoughts are far more stimulating than our poor seminar, but if you could bring yourself to shine the light of your intellect on Auden, we are discussing one of his poems and I have twice asked you for an explication of the closing lines."

Something about me annoys my professors in the department of English, even when I am unpolitical and trying to please. I am the wrong sex, wrong class, wrong ethnic mixture, wrong size, wrong volume level. Even when they give me A's, they tend to be sarcastic and curt. Perhaps they suspect years in advance what I am going to do—write what they will never admire but will have to endure years of students who do. All time is an illusion: as I sit in his seminar my professor is punishing me for how annoying he will find my work in twenty years.

Tonight I am supposed to go to a PAF party. I'll develop a headache at ten thirty. Not sleeping with Gerrit has some advantages. He'll take me home from Dick's and I will promptly slip out again.

At supper Donna bolts the table. I follow her. She is throwing up. Afterward she lies on her cot weeping. Minouska kneads her shoulder, trying to comfort her. I hold her limp chilly hand. "If I keep throwing up this weekend, he'll make me see a doctor. Then I'm done for! It's all over then. I want to die!"

"I'm getting the money. For sure! You go ahead and make the appointment for a week from now. You have the deposit. Give him your hundred down. Next Wednesday or Thursday."

"How are you getting the money?"

"When I have it, I'll explain." Invent something.

She sits up, staring. "I don't want money from that hoodlum. Don't you borrow it from him."

"I'm not planning to borrow it from him. Don't worry."

"It's that rotten self-destructive streak in me. Just when I have a chance at being happy, at getting what I want and need . . ." She strikes herself in the side of the head. "I can't believe I went and did that. With that goon! If only you'd broken up with Peter sooner! If only I hadn't gone! If only I'd broken my ankle instead!"

"Does Peter actually make you happy?"

"Can any human being make another human being happy?"

"Can a rhetorical question answer a personal question?"

"Of course he makes me happy. He's what I always dreamed of being. Only this thing is gnawing at me. I feel guilty with him all the time as if I'm putting one over on him. I have nightmares, Stu, where I hear myself telling him. In nightmares my tongue starts to move and I hear myself telling him and then it's all over. He just walks out and leaves me and it's over. I'm all alone."

"You're not alone right now."

"In my nightmares I'm absolutely alone. . . . In bed I keep worrying he'll notice something. Every time he touches my belly I'm scared." She unzips her corduroy skirt and pulls her panties down. "Can you tell yet?"

"You're flat as a soda that stood overnight. Nobody could tell. In fact I think you're skinnier."

"I can't eat. Even when I don't feel nauseated, I can't stand putting things in my mouth and chewing them. I feel gross."

"Donna, you're skinny. You weigh less than a hundred

pounds. You look better to me when you carry ten pounds more."

She shrugs. "I can't stand fat."

I remember Mother telling me you can't diet a baby away. "Make the appointment. Trust me. I'll have the cash."

"Sure. You're going to buy a little press and set it up in the basement and run off my three hundred."

"If I have to."

"I do trust you. But you have less money than I do."

"Not by this time next week. I promise!" I will never tell any woman how to do it herself; I will never let any woman around suffer a baby unwanted, unloved. That is a promise I make to my own survival. I will get the money.

"I have to get cleaned up. He'll be here any moment." She drags herself across the hall to the bathroom. "Go finish your supper."

I wish I could say I too was not hungry, in solidarity, but I am always hungry. I run downstairs to grab what I can while there is still something to grab.

THIRTY-ONE

At the Center of Fear, Exhilaration

HOWIE COMES IN to Dick's apartment with his arm around Stephanie's shoulder in loose possession, their faces flushed as if they have just been laughing or making love.

"They did what?" I ask, only half listening. Gerrit is upset about something he saw on the evening news. We don't have a TV in the co-op and I haven't seen a paper in several days. People in my classes have been talking about who will get honors in English.

"The Soviets invaded. Tanks in the streets of Budapest. It looks like World War Two footage, except instead of the Nazis, it's the Soviets invading another Communist country."

How vivid is the embrace in the hall after that unhappy party. Jealousy squats on my liver and howls. My mouth tastes of bile. Gerrit assumes I am upset about the Russians. How embarrassing to be so trivial, unable to join in the political argument that is raging. I slip away from Gerrit to get myself another drink, but there they are in the kitchen. By the stove where Carole Weisbuch is making tacos, Howie and Stephanie stand pressing so close Stephanie's full stiff skirt is crushed and rustles with each movement. She is picking up packages of spices, holding them up for him to sniff. Her arms are bare from the shoulders. "And this is oregano. We use that in tomatoes and lamb—oh, wait till you have a real Greek leg of lamb!" She presses with the flat of her hand on his midriff, "I'll make you fat!" while he bends toward her laughing and the skirt rustles wildly. "These are cloves you stick in ham."

"Cloves *you* stick in ham." He sniffs the package. "They smell like you."

Analytically she tilts her head. "A little like my bath powder."

Bolognese leaning against the refrigerator is watching me with a somber gaze and in shame I realize he reads me clearly. I cannot keep my eyes off them. Their nonsense burns me. I've never seen that shimmer on Howie. With me he is serious or teasing or argumentative. I cannot kindle that face. I cannot make him laugh that carelessly. Though I talk and understand till my brain smokes, I cannot set round him that lion's mane of joy.

"And this is rosemary and this is basil—male and female created he them—and this is thyme."

"Put the jar in your purse." His arm encircles her. His hand slides down to her buttock. "We never have enough time."

I spin back to the living room and attach myself firmly to Gerrit's side, the way I never do. Finally through my haze the news begins to penetrate. Something shocking has happened, bad news for the Left, bad news for the world of future possibilities.

It is easy to leave the party early. Gerrit is too involved to miss me. I go off alone and arrive home just after ten. If I dared I would get drunk, but Kemp has a right to my full and sober attention. I feel grateful to him as I wait, grateful because he has given me something compelling and frightening to do that draws my attention from my obsession, grateful because I will come through for Donna. Grateful because I will assuage my raw loneliness tonight with him.

As I watch the clock I feel lost. How do people know who they are? They are the work they do. I am still a student. I call myself a writer but nobody else calls me that. If I knew how many years it is going to take for the world at large to ratify my vocation, I would kill myself on the spot.

My mother is Mrs. Stuart: the mother of sons and incidentally of me, but firstly and always my father's wife. That's what her food and her few clothes and her hardwon gristle of security issue from. Donna wants to be Mrs. Crecy. Being Donna has scared her. I am Donna's friend. That was part of my identity, that there were two of us struggling to make our way, conspirators and mutual advisors. We formed a small female government not in exile but underground. We made our own rules; now I lack them.

Once I was Mike's lover and that defined my world. When I was Peter's lover, that defined only the content of certain evenings and what I did for sex. What I do with the men I see now is even more peripheral. I don't know if that's good or bad. My society tells me it's wrong, my relationships are promiscuous and I am a bad woman who will come to an early and quite nasty end.

For Stephanie the real work she does is Howie. Her classes are secondary. She piles up incompletes. Her friendships fit into the small accidental cracks of the day. She has no politics. I do not know if she holds any opinions she would not change for him aside from those she has evolved on how to attract, get, keep and manage men. Her love for Howie and her need for Howie provide her with a massive and intense purpose. Of every event and possibility that rises she asks herself, Is it good for the Relationship?

To myself I feel small, fragile, lonely and very scared. I try not to think about what we are about to do, forbidding myself graphic images of stealth or violence. The hands close on each other toward eleven. I change into my black pants and black sweater, pin my hair up under Francis' old cap as I did on my high-school forays. I put on my battered suede jacket—that rummage sale half of a riding habit—and slip out of the house through the kitchen door, fixing it so it will lock behind me. Quiet on my sneakers I come around and there is the silver convertible waiting for me.

"What did you do to your hair?" he demands.

"Pinned it up."

"How come?"

"I don't know. Guess I wanted it out of the way."

"Not a bad idea. Long as you keep that jacket on, you could be a kid. Here's the list." He hands over a typed sheet as the silver barge churns off.

"I'm supposed to make sense of this stuff?"

"You're good at studying. Just learn it. Tomorrow you find the stuff. It ought to be labeled. You'll have a flash. You locate the stuff and Buddy and Ray will move it out."

He parks two blocks from the dental supply house, in an industrial section along the river. Friday night it's quiet in this district. The air is cool and damp like stone against my face. A train is passing. We walk around the block. Then we squat behind a big trash container while rats crawl over my mind, waiting for the night watchman to make his rounds into our building so we can make a final check of his habits. A car speeds by. One of my tasks in childhood was to take out the garbage to the galvanized tin can by the alley. Garbage went into the covered container and trash into an open oil drum. Occasionally when I took out the garbage after supper, a rat would leap out and scuttle away. Whenever we were between cats, we had mice in the house. That never scared me but the rats ran over my nightmares. They moved like menace personified, close to the ground, fast, furtive, muscled and alert to attack.

I hear footsteps. I am convinced we are visible, glowing radioactive through the wall of the igloo-shaped container. When I shift position, the folded-up list crunches in my pocket like a string of cherry bombs going off. Why do I think Kemp knows what he's doing? Because I believe men I fuck. A perfect basis for getting involved in a burglary.

Never again, I promise myself. Never again will I be without enough money for an abortion for me or for a friend. Never. I swear it, I promise it, I want to carve it into my arm. Never!

The door has closed behind the watchman. We peer around the side of our bin. Lights go on and off. Ten minutes later he reappears and walks to the right toward the next building. I am getting chilled and I have to piss. Blood no longer moves in my veins. I cannot even see Kemp. He lights a cigarette and passes it to me. Twenty minutes. The watchman comes out and goes to the right again around the corner, scratching his ass as he walks.

In another five minutes Kemp rises, leaving me behind the bin, and tries the key he had made. The question is whether it will set off the alarm. We assume they have one. I cannot see Kemp in the doorway. If I had to run I could not, for my knees are frozen. Then he comes strolling across to me. "Come on. Let's head for the corner. We can see just as well from the next block if anything happens."

"Does the key work?"

"It works. Now we'll see if it triggered a signal."

"I don't hear anything."

"No, but that don't mean there's not some kind of alarm that isn't a fucking stupid bell."

We march down the street, wide as the Champs-Elysées, wide as a football field. He will not let me run, gripping my arm. "Take it easy, Julietta, easy does it." Kemp doesn't believe in running if you aren't being chased. A car crosses the block and my heart kicks in my chest. Every car that passes is the police. We keep walking. Halfway down the next block we squat behind a truck. Five, ten minutes. My bladder hurts. I am not cut out for this.

Finally Kemp agrees that nothing has happened and we are free to stagger back to the damned igloo to wait for the watchman to reappear in one hour and forty minutes—we think. I have discovered the route to instant arthritis. I piss behind a truck and then trot awkwardly to catch up with him. My knees no longer work correctly.

When at last we reach his shack, Kemp is moody. We go

to bed without having sex. I suspect from his body scent he has already been with a woman tonight, but I am indifferent. I curl like a mouse with a hard nut around a solid and permanent-seeming kernel of fear.

Will I have enough nerve tomorrow? Will I disgrace myself by panicking? I know Buddy and Ray resent my being involved and think Kemp is crazy to include me, which may be true. My fear of being financially dependent on a man and my constant need of money interact to coerce me into trouble. I am so frightened I cannot grasp myself, cannot find a core of self in the murk of fear. It is as if I had dissolved in a cold swirling fog. Whenever I drift toward sleep, I wake suddenly with a jolt as if falling. Who am I? I feel lost and invisible. Nowhere can I find images that give me aid or comfort in determining what kind of human being I must try to be, what is a woman fully enabled and alive.

After a silent eggs and sausage breakfast, he drops me at the co-op. I type a paper, put in my time cleaning the bathroom, go off to the library to work in the periodicals room. I perform jaw motions usually related to talking as the day proceeds in swift jerks and long stretches when time stalls utterly.

As I lean on the bastion of desk in the periodicals room counting the afternoon's fine money and yawning as I wait for my replacement to come on duty, Howie enters. I hate the jab of these unexpected meetings. Just time as he walks the length of the room to put together a face surprised (not too) and pleased (mildly). He hails me, "Where have you been?"

"Working here all afternoon, as usual."

"Been studying upstairs. I'll wait till you get off and we'll have coffee in the Union. It's been awhile."

Our voices murmur conspiracy against the turning of slithery pages, the coughing and shuffling, the beat of the rain on the long windows. "Not this afternoon. I have to study."

"You can't spare half an hour? You're avoiding me."

"Why? Do I owe you money?" For all the exchange of

smiles, I will have to go with him. I half rejoice, for I have been parched for his company. "You've been busy yourself." My voice, is it bitter? Here comes the woman who takes over. It has been raining since noon and we pause on the library steps before plunging into the downpour. Campus is dotted with bright yellow slickers. As we agree by nods to venture out, he takes my arm, then with sudden awkwardness becomes conscious of the automatically intimate gesture that belongs to Stephanie.

Pell-mell we run through the storm to the Union. At a table I stare at him covertly. Unlike Kemp who moves with grace that is conscious but conscious as Minouska is when she stalks a bird through the windowpane, unlike Gerrit who often pays no attention to what his body is doing and walks into a chair while involved in arguments or puts his glass down where the table isn't and looks astonished as it splashes below in a small explosion of shards, Howie's movements seem drawn from a legion of possibilities by minute but conscious decisions. Subtle bulldog. He was not subtle in Dick's kitchen with Stephanie. As we sit with our coffee, his strong hands with their blunt spatulate fingers crouch on either side of his cup. Deep inside, my hopeless desire sighs raggedly. I am feeling sorry for myself, indeed. I imagine myself arrested, shot tonight. I would like to pin the blame somehow on Stephanie and him, but it won't wash.

He gauges me over his glasses, tilting his chair back with a muscular arm on the table steadying him. "You've been avoiding me, and I know why."

My ribs contract fearfully, a wheezy concertina. "Oh?"

"Because you know both of us so well, you're afraid of getting caught in the middle. Of being a double agent. Of interfering."

I feel as much disappointment as relief. To have it out! "More cowardice than scruples, believe me."

"But we want to go on talking to you. We're not so delicate you have to tiptoe around watching out for us."

That *we* grates on me. "This is a committee report?"

"Stephanie feels as if you close up. I see you duck out of

PAF meetings before I can speak. You never have coffee with Dick and Bolognese and me anymore."

Their wills trapping me. "Let's not overanalyze this. I've been busy."

"Not too busy for Herr Professor."

"Oh, Howie, there's no great romance going on."

"You show up with him at every party. And you leave with him. After meetings you go off with him. You stay on in his apartment."

We glare. I say, "Gee, I forgot I signed that total-abstinence-from-men pledge. When did the Central Committee send that through? It must have slipped my mind! Of course you live in a monastery these days yourself."

"I just don't see what you're getting into. You don't ask enough of men!"

"I ask too much!" I push back my chair. "I get nothing I want!"

"Oh, sit down, Jill, sit down." Visibly he puts a lid on his temper. "People always think they could run their friends' lives better than their friends do."

Ashamed of letting my bitterness flash out, I sit. "Want to run my life? This government is ready to resign." I do not want to quarrel with him. Am I trying to force him to guess? To drive him away? They want me as a pendant to their intimacy, so I should display a healthy calm interest. "So you're serious about my roommate?"

"Everything I do is equally real." He rocks back. "People like to fool themselves that only certain parts of their lives count."

"People like to fool themselves that some abstract nonsense said loud enough answers a personal question."

He waits for me to look up from my coffee, his eyes a hard enamel grey. "Let her make what she can of me."

I catch his gaze overintently. What did I used to do with my eyes when we talked? "What do you mean?"

"She'll have what she wants from me. She'll define it. You know what I am. She has to figure out if that's what she wants."

And you, what do you want? I know my desire, a friend

whose secret wish is disaster while jealousy's dark rheumatism attacks my joints.

When I leave the Union, the rain is lighter. The town has a damp smell of earth and earthworms, of drains. The wooden houses strike me as excessively pastel, never the iron greys or grime of the city, but light grey, white, pale yellow, the sodden green of lawns. I am tired of lawns and classrooms. I can see a path composed of many flagstones of a pearly opalescent grey under the faintly raining sky, leading me on to teach in my own classroom the work of other poets to students almost involved enough to care. What I do tonight is a prying of myself away from that security, classes leading to classes leading to classes.

But when I arrive home there is a message to call Kemp, who is terse and to the point. "Game called on account of rain. See you tomorrow, Julietta. Same time, same place."

What a letdown. I cannot endure the hours I have to drag through. And suppose it rains tomorrow too? Who ever heard of a burglary called on account of rain? In Ann Arbor it could rain until it starts to snow in early November. I *promised* Donna.

Sunday afternoon as I am returning with my duffle bag of clean laundry over my shoulder, I glance automatically into the living room and stop short: Peter and Donna. They sit on the couch both blond and fair and slight and tense and wiry. I cannot believe I ever fitted between them, each with elbows tight in to their slim sides, arguing in low charged voices. I receive an electrical shock as they look up at me, both together.

Donna becomes vivacious. "Oh, you're doing laundry—how completely virtuous! Everything I own has stains. I've been in an orgy of coffee spilling for weeks!"

His head bowed, Peter manufactures a sick glassy grin. "How are you?" he asks with paralyzing earnestness. How alien he looks in a neat flecked grey Harris tweed sports coat and properly contrasting flannel pants all knife-edge precise, yet the face of a beautiful pale rat at bay. He shines with icy tension. My flesh denies him. With a curtsy I reshoulder the laundry and flee.

I am haphazardly sorting my socks and panties when Donna slips in to whisper breathlessly, "Do you have it?"

"For sure." I lie and glance past her out the window. It is only drizzling. Tonight has to do, it has to.

"I can't sleep anymore. I haven't slept all week."

In fact the skin around her eyes looks like crinkled carbon paper. Her hands that close hard on my arm are cold. Her face is beyond pleading to a demand. She is drowning in her fear as I have been stewing in mine. I force my voice hearty. "Sleep long and hard. It's all right."

"Can I see the money?"

"I don't have it here. But it's okay. I'll have it by the time we go. Wednesday, right?"

"Wednesday at nine in the morning." Her hands wring my arm. "If we don't have the cash, he won't do it."

"No problem, Donna, no problem. We got it. You can take my word." And flush it down the toilet.

My word. I sign out for Detroit and Kemp picks me up for a late supper. We eat in his favorite Italian restaurant in Ypsilanti. About halfway through the meal he begins to come to life. We are sharing a bottle of the house Valpolicella.

"Come on," he says grinning. "What are you scared of? We pull our deal tonight and get our money cash on the barrelhead. In the meantime those bozos in Washington decide it's time to flex some muscle and show the Russian boneheads what's what. So we wake up at two A.M. with everything bright and before we know it we're just hot ashes."

"But I am scared. I've never done this." And I'll never do it again. However my appetite begins to wake and unwind its shining coils, to taste the smells and flavors with flickering quick tongue. Maybe we'll all be dead by the end of the week, squandered like my mother's teeth.

"Being scared is a waste of time. What does it do you? Makes you stupid. Makes you careless."

"Aren't you scared?"

He shakes his head no. "I stopped in Korea. I went over for the end of it and I figured after the first month, what the hell? If I get blown to pieces, I won't know what hit me. Nobody asked me, please, Mr. Fuselli, do you feel like dying today? When your time comes, you buy it. Right now some miserable real-estate salesman is boozing on route twenty-three. We waltz out of here and he plows right through us. Or I just ate a cancer germ. My mom's old man, he keeled over one day. Never sick a day in his life, just like me. Then one day he was picking up a sack of cement and pow, he died. His heart burst. What good would worrying have done him?"

At Kemp's shack I change, just before Ray and Buddy arrive. In my pocket the list is wadded up, but the ability that lets me pass courses like botany with A's by memorizing the book the night before is with me now.

We pile into Ray's Studebaker and drive into town, where Buddy and Ray pick up a bread truck their friend Ace is driving. Kemp will not drive his car because he used it to scout. We wait a block distant till Buddy trots back to signal us that the night watchman has just gone around the far corner. Ace drops us in front of the dental supply house and continues on to park his truck around the corner and then return for the Studebaker. I feel like a brass band. How can anybody miss us, four of us shuffling around on the step while Kemp unlocks the door and glides into the fluorescent-lit hall to check things out.

He is back quickly, opens the door and beckons us inside. We follow him down the hall through a reception room. The door beyond stands open into darkness. We dog him closely, tripping over each other's heels, down a corridor past the doors of offices to another door, also open. Now we are in the warehouse. I suffocate in black air thick as glue. I find myself panting. They will read that as cowardice. Which it is. I control my breathing.

"All right, Julietta, move it. Find our stuff!"

I fumble with the flashlight he gave me. My mind goes a complete blank. Steel shelving reaches to the ceiling. The room is divided into narrow aisles with a cross aisle halfway down. I drop the flash, scramble for it and then Kemp turns on the lights.

"Hey, Kemp," Ray says, wincing.

"They got no windows." He shuts the door to freedom. "We'll work much faster."

"Here's the instruments," I squeak. I am a mouse pittering along the aisles from box to box. I was happier in the dark, but Kemp is right. What I point out, Ray piles by the door. Kemp has gone back out to stand watch and supervise. Buddy treks each box out through the maze of corridors to the outer door. When we are ready, we'll send for the truck.

Kemp segues back and forth to keep an eye on the operation. "If I whistle, drop out of sight and keep still. Douse the lights. If I whistle twice, make a break."

What I always wanted was to get shot by a night watchman for stealing dental instruments. Maybe it's Mother's dentist who's buying this stuff hot, so he can expand his humanitarian practice. At first I worry about taking the wrong items. If I mess up, I don't think Kemp will take it lightly. After all, we're in business together.

But a rhythm develops and when I look at the watch I borrowed from Wanda, time glides by. I worry whether we are moving the stuff out fast enough, before the watchman's next round. I have a sudden sense of our balletic movements, of beauty in the coordination and the speed. Nobody talks, except for an occasional grunt or an exclamation when something is heavy. I carry a few of the lighter boxes to the hallway myself. I realize I am no longer sweating fear; I am not even afraid. We move too fast. Fear is around me like fog outside the walls, but I am inside the action and I have no time to notice the cold white bank of fear. What we do provokes its own exhilaration, this nighttime dance deep inside a place we are not supposed to be.

We swirl through our paces. I find the objects and the boxes and the crates, which then are carried through the hallway to the outer door. As I find items, I try to take time to check them off on the list.

Suddenly Kemp is at my elbow. "Speed it up. Five more minutes in this stage. That's all."

"But we haven't got everything."

"What we've got, we've got."

Ray and I scuttle faster. Now it is close to comedy, my sense of us sweating in the barely heated room rushing the boxes, me dashing ahead down the grim high aisles and grabbing sealed boxes of instruments, of alloys, of drills and pumps. To tote out a chair takes Ray and Buddy together. I am sweating again from haste.

"Okay. That's it. Out!"

We follow him. Ray helps Buddy cart the last stuff to the outer door as Kemp sends me for Ace and the truck. Kemp never relaxes his grasp on the scene; we are his hands, his legs, his muscles. Around the corner Ace guns the truck. I climb into the Studebaker to sit quietly, the key in the ignition but the engine off. After Kemp's lessons, I could drive this car, I think. Nervous again for the first time in at least an hour, I lock the doors and lie down to make myself invisible. In ten minutes they must have the truck loaded with all those boxes. That gives ten minutes more leeway before the night watchman is due around the far corner to begin working his way down the three buildings on this side of the block. I turn the engine on, pull slowly around the corner.

They are still loading. I pull up abreast. "It's time!"

"Shit," Kemp says. "I know it. Faster!"

Now my hands sweat so profusely my gloves are wet and slip on the wheel. The men move in slow motions, large figures underwater who push against high gravity to force the leaden boxes through the murky atmosphere, three men (Ace still at the wheel of the bread truck) frozen in instant replay. I stare at the far corner around which the watchman will march any second. The truck is facing back the way we came. Laboriously I turn the car around to face the same direction, then sit with my eyes fixed on the rearview mirror watching that pool of light into which the watchman will step.

Kemp has given the high sign. They shut the doors of

the bread truck as Kemp comes around to our car's driver's side. With the engine running, I scramble over and he slides in, slamming the door with the same gesture as he heels the accelerator and we are off with a screech of rubber down the street, leaving the bread truck to amble after us.

We drive straight to Livonia, a near suburb of Detroit, where we park in a garage behind a row of garden apartments. As I sit in the Studebaker, Ace, Buddy and Ray unload, much more leisurely than they loaded. They are tired and clumsy. Kemp goes into the apartment building with a thin grey-haired man who tells us to be very quiet, for this is a respectable neighborhood. Kemp returns for my inventory and then disappears again.

When he comes back at last, he brings a six-pack of beer and the unloading goes on. When the truck is finally empty, Ace drives it away, after Kemp peels off bills into his hand. Then Buddy climbs into the driver's seat with Ray beside him, while Kemp and I curl up in the backseat.

There he makes five piles of money. Ace got a hundred and fifty off the top. Kemp gets two shares; the rest of us one, in twenties that crackle in Kemp's hands. As the car is stopped at a traffic light, he passes Buddy's share to him. Ray reaches over the seat for his money. Last, Kemp hands me mine. I would like to count it. I don't know if this is polite. It feels fat, but I don't know how thick a pile the three hundred I need for Donna would make. I stick the wad in the pocket of my suede jacket and try to count the bills surreptitiously with my fingertips, but I keep losing track.

When Kemp and I are finally dropped at his house, I shut myself in the bathroom and count the bills quickly. One hundred, two hundred, three hundred, four hundred eighty. Abruptly tears start out of my eyes. I wash my face and comb my hair down.

"Not bad for such an easy job." Kemp rummages in his refrigerator. "See, I told you it was a piece of cake. Are you hungry?"

I nod.

"I've got some minestrone. Good and thick. While it's heating, let's fuck."

It is one of our good times. We are both greedy and easily roused, tired enough to take the time I need, keyed enough for my time to be shorter than ordinarily. By the time we are done the soup is boiling. He steps into his pants without underwear, hastening to the kitchen to see to it, lest it boil over. Yawning with pleasure and relief and deliverance, I pick our scattered clothes off the floor. As I lift his jacket, the weight puzzles me and I touch the pocket gingerly. It is a gun. Carefully I replace the jacket on the floor and sit on the bed's edge.

He lied to me. He told me he never carries a gun. I am sweating again as I sit there and my teeth abruptly chatter. I put on his terrycloth robe, twisting it tight around myself as I consider whether to challenge him. It is over. Nothing had happened, so far at any rate. I do not expect us to be caught. Still, I feel tricked. I would not shoot any working person for money. Why did Kemp bring it? Inner security? Feeling like a professional, a big shot? Superstition? Or to use if necessary? I feel less safe with him than I have since that first time I got into his convertible.

In the morning Kemp calls in sick to the optics factory, I cut my classes and we sleep till eleven. After breakfast I walk to town. The sun is sunny, many leaves torn from the trees by the recent storm and clear sunlight lancing down unobstructed on my bare black head, warming me like a motherly hand. Briskly I hike, contemplating how much I enjoyed the burglary and how frightened his gun makes me. I probe and probe my reactions, aware I am truly frightened and yet truly fascinated: by myself, by the night's adventure, by Kemp still.

As I enter town I pass a field overgrown with tall weeds, gaunt brown stalks and still living grass, strewn with broken bricks, cinder blocks, aluminum cans, pop and beer bottles, rotting trash. A man who must be a professor strides briskly across the field, taking a shortcut toward the street that leads to the university. He trots along carrying a black umbrella tightly furled and swung like a walking stick. Under his arm is tucked a leather attaché case. Among the broken bricks and strewn condoms and mudholes he swings along evenly to his one o'clock class. Perhaps he is running over his lecture in his head, for he does not even see me. He reaches the sidewalk on the far side of the garbage jungle, striding along the neat residential street without altering his pace. I smile as I fall in behind him. What class do I belong to? His or Kemp's? To whom is my loyalty due? I am a creature of this vacant lot, like those I grew up playing in, but even this one is no doubt due to be built on soon in this prosperous and ever-expanding city. In my pocket I carry Donna's liberation.

THIRTY-TWO
In the Snow King's Palace

THE ABORTION IS performed in a house that is a clinic inside, clean and efficient. The catch is that because of the illegality, no anesthesia is used. It is an operation done raw, Donna cut open and feeling every stroke. The doctor, unusually kind, permits me to remain in the room. Donna holds my hand. When he is finally done with the D and C, my hand is bleeding.

This doctor is also unusual in that he has the patient wait and recover on his premises to make sure no complications seem likely. Donna is put to bed in a small upstairs room, in pain but happy. I sit by the side of the bed, giving her my uninjured hand. She is bleeding heavily but at peace. As I watch her, I feel a sense of victory. Even with her being in pain, locked in like prisoners, unable to use the phone, this is the best our time has to offer.

Buhbe had twelve children and at least five abortions; Mother three children, at least two abortions and a miscarriage that almost killed her—doctors can't help you when you're miscarrying until the fetus is out, for fear of being an accomplice to abortion. My buhbe, my mother and their sisters always chose illegally and dangerously which of the endless possibilities for fecundity they would bring to birth, which of the multitude of possible children they might feed, clothe and love. So women have always done in all societies everywhere, with or without male knowledge or aid, with or without the help of official medicine and law. Such was the province of midwives and witches.

Buhbe was born into hunger and danger and sailed in steerage into poverty and danger. Survival was an end in itself. Yet what a storyteller she was, carrying like seeds in a watermelon stories of the vanished past, of history burnt down, of the murdered and lost, the dense maddening lore of the shtetl.

Mother was born into trouble. After I was pregnant that first and only time, she taught me to touch my womb and tell what time of my cycle I'm in, how close to ovulation, how close to my period; she also taught me that a menstruating woman turns fermenting wine sour and that cats understand everything you say about them. One of those dicta is a superstition.

Sometimes I see her as a blood sacrifice to the ordinary confines of working-class life for a woman, robbed not only of her teeth but her chance to live out the hunger, the vitality, the rich imagination and passion in her. I am one strand in a fabric of women, Donna and Theo and Stephanie and Alberta and many others as dear or dearer to me who do not fit into the particular pattern of this story but live with their lives stitched to mine. Were I pointing out a different pattern in this crazy quilt, it would be their stories I would tell you as another story of my living.

"I'm bleeding . . . rather heavily," Donna says tentatively.

The blood is running out so fast that I summon the nurse. The nurse gives her an injection and props her legs up. Finally the flow lessens. I am profoundly grateful to them for not sending us out where she would bleed in the street. I know what happens if you go into a hospital emergency room bleeding from the uterus. It is like going in with a gunshot wound; the criminal aspects come first and the medical treatment second, if then. I know how rare this doctor is to do follow-up care.

He does not release us until the end of the day. The co-op presents a more difficult situation. Normally we might have toughed it out like Wanda when she had her abortion and announced it, but if Peter is to be kept ignorant, nobody else must know. Donna has the stomach flu. Rosellen and I take turns nursing her. By Friday she is up, her face a dead chalky hue but more animation in her eyes than I've seen in weeks.

Friday afternoon she comes upstairs to my room and hugs me as I sit at my desk. I am startled. She has given herself permission at last to touch me. When she comes into the room she kisses me, and she kisses me when she leaves. They are dry soft kisses but kisses of affection. She never touches anyone but Peter, and I doubt if they walk entwined. Lennie was probably the only physically warm person she has ever been with—except for me, who hardly counts since till now I have been forbidden expression. I respond timidly, accepting these sudden offerings like flowers out of the snow that has begun to fall, large damp white circles like dogwood blossoms floating down and resting everywhere with an air of delicate surprise.

I want to be loved, I drink it in, but it feels fragile, born of the surcease of fear. When I wash my hair Saturday before supper, she insists on putting it up. As she does elaborate things with her curlers, I suffer the twisting and piling and the session under her hair dryer.

"You have dramatic features," she tells me. "I'm a canvas I paint a face on. But you should play up your darkness."

"Absolutely," Stephanie says from the rocking chair, where she observes with a mixture of jealous alarm and curiosity. She has told me she thinks Donna wants me back as a roommate. I assure her I have no intention of moving out. I am tired of that drama of living together and not living together and almost convinced that we have grown closer without the constant bickering over mine and yours and who used what and left it how.

"Jill takes all the wrong tack with men," Stephanie says, applying orange polish to her toenails. "Instead of waiting to see what a man wants, you tell him who you are."

"If someone can't know me and still love me, let him clear out." I am annoyed. Where her robe slips I see a red love bite on her shoulder. The insult lies as much in her blunt instruction as in her assumption of superior fire-power.

"You have to be honest," Donna says loyally, who has just spent a month lying to Peter. "We both believe in the primacy of communication. Making love is a form of dialogue."

"Oh? In French?" Stephanie snorts. "You know how to get round Jill, all right. You just agree with her silly moral notions."

"I believe in acting clearly." Donna handles my hair roughly with the effort of keeping her temper. "Our acts embody our values."

"Acts? Like scratching myself? Brushing my teeth?" Stephanie jams the cap back on the polish bottle crooked.

"Why are you in such a bad mood?" In part they are pleasantly fighting over my platonic favors, but I think Stephanie is upset. "What gives with you?"

"Howie's going to medical school at Columbia."

"Sure. He likes New York. Columbia's a good school. And it'll put some space between him and his family. He needs to be farther away."

"But I have too many incompletes to graduate. I'll have to finish up in the fall."

"Do you care about your degree?"

"My father would kill me. Howie says I have to get it. He doesn't want to get married till I graduate," she wails, scowling at her fresh orange nails. "My feet! They're funny-looking and yellow."

"What are you afraid of?"

"I know what she's afraid of." Donna adds another layer to her construction and nails it in place with a mock tor-

toiseshell comb. "When your guy is living someplace else,
he's meeting other women—at work, every time he goes to
a friend's house. If you aren't on the spot, he's fair game."

Over my piled-up hair they grin at each other, sharing a
moment of comradeship while I suffer a sense of being
another species.

What Donna has wrought on my hair certainly makes
me look older. I hardly dare nod or sneeze for fear of its
all tumbling down. Tonight PAF debates free speech on
campus. The university screens lecturers. We're always getting our wrists slapped for desiring outside speakers. But
under this debate another is surging. Hungary, Hungary,
the betrayal of the Left, revolution, counterrevolution,
anarchism, bourgeois liberties, nationalism, imperialism,
they're worse than us, they're as bad as us, they're all there
is, they're irrelevant. The speeches on responsible leader-
ship in loco parentis ring false. People contradict each
other nastily. It feels as if we are falling apart from an
invisible center that has rotted out.

Tonight after the forum there is no party. Somehow no
one arranged it this week. I end up at Gerrit's apartment
by default. The time has come to make this attraction real
or dismiss it. Bolognese, Gerrit and I sit in Gerrit's tidy
kitchen. *Die Deutsche Ideologie* lies on the dish rack with
a knife marking his place. Bolognese leans all the way back
in his chair. Gerrit sits loosely forward, his elbows resting
on the table, as we drink coffee I made.

"The truth is, the better students are always displeased
by their education," Gerrit is saying. "They complain it's
too hard, but it's never hard enough."

"Bullshit," Bolognese says. "We don't want it harder, we
want it truer. We want dialogue, but we're just statistics on
a curve."

"You think you don't crave answers?" Gerrit sits up
almost straight so I know he has thought of something he
is going to enjoy saying. "What we all want from our
education is to be one on one with Socrates. We all want to
be fucked by Socrates."

"I bet you wouldn't, actually," I say. "The ugly disreputable old geezer. A lower-middle-class failure who only flirted, then went home to his bag of a wife. You're thinking about Plato. The poetic young man of good family and interesting attitudes."

Gerrit is looking at me, eyes glowing with interest. He likes me when I am his good, good student. Why doesn't Bolognese go home? Am I allowed to seduce Gerrit or forbidden? I want Gerrit to save me from Kemp and my taste for low adventure. Gerrit, make books as exciting as my underworld journeys. You're a moral man: make me moral too.

I waver. I want to take Gerrit's handsome leonine head between my hands and waken him to my potentialities with a kiss, not one of those chaste dry-lipped pecks he gives me in his car when he is about to deliver me to my house like a penny into a piggy bank. A moment later I want things simple. I want to be his student/friend/comrade as unambiguously as Howie and Bolognese are, without sexual vibrations to trouble the air. He started pursuing me, but only to a point where I hang flapping idly like a newspaper caught on a fence.

Finally Bolognese leaves, but only after Gerrit has dropped a few hints that the hour is late. Is he going to take me back immediately? He doesn't. Instead we sit on the couch. With his head in my lap, I pet his hair like a cat's fur while his feet in hand-knit argyle socks hang over the far arm. His mother knits them. She also knits him sweaters, mufflers and an afghan that covers his bed instead of a spread. He is his mother's darling boy, the oldest, brightest son in a family of five. His father is a corporation lawyer. I suspect his family has almost as much money as Peter's but he cares less. It never occurs to him he is not important and successful in himself. He lays his head in my lap and soaks up female attendance and adoration without ever considering that this is not a service provided by the city like water, I think, but I am still charmed.

A. You cannot easily seduce a man who does not touch

you. If I sat down suddenly in his lap, he would assume I had mistaken him for a chair.

B. He does not get drunk. He drinks wine only to the point of an even greater ease of the tongue.

C. I could ask him. Hey, Gerrit, you wanna? Want to what? You must define your terms. Nowhere in any staged miniature drama in my head, one-act revue, can I say, Hey, Gerrit, want to fuck? I am too respectful. To put anything into such blunt words would alter our delicate rapport. Gerrit, do you love me? Of course he doesn't; I myself suffer only from a four-year crush.

D. Hey, Gerrit, I'm in love with Howie, so let's go to bed so I don't mess up with him and Stephanie. That lacks appeal.

At the moment what I want is to get him to pay attention to me: intellectual attention. Maybe I want the answers he accuses students of longing for. Tell me how to put my life in order. Show me how to be just and political. "Sometimes I don't know where I belong," I say, thinking of Kemp's shack, which is so much more comfortable to me than this apartment. "If I belong anywhere."

"Anomie," he murmurs. "The center doesn't hold. Invisible stresses. Unresolved contradictions. A bridge stands until one day it falls into the river, that bridge in Puget Sound, suddenly we think, but the stresses were built into the design."

"Other people my age know what they want. They want X other person and they want to marry X and have three children and live in Bloomfield Hills. They want to earn so many thousand a year and have two specific cars and a specific model boat and a summer home on one of two lakes."

"They're just deferring the discovery that you cannot define yourself by things you own and surround yourself with."

"But I have to belong somewhere. I get scared. I don't fit into anything. What can I join myself to?"

"But the price of joining, of belonging. The price!" He frowns up at me. "You were close to Alberta."

"Still am." Astonishing. He mentioned her name of his own free will.

"She talked to you about her life?"

"You, you mean, or her life otherwise?"

"And her family?"

"Mostly her father. But yes, her family."

A silence. Then, "I wanted to be sure. . . . I never joined. Maybe I'm too bourgeois. Too attached to the intellectual freedom I prize which Ralph—Alberta's father, did you ever meet him?—calls the candy with which petit bourgeoise intellectuals are bought off. The power, he'd say, to publish radical academic papers no one reads and write all the jargon you please as long as nobody can understand it who works in a factory."

He never joined what? Then I know what I halfway guessed. Alberta's father and mother are in the Communist party. "Well, aren't you glad now you didn't join?"

"After Hungary? Yet I don't feel spared any disillusion. Spared some sense of complicity, perhaps, but perhaps not. I wonder if I just refuse to take any chances—do you think so?"

"Without you there wouldn't be any PAF and thus no progressive presence on this campus not closeted or tiny and sectarian." I am deeply flattered by the question. Oh, give me your intricate and beautifully constructed Wasp conscience to handle reverently. I won't hurt it.

"But is it enough?"

That seems a rhetorical question and I wait him out.

After a while he mumbles, "I feel guilty about her tonight. As if I ought to be comforting her. I know how she'll hate what's happening and yet feel wholly supportive of her father."

"You could call her."

He snorts. "I'm sure her phone is tapped."

"You could say you're thinking about her. You could say that with the FBI listening. Really. If they watch her, they know you were involved."

"They used to follow us sometimes. She had her first

scary experience with them when she was twelve. . . . Should I really call her?"

"She might not be home," I offer. "Why not try?"

After another ten minutes of debate he goes into his bedroom and shuts the door. I hear the murmur of his voice. Half an hour passes while I read his latest *Dissent*. There's a great article by C. Wright Mills. By the time Gerrit emerges, I have lost my desire to seduce him. Any strong reminder of Alberta's feeling for him turns me off. He looks as if he had been pummeled into some kind of feeling, and we start where we had left off, trying to talk about how we each feel about the Communist Party of America and its clandestine embattled glamour. I spend the night, but on his couch.

Saturday afternoon in January. Yesterday snow sifted down and today the sky is a basement ceiling. Cellar light. The wet snow is mounded over everything, censoring all garbage and details, the old tires and bottles around Kemp's shack. It looks pretty and yet the clammy light saps any desire to venture out. We drink cocoa and eat little lemony cookies Kemp's mamma baked. I study for my finals as Kemp works on an old hunting rifle he has taken apart on the kitchen table. He picks up old guns and refurbishes them for fun and profit.

We hear the car drive up. With a leisurely shuddering yawn and stretch, Kemp goes to the window. I hope it isn't Buddy. Kemp glides past me to his room and opens a drawer. I look out then, suspicious because of the tension of his stride, the silence. It's a red T-bird I know I've seen parked downtown. It's so red I always noticed it, well kept and polished except for one crumpled fender which I used to wonder why the owner didn't fix. The man who gets out and squints carefully at the house is Black.

"Who's that?" I ask with part-real and part-feigned innocence.

"Nobody." Kemp sits at the table and works on his rifle as if he had heard nothing. "Take your book into my room. You can study in there."

Slowly I walk to the bedroom doorway. I can see the Black man finish a careful survey of the locale and approach the door. "How come? Who is he?"

"Shut the door. It's nothing I can't handle, but I don't want to be worrying about you."

I shut the door and stand just inside. Another fence? Another little job? It's none of my business, but as a writer, don't I have to study everything? There is a loud insistent banging on the door.

"Don't break it down. It's open," Kemp says in his cold, nasty, don't-mess-with-me manner. "You just turn the handle and pull."

The door opens and shuts and nobody says anything. I press my ear harder to the door. Finally the Black man says, "What'd you do with your girl? The one standing at the window giving me the once-over-lightly?"

"I sent her home."

"Sent her in the bedroom, you mean. You call her right out. I don't want nobody in this house I can't watch. Don't fancy being shot in the back by no white floozy."

"She's a college girl. She's doing her homework and minding her own business."

The bedroom door kicks in with such suddenness it catches my arm as I jump back. "Get out here where I can see you," he barks.

I slide along the wall and sit at the table opposite Kemp. I still have my Schopenhauer clutched in my hand. The man's eyes fall on the book and he grins. He is an inch or two shorter than Kemp, maybe five, six years older and built strong like Howie. His hair is in a long smooth conk and he is wearing a light grey suit as fine and conservatively tailored as any of Peter's. "Missy Coed, no lie. You Chinese?"

"No, Jewish." Surreptitiously I rub my bruised arm.

That always stumps them. Kemp seizes the moment to try to regain his lost dominance. "Okay, Mercer, what gives? I don't remember issuing no invitations to come drop by and chew the fat. But now you're here, sit. You want a beer?"

"Let Missy get it. I don't turn my back on lowlife."

"This here pimp is calling me a lowlife. That's some joke." Kemp nods to me to get the beer.

"Yeah? My girls come to me because they like my loving and they want my protection and they got it. And they need some protection with lowlife like you and your little creeps scuttling around."

I sidle to the refrigerator and take out two beers. Facing Mercer, I open the bottles and place one in front of each.

"I drink from a glass," Mercer says. "Unlike lowlife."

I get him a glass from the cabinet and sit again.

"Sure," Kemp says. "We can break it after you leave. And that blessed moment should come real soon." He drinks with his left hand. His right is under the table.

"I'd be pleased to leave real soon with Rinda's money. Your little creeps took two hundred off her last night. I also want fifty for her doctor bills. Plus I'm giving you a warning. You lay mean hands on one of my girls again, I'll cut you into pieces so little a pussycat can eat them out of a dish."

"Kemp was with me last night from seven on all night," I say truthfully and with great relief. "Honest. There must be forty other people who saw us together including my whole co-op."

"But his two little creeps weren't with you, college, Buddy Rayburn and Ray Koszieski. They busy down on Liberty, shaking down my girl and beating her till she bleed."

"Buddy and Ray beat up a prostitute and took her money?"

"Shut up," Kemp says to me. "A Black whore so ugly she ought to pay them to fuck her."

"Sure, she so ugly and so Black she make two hundred dollars by one A.M. sure as clockwork. Your girlfriend don't think it's so great they gang up, two big fat crackers beating on one poor skinny piece and knock her around and take her hard-earned money."

"You stay in your own part of town over on Detroit Street. But you were on our turf. If she wants to walk our streets, she pays us. She owes us, and we took it."

I am shaking with anger. "And Buddy likes to beat up

women. He likes to leave women all bruised and bloody. That's better than the money they took off her." I stand and they both look at me with surprise. "Please, Kemp, give him her money. It's hard being a prostitute, real hard. And if they hurt her, give him money for a doctor. I remember what Donna looked like after Buddy raped her."

"Shut up!" Kemp pounds his fist on the table. He stands. "Go in the bedroom and shut up. This is business. I don't have a thing to do with that whore of a cousin of yours. This is a nigger whore and if she wants to come on a white street, she's going to pay."

I grab my purse and throw my wallet down on the table. I pull out my money. Twenty-eight dollars. "Take that for her. She's a woman, and do you think I'm so fucking white? I won't have any part in this. I won't." I take my coat from the hook by the door and run out. I pull my coat on as I run, stepping into my boots and stumbling through the car tracks toward the road.

Nobody follows. For all I know they may kill each other. Already as I go I think how I will miss him.

Kemp stays away for a week and then comes around, but I find it easy to evade him. I have a whole houseful of women to answer the phone and door and say I'm in Detroit. He is too proud to persist, and after a week of siege he exits my life.

I can't tell you what happened to Kemp. When I used to travel west to Ann Arbor regularly in the middle sixties on antiwar business, nobody had ever heard of him and he wasn't listed in the phone directory. Yes, I looked, I admit it. That was the year Francis died, presumably of a heart attack incurred while "resisting arrest" in Los Angeles. The body was covered with bruises and there were marks on the neck. Neither my mother nor I had the money to pursue the case, and the movement people I talked to in L.A. could not see how it could be political and thus their business, this middle-aged bum living in a Chicano neighborhood who was mixed up with a car the police said was stolen and he said he'd bought. Two different women in-

troduced themselves to us as his widow. Both were attractive, brown-skinned and grief-stricken, and each told a different story about why the police had it in for my brother. Mother was equally consoling to each and equally convinced that he had not married her. Probably not. Francis was an anarchist to the finish line.

Curiosity, as well as lust and nostalgia, made me try to find Kemp in '66. I was still mourning Francis. To this day I think of Kemp oftener than any other man of my college years, except Howie, usually when I am cooking one of the dishes he taught me.

THIRTY-THREE
What's White and Falls, What's Black and Stays

Friday, MY LAST final over and a dry pellety snow hitting the sidewalk like uncooked grains of rice, I saunter home into the sounds of Mozart and Miles Davis and the clatter of dishes from the kitchen. Rosellen bounds down the steps to seize me and swing me around the hall. "Donna's getting married! Donna's getting married!"

I hold her still with the force of both hands. "When?"

"Day after tomorrow. They had their blood tests. They got their license. Donna just called her mother and she's bawling—her mother, I mean. Isn't it wonderful? I've never been so excited."

I take the steps two at a time. Wanda, our house president, charges out as I enter. Donna's eyes shine electric blue with anger as she pulls books pell-mell from the shelves and hurls them into a box. A worn sleazy slip hangs on her, her arms are smeared with dust, yet energy crackles out. "Cat! Get out!" She hauls Minouska from a half-packed box.

"You're getting married?"

"Yes. Can you take that print down without tearing it?"

I kick off my shoes to clamber on the bed, seeing with a jab of regret that it is the Gauguin of the woman with melon and flower that always hung in our rooms. "Why the big hurry? You aren't quitting school halfway through your senior year?"

"I'll drop whatever I don't require to graduate, and I bet I can finish up the last course or two at Wayne. I have oodles of extra credits from summer school. . . ." She laughs, trying to cram books in sideways on other books. "That's one advantage of avoiding going home that I never anticipated."

"What were you fighting with Wanda about?"

"She wants me to pay next semester's rent. But why? I'm leaving now. It's not fair. You can get somebody else."

"This late I'm not so sure."

A brief flush of hope warms me. Maybe if the house won't release her from her contract, she can't marry Peter yet. Anything could happen to a semester. He could choke on an olive pit or fall into a reactor model. Big Sal could come back and carry her off. I prefer him to Peter, I decide, for he didn't take up nearly so much of her time. "Of course I'll support you." The rub of it is, I will. "Does Peter's family know?"

"We'll send them a telegram right afterward. The idea is to do it, then let them react."

Rosellen surges in with two cardboard boxes. "I found these down the basement, but that's all."

"I need at least five more. Can't you try the supermarkets?"

Rosellen feigns mopping her forehead. Then she grabs her double-breasted cashmere coat. "Back as soon as I can!"

Donna shouts after her, "And a good strong box for Minouska, don't forget!" Donna gives Minouska's black head a quick caress as the cat sidles through the maze of boxes, sniffing and putting her small paws on top of each to peer in. Occasionally she gives a querulous, "Meow?"

"She'll be scared of the car ride, I'm sure." Donna wipes her dusty hands on her already dusty slip. "After the wedding, we'll stop back here, load the car and then she only has to put up with an hour or so."

"Where's Peter?"

"Out trying to cash a check." She lets an armload of books drop and stands overwhelmed and suddenly becalmed. "What will he say when I tell him Wanda wants to make me pay next semester's rent?"

"You look worn out. Stop and have a cup of coffee with me. Please."

She gives me a tiredly inquisitive look, then smiles. Across the dining room table from me in her plaid bathrobe, a checked excitement simmers in her. "My trench coat's at the cleaners—I mustn't forget. And mail forwarding. And how many sheets should we have to start?"

"I suppose three sets minimum." I shake myself. "Donna, Donna, why are you obsessing about sheets? Don't you suppose Peter has sheets on his bed?"

"But not *our* sheets. Who knows who else he slept with on those sheets?"

Well, we both know at least one person.

"I'll have to crate the books and have Rosellen ship them; they'll never fit in the Sprite. I told you, I want to get married. I want to be Donna Stuart Crecy. . . ." She pronounces it French.

"Why so fast?"

"Fast is painless. Like pulling a tooth." That small crooked grin. "Less time for the enemy to head us off. Anything could happen with him in two months. Leaving him in Detroit alone weekdays is far too dangerous, with all those old society girlfriends hanging around like hungry piranhas."

"You've hardly had time together to try things out. Why not wait till you're surer of yourself. Of him."

"When would we get the chance, with him bustling around Detroit and me stuck here?" She brushes cobwebs from her forehead. Her voice has the sweet timbre of decision. "He needs me to get him away from his son-eating family. Marrying must always be like jumping off a bridge. We have our license to jump." She stands. "I must go pack. He'll kill me if he comes back and I'm sitting around."

I follow her. "I'll help."

"That's a real kindness. Could you pack my socks and nylons? And see if you can find me one pair without a run."

"Will try." All the time I feel that she is listening for Peter's voice in the hall. I want to jump up and down to compel her attention. "Donna . . . I'm afraid for you."

Her eyes crinkled up, she gives me a quick hug. The ability to express affection has stayed since the abortion. "Stu, I'll be much better off, much safer. You'll see how calm and happy I'll be. My therapist says I'm acting much healthier as a woman now. A man who belongs to me, a place I belong—we'll be real people. I'm tired of being a student. Students are nothing! It's time to live, instead of interminably studying other people's lives."

"But your life has to center on some good work you want to do."

"Oh, all that running around fiercely trying to be some-body else. Imitating you, imitating Lennie, imitating Sal. Now I'm going to be Peter's wife and be happy and make him happy. I've grown up. I'm accepting my destiny as a woman."

"Keeping house in that two-room apartment?"

"We won't stay there long." She frowns at her slip, pinching the flimsy rayon. "So help me, I won't take this ugly old underwear. I'll be married in none, sooner. I'll throw it away." Seizing the slip in clenched hands, she rips it down the center, steps out with a pleased giggle and tosses it in the garbage.

"You have this." I hold up a black satin slip. "Sal bought this one. It's still pretty."

"I'll wear it. Black for the bride. Actually black is for the mourning and protesting parents, right? The howling mother of the groom. The threatening father brandishing the trust fund papers. I'll travel in my grey wool suit."

I act as her maid, brushing the suit, my hands sketching

arguments on the flannel. What can I say? Donna, he's a little shit, please don't marry him. Your darling is a trap. Nothing you give will be enough. His discontent will destroy you.

"I'll write, Stu. Are those nylons okay? Give them over. Now a clean blouse. And check it has all its buttons. Do you suppose he suspects how like an orphan child his wife is arriving?"

"Would you like some indecent underwear as a wedding present?"

"That'd be perfect, Stu. And please, talk to Wanda for me. Sway her. You can do it." As I turn, she adds a quiet sentence, tilting up to me a face suddenly devoid of expression. "Stu, *don't* try to make the wedding—all right?"

Donna is encased in wedding. At a special house meeting, the women in a wash of sentimental excitement vote that we shall absorb the cost of her room among us if we cannot find someone to move in. I cannot see Donna alone and neither can Peter, for she trots with a wake of helpers, in a gale of errands and messages, of boxes and wrapping paper. Donna's sister, Estelle, arrives from Detroit to run up and down the stairs with a distracted frown, an electric mixer under one arm and a pencil in her teeth.

Off to Flint they go. Minouska and the boxes await their return. They are to stay with Donna's parents. My parents are going to the wedding too. Obviously it is getting slightly out of hand.

My mother calls. "Now, Jillie, you have to go. You're behaving like a jilted female. You have to stand up proud and hold your head high so nobody can say she got the best of you."

"Mother, Donna asked me not to go."

"Well, I never." She clucks her tongue. "She knows you'd outshine her as the sun outshines the moon!"

"Mother!" I cover the mouthpiece, giggling. "Me? Since when?"

"Aren't you my daughter? You go anyhow. We'll get you a dress. Come in on the bus and we'll find one on sale."

"Mama, I can't. I promised her. You go for me."

"What should I tell them, so it won't look like you're sulking?"

"That I'm working at the library."

Mother calls back after the wedding, before Donna has returned. "So the only person from *his* side was his sister. a poor woebegone bean pole of a girl, looking as if she was smelling a skunk all the time and *so* nervous. Chickie, she jumped every time anybody spoke to her, like a mouse the cat's caught. Imagine, his parents didn't come."

"Mother, I don't think Peter's told them."

"I wondered." She pauses, rolling that around in her mind. "So he didn't tell them? Just his sister because she's got no spine anyhow. So what will happen when they find out? Will they get it annulled?"

"Peter's twenty-six and Donna's twenty-one. How can they?"

"And carried on all the time he was your so-called boy-friend."

"I should be marrying him? That's what you want to wish on me?"

"Ha! With your free-and-easy ways with men, none of them will ever marry you. Why should they, when they can get what they want from you for nothing?"

Donna returns from Flint in a russet knit suit with her skin glowing as if a candle were lit inside and with a twisted gold band on her proper finger. Peter wears a simi-lar band as he sits disconsolately at the bottom of the steps, still center of the reconstituted cyclone.

"Peter!" Donna races down. "Help, please!" She tugs him upstairs. The boxes of books and records Rosellen and I will ship are stacked along one wall. Donna has piled up to go two old black pasteboard suitcases, a plastic ward-robe containing coats and her good cocktail dress (from Big Sal) and a new piece of blue Samsonite luggage con-taining the presents of the last few days. "Peter love, here's the best box I was able to find for Minouska. What should I do with her shitbox? Would it be better if I put her in the box or if I just hold her on my lap in the car?"

I stand with the water dish in my hand waiting a decision. Peter lounges in the doorway. Slowly his eyebrows rise. More slowly he strolls in with exaggerated astonishment, poking the two battered black cases. "Do you expect these to hold together till we get downstairs? I can see us driving down the highway, leaving a wake of old lingerie like dust bowl refugees."

Donna laughs nervously. "Should I put Minouska in the box or not?"

"In my car? Look, Donna, we are not traveling with that beast. Where are we supposed to put it when we get there?"

"Lots of apartments allow cats. I can't just throw her away. She's mine!"

"You found her in an alley, put her back in an alley. We have a tiny apartment and I'm not sharing it with something that shits in a corner."

"She's nice, Peter. You'll love her once you know her. She's very clean."

"Cats fend for themselves. Will you stop anthropomorphizing? And look at this crap!" He surveys the boxes, striding back and forth. "You've got more junk than a ragpicker. I can see us now arriving with this mess and carting it past the doorman. Hello, Mother, I want you to meet my wife—not the one with the mange, Mother—"

I expect her to blaze out but she shrinks, fingers smoothing the russet skirt across her thighs. "She's met me already."

"Not as my wife." He turns to Rosellen, all good sense and downright winning charm. "Now tell me, do I have to be cast as a villain because I don't want a flea-bitten cat on my honeymoon?"

Rosellen blushes and stutters and says she's sure she wouldn't know.

"But I can't just leave Minouska. I can't throw her away like an old tennis shoe."

"I'll take her," I say. "She was both of ours."

"Would you?" She looks at Minouska, who lies very flat on the bed with her ears pressed to her head and her eyes wary slits. Minouska knows she is being talked about and she is scared. I knew it was too good to last, she is thinking.

"Sure," I say.

"Just for a while. Till Peter and I are settled. I don't think she'd mind that so much."

"Let me have her, then."

Peter expels his breath in exasperation. "The two of you and your baby substitute give me a bellyache. Okay, hand over your black baby and let's get on the stick."

In blind haste Donna and Peter gather the luggage, shout their good-byes and go clattering out. Then I am standing on the porch, jostled by my housemates, and she is gone. Slowly the women disperse but eddies of excitement disturb the house, preventing all work by making it trivial. Minouska leaps up on Donna's stripped cot and sniffs it, turns and paws and turns again, plumps down in a neat coil to wait for Donna and supper.

Upstairs in our room, Stephanie plucks her brows with a tweezer, frowning. "She made it. How did she get him to do it? There's something heady about a wedding, like a parade. No matter whose parade it is, you find yourself wanting to march too."

"Where? Off the edge?"

"It's all these affairs that waste you." Stephanie sighs deeply, staring at herself in the mirror. "All that work and it goes nowhere. What'll happen to me if Howie doesn't come through? Who will I meet once I'm out of college?"

I lie on my bunk facedown. I can see it, the wish for the seal of approval of marriage that comes while standing between the mirror and the bed in a litter of cosmetics and mended underwear and all the miracle-working creams and lipsticks that wrought no miracles, when you see with a stealthy chill that the smoldering evenings, the cozy mornings, the conversations like chess games, the words that filled you like a clear glass with chámpagne, the words that ignited the air, have all left you hungry as a girl lighting candles on her thirteenth birthday, have left nothing but chaos to be structured in confession. Only let me remember what more I know, that a great-grandmother too has only her skin and her hunger.

I hate this marriage! I wanted her to finish with Peter. I wanted anything but her gone and my side bleeding as if something I had taken for granted, taken to be my own skin, turns out to be hers and ripped from me. He could not resist that jab. Men never believe in the friendships of women. But we are not over. Her books to be mailed first. She writes, thanking. I answer. She'll be lonely in Detroit. Put in a poem or two. She has not seen my work in a while—surprise her. News and gossip. Minouska. Visits back and forth. She is not dead, just married. We have plenty of time. We will continue.

THIRTY-FOUR

In Your Commencement Is Your Ending

WE EXPERIENCE A week of perfect spring in mid-March and then the snow comes down in a wet fury as if to abolish even the memory. It's an early April Sunday around noon and I am reading my notes on *Dubliners* for my honors thesis, when someone knocks on my door. "Approach the presence," I bellow.

The door opens and Donna comes in, snow melting on the shoulders of her tailored black coat, her little fur cap. I shriek surprise, repeating her name three times.

She shivers, her high boots leaving a wet trail. Shyly she laughs, patting the snow off. "I was home for my mother's birthday. I decided to stop by. I have to leave by two thirty, at the latest." Minouska trails her sniffing, sniffing, giving puzzled cries of query. It has been two and a half months.

"Wonderful. . . . Is Peter with you?"

"He couldn't get away." Circling the room she looks at everything blankly, pauses over the typewriter. "Did I interrupt you?"

"I'm trying to figure out how Joyce gets his effects with language."

As she sits in the desk chair to look, Minouska leaps into her lap, sniffs upward toward her face. The wet spider-silk hair clings to Donna's cheek as she bends to read a page. "It looks very technical."

"I was trying to see if I could be as precise about prose as I could be about poetry, or anything in that direction. . . ." I trail off.

She is not listening. Her hand lingers on Minouska's narrow head.

"Will you be taking her with you?" I ask.

She laughs. "Don't worry! She's yours, now and forever. Though I should never have left her—no, I shouldn't have." She hugs Minouska suddenly. Startled the cat slips from her, leaping to the window ledge where she balances warily with flattened ears.

I say lamely, "You moved too suddenly." Minouska spent the first month after Donna left wandering the halls of the co-op yowling with her tail straight up. My fellow housemates almost made me get rid of her; only I delivered an impassioned speech about grieving for lost love as a basic mammalian trait. Then I had a serious talk with Minouska about survival. She began to eat again. I stole her delicacies to win her affection, but we have settled on cat food and kidney. While I work she lies black paws crossed on my desk, blinking sensuously. She has the manners of a grand coquette, but I find under her fur the remains of old lacerations. We please each other.

Donna rises, brushing cat hairs from the sleek coat she has not removed. "It's chilly in the house, isn't it? Have you had lunch?"

I shake my head no. "I can make you some soup. Or scrambled eggs."

"Let's go out. I don't really want to see anyone else here. I feel guilty, but we have so little time." She turns in a slow circle as if looking for something she does not find.

As we leave she nods at the bundles piled in the hall. "What's going on? Somebody else getting married and moving out?"

"We're collecting clothes and food for Mississippi."

"For Mississippi?" She laughs. "Like children's war relief?"

"Just about. They're starving the Black sharecroppers down there, who've got involved in a voter registration drive."

"It's nice something political's happening," she says vaguely. "I should register, now that I'm finally in the eyes of the state a certified goddamn adult."

The snow thick and wet encircles us, lining our lashes and clinging to hair and brows, to the fur of her cap. She has the little white Sprite parked nearby and with a sense of ashen familiarity I clamber inside. "You borrowed Peter's car! That must be true love."

"Rather it must be that Peter's father gave him a Porsche finally, for getting his Ph.D. As promised. This is my car now. I love having a car. I took driving lessons from this weird cowboy. Whatever happened he never raised his voice. He just chewed gum and looked bored. I'm a real adult, Stu, with my own car and my own husband and my own life!" She drives with careless dash, skids at the corner, pulls out of it and slows down slightly. "What's with your love life?"

"I neither love nor live," I declaim. "I am immovable as stone."

We eat at Metzger's. She orders a large lunch for us, urging choice on me as if the eating itself were the reason for our being together. As we drink dark beer, awaiting our food, I question her, "How's Wayne? Do you like it?"

"I'll get my degree in June. I can't tell you how I hate going to classes twice a week. It's a complete bore. In my own head I've graduated and I'm done with all this. What I want to learn, they can't teach me here."

"And with Peter? How is it going?"

"His parents want to buy us a house. If they do, he'll never leave Detroit. There was an opening at Argonne but he decided he hates Chicago." She gives me a sliver of grin. "It's a struggle."

"Then his parents have accepted you?"

"Let's say they've accepted me as his first wife. But they're putting the screws on about kids."

"And Peter?"

"Oh, he adores children."

"The hell he does. Since when?"

"Since we got married." The food arrives. She stares at her sauerbraten without recognition, picks at it, nudges it away. "But it means he's serious. Committed. Of course we'll have them eventually."

"You never wanted children."

"Stu, you know how immature and self-destructive I used to be. . . . Julie's baby was born last Tuesday. Five pounds, four ounces. A boy, Carl, junior."

"I ought to go see her. It's just impossible to get there."

"She's euphoric. I wonder if it's some drug? Slaphappy."

"What are you doing besides school, Donna?"

"We socialize a lot with the other physicists and their wives. I think of it as the Beef Stroganoff War. Who can make something fancier every Saturday. Sundays we spend with his family. Today I'm missing that. Pity! Stu, they make me aware of how much I have to learn to be his wife. All the social things I don't know. Innuendo of phrases and addresses and schools."

"But he didn't marry that. He had girlfriends for years from that world and he felt stifled by it."

"Every man wants it both ways, right? And I'm studying conversational French at Berlitz. We're going to France at the end of the summer. Do you believe it, Stu? We're going! That's our belated honeymoon."

Conversation stalls. A sense of something wrong, a quiet agony ticking like a jeweled watch inside her forehead. I ask automatically of my aunt, her mother.

"She does love me, she really does!" Donna speaks vehemently. "It was like being in a warming oven, there. I got her a pretty shawl—I've never been able to give her a real present before." She speaks of her nephew, Estelle's son. "It's ghastly, seeing him play with his armory of guns and death rays, his jet fighters. He has everything but a toy H-bomb and a little fallout shelter."

"Sure, baby dolls for the girls and guns for the boys. Toys for adjustment."

"But they don't really prepare you." She stops poking at her food to grin at me. "I was watching baby Gloria with her board with the different-shaped holes and the blocks that fit exactly."

"Toys for frustration? That'd prepare you for the world. A pegboard with all round holes and nothing but square pegs to smash in."

Her laugh barks out. "And instead of cute cuddly dolls, dolls that keep shitting like real babies. Dolls that cry like hell all the time, an awful terrified squeak. Walking dolls that limp."

"Marbles just a little flattened on one side. Guns that misfire or blow up—"

"And a dollhouse with an almost sealed basement full of roach eggs. Just a little hole left where they crawl up as they hatch, so you clean and clean and never can be rid of them!"

We can still improvise together, but in such a way as to kill my appetite. She insists on paying, murmuring without any sense of letting out secrets, "I'll just tell Peter I had to eat on the road. He won't even know I stopped or saw you."

It is only I, following her out, who am embarrassed.

Exasperation having conquered tact, lust having conquered timidity, I say loudly and bluntly, "Well, why not?"

Gerrit's hands lace over his cup, as if protecting his coffee from me. "I can't take advantage of you."

"But can I take advantage of you? What's advantage? Seeing what might be nice? I'm not a virgin and I turned twenty-one two months ago."

"You wouldn't respect me if I let this happen."

I giggle. "At least you don't say you wouldn't respect me."

"I don't know if I would. It seems . . . unnecessary."

Does he have any sex drive at all? When I cry in front of him, he thinks there's something wrong with my eyes. He can only view expression of emotion as aberration or sickness. What is his mother like, I wonder, knitting, knitting? She smiles as she knits. Beams on her beamish boy. "Does everything have to be done out of necessity? You need to eat to live but you don't need steak. You could live on soyburgers and dog biscuits." Then I am afraid I may have given him an idea.

"I don't get involved with students. I don't approve of the jerks who do. It's using position."

"You aren't my professor. You haven't been for four years. You aren't even in my department. You can't even put a letter of recommendation in my file. American history, they'd say, what's this?" I am pushing him past any real thought of consequence because what is happening is interesting. I don't think anybody has ever pushed him quite this way, or maybe Alberta did. "Wasn't Alberta your student at CCNY, before you got this job? She followed you here."

"Well, and look what happened!"

"What happened? You almost married her? That was a close call."

"I almost fucked up my whole career!" he says and jumps up, pacing to the other end of the tiny kitchen.

Oh. Of course. Having a Communist for a girl friend is bad enough, but marrying one! To be a Left lib without a label, that's the ticket to survival. Dissent but not subversion, forums but not fights, exactly how far you can go without losing your job. In spite of Mike's predictions two years ago, Donaldson marches on. There is no use being snotty even as I sit in his kitchen drinking coffee I made in his pot: he is the best of the bunch. At least he stimulates thinking in his students. Because of what he just blurted out, he is glaring at me and it is time for me to go home in the rosy May evening.

Howie hauls Stephanie's black steamer trunk up from the basement, and out of a whirlwind of skirts and dresses and sweaters, two piles emerge to restore us to hers and mine. "Why are you going home for the summer to Port Huron?" I ask.

She speaks from the depths of the closet, throwing shoes

out behind her like dirt from a hole she is digging. "You sound just like Howie! Really!"

"He's right. You could finish up your degree at summer school."

"Nonsense. Most of my incompletes are papers I haven't written, and I can work on them just as well at home, and a lot cheaper. Stu, you just don't understand. You and Howie don't have real families."

"My parents are pretty real. Howie gave a whole year to his."

"They don't seem to care what you do, where you go. You're off to New York, and you don't even have relatives there."

"It's not true they don't care. They try to control me. I left home so that they couldn't."

"If I didn't come home for the summer, everybody in the neighborhood would ask where I was. My father expects me to work in the store. They pay for my schooling and they expect me to come home when they want me home. They'd never agree to summer school." She tosses my black turtleneck to me. "I'll have all summer to work on my father and my mother, separately, to persuade them I can go to New York to work. I do have an aunt there in Astoria. . . ." She pronounces it as if it were Greek—Ahs-tor-ree-yah.

"At some point you're going to have to go public about Howie—tell your parents."

"Ummm. It'll be trouble." As she packs, the room looks bleak and bare.

"I can see you after the fourth kid finally telling them it wasn't a virgin birth after all."

"My father's not naive. Just possessive."

"Is it because Howie's Jewish you're afraid?"

"He doesn't look very Jewish. But he's clearly not Greek. . . . Is this yours or mine?" She holds up a Liberty print blouse.

"Never saw it before in my life."

"I swear it isn't mine. . . . Stu, what's the point causing trouble when we aren't about to marry yet? When we're finally going to do it, I'll fight those battles. Suppose I went through all the fighting and suffering and then we didn't get married? They wouldn't trust me anymore and I'd be nowhere."

I pack, dividing my stuff into what will go into temporary storage in Detroit, and what I'm carrying along to New York that will wait in Ann Arbor while I say goodbye to my parents. I will be staying with Alberta at first, on Horatio Street in the Village. Today my father will fetch me and boxes. Wanda will feed Minouska. Then I come back, collect the rest of my stuff and head for New York by train. Alberta will meet me next Friday. To my naive surprise I have learned my parents do not give a damn about my graduating with honors, and would only go to the commencement in the spirit of attending a funeral out of obligation. We will none of us go to commencement.

I have not been able to write Donna. I can't endure the idea of Peter picking up my letters. I think of her daily as if an unanswered phone were ringing in me. Oddly enough we communicate through Mother. Estelle calls my mother frequently, too frequently for my mother's pleasure, to complain of how unfriendly and superior Peter's family acts. Donna calls my mother to complain in general and to pass messages to me. I give my mother messages for Donna. Mother is switchboard central. "I call when *he* isn't there," she explains. "It's easier on Donna."

I ask hopefully, "You know his schedule?"

"I just concentrate before I dial." She smiles serenely. "I can tell."

Mother has arranged a rendezvous for tomorrow noon at the house. I would rather meet Donna downtown or at the Art Institute, but if as it seems I can't call without tipping off Peter (am I to assume he has forbidden her to see me?), I have to take Mother's arrangement as a given.

Mother is on Donna's side now. I can't believe how Mother approves of my ex-roommate, my cousin, my old conspirator. Does that mean she is accepting me more? I never give up. In a chamber of hope deep in the sinuses Mother opens her arms wide as a queen-sized bed and gives me a salute of victory and cheer, crowning me with roses. Mother bursts into a full operatic aria entitled What a Great Daughter I Have! I sing loud as a chorus of three hundred, Oh, Mother, You Are the One! My One and Only Mother! All images I have of deity are based on early perceptions of thee, source of milk and mothering source of joy and sorrow, source of sweet caresses, random blows and fearful absences! Never grow any older and adore me again. The universe is just as tricky and just as arbitrary as thou, and almost as beautiful.

Detroit in the summer gives me a hunger for any kind of love, like a drug I could take to quiet this pain which is not entirely memory, both rock and shadow. The smells of asphalt melting under the onslaught of the dirty sun, of burnt rubber, of cooked cars, of brains baking, of angers stewing, of violence on the boil, mix with the fragrance of iris and cut grass from a neighbor's lawn, of the red roses that bury the fence under their perfumed tresses, the odor of parsley and sage growing just outside the back door in what was once my sandbox. I go about staring hard at the row of stores on the corner with their stamped-tin ceilings, the cinder block bars, the gasworks and the four-whore house on the next block. The neighborhood is turning all Black. My parents talk of leaving. The Djordejevicks sold their house to a colored bus driver and they got ten thousand, my mother says, ten thousand and the roof leaks. I walk fifteen blocks and see only two kids I knew. Kids. One of them is forty pounds heavier than when I last saw her and two babies lighter, one hanging on her skirt and the other in a buggy.

Running up the outside staircase to Callie's, I bang on her door, but the man who answers is Black and suspicious. The room I glimpse past him has been repainted and paneling added. Something in me repeats like a mourner that this place I have hated is now, because I am leaving it, precious and necessary fuel to me.

I am lying on the old glider upstairs staring at the boxes I have packed and the odds and ends I have still to pack, when I recognize the car engine outside and run the length of the attic to peer out. White Sprite. Donna climbs out, silvery hair, dark glasses. I lunge down the stairs but cannot beat Mother to the door.

"Put on a little weight, um?" Mother pinches Donna's upper arm. "Never mind. You look better. You were too scrawny before. Did your mother-in-law buy you that outfit?"

"Marriage is fattening. All that entertaining." Donna gives a high giggle and Mother chimes in.

"Now that's too true!"

Donna is tanned: I cannot remember her being tan before. The slacks are linen and fit well; the polo shirt is narrowly striped turquoise on black. She says it is French. Her hair is not curled but cut in layers that make it fuller. No doubt about it, she looks good. Mother nudges us into chairs and bustles into the kitchen for lemonade. I have not had lemonade since I left home; it is the taste of summer in my mother's house.

"So you're done with school now, the same as me," I say, although even as I say it I feel little is the same.

"Finally! But how come you're not going on to graduate school?"

"I'm going to New York."

Donna sighs. "It was hard, enduring classes to the end. I felt years older than everybody else. I kept looking at the girls in my classes and thinking, At least I'm done with that. The meat rack."

"Don't you think it was a waste of time and money?" Mother says. "After all, you're married and what good did it do you?"

"I'd never have met Peter if I hadn't gone to Michigan," Donna says firmly. "And I was really stupid and naive before."

"Take off your sunglasses in the house," Mother urges. "You'll ruin your eyes leaving them on."

"Oh, they're prescription." Donna tilts them to show us. "Peter wants me to get contact lenses, but the idea of poking things in my eyes terrifies me. I can never put drops in."

"But if he doesn't like you in glasses," Mother said meaningfully. "A thing like that can put a man off."

Donna grimaces. "I'll have to try them. I keep postponing the appointment."

"How are you?" Mother asks, staring at Donna's midsection. "Are you . . . ?"

"God no!" Donna blurts out. "I'm careful!"

"Good, don't be in too much of a hurry. Remember after you have babies, you're never alone, not for years. Not in the morning, not at meals, not at night. You understand me?"

Donna nods. "It would be disastrous now."

"How are you getting on with his folks?" Mother asks.

I am feeling left out. I will sit silently and pout and then they will see how they have injured me, bonding against me, the two of them, married women conspiring about The Husband together.

"I try to keep my mouth shut, I try and try. But I can't sit through whole dinner parties without saying something, and then I do it! An idea comes out of me. An opinion. Something that actually demonstrates I'm a person and I read the papers every day and think." Donna is looking at me now.

I can't resist answering. "You get in political arguments?"

"You'd be surprised. We can get into one from a comment on how hot it is."

"The weather," I say, "is it the Russians' fault?"

"When summer hit they made some snide remarks about quote the colored unquote opening the hydrants and how it showed they had no sense of civic responsibility, so there was no use pouring money down a rathole. I said I thought a rathole was an accurate description of some of the slums in Detroit and didn't they like to use their pool when it was hot?"

"The rich are all fascists at heart," Mother says succinctly, her hands on her knees. "We're just laying chickens to them."

She startles me, when out of her comes a pure political

remark from her distant past. "Where does Peter stand in all this?"

"Oh, squarely in the middle." Donna laughs. "I'm always making resolutions that I won't get into a fight over there. . . . But you know in a way he likes it. He likes them focusing their discontent on me. I'm a lightning rod. He can mediate. It makes him feel mature and superior."

"But he's awfully dependent on what they think," Mother says.

"I've got to get him out of here. He's been offered that job at Brookhaven, finally, but at less pay. He said if I agree not to go to France, he'll take it. So I said I'll give it up to move to New York, but he's still dillydallying. I've been trying out a line on him that his father remained in Detroit all his life because he was scared of New York. I think it's having some effect." Donna sighs. "But marriage is great, Stu, absolutely great."

"Come on, Donna, marriage is only the sum total of separate events. It's not a thing."

"You don't understand," Mother snaps and Donna nods. Then the teakettle whistles from the kitchen. Mother bounds up to bring back the old tabby teapot on a tray with small cups.

"No tea for me, thank you," Donna murmurs. "I'm half cooked."

Mother holds out a cup to her. "Wouldn't you like me to read your leaves? I haven't since you were a toddler."

Donna's face contracts. She glances around as if beseeching me, the wall. "Oh, don't bother! Please."

"No," I say. "She doesn't need that."

"Please. I don't think I want to know my future." Donna resorts to a weak giggle.

Mother looks at her with a measuring stare. "Perhaps some other time." Her voice is sharp with disappointment. "If ignorance is bliss . . ."

"Donna, could you take me for a drive? I'd love to see Belle Isle again."

She agrees instantly. I know Mother is miffed at our leaving, but I will deal with that later. Donna drives with style. In fact she handles the car better than Peter ever did.

Does that bother him or doesn't he notice? She has caught his daydream and outperformed, and in what else? For she is quicker, brighter and more desperate. I say, "When I was growing up and used to take the Tireman or the Joy Road buses downtown, I used to sit at the dirty bus window trying to figure out why the objects that gave my eyes the most satisfaction, the most to work on, were grimy tortured rooming houses and slum tenements with broken grandeur, the posturing of dead Victorian egos among the burning stench of people wasting. How can you come from Detroit and not think beauty must contain grit and rake you while it delights? Without an aesthetic that gives a place of honor to the power of incongruity?" I am surely trying to impress her anew.

"Peter has that Grosse Pointe mentality, all right. Try to get him to do anything in Detroit. If he knew we were going to Belle Isle, he'd lecture me for an hour on how dangerous it is." A red light halts us in the world that feels as if it is made of melting plastic. "Marrying me was his big act of rebellion."

"Why do you think marrying a man is any better than living with him?"

"He isn't committed." The light changes and she drags a Corvette. "He doesn't have to work things out. You think Peter would move to New York if we weren't married?"

"He was thinking about it a year ago."

"I'm talking about doing it. I'm his wife. That means I come before daddy and mommy and all the twirps he hung around the fucking country club with. . . . Oh, I'm taking tennis lessons. I dropped the French, since we're not going."

"Are you terribly disappointed? I'd consider a murder or two for a trip to France."

"I have to think of the bigger picture, getting him away from the poisonous influence of his parents. Marriage means taking your decisions seriously, Stu, not just bolting off the way we used to."

The sun steel-clangs on streets that smell of tar as she whips the car through traffic. Behind the dark glasses her eyes are squinted against the glare. I experience a moment of pure loss thinking of Kemp. It was impossible because of his violence, his racism; it was impossible and yet I miss him. Physically, irrationally, I miss. It's driving in the car that brought him back to me.

"The scary thing about affairs," she is saying, "is you put everything, all of yourself, into every one and lose."

"Doesn't have to be that way. I want more friendship and less clawing and gouging."

"But if you love, I mean. You're burned afterward. So you do it again. A little less of you is left. Then a lot less. Marriage is different."

"Yeah, divorce is worse than breaking up, I hear. I don't see a neat progression and I don't think there's less of me. I open up differently with different people. Different selves emerge."

Belle Isle is very flat out in the middle of the vast Detroit River, with episodes of little bridges, lagoons, flat open playing fields, groves, what I think of as casino architecture. It's crowded today but there's room for more. The yacht and powerboat clubs face Detroit, but on the side toward Windsor, Canada, people are sitting in chairs they've brought, sunning, listening to radios, drinking beer, fishing. It's always cooler here. We park downriver, under the shade of a big weeping willow. She shades her eyes. "I'm always the same self. Me. The dumb scared child who shits in her pants. That's what I've learned in therapy, Stu. You need a good therapist."

I refuse to rise to the bait of our fortieth argument on therapy. "Sometimes I love Detroit." I gesture toward downtown. "How it steams and throbs on a June day like this, an enormous wounded heart."

She stares at the river flowing away from us downstream. "Do you remember how when we were freshmen we'd talk about when you ought to sleep with men and what was promiscuity and we were very grave and anxious?"

"We tried to make a new morality that works for us."

"So I noticed how at first I thought three affairs meant you were promiscuous. Then I had three, so I thought having sex with somebody you don't love is promiscuous.

Then I had an affair with Charlie. Then I thought being involved with two men at once or taking somebody else's man—so I broke every rule I made. It's like there are no rules, really, and you can just drown in it."

"But there aren't rules. You do make up your own or just accept what somebody else made up for their reasons." I feel shed like an old sweater. I get out of the car and walk toward the water. She follows me. I say, "I feel as if you're more married than you are Donna. Marriage wraps you up like cellophane."

"But it's the thing I'm doing. The most important thing in my life. Everything else has to be secondary. Everybody sees less of her girlfriends after she's married. Grow up!"

"Damn you, Donna, fight it! You need me in your corner."

"He's in my corner. You've been afraid to fall really in love after Mike. You'll see." She smiles, her gaze turned away. "You're jealous."

"Yes, I know. Donna thinks Carl and I are the Jukes and Kallikacks of our generation." Julie pats her belly. She is pregnant again. "It's far more practical this way. Get it all over with. I mean, I can't do a bloody other thing now anyhow, so I might as well make babies while I'm raising babies, don't you think?"

"Are you happy with Carl?" Has he stopped saying women are made for love?

"Of course! I have what I wanted—a husband, a house, my own family." But the rest of the two hours she complains. He isn't ambitious enough, he doesn't listen to her father's advice, he spends too much time in front of the TV too much money playing golf. He never cleans the bathtub after himself. He doesn't pick up his socks. He won't brush his teeth before they make love.

But Julie adores her children unstintingly. Carl, Jr., is sweet and chubby, hauling about an immense once-white rabbit. The baby is featureless to me but beautiful to Julie. Julie as mother is Julie without sarcasm, rid of the necessity to make the first put-down. I feel she has developed a contempt for Carl already, based on conviction that anyone she can have isn't worth having. "The major advantage to marriage as far as I can see," she says when I repeat my conversation with Donna, "is, one, you get to make babies and they're dumplings and they have to love you. And two, when you're dating a man and you start having sex, you always have to. But once they're married, they stop making a fuss. Five minutes once a week and you're let off bothering about it the rest of the time."

Like the Victorian house in Cold Springs, Julie's split-level has two living rooms, a formal parlor done in white and blue for company (not including me) and a family room where they actually spend time. About Donna, Julie declaims, "She can't go on fiddling. Either she has to produce an heir, or go back to school, or go to work. No other choices. She's a fool if she doesn't pick babies." Then she tries to condole with me on not having nailed down Donaldson. "He would have been a real catch. Then you could have stayed in Ann Arbor."

I almost shudder.

The night is hot and thirsty. The elms stoop under the burden of dusty slack leaves. Around the streetlights flying beetles and moths form speckled halos. Detroit stirs and seethes around this quiet street. It is crackling and sputtering, slamming cars together like crushed tin cans, rushing ambulances through the night, shooting off Saturday night specials and cherry bombs, racing its engine, bursting into rhythm and blues or country music from rival car radios as they squeal down the street in a movie chase and then halt with a screech at the stoplight, their radios blaring even louder. Everywhere people are fucking and fighting and blowing off the anger of the grim and grimy workday. The whole city is on amphetamines. On uppers and booze. It sings funky and grinds its teeth, cool and hot at once and hungry for something to kill the pain.

"New York," my father mutters with deep suspicion, rocking on the porch. "I was there once. They don't have one hotel, they have two miles of hotels. They don't have one pawnshop, they have two miles of pawnshops. Streetcars up in the air too noisy to hear yourself. It's a dirty place. No trees. No light."

Every day Mother marks the newspapers, circling with red crayon jobs for secretaries and receptionists. "We're looking at houses," she says. "We'll get a bigger house. One with plenty of room for the boys when they come home and you can have a room all to yourself. You could save a lot of money with a good secretarial job and living at home. Get yourself some clothes and have your hair done and see Donna whenever."

She works hard, my mother in her little house. The soot floats down day and night. Sheets on the line yellow in the acid rain from the factories. Every two days the sills must be washed. My father tracks in grease from work and his clothes have to be prescrubbed at the washboard before they go into the washing machine with its wringer where she catches a finger at least once a year.

She sits nearsightedly squinting at the old sewing machine, shortening a coat she bought too large at a rummage sale. She is always making over, trying to create something nice and pretty or at least serviceable out of what somebody with more money has discarded or sold off cheap. Things break and she fixes them, mends the old chair, glues the cracked plate, darns the worn sock. All day she scrubs and cleans and mutters. The bills come in and she mutters. She wants it nice, the house, her life. She irons even the sheets and towels. She wants to be a baleboste and she is still showing her mother she can do it better. She was angry at her mother; she stayed angry. Not enough in a family of twelve for any particular girl-child.

He works hard, my father, long hours. His hands are relief maps of burns and scars. His back is stooped from peering forward into engines. He has a permanent hacking cough from smoking and from breathing exhaust fumes. His light grey eyes are squinted as if against a glare; they have the air of having wanted to look into distances rarely offered them. At fourteen he worked evenings and weekends and he has worked ever since.

With my books and my papers and my ever more pe-

culiar interests and passions and ambitions, my friends
they mistrust, I come into this house like a hot wind,
casting dust in their eyes and spoiling their food. I want to
make them happy. I pursue them around the house trying
to share my ideas, to please, and I terrify. I am nothing
they know what to do with. They tell me about the daughters of their friends, the girls of the neighborhood. Audrey
had twins, both boys. Joyce is engaged to a pipefitter.
Neighborhood news. Freddie is in prison at Jackson not
for the still but for a robbery Mother thinks he didn't
commit. Sharkie is in the army in Germany. Callie is working at Awrey's Bakery, along with Le Roy next door, who
told my mother.

"Where's Francis?" I ask.

"He shipped out on an ore boat," Dad says. "Got his
union card. Working the Great Lakes up to Duluth."

"At least he's working regular," Mother says. "It takes a
load off my mind, chickie, to know where he is so I don't
lie awake all night stewing and fretting about him, like I
did when he was you-know-where down in Mexico."

I want to say, *Look, I love you*, but it comes to me that
is the last thing I can say directly. It is not said in this
house. The flimsy walls would crack with shame if I spoke
it. We have channels between us for insult, channels for
negotiation and innuendo, for push and pull, even for comfort after injury, but none for affection. I am a daughter
who does not fit into the narrow slot marked Daughter and
they cannot rejoice in me.

Mother calls to me. She squats in front of the tall secretary dragging out the old album. She folds back the tablecloth Buhbe crocheted and plops it down on the plastic pad
underneath. "You'll want some of the family."

I find she is right. Leaning on a plump elbow she turns
the cluttered pages, touching her forefinger to her tongue
and tapping fading snapshots of her family, frowning with
a sucked-in muttering, nodding with a bittersweet pucker.
Boys in knickers girls with huge bows perched on their
curls pose in ranks on the steps of dreary frame houses old
even then. Mother's face beautiful and heart-shaped turns

up with a shy and pained smile as she sits on the grimy stoop of a tenement, one tentative hand still protecting a book and her long muslin dress brushing her high shoes. She was so beautiful, my young mother, that my heart throbs like a rotten tooth.

"There's your grandfather with some of his friends, just before they killed him." In a group of pickets, Grandfather puts his arm around a fat man with his arm in a sling. "Wasn't he a man and a half? Look how he stood, like a king."

With two young women, arms around each other's waists, Mother in white shirtwaist and stem-narrow black skirt stands outside Wanamaker's where she worked. Mother is on the left. With a corsage on her starched bosom and her leg nicely turned out, she waits hopefully in a model's pose for the attention that will transfigure her world of trouble, poverty and sorrow.

"That's *him*," she whispers loudly. "Didn't think I had any left. I thought your father ripped them all up." A stocky man grins on a seashore in a striped thirties bathing suit. Dad passes us with a beer in his hand and says nothing.

"Who's that with me?" Grinning through a missing front tooth I hold my skirt out daintily and embrace a spindly flaxen tot who stares not at the camera but at my cat washing himself. One thin arm extends futilely toward his furriness.

"Donna. You were four. Oh, you were such a sweet-tempered baby, Jill!" Her eyes rake my face accusingly. That baby, where?

Father's face at his high-school graduation peers bright-eyed as a squirrel from lowered face, chin warring with stiff collar. Photographs grey as the gnawing rat of time. Albums should come engraved with grim Latin mottoes. Buhbe huddles spent and confused in the hot July sun on Belle Isle. Did she smell death in the dusty picnic air? What determined that she spoke Yiddish to me and I answered her in English? I will learn Yiddish and hear her voice again, reborn.

Mike and I drink soda on the steps. "Let me have that one."

"Holding on to the past! That nothing—a hero made of straw! A schtroyene held!" She slams the album shut. "Enough! You're never satisfied." She glares at the photos she gave me. "Give you an inch and you take a mile."

In a moment we are quarreling loudly, dissipating the smell of death and defeat in the only ritual we have.

Beyond the tracks the Huron glides by, gunmetal grey under high clouds. The hills of town rise behind the red-brick station. No one comes down the path to see me off. What a lot of self I expended here. So, you half-assed martyr, who do you want to gather on the platform with a band? A delegation of ex-lovers with bouquets of poison ivy?

The train coils round the bend of warehouses coming, so soon. Out I go as in I came and the town nestles on its green wooded hills puttering and intent on itself. I touch my battered blue suitcase for comfort, the same one I brought to school and put down in Donna's room. Type-writer. New fiberboard case holding one cat doped into submission. Supper in a bag. The engine looms past, taller than I expect. The cars settle to a halt. Coach to New York? Steam tickles my legs as I drag my load on board.

Midway down the car I stow my luggage in the rack and the box of dulled cat at my feet as quickly, time ebbing, I press my cheek to the dirty glass. Good-bye to the vaude-ville where I learned my pratfalls. The coach lurches for-ward, pauses, glides with a high springy feel past the sta-tion. In five minutes we are out of Ann Arbor, heading eastward. I have made a plodding beginning at learning my craft, my politics, my needs. I have acquired a dependent. Across the deepening twilight of the rippling belly of mid-America we glide through little towns and middling towns where cars crouch on the far side of zebra-striped barriers, their headlights brushing me as I flick past, toward loneli-ness and beginning again. East to the ocean I have never seen.

THIRTY-FIVE

A Life Alone Is Not Necessarily Lonely

BY AUGUST FIRST I am settled in my own apartment on East Twelfth Street just off Second Avenue, in a big living room that serves as my study and my bedroom and a small kitchen just twice the size of the full bathroom I have learned is a luxury on the Lower East Side. From the previous tenant I inherited the table and three kitchen chairs, a chest of drawers and a machine-made Oriental, along with a permanent supply of small tan and mahogany cockroaches and large shiny coffee-colored ones. At first Minouska pursued them, but I gather their flavor is foul.

I have already established a pattern of doing temporary office work for an agency and posing for art classes, part-time jobs that give me time to write. My apartment is an oven on hot nights, when I trek over to Alberta's to sleep, about a ten-minute walk. Alberta has an air conditioner in her three-room apartment, which feels much more spacious now that Minouska and I are not clogging it up. My first purchase was a double bed (I am as usual full of hope) and my second, some curtains (one of the men across the hollow court of the block uses binoculars). Minouska lets me know that what she always dreamed of was a nice apartment, the two of us, with ledges that catch the morning sun and a bed heaped with pillows to sprawl on.

I have the fourth-floor walk-up in the back for which I pay $67.50 plus utilities. For the first time in my life, I live alone. My plates from a junk store, my silverware stolen from the Union, my glasses from Woolworth's, my door from the brownstone's basement, on legs that I myself attached, my pans from Goodwill and my mother, my books shipped from Detroit, mine! I course with the same euphoria of freedom those first weeks in my own, my first, my paradise of little hotbox apartment that I did when I first came to Ann Arbor. From my six weeks as her roommate I got closer to Alberta than I ever had been, but I could not write there and I was always aware how much space Minouska and I took up. Like my mother, Alberta would point out to me better jobs than I wanted, thinking I should prefer a job in publishing to three days in a dress house, two days in a cosmetics mail-order business.

On Second a few blocks south is a market whose stalls offer still lifes of fruit and vegetables, barrels of oysters and clams, ripe Sicilian olives, ropes of smoked fish, smoked eels from Long Island. Cooking is an activity Alberta took up at one time, perhaps for her husband of a few months, perhaps for Gerrit; considered and dismissed. She is a believer in take-out and restaurants. Her idea of cooking is to purchase a barbecued chicken from the Jefferson Market and stick it in her oven for ten minutes. When I moved out, she gave me an old *Joy of Cooking* from her brief domesticity, and I had my first cookbook affair.

The pleasures of a single existence are intense but unexpected. I have never read poems about the love of one's own kitchen, pots, towels, cat, books. I meet men in the city as easily as a finger stuck in water comes up wet; friends of friends, people I knew slightly in college, men I fall into conversation with. I spend enjoyable evenings but decline to become involved.

* * *

I am cooking a rice pilaf with chicken for Alberta, who reclines on my bed/couch smoking a miniature cigar, a habit that drives her father crazy. She is leaving his law office. Professional intimacy has not proved comfortable.

"I interviewed at Corbett, Corbett, Bates and Bernstein."

"Alberta! I know that's supposed to mean something, but not to me."

"They're a firm specializing in domestic cases."

"What does that mean? Not foreign?"

"It means low ranking. It means my father screaming at me and storming out of his own office and slamming the door and then having to walk back in because of course it's his office. It's divorce. Separation. Child custody. Women, bubeleh, women."

"I think it sounds a lot more interesting than corporations."

"Me too. But I know it shouldn't. It's declining real power. My father says it's not political, and of course it isn't." She sighs.

"You can't say it doesn't matter if a woman has to stay married to some man who beats her. Or if she loses her kids. Or if she has to go on welfare."

"I feel pulled to it. It is more interesting to me, Jill, even though the law involved is less exciting. He—Bernstein, that is—offered me the position and I took it. I didn't know I was going to till I heard myself accepting."

We eat in the nook part of the kitchen, opening on the courtyard from which a faint breeze touches our faces. She has brought Frascati. That summer I decorate, as do all bohemian graduates, with candles in wine bottles and cheap art reproductions of Miró and Chagall. What my guests have been bringing me to drink sits around in the form of empties with crooked candles dripping down wax that is supposed to hide the labels.

Often we promenade the Village, looking in windows of earring shops, wandering through small galleries, stopping for cappuccino. Sometimes we go uptown to a meeting about civil rights called by CORE (the Congress of Racial Equality). We sit on a blanket and listen to chamber music concerts in Washington Square Park. We go to French and

Italian and Japanese movies. We listen to debates about nuclear weaponry and disarmament and socialism. At the coffee hour afterward we meet more young men, with whom we go out sometimes together and sometimes separately on weekends. We are united in the desire to avoid spending money on our jaunts. Although Alberta makes three times as much as I do, she spends three times as much. Her rent is high. She dresses well in crisp suits, has her hair done once a week and eats in restaurants. We are both always short.

My next-door neighbor is an earring maker named Conrad who has a basement shop on MacDougal the size of a shower stall. A follower of Gurdjieff, whose book he lends me for a weekend ("Forty-eight hours. It shouldn't take you longer than forty-eight hours to read it"), he explains he is becoming a superior machine. He is on a higher plane of being than I am. He sports a bushy blond beard, wears a red shirt and whines about how bohemians are spoiling the neighborhood. Quiet (I imagine him sitting in the dark all evening with his arms folded practicing inner discipline) he complains about my noise—typewriter, phonograph, friends.

Under me is a gay waiter who tells me his motto is never the same one twice. He frequents the St. Marks Baths and has a myna bird named Gorgeous George who cannot learn to talk. I hear what my downstairs neighbor is trying to teach him and maybe the bird is simply a prude. Minouska saw it once and began to sing with lust.

Across the hall from the waiter are two women studying art at Cooper Union, a local art school. On the floor below are a Puerto Rican couple with a baby and an old woman whose mother is in the nursing home, The Sons and Daughters of Israel, down the block. The Black janitor lives in the front apartment below ground level. The garden apartment is inhabited by a professional couple (both leave in the morning in suits, carrying attaché cases) who scream in a language I will not learn till next year is Hungarian, and a poodle who yaps. I try to practice my Spanish on the young mother when I catch her alone at the mailboxes.

The freedom to work ignites me. The best thing about being a writer is that I get to sit down and write. I love the luminous cone of concentration. I love stopping and then taking a moment to remember who and where I am. What I do not love yet is what I write. Something awkward, inert lurks between the vision and the word. I cannot yet say what I mean.

Every couple of weeks I type poems and send them into limbo—some little magazine where they age for three to five months come back coffee stained, to be retyped and sent out again. I have a big chart of where my poems have been and are to give me the illusion of progress. The Tuesday my first poem is accepted by *Fugue*, Alberta brings a bottle of California champagne and I discover I can get drunk in twenty minutes.

Some days I work for money at boring jobs in offices where I steal paper. Some days I sit at my trestle table and work on my poems. Already I feel as if I left Ann Arbor a year ago, for the melancholy and sense of defeat I carried in my chest like a glacier have more than melted, wholly evaporated. This is my own, my adult life.

It is then with a pang of dismay I answer the phone on a Thursday at five forty-five in late August as I walk in from work, with my newest affectation, a clipped, "Stuart here," and in my ear Howie drawls, "Well, I'm here too, what do you know about that?"

"Oh." I choke. "You are," I add, and the woman who chats in sidewalk cafés and dim bars and spaghetti joints and French restaurants about abstract expressionists, Sartre and nuclear disaster, quite wilts. "Oh, you're here. In New York. When did you arrive?"

"Yesterday. I'm staying with my aunt Manya on West End. Why don't you come up and see me sometime? Like now?"

"Why don't you come down and see me sometime, like now? I don't live with my aunt anybody. I live by myself and my neighborhood is marvelous to walk in." I am a Lower Manhattan chauvinist. I believe real life stops at Fourteenth Street. Up north is where I work for money.

"Give me the address."

I do. "Shouldn't I give you directions? What cross street are you near?"

"Now hold on, landsman. I lived here for two years, remember? I'm the expert."

"Oh, Howie, they tear it all down every year. It's just a concrete stage setting." We are so sophisticated, two transplanted Detroiters, that I grin to hear us and then I am pleased he called. Old languors have no place in my busy city life. Why moon over any man? Pooh, I had my choice of seven this month and bit into none of them. I have outgrown this weak and woozy longing and am prepared to be wholly a friend. "So come. My name's on the bell." (J. Stuart.) "Is Stephanie with you?"

"No. She's in fucking Port Huron. You'll hear my complaints soon enough."

He comes to supper and does complain, while I cook him the identical meal I made for Alberta last week—practice makes perfect—till I send him out for wine since it didn't occur to him to bring a bottle. He gets a white Rioja we sip as I finish putting our meal together.

"Stephanie didn't make up her incompletes. Now she has to go back and put in another term. I ask her, What did you have to do this summer that was so damn important you couldn't make up your classwork? She rattles on about her family and working in the dry cleaner's. What it comes down to, is that when she's home she blends seamlessly into the world she came from, and I'm just not real to her."

"Parents, her sister, her grandmother all in that house. It might be impossible to work there."

"Then why didn't she go to summer school? It's a case of being adult enough to know what you want and pursuing it. But she's acting half the time like a woman and half like a child. I come last."

I have to soothe him for her absence, the irony making me glum. The next week I do the same things with him I do with Alberta. It's almost the same, isn't it? Almost. After he leaves me, I never sleep.

Labor Day weekend the city broils. If I wasn't seeing Howie, I'd go stay at Alberta's. She's out in Bridgehampton

visiting friends, but I have the key to her apartment. Tonight, Sunday night, maybe I'll carry Minouska over after
Howie leaves. Minouska would follow me into the subway
if I'd let her, with her passionate loyal fixation. If not
watched, I may at any moment disappear, like Donna,
from whom I have received two enigmatic postcards.

July 15, 1957

Dear old Stu:
It's warm in the cocoon and sometimes dark too but
they say darkest before the dawn. I'm delivering ultimata
but out of strength or desperation only the Spirit of
Christmas Future knows. Nymph in thy orisons be all
my sins remembered—so I can forget them.

Donna

August 12, 1957

Dear Stu:
It's closer, but to what? May the next you hear from me
be a local (nontoll) call but don't hold your breath. I'm
turning into a high-class infighter. The slimiest innuendo
in the Middle-Worst.

love & angsts
Donna

I return a postcard with my new address and phone number and a quotation from Proverbs: "Hope deferred maketh
the heart sick." I hope we are not sending cute postcards
back and forth for the next ten years or until she gets
bored with her husband.

The air is sulfurous and fills the lungs with pillow stuff-
ing. The city smells like an old ashtray. Clouds pile up over
the East River while the air clots. I am trying veal paprika
on Howie, with spectacular success. He even wipes his
plate with his finger after the bread has removed the last
trace of sauce. It has turned dark early. I speculate, "Feels
like fall already, the days suddenly shorter."

He squints out. "I think it's just going to rain."

"That would be lovely. Wash the city. Wash the air."

Howie has found an apartment with two other medical

students on 109th and Amsterdam. He moved in yesterday and spent today unpacking and putting up shelves. "I don't have enough energy left to go out. I wish you had a TV."

"I do have a kind of TV." I turn out the lights and motion him to sit on my couch/bed facing the windows, whose shades I raise. "I got the idea when I saw the man across the way watching me through binoculars. I'm serious, Howie. Just look."

"At what? Hey, what's going on? Are the cats killing the dogs or are the dogs killing the cats?"

"I have counted eighteen different and recognizable cats, who all make love or fight every night. Think, Howie, how quiet the nights would be if cats practiced oral intercourse! Then there are all the dogs chained up in yards of garden apartments who bark at the eighteen cats."

He points at Minouska, lying on his belly. "Does she get jealous and want some too?"

"She listens, but she views them as the slums from which she rose." She will not go out unless I take her.

"There's a bald guy playing guitar." Howie is getting involved in my program.

"He has a friend with a banjo and another with an accordion."

"Who are those two guys who walk around in towels? Don't they ever pull the shades down?"

"They never wear clothes and they never pull down the shades. See, there's Binoculars. But the man who sits at the kitchen table with his hands over his ears while his wife yells, they're not home. And the Pureto Ricans who play dominoes are off someplace. The old man always wins. And the woman who yells Shut Up that Noise, she must be on vacation too." I kill time looking out whenever I am stuck. Red and yellow bricks, bricks plastered or painted, walls crowded with side-by-side windows. Flowerpots, flower boxes, plants on ledges and fire escapes. Clotheslines on pulleys to windows. Small patches of gardens sport a statue, an outdoor grill, rusting metal chairs, graveled paths.

"Why are you living way down here, Stu? And why alone?"

"Don't call me that!"

"It always grated on me." He frowns. "How did I pick it up?"

Three guesses. "I like living alone. You used to enjoy it yourself."

"I didn't enjoy it. I was just too lazy to move."

"How hot it is." I tug at my dress. "You're always talking about your laziness, when you work harder than anyone I know."

He stretches his arms over the pillows. "I'm talking about a deeper laziness."

I gather Minouska nervously into my lap to be caressed. "I'm tired of so many lives impinging directly on me."

"Whose fault is that? You love gossip and intrigue. You have to be involved with everybody. Now you're playing hermit."

"Hardly!" Caressing the cat feels suddenly too seductive so I put her down. A heavy sigh of wind moves through the room. Far-off thunder rumbles on the edge of hearing like a half-understood warning. "I've just never had a place of my own. Why are we glaring at each other?"

He falls back, passing his hand over his face. "Why can't it rain and get it over with?"

Afraid he will become bored and leave, I search my life for anecdotes that can be rendered amusing. I cut myself into hors d'oeuvres. What does he think, hands crossed on his belly and only a grey glint under his lashes to show he is awake? I am his clown, while he imagines Stephanie. I want to fall on him in an attack both hostile and sexual and chew through his thick throat.

With a clap of thunder, the storm strikes. I find myself crouching on the floor with my hands over my ears. Minouska rushes under the flap of bedspread to cower there. As the curtains blow in a surge of rain, Howie trots to shut the windows. A stab of lightning blazes over the housetops, the ailanthus trees dash and bow. He stands grinning at the lightning that crackles in a cascade of tumbling thunder blocks and driving rain. "Turn out the light again so we can watch."

A river coils through the air bearing leaves and twigs

and paper, beating the treetops sideways and pouring over
the roofs. The phosphorescent violet blaze of lightning
turns the world on and off like a neon sign. Gradually the
rain quiets to a steady downpour. He turns with a grunt of
saisfaction, finishing his wine. "That was fun."

"Lucky that storms aren't like fires. People who think
they're pretty can't go around setting them." I put on a
record, Bach concerto for violin and oboe, but leave the
lights off. "The wall's hard," I say. "You can put your head
in my lap if you want." Like, take a cookie.

"Sure," he says with bland amiability and moves his
head. As the music winds around us, joy melts through me
to have him here, no matter why, dimly perceived in the all-
mothering dark: his wide Slavic face, his grey eyes, his
chest with the breath that gives a little ride to the glasses
perched there. Love turns me to a lump, while the music,
rich and sinuous, gives cover to my silence.

When the record finishes, he lights a match to look at
his watch. "Late. Damned late. I've overstayed. With the
rain still coming down and I'm tired. Two subways and a
hike on each end."

"You'll get soaked. It's coming down buckets."

Together we stand looking at the rain while we gravely
agree that it is plentiful and wet. "You could look for a
cab. If you think you can get one in the rain. Of course,
you can stay if you like." I switch on a lamp and we stand
blinking. I hope that in the light my proposition will sound
innocuous.

He stares at the rain. "I can't hack the subway tonight.
It's too damned far. . . . A cab is my food money this
week."

"Whatever your prefer. . . ."

"I'm tired. I moved twenty-five boxes today." He opens
the windows on the rain and sticks out his hand. "You
wouldn't mind if I stayed? Really?"

"Why should I?" I ask lamely. "By all means." I hardly
know what I am saying.

While he is in the toilet I make up the bed with clean
sheets. Nothing is more innocent than his staying. I slap

the pillow flat. I don't care! From my jewelry case I take my diaphragm and slip it in the pocket of my robe, putting that over my arm.

When I come out of the bathroom in my turn, he has tossed his trousers and shirt over a chair and lies with only his arms above the sheet. He offers with gruff shyness, "I can take a blanket and sleep on the floor."

But he has already got into my bed. "This is fine," I say loftily, turning off the light and hanging my cotton dress over his clothes. "The mattress isn't bad." I lay me down and there we are eighteen inches apart. I cannot tell if it is still raining out or only dripping on the roof.

"Good night." There absurdly we lie. I am stiff awake, too overwound to keep my eyes shut. My eyelids keep jerking open, window shades on too-tight rollers. I wish I could think of something provocative to discuss that would keep him awake, but I cannot stick two words together. My flesh prickles with nervous itches. The side toward him burns. Is he asleep? His breathing is deep and regular, but suspiciously so, as if overacted. My lungs have stopped working; they are stuffed with down.

Desperately I want to sneeze and kick and scratch and buck and roll, to make him as uncomfortable and as insomniac as I. Why did I invite him to stay? I am sufficiently punished for my conniving. I am weary to tears and the traffic in the street seems to whine in my head. I will never sleep.

Yet, late, hours later, I do. At least momentarily we both sleep because when we wake it is together at the same time locked in each other's arms. With a sharp, wholly awake groan he tightens his hold, as our mouths find each other. I know immediately like the cutting of a veil that we have been involved in the same conspiracy; the readiness that meets mine is also from something long held back and rendered forbidden, except in the borderland between waking and sleep. We pull at the shields of underwear, separating only to shove those oddments away to the foot of the bed and close again.

With heedless impetus he turns me on my back, his weight shifting over, and butts blindly till I part my thighs and move down to take hold of him, hard and stumpy, and slide him into me. Together we exhale a long breath and our mouths join more gently. Like someone exhausted after a long climb, he lies unmoving in me, just the pulse of him. Then with a sigh he takes his mouth from mine and settles up, nestling my face between his neck and shoulders, and slowly we begin. Out of my mouth pressed to his salty skin a soft thick cry escapes and hovers over us.

"I don't mean friends," Karlie said. "Look, you don't have to act protective with me." She leaned back on the table, ever closer to the butter dish.

I moved the butter to safety. "But that's what survived. I value friendship a hell of a lot—"

"Then you weren't really in love with him, you're saying?"

"I was, terribly. That never wore off. He had . . . tremendous physical presence."

"I've seen photos. He wasn't exactly tall, thin and handsome."

"What makes a man a good lover isn't looks or leanness. Maybe it's the opposite." I patted my belly. "Thin is not my ideal, anyhow."

Her foot swung in its scuffed running shoe. "Was he the great love of your life?"

"No." I grinned like a pumpkin. "Josh is. Haven't you guessed?"

She glared at me. "Did anybody at all really love him?"

"Stephanie and Sarah and I—we all did, Karlie. He liked women who were scrappers—we all had a more tenacious grip on living than Howie ever had. We survived him very well—we couldn't help it. But we all remember him. Strongly, fondly."

"And you're all friends. That's weird."

"Not to be friends would be weirder. In a political context, it's easier." If she wanted my life on a platter, she had to learn that only roasted piggies come that helpless, with apples in their gaping mouths. I used to confess Karlie; I used to talk myself out all night. I wanted friends and lovers to accept me, to accept the things even I could not

*yet swallow or stomach. I suspect I wanted them to give
me back to myself neatly structured and in luminous order.
I have learned to do that myself fictitiously, the structur-
ing, the order.*

"Nobody else has a Black aunt and a Jewish aunt and is
supposed to be Greek and her father is a political saint!"

Then I realized of course she didn't want me on a platter, she wanted herself. I might be useful to her, this fuzzy
pubescent girl-child in whom I began to see a little of
Howie, his bulldog persistence. "Why not stick around for
a day or two? I have some photographs. Some letters."

"You'd show me the letters? Love letters?"

"There's love in them. But more discussing what we
each were doing politically. Arguments about civil rights
versus the war—the war in Vietnam," I footnoted, "as a
priority. The letters of writers are never truly private.
Somebody's going to edit them someday and everybody
knows that." Maybe Howie didn't. I'm not sure he understood what I meant to do.

"Can I see them? I don't want to go home yet anyway."

I took her upstairs and rummaged through my files. I
gave her the folders and sent her down to the tent to read
while I went to work myself.

In midafternoon Josh loomed over me with that tasty
expression he gets when he feels I am not being correct,
moral, generous enough and he is about to set me straight.
"You have to open up with Karlie. She is his daughter."

Why didn't I tell him right off about the letters? Partially
I didn't want him to waste the evening reading them and
then twisting and turning in futile jealousy. Partially I
wanted him to take me more on faith. We both get into
that, wanting great love to be greater and absolute as a god
carved from rock on an Egyptian hillside. "Everyone turns
up again, Josh. Even the friends who went underground or
moved to Japan to study Zen or married revolutionaries
from Namibia all turn up except for the dead and sometimes even they come back. I've seen her three times—once
in Truro in the fog I met her, out on the moors in a spot I
try to avoid now when I'm alone."

"Did you ever see him?"

"Howie? No. We mourned him so thoroughly. It was all talked out."

"Because he was a hero."

"After somebody's dead you think of them as always dead, as if the story wouldn't have come out all different if he'd not gone out that night and fallen into the ambush. The call said a sick child and the Klan was laying for him at the crossroads with shotguns as if murdering Howie could make a generation content to be pissed on. Now they're all over the papers again."

"You should say all that to her."

"I guess so. I always think the young ones know more than they do."

I was making paella for supper when she asked me, *"Did you and my father ever get together again after he married my mother? I mean, weren't you ever lovers again?"*

I stirred and stirred the rice as it became translucent. *"You know, Stephanie never asked me that. How come you ask?"*

"From the letters, I wondered. Didn't you ever do it?"

Only the living hurt; the dead don't worry what you say about them. Their ears are full of mud. *"No. I would've, but he was too loyal to Stephanie. He loved her too much."*

She fixed me with a level skeptical gaze in which too I could read something of her father. *"He wasn't too loyal to have an affair with Aunt Sarah."*

"It wasn't an affair. They were working together and they were in danger together."

"Mmmm." She stared at me, lowering her chin. *"You people were all crazy, weren't you?"*

"Honey, we were the sane ones. We still are." I tasted my seasoning and added a few more threads of saffron. Alberta and clan were coming to supper and I determined to enlist Alberta in a history lesson. I began to get excited. I bet I had that old clasped-hand SNCC button in a drawer someplace and the songbooks. I bet she doesn't even know SNCC was the Student Non-Violent Coordinating Committee. *"This Little Light of Mine."* If only Alberta still played her banjo. *"In the fifties we were all a little crazy,*

but we've been getting clearer and clearer ever since." Even Josh didn't have a grasp of the political history of the early sixties. For Alberta and me to share our common web of work and friendship with Karlie, with Josh, with her own kids, would be the best home movies we could dream up. And the paella was going to be superb.

THIRTY-SIX

One, Two, Three, Many

So WE PASS the night and Labor Day morning able to be gentle and inventive and curious now that the violent closing has torn the modesty long knit between us. I know too as I touch the corners of his wide mouth that we still ride the wave of impetus, before the slack when we have to talk. This shall be an only time, or else it represents the end of whatever innocence impulse can claim. No matter what happens, the sun has come into my flesh. I bask in his arms. Behind his half-closed eyes, a glint of milky blue-grey in the light spilling over us, a decision is made and I resign myself to it even as I argue and wheedle and promise with my body. From the ledge Minouska contemplates us. I want to incorporate this joining whole, drink it through my pores and reassemble it, already memory as it happens.

Finally we rise. I could sacrifice a boar to him, decapitate an ox. I only make scrambled eggs, toast, drip coffee. He sits back from his breakfast yawning. Suddenly his posture stiffens. "Forgot to use anything! Is it too late?"

I have always told him the truth. This would be a poor time to stop. "I have an evil mind. I put in my diaphragm."

"Oh." He squeezes his nose. "I wish you hadn't told me. We could use the myth that it happened in the dead of night. Slambang surprise."

"It only implied *my* readiness."

"Gee thanks. It was a long time coming."

With a chill of disappointment I look at his young slightly sullen morning face, realizing the decision I had imagined in his eyes is unmade. Thus far I have come with at least the shadow of Stephanie's permission, the evening, the impulse. To ask more is to take what she would not permit if she could stop me. Nor am I sure I can reach him. I step around the table. "Surely you've made me pay for every bit of blindness, every bit and then some."

With a grunt deep in his chest he takes me on his lap and rocks me against him, hiding his face in my breasts. I feel rather than see the grimace that pulls it rigid. His breath touches me through the cotton. I stroke his sandy hair, thick and coarse as dune grass, curly as moss. A beach where we will go today to lie under the sky and stare at the lashing water.

Tomorrow his classes begin. Tomorrow I call my temporary agency for my next assignment. Tomorrow we resume or we abstain. Today we pack a picnic lunch and ride the subway out to Rockaway, through Brooklyn and across the marshland. The day is flat and intense, like a photograph of itself, an effort of intense color and hollowness, not of emptiness but of strangeness, as if the little houses were secretly filled with arcane light, a sense I will associate years later with acid and with danger.

Everything moves me. Everything is pregnant with words we do not say. There is an aura of silence about us as we move through the slow afternoon past the trim, the gaudy little houses, through the sands littered with thousands of bodies in little scraps of latex and nylon. We walk in a magnetic field of intense lust. His body has become sex to me. I feel as if my cunt were full of warm honey all the time. Every touch jostles me into wanting. The center of gravity in my body is about two feet lower than usual, right in my crotch. I am so distant from the practical, the day is almost over before I think to ask him why he didn't

drive last night, and learn of the death of his car the
week after his move. It threw a rod, and he stripped it of
identification and plates and reported an abandoned ve-
hicle. He feels guilty, of course.

When we stickily part Monday evening, exhausted with
sex and talking about everything but what we are to do, I
work on a poem. I write, rewrite, work through draft after
draft.

                                        Rockaway Beach, Long Island
1. *The Town*
On Rockaway Beach, bargained from the sea
by timely dumping of ancestral garbage,
jostling for space the houses preen,
rococo cages decked by lonely wives.
More birdbaths than birds adorn the tiny yards
with cookie cutter shrubs instead of trees.
The retired rock on tiers of porches
watching the couples pass down to the sea.
They sit into the dusk. Their faces hang
waning in the gloom like wrinkled moons.
Cards are fanned out under table lamps
along the rows of humid living rooms.
Talk somnolent as honeysuckle
thickens the air and drowns
                              the sound
                                        of waves.

It goes on to 2. *The Beach* and 3. *The Amusement Park*.
I work it over and over, wanting it to say something that I
cannot force it to mean. I write the objective, observational
poem I have been taught, carefully ironic and containing
nothing of what burns a hole in my body like a sun shut up
in a paper bag.

Tuesday passes. I go to work in midtown. I come home
and rewrite my Rockaway sequence some more.

Wednesday passes. I come home and Howie is sitting on
my stoop. As soon as we walk into my apartment, he
throws his arms around me, before I have time to put
down my big canvas purse, convenient for carrying off

supplies. As we kiss it falls on my foot. In about two minutes our clothes join it on the floor.

Just as well he is a medical student. Just as well or I'd be sore all the time and get nothing done. The last thing I expected was that under the conversation and the political work and the friendship runs this immense river of lust. Neither of us knows quite what to make of this vast powerful sweating body we become together. We spend a lot of time in bed. Then we feel guilty. We cuddle and stroke and caress and fuck. We fuck for a long time. We fuck two or three times in a sequence of night and morning. Then we run off from each other to the rest of our lives, a little frightened.

As I do my marketing, suddenly I have to be careful of men. I have never before had trouble, walking quickly, sidling through the city like a cat through the labyrinth of courts and alleys. But now I dawdle, float. I exude something that is dangerous. Fortunately the weather is crispening. I can wear my old sude jacket or a raincoat.

Today, early October Wednesday I am not working and the sun is hot and rough on my arms and face as I return from the market. Howie has given my body back to me. I feared Mike's boast: that only in that tortured dominance would I ever love and enjoy fully. An obscure dispensation allots the full orgasm here and not there; denied importance when it's missing; largely beyond control; when it's given, like a sun of amoral rightness crowning my acts. I feel complacent with sweet roundness like a pear.

Coming home with my shopping bags heavy with yellow apples, purple broccoli they call cauliflower, white fillets of flounder, bouquets of ruby lettuce, I see at once angling into a small parking space up the block, the white Sprite. My heart catches, a phonograph needle hitting on a scratch. I sink on the stoop with my packages and wait for her to arrive.

She wears a cobalt blue sheath almost too tight to walk in, giving her a hip-heavy waddle as if she were a much bigger-bodied woman than she is. She is no longer slender, not overweight but filled out, squinting at me in the shadow of the stoop. She takes off her sunglasses and I see they are only sunglasses, not the prescription lenses of before. "It's me," I say, wondering if she can recognize me without her glasses.

"Waiting for your true love, Stu?"

"Or a bus. Or something. Maybe you."

She follows me up the steps, at about half my pace in the hobbling skirt. Inside, she surveys everything. "I love your place."

"You won't lecture me on living here? All our friends from college faint when they see it. They won't come east of Fifth."

"I love this neghborhood. I envy you, Stu." She sits at my table as I put away groceries.

"But you're here now too. Obviously you made it."

"Well, yes. I won. But the trouble is, New York State isn't New York City. I never knew how long Long Island is. I mean, do you grasp it? Have you ever been out there, in the great beyond? It must stretch halfway to Maine. Hours and hours of bumper-to-bumper late-model cars and jowl-by-jowl tract houses."

"You're out in the suburbs somewhere?"

"Oh, you got it, kiddo."

"In one of those houses that look like all the others."

"You think that's a joke, something from the Malvina Reynolds song, 'Little Boxes.' No, we have an apartment in an apartment complex. Not a real apartment like this. It's my mama's dream come true. Everything's electric. They haven't yet got those windows like in Peter's father's Cadillac where you press a button and they go up and down, but that's 'cause the windows don't open at all. It's air-conditioned. You don't even have garbage, like ordinary people. There's a machine in the kitchen that eats it. You wash it down the sink and it makes this dreadful suffering noise and grinds it up. And a dishwasher. Even Peter's mother doesn't have that—just a Negro maid." Her voice and gestures rise and dip with a mixture of enjoyment and dismay.

I ask, "But what do you do?"

"I play the machines. I put the garbage in the disposal and the dishes in the dishwasher and take the laundry to the laundromat. I play house."

"He works and you keep house?"

"Don't look at me that way. It's every bit as boring as you imagine. I thought I'd be in the city and I could spend a hundred years just going to museums and galleries and concerts. But Peter and I are both in analysis. Peter's analyst is out near Stony Brook, but mine is on Park Avenue. God, my analyst, he's intense. I adore him. He shines in the dark, Stu. Transference, phooey, I worship him! Besides that I find him one of the most stunning minds I've ever encountered, it gives me an excuse for coming into the city three times a week. . . . Do you think I should go back to school, Stu?"

"In what?"

"Oh, physics maybe. Or psychology." She grimaces, idly patting Minouska, who has settled beside her. "I don't want to. I want something real to do."

"Donna, have you ever felt sexually besotted? Just obsessed with making love with somebody till you felt slightly nuts?"

"Of course. I go a little crazy at times. Grab a stranger. Then wallow in all kinds of Catholic guilt. Dreary cycle."

"I don't mean when you aren't involved with someone. I mean when you love somebody and you're involved."

"Isn't that kind of electricity necessarily a phenomenon of not knowing the person yet? So that you can invent marvelous fantasy figures to inhabit that momentarily charged body."

"I guess, not for me. It's Howie."

"You're sleeping with him finally? But you've known him forever."

"Exactly."

"Maybe it's the breaking of a taboo."

I'm unconvinced. "I'm afraid I'm turning stupid. Utterly sunk in the flesh."

"Better than being sunk in East Setauket," she says glumly. "We started out sexually like lightning. Now Peter comes home muttering about his work every night. He feels he's over his head technically. It's my fault, of course, for making him leave Detroit."

"You aren't making love?"

"Not nearly as often. We're both having some problems. I'm going to work on it in analysis. Dr. Evans says that one of my key areas of conflict is my sexual identity."

"I thought analysts weren't supposed to say anything but mmmm."

"He isn't that kind of classical Freudian. Peter's analyst is interchangeable with a stuffed owl, as far as I can tell, except for what he costs. I can tell it's going to take Peter years."

"Then what?"

"We have children. We've agreed not to have babies till we've both completed our analyses." She grins at me. "I'm sure I'll want them by then. Dr. Evans says my fear of having children is related to my sexual identity problems."

The next letter that comes from Stephanie, Howie brings to me and hands over wordlessly.

Dear Howie,

I went shopping yesterday with Sophie. I've been meaning to ever since I noticed at the picnic how pretty she is. It's jealous-making, buying pretty things for another female even if she is only 14. But she is shaping up fast! Too young for you, though. My cousin Marina got married last week. I danced till I couldn't stand. What food! She is six months younger than me and now she's married already. You know I can't come to New York yet, why ask? It's been a long time and maybe we fade for each other, a little. Or that's the impression I get, trying to squint across. But we'll see each other Thanksgiving—won't we? Is Jill's place nice? Are you coming to Detroit Thanksgiving? Missing is a great pain—in every place. If you come early we can meet in Ann Arbor. I'm sure I could find someplace!

Your soon
love XXXX
Stephanie

I cannot in turn show him the letter I got. She must have written them one after the other, I imagine, first his and then mine.

Dear Stu,

Sorry to be so slow answering. Howie's complaining too. I feel incapable of writing. I feel too lost, desperate, confused—I tell you this in strictest confidence! So you have been seeing much of him, to judge from both of your letters. Tell me, does he love me? You must know by now. I can't bear doubt, although I am full of it. Perhaps that's why I must know he is sure, although I don't believe it.

I hate my classes. I'm working for a Greek friend of my father's who has a printshop in Ann Arbor. It couldn't be more boring! I work every morning for him, doing my dreadful typing. Is this all worth it? I hate my life. Should I go to New York? I have a chance for a good job in Portland, Oregon, where my uncle Teddy manages a hotel. George, the son of my father's friend, runs the office. He's dark and big built and handsome as hell. The type bred in my bones as attractive. He tries to seduce me, so slyly, so convincingly, without his father ever catching on. But my strong will saves me a day at a time. I couldn't love him, it's too much like looking in the mirror. Except he's good looking and kisses so well. . . .

Howie's letters are so banal. I tore one in a rage. I envy you living there! I feel years older than the good girls around me. What does Howie say about me? I wouldn't be surprised if he had someone he was involved with for a while; I wouldn't be surprised at all. I know him that well! Never tell him what I said I hope for with him, don't you dare! I'm going out to a movie with George and I have a headache. Maybe his father does know he's after me. Maybe they all know and it's a plot.

love,
Stephanie

Her head aches. My stomach turns over. I wish she had not written brightly to him, emotionally to me. I want her to guess all and not to care. How far that is from fact sickens me. I tell him only that she has written. When he waits expectantly. I flare up. "It's too much, reading each other's letters. You have to leave me free to deal with each of you as an individual."

He shoves his hands into his belt and looks out into the hollow center of my block, resting his forehead on the windowpane. "She mustn't know. She doesn't have to know."

The knife edge at my throat. "End it now?"

He swings around. "End what? Knowing each other?"

"Sleeping together."

"Want to hire a chaperone? An out-of-work house-mother? Want to go back to pretending we're just two of the boys?"

"It wasn't all pretending." I stand. "What do you want, then? To see me for an evening now and then, secretly?"

"Don't be obscene." He sits on the couch/bed, smoothing out the coverlet absently, picking off one of my long black hairs. "I don't know. I don't know what to do."

"You love her?"

"Damn it, don't talk about that." He scowls, haggard. "You haven't asked how I feel about you. Don't ask about her. This has nothing to do with words."

"What has it to do with?"

"Responsibility."

"Ah." I stand before a glass wall. "If that isn't a word. You feel responsible for her?"

"For both of you. For how I am." His head hangs.

"Don't feel responsible for me. I'm responsible for me."

"She's a kid trying on Halloween masks. She plays gypsy, she plays housewife, she plays femme fatale—and bang, she gets hurt." He scratches his head punishingly. "At the same time, that she was a virgin gets me—"

"She was?" I compose my face. "Are you sure?"

He glares. "Well, of course!"

"I mean, I didn't know."

"Oh, she said she used to tell her girlfriends stories to make herself out experienced. I've done the same."

I wonder. No, this I can't accept, this marvelously renewable virginity no traffic can dent, a hydra whose heads grow back as rapidly as they're lopped off. I am furious with her for denying her self, her past, her choices, yet I am touched by her belief that this fraud is necessary, her willingness to perjure herself so that every man may be the first. It has a symbolic reality, but I am dazed by her. How must she have felt in his arms acting out ignorance?

But he is snagged on my questioning. "Why were you surprised? You were her roommate. You're awfully close not to know that."

"We didn't discuss men much."

"It wasn't just that she told me, it was the way she acted—"

"It's just my silly assumption that when people see each other, they're sleeping together."

As if in gratitude at providing him with a way to let the matter drop, he puts his arms around me. "Bolognese's in town. He's found an editor's job with Macmillan's and he's living in Chelsea."

"Ann Arbor's reassembling here."

"He didn't get the fellowship he wanted, so he's working for a year. He asked how you were and I half jumped out of my skin. All I could think of was that he knew. Then I felt a funny sort of jealousy, with him asking how to reach you, and I wanted to tell him about us. I had to force myself to give him your phone number."

"I've told no one." Except Donna and Alberta, it occurs to me, but they're my friends. Of course his two roommates know where he sleeps half the nights. Actually a fair number of people know, when I consider.

He rests his chin on top of my head, sighing with weary satisfaction. "It's hopeless, hopeless." He has an erection.

Maybe she'll never arrive. Maybe she'll fall in love with that guy George. I don't believe it for a minute.

The weeks chug by. This is a drier, sunnier November than I have known, more fall than winter. Sometimes when he is studying late at night, he calls me, waking me. "I must be a sadist," he says in my ear. "I enjoy waking you. Like touching you with the phone. It's clumsy but it works."

Should I turn on a light? No, he is vivid in the dark. "I'm missing your anatomy." In my drowsiness words come slowly.

"Tell me how you're lying. Is the sheet over you? Did you dream yet? What did you dream about?" When I wake into sunlight, that brief conversation in the dark feels more dreamlike than my real fragmentary dreams.

I march through the streets of my day with that bodiless caress around me like a shawl of light. It amazes me that we can pass through our lovemaking as through the sun's heart, that I can touch his body good and real as table or bottle of milk and please him and all seems natural. It amazes me that I do not perish of intensity and fullness but go on breathing and working. If I lack anything in November as the earth cools around me, it is a cult, an archaic goddess simple and ambiguous and powerful as blood to whom I could carry my love like a naked votive figurine, crude, the genitals exaggerated and the expression almost appalled, the arms upraised in supplication.

A crisp Saturday in late November. Last night when we went with Alberta and her date to see *The Threepenny Opera* in the Village, it snowed but did not stay, a dusting, fragile, evanescent but clear in its portent. Now the sidewalks are dry and the temperature around forty-five. Howie is arguing against the Staten Island ferry, claiming it will be raw out on the water. We are half naked and entwined on the floor eating slices of pear and Havarti cheese. When the phone rings, too lazy to struggle free of his grasp, I lean way back and drag it to me thumping along the floor. "Stuart speaking."

He mimics me, tickling my bare sole.

"This is Bolognese. I just saw Stephanie, and I gather she's on her way over."

"Oh." I fumble the receiver. "How did you know? I mean . . . thank you."

"Howie's there, isn't he? What do you mean, how did I know? I knew before you did." I can imagine his sardonic olive face.

"That was Bolognese," I say. "Stephanie's on her way here."

"God!" He lets go my ankle and jumps up. "Let's get out of here."

"Don't panic." I grab his extra shirt and sneakers to stuff them in a drawer. "Help me make the bed."

"What are you going to tell her? What does she mean by not writing or calling? Why the hell didn't she let us know she was coming?"

He had fifteen good reasons for not flying home at Thanksgiving, but they amounted to me and cowardice. This is the immediate response. I throw my arms around him. If he cannot choose, I will fix things so he won't have to. "We'll tell her. We can't treat her like a child. Somehow we'll manage, the three of us."

"Manage what—a massacre?"

"Stephanie will accept it." I am surer than I can bring her to it than him. "Talk to her. Tell her what happened—or do you want me to?"

He goes frowning to the window. "Of course. Only I'd be pretty rotten if I let you."

I dare not approach for fear of irritating him. Instead I hand him his shirt and then wash dishes, dry my hands and comb my hair. I would like to advise him on introducing the subject properly but how angry he would get if I tried, effectively prevents me. I am poised with my hands clasped, trying to think of something magical to say that will overwhelm him with the realization of how lovable I am in this last paring of our time as a couple when he says with dismal relief, "Your buzzer. That's her."

I buzz back to let her in. Smooth my sweater and skirt. Brush crumbs from the tablecloth. Why doesn't she knock? Howie rubs his jaw, sitting gingerly on my desk chair. Finally, there she is. I open the door, my face twisting into a smile that must look as if I had just tasted milk of magnesia. "Hello, Stephanie. Welcome to New York."

"Hi, Stu." She strides in jauntily, swinging a feed bag

purse. Something in the last months has changed her style, discarding weight and accessories. "What a time I had getting here! Bolognese gives rotten directions!" With a half swirl she perches on my couch / bed, apparently only then seeing Howie with a bright smile and nod. "Hello, hello. . . ." She has had the bronze satin of her hair cut quite short and the effect is handsome with her ears bared to the silver drip of earrings. She wears a slim black skirt and a striped overblouse. She has dressed to emphasize the time passed as well as to present a Stephanie enhanced. Gallantly she hales us, "Don't stand there gawking as if I'd fallen from Mars. It's cold out there, no matter how balmy it may look. Give me something hot—do you have some good tea?"

While I make tea, he looks at her with monumental impassivity. I am afraid his lack of response will hurt her. I am afraid his silence conceals a renewal of older, stronger feelings that will sweep me away. Glancing up from a pear she is treating to the dignity of a knife and fork, she prods at him. "Have you eaten already? Good, you can talk. I checked in with my aunt Efi yesterday. I'm staying with her, in Queens. I have a room of my own with its private john, so it won't be bad. It was her son's so it's a bit butch—model airplanes and *Playboy* pinups and old smelly catcher's mitts in the closet—but I'll endure it cheerfully."

"If you'd let me know, I could have met you."

"I wanted to surprise you." With a guileless smile. "Being met is so artificial. Besides, you know me—tons of baggage. I thought my uncle would be better equipped. He has a van."

"But you know I hate surprises." His voice rises gruffly from his chest through layers of inner wool. "I'm too slow moving."

"Still a porcupine?" She glances from under thick lashes.

A cautious look passes between them intimately questioning. Reluctantly he answers, so I know this is one of their shtiks, "And you're still a bobcat. So. Did you finish your incompletes?"

My superfluity runneth over. "I have errands. Back in an hour."

I wander in a daze limp with self-pity till I pass the Strand Book Store and am sucked in. I browse. Melville. I took English honors, but I never had to read him. A squat *Moby Dick* in blue binding draws my hand. Sitting on a short ladder I skim. An hour and ten minutes later I blink up from a school of suckling whales and fathoms of green water, while the present falls over me with the soft weight of a ton of blankets. The small miracles of concentration. Rising I shake the wrinkles from my skirt to exchange two dollars with a hunched man behind the cash register for the sure weight of the book under my arm and drift onto the cold blowy pavement toward my occupied apartment.

Hesitating, I knock. Stephanie flings open the door with an exuberant bang. "Such politeness! I hope you didn't think . . ." With her bubbling laugh, her old robustness of movement. "We'd been wondering what had happened to you—run over by a bus, carried off by white slavers. Now, Howie must go home." Mock severity. "He has studying to do. You and I can chat—unless you're busy?"

"No, no," I say weakly, searching for his gaze. He gives it to me with bland incredulity.

"Now march." She takes firm hold of his shoulders. "We'll have supper together on the early side. We won't eat till you come."

"I'm going. Think kindly of me." With gentle bashfulness he flees.

When the desire to bolt after him has subsided, I turn to face her. "You know."

"Well, rather." She passes her hand over her neatly cropped hair. "His delicacy is extreme. Why don't you give it to me straight?"

A grin tweaks my face as I imagine his mumbled oblique recital. "We've been sleeping together."

"Ah." She sinks back on the couch. "I wasn't quite sure."

"I'd hoped he'd told you that."

"Who knows what he told me?" With a tense forced smile. "At no small cost I'll relinquish saying I told you so. This happened recently?"

"Sort of. Labor Day."

"Labor Day? Right after he arrived. Oh. Go on."

"To what?"

"What did you plan to go on to?"

"I didn't plan. I leapt."

"Into bed." With a sharp giggle. "The usual leaping place for the likes of us."

"Worse I meant it. I love him."

"Of course." Judgment serrates her voice. "But I too love him. I'm standing back taking all this in. Don't think because I didn't fly at you, I'm vacating the field."

"I'm not trying to push you out."

"No?" The sun catches the flecks of green in her wide-spaced eyes in which anger dances. "What, then?"

"We're a triangle. Given. Supposing of course that he'll accept the situation, dubious even though he created it." I feel as if I am forcing my will on her through a burning glass. "We're three peculiar individuals with odd connections. How else can we proceed by trying to find out what we want and need from each other?"

"Mmmm. You think if forced to choose between us, he might throw the whole thing up and decide to study extra hard?"

"That's my guess. I won't ask him to choose. It's your freedom to put that to him if you want to."

"Do you have anything alcoholic? I really am dry as a bone. Anything long and tall?"

"Nothing but wine and cider."

"You? I don't believe it. I thought you'd have a bar set up."

It occurs to me I've been drunk only once since I left Ann Arbor. In my new regime of laboring to buy writing time, I have no desire to waste myself. "I could mix wine and seltzer for you."

"Okay. But I learned to drink gin and if we're going to have a ménage à trois—what does that mean, exactly?"

"Housekeeping by three."

"Don't think I don't envy you this apartment! It gives you an unfair advantage. You won't mind if I make myself comfortable?" Squatting she wriggles out of her girdle (how the hell do you suppose anybody wore those skirts?), unpeels her stockings. Then she sprawls on the mattress reaching up a lazy plump arm for the wine. "I hate girdles, but you must admit it improves my figure unutterably!"

Kicking off my shoes I sit propped against the wall. "You looked elegant when you stalked in."

She laughs throatily. "And you two looked like dying fish. Did you think I'd make a scene?" She shakes her head, setting the silver earrings tinkling.

"I like those."

"A present." She touches them. "After holding on to my virtue for months, I succumbed to George one night. Moonlight's a dangerous commodity—trickier than whiskey. Tell me how it happened between you."

I hardly think I am meant to believe her. "It rained hard one night so he slept over."

Vulgar as blue jays and as wary we pass the darkening afternoon. At six Howie returns, pausing in the doorway as if hesitant to enter. She pinches his cheek. "Come on. I'll take you both out. My treat."

He frowns. "That's pointlessly extravagant."

"I want to!" With stubborn vitality. "I have money now. Tomorrow I have to look for a job and I mean to land a good one. Tonight I want to eat real Italian and drink red wine.

He gives in gradually as we meander looking for a restaurant to match Stephanie's fancy, ending in one south of Houston. In the dark booth he sits like a bulldog tormented by a butterfly.

Leaning flirtatiously over the table she gives him a clam from her appetizer. "You lucky man with two devastating concubines. Show one shred of bumptiousness and we'll beat you up."

"And the two of you will live happily ever after?"

"Why not?" She flutters her bronze lashes. "Just don't ever, ever let me hear another word about a brother-sister relationship or I'll climb up on a table and scream."

"I told you I always wanted a sister—I just never explained what I wanted her for."

Eating my supper I feel decades older. I had forgotten how she brings out that awkward playfulness in him (al-

though remembering the scene Bolognese's phone call interrupted, I feel absurd in my aloofness). Not with the
jealousy of the afternoon but with relief I'll go home after
supper and leave them to each other. At least we have
purchased a time to find out what questions we have to ask
one another. I mean to be patient and daily as grass.

THIRTY-SEVEN

Till Someone Takes It Off, You Don't Know There's a Lid

PERHAPS IF STEPHANIE and I still shared a room, the flurry of day and the rumination of evening, we could hold in balance our separate needs. She spends time in my apartment primarily to prevent my being alone with Howie more than she considers necessary, and the harder she tries to conceal her anger, the more I feel it permeating every interchange.

As for me, I have more time for Alberta, for Bolognese and for the subworlds of New York I explore with each. With Bolognese I go to readings and bookstores and coffee-houses. With Alberta I go to political lectures and meetings, to parties among the young people we have met. In January we take part in a demonstration. About three hundred people carry placards in the cold against H-bomb testing.

Alberta is used to demonstrations, so I do what she does. Refused a permit to use the streets, we walk on the sidewalks round and round with our signs. I feel frankly silly. It seems futile to march around Times Square with our placards as if to persuade the few prostitutes on the job in the afternoon not to drop more H-bombs. I am reminded of the Jehovah's Witnesses of my neighborhood with their *Awake* magazines, their intense uttering of The Message. I have become a member of a little sect, the antinuclear Left. *As I describe that lonely march* The Times *today carries an article about people who lived near the test sites then and who were invited to come outdoors and view the fireworks, local schools being let out for the occasion. Now the survivors are trying to sue the government because they have lost many in their families to cancer.*

Alberta is cheerful, pleased with the turnout and spirit. People march in knots of friends and comrades. Alberta has no trouble telling the Labor Youth League from the Women's International League for Peace and Freedom from the Quakers. We march with people our own age we have met at forums, less sectarian than the older people. Those bloody internecine battles of the thirties that estrange them are quaint to us. Perhaps we need a larger mating pool than any one party would provide, I think sardonically as we march round and round.

I ask Alberta, "Do you think this does any good?"

"Not doing it would for sure not do any good, right?" She winks at me. "If it makes a few people think about the issues, isn't that a gain? It puts a little pressure on the powerful."

I stop to pee in Longchamps. I'd like something to eat, but my budget won't permit it. Then I rush back, half tempted to fade into the tourists and passersby but making myself locate Alberta. You have to say what you have to say however you can manage to say it, I tell myself, waving my placard and marching by her side. It occurs to me she does not march with the CP people, although she says hello to many of them by name. Alberta has not joined the party and will not, although she will always defend her parents' choice. I wish I had warm fur-lined boots. I wish I had warm gloves. BAN THE BOMB!

Howie never takes part in protests about nuclear weapons, but he comes along to meetings about the Negro voter registration drive beginning in the South.

"Do you think voting is more important than the possibility of getting blown up?" I ask, curious. My apartment is hot; the temperature inside apartment buildings in New York seems fixed at eighty. Outside the wind rattles the windows, blowing down from a flat black sky like painted cardboard. When I bend to kiss him, his mouth tastes of cocoa.

"Protesting technology is stupid. Like weavers breaking up machines. You have to imagine people crusading against gunpowder."

"Gunpowder can't wipe out a world."

"Tell that to the peasants during the Hundred Years War." He groans, rolling onto his back. "I don't want to be political. . . . It's a mug's game. The Left never has a chance. But I can't help getting involved. We both grew up in Black neighborhoods and we can't ignore what we know. We were born implicated."

"That's true." I sit up. "Do you remember the Detroit race riots?"

"Jill, I was too little."

"I remember. I was in day care that summer. The whites started whispering that the Blacks had knives and the Blacks started whispering that the whites had knives. All the whites congregated on one side of the room and all the Blacks on the other side, and me and Sarah Altweiler were left in the middle, the two Jews. Then the mothers started arriving to fetch us."

"Sarah Altweiler. Why does that name sound familiar?"

"One Sarah Altweiler is speaking next month at the Young Progressives Forum. I wonder if it's her? It can't be." But I want it to be: some link with my burned-down childhood.

His eyes are grey wilderness as they look at me with a question that could be simply, Do I want to? Or as complicated as a summation of six years' knowing. My cheek rests on his chest against the tree of hair and the heart telling seconds. "Do you ever think suddenly about death when you're happy?"

"I'm not Mike striking poses," he answers brusquely.

Hello old sore: still open after all this time? "Howie, you miser, you never forgive or forget a thing."

He shuts his eyes and I watch, hungry for that change into a younger, harder-looking, impulsive Howie whose face has an imperative beauty that is the precise mask of his need. Like his body slumbering in faded khakis and coarse work shirts, does that vulnerability live in him behind the constant decision-mongering of his daily life? I feel in love with the man I have known, but I love this man with the immediate yes of vision. Could he be born tonight from this bed, his boredom would rip like cellophane before his first step; with an infant's fierce curiosity he would seize the choices before him and tear into them, know them. His ungrounded intelligence would move freely.

He quickens in me, totally alive. Febrile mumbles. Whorls of damp hair, flushed eyelids. A dark bloom throbs around him. I let my arms loosen in gentle laxness and then close them again above his broad back. "Oh . . . I love you . . ." hardly realizing in its truthfulness and familiarity that the saying of it is new, until he rolls to one side looking past me with lines back on his forehead, that seam of worry already habitual.

In a deliberately mocking voice, he asks, "How? Like you loved Peter? Like you love a good steak? We can't use those words."

I am too naked. I pull the sheet over my breasts. "Why can't we use those words?"

He digs his chin into his chest, pushing back with his shoulders against the wall. He frowns as he pinches the skin of his abdomen into folds. "No, you don't."

"Is it supposed to give me a nice protective coat of dignity to pretend I don't? You can stuff that. I didn't mean to say it, but it's true. It's been true for months, at least."

He shakes his head no, leaning back with his hands braced behind his neck. "You don't need a protective coat and you don't need me."

"If we lived together for a year, I'd need you."

"No. You'd be used to me. You'd never need me."

I hug myself in exasperation. "Babies need, but anybody can live without love. It's bitter and mean but you make do. If you can't love me, why argue about need?"

"Oh, I used to put it on for you. Years ago. I used to stand on my head to impress you that I was a regular solid gold genius. You were the only girl who'd paid attention to me and I was scared silly of offending you, you were so abstract and high-tempered. The name-dropping I did of books you hadn't read." He grins. "You made me sweat."

He was so calm and flatly argumentative, that fat kid, I hate to believe behind his yawns and theorems he cared for the impression he was making. It is time I guessed other people are human too. I take him by the shoulders. "A long way from the boneyard, kid."

He folds the sheet around him, sealing me off. "When you say love, you mean that we have a good time in bed—"

"You think fucking like this grows on trees? Yes, I value it, you, what happens between us."

"It wasn't that way with the others?"

"Nothing like. That's bare truth."

"Anyhow, you just mean sex and some pity, loneliness. If it depends on that, it can go away overnight."

"Anything human can wear out. I get the feeling you want me to present you with myself like some bill you can pay."

"I don't see what you want me for. Do you see me, this slob? Once you figure out who I really am, you'll get disgusted just as you did with Mike."

I sit forward, glaring. "What are you doing to yourself? This business of going to medical school. You don't want to be a doctor."

"I've taken my bobishe's money. I can't back out now."

"Why not? She's had her life. Why give her yours too."

"What she's paying for, she'll get: a doctor in the family."

"Howie, you can't go around with a load of guilt from childhood. You have to do what you want."

"What's to want? I should follow my nose and end up in physics like your old boyfriend? Physicists do such a lot of good in the world. Scientists are truly noble people—you only have to ask one of them. Pursuing truth and government grants. If I crave to work for the Department of

Defense, I'll join the army. Doctors are out for money and everybody knows it. But at least you only kill people one at a time, and you aren't trying to do that."

"Don't do anything, then. Be a bum. I'd like you as a bum."

He turns on me, his face blanched. "I can give my bobishe what she wants, don't you see? She doesn't want me. She just wants a doctor, any doctor. Okay. My mother too."

"All this feeling guilty. I swear if I complain about the weather, you apologize. What use is it? You aren't that important, my love. It snows whether you want it to or not. We are in this, all three of us, because we want each other. You aren't getting away with anything. If we don't want you, we are each free to depart by the many available exits."

"I ought to choose. I know it. This isn't any good."

"I don't think it's so bad," I say truthfully. "Half of you is worth two Peters and then some. But if you want to choose, choose, it's your right. Even if you choose her, I affirm your right to want and each of our rights to want." I bang my fist on the mattress. Not satisfactory. "Want! Demand! Choose! Choose everybody. But don't sit there between us probing old guilt like a bad tooth."

"Is that what you want, what you really want?" He takes hold of my shoulders in a bruising grip.

"I want you to do what you want. Because I sure do what I want."

He stares a moment longer, then lets go, falling back again with his hands behind his neck. "For a person who hates to cause pain, I'm always getting into corners where the only way out is stepping on somebody's head."

The first daffodils of florist's spring are artfully arranged in a cobalt vase on Alberta's seldom-used television, which is on to the Channel 11 news. Alberta and I eat the chicken cacciatore I cooked in her kitchen in which I know better than she does where the garlic press and the clam knife are stored.

She grumbles, "Do we have to watch this?"

"Yes. We're waiting. . . . Look, ay ay ay, it's her!"

Alberta squints. "Don't be absurd."

"Yes. That's Donna in the tutu."

"It isn't really a tutu."

"Whether skies are blue or grey, we're bringing you the weather today," Donna murmurs in a breathy treble. "Tomorrow, folks, we can look forward to a nice sunny day, a little foretaste of spring and pleasant things to come. The high is expected to be in the mid-forties, with temperatures dropping into the low thirties in the nighttime. We can expect breezes of ten to fifteen miles an hour from the southeast. There'll be a few wispy clouds but mostly the old sun will shine on us all day." Her manner suggests this information is sexually exciting. She wears a low-cut blouse in which somehow they have produced excellent cleavage. Her skirt is not exactly a tutu but it is not exactly anything else. She wears stiletto heels and a lot of dark eye makeup. Her eyes look enormous.

I shut off the set. "Well, it's better than sitting in a box in East Setauket," I say. "Isn't it?"

"I suppose so. . . . If she can move over into covering news . . ."

Alberta and I chew glumly on. Alberta is offended by the vulgarity of the costume and the performance, I by what I have to see as a total waste of Donna's intelligence.

We are walking down a street in midtown, Donna and I, fresh from window-shopping and a pushcart lunch when I see us framed in a mirrored window. Donna is dressed like the mannequins: pencil skirt, wasp waist, gloves, matching hat, belt and purse, a matronly armored style hard as the carapace of a beetle, but too lacquered to bear wind or water while it proclaims that the woman within is immutable as marble. Beside her I look childish, wearing my student uniform of plaid skirt, sweater and loafers with dancer's black tights. To be an adult woman means to be in pain, for that clothing hurts. When I see the Fifth Avenue bus and start to run for it, I have to stop, remembering Donna cannot run.

Donna's clothing is part of being married and part of

going to work at a television station, even though when she goes before the camera she puts on her absurd outfit. When I go to work in offices, I have to pin my hair up into a bun, for loose long hair seems immoral to people. Only Brigitte Bardot looks like that, rumpled, hair wild. I go in my student clothes or a wool flannel princess jumper out of a thrift shop. At home I have only to let my hair tumble down and I am no longer respectable. If we dip into Bonwit's or Henri Bendel's because Donna must have a new pair of gloves to reach halfway up her arms, the salesladies ask her at once what she wants. They never voluntarily speak to me. They look at me and glance away. The clothing they share speaks an extreme fear of the body, of flesh, of mortality, of desire. To be "well-groomed" is virtue itself. The clothing says a woman has nothing to do but maintain herself like a perfect white living room for company. The clothing says she is a lady: she doesn't labor or sweat.

"Phooey," Donna says in my living room, her crossed leg vibrating annoyance. "I'm damned lucky to get the job. Without Emil, my analyst, I'd never have gotten my foot in the door. Really! You and Alberta are naive. Are you under the illusion I could walk in and say, I'd like to try out for John Cameron Swayze's job? Not only am I doing the Weather Girl slots Monday through Friday, but I'm working on the kiddie show at five."

"In the same costume?"

"No, a long blond ringlet wig and a lot of white gauze. I'm the good fairy Tintoretto."

"Tintoretto?"

"You imagine no one has a sense of humor around there." Donna gives me her old crooked grin. "Look, it beats any other job I've had. Would you believe I get fan mail?"

"Your analyst got you the job?" I wish I could remember when he went from being Dr. Evans to plain Emil.

"Just the interview. I won the job myself. He has dozens of patients in the media. The Weather Girl before me was an actress and she got the lead in a road company production of *Kiss Me Kate*."

"So how come Peter finally let you take a job?"

She grins again. "We're three thousand in debt."

I whistle. "How did that happen?"

"Partly because his old man faked him out and per-suaded him to reinvest the income on the trust fund au-tomatically. Which I think is pretty dumb, but nobody asked me. Partly because I let it happen. It was easy."

"Are you saying you did it intentionally?"

"Not exactly and not on the record." She kicks off her spike heels to massage the bottoms of her feet sensuously. "But I didn't kill myself to keep it from happening. He's used to spending money, face it. We can't live on his salary in any kind of comfort. I just let him find that out without trying too hard to put off the inevitable."

I can't believe they have trouble on Peter's salary. I am paid a dollar fifty an hour, more when I pose, and work an average of twenty-four hours a week. I don't save much but after the rigors of putting myself through college, I feel I live quite comfortably. I have a privacy, time to write, sex, food, even some pretty dresses. "What costs so much?"

"Everything! Our analysts. He'll eat hamburger once every couple of weeks if I barbecue it. But basically he believes in steak and prime ribs. And I went through the gourmet fantasy and out the other side. You spend two hours shopping, six hours cooking and it's all over twenty minutes after you put it out. . . . Both cars cost a hundred dollars whenever a mechanic does a laying on of hands. Insurance. Scotch. Decent clothes."

I shake my hands limberly. "Didn't take you long to get used to Peter's standard of living."

"Damned right. About five minutes, I think."

"But you're working for the freedom, not the money."

"The money means something. A lot in fact. And they like me at the studio, they really do. My producer Guy says they've had very good response to me. I have high viewer recognition already. Jill, Monday for the first time, a boy recognized me on the street. I was trying to hail a taxi to get down to Emil's from the studio in between my five o'clock and my seven o'clock, and I was running late as usual."

"To tell you the truth, I think you're doing okay. It's just so exotic, as a job."

"Nonsense." She paces. Her energy level has risen to what it was at eighteen. She has burned off fifteen pounds to leave her slight frame bone-thin. While she is in my apartment this afternoon, the phone rings for her twice. She speaks in that breathless seductive voice. "Yes, this is a perfect place to call me. You can always leave a message here for me, angel. It's my old roommate from college."

She could at least have said cousin. She does not want to claim me fully. Yet I don't think she is talking to a lover. Her calls have to do with internal maneuvering for place and position. Her job has given her a microcosm she finds more vibrant than that of her marriage. If I guess that so readily, Pete will guess it too.

"What does he think of all this?"

"I try to keep it out of the house." She grimaces. With her nose screwed up, she is a rebellious awkward child. "I try not to take my calls there. I don't talk about the studio —I pretend to think it's silly and only good for the money."

"But you don't think that."

"No, Jill. In our little bohemian enclave, maybe people don't adore the tube, but everybody else does. It touches people's lives like nothing else. I mean to make a career in television. For once my face has got me something besides laid. I'm told I look vulnerable."

"Hey, Donna. Eh, where does the seven o'clock cleavage come from?"

"Tape. Besides, everybody looks fatter on television." She eyes herself critically, probing with a hard middle finger at her midriff. She refuses my offer of supper or even cheese. Tea with lemon is all she takes. "That and white wine. I drink only white wine. It's non-fattening."

One night I go with Alberta to a reading of beat poetry, mostly because we heard through our civil liberties group about the attempt to ban *Howl* in San Francisco. We have seen enough parodies of beat poetry to give us a simulacrum of familiarity. We think we know it because we have read about it in *Time*. Bolognese is scornful and uninterested. If it were not that Sarah Altweiler is in jail in Georgia and thus cannot address the Young Progressives Forum, we would not be sitting in this large audience. I have attended many poetry readings at the university where a hundred people was a good crowd. Eight was a small crowd. Here we have six hundred people, some of whom are as overdressed as if going to the opera.

There are several readers, loud rather than good, but you are about to witness a conversion experience. The last reader is Allen Ginsberg, thin and clean-shaven. He wears a plaid lumberjack shirt and radiates gentleness, patience, an almost motherly caring. I like him, although I recognize whenever he mentions women in his poems, it is with a casual and unexamined disgust. The subject matter is not the hook that snags my vitals. I have been afraid of drugs since a friend ODed on horse when I was thirteen and she was fifteen. The mysticism bores me. But certain poems cause me to sit bolt upright, breathe rapidly and experience the lifting of iron bars from my brain.

The meter moves me. I begin to think critically about what I've been taught about prosody. I begin to wonder about an English education for an American poet. The conversion experience, the sense of fire descending, strikes because I realize as I listen that it is possible to write with the whole entire live self. My self. It is possible to dare to write poems starting immediately tomorrow morning about what I care most for.

I sit there stunned. I started out doing that. Yes, in high school, when I first came to Ann Arbor, yes. But I unlearned to. I was taught to distance myself from my work. To write with a tiny part of my intellectual and emotional equipment. I was taught to see poems as complicated intellectual constructions full of carefully layered ambiguities, ironies and ironically treated myths, alluding in a complex web to other similar works. But you can write about fucking, you can write about supermarkets, you can write about your mother, you can write about the Bomb. You can write your politics. You can actually write poems that say what you feel and think.

I cannot speak. I want to run off and stare into my

brain, opened suddenly from above and shining blue. I rush out followed by Alberta and cannot even take the subway. We walk miles downtown through the spring night. I have to work off the energy that chafes me.

Will I ever be visible? Will I ever be real? I want to be discovered into reality; yet I have not created my self, my work. I am inchoate, unborn. Who am I to assume that what I feel and think and experience matters to anyone else or ever could? I am too weird and strange to shape the dreams of others. My professors droned on of the universal in college, but they seemed to mean only notions, emotions, interests common to white men with money. I carry hope, born from a man who proclaims himself proudly Jew and queer, that I can write out of me, that I do not have to pretend to be an English gentleman to create.

Spring 1982, Bloodstone Review

Miss Stuart's seventh volume of poetry is crammed with reductionist simplistic snippets of women's lib cant. In describing a series of male/female encounters in which women are injured, raped, maimed, Stuart is unsympathetic to male needs. Individual poems stress only the woman's role and anguish, instead of taking a balanced view. Only the poems about good sex transcend this morbid polemical bias. When we men denigrate women, compare them to mud, death, meat, sows, sloughs, sewers, traps, toilets, when we equate them with mortality, contingency, nature, when we put down women who put out and women who don't, we are merely being universal. Miss Stuart is guilty of special pleading. In art there can be no special pleading for women. Her poetry is uterine and devoid of thrust. Her volume is wet, menstruates and carries a purse in which it can't find anything.

Sydney Craw

Howie could be considered the center of our triangle, the obvious fulcrum of desire. Stephanie could be seen as the center, the sensitive and often sore spot. She feels most put upon and must be catered to, pleased, courted. In another sense I am the center: as the most content in the triangle, I put the most effort into making it work. I try to monitor everyone's level of conflict and annoyance. I negotiate. I tell Howie that Stephanie needs more time with him that week. I tell Stephanie that Howie is frantic with his exams, meaning we should let him take a vacation from both of us.

We are a minor scandal among our friends. Alberta puts up with it, for my sake, but it strikes her as unaesthetic. As a divorce lawyer she passionately believes in monogamy. The more she unglues couples by day and ministers to the problems of the incompatible, the brutalized and the rejected, the more firmly committed she is in her evening and weekend life to the search for Mr. Right. Sometimes when we are sipping bourbon on a quiet night she tells me she will never meet the man for her. Gerrit was It.

Bolognese is ribaldly amused. Donna is fascinated, half frightened, half intrigued. As June heats up the city, our primary problem is Stephanie's job. She has been working as secretary to her second cousin who owns a furniture store in Queens. She wants a job in Manhattan and I go to work on Donna.

"But why?" Donna asks me. "How about we get her a job in Alaska instead?"

"She wouldn't go. Besides, you have to understand. If one person in a family is unhappy, everybody in a family is unhappy."

Donna eyes me with a faint smile. Ever since she took the job at Channel 11, she is more at ease with me than she has been since she fell for Peter. I wish I could understand why his cold mercury presence no longer pollutes our communication, but I accept the miracle. She says, "You want to bribe her not to fight you for Howie. You think you couldn't win."

"Wrong guess. I don't want to think about winning. After a year of lusting after him futilely, a piece of the action is amazing grace. I rather like the triangle. I know I'm not supposed to, but it gives me a lot of time to write."

She laughs. "Don't ever say that to Howie. He'd never forgive you. I can't imagine any man who would."

"I should seem to be suffering? But that ought to be guilt-provoking. He can feel guilty about anything—the gross national product. The average mean income in Tobago. I'd like to iron the guilt right out of him."

The phone rings. It is for her. She takes the receiver from me. "Ta, Liz, you're an angel! Give me the address. How should I dress? No, I won't be recognizable. Two twenty-two Lex?" She motions wildly at me, pointing to her purse. "Appointment book," she mouths off-phone. "Who do I ask for?"

With the privilege of old friendship I open her purse and hand her the red leather appointment book. The purse is crammed with vials and jars and compacts of makeup and various pills: diet, headache, whatever. When she hangs up she turns to me insistently. "I'm trying out for a commercial. Should I? I'm curious. But, Stu, isn't that completely selling out?"

"What's the difference between being Weather Girl and selling . . . what is it?"

"Floor polish."

"So what's the difference?"

"Weather's a service, Stu. I'm just the visual equivalent of dialing weather on the phone. Lots of people depend on that information. Travelers. Bus drivers. Baseball teams. Farmers. People planning picnics." She paces to the window, looks out at nothing, paces back. Her face is painted into hard edges, precise sculpture of shadow and light; her hair is a fluffy cloud. "I'm studying meteorology on my own time. What's the difference between giving accurate forecasts in a long skirt or a short skirt? But a commercial . . ."

"Look, half the time when you get me to watch, I can't tell the difference between commercials and programs anyhow, except that a lot of the time the commercials are better photographed."

She seems disappointed, as if she wanted me to talk her out of going. "But, Stu, for the first time in my life, I'm somebody."

"I see that. Donna, your ideas haven't caught up with your life. You keep talking about fulfilling yourself as a woman and adjusting to sex roles, and yet, when you stayed home and did nothing, you were bored silly. You like working."

She gathers herself to leave. I frighten her if I challenge the ideology she is supposed to live by, but clearly doesn't. She has a need to pretend that her job is a temporary aberration to be washed away with all other neuroses when she is healthy, which is defined as wanting nothing but Peter and domesticity. Maybe she has to pretend that with him, but with herself? With me? Looking at the door she has just departed at full speed, I ponder and shrug. After all, that ideology is no different from the religions of most people, pious moralities shielded from the abrasion of actual use. If she wants to go on believing in transubstantiation or the immaculate conception of Mary or the Freudian biological destiny of women, what difference can it make when she is careful to live her daily life by quite practical criteria? She shares that set of beliefs with Peter and perhaps to unravel that fabric would threaten their marriage. As long as her ideas don't interfere with her activities, what harm can they do?

Within a week, Donna comes through for me. She gets Stephanie a job typing invoices at Channel 11.

THIRTY-EIGHT
The Three-Legged Race

BOLOGNESE CANNOT LIKE my new poems. "Irrational," he calls them. But neither can he dismiss them. They command his respect even as they annoy him. As a slush editor, he is used to going through dunghills of rotting hopes in the form of unsolicited manuscripts every week, making snap decisions and moving on. My poems detain him. He knows they are bad by every criteria we were taught, yet when he finishes lashing me with the scorn informed by our common education in English honors, the poems still stand there. They are raw, they are often too long, but they are in a voice I know is mine. They are real as potatoes.

Sunday brunch at my apartment: bagels, cream cheese, bialys, Nova Scotia and orange juice. I did not buy the food, of course. Stephanie, Alberta and Bolognese kicked in and Howie went out and actually purchased it. I contribute the strong black coffee, the butter, the plates, the Mozart.

Bolognese finally stops worrying at my poems and slumps back, lying flat but for his head propped against the bed's edge. "No, I just get two weeks' vacation," he answers Alberta. "My parents have a cottage on Crystal Lake in Michigan. They sent me plane tickets and it'll all be free and no more, although just as, boring as if I went out to your playground."

"I love Sag Harbor. It's not spoiled yet. We rent a funny dear falling-down house. We could easily fit in more people or so if any of you reconsider staying here stubbornly to broil," Alberta says.

Howie sighs. "I want to get out of the city. But with the orderly job, the only days I have off are Mondays and Tuesdays. At least Presbyterian is air-conditioned."

"And when it gets really hot this August, I'll just hike over to your apartment, Alberta. Your pad is my country air." After all, I have a key. I'm supposed to keep an eye on things, bring in the mail, satisfy the minimal needs of a flowering cactus a recent suitor gave her. I think it was supposed to represent a symbolic protest, but Alberta likes it. It's the only plant she's ever been able to keep alive in her apartment. "And Mondays we can make a determined effort to take a bus to someplace green."

First Bolognese leaves to work on his latest short story about a man who eats himself to death. Then Alberta is off to stuff envelopes for CORE and then meet her newest held-at-arm's-length young man to go rowing in Central Park. I am at the disposal of my family, uncertain how we are to pass the hot hazy day. Stephanie has been quiet, not a good sign. She has been liking me better since Donna got her the job at Channel 11, for she too is excited by the romance of television. But whenever Stephanie warms to me, she shortly withdraws, sure I am fooling her.

"What's wrong, sweetheart?" Howie asks her. "Do you have a headache?"

"A giant one. Does it ever occur to you that when you say 'sweetheart,' you're not being specific enough? Never mind, this morning was boring beyond endurance."

"I thought you liked Alberta and Bolognese—" he begins.

"They're *her* friends. Who else would go on about her poems for two hours? As if anybody couldn't write like that if they were willing to strip in public. You could do it. I could do it. But we wouldn't. It's the ravings of somebody who's willing to rave!"

"It wasn't two hours. Maybe forty-five minutes. And nobody was being exactly complimentary," I say defensively.

"You don't care what they say as long as you're the center of attention. What you can't stand is when you aren't."

"Steph, I can talk to Bolognese separately about my work—"

"Work? You call that work?"

"I didn't realize it annoyed you. I guess it can be boring for other people."

"My goodness, you've noticed there are other people! We may be getting someplace yet."

Since I am The Other Woman, I am no longer The Poet to Stephanie. She dismisses my work as if it were some outré form of flirtation or self-decoration designed to seduce impressionable males. Since viewing me as a rival, she cannot credit me with any real ambition beyond possessing Howie. Yet frequently she forgets to scowl and we have wonderful times, the three of us, even she and I. The truth is that Howie has little time for either of us, and we make each other's life easier and pleasanter in the city, if only she could acknowledge that. I want Stephanie to love me, but she won't.

"With her old apartment," Stephanie says with a mock-pout that is too real, "it's as if Stu were the wife and I were the mistress."

"Let's do something nice before I go to work," Howie says. "Like take the subway down to Wall Street and walk south to the Battery. I love the financial district on Sunday."

Stephanie examines her almost black nails. "Can't. I'm seeing Brian from the station, and he's picking me up in Queens."

"That balding jerk? Even on screen he slobbers."

"Aren't we touchy? And who started searching for variety?"

He tries a smile. "Not having a right to be jealous doesn't mean I can turn it off like a faucet."

"It's getting more and more unfair!" She crosses her arms as if holding herself in. "I have to work Monday through Friday. That's the only time the business office is open. You work Wednesday through Sunday from two to ten. I see you weekend mornings and Tuesday evenings and maybe one evening a week after ten. *She* switches her schedule around just as she pleases and hogs you all your time off."

"Actually I only take Mondays off with Howie. Fridays are for me," I say. "And Monday I write till three."

"But no, she has to use up Sunday morning with this egoistic brunch with all her friends and now she's talking about going off with you on Mondays while I have to work!"

"But, Stephanie, I work too. It's hot in the city. I get tired. I don't have that much time alone with him either. Do you think I don't suffer from a feeling of wanting more too?"

She crosses the room with edgy nonchalance to the good chair. "Keep it to yourself for a change. You always are suffering about something at the top of your lungs. Who asked you to be so damn honest? Not me."

She is right, of course. An awkward smile pulls down the corners of my mouth.

"Which of us used her good friend's absence to start having an affair with that friend's boyfriend? When I arrived, did I find a welcome? No, the two of you slinking around, you with your stricken face hanging out and Howie tied in knots saying, we must reassure Jill. I've leaned over backward being civilized." With her legs crossed, her ankle swinging in an arc, she gives off a vibration of anger like the whine of a small but high-powered saw.

Howie rises slowly, rubbing his knees. "She says she loves me."

"She would!" She flicks at her short hair indignantly. "Just because Jill's loud about her so-called grand emotions, does that mean she feels more? She's an exhibition-ist!"

"I loved him for a year with my mouth shut!"

"But you couldn't keep it shut, could you? You're always loving somebody to death."

"You've had a few trial runs yourself."

"Shut up!" He slams his fist into the wall.

We do shut up. We stare at him. Minouska crawls under the bed.

"So the two of you won't be satisfied till it's blown up! Push somebody downstairs! All right, all right. I'll flip a coin. Will that please you? Will that shut you up?" He rummages in his pocket and throws down a quarter.

"You ought to use Milt's silver dollar but you spent that on your first whore. Now you want us two for a quarter?" I am trying to jolly him into backing down.

"You think it means something, all those years," she shouts, "but you never wanted him till I had him!"

"Peace, Stephanie. Heads or tails?" He is drunk with emotional exhaustion. I can feel the high pitch of worn nerves off him. I am a good conductor; at once I ring with his overwound excitement as I used to with Donna's highs and lows. He shakes the coin in his cupped hands.

She bites her lip. "Do you think I'm something you won in a crap game?"

"Let him," I say. "Let him. You don't want to continue."

"Heads or tails, Stephanie." His face is berserk with strain.

"No!" She grabs at the cage of his hands.

Our faces seem soaked with light. His lips draw back from his teeth in a feral grin. He looks at neither of us but only at his cupped hands. Stephanie seizes his wrists and tries to pry them apart. He yanks free, backing away. We have at last wrenched him from self-control. "Heads for Stephanie, tails for Jill." He tosses the coin. It spins and arcs over to land between them on the rug. She covers it with her foot. "Let me see it," he rasps. "Get your foot off, Stephanie."

"Do you think you can get rid of me like this? You big fool, I ought to let you. Don't you see how she controls you? It won't take you a month to get her out of your system without me to coddle you, but till you do, you're no good to me."

His voice is quiet. His hands hang at his sides. "You're walking out?"

"You bet I am. You're free to look me up, Howie, when you are free. Would you be a lamb and just stay put until I'm out the door? I don't want tearful good-byes because this isn't a permament parting. It's just bye-bye till you come to your senses." She drops the quarter on my bed. "As for you!" She turns glaring. "Don't you ever pretend that you haven't been shoddy!"

"Don't you pretend you didn't look before you covered the coin with your foot. I don't want to hurt you—"

"No, you just want me to pretend I'm not hurt."

"Touché. But I'm fighting for survival too."

"You ask for a hard time. Until you learn to compromise your damn principles, you'll be dying every week and who cares? You've been honest and honest, and I've been tolerant and tolerant, and now I'm through. I've had it. I quit!"

The door slams. He throws himself on the bed, face to the wall. I sit cowardly and still. Minouska creeps from under the hem of the bedspread. Her ears prick up as she sniffs. Screaming over? Then she comes strolling to my lap, leaps up, turns around kneading a safe nest. I wait and wait, watching Howie slung there against the wall inturned on his agony and sucking it like a sour bile-flavored candy. Finally I must speak because it is time for him to leave for work. I clear my throat.

Then he sits up. "We staged that. You and I."

"Only in the sense that two people who know each other well can talk without words." I skirt him cautiously.

"No!" Brutally he scrubs his eyes with his knuckles. "That was ugly." All his movements are heavy as he hauls himself up, gets his gear. "We're a bunch of pigs."

I force myself to keep quiet. I have to let him heal. Shifting the cat to my shoulder, I walk after to stand watching him down the dark flights.

* * *

Donna tumbles in, wiping at her forehead.

"But you look marvelously cool," I say. "I'd faint in that outfit."

She wears a white shirt with high stiff-winged collar rising on her neck and disappearing under her hair. The sleeves are long and crisp. Moving slowly, she takes off her blouse. "I need your help. You have to put makeup on my bruises."

"What happened?"

On both sides of her neck are livid bruises. Each thin upper arm is circled with more. "Peter and I had an argument."

"He did that?"

She nods, matter-of-factly. "He has an incredible temper. You know that."

I remember the last scene in his apartment and nod. I imagine sinking a knife into his narrow chest. "Will you leave him?"

"Leave him? Stu! Don't be silly. I adore him. We have a fight every so often, that's all. Everybody does. You don't walk out on a marriage because of a couple of fights." She sits on her bra on the toilet seat and hands me the makeup, spreading one of my towels over her tight blue linen skirt.

Carefully I wash away the layers of old makeup, dry her and begin covering the bruises freshly. "What was the fight about?"

"Supper. It doesn't matter." She speaks calmly. "He's the center of my life. What I always wanted in a man: Beautiful. Cold and hot at once. I never get past him. I never get away from him. I just need a tiny bit of freedom to make something of myself. He's a physicist, a scientist. Everybody admires what he does. I just need something that balances things a little bit. To make some money on my own."

"But he hurts you."

She looks at me with pity. "When you love somebody, he always hurts you. Because he can. If you don't love him, he can only annoy you."

"That seems to me utter bullshit, Donna. A rapist in the

street can kill you dead. A mugger can leave bruises on you too." I finish the paint job.

She sits on my bed/couch waiting for the makeup to dry. "Stu, you know a bit about drugs, don't you? You had a girlfriend on heroin, you told me once."

"Yeah . . . but I know zilch."

"I wonder . . . have you ever heard of anybody getting, you know, kind of addicted to Dexedrine?"

"The stuff kids who hadn't studied used to take during exams? No."

"I didn't think so. I've been on amphetamines for a while."

"Why? You always had plenty of energy."

"I wanted to lose weight in a hurry. And the commuting was getting to me. It's an awful drive. I was coming home dragging in the door at the time of day when I have to be fresh for him. . . . And I know he finds me attractive again."

"But he always found you attractive!"

"Oh, sure, Stu. When a man wants to marry you, you're beautiful. After he's had you at home for a while and you're a servant and chief bottle washer and cook and laundress and cleaning lady, it's like you've lost rank and status. He actually begins to perceive you as less attractive."

"But that's the job, not losing weight."

"Maybe." She smiles. "Our love life has certainly heated up. I wonder if it goes in cycles when you're married. I'd like to imagine us still going at it like animals when we're sixty."

"I bet it's the job. I like you better with a few more pounds."

"Oh, Stu, you like plump women. Like your mother."

"You're right." I am a little stunned. "How long would it have taken me to reach that insight in analysis?"

"With Peter's analyst, five years. With Emil, there must be some pill you'd take that would do it." She sounds a little sour. "Oh, Stu, we've known each other so long, through half a hundred changes. Who else do I trust the way I trust you?"

* * *

Monday night, eight days after I have last seen Howie, eight days without speaking, I am cooking spaghetti when Minouska marches tail high and nose pointing to the door, meowing insistently. "What is it? A mouse?" I come to stand beside her. Is someone outside the door? Six is early for a prowler in the hall. I cannot bring myself to open the door but neither can I walk away. Finally there is a knock. I know then. "Howie?"

He has been standing outside the door unwilling to use his key. He sniffs the kitchen air. "You're eating?"

"It's almost ready. There's plenty. Won't you have some?"

He hesitates. Argument of the supper air. "You really have enough?"

Liberally I add more hamburger, more mushrooms. I celebrate as I can: he stays the length of a meal.

Sitting, he surveys the room—playing stranger? His face is neutral. I hoped he would return torn and I would love him together, but he shows no unravelings. Minouska sits before him wanting an invitation to his lap but he ignores her, pretending he does not feel her begging gaze.

As I set the table I wonder, would he take food if he meant to end us? Yes. Gently pry off, old friends parting with full rational discourse. When I sit down across from him, I am aware of Stephanie's empty place. My appetite has evaporated but he eats steadily.

As he takes a second helping, he asks, "Wonder why I came?"

"When you don't I wonder why."

Not a ripple. His eyes are a winter color. December in his skull, too. Once again he stares around. "What have you been doing with yourself?"

"Writing. Reading. Amusing my cat. Working for peanuts."

His face hardens, my flippancy annoying him. "And looking for another man?"

"Not yet." If I could only touch him. "That's a nasty question."

"You don't usually believe in lying fallow long. You don't expect me to be polite?"

"You told me once I expect too little and I told you no, I expect too much. Shall I make coffee?"

"How long did Mike last?"

I stand backed against the stove. "January to September."

"So you'd offer me six months."

"I offer myself."

"No, you don't. You offer me a little piece and you keep your distance. You liked the triangle. You don't want all of me."

"I wanted you to come alive! To do what you wanted for once."

"Got your wish?"

"Leave me alone!"

"I hate the men you've been with. Bastards all. They'll get worse."

Kemp taught me to make the spaghetti sauce Howie likes so much. "No. Not true. Every friendship, every intimacy teaches. I'm learning."

"What? To fuck crocodiles? How much less does each leave?"

"That's not true. Mike almost killed me. I knit slow."

"What for? Is pain so much fun?"

He fingers my bruises like a brother. Under his knowing jabs my fears light up until I cannot see his face. "Take your stuff. Get out, get out, before you undo everything!"

"I'm not some appendage to your life. I don't come easy, Jill. But I don't let go easy." He takes my arms. "I didn't mean to make you cry."

"Yes, you did."

"Okay. I'm sorry. But I'm not done yet."

"Be done! Get out. I won't listen."

"Stop reacting and hear me. I don't want to break up with you. I'm besotted with you. I dream about your body at night. When I jerk off, I think about you."

"You do? Then if you want me, what's wrong?"

"The way we've been. We started wrong. It went on all crooked. Now we have the chance to start again right and clean. No hole-in-the-corner affair. None of this stop and start and mess-it-up crap. A new life."

"We'll see each other?"

"More than that. We'll get married!"

"What?"

"You heard me." He takes hold of my chin. "I've been thinking it through all week. Let's do it."

"Get *married*?"

"I won't settle for half a loaf. A piece or a part of something. You need me, Jill. The way your life is going, you're wasting yourself."

"You mean . . . all that nasty yelling and all you meant was, you want to marry me?"

"How much more do you want?" He laughs, letting go of me. "Did you ever make that coffee?"

I swing around. I poured water through the drip pot, but I never added coffee. "We can have some hot water. Unless you're prepared to go buy some champagne."

"Later. Make the coffee."

I spoon in grounds. "But why didn't you just ask me? Like, ask me nice?"

He gives me a look of bland disbelief. "Just strut in saying, Well, how about a little marrying today? Are you crazy?"

I clutch my midriff. "Couldn't you just move in? We could live together fine without all the official glue."

"No. And watch the coffee."

"Why not? Common law. Do it yourself."

"Because of family. Medical school. Taxes. And the need for you to stand up and commit yourself absolutely."

When the coffee is done I sink in a chair, my thighs watery. How buffeted I feel. "Say it again to me."

"That you have to commit yourself."

"No. The big thing."

He grins. "That we're getting married?"

"Better. But you really think I'm a good woman—all that? And you love me? Or do you? You never said so, ever."

"I love you."

"Finally! But just as I am—me? You don't imagine me turning into somebody different after the ceremony?"

"Nonsense. I expect you to turn into a little old lady eventually."

"I guess under the skin, subliminally, I believed my mother. That nobody would ever want me."

He gives me a slow amused smile, sipping his coffee. "I never believed your fulminations against marriage would survive a proposal."

"Don't bet. Don't think I'll take an old hand-me-down marriage. I don't want any marriage I ever saw."

"I'm only offering you one. With me." He pulls me into his lap. "I asked and you took me and we're doing it. For real."

I feel light as crumpled paper. I am going to be happy; I am going to make him happy. How extraordinary. How ordinary. I have arrived in a central safe spot where I am loved.

THIRTY-NINE

Of Champagne and Blood

ACTUALLY IT IS with Donna I have the champagne, real French and bought with her money. "We're celebrating two victories," she says in a happy rush. "Your getting married. And I know you'll be just as happy as we are. Marriage is wonderful, Stu, the only way to live. It will be absolutely *healthy* for you."

"Tell me what the second thing is. . . ." I do not know why I continue, it is nothing I think consciously, but a voice somewhere in my body speaks up. "Are you pregnant, Donna?"

She visibly jumps. "Whatever made you ask?"

"I have no idea. Are you?"

"I sure hope not. Actually I found a tiny hole in my damned diaphragm a couple of weeks ago. I went immediately and got a new one. Not to worry, Stu. Just keep it under your hat. If my luck is rotten, I'll deal with that problem when I come to it. What I had in mind was something more positive. I've been offered a job on the twelve noon news on 5."

"Doing weather?"

"No, Stu. Real news. A giant step into seriousness. I know I won't get the big stories, I won't get to cover the mayor or even the city council. But no more leggy little costumes. No more cleavage. I've made it! Fashion, women's stories, human interest."

"The noon news. How will that work?"

"I'll get up early and commute in. And I'll be home every evening when Peter arrives. He's really pleased."

"When will you see your analyst?" I am really wondering when I will see her, because I do my office work nine to five.

"Emil can shove it. It's Peter I need to work on communicating with, not some Park Avenue doctor. . . . I'm having a little trouble getting off those pills. If I want to see him awhile longer, I'll get him to give me an earlier appointment."

"Is Peter giving you a hard time for wanting to quit analysis?"

"He's very superior about it. How it's a real commitment and an ongoing process you don't just dip into. How if I had really completed the analysis process, I'd want to have kids."

"Have you told him about the hole in the diaphragm?"

"No. . . ."

"Won't he be suspicious if you are pregnant?"

"How will he know?" She pours us both more champagne. "My diaphragm was only a year old. My gynecologist changed my prescription last summer. . . . I'm going to need a new car soon, the Sprite is aging."

I clink my glass against hers. "I'm very happy to drink to the news on Channel 5."

"Stu, I've got to succeed at it. I feel as if this is my one real chance. Something I found myself. I'm not imitating you or Sal or Peter even. Nobody else thought I'd be any good at it. But I know Peter respects me more since I'm doing it, even if he gives me a hard time about working. . . . Five's a network station, its ratings are decent. . . . When's the wedding? Shall I go?"

"We're going to have to tell the parents first. We're visiting them all in Detroit in two weeks."

"Really? Why not do it first the way I did?"

"Howie says I won't believe I'm married if we don't do it head-on. He's saving me."

"He probably is," she says, pouring more champagne. "Here's to being saved. Peter saved me."

"From what, exactly?"

"My bad patterns. Destroying myself. Ending up alone and crazy. Winding up a two-bit whore or hanging around bars to pick up truck drivers."

"Donna, those images come from B movies. It's like my mother who only knows of wives or old maids. Are we in the Middle Ages—marry or go into a convent? Do you know a lot of women who've gone through four years of a good college who are two-bit whores? I've known more whores than you have, and it's a boring job. You do it for money—to support yourself or your kids or a habit."

"Peter's friends keep asking me when I'm going to have a baby. All their wives are pregnant. Sometimes I feel as if every woman my age on Long Island is pregnant. But we can't live on what Peter makes."

"Well, you arranged that, right?"

"I was flip about it, as if it were all my clever plot, but the truth is we spend more now than we did then. He'd move to Detroit tomorrow, Stu. He could get a better paying position with Edison. Then his parents would build him a house. He hates being his father's son, but he's used to trading on that, and he can only do it in Detroit. Here nobody but a few modern architecture buffs ever heard of his old man."

"Don't move back! I'd miss you like hell."

"I won't! He'd be right back under their thumbs. All the work I've put into him would go down the drain. His father charges him in disrespect for every cent he gives— and our marriage will never survive if we're near them. I'm allergic to his mother's hair dye."

Minouska sits purring between us. Now that she has forgiven Donna, she always comes to sit near her, her eyes yellow slits of ecstasy.

"I feel as if marrying Howie wipes away that old pain

when Mike saw me as something my parents were trying to palm off on him."

"Aren't you glad now he didn't go for the idea?" Donna pours the last of the champagne, her movements clumsy and loose. We are both well on the way to being drunk. "Somehow I never imagined Howie for you. Thought you'd go for someone . . . more glamorous."

"If we live to be ninety, Donna, and marry five times each, we'll never think each other's husbands are good enough."

"Will his family be nice to you?"

"I can't imagine why. I can't see why any family would want me in it, to be honest."

"When are you going? Into the lion's den."

"First week of September, before school opens."

She pats Minouska. "Who's feeding her while you're gone?"

"Alberta'll be back. I thought I'd ask her to come by."

"I'll do it. As long as you're gone weekdays."

"We're going Saturday afternoon and coming back Wednesday."

"I have to come in to work Labor Day, so I'll feed her Monday and every day till you get back. No problem. I'd enjoy it. Just remember to give me a key."

My instant respectability stuns. Even Bolognese seems mellowed by the news. Julie sends me a chatty letter stuffed with pictures of Carl, Jr., baby Constance, and herself big as a house in the background. *Five children in a row. I counted them on my fingers just now. Julie loved having babies. She enjoyed pregnancy; after the first several she became involved in natural childbirth and the La Leche League. Like my own mother Julie was terrific with infants and young children, but about the time they started bringing home report cards and having social problems in school, she would begin looking at them with a colder eye. Her children after seven all wore a bewildered sulky air, ex-angels in exile. Carl had affairs from year one of their marriage but Julie ignored them, rightly considering them triv-*

ial. In '68 Carl started smoking dope, growing his hair, running after teenyboppers, saying groovy and far out. He quit his job to develop his soul and at one point turned up on my stoop in New York. I was in my combat boots, down-with-the-running-dogs-of-imperialism phase, so I didn't communicate too well with this oversized hippie sporting a Beatles haircut, a beaded headband and good leather attaché case full of drug paraphernalia. Julie had an official nervous breakdown. Carl was busted in Cleveland. His family's lawyer got him off on condition he return to Julie. Julie was allowed to have one more baby in 1971, number six. Karma, Carl named her. Julie stopped sending Christmas cards and notes with photos about the time some of her friends began to have heard of me. She was insulted by the fuss. After all, she knew who I was, putting it over on everybody else. Quite so. I was sorry to lose touch.

Our wedding plans please everybody as if we were fertilizing the earth and creating social luck. Was this all I had to do to make the whole world love me? I wish everyone I meet may soon be as happy: only in a world forested with lovers would I feel safe. In the bush of my head small drab birds warble fearful guilt about Stephanie.

Sitting in the laundromat watching Howie's clothes flash by like domestic television, his bright socks, his drab work shirts, I try to imagine marriage. I see us both working, a hum of productivity rising. He is healing; I am writing. We tell each other our useful busy days. In my wallet in the laundromat I am carrying a scrap of paper I found on my pillow two mornings ago. "Jill, I love you. We will have a life that shines." Secretly I carry it with me folded to a soiled wad. Whenever I pay for anything, I touch it. I am loved. What could be more important? I ripen in that sun.

"We'll start looking for an apartment as soon as we get back from Detroit," he says over fettuccine. Lunch is our big meal, with him eating a cafeteria supper in the hospital.

"Why don't we just live here?"

"I can't waste that much time commuting. I'll have a heavy load in the fall."

A stab of regret, which I squash guiltily. My first home, my dear private place, my own.

"Besides, everybody drops in on you here. I couldn't study with all that ya-ta-ta-ta. . . . I hate living with Robbie and Steve. They're the world's biggest slobs. The bathroom smells like a subway urinal. The kitchen smells like the subway. We'll live like human beings."

I'll be an adult. Grown-ups. A sobering thought. I don't believe it: we will play house.

He holds my face between his palms. "I see the waif in you. The child who craves a home. The woman battered by the callousness of unfeeling men."

A tear forms in my eye. I feel frail. Of course I need taking care of.

"We'll have a few hard years. Then you'll never want for anything. You'll be able to do the things you dream about without getting kicked in the teeth. And I know you'll keep me honest. You won't let me take a suburban practice and push placebos to people who have nothing wrong with them diet and exercise wouldn't cure."

We will be together; I have not since early childhood known the taste of certainty. He is promised to me like dawn and dusk. Those broad bones in his thighs and forehead, the mossy hair, the wintry eyes and stubborn mouth: he will not walk away. All my brambly ways now stand revealed as roads leading to him. All accidents and blows I gave and got, needful preliminaries. We've grown out of each other and now we grow back together, round as a poem.

"How's he going to support you? Some people when they think they're in love believe the moon's made of green cheese and they can eat it with a long-handled spoon. Listen to me, Lady Jane: life in a cold water flat will be hard on a girl who's been taking it easy in college all these years instead of out earning a decent living." Mother's hair bristles and flutters like black flames. Her small plump body prances on alert. To and fro she marches banging pans on the stove and dishes in the sink.

"Mother, who supports me now? Me. I'm not about to

quit work." At the wobbly kitchen table I pause with knife in midcarrot, struck by how much she is enjoying this drama. Before her energy the house feels rickety, as if she might break through its walls, flimsy as stage scenery: but she never does.

"What do you know about keeping house? You'll be scrubbing your fingers to the bone for a boy younger than you who'll be tired of you in no time and chasing after high-school girls." She grasps me by the upper arm. Dark eyes scrape my face. "Are you in trouble?"

"No. I'm not pregnant, I do not plan to be pregnant."

"Ha! How many women plan to be caught? There'd not be half the people on this street if babies listened to planning!"

I laugh. It strikes me that she can be salty. If she were not my mother, would I appreciate her more?

She intones mournfully, "You're too young to settle down."

"You were younger. The first two times."

"Shhhh! Oh, in years. But I knew the world, chickie. I'd boiled water for my brothers to be born and wiped their bottoms and bargained with the undertaker for coffins—they'll rook you every time. How can you marry into a graveyard family? A father to bury his mistakes, now isn't that something?"

It is one of her virtues that she never for a moment considers Howie a good catch. "His father's been dead for years, Mother. They kicked his mother out of that house. She lives in a three-room apartment with his grandmother."

"Poor boy!" She clucks her tongue. "He lost his papa young, the way I did. Poor woman! To be uprooted and stuck in a little bitty apartment with no yard or garden and I bet the neighborhood isn't safe."

It's supposed to be safer than this one, but I keep my mouth shut. Take any source of good feelings available.

When Howie comes to dinner, mother is a steel kitten. Defiantly she wears an old housedress when he arrives. Then she disappears. Dad is hearty and miserable. He huddles in his armchair smoking furiously, his eyebrows meeting in embarrassment. His hands harden into the bole of a gnarled winter tree. Alone with me these days, he talks about last night's game between the Tigers and the Yankees. He seems primarily worried I may have become a Yankees fan.

Mother emerges in a purple frock festooned with sequins. As we march toward the dining room table three feet away, she pinches Howie's arm. Under the lopsided chandelier of four light bulbs we sit down to pan-roasted chicken. Relax, everyone! If I did, I would slide under the table. LOVE THY DINNER PARTNER, a neon sign flashes over my head in hearts-blood red and truelove blue. Howie is ensconced on his dignity like a hard cushion. Mother tilts her head coquettishly, fluttering her lashes; then throws him dark musty glances of scorn and mistrust. Dad daydreams of fishing in an icy mountain stream a mile above our plates.

"A civil ceremony with some justice of the peace you rout out of bed—call that a wedding? Bad start, bad end." Mother nods sagely over the chicken breast.

"We'll need the money after we're married." Howie is practical and foursquare here, everything battened down. Wise but distant—his medical manner to be.

"We'll see what your mother says." She cocks her head as her black eyes needle him. "What will people think if you have some hasty hole in the wall wedding?"

I say quickly, "Nothing they'll still be thinking in a year. We don't want a whole Fourth of July parade and fireworks."

"Why not?" Mother tosses her hair back with a queenly nod. "You won't get another chance. Of course these times you never know. Some people get married every other year to a new person."

A smothered groan escapes Dad: he sees this going on, every two years a new suitor he must play the father for.

Howie and I avoid each other's gaze. He has a sentimental preference for my father, who speaks American, has a regular job, watches the ball games. With my mother Howie turns political, searching for weaknesses on which to rest an alliance or push an advantage. He disapproves of

her for not resembling his own pallid suffering refugee
mother. I want him to admire her sass, to understand how
a lack of scope for her energy and imagination has warped
her, to gauge the richness living has withered but not without traces, like the fossils of vanished jungles in rock. I am
the product of her imagination and her poverty of outlets. I
watch them try to manipulate the other, wanting each to
catch at least a glimpse of what compels my love.

We expected trouble from his family, but I am the compromise candidate. At first his mother is stiff with me, her
eyes plowing my face. But once we have eaten together,
she begins to thaw. I have the feeling of a breath held and
held, now let out in a long sigh. As Howie explains later,
his mother said, "We were afraid you'd marry the other
one. The Greek."

For hours measured by the drip, drip of an old cuckoo
clock, stalactite of time leaking to stone, I sit on the flow-
ered couch beside her. His grandmother twisted with arthritis crouches in the armchair before us. Across the room
Howie has the TV on.

"After the chasseneh, you can get, eppes, a better job, a
smart girl like you," Grandmother urges.

"Then Howie won't have to work long hours in the
hospital every summer," his mother chimes in. "He needs a
vacation."

"Going to medical school is enough work for him,"
Grandmother says in her turn. "Let's talk tachlis, you can't
get a full-time job?"

I look to him for help but he watches TV, shutting out
our voices. At night his mother sleeps on this couch. She
gave up her twin bed to Howie, while Grandmother sleeps
in the other twin. "I write. That's the real work I do. The
jobs I take are to make a living so I can write."

"Writing poetry, that's fine in college. You did well in
college, I remember." His mother nods encouragingly at
me. "You had a good scholarship. Poetry, playing music,
it's nice. Later you'll have something to give your children."

"But now you're getting married, nu. You have your
husband to think about. No children till he's settled in a

practice." The grandmother waves her swollen forefinger at me.

"It's your job to watch out for that," his mother whispers.

"Oh, absolutely, I agree. No children for years."

"I'm a grandmother three times, I'm in no hurry already," his mother pleads. Her voice is gentle, caressive. Although she has no accent, it is the softness, the texture of her voice that are foreign. All her sentences rise on the ends. Even when she is trying to bully me into becoming a proper wife, her rising inflection makes the remarks sound like wondering questions. "Later on you'll give me grandchildren."

"Not too much of this later. I'll hold on, halevai, but I'm not seventy anymore," the grandmother says.

"He must be settled in a practice first," his mother says. "He'll start out in debt. You can't give them more money. Your savings will be gone by the end of his schooling."

Grandmother mutters something inaudibly, glaring. Her savings have meant power and she does not want ever to see the end of them.

Now his mother brings out a fat album. Hours of Grandmother's children, aunts and their husbands, of grandchildren, of Howie's father who was once a baby in Poland, a child in Germany, a teenager voyaging across the wild wide ocean. Hours of Howie's brother Milt. I suspect his mother prefers her older son, for with him the ground is certain. He lives half a mile distant. She talks to him every day. I want to thrust the album from me. That child in faded sailor suit dragging a wagon, what can I do for him? Then suddenly Howie's sixteen-year-old face glowers from its veil of fat. With a pang of queasy guilt I meet its squinted wary stare: was marriage what we meant? Are we wiser or more foolish?

My days are run like an airport, appointments just missing collision. Mother plays traffic control. Forced to choose between Yahweh and the God of the County Court, we go off for a nervous chat with a reform rabbi who

married Dick Weisbuch five years ago. The families have
negotiated over our heads that we are to marry in Detroit
at Thanksgiving. The wedding is clearly not going to be
quite as simple as we had imagined; on the other hand, it is
not going to happen immediately. I suspected when Howie
took control of my life that we were to be married in
Detroit as soon as we told our respective families. Mother
gives me to understand preparation takes months.

    electric toaster
    6 towel sets, assorted colors
    7 linen dish towels
    canister set
    wall can opener
    good knives

Father has removed to the basement, where the protesting
whine of his saw accuses us as it bites wood to soothe him.
That night Howie said we would marry, I did not dream of
aluminum bread boxes.

"Donna never writes me any longer," Mother complains.
"Out of sight, out of mind. Thick as thieves when she's in
town and then kiss her good-bye."

I cannot tell if Mother grew to like Donna or if she
simply wants to be in on the story. With hindsight I know
that Donna forced the intimacy to fill the gap of doing
without me. Now that she has worked out a way to see me
without Peter being aware, she has forgotten my mother.
Donna is narrow in her passions, whether of love or friendship, but long-lasting.

"Howie may not be as showy a catch as Peter but he's a
good boy and Jewish. When you come down to it, Donna
should marry her kind and you should marry yours. That
way, you both know what you're getting. . . . Is he *affectionate,* Jill?"

My skin crawls with memory. In my room, sultry summer. I stood squirming, trying to hide my love for Mike
where she could not damage it, while she probed. For a
moment I feel wary and defensive as one of my apartment's roaches. I want to turn with my teeth bared and

shout, look I am playing this bloody stupid family game but don't push me too hard. Blandly I say, "Yes, Mother. He has a pleasant disposition."

"Um." She sucks on it. "Well, he's more of a mensh than that Mike Loesser you brought home." As if the same memory had been triggered in her. What makes me feel betrayed are the little comments that reveal she too imagines that I will buckle down to the boring routine she calls being a woman and give up everything I want to do. "You can always write an evening now and then. Once the children are in school you'll get a little time for hobbies again."

My mother: the miracle is that in middle age we are friends. As I get older, she admits to being older and older. I still do not know how old Pearl is, but I know she took a big risk in having me. Actually the story of her early years makes more sense if you have an extra five years or so to play with. Why did she stop disapproving of me? She likes the row of books. A couple of years ago, she began to talk about dying. She said that she is sorry she could not love me when I was younger, but that she can love me now; except that she still can't use that word with me. She still asks me if men are affectionate. She asks me that about Josh: "Is he affectionate, Jillie?"

I am finally not embarrassed. "Yes, Mother, he is. He's the most affectionate man I've ever met." I mean that; I also mean the other if affectionate has been all these years a code word for sexual passion. I am still not sure.

Mother, the romantic still and eternally, in her mideighties preferred Josh to all my other men because she found him more attractive herself than any other man of mine she had met. "Age, phooey," said my mother grandly. "All the women in my family marry younger men. If he isn't ten years younger, you aren't properly matched. They wear out sooner, and who wants to be left a widow? Don't you have to train them no matter what?"

Now that I am in my forties, she tells me I'm beautiful; now that I am in my forties, she sends me presents and we have the long, personal and even remarkably honest phone calls I always wanted so intensely I forbade myself to imag-

*ine them. How strange. Perhaps Shaw was correct and if
we lived to be several hundred years old, we would finally
work it all out. I am deeply grateful. With my poems, I
finally won even my mother. The longest wooing of my
life.*

Howie and I are silent on the plane and on the airport
bus. We are stuffed, glutted, talked out. He goes up to his
apartment near Columbia to get his gear together for registration. I head home. I'll call in for a work assignment
tomorrow morning, but I may have to wait till next Monday for a job.

As I go up the steps Conrad, the earring maker next
door, sticks his head out. "You have to do something about
that cat! It's been crying all day and all night. I'm going to
call the SPCA."

"I'm sorry. I'm terribly sorry. I've been out of town. A
friend was supposed to feed her."

"I can't stand that howling."

"She won't do it ever again, I promise!"

Damn Donna! After she volunteered, too. Alberta's Sag
Harbor rental was up August 31 and she would have fed
Minouska efficiently, even though she has a political objec-
tion to pets. As I unlock the door Minouska bursts into the
hall. I have to chase her down four flights to the bottom
while Conrad peers out through the crack of his door.

"Minouska!" I grab her. "I'll feed you. Don't be crazy!"
She scratches my arm for the first time in two years. I
carry her stiff and protesting in yowls back up the stairs. I
dump her inside, grab my suitcase and slam the door.
What's that smell? Like spoiled meat.

When I step to the door of the living room I see her. She
lies on her back tangled in my quilt, one arm raised on the
pillow, one arm stiff off the bed's side. The quilt, the mattress, the floor are soaked, puddled in dark congealed
blood. Even at the first instant as my knees buckle and I
clutch the doorjamb, I know. Even as I call, "Donna!" and
run to her to kneel clutching her cold arm, looking into her
eyes pale, open and jellied, I know. Her skin is blue. Her
mouth is colorless. She is dead. A cry leaks from my throat.

I tug at her, wanting to find some warmth, some life, wanting to beat her, to pummel her back to breathing. The sheets are stuck to her with dried blood from her womb. Did she abort herself? But she had money. She must have found a doctor. Why didn't she tell me? Why? I moan with rage.

I am sitting on the floor. I have been crying a long time, so long I feel drunk. Her death forces itself through me like raw grain alcohol, white lightning, leaving me dizzy. I gasp for breath. I know I cannot just sit here. I see by the clock that it is seven and I must do something. What do you do with a dead friend? I feel she is mine, yet I reject her death, I will not forgive it. Not this stupid, stupid dying into meat, not the people who killed her with their law-armored hatred of women.

I wash my hands and face. I feed my terrified cat. I walk back into the living room, feeling hollow. She died alone here hemorrhaging violently. Beside the bed is a cup with tea in it and a teapot. A wet towel. She must have tried ice cubes. The phone is off the hook and dead. I put it back. Now the tears run down my face steadily as a faucet left dripping.

I cannot go on sitting here with her. I feel crazy, empty. I must do something but cannot think what. Her hand rigid in midair beside the mattress is the left hand with a gold band. She belongs to Peter in death. I call her number. It feels strange to call in the evening. "Peter, this is Jill—"

"What do you want? Are you calling for her? Where in hell is she?"

"I just came back from Detroit. I found her here. In my apartment. Peter, she's dead."

"What?"

"She bled to death here."

"What did she do, get an abortion? The two of you! I knew it. That bitch! That bitch!" He is sobbing with anger.

I actually understand. I am angry too, although for different reasons. "I don't know. I just walked in from the airport."

"That's your story. What do the police say?"

"What police?"

"Haven't you called the police?"

"No. I didn't think of that."

"Well, you're in trouble. I'll call them now. I reported her missing when she didn't come home last night. . . . What's your address?"

"I'll call them." I hang up. That was a consoling conversation. We were able to offer each other a lot of comfort. I phone the police and say what I have to say three times, spelling my name, spelling her name. It occurs to me that Peter guessed about the abortion right away, that he was not at all surprised she was pregnant. Whereas Donna thought he'd never guess. A small hole, like a pinprick.

I feel cold, cold through. Not as cold as my poor dear. Her purse is lying on the floor. I pick it up to go through it. The piece of paper I expect is folded neatly inside, written on a Channel 11 memo. Her job at Channel 5 was to begin October 1. I memorize the doctor's name and address before I burn the paper at the gas stove and wash the ashes down the sink. That doctor may or may not have failed to save her, but it is the law who killed her: the people who make the laws that try to force us to bear unwanted babies and force us into crudely botched abortions instead, the legislators and the judges, the people who pressure the lawmakers, the people who enforce the rotten laws. I will not help them. I will not open her to them. I put the purse back where I found it. Suddenly I realize I should call Howie. I am still telling him when the buzzer sounds. "That's the police," I say. "I'll call you back."

"I'll come right down. . . . Or should I? Being a medical student, they might think I'm implicated."

"I'll call you back." I am numb.

They are two voices. I can barely distinguish the police detectives although I know the roles they play are distinct. Too much fog. I stand by the stove where I don't have to see her. Minouska is cowering under the table. The questions rise before me like large carp out of a cold somber place where no light ever shines. I hold myself, chilled to the heart.

"No, she didn't say anything to me. I gave her the key because she offered to feed my cat while I was in Detroit seeing my parents." I show them the plane ticket stub. They look at it very carefully. "The cat used to be her cat, before she got married. I took the cat from her." I show them Minouska cowering. "No, it was in Ann Arbor. No, she never mentioned being pregnant to me. No, I don't believe she was having an affair. She was very much in love with her husband. Her cousin, yes. Didn't I say that?"

Then a second set of police arrive, apparently in response to whatever Peter did after I called him. They are even more suspicious of me then the first batch, and carefully examine my plane tickets. I hear one of them calling in the next room to verify I took the plane. "I went with my . . ." I start to say boyfriend, then change to fiancé. That sounds respectable. "We were visiting our parents— they all live in Detroit—to tell them we're getting married."

"Let's have his name and address."

They go through her purse, they go through my drawers, they read the papers on my desk, questioning me about my poems. That I write poetry seems suspicious to them and my stock sinks again. "No, she didn't usually have a key. I gave it to her when she offered to feed my cat while I was in Detroit. I gave her the key last Friday. No, we didn't leave until Saturday, but she doesn't come into the city on Saturdays. My parents can confirm I was in Detroit constantly from Saturday at four when they met us at the airport. No, I left my boyfriend at the East Side Airlines Terminal. We took the bus from the airport together. He went to his apartment, I came home. No, she just said she would feed the cat Monday and Tuesday. I said I'd get home today to feed her in the evening. I left a lot of food out Saturday for the weekend. I've known my boyfriend since I was sixteen. No, my cousin."

It takes me awhile to understand they ask the same questions over and over because they expect to trap me in some inconsistency. The phone rings. The heaviest policeman answers it. His name is Muenster, like cheese. "It's for you," he says. I'm glad. I don't want to explain that Donna used to get business calls here. "He says he's your boyfriend."

"What's going on?"

"The police are still here. They seem not to believe me."

"I'll come down."

"No. I'll call you when it's over."

He argues with me, pro forma. I know he doesn't really want to come. He's exhausted, he has to be up early and he never liked Donna. They were jealous of each other in a quiet unemphatic way. I am wary that in my need to blame somebody, I could blame him because I was in Detroit and not with her.

"Why did she come into the city all the time? Did she have a boyfriend?"

"She had a job." I explain the job.

"Hey, that's her. I know her," says one of the other cops who have come to crawl over the room. "She does the weather on the TV. Channel Eleven."

"I never watch that. I do Huntley-Brinkley. They're the best."

"It's the local seven o'clock news. She's a looker. Or she was. Jesus, I didn't recognize her."

"Why didn't you tell us who she was?" Muenster asks accusingly.

"I did tell you. Donna Stuart Crecy. . . . You never asked me where she worked."

They are intrigued. The case for the first time holds some interest. "Probably balling some guy down at the studio," one of them says to the other. To me, "Did she have any special friends down there? Any guys she talked about?"

"No. She liked her job but she didn't talk a lot about it. She worked because she and her husband needed the money." They think the crime was the abortion, not her death. I am turning to ice and ashes. Like Donna.

Three of the detectives have retreated into the hall for a conference. My neighbor Conrad is confiding in Muenster: "So with the damn cat yowling all the time I knew something was wrong. I should have called the SPCA."

"Yeah? You ever seen a little blonde coming in and out?"

Conrad has seen nobody, but he has heard the cat. No, she doesn't give many parties, but has a lot of male visitors (am I suspected of running a whorehouse?) and plays records too loud. A doctor comes to examine Donna. I hide in the kitchen. Men keep arriving, consulting each other, departing.

The sandy detective has something in his hand. "Amphetamines. Speed. You know what these are?"

"No."

"Did your friend ever talk to you about drugs?"

"No. She didn't even smoke."

"Smoke what?"

"Anything. She drank very little." This time I have a memory I'm willing to share. "She did talk to me once about diet pills. She was wondering if they were addictive."

"Diet pills? These things."

"I never saw them. She said they were like Dexedrine."

"Where'd she get them?"

"Her analyst prescribed them."

"You know his name?"

"Dr. Emil Evans. He's on Park Avenue. That's all I know."

"If he's an M.D., he can prescribe them. If not . . ."

"She talk about any hanky-panky with him?" Muenster asks.

A couple of other policemen arrive, one to take photographs. I sit at the kitchen table. Muenster sits with me, suddenly sympathetic. "Guess you knew each other a long time." The same questions hit me dully from another angle. This feels like a grim and boring dance, a high-school dance where I had to follow the clumsy lead of some huge and sweating boy round and round while he stepped on me and his belt buckle pressed into my Adam's apple.

Peter arrives. "You're responsible for this," he snaps at me.

"She says she was in Detroit," Muenster says. "Why do you say she's responsible?"

"She always tried to break up our marriage."

I realize that Donna never confessed to him about the abortion in Michigan; that remained our secret. Peter is tan, oddly handsome, tiny next to the cops. They take a fast dislike to him because he attempts to manipulate them, telling them whose son he is, which might ring a bell in Detroit but means nothing here. Then men arrive with a stretcher to take Donna, and Peter goes off with them and the sandy detective. Suddenly I realize I cannot remain. I can't very well stay at Howie's with Steve and Robbie. I ask the detective if I can call my girlfriend Alberta so I can sleep at her place. He says he thinks it's a good idea.

He listens to that conversation too. I realize that he has moved in, that I will conduct the rest of my life with Muenster sitting in the room watching me write poems and make phone calls. He will follow me to work and sit nodding and smoking in a corner while I type letters and inventories.

Detective Muenster drops me and Minouska with her cat box and some cat food at Alberta's. He says they'll be in touch. Minouska shakes all the way across town.

Lying on Alberta's bed I cry slowly until I cannot breathe, whereupon she feeds me an antihistamine. She calls Howie for me. My throat is too swollen for me to talk. Finally from her precious supply, Alberta gives me a Seconal, which knocks me out at three A.M.

When I wake, she has gone to her law office, leaving a note of comfort on the other pillow. She slept on the couch. Minouska is in bed with me, under the covers, pressed taut to my stomach. I turn on my side and begin to cry again.

FORTY

Crazy Is as Crazy Does

"THERE'S THE UNDERTAKER'S," Dad says. "We were by last night." He drives around the side of the big Tudor mansion, following a Gothic-lettered sign advising Ample Parking to the Rear, where an attendant relieves us of the car. The sun casts shadows of hemlocks across the lawn wet from a sprinkler.

I grasp at Howie's dark arm, let go. We shuffle into a paneled vestibule, lining up to sign a book. Howie straightens his tie before his reflection. When Dad hands me the pen I know what I want to write, Donna Stuart. I make myself write my jagged name.

Mother joins us. "Oh, Malcolm, you didn't sign! I signed for us all already."

"You shouldn't have." He lowers. "That's a husband's duty."

Mother picks lint off Howie, straightens his straightened tie. "You've got on a suit. Good. I wasn't sure you had one. You look good enough to meet anybody's relations." She grips my arm, urging me into line behind her. "Hurry and view her. They're about to begin. It would have been so embarrassing if the two of you were late, in front of them all. Your aunt Jean is here, she flew in earlier. Shhh!"

The creamy casket shines like a new convertible. Dad halts over her, chewing his lip. Mother's head ducks and bobs up, lips moving. I slip forward. For an instant I think it isn't Donna. The face looks like china smashed and carefully glued. The bones have melted into a pudgy smoothness. They have applied makeup heavily over the blue skin. Rouged baby unconvincing on the satin pillow as a bowl of wax fruit.

Mother's fingers meet in my arm. She is yanking at me. Howie prods me forward, his jaw locked. I let myself be pushed. Did I nod out over the coffin?

Aunt Louella looks thinner, her face drawn toward her nose. She dabs at her pale eyes. Grief rises from her like sweat; I smell it and am put at ease. I take both of her hands while she grasps mine and something real is momentarily exchanged. "Oh, Jill, it's not right," she murmurs.

"It's wrong," I say in litany. "I won't forgive."

"No, all wrong. Don't ever forgive."

The line pushes us apart. "They did a beautiful job, Louella," Aunt Jean says piously. "She looks so peaceful."

Dad is shaking various hands. They materialize around him, hands to be shaken. Howie stands at his side. I take refuge behind them and manage not to pass on with the line to Peter's clump. On the wall is a plaque from Thomas A. Fairweather & Sons of Fairweather's Memorial Chapel to themselves in appreciation, calling attention to air conditioning, a pipe organ, ten public rooms, a fleet of modern vehicles (unspecified: go-carts? fire engines?) and Over a Quarter of a Century of Dignity and Reverence. I nudge Howie. "Reverent for twenty-six years and what do they get? A lot of stiffs."

His face softens with a suppressed smile. That is the first thing I have said in three days he has been able to relate to.

Mother tugs on my elbow. Peter slumps near the archway. Our eyes meet with a shock of pure hatred. Then he sloughs off my glare, turning away. I want to kill him. Slowly.

"What did you say, Jillie, don't mumble. Aren't you going to offer your sympathies to Peter?"

"No."

"Everybody will notice. Go over. People will think you're still jealous."

"Mother, he tried to implicate me with the police."

"Oh, he did, did he? You stay away from him." She sits me down firmly. "Just let that no-goodnik try." She takes Howie over. "This is Jill's fiancé," I hear her lilting. "He's in medical school at Columbia. Oh, you've met? We're so very sorry, Peter." Handshake. Pump, pump. Howie and Peter jaw to jaw.

The organ begins emoting. Aunt Jean leans over the row to me, her weathered-pine face drawn tight. "They brought in an Episcopalian! The Stuarts are all Presbyterians. Except for her mother, who's a Papist."

"Donna was a Jew. Like me." To seize her body and run. Dig a hole in Rouge Park, in the Arboretum with my nails, faithful dog.

Velvet, marble, mahogany pews. The organ farts purple. Gladiolas, carnations, lilies. Peter's mother is saying to Aunt Louella, "Oh, but I understood your whole family was High Church. Donna led me to believe that. . . ."

I slide over for Howie, wedged between Mother and him. Everyone looks up expectantly out of folded faces. The minister is bald, but for a patch of brown hair that has taken root over each ear, on the protected side slopes of his high slick head. Though his voice has great resonance when he lets the bass boom forth in a phrase of scripture, for the most part he does not pitch to the back but offers it round urbanely, like a tray of canapés.

We are supposed to follow the service in a red book and we keep being supposed to get up and sit down and kneel. Perhaps twenty people in the room know what is going on. After a while the rest of us are hopelessly lost, asking each other, what page was that? popping up at the wrong times, sitting out a long prayer when we are supposed to kneel. Mother gives me a look of complicity in total incomprehension.

Finally he settles in to preach, using a text from Corin-

thians. " 'But some man will say, How are the dead raised
up: and with what body do they come?' " His voice turns
clever and silken. He reminds me of English professors
who defend the absolute sanctity of tradition—a tradition
of which they may be part but not I and never Donna—by
wit, by quotation, by making opposition appear oafish and
uncivilized. On his voice the corpse is borne forward hung
with dewy ribbons like a Paschal lamb. He alludes to the
car crash supposed to have killed her.

Donna was, Donna is not. Just in front of Howie, Donna's nephew sits next to Estelle. His head, tilted back,
moves slowly as if he were reading something written on
the archway. Then I see too. From the coping overhead a
small brown spider is spinning downward, riding up into an
interstice of the carving, then gliding down again. I watch
the spider stitching.

Aunt Louella sobs. Uncle Hubie rubs his hands in emotion for which his set of acceptable faces provides no exit.
And Peter, he is a finch given an auk's egg to hatch. He sits
on her death flapping his elbows.

" 'The first man is of the earth, earthy; the second man
is the Lord from heaven,' " the minister quotes. She was of
the earth, earthy but not man, of the light, burning, of the
wind, fierce, of the water, swift flowing and now spilt. My
friend in a whirlwind of words, the friend I failed and love
still, uselessly. Sharp ivory doppelgänger with a laugh like
something breaking: are you already fading a little that I
make up phrases to try to hold on to you?

"Howie," I whisper. "I can't take this." His face freezing, he glares at me sideways. His eyes of a changeable sky
are grey and cold.

Mother's hand darts out too slow, scoring my elbow.
Then I am out in the aisle. The minister's full voice knocks
once as if a cylinder had missed as I stumble past him. The
funeral director looming beside the exit starts toward me,
his lips pursing to whisper, but I dodge around him and
out the heavy door. On the lowest step I sit and am sick,
violently.

* * *

"Since you're evicted, you have to find a place to live anyhow." Howie scrubs the top of his head with his nails. "Let's get moving on it. I can get the apartment section of the Sunday *Times* early from my newsdealer."

"I can't do it. I can't look yet." Head propped against the wall I lie on Alberta's bed. Something squats on me, cold and heavy incubus. I see you with snow on your fine hair coming flushed from Lennie, hugging yourself, uttering joy in harsh high sea gull cries: a girl six years younger than the woman who died.

"All right, you're sorry. I'm sorry too. But you aren't helping by turning yourself into a bag lady."

"I have to wear her out, don't you see?"

"You have to wear both of us out. You're giving yourself to it. You're enjoying it." His bulldog jaws are clamped in recoil.

"She's really dead. I'm knowing that all of the time. I can't get past it yet."

"I hear you being sloppy and mystical. Okay. Donna was your cousin—you carry on about how stupid it is that you have to be polite to mine. But she was married to that nebbish Peter. She was his, not yours."

"She was mine too."

"In the meantime you abandon me."

"I know you saw Stephanie yesterday. Her cologne stuck to you. I can't help it, I have a keen nose."

"We're never alone. At my place there's Steve and Robbie, and you're holed up with Alberta and a cat."

I say nothing. Alberta is more tolerant than he is. I am not yet able to start playing house with him.

"Do you think I'm sneaking around to see her? I felt I owed her an explanation. I wanted her to hear about our marriage plans from me. We treated her shoddily."

Stephanie's word. "To be sorry means nothing when I'd do it again."

"I wonder. You have little enough use for me now."

"Howie, you can't protect me from mourning."

"What am I supposed to do, put myself in storage? Climb into a box while you decide you want to pursue some damn experience? When we're married, you can't just duck out." He holds himself around the belly as if he had eaten something poisoned that swells inside. "Jill, all night long I watch the bodies come in, teeth knocked out, heads smashed in, one arm held on by a shirt. We're meat! You get used to it."

"Used to it so you don't feel. For each of them, it's pain. People aren't replaceable meat."

Ever since the funeral he has a way of looking at me when he thinks I am not observing. "You know, Jill, people get brought into the psychiatric unit who aren't acting any crazier than you are. Yet I keep having the feeling you could stop if you wanted to!"

We are running down a narrow way between Djord-jevick's garage and a scraggly hedge smelling of dog piss, running hard but holding hands. The gate sticks. I pull and pull at it. She is small and her face is dirty. They are close behind, their footsteps pounding, metal clinking. I yank at the gate. Callie hides her face, cowering against the blotched grey wall of the garage. I tug with both hands. The gate bursts open, letting us crowd through to race down the alley and cut across a vacant lot. She grips my hand too hard in flight. They chase us across hillocks of snake grass. We hide in the prickly bushes. They are crashing through the weeds, making the ground drum against our knees. Her heart throbs in her thin throat. A smear of rust or blood rims her pale mouth. *Run for it! Upstairs*, I urge. She runs so slowly I am sure they will catch us, up the back stairs, up to the huge dusty attic. We crouch in the middle of the floor. Afraid of the rats she hides her face in my shoulder. Her nails hurt me. Her tears are cold pebbles. *The rats won't bite us, Donna*, I promise. Steps encircle the house. I hold her saying, *We're safe here*. She shivers. I see there are no doors or windows in the attic.

On the night of no moon, rain comes down like the sky falling in skeins and yarny drifts. At sunset I go out to walk all evening. Often she is with me. We stroll, we argue. Our voices soar like toy hawks, high-pitched, shrill, excited as they climb and circle and hunt. I lose her and come upon her.

Frozen ruts of car tracks underfoot. Snow makes the air heavy. She takes off her mittens and bends to the snowbank that slopes in on the road, dabbling her fingers. Playing with the snow she laughs at me. Blood frozen like raspberry sherbet. I touch it to my tongue, but the taste is foul and salty. My breath steams because I am too hot, feverish with wanting. *You're always wanting something!*

After dark, among the trees, teenage boys surround me, but then they fall back. I frighten them. I walk encased in something that protects me. Far into the park in a glade, I find her waiting. The claws of her hands dig into my arm, the nails black with dried blood piercing to the bone. "Is this what you want?" She laughs at me. "Leave me alone! Take me with you! It's cold and it hurts. It's getting colder. Mother. Make it stop! Momma! Momma!"

"I will take you with me. I will!"

"Take my death inside. Give birth to me!"

"I will."

A horn blasts. I scramble out of the street as a cab whooshes past. The street is once again warm and the soft rain soaks into me as if I were a fallen leaf. Wet through and through. My knees are trembling, my calves and thighs weak. Although I have no idea of the time, I can tell by the streets it is well past midnight. If I had my purse I would hail a cab. I am on Central Park West, near Eighty-first. I walk home nervously, fast as my fatigue will carry me. In my hand I hold a wet branch. My palm and my arm are bleeding. On my arm like stigmata are the imprints of nails, deeply scored and bleeding. My own nails are bitten short. With great urgency I hurry home. Whatever protected me tonight has worn off, and I have work to do.

When Alberta gets up to go to the law office (I have given her bed back and sleep on the couch), she finds me at her small tidy desk with bough still wet, my hand and arm bandaged, and several sheets of paper surrounding me covered with drafts of a poem.

Tunneling

I entered the black bough
(lizard scaly, weeping dark snow),
plunged down the sapless trunk
through roots whose fine hairs groped
in the ice-locked mud,
through the pebbly hide of sleeping toads,
their cold hearts almost still,
through the bones of butchered
Indians and mastodons, through
the frozen thunder of granite,
the hidden cave waters sliding
in peristalsis, I dived headlong.

In a cave the color
of the inside of eyelids
I found you crouching, knees drawn up.
I've come to take you back, I said.
Where is back? you whispered,
*I love nobody, and what you love
crouches inside you in a cave,
now, pearl or tumor or child.*
You broke off the middle finger
of your left hand and offered me it.

Scrabbling back to the light,
Oh, it tells time for me
and the time runs fast
like water downhill
to the earth.

"I see you've been eating at last." Alberta pauses in her
royal blue robe on the way to the bathroom, her hair in a
single braid.

"Yes, I got hungry."

She looks hard at me. "Welcome back, kid."

"It's not back, exactly. But thank you for your long
patience."

*   *   *

I mutter of mortality like a medieval monk. Donna has torn an innocence in me that believed there is always another chance to make good what has lapsed, always a fund of time beyond the next heartbeat. Calling Channel 11, I request of Stephanie that she visit this evening, while Howie is at his medical students' study group and Alberta is seeing her newest, earnest and rising young lawyer-accountant-advertising man-editor-broker-professor of economics. Stephanie is sarcastic, yet clearly intrigued. Breaking through the surface of her bright hostility is the shock of Donna's dying. Before Stephanie arrives, I bake her favorite chocolate cake and chill a bottle of Mosel. They won't go together, but I aim somehow to please.

She locks her fingers. "I tried out for her job. I mean, everybody did. I didn't get it. But I'm glad I tried, because I'm moving over into a production job. Guy is taking me on probation as script girl."

"No more invoices. I'm glad."

"You sound it. Why should you be glad?"

"I wouldn't want to type invoices all day every day. You're smart and it's time you got a better job."

"What about you? What are you doing? Temp work is hopeless. You never get promoted. The agency takes more than half of what they charge for you."

"I need time even more than I need money."

She shrugs. We sit on the couch I sleep on every night, Minouska spread like a boa along the back. Stephanie cuddles up, sipping her wine, while her shoe dangles, dangles and finally drops. She coils like an odalisque, occupying two thirds of the couch. "The police swarmed all over us. I mean, you'd think she'd been murdered. What business is it of theirs whether she was having an affair or happy with the creep she married?"

"They think it's all their business. They even read my poems."

"They can't think it was suicide. Nobody commits suicide *that* way. It's because you're trying to live you do it. . . . I think it's horrible you found her. When I had my period last week, I kept imagining how she died and thinking that I was bleeding too hard."

"If we hadn't both got involved with Howie, we'd still be friends. I miss your company."

"You should have thought about that before! About us being friends."

"But, Stephanie, I'd been friends with Howie even longer."

"I never believed in that business of men and women being friends."

"Stephanie, half the time you don't believe in this business of women being friends. I guess that's all I believe in: friends of one sort or another. Almost always there's some sex in it but it's only one item among many." As we drink, I remember the champagne Donna brought me. All the words, all the damn words that sometimes seem to kill but never save. Can poems save? What—memories? A poem as an engine to create a momentary flash of Donna.

"An item, hmmm? That's one way to put it. . . . I used to wonder if you hadn't ever gotten it on with Donna."

"Were we lovers? No. Only once when I was thirteen. Never since. She was afraid of it."

"You sound as if you're sorry you didn't."

"It's minor among my sorrows. But yes, I regret being scared out of my love."

"Did you love her more than you love him?"

"When you really love people, there's not more, there's only different."

"Love, love, love, Jill. It's just words, like your poems. I want something real. Something I can grab hold of and feel." The lamplight catches the green flecks in her eyes like beautiful marbles, the best agates I never wanted to play with but hoarded to hold in my hand.

Without thought, on the push of momentary impulse, I kiss Stephanie on her long mouth with the corners I know will be sensitive. It is not a passionate kiss; simply inquiring. But she kisses me back and I find I had forgotten the soft squirmy sensual delight of holding another woman. We kiss and kiss on the couch, our mouths turning into peaches and mangoes, our breasts rubbing through the thin fabric of her shirtdress and my blouse. I am not pushing anything. I had not decided to do this and I am deciding nothing. The heat and the moisture envelop us, a small sweet orchard of rampant fruiting vines. We are grapevines clustered with purple fruit ripe among the trailing tendrils and thick leaves. The grapes burst on our tongues.

Suddenly she pulls back and jumps from the couch, going to smooth her hair at the mirror over the tiny fireplace Alberta loves, although she never puts anything in it but three very clean birch logs for decoration. "How did that happen? It's very dangerous."

"Not really," I say. "No more so than the chocolate cake."

"But how could you do that?" Howie stares at me. Alberta has left without us for the Young Progressives Forum, where Sarah Altweiler's speech is postponed again because she is still in the Macon County Jail (*so that Howie will not meet her until three years later, to be recruited*). Howie and I are not going, for we are stuck in the kitchen area of Alberta's apartment arguing. We have our most intense scenes in kitchens. "When Stephanie came to me, I couldn't believe it."

"I wanted to be close to her. I wanted to take her as seriously as I take you, I wanted to make that happen—"

"So you do a sick thing like that?"

"It was nice, actually. I baked her a cake—"

"Did you think she wouldn't tell me?"

"I didn't worry about it. Howie, there's a slice of cake left. Alberta had some. It's my best effort to date in the chocolate cake masterpiece category."

Taking me by the shoulders, he shakes me hard. It hurts. Afterward my shoulders still hurt. "Are you crazy? Are you trying to destroy everything?"

"I think I was crazy right afterward, Howie. But not now. I don't see anything that isn't in the room for other people. I have to go back to work anyhow. Flying to Detroit and losing my security deposit and all have left me in debt to Alberta." I know I am annoying him. I touch his cheek gently, trying a little body argument, coming up

close. "Now that I understand, really understand, that we
all die and at any moment, suddenly, I'm living my life a
little differently. That's all. I mean to express my caring all
the time. I sensed an old jealousy in her I wanted to speak
to directly. . . . Kissing isn't fatal, dearest. No harm done.
Stephanie just feels a little superior."

"No harm done, no harm done!" His fists clench. He
throws himself away from me, bringing himself up against
the refrigerator. "Do you believe that?"

With a wave of ice gliding up my trunk I see that things
are chilling quickly. A good energy is escaping through
every pore, leaving me with empty folded hands. "Howie,
can't you imagine sometime you'd be with a close friend?
Say you're with Bolognese and he's upset or grieving. Can't
you imagine putting your arms around him and holding
him? Can't you imagine having sexual feelings?"

"What'll you do the day he makes a pass at you? It may
take him five more years, but sometime when the two of
you are sitting up past midnight nitpicking on each other's
work, he's going to strike like a snake. Will you feel sorry
for him? Will you have some of those momentary sexual
feelings you're touting?"

Just enough truth to hurt. Bolognese's long olive face
bent over our pages dances in the room between us. "He
wouldn't."

"You're lying." He holds himself. "Jill, you have to give
it up. All this chasing and tree climbing. Look, if two
people are walking down the street and they come to a
corner, they can only go one way."

"And sometimes they can't. Why not have a coupling
where I can now and then walk around the block by myself? You don't trust me."

"That night I came back to you, I didn't say I was
moving into your life, Jill. I said I don't like your life. It's
sloppy."

"Come in the living room. Sit down." I take his hand.

Reluctantly he follows me into the living room but will
not sit on the couch. He stops at Alberta's desk, looking at
my poems without reading them. "What's this?"

I walk over. "The name of the doctor who did Donna's abortion."

"I thought you didn't know it."

"I wouldn't tell the police. I wrote his name and address down so I wouldn't forget. I have an idea about setting up a way women can have after-abortion care."

"A doctor has to report an abortion, if a woman goes to him for care."

"I know it's not legal. But it has to be done."

"Jill." Now he is standing right in front of me. "You can't marry me and do all these things."

"When you scolded me, I always heard the affection in your voice. I told you I didn't want any marriage I'd ever seen. I thought we could invent our own."

"Like a circus tent, three rings going at once and a freak show on the side."

"You don't want me," I say quietly. I feel like an exploded clock, my works all over the couch. "How can I afford you?"

"Of course I want you. Even standing here, I have an erection."

"But not the me inside." I look up into his changeable eyes of a cloudy day. For a long time they have been watching me and I have watched him back.

"I won't let you make a fool of me."

"I can't kill myself to become your wife. You have to want what I really am." I stand up and put my arms around his strong thick neck. I brush my mouth against his. "Howie, I love you. I love to be with you. Why isn't that enough?"

"Enough for what? Let go, now, damn you. Let go!"

"I don't want to. We're friends. Howie, you can't go from loving me to hating me. I won't allow you. I won't!"

"Then let go. Let go or I will hate you."

I let go and step back. He picks up his khaki jacket and a moment later he is gone.

A slow loosening goes through me, a desire for him so strong I think I will fall to the floor. It passes. "Why are you so fucking scared?" I scream at the door.

I give Minouska some chopped-up gizzards and then slowly strip and put on my bathrobe as if I were ill. My love glows uselessly as a bulb left on in a locked room in an empty house; outside the meter slowly turns and that is the only product of the wasted energy, the spent light.

Scouring the tub, I find myself humming a sad modal melody. Listening, I stop cold. Then with a shiver I clearly hear Donna singing behind me:

> *"How shall I my true love know*
> *From another one?*
> *By his cockle hat and staff,*
> *And his sandal shoon. . . ."*

My neck bristles. I do not turn. I had forgotten how she used to sing, her soprano thin as mist. She sang enough off-key to offend Peter's good pitch. Then she did not sing anymore at all.

The way it worked was, you called a number and asked for Donna. That was my idea, the name. You left your name and number. One of the eleven women in the group called you back. We'd talk a little on the phone, then arrange for you to come to a meeting place. From there you'd be taken to the office, where one of us would counsel with you. The whole procedure was explained. Then we'd set up an appointment to meet again on the same corner. That day you'd be taken to the clinic. Aftercare was available on the spot or by calling the original number. We provided the cheapest and safest abortions available.

The original contact was based on blackmail, but soon we didn't need Donna's doctor. Maybe three thousand women, mostly poor, many Puerto Rican and Black, a lot of them married with more kids than they could handle already, three thousand women over the years remember Donna who got them out of trouble; who brought them better lives for themselves and the kids they had and could try to love. Finally our demonstrations and pressure, our unremitting pressure, those dreary bus rides to Albany and Washington legalized abortion and Donna was retired.

For how long?

* * *

If you had been dropped from the moon into our bedroom, you could have told it was in the Northeast because of the temperature. In no other part of the country do people have to keep their houses as cold. But our land was beautiful, with the wet snow dragging down the branches of the pitch pines, with the cardinals, the jays, the finches jostling around the feeder outside. Bird food was expensive this winter. As Josh filled the feeders, he announced the cost; but when the next blizzard arrived, he pitied the birds again. The summer people always say, oh, it never snows on the Cape. They read that in a book someplace. We were snowed in at the end of our road, waiting without impatience for the town plow to clear a path to us, while the cats slept in a pile like a patchwork fur quilt, keeping each other warm at the foot of our big bed.

"I get scared. I get very scared," I told Josh, sitting up in bed.

"But you aren't trying to be a poet now. You are one."

"I was writing poems then that everybody ignored. Now I write poems enough people read for them to survive. It feels fragile. The poems have to get printed for people to find them and like them. They have to get distributed. Writing is only the precondition to the life of the poem, but writing is the only part I control."

"No matter how much you love me or whatever happens between us, you aren't going to give up. You've written for years. And what would pay the electric bill? Together we just make it."

"Together we make it just fine. Sometimes," I added ominously. "When you aren't being impossible."

"You're never impossible, of course."

"I'm merely difficult. I've always been fearful, all my life. I get it from my mother."

"Are you more scared of the economy or the government?"

"Don't know if I can differentiate. It sure is cold."

"Well, sweetie," said cheerful Josh, "you want them to warm it up with burning witches and women's clinics or with a nice war?"

"What's that?" I ran to my office window to look out. The plow blinked its lights like a toy locomotive as it bludgeoned along. I returned to Josh, still sprawled in bed. "I'll carry the compost out if you'll take the trash to the dump. You'll have to dig out the blue car."

"I'll get get the mail if you'll call the plumber."

"Okay. And while you're in town, get milk. And yogurt. And the papers." Together we wrangle and bargain our way along. Scared. I am running scared, I am running. The times tighten, harden on us. I am not quite as tough as I used to be, accustomed as I have become to loving, to eating regularly, to drinking wine and having music canned at hand; although in some ways I am stronger. What I want is clear to me as counting. We worry together, singing our fears like the chorus of spring peepers that in a month we hope will cheer our evenings from the marsh. They only want to get laid. We also require that. How dangerous is it to want each other as the temperature drops and friends dry up and blow away? In wanting each other we each want a world in which we and our work can survive, and that's where the trouble starts.

I have moved into a small but sunny apartment on Second Avenue. I am doing more posing and less typing this fall. I have a new secondhand mattress and some of my old furniture, but the rooms are sparsely furnished. With my notebook under my elbow I lie on the floor nose to nose with Minouska, who is telling me how this is the apartment of her dreams, best of all with its fascinating musky smells of previous tenants. I begin to realize that contrary to the popular belief about cats, Minouska likes to move with me. How many apartments in the slums of how many cities will we share, each one as we settle in, pronounced by her delightful? She will live to spend her old age with me and other companions, human and animal, on our own delightful and hardworked couple of acres. My familiar, who will die in my arms on the Cape and be buried under the wisteria.

For my totem, the alley cat. All cats really want to live with me: this is one of my quiet secrets. Sensuality speaks to sensuality. We blink. They allow the approach of my hand and their sleek flanks delight me in return. We find each other beautiful and each of us means by the hand as well as the eye. We share too the situation of small predators who easily become prey. I have my equivalent of claws and teeth, and indeed my arched back and loud hiss are my best defenses. When I need to hide my size and weakness, I can look fiercer than I am, but when I cannot talk or threaten or argue my way out of trouble, then I am in a lot of trouble. We are scavengers in the alleys and streets of a society we do not control and scarcely influence. We survive and perish both by taking lovers. Freedom is a daily necessity like water, and we love most loyally and longest those who allow us at least occasionally to vanish and wander the curious night. To them we always return from the eight deaths before the last.

About the Author

Marge Piercy has written eight previous novels and has published eleven collections of poetry. Her most recent poetry collection, AVAILABLE LIGHT, was published by Knopf in March 1988. Her work has been translated into fourteen languages. She lives on Cape Cod with her husband, Ira Wood, the novelist and screenwriter.